BONE FROG
BACHELOR

Books 1–4
Includes Prequel

SHARON HAMILTON

SHARON HAMILTON'S BOOK LIST

SEAL BROTHERHOOD BOOKS

SEAL BROTHERHOOD SERIES
Accidental SEAL Book 1
Fallen SEAL Legacy Book 2
SEAL Under Covers Book 3
SEAL The Deal Book 4
Cruisin' For A SEAL Book 5
SEAL My Destiny Book 6
SEAL of My Heart Book 7
Fredo's Dream Book 8
SEAL My Love Book 9
SEAL Encounter Prequel to Book 1
SEAL Endeavor Prequel to Book 2
Ultimate SEAL Collection Vol. 1 Books 1-4 /2 Prequels
Ultimate SEAL Collection Vol. 2 Books 5-7

SEAL BROTHERHOOD LEGACY SERIES
Watery Grave Book 1
Honor The Fallen Book 2
Grave Injustice Book 3
Deal With The Devil Book 4

BAD BOYS OF SEAL TEAM 3 SERIES
SEAL's Promise Book 1
SEAL My Home Book 2
SEAL's Code Book 3
Big Bad Boys Bundle Books 1-3

BAND OF BACHELORS SERIES
Lucas Book 1
Alex Book 2
Jake Book 3
Jake 2 Book 4

Big Band of Bachelors Bundle

BONE FROG BROTHERHOOD SERIES
New Year's SEAL Dream Book 1
SEALed At The Altar Book 2
SEALed Forever Book 3
SEAL's Rescue Book 4
SEALed Protection Book 5
Bone Frog Brotherhood Superbundle

BONE FROG BACHELOR SERIES
Bone Frog Bachelor Book 0.5
Unleashed Book 1
Restored Book 2
Revenge Book 3
Legacy Book 4

SUNSET SEALS SERIES
SEALed at Sunset Book 1
Second Chance SEAL Book 2
Treasure Island SEAL Book 3
Escape to Sunset Book 4
The House at Sunset Beach Book 5
Second Chance Reunion Book 6
Love's Treasure Book 7
Finding Home Book 8
Sunset SEALs Duet #1
Sunset SEALs Duet #2

LOVE VIXEN
Bone Frog Love

SHADOW SEALS
Shadow of the Heart
Shadow Warrior

SILVER SEALS SERIES
SEAL Love's Legacy

SLEEPER SEALS SERIES
Bachelor SEAL

STAND ALONE BOOKS & SERIES
SEAL's Goal: The Beautiful Game
Nashville SEAL: Jameson
True Blue SEALS Zak
Paradise: In Search of Love
Love Me Tender, Love You Hard

NOVELLAS
SEAL You In My Dreams Magnolias and Moonshine

PARANORMALS

GOLDEN VAMPIRES OF TUSCANY SERIES
Honeymoon Bite Book 1
Mortal Bite Book 2
Christmas Bite Book 3
Midnight Bite Book 4

THE GUARDIANS
Heavenly Lover Book 1
Underworld Lover Book 2
Underworld Queen Book 3
Redemption Book 4

FALL FROM GRACE SERIES
Gideon: Heavenly Fall

NOVELLAS
SEAL Of Time Trident Legacy

All of Sharon's books are available on Audible, narrated by the
talented J.D. Hart.

ABOUT THE BUNDLE

Bone Frog Bachelor (Prequel)

I have done it all. I have built three global security companies, including foreign subsidiaries which include an airline company and a shipping conglomerate, partnered with some of the biggest industry titans in the realm of international trade. But my love is in protecting and securing the safety of those I care about.

And I've done this, as it turns out, at the expense of my own security and fortune. I've cared for everyone else's assets, and left mine wide open to plunder.

Well, that was then. This is now. This is me fighting back. I'm going to screw that b**** of a former wife, who, while she was screwing me in my own bed, was slutting with other men. I was naive, but now, fully awakened, I will have my revenge.

And it will be sweet!

Unleashed

Armed with new focus and passion for restoring his rightful place atop his shipping, consulting and private security empire, former Navy SEAL Marco Gambini takes his new love on a dangerous and romantic pre-honeymoon to the Pink Pasha on a private island owned by the Sultan of Bonin.

Shannon Marr is up to more than just being Marco's sexual distraction and future bride. She inserts herself into the mission being planned to protect two of the Sultan's sons as they endeavor to grow their development business in West Africa.

The stakes are high but the rewards, both physically as well as emotionally, are worth it. Shannon is determined to earn her keep by helping Marco claw his way back up on top by exposing the strengths of her soft and warrior-strong womanhood. Together, if they can survive and overcome their new enemies, their partnership could be unstoppable.

Or they could go down in flames together.

Best read in the following order: Bone Frog Bachelor, Unleashed.

This series involves the same couple: former billionaire and Navy SEAL Marco Gambini and his new love, Shannon Marr, as they traverse oceans and play in the dangerous world of assasins and mercenaries while clawing their way back from the brink of destruction, restoring Marco's powerful fortune earned through his successful shipping, real estate and protection businesses. With each book in this series, Shannon grows into the partner he's always wanted: someone worthy of his trust as his right-hand woman, as well as the woman who can match him in every way in the bedroom.

Restored

Marco and Shannon's hot liquid romance scorches the Florida Gulf Coast

Marco Gambini's Bone Frog Development begins building the Trident Towers project on the Gulf Coast of Florida, managing a diverse team of characters including the two princes, Khalil and Absalom, sons of the Sultan of Bonin... but Rebecca, his vindictive and controlling ex, is doing everything she can to sabotage the project and his relationship with his fiancée Shannon.

Marco also begins building Shannon's dream home nearby. But this former SEAL finds hosting two pampered princelings, who have never in their lives lived without servants and have never done any hard labor, proves more problematic than previously thought.

Shannon finds exciting new challenges, learning about Marco's unique sexual needs, and experimenting with her own triggers and desires as she explores her limits. Their love burns deeper in all areas as they plan a lavish and eccentric wedding at the Pink Palace.

A quick trip to Central Africa to check on the approval and permitting process leads to sudden danger and near-death for part of the team. Shannon learns even more about how her trust in Marco could save them both.

But be warned. There are storm clouds brewing. All is not as it seems. You'll want to continue with Book 3 coming next Spring, *Revenge*.

Revenge

They've planned the wedding of a lifetime – but will enemy forces keep them from reaching the altar?

Marco is a former Navy SEAL who now oversees the construction of veterans' housing. He's counting down the days to his future with Shannon, the love of his life. However, the bomber whose blast injured Marco and destroyed his headquarters in Florida is still at large and still holds the potential to affect all areas of Marco's life.

Shannon can't wait until the day of her lavish wedding, which will take place at a Sultan's palace in the Indian Ocean. All the RSVPs have already been counted when unseen forces threaten to destroy Marco's vision and sabotage his company. With Marco fighting ruthless warlords halfway around the world, it's up to Shannon to support him on the home front.

But is Shannon equipped to help Marco when danger engulfs them both? Will they succeed in their respective missions and arrive on the Sultan's paradise island kingdom in time to walk down the aisle?

Revenge is the third book in the Bone Frog Bachelor series which follows Marco and Shannon's steamy hot romance from the first time they cross a scorching hot path on Florida's Gulf Coast to exotic locations around the globe.

Legacy

Former Navy SEAL billionaire Marco Gambini and his forever love, Shannon, are back together again after a harrowing rescue of Marco's advance team in Africa, threatening to cancel their long-planned wedding at the Pink Palace owned by the Sultan of Bonin.

He has hosted the Sultan and his entourage for a month, and now they leave to return home to their Indian Island kingdom, to prepare for the big wedding. Plans for building the housing project in West Africa are on hold, temporarily, while they ready themselves for the biggest adventure of their lives: their wedding day.

That is, if the bad guys and dangerous militia in Africa will leave them alone. Armed with vengeance and hatred, the terrorist group plans the ultimate revenge, putting more than just Marco's company in jeopardy. They attempt the unthinkable.

Only Marco and his team are up to the task of not only saving their special day, but preserving a dying man's legacy.

AUTHOR'S NOTE

I always dedicate my SEAL Brotherhood books to the brave men and women who defend our shores and keep us safe. Without their sacrifice, and that of their families—because a warrior's fight always includes his or her family—I wouldn't have the freedom and opportunity to make a living writing these stories. They sometimes pay the ultimate price so we can debate, argue, go have coffee with friends, raise our children and see them have children of their own.

One of my favorite tributes to warriors resides on many memorials, including one I saw honoring the fallen of WWII on an island in the Pacific:

> "When you go home
> Tell them of us, and say
> For your tomorrow,
> We gave our today."

These are my stories created out of my own imagination. Anything that is inaccurately portrayed is either my mistake, or done intentionally to disguise something I might have overheard over a beer or in the corner of one of the hangouts along the Coronado Strand.

I support two main charities. Navy SEAL/UDT Museum operates in Ft. Pierce, Florida. Please learn about this wonderful museum, all run by active and former SEALs and their friends and families, and who rely on public support, not that of the U.S. Government. www.navysealmuseum.org

IF YOU GOT ANY CLOSER, YOU WOULD HAVE TO ENLIST

I also support Wounded Warriors, who tirelessly bring together the warrior as well as the family members who are just learning to deal with their soldier's condition and have nowhere to turn. It is a long path to becoming well, but I've seen first-hand what this organization does for its warriors and the families who love them. Please give what your heart tells you is right. If you cannot give, volunteer at one of the many service centers all over the United States. Get involved. Do something meaningful for someone who gave so much of themselves, to families who have paid the price for your freedom. You'll find a family there unlike any other on the planet. www.woundedwarriorproject.org

TABLE OF CONTENTS

BONE FROG BACHELOR

Bone Frog Bachelor Series
Prequel

SHARON HAMILTON

CHAPTER 1

Marco

I HAVE DONE it all. I built three global security companies, plus foreign subsidiaries including an airline company and a shipping conglomerate. I used my skills and training as a former Navy SEAL and partnered with some of the biggest industry titans in the realm of international trade. But my love has always been in protecting and securing the safety of my country and those I care about.

And I did this, as it turns out, at the expense of my own security and fortune. I cared for everyone else's assets and left mine wide open to plunder.

Well, that was then. Now I'm fighting back. I plan to screw that bitch of a former wife who, while she was screwing me in my own bed, was slutting with other men. I was naive, but now, fully awakened, I will have my revenge.

It's a very simple two-step process: One: Get even. Two: Create massive success by re-capturing the wealth I lost playing the marriage game. Payback and wealth creation are the best forms of revenge a man can conjure up. Maybe it wasn't the road to happiness, but it's the road I'm taking, with my team of specialized agents. My revenge would be sweet, and the screwing her over wouldn't have any bedroom on the horizon.

Happiness was an illusion. I believed being happy was running hard and screwing harder next to a woman I thought was a racehorse, like myself. She ran a lean takeover operation of my assets. Maybe she would have upped it to the optimum level, since we had no children. She would have been my sole beneficiary. While I wasn't looking, the person I thought I was closest to dug in deep through opportunity and, yeah, because I'm a good guy at heart.

No more. Fuck Mr. Good Guy. I'll be taking no prisoners. I'm a vacuum cleaner in a phonebooth full of million-dollar bills. And yes, they do exist. The Treasury Department printed some for me so I could frame one to hang in my office.

Tony Abruzzo told me about The Bachelor Towers (lots of sound effects there…or at least there were every time he spoke those words). He said it was mostly inhabited by younger men of my ilk. Up-and-comers and monied trust fund babies who could be my sons, if I'd been a bad boy in high school and knocked someone up.

At first, I wasn't interested. I was still seething from the betrayal Rebecca had played against me, taking half my wealth and costing me most of the other half defending what I had left. The anger was fresh with me. And since I never gave up, I knew it would never go away until it was satisfied. Those fires quenched.

I remembered that conversation well—when he "sold" me on the idea just like he'd sold me Bentleys over the years.

"Marco, one thing's for sure, with the average bachelor age being around thirty-five, there won't be many women over that age. Ripe, beautiful. Looking for love and money. And I'll bet many of them are tired of boys—or boys trying to behave like real men. You've got the experience they crave. Been a Navy SEAL and have the scars to prove it. You came from nothing and carved your way out with years doing hard time on the battlefields and used it to your advantage. You're smart. You're lean and primed for some old-fashioned good times you so richly deserve."

"You're forgetting one thing, I'm focused on revenge," I told him that day.

"Even better. They love men who are driven to obsession."

"Why would that be?"

"Because a man who can't fight can't fuck. You remember that quote from Patton?"

"Yeah, we used to say it every night in Coronado after we got our leave."

"Women love to be the object of desire by a man who knows better. Not a man who is beginning to get the lay of the land. They want an experienced lover who will ride them wet and leave them panting for more. You're the original Italian Stallion, Marco. You're the guy they've been looking for their whole lives."

I must have looked skeptical, but I was seriously chewing on the idea.

"Here's an added bonus," Tony said as he sipped his purple martini that looked like it could be a Dr. Death cocktail. "You don't even have to tell them to flaunt it in front of your ex. Women love to do that shit all the time. It's human nature to them. It's the, "'see what a prize you threw away?'" stuff. Wars were fought over this, Marco. You know I'm right."

He had several valid points, and then I investigated.

So here I was, walking into the marble foyer of the Bachelor Towers in Boston. It wasn't much to relocate from New York City proper, and I was done with that whole life anyway. Boston had plays and musicals, opera, art galleries, museums and parks. And before I decided, I spent a day just walking around the city, finding its people were real, gritty, and not snobby like New Yorkers could be. It had great restaurants, lots of movers and shakers there. I would still maintain my apartment in D.C. so I could slip in and out without detection and with the security and anonymity I required since a lot of my business was generated there. Rebecca didn't know about the safe house in Coronado and the lot in Florida, if the shit really hit the fan.

And it almost got that bad.

Everything that was important to me was in the small black leather duffel bag with the Bone Frog logo on it in my left hand. My right hand held a half dozen hangars of suits I couldn't bear to part with. These had been specially made for me in Hong Kong and South Korea, sewn of the finest wool and linen blends, the seaming thread so lightweight it almost floated. Everything else I left with the brownstone in New York. I even left her my jewelry and my wedding ring. I didn't want any taint of it permeating my new life as a bachelor.

Since the reception desk was empty, I looked for the person whose job it was to greet the residents of the Bachelor Towers, the person who I would probably get fired. I crossed the lobby to the neat bar sparsely packed with couples and three-somes, speaking in hushed tones. A piano player tinkled the ivories in the background. The bartender, Oliver, I'd been told had been stolen from the Waldorf. Hired for his discretion, he knew the tastes of just about any living legend, down to the number of orange peel slices, shavings or sizes of the ice cubes. I needed a drink badly.

"Sir? What do you require?"

I liked his attitude right away. His green eyes and slight brogue were charming. He'd taken this job to come home, I deduced.

"Something muddy, smokey, with an orange aftertaste. Not too sweet. Give me my next favorite signature drink, please, Oliver, if I may call you that?"

He surveyed the clothing I was carrying. "You may indeed." Placing a coaster on the countertop he snapped his fingers. A young, handsome Filipino bellman relieved me of my load, moving in the corner of the bar, in the shadows like a clothes tree, awaiting further instructions. Again, very impressive.

"And what may I have the pleasure of calling you, sir?"

"I'm one of your new tenants, Marco Gambini." I hesitated to mention the vacant front desk, knowing it might be career-ending, but I decided to go with truth. "And your front desk is missing an attendant."

"Yes, Brent is attending to a little escort out the back of the building. It's where we deposit the detritus, and it's unfortunate you happened to come along during that moment. I'm sure he'll be back shortly. And I apologize. This is on the house, Sir."

He pointed to a deep purple/cobalt cocktail floating with some heady orange cream liquor, the red pitchfork plastic stir had skewered a bright red cherry. I liked the visual of the screwed cherry, though I didn't like things too sweet. I sipped. Hint of fizz. Orange and roses aftertaste. Pure sex. I was hooked.

I held the squat etched glass up to him, "Perfect. What do you call it?"

"Midnight in Manhattan, sir."

"I like it even better."

I loosened my tie and unbuttoned my shirt. I felt comfortable studying the room. A young, very lean, blonde girl came up to me, sort of like the house pussycat. With practiced grace and subtle fragrance in a form-fitting dress that revealed how perfect her body was, she joined me at the bar.

I usually like to talk last. This time, I was going to tell her I wasn't interested, but she beat me to the punch.

"So you are the legendary Marco Gambini, the billionaire SEAL?" She interrupted my possible answer to give her command, "Ollie, another one of those for me, with two cherries, please, and don't let him pay for it."

That's when she turned to me and I did like what I saw.

"You're timing is poor, sweetheart. I'm no longer a billionaire."

"Oh, I think not. I don't judge men by their performance but by their potential." She glanced me up and down like a man does to a beautiful woman. "I'd like to be your first date, sort of a "'welcome to the family'" kind of fuck, if you'd do me the honor."

She got me laughing right away, and that was a good sign. I liked women forward, assured, and beautiful. She was nearly half my age, and that worked too, in all sorts of ways.

Brently Morrison, the front desk manager, burst into the bar, his hands wringing, breathless. "I'm so sorry, Mr. Gambini. We had a difficult situation, and I was pulled—"

"Brent, I think we're good," interrupted Oliver. "If you can show Lujan here to Mr. Gambini's room, he'll hang these things up for our new resident." He turned to me. "Is that to your liking, sir?"

As I leaned back into the bar, the blonde moved close enough that I could feel how her body breathed, something I always loved about a woman. "Just one drink, and then I'd like to get settled. It's been a long day."

With another couple snaps of his fingers, Ollie sent Lujan, my suits, and duffel with Mr. Morrison. I still had the Glock tucked into the back of my pants since I never could get the feel of wearing a holster for the animal. I turned and caught her forcing a stabbed cherry between her red lips, biting and chewing it while gazing at me with steely light blue eyes.

I figured Oliver would have warned me if she was a working girl. I had always thought sleeping with women other than my wife to be a stupid hazard many a man regretted later. Especially without a blood test or background check.

But I was getting reckless in my old age. In my rage. Or maybe I was mistrusting my new-found freedom when it came to women. I'd always been tightly bound in my commitments, still fingering the groove left behind from fifteen years of wearing a wedding ring. Moving in here would be a doorway to my new bachelor lifestyle and I liked to stake out the terrain, notice the little things that could result in a failed mission to guard the safety of my men. I turned around just to make sure Rebecca wasn't there watching me take the morsel dangled in front of me—someone I knew I'd thoroughly enjoy.

But the coast was clear. I was ready to launch.

Permission to engage, you bastard. Make it so! I told myself.

She was lovely to look at and I allowed my heart to melt just a little at the edges like a dark piece of chocolate on a warm plate.

"I know the name of this building. I know the name of this drink. I *don't* know *your* name," I whispered, leaning into her.

She didn't answer right away but devoured the other cherry in front of me, tearing at it with her bright white teeth, daring me to grab her and kiss her sweet lips, which of course I wasn't going to do in public.

But I thought about it.

In my fantasy, she was naked, displaying her perfect ass as she lay a path of rose petals in front of me while I walked barefoot, crunching them with each step.

She gave the perfect answer. "You don't need that, Marco. I know what you need."

Well, all right then.

CHAPTER 2

Marco

B RENT BROUGHT ME my key card. "We will have your touchpad completed tomorrow, if that suits you, Mr. Gambini," he said, handing the platinum key to me.

"Thank you."

"I have a bit of orientation to give you, when you are ready, so just ring me up." He handed me his card. "That's my cell, and I answer it twenty-four hours a day. It's a special line for our residents here."

"Thanks again," I said as I slipped the card in my breast pocket. She was still rimming her drink with her forefinger. Ollie was waiting on a pair of young bucks halfway down the bar.

"We've taken the liberty to stock your apartment with some staples. We understand you prefer Coppola, so we've had it flown in. You'll find a case of it waiting for you. We have some cheeses and specialty fruits in season from our farmer's market. Next to the basket is an order sheet for anything we left off. We know you like Black Rifle coffee and drink it with half and half, so that's all provided for you, along with a grinder and French press."

I continued to be impressed, although it violated one of my cardinal rules.

"I'm going to have some boxes delivered in the next day or two, mostly clothes, but a few other items I've purchased, including a big screen for office work. I don't like anything delivered to my quarters without me being present."

"Of course, Sir, for security."

"So this will be the last time this occurs, is that clear?"

"Yes, sir. We have storage upstairs outside your quarters. Would it be acceptable to leave things there, or would you like to approve them first?"

"I'd like to see them before they're placed anywhere near my front door."

"Very good, sir. Will there be anything else?"

"No, I think you've done a fine job, Brent." We shook hands. As he began to walk away, I called out, "What sort of problem was it that involved the rear entrance?"

Brent blushed. "Of the female kind, sir. It happens." He shrugged. "It was a request of the resident. Nothing we couldn't handle, although we don't make a habit of it." He finished his sentence without looking at the blonde.

Good on you.

Oliver approached and asked if we wanted a second, just in case I'd changed my mind. "Not for me, although it was delicious," she smiled, pushing her empty glass forward. Her red fingernails matched her lips perfectly.

"I'm good. I'm going to be addicted to Midnight in Manhattans," I said.

"In the morning, we'll make you my orange juice wake-up elixir best had with fresh biscuits and strong black coffee, Breakfast in Boston. You'll like that one too, Mr. Gambini."

I took her arm without asking. As we crossed the marble foyer to the elevators, it occurred to me I hadn't eaten in several hours. The drink had been strong and I liked how it kicked in. But my mind was far from food.

She was easy on my arm, adjusting herself as we stood in the elevator just so her left thigh lightly pressed against mine and my forearm grazed her breast. It had been a long time since I'd dated, and even though my libido heightened, which I liked, I didn't want her to see me nervous, which I didn't like.

On Floor Twelve, we exited, walking into a mini landing room that doubled as a small sitting area. Several locked doors were lined up around the room, probably my personal storage areas Brent had mentioned.

I tapped the key card against the glass square on the door marked 1212, heard the click, and entered my new apartment.

The drapes had been opened, and a stunning view of the Boston city lights displayed before me like a tray full of jewels. I'd seen pictures of the scenery in the daylight, panoramas of the harbor and surrounding area, but not at night. This was every bit as beautiful as the glistening columns in Manhattan I called home for fifteen years.

A large bouquet of flowers was on the coffee table in the living room. Off to the side and open to the huge room, was a stunning kitchen with black granite countertops, appointed with black-tinted stainless steel appliances, just as I'd ordered. I had decided I'd learn to cook, and I supposed it wouldn't be something most the men in this building did, which didn't bother me one bit.

She was behind me, telling me she was ready whenever I was. And I was.

My arms encircled her waist as I pulled her into my body. I arched her backward, feeling the heat of her quivering mound. Her soft face looked up to me, her arms up over my shoulders, her lips slightly parted, ready.

I dove in with a kiss I wanted to remember. The first of many. I knew by the way she sighed and moaned that she'd be good for me, to help me forget—just for the evening—that I was a mean motherfucker bent on revenge.

I took her hard, but was careful not to hurt her. We went over the threshold together. The two of us. In a barrel. Over the Niagara Falls.

In her arms I found solace. Her legs spread wide and her sweet moist sex restored me to the man I'd always been. I was grateful for the anonymity, the lack of competition in the fucking I'd told myself I loved with Rebecca. She was no comparison to Rebecca. She matched me in every way, sometimes leading me gently into rooms I'd not been inside during my long monogamous marriage. I was thrilled to be bridled by her beauty, her strength. It was long and sweet and I was fully satisfied, but not totally sated.

I think she was surprised how quickly I'd undressed her outer shell, peeled the layers of whatever had begun to build in her young life. She probably wasn't prepared to have any feelings for me whatsoever. But I could tell she did. As I came inside her the first of several times, savoring her shattering body beneath me, she turned her head, and I, always the gentleman, pretended not to see her soft tears. It was a surprise to me, too, that I liked seeing those tears.

My last memory of the night, before I dozed off to sleep, was the lovely lady tucking herself into my chest. My arms naturally cradled her body as if she needed protection. But she didn't beg. She just accepted the strength of my arms and my chest, with her chin tucked down, her hands up to her lips in fetal position.

She didn't ask for more than I gave and I didn't give more than she asked for.

SHE WAS GONE from my bed when morning sun shone through the sliding glass door in the master bedroom. I'd always thought it better to send a woman away with something more than she walked into my life with. I used to think that way before Rebecca. And she was the only exception to this rule.

As I lay there, still smelling her sweet scent, I thought about what was fair. Rebecca had made the mistake of taking first advantage. I'd now start yanking it all back, and then some. I wanted her to rue the day she first met me.

I rose, throwing on the new silk robe left for me draped over a burgundy leather occasional chair. Cinching the waist, I padded out to the living room and open kitchen, looking for her. Her perfume still lingered in the air.

"Hello?" I asked.

But there was no answer.

"I would call your name if—" But I knew she'd gone.

It was a first-class move and made her easy to be desired, a mystery to be pursued.

Picking up the house phone, I ordered the biscuits Oliver had recommended, some fresh jam on the side, and a bowl of strawberries.

"You want the Breakfast in Boston as well?" he asked me.

"Well, of course."

"And how was your evening, sir?"

"Spectacular. Do you know how to reach her?"

"She left her phone number with me in case you asked."

Another nice touch.

"Who is she?"

"I do not know. Have not seen her before, Mr. Gambini. But she came looking for you, that I know for sure. Brently has her personal information. Her address and place of employment were verified. I'll ask Mr. Morrison to send this up with your biscuits. Would that be acceptable?"

"Of course, I'd like that. Any guesses?"

"Well, your residency isn't exactly a secret in Boston. Neither is your divorce."

"But, this isn't Manhattan, so I thought—"

"The old money lives here, Mr. Gambini. But I'm sure you've been told this before. We make it a habit of knowing everything about our residents and their guests. Guests, especially the ladies, have to be vetted first to hang out at the bar, unless accompanied by a gentleman of the house."

After grinding my fresh Blackbeard's Delight coffee and pouring the boiling water into my new French Press, my doorbell rang. My order of fluffy biscuits—accompanied with three small bowls of apricot, blackberry, and strawberry jam, along with whipped butter and strawberries and cream arrived. A plain brown manilla envelope was sealed on the side, with my name on it.

Her name was Shannon. And she lived in Florida, of all places. She was fifteen years younger than I was. She had pursued a modeling career but was working at a Tampa television station,

TMBC, as a stringer and part-time weather person.

I touched her picture, as if my forefinger could somehow pick up some of the missing pieces of her life. But the connection, if there had been any, was not there. I would have to find out because I certainly intended to call.

Beneath the envelope was a folded Boston Herald newspaper. My picture was front and center.

D.C. Power Boss Retreats to Boston. Tail between his Legs.

It was the sort of headline Rebecca would have written. I picked up the silver tray and threw it against the wall. Biscuits, jam, and the lovingly prepared Breakfast In Boston drink flew in all directions.

I ran in search of my Glock.

This. Meant. War.

CHAPTER 3

Marco

I WAS IN the shower when the cleaning service let themselves in and began removing the mess my anger had created. I did give permission not to be the one to let them inside, as long as Brent did it. I felt a twinge of embarrassment, like a piece of my dirty laundry had been exposed, but I wasn't going to ask for forgiveness. It was a lesson to myself. I had to make better choices, better decisions than the ones I made leading up to this fiasco. And life would change, eventually. I would have my day.

Until then, I did have to control my anger. Note to self: Stay in control or something else will slip.

The ladies worked quickly, apologizing for turning on the vacuum which I swished away with my hand.

They had the newspaper, still folded, tucked into my wastebasket, along with the broken plate and glasses. They replaced it with an identical wastebasket, bowed and exited my apartment.

I was famished but refreshed from the shower. It was time for action, but first, I needed to eat.

My CFO for Bone Frog Security was meeting me in an hour, but he'd arrived last night and was staying downtown. I picked up my phone and dialed him.

"Marco," he said. "I hope we're still on for—"

"Change of plans. This will be a breakfast meeting. Downstairs, in the dining room here at the Towers. I'm headed there now, so anytime you want to show up works for me."

"I was just about to step into the shower, so I'll be over in about fifteen minutes."

"That'll be fine."

The dull pause and heavy breathing on the other end of the line told me Frank Goodman felt apprehensive about the meeting. I knew he'd been sending his resume out, thinking that my change in financial fortune might cause me to cut back on non-essential personnel. It always amazed me how people could self-sort for a downsize. It hadn't been what I had planned to discuss today. But his behavior got my attention.

"Did you bring the reports I asked for?"

"Of course, Marco. It's quite a lot to digest."

"I'll bet." Fuckin Rebecca was good at looting. She was good at everything, including fucking me senseless. I hoped she would be a very sore loser, because it would be so much more pleasurable for me to watch her total meltdown. I wanted her destruction to be a public, ruthless event so that no one ever considered doing such a thing to me again. Yes, I knew that made me a hard man. But it also would make me bullet-proof.

"Well, Marco, see you in a few." His voice wavered with nervousness.

"Yes. You. Will. And by the way, will you join me for a Breakfast in Boston? It's some specialty drink the bartender makes here. I'm going to try one and want you to join me."

"Whatever you like, Marco."

"And I understand the bacon is specially cured, comes direct from a hog farm in Nebraska, too."

"Marco—I don't—"

"Oh, that's right. You eat Kosher."

"I try. If there is a reason I am to eat bacon, like are you considering purchasing a meat packing plant, I can justify some things, but…"

"No. Bacon for the greasy goodness of the fat sizzling in the pan. That kind of hickory-smoked bacon. I'll enjoy it alone, then. But you can drink."

"Yes, I can. But I usually—"

"Today is a new day, Frank. We're going to do a lot of things differently from now on. We have a lot of territory to cover, and the enemy has had a head start on us."

"Exactly. That's the Marco I knew would show up. And I'm greatly relieved to see it too, sir. We're taking no prisoners, is that right?" The timbre of his voice didn't match his words, but they were good words, nonetheless. It meant he was trying to keep up.

"You've got it. I hope you have the taste for war."

Frank didn't answer that one, which bothered me a little. I knew he wasn't a wartime CFO, but he was an excellent forensic accountant, which had been his job as a department head at the IRS for nearly twenty years before he joined my firm.

"See you shortly, Marco."

I scanned the cityscape, following cars traveling along the seaboard. This wasn't the commercial or shipping district more for tourists. A few regular sport fishing outfits and even a pirate ship for roaring drunken parties were docked and sparsely attended. Tugboats and tour ferries crammed into the harbor too. A steady stream of delivery trucks and caterers worked along the docks. A couple stainless steel breakfast burrito trucks honked and attracted workers from the nearby warehouses.

After one last check in the mirror, I headed downstairs, ready to do battle. It might have been my imagination, but I thought I could smell faint traces of her scent lingering still in the elevator. I guessed I was only the second or third person to use it after her early morning departure. It was nice lace on an otherwise steel-cut day.

I nodded to the bartender. He motioned me over.

"Everything okay? Was something not to your liking, Mr. Gambini?"

"No. It was the headline that bothered me some. Nothing to do with you."

"I want you to know I will re-create that breakfast for you if you'll take a seat."

"I'm meeting a colleague in the dining room. Make it two, but hold the bacon on his. And two Breakfast in Bostons please."

"You got it. Just have them seat you and I'll be right over with the drinks. And the envelope—do you need duplicate information? I can get another copy for you, if you need it."

"Yes, that will be good. Sealed again, like the first time."

"Yessir. Coming right up."

He spread his hand, palm up, out over the bar and Marco followed his direction to the small dining room. Even at nine in the morning, the lighting was dimmed and intimate.

Within minutes my refreshed Breakfast in Boston drink was sitting in front of me. Just as my biscuits and jam arrived, Frank Goodman walked into the dining room with his black briefcase in tow. I'd always thought he was a good-looking guy hiding behind those big glasses. He dressed so conservatively, nobody ever remembered him. I wondered what would make a man do that to himself.

He sat across the table from me, set his case on his knees and flipped open the brass locking devices with two loud clicks, releasing the top.

"Frank, Frank. Let's eat first. I'm sure we can delve into all the financials after we get something in our bellies," I said, stopping him.

He was flummoxed for just a second.

"It's going to be bad news, anyway. Have some biscuits, coffee, and this drink is to die for. A little orange juice and alcohol is needed to digest this stuff, right?"

He pushed his horn-rimmed glasses back on his nose, closed the case and tucked it beside his ankles under the table.

"Very well." He took his lay of the table, draped his lap with a linen napkin, chose a fluffy biscuit, and covered it with soft whipped cream cheese. Then he added blackberry jam.

"Really? Cream cheese and jam?" I asked him.

He hesitated before depositing the entire top half of the biscuit in his enormous mouth but smiled with lips closed as he consumed the warm delight, nodding. Covering his mouth, my CFO mumbled.

"Excuse me, Mr. Gambini, but it isn't often you get whipped cream cheese. I thought it could be butter at first, which would have worked just as well. Trust me, the combination is outstanding, assuming you don't have a hockey puck for a biscuit. These are fabulous."

I could barely understand him.

"They are," I said, matching his combination. "And I agree with your choice. I'm hooked on something new."

"No doubt you'll work it out in the gym later. I'll just keep adding it to my pregnancy," he said, patting his small but developing paunch.

The brew was not as pleasant as my Black Rifle coffee upstairs, but with the cream, was acceptable. I made a mental note to inform them I'd like the Towers to support my Veteran-owned coffee company friends.

"How was your trip up, Frank?"

"My dad used to take a room at the Seaton Arms years ago when he wanted to get away on business. But I think he really wanted to get away from my mom and all us kids. God knows what he was up to there. It was like deja-vu staying there last night. I thought I could even smell his old cigar smoke."

"Your father was a good man, Frank. As you know, he was one of my first investors. In those days, it meant a lot too."

"He was. And I miss him, that's for sure. I'm a better businessman today because of all his yelling and prodding he gave me over the years. He never liked that I worked for the IRS, until he had a big audit himself. And then he accused me of orchestrating it so he'd get off my back. But in the end, we both weathered the storm. He drilled that entrepreneurial spirit into me and trained out the wild side somehow. He was right. Made me a better man. You remind me a little of him, sir."

"Please, Frank, we are the same age. Don't call me sir. It makes me feel old, and I don't need to be reminded I'm not in my twenties. It's been how many years now? Let's not be that formal."

"No, I understand. Just showing some respect and wanted you to know how grateful I am to have a job with Bone Frog."

I figured that was a little cover his ass in case I knew about the resumes being sent out. He was smarter than he looked sometimes.

"Duly noted."

He finished off his Breakfast in Boston, and our waiter asked if he wanted another. He put up his palm, no, before checking in with me. He asked for scrambled eggs on the side, and watched as oatmeal was delivered to me, covered in strawberries.

"Wait. I'll have one of those," he changed his mind, pointing to my bowl.

"Very well, sir," the waiter answered and left without a sound.

"I slept like a baby last night. How about you, Marco?"

I smiled, but my stomach gurgled and my groin got hard just thinking about the delightful romp I'd had.

But right now I had raw meat between my teeth and I was ready to tear apart the animal who had caused me pain. Now wasn't the time for screwing or rising to new heights of pleasure. Now was the time for getting bloody, preparing for combat. I always carried my Glock, even when I was in cities where guns were outlawed. I had every license and clearance known to man to conceal carry. It would be like showing up naked to a cocktail party not to have my favorite sidearm, which had been with me longer than even my former wife.

We completed our breakfast and the table was cleared. Frank opened his briefcase and placed a sheaf of papers in front of me. Some were reports. Some were graphs attached to supporting documents. One was a subpoena.

"What's this?" I said, holding it up between my thumb and two fingers like it was a piece of dirty laundry.

"Came in last night just before I was leaving the office. By courier."

"Nice touch. Just before you're to come report to me. Who

leaked?"

"I think it was a coincidence, really. Your gal, Jennifer, seemed very surprised."

I glanced at the cover page. It was an order to appear and bring records, at Rebecca's attorney's office.

"When it comes to Rebecca, there are no coincidences," I said. "She shits on a timetable. I don't think she's been surprised since that fuck, she got at her daddy's horse ranch when she gave her virginity up to a man she thought was a crown prince who turned out to be a royal con man instead."

"Wow."

"Oh, don't be surprised. She grew up hard. Not a lot of love in that home."

"Well, that's harsh. I mean, sorry for her."

"She'd slit your throat if she heard you say that, so be careful."

Frank adjusted his tie, touching his neck right where the knife would go in smoothly for the kill, and looked at me warily. "Marco, you're going to have to make some tough decisions. What they're asking about is your construction project in Florida—the veteran-ownership venture, building homes for injured vets"

"Bone Frog Development. The Trident Towers project."

"Exactly."

"Makes perfect sense. She'd want to hit me where it hurt the most. Odd that she would go for a non-profit like that. I don't expect to make a dime. I'll probably lose my shirt on it. Why the hell would they care about that?"

"You're asking me? You were married to her. Anything I've heard would be just gossip."

I pushed the papers forward and leaned back in my chair, folding my hands together over my chest. Now we were getting to the good stuff. The truth.

"Try me."

"Excuse me?" His eyes were wide and his glasses slipped down his nose, needing to be pushed back again. From years of interrogating bad guys and judging tribal leaders as to whether or not they could be trusted, I saw the dilation in his pupils, along with a slight worry line crop up between his eyebrows. He knew he got caught.

"What have you heard? Spill it, Frank."

When a subject looks down at his hands with fingers locked together, I knew he was looking for a way out, a friendly hand to give him a solution to wiggle free.

He was out of luck.

I'd already been told he was saying to others he doubted I would survive the coming months. This was about whether or not I could trust him. I didn't begrudge his opinions, but I damn sure better get the truth to a direct ask. This was his chance to keep his job, if he still wanted it.

"I'm a numbers guy, Marco," he said as he raised his gaze to meet mine. He was fortunate he didn't look away as he spoke his truth. "I've seen all these things coming and going, and you're going to have a huge cash flow problem in a few months. All these audits and attorneys' fees are drying up your liquid, not to mention the settlements you've agreed to. And the public comments in the news, well, I've been asked by several people if they should start looking for work elsewhere. And, although I haven't heard it directly, some have said that the contracts have started to dry up. You know how the government works. They don't like controversy."

"Even though they specialize in it."

He kept his eyes locked on mine, thankfully. "Exactly. But even you have to admit, the numbers don't lie."

I leaned forward, placing my palms on the table, and then grabbed the paperwork to start reading over the fine print. I wasn't going to tell him not to worry, because he was right. The numbers were worse than I thought. I was going to have to study these and then give clear direction.

"Where would you suggest I begin?" I asked.

"I'd sell off one of the entities. The airline, the shipping company, or the leasing agency. I'd boost your personnel security contracts since they are the most lucrative, and frankly, they are the most vulnerable. You might consider using some of your sales to hire a Washington PR company."

"I've never had one before. You think it's wise to do that now? Start a new project?"

He shrugged. "You need to protect your personal connections with your higher ups. You need those contracts. It's the fuel that makes everything else run smoothly. Your friendship with the Vice President, the Secretary of State—you need to make sure they are solid."

He was right. I needed to reassure myself things were that bad, first.

"And," Frank started, placing his hands on the table. "I know you've never considered this, but it would be a good idea to cultivate some contracts with the Kingdoms."

"No. No non-US."

"But Clearwater and Red Dog are making big inroads into that," he argued.

"You don't know their numbers, Frank, or do you?"

"No, sir—Marco. I don't. I have nothing to go by except what I see in the papers, and the contract bulletins."

"And you don't know the casualties they are suffering, do you?"

"No, Marco."

"They put their men and women in bad places. I won't do that. I don't care how bad ass we are. I won't do that."

He leaned back in the chair, and I knew there was something else.

"What is it?"

"Yesterday, I got a call from Senator Campbell. He asked me point blank if you were interested in meeting with a delegation from the Kingdom of Bonin. They have just signed on to bankroll a housing project in North Africa. They are going to need security for their royal family as they negotiate and follow-up on these projects."

"So? I'll meet with them, but I've never had to take one of those jobs before. I usually collect a referral fee and send it to someone else."

"I understand, but Senator Campbell said he was hesitant to refer them to you. He had questions. He asked me if your recent setbacks had caused you to lose your nerve."

I was ready to toss the paperwork, the table and all four chairs out the large window overlooking the bustling street outside.

Hadn't Frank ever heard the term, "Don't shoot the messenger?"

CHAPTER 4

Shannon

I WAITED TWO days before flying home to St. Pete. My body still rumbled—shaking, really, from the insides of my core all the way to my toes. I'd stepped into forbidden territory, yet something was so satisfying about it, I was a moth to the flame. It might destroy me, but I'd accomplished what I set out to do, and now, unexpectedly, I wanted more. So much more.

After Emily's death, Mom and Dad moved to Florida once I left for college a few years later. They joined an active adult community in order to fill that horrible void left with Em's passing. I was grateful the burden didn't fall on me, because I was also reeling from my older sister's untimely death. Those were strange years, finishing up high school and then applying to colleges with as much direction as a rudderless boat. The house had been so quiet without her. My mother rarely smiled, and my dad drank more. Never one for many words anyway, he retreated into a darkness that was so black it threatened to take me with it.

I became invisible. I never knew how much light Emily shed on our family until that radiance was extinguished. I was careful not to upset my parents, and they tried very hard to shield me from the hurt and pain they were feeling and could not help but show. It was a standoff with no winners.

I finished my degree in California, at Sonoma State, in communications and started exploring my options for future television work, which had been my long-term goal. I learned how to look and act professionally and took on an acting coach. A small low-budget indie film even cast me, giving me screen credits only. I modeled some, but when I was encouraged to go to near-starvation levels to get my weight down, and I refused. Plus-sized jobs started booking me, even though I was normal weight. My self-esteem plummeted and at my lowest, had an affair with my drama teacher in college. That lasted until his marriage broke up over his affair with another student.

I vowed that would never happen again to me. It was not a part of my life I felt very proud of. Lesson learned.

But it whetted my appetite for older men.

Em would have married Marco Gambini if she hadn't been killed in that car accident that took her life with three of her sorority sisters'. My mother and I had hoped the accident would curtail my father's drinking, because the drunk who hit them walked away with just a broken nose. He got some jail time, but not enough to satisfy our revenge and anger.

And that brought the other heartache into my life. Marco Gambini, my older sister's fiancé, was my imaginary lover, my girl-crush, the man I compared every other man to when I dated. I guess he could even be considered a father figure since my father became a mere ghost, albeit a ghost who played golf every day and liked to sit and watch my mother play Bunko and Pinochle. After the funeral, I never saw Marco again, until two days ago when I walked into the Bachelor Towers, took up a seat, and became my sister for one whole night. It was a gift to myself, something I think Em would have approved of if I'd had the ability to ask her. I needed to know I could play for keeps with a man like that.

I walked away knowing that it didn't work that way. He wasn't a man like that. He was the only man in the universe for me. My teenage radar had been spot on. He was a keeper.

Now I had a problem.

So when Marco didn't call, I knew I had to go back to the beach retreat I'd purchased with my own savings, the little one-bedroom place painted bright yellow with turquoise trim, nestled in the bluffs overlooking the white sugar-sand beach of the Florida gulf coast.

Some might judge me, and they should be careful. I've never been the girl to resurrect my dead sister's life to make it my own. That's not me. I needed to revive my own life, not Em's. Sort of my right of passage.

Call it my empathetic nature, but I knew I could help heal his wounds, temporarily. For one night. For one night, I could pretend that the confluence of events between us had never happened. That we had no history. I wasn't looking for a future. I was looking to bury the past once and for all.

Everything about him was familiar. His scent, the way he smiled, kissed. The way his fingers explored. The little grunts and deep grumbles in his chest, even his whispers and sighs as I rose for him, bloomed for him, showed him my insides—that place I'd never shown anyone else. Oh, I wasn't a virgin, by any means. But I was new to love, to what Em had in her life. I had begged for just one taste of him, and now I would be tainted forever.

Did it bother me he never called me back?

I didn't expect it. I suspected he wouldn't.

Would I try to chase him, duplicate that night of passion again?

I told myself that, no, that wasn't the agreement I'd made with my better angels. With Em. With him, even though he was completely unaware of it.

Did I expect he'd recognize Em in my eyes?

I wasn't sure, but I'd hoped not. They were my eyes needing his examination and determined lovemaking. It was my body he pleasured, that I gave to him. It was for and about me. And I would be forever grateful, even as the remembrance of that night would leave me breathless, haunted, and wet for weeks. Possibly months or even years. I might never find that intensity again. But there was one ground rule I would never break.

I would never chase him. I found him. One time. Now it would be up to him and only him, to go beyond that. As my female parts recovered from the long night of lovemaking, the ache inside remained.

Only way to deal with it was to call it delicious, rare, and tuck it away in my wine cellar of experiences where it would remain a vintage release consumed sparingly.

After all, a good wine was meant to be enjoyed, not stored forever. That's exactly what I did.

THE TAMPA INTERNATIONAL Airport was a dose of reality that came on me like a firehose. Retirees flocked in groups as tour operators collected them all with brightly colored guide signs held high above their heads. Families were reunited. Young couples arrived to join the throngs at the Gulf Coast beaches. Businessmen in suits sweated under the heat, unaccustomed to the humidity. Children ran around everywhere, and pets were released from their crates.

I passed long lines of passengers waiting to escape from the Florida sun or begin their trip home after a vacation. It was a bustling society of everyone coming from and heading to different places, and for a moment in time, all residing within the confines of the terminals spilling out into the hot parking garages or hotel passenger vans.

I retrieved my one bag, then found my car in long term parking, and headed for the refuge of the coast.

My shoulders relaxed the closer I got to the water's edge. Just before I arrived at Beach Trail Road and the driveway leading up to my little beach bungalow, my phone rang.

"Judie. I'm back, almost at the house. How has everything been?"

My best friend reminded me so much of my big sister Emily, it was uncanny. She had been the one who found Marco's headlines and placed those news printouts on my desk in my cubby.

"You know, sunny with a chance of rain. They hired and fired a new intern…"

"Already? That's got to be a record."

"I think so. Apparently, her dress attire was not appropriate. It got her the job, but it's what got her fired."

"Oh, I get it now. Clarence."

Clarence Thompson was our evening anchor personality, complete with hair plugs and makeup, even when he wasn't on the air. He was getting long in the tooth, with habits that weren't aging well with the female population at TMBC. It was only a matter of time before he'd be forced out by a sexual harassment lawsuit. But this train wreck of a man just couldn't keep his hands and his mouth under control.

"Fucking Clarence. The cat that ate the canary."

"The one and only. So, Shannon, mission accomplished? Did you meet him?"

I hadn't told her everything I was planning, and now I was glad I hadn't.

"Yup. He's still as handsome as I remember. A real gentleman, too," I lied.

I could still hear the words he growled over me, "I love fucking you." My badge of honor. I nearly came in my car seat just re-calling how he commanded my body while I was powerless to refuse him anything. In my mind I told him to fuck me harder, take me from behind, from the side, upside down if he wanted to. I could still feel his grip on my hips almost to the point of bruis-ing, clutching me tight as he skillfully drilled me a new meaning of the word *fuck*.

I checked my rear-view mirror as I pulled into my driveway.

Yup, I had perspiration on my upper lip. Good thing Judie couldn't see the flush on my cheeks too.

"So did you tell him who you were?"

"Not on your life."

"So that's it? You met him, what, and then walked away?"

I saw myself hanging off the bed as he buried his face in my crotch. I could feel the smooth grey carpet with my fingertips, my back arched, my knees bent and spread wide for him. I didn't walk away. I *floated* away. I vibrated all the way down the elevator. If I'd bumped into anyone, we would have both burst into flames, with how hot I was.

"Yes, I met him, and left my phone number. If he wants to see me, he'll call. But the next step is up to him. I just wanted to meet him and not have him feel obligated to talk to me because of Em. And he didn't figure it out. Like I said, he was a real gentleman."

I had him in my mouth as his fingers lazily messed my hair in all directions. I pretended to hear him whisper, "Oh, sweetheart," which of course didn't really happen. But I got him harder again after our second or third round, and he showed his appreciation thoroughly afterwards.

"You surprise me, Shannon. From all the talk—"

"What do you take me for, Judie?"

Again, my lies were making me a bit careless. But I couldn't help thinking he'd recognize the scent of my body, too, if I were to casually pass him by in some hallway. That he'd be moved to slip me into a broom closet or bathroom for something dangerous and quick.

I was every bit the slut she was thinking of. I was desperate to prove it too.

No, something had been unleashed, and things were never going to be the same again. But that had been what I was looking for all along. I walked around like a marionette, my wrists and ankles tied with invisible golden threads pulling me back to Boston where I would watch the twinkle lights of the city until I could no longer focus.

Judie paused. "You're kinda breathing hard, Shannon. Are you okay?"

"Never better."

CHAPTER 5

Marco

I TOOK TWO days, reviewing the numbers carefully, and could see how Frank would come to the conclusion I needed to unload one of my entities in order to save the rest. My net worth was *less* than half what it had been before the divorce and resulting proceedings, something I hadn't wanted to look at in black and white until now, but the biggest problem was that my much-needed cash flow had been consumed with legal fees and other restructuring necessary to protect me and the rest of my assets. All that would be on-going. And now she wanted the Florida project, the one entity that wasn't going to make me money, but was the one thing I felt the most passionately about: getting homes for disabled Navy SEALs.

I scoured the balance sheets, searched my records for details he'd given me online, backing up the summaries he'd presented. I looked for a flaw in his analysis.

I didn't find one.

As I'd learned from my training, I began coming up with a plan by first filling out the knowns and identifying the huge gaps and unknowns before coming up with the plan I could dive feet first into. The list was growing the more I brainstormed. Prioritizing the most important, I began checking off the items as fast as I could re-allocate them, sometimes even changing their value. We used to do this all the time on the Teams, checking and re-checking targets and assets, evaluating and re-evaluating methods and task details. A successful mission was all about identifying the strategy needed so we wouldn't have to think—we could just execute the plan. And all of it was always heavily dependent on the quality of the information used to create the plan in the first place. That's what I was going for. Accuracy. Facts. Looking for problems and potential pitfalls so nothing would be unaccounted for.

I spoke to several department heads and called a board meeting in D.C. for early next week, when I hoped to have a decision made so I could announce our new direction. I needed to touch base with my attorney about the new subpoena. I toyed with the idea of flying down to Florida to meet with the non-profit group working on the housing project, just to take their temperature and perhaps warn them.

The comment Senator Campbell made bothered me, and I knew shirking that phone call would be a mistake. My heart and my gut weren't up to it, but I manned up and dialed his personal number.

"Hey, Marco. Long time no hear. You still got all your arms and legs intact?"

I had been trained never to show emotion, so, even on the phone I wasn't going to wince because I knew he'd hear it in my voice.

"I picked her for all the wrong reasons, Senator. Thing is, I can admit a mistake when I've made one, and this one was colossal. But not fatal. You know what they say about a wounded bear?"

Campbell had a belly laugh at that one. "Glad to say I don't share your experience, Marco, knock on wood. Beth and I have been happily married for nearly twenty-four years." He paused carefully, taking in a deep breath. "Frank told me about your meeting on Tuesday, and he mentioned he brought up my offer to make introductions to the sultan of Bonin. He said you might consider speaking with him."

"I am willing to listen. No promises."

"Of course. I think he's been around long enough to understand this. But he is rather persistent and insisted that the two of you discuss your mutual futures *in person.*"

I suspected the sultan was a heavy contributor to the senator's re-election campaign. Whatever mutual future there was between the sultan and I would no doubt include the senator as well.

"As I said, no promises. But yes, I'll speak with him."

"Good. That's good, Marco. I know you are busy, but when can I tell him you'd be available and are you willing to travel?"

It would be far easier for me to travel with a small contingent than for the sultan to come with his harem, his princelings and several of his grandchildren. I could slip in and out easier than he ever could, so our meeting could truly be done in secret. I agreed to let the senator arrange a meeting at one of the sultan's properties, a luxurious palace on one of the islands in the Indian Ocean. Once when I was still on the Teams, we had helped with a sweep of the grounds when a suspected terrorist was smuggled there. We captured the bastard in a storage closet inside sultan's enormous kitchen. The terrorist saved us a lot of time and trouble, too, since his interrogation was done in secret aboard a Naval vessel nearby.

I could arrange the transportation, thereby ensuring my safety, if the sultan could agree to the airdrop and the exact timing. Senator Campbell promised to get back to me within twenty-four hours. I asked him for permission to use Naval assets if need be for landing and he said he'd arrange it.

Checking contract scheduling, I noticed I had Little Bird, my pet nickname for one of my favorite little Sikorskys, safely stored in the Maldives. That might give me some luck with Diego Garcia friendlies, and besides, the Navy owed me some serious favors. If I could piggyback, an Indian Ocean meeting was entirely possible and wouldn't require much in the way of expense.

So I was boxing myself in, fixing myself up not to be able to say no, since Senator Campbell had some enviable Armed Services creds. But more importantly, his wife was the younger sister of the First Lady, which had even more weight.

Barely four hours went by before I was contacted by "Harry", the sultan's gay bastard son, born of a favorite harem girl and never in line to the throne, partly because of his birth lineage but most certainly due to his sexual preferences. I'd worked with him before. He'd grown up as close to an American kid as possible, even attended NYU film school while living with his mother in a purchased brownstone in Brooklyn Heights. The sultan hired him right out of college to be his social secretary and trusted the kid with his life. In return, the son lived a lavish lifestyle he'd have never had and promised he'd never disrespect his father.

"Well, Marco, I guess we'll be working together again. My father is most anxious to get caught up."

"I'll bet. So, which one of your idiot brothers is heading the project in Africa?" I asked. Harry, short for Hanarabi, and I had always been on close terms, not dissimilar to how I used to joke with my Teammates.

"Oh, that would be Khalil and Absalom. You know they both graduated with advanced degrees in engineering and architecture at MIT."

"How many buildings did that cost the sultan?"

"No, I think there might have been some help, but they earned it on their own, with some extra tutoring, of course. But it was earned fair and square, just how you like it."

I got the dig about me being the square one, but let it go. I didn't like the joke, but he had to put up with a lot of stuff from me in the past, too.

"Glad to hear it. I was afraid they'd be tossed before they could finish."

"Hardly, Uncle Marco," Harry resurrected the name I'd not heard for over five years. "They were way more serious about their studies and their legacy than I ever was. I'm still looking to make my directorial debut."

"Which means your father has turned you down another dozen times."

"Quite right. He isn't into a gay West Side Story." He sighed. "But in the meantime, all this work takes the place of the bright lights on the marquee in Times Square. Someday, if my father doesn't manage to live to be a hundred like his father, I might actually get a chance!"

"In his line of work, that's a good thing, Harry."

"You mean being sultan?"

"I know men who would consider it a full-time job to keep all those women happy in your father's stable. And I mean him no disrespect, Harry."

"Oh, I get it. But he pays to play. Look at all the family he supports. So now he wants to see my brothers become successful businessmen, something he was not allowed to do by his own father."

"Do they know?"

"Do they know what? Oh! That I am their brother? Oh heaven's no! There are always palace rumors, but nothing he can't quickly quash. My mother's life would be in danger, and she has no protection."

"So he's still kept that golden leash on you."

"Oh, Marco, you know I love the man. He's always been good to us. I am a devoted sycophant, and he knows he can trust me with his life. I don't think he'd say the same about any of his wives."

"Bingo. Women are complicated. I learned that lesson the hard way."

"I've heard."

I knew they'd have done their research before reaching out. "So you have the dates and the arrangements figured out?"

"I have them coming to you over a secure link, encrypted with your mother's birthdate added to the date of your wedding."

"Grrr..." They really had stepped up their game.

"Oh, stop it, Uncle Marco. She can't be *that* bad. You were with her for a long time."

"Too long. Tell me she hasn't made any contact with him."

"Haven't heard a peep. So you'll be coming alone or is there a new Mrs. Gambini in the wings?"

"I'm solo. Probably going to be that way for the remainder."

"So we're more alike than you realized, Uncle Marco."

"Watch it, kid."

We wrapped up, and several minutes later I got the encrypted files giving me the time, place and several letters of permission and introduction to any of the government entities I might have to deal with to travel.

At the bottom of the document was a figure the sultan was offering, which I knew I could bump up if I needed to. But it was a figure that would pay for all my business expenses for the next three years.

I smiled, not at the number, but at the idea that I didn't have to share one penny of that with Rebecca.

If I took the job, of course.

CHAPTER 6

Shannon

T HE NEWSROOM BUZZED with local discussions and issues related to voter registration and challenges to politicians running in various runoff elections and pivots for posturing in the next general election, which was thankfully several months away. Of course, weather was more important as residents of the greater Tampa area and beach communities planned their vacations, their fishing trips and outdoor events.

I allowed the makeup artist to finish, curling my hair and doing a soft blowout, when I removed the drape and stepped into the green screen. I demonstrated that the next hurricane would be heading west of us, heading right up the middle of the Gulf to land perhaps on New Orleans or Galveston, and not anywhere near my sleepy beach bungalow. I gracefully pointed to the string of "recruits" as I called them, lined up to run in and wreak havoc right behind Hurricane Eloise. Everyone was praying that Eloise would change her temperament and become a tropical storm. I told my audience that I was hoping she'd be a good girl, and winked. The Program Director gave me a wide smile in return, followed by a thumbs up.

Of course, I couldn't get off the stage fast enough to avoid bumping into Clarence Thompson, who pretended he didn't see me. It gave him a change to feel my tits with the flabby upper chest of his. If his hands had been used to stop his forward momentum, I was prepared to slap him. Hard.

Luckily, Clarence was creepy, but somewhat on his better behavior. Besides, there were ten sets of eyes staring right at both of us.

"Shannon, glad you made it back to our beautiful little paradise. How was Boston?"

I was surprised he knew anything about where I was going.

"Colder," I said, making sure it sounded that way too.

He blushed pink from my subtle insult and then broke out in a wide smile. "Well, we're all very glad you're back. Things are just never the same when you're gone." He had placed his palm over his heart. He should have just been honest and grabbed his dick.

I imagined the scent, the feel of Marco's strong body on top of me, beneath my undulating hips, and how he made me feel. I took secret pride in the knowledge that this cretin couldn't take any of that beautiful memory away from me. It would forever be my secret, the most valuable thing I owned, at least for right now.

I ignored the comment and walked back to the green room for something to drink, awaiting my next performance. The room was plastered with big screens—which not only showed the content of tonight's broadcast in three sizes, but several other news channels'. The mix of national and cable kept us current.

One of the stories a competing station showed was on the housing project Marco Gambini had started in Belleair Beach and how there was some concern the project would no longer be built, due to complications resulting from Marco's recent financial setbacks, without mentioning the contentious divorce. I walked closer to the screen with my water bottle as the newscaster played a quick clip of Rebecca Gambini's interview done earlier that day. I observed the woman with new appreciation for what a mismatch she was for him, and it made me smile.

"Yes, well, there have been some restructuring measures taking place at the present time. Some of the Bone Frog Industries projects have been sadly neglected, and I'm rushing in to see what I can do to rescue them," she said, her lying eyes trying to look all wide and doe-like. I knew exactly what kind of poison brewed in her belly, and I said a secret prayer that those acids would become lethal.

The interviewer asked her a question. "Forgive me, but wasn't this a project your former husband had been working on alone? So now you've been given authority to carry the ball, so to speak?"

Rebecca clearly didn't like that comment and glared at the young interviewer. She throttled the microphone placed toward her, squeezed her fingers over the young woman's, leaned in, and said, "It's called *fruits of the marriage*, Gaylee. I'm passionate about this work and how it is to go forward, so that's why I'm here." She outstretched her many-ringed and diamond-encrusted fingers with the bright red nail polish, motioning over the vacant lot that had five acres of palm trees cut down behind her.

The woman was here! She was in this area, spreading her venom all around her. I shouldn't have been surprised.

This gave me an idea.

MY PROGRAM DIRECTOR, Jared Newsome, was shutting down his office when I arrived after my third weather report. His warm, handsome face didn't hide his appreciation that I'd graced his doorway.

"All done tonight?"

"You know I am."

He shrugged. "Care to join me for a cocktail? You can tell me about your trip."

Why was everyone at the station riveted on my personal life?

"No, thanks. I appreciate it, but I'm going to lay low for a few days and get my land legs back. I really don't like flying."

"Really?" He gave me a quick look over and then shut his eyes tight. "I'm sorry. That was—"

"What I would have thought too," I answered for him. "And no, it's not a sexual thing like they say. I'm just tired from the travel and being jammed into small spaces. I always get this way when I come back from a trip."

"Of course. So what's up?" He closed his laptop, pushed it into his padded case, tucked his rolling chair into his desk, and came around to stand in front of me. I could tell he was going to ask me again, and again I would be turning him down. But I liked him. I genuinely liked him, and I was hoping that we could maintain the good friendship and trust I felt we had together. I considered him sort of a mentor. "You've not been looking for greener pastures, have you?"

Now I understood his concern. He was wondering if I'd interviewed at the larger Boston market. It would be an obvious step-up in my career, although perhaps a bit soon.

"No, Jared. You don't have to worry about anything like that. I'm extremely grateful for everything you're doing for me here at the station. I'm not looking."

Well, it wasn't a lie. I wasn't looking for a new job, at least.

"Okay, that's a relief. We think you fit in nice here. We'd certainly hope you feel the same way."

"I do, Jared."

"Clarence isn't bothering you too much, I hope."

"You don't have to worry about that. If he comes on to me, I know how get rid of him, as I've continually done since I started. I don't blame him, even though you know I don't like him very much. He's wired up wrong. He's like a dog you want to rescue but he keeps biting the hand that feeds him. He's his own worst enemy, and I honestly don't think he'll stop until he does something big."

"Very astute and mature of you, Shannon."

"He's *your* problem, Jared."

"So we aren't going to have a drink, Clarence is minding himself for now. You aren't looking for a job. Why are we talking here?"

He was good at getting right down to things. That gave me courage.

"You know I've always wanted to do more things related to the news, not just weather. And I have a couple of ideas about stories I'd like to pursue, with your permission. I don't want to give up my weather duties, but I'd like to tackle a real news story."

I could see he was intrigued. His eyes sparkled as he studied my face. I found it difficult to look him straight in the eyes because I wanted this so bad. Finally I looked up and decided to just go for it. All he could say was no, anyway.

"I watched in the green room about Rebecca Gambini's trip out here to assume duties related to the Navy SEAL housing project that was proposed at Belleair Beach. I think I could do a kickass interview of the woman, her plans, and her position on this. It has a lot of human interest, not only because of the divorce but the need for housing for these Navy heroes. Plus, this project would impact the local economy. It has all the earmarks of a series of special reports. I'd like to help her champion it a little bit."

Jared rolled back on his heels. I could tell he'd never considered this coming from my mouth.

"You've really thought about this, haven't you?"

"I have."

"Do you have any special insight?" His eyes looked unremarkably calm so I didn't suspect anything Judie and I had discussed. I decided to deflect a bit.

"I might need your introduction to her. I don't know her. But I think she'd like another story. The last interviewer got several things wrong, and I can tell she perhaps offended the woman. I don't think I would do that."

I hoped that my insides didn't give me away. And I really had no ulterior motive with the interviews. I was just a moth to the flame, powerless to walk away from an opportunity, even though my better judgment was nudging me in the gut. I didn't care. I had to try this, just like I had to meet Marco after all these years. I just couldn't stay away, seeing as how she flew right into my neighborhood as if it had been predestined.

"You might have something there, Shannon. I agree that there's a story under all that drama. Made for someone with some considerable journalistic chops, though. Are you sure you want to step into the fire pit?"

"Are you saying you don't think I can handle it?"

"Oh, I think you could handle the interview well enough. But I'm wondering how you'll handle Clarence or some of the other groupies trying to claw their way up the ladder. You could become part of the story, you know, if it doesn't go well. Are you prepared to become part of the drama? Really?"

I was shaking, brimming with excitement. He was at the edge of letting me do what I'd dreamt of doing.

Was this really happening?

"I'll say you warned me. But one thing is for sure. If it goes badly, you'll not only have a weather girl, you'd have somewhat of a celebrity. How bad would that be for ratings?"

Jared chuckled, studying his shoes.

"Shannon, I wish you'd let me buy you a drink…"

"No."

"You'd give up this chance?"

"I won't do it for a drink with you. That's not how I work. If it's no, it's no. If it's yes, then it's a solid, no-holds-barred yes."

I watched the softness in his eyes, the way he licked his lips and studied mine. He wanted me. I didn't shirk from showing him I knew. But the answer was still no. Sure, I could cajole him, have a good time and make myself believe I could convince him with my sexual prowess. Then he'd pretend he hadn't lost all respect for me, just like he'd lost any respect for any other woman to take advantage that way. And he'd hate himself too. And me.

It would be easy with him, because he was attractive and he wasn't begging, just leaving the door open. But I wanted more than that. I wanted the chance to earn something on my terms. I wanted to prove to myself, to the part of Em that still lingered all around me, that I was ready to step into the real world. I could sing at the top of my lungs, a full-on opera singer who had hidden her talent.

It was time to take the gloves off.

"Then it's a yes. God help me, Shannon, but I believe in you. If it doesn't work out, then can we have that drink?" He winked at me, standing a little too close.

"Ask me when it's over, Jared. Don't ask me now."

"Okay, then. I'll make some calls and see if I can get you an interview. Go prove me a discoverer of brilliant talent, Shannon. Make me proud. Take that brass ring all the way to the bank. I'll cover where I can, if I'm needed."

"Thank you." I could have kissed him easily.

I gave him a flirtatious smile instead and slipped out of his office and back into the bullpen where I could breathe at last.

ALL THE WAY home, my body buzzed. I listened to country music then switched it to New Age then classical. I held my head high, and imagined the To Do list I'd stay up half the night to complete. I wanted to list all the questions I'd ask her. I wouldn't mention Marco. I'd wait for her to do it, and then I'd ask for more information.

By the time I reached my bungalow, a worry had slipped into my head. What would I do if Marco saw the interview and remembered me? What would he think about me stalking him in Boston and inserting myself in his affairs in Tampa? If he sought me out, would I even be able to answer that question?

"I don't know," I said out loud.

But then storm clouds began to lift. I was standing on the beach all of a sudden, long after sunset, feeling the glow of what once was. The sky cleared and all that was left was the heat generating from a full moon at my back. I didn't even remember locking my car, unlocking my house, slipping on my sweats and flip flops, and making it outside to the fresh air and the beach. It was almost like I'd floated here.

It felt like a crossroads, a point of no return.

Was Em behind all this, weaving a tale and cinching me down with those golden cords of hers? Was this her way of living inside my body somehow while he pleasured me? It was ridiculous for me to consider.

It was even more ridiculous to doubt that there wasn't some sentient being out there making it all happen.

Maybe I better start going back to church.

CHAPTER 7

Marco

MY ADMINISTRATIVE TEAM readied for the big meeting in D.C. that was to come in just two days. I informed who would be accompanying me to the Pink Pasha, the sultan's palace on his private island, and we discussed logistics and security issues. Ryan would travel over to inspect the Sikorsky, which hadn't been flown in thirty days and would needed to be re-checked. He'd remain there until our mission details were finalized.

Our online call, which began at four A.M. due to where my team was stationed all over the world, was productive, and we covered a lot of ground. I managed to cross nearly everything off my agenda list, which always brightened my day.

I created a flurry of phone calls, mostly leaving voicemails that would be answered when people arrived at their desks in the US, setting into motion new restructuring plans and reviewing upcoming contracts, bids in the pipeline, contract negotiation procedures and strategies for the next several months. I needed a breather, so I took a break and went for a run.

I always think best while moving, so used this thinking time to get acquainted with the downtown and Harbor areas in Boston. My run through the city was still in the early morning hours before the commute started—my favorite time of day. I returned to my suite, took a shower, dug into more paperwork, and answered phone calls.

Later, I took a late lunch and frequented a couple of favorite haunts I'd been told about and swept through several modern art galleries on my way back to the Towers. I found stimulation in the colorful abstract artwork, my favorite being Italian fusion art glass.

I wanted to plunk down my platinum card, prepared to purchase every piece in that little gallery, since my bare walls at the Towers were driving me crazy. Instead I hesitated, purchasing just one large abstract instead. It reminded me of a woman's nude torso, a sensuous view from the rear. I had a perfect spot for it— right over my bed.

It was everything I could do to stop from having the gallery concierge throw in half a dozen other matching pieces and a bronze I liked to fondle. Being sensitive about my funding dilemma pissed me off, but I stuffed it back down, planning to use it as fuel for the bonfire I was building under Rebecca's reputation and comfortable lifestyle.

Did that make me a dangerous man?

I hoped so.

One of my Manhattan bankers asked me to stop in at a local Eastern Bank & Trust to review and sign papers, authorizing a transfer of funds that usually happened later in the month. I decided to set it up so that in the future these could happen automatically up to certain limits, but I did wonder why this was coming so soon in the month.

The Bank & Trust office was sterile, just like I found most banks. I remembered the first time I went in to get a loan as a newbie frog. They turned me down—and not nicely, either. Funny thing how banks don't like a lax attitude toward making car payments. That first red Mustang I bought had burned a hole in my credit as fast as it gobbled gas driving up the California coastline in those days.

The next time, a year later, I walked in with Rebecca on my arm. Maybe she was the magic sauce that made it all happen, but that day, we walked out with the promise of being able to buy something in Coronado. It was to be our forever house, until kids.

And that never happened either.

I still owned that house—paid it off in record time. Oddly enough, she'd left it behind, just like I did with our wedding pictures, in the divorce settlement, almost as if she'd forgotten about it. Since most of my operations were on the East Coast, I didn't use it very often and, instead, had someone run a VRBO, which made some cash that I had stashed in a savings account for a rainy day. Selling that house would net me a cool couple of million, as if that would solve all my financial problems. Otherwise, I'd liquidate it in a heartbeat since the place meant nothing to me.

It was a lush little corner lot with a beach access trail, but no water views. I'd expunged all my memories of how it made me feel to own my first home—to plant palm trees and things in the yard I could go back to in fifty years as an old man and see them standing tall and invincible—just like how I felt at the time.

A little tweak of regret stabbed my stomach as I thought about those days of being drunk on sex and running around being a Boy Scout with my buddies on the Teams. The whole world had been my theater, doing things no one would ever believe, having more fun than I had a right to and coming home to a woman who liked to screw hard and was just as intense as I was. I was a God then, a force for good.

When did it all change? When did life get so dark and difficult?

But I still was that force for good as I left the Teams and started my passion for business, protecting the innocent and getting paid a lot of money for it. It was just on a larger scale. With more at stake. And solo. Maybe that was how it was supposed to be all along. God sure kicked my butt to remind me I was just a dumb frog at heart. Being a billionaire was just a trapping, an extra piece of equipment to strap on and enjoy for a few moments of my life.

Because that's how it turned out to be. And it would be that way again.

Today, I sort of felt just the same as I did fifteen-plus years ago when I first walked into a bank and got my ass handed to me. No one had to remind me I wasn't in a position of strength and these new "clothes" I was wearing somehow didn't fit to my liking. But I told myself it was only temporary.

Story of my life.

Serena Bolton was the vice president's secretary. She wore a brightly colored yellow and fuchsia dress which belied this time of year in Boston. Her dreadlocks were pulled up on top of her head, woven with yellow satin ribbons, making a striking pattern of rows and zigzags. Occasionally, a tiny pink flower would poke through. Her skin was as dark as the macadam roads I traveled on by taxi, deliciously highlighted with her bright pink lipstick and purple eyeshadow. She resembled one of my Italian fusion glass pieces and was just as lovely to look at.

"Mr. Cullen is waiting for you inside, Mr. Gambini. If you'll just follow me, please."

I sauntered under a large second-story balcony with glass partitioned offices above. She tapped on the vice president's door and I watched my intended target push back his wire rimmed glasses, straighten his jacket, stand, and come to the door. He held out a beefy hand, stubby fingers splayed.

"Mr. Gambini, nice to meet you. Welcome to Boston."

"Thank you, sir," I replied.

He waddled to his seat while motioning to his secretary to return to the lobby area from which we came. He sat down with an audible crunch, directing me to sit across the desk in the single, wooden and very Spartan-looking chair. I noted that most of his meetings were intended to be short and uncomfortable. I girded my loins.

"It's been brought to my attention that we have some cross-collateralization issues, Mr. Gambini. Most of this coming from your recent, unfortunate separation." He frowned into the paperwork in front of him in one very neatly piled file about a half inch thick. It wasn't lost on me that "unfortunate" wouldn't be the proper word for this and could cut two ways. Did he mean unfortunate to be divorced, because I felt freed? Or did he mean unfortunate because of what it had gutted from me and my businesses? I decided to ask.

"*Unfortunate* is a relative term, Mr. Cullen. I assure you, the best is yet to come. This was just a matter of pruning and tidying up." I tried to sound confident.

He wasn't buying it.

"I'd say it rather looked like having to give up one of your children, Mr. Gambini."

"Which, luckily, I don't have."

"Lucky for them as well, wouldn't you say?"

He'd just smacked me, and I was resisting the urge to see how flabby that belly of his actually was.

"I'd call it a haircut with a dull blade, Mr. Cullen. She was a bitch."

I decided to see what kind of metal he was made out of. His single eyebrow-raising gesture told me he didn't approve of my disparaging a woman. I normally didn't either, unless she deserved it. Rebecca certainly did.

"As you say, she could be, but she has a smart lawyer. I'd be careful who you go expounding your feelings to, Mr. Gambini."

He was a poser, and I salivated to dig my teeth into him.

"Is that a threat, Mr. Cullen? While we're being so helpful to one another, can I suggest you not say things like that to me? I could easily do business with someone else."

And then I felt brilliant as I saw the fear cross his face.

I stood up. "Don't answer that," I said to him, holding out my palm to his seated form. "I've just made my twentieth executive decision of the day. You can call Mr. Halliday in my accounting department and tell them you've gotten your bank fired."

He hadn't been prepared for this and started to stutter.

"With me, it only takes once. I don't give second chances, and I don't like threats. In case you didn't know, you just issued one."

I left.

It took me thirty seconds to catch a taxi. I'd just gotten seated when Frank dialed me.

"Not here—I'm in a cab," I barked.

"Marco, have him wait. Step outside so I can have a conversation with you." He sounded serious, with a dash of panic on the side.

"Just tell me, dammit."

As we sped toward the Towers I learned that there had been a call on one of my loans and cash was needed to keep the bank from foreclosing on me. My commercial dealings in Florida had been compromised by the recent filing of an injunction against the housing project on the beach for old frogs. Calling around, my CFO had only located one bank willing to extend me a line of credit, based on my reputation and personal guarantee.

And I'd just pissed off that one bank willing to help me out.

"Just go back in there and tell him you made a mistake. It was a misunderstanding," Frank told me. I could tell he was pissed.

"Not on your life. Bankers get rich not by saying yes but by saying no as much as they can to cover all the bad yesses they make. I'm not going to give that sonofabitch the satisfaction."

"Marco, you have to face the facts."

"Fact is, Frank, I'm swimming with alligators, but I don't have to become a fuckin' yellow-finned tuna in the middle of the swamp."

"Yellow-finned tuna don't live in the swamp."

"My point exactly. I wouldn't make him that lucky and bestow on him such a miracle. Let him live on worms and rodents. There has to be another way."

"Marco, there is no other way."

"There always is another way!" I yelled. "Now don't call me back until you figure that out!"

I hung up. I felt the cabbie's eyes on me while I fussed. I wasn't proud of my anger or that I'd yelled at him and been abusive. I dialed him right back.

Before I could say anything, he blurted out, "I've taken another job, and I'll be leaving on Monday. Maybe one of the sultan's daughters needs a good husband. You're that lucky, Marco, and way better looking than I am, so I think you could pull it off. But then, he'll own you. Have a nice life, Marco."

CHAPTER 8

Shannon

JARED WAS AS good as his word. He nailed the location of Rebecca's hotel in Clearwater by nine P.M. I called the hotel and got through to her right away, which surprised me.

"Your program director speaks highly of you, Shannon. He also stated you thought my interview this morning had been botched."

I was impressed Jared had the clout to be able to reach the ex-Mrs. Gambini, and even more by the fact that he told her about our conversation.

"I think she did a great disservice to your project, Mrs. Gambini."

"Oh please, I've been going by 'Hey Slut' now for the past year or more. You can call me Rebecca."

She did have balls the size of his. Okay, so much for one wrong mismatch. Maybe hers were bigger? I couldn't believe I was even thinking about his balls, and I certainly hoped she couldn't tell.

You really have the chops to make it if it doesn't go well?

Jared's question hung upside down in the bedroom of my belly, somewhere dropped around my ankles where my underpants went every time I thought about Marco.

"Thank you, Rebecca. In short, I think she dissed you."

"She totally dissed me, Shannon—or did I get that right?"

"It's Shannon, correct. I thought her comment about you taking over was disrespectful—almost as if she wished you'd fail."

"Well, I've dealt with little sluts before. Takes one to know one. If I didn't know it, I'd almost believe she was one of my husband's floozies."

"Oh, I'm so sorry. I didn't realize that—"

"Don't be. It's just my wild imagination. I can only imagine what he's doing and how many women are hitting on him now. He was a Navy SEAL, you know."

"Yes, I—" I had to stop myself or I'd send a vibe Rebecca's way that she was keen enough to pick up on. "I've read that was the inspiration for the project. A home for homeless SEALs. I didn't know there were any."

"A lot of people don't know how haunted they can be. Some are driven. Some are haunted by their past." She sighed.

I surmised she was examining the grey clouds in the sky, detritus of the sunset nearly wiped away by now.

"You want to join me for a drink, or is it too late? You're a weather girl, right?"

"Actually, I'm a full-fledged reporter on a string to become a news reporter. They've just not discovered me yet."

That was the truest thing I'd said to her so far. I was jumping at the chance to join her but didn't want to appear too eager.

"Well, come on over. I'll grant that interview. Who knows? Maybe we can help each other out?"

"Thank you. Hope it isn't a big imposition."

"Not at all. I don't sleep well these nights. If I'm going to get drunk tonight, I might as well have company."

"You're on, then. So, you're at the Wyndham?"

"Yes, ma'am. Penthouse suite. Nice view of the Gulf, which you won't see much of at this hour of the night."

"I'll be over as fast as I can."

My fingers fumbled, my nerves buzzed throughout my body as if I was on a blind date with a Martian. This wasn't that kind of encounter of course, except for the fact that I had done all kinds of nasty things with her husband—rather, her *EX*-husband, the one she discarded and left up for grabs. And not only had I done those things, I wanted to do them over and over again.

I dropped my lipstick on the bathroom floor rug and had to toss it in the washer. I fluffed up my hair, pushed my boobs down in my minimizing bra and wore my sloggy black slacks under the oversized shirt that did nothing for my figure. One way to *not* win the trust and friendship of another woman is to do the "whose boobs are bigger, whose ass is tighter" thing, and reality didn't have anything to do with it. If she even *thought* I was prettier than she was, I'd be cooked liver without the onions.

I took a cab over since I knew I'd be drinking. He recognized me immediately.

"You smell as nice as you look Miss Marr." His wink was genuine and non-threatening.

"Thank you—" I checked the badge swinging from his rear-view mirror—"Carlos. Those modern flat screens have everything. I'll have to be more careful tomorrow tonight when I come on. Don't want to overpower the audience with too much perfume."

We both laughed.

The newly remodeled pink hotel was still pink in the late evening air, enhanced by rose-colored floods and a swarm of Flamingos who graced the lake and waterfall in front of the entrance. I was surprised they didn't put themselves to bed like chickens.

Inside the lobby, the night desk manager recognized and greeted me. He escorted me to the penthouse elevator, pushing the button and then stepping back. I fumbled for a couple of bills from my purse, but he smiled and shook his head.

"We're just happy you're here this evening, Miss Marr. Mrs. Gambini is expecting you."

About halfway up the floors I was struck with a sudden sense of impending danger. Just what in the hell had I gotten myself into, I wondered? I felt like a kite that had lost its tether, looking for a safe place to land (which was impossible for a kite).

Every story and scenario running through my brain was messed up. It was so bad that, if she hadn't greeted me in the hallway outside her suite, I might have pushed the button to go back down and caught a cab to run home. Maybe have a good cry on the beach. Find some of Judie's Scotch she left the last time she visited. Should I have called her first, just to make sure that if Rebecca murdered me when she found out what I'd done that someone could notify the police? Would I be afflicted by that talking disease that would make me blurt out something like, "He sucked me good, Rebecca. He screwed me so hard I couldn't sit down for days, and honey, I thought about him every time I crossed my legs and hoped his tongue was buried deep inside me."

Surely something nasty and venomous would come out of my mouth.

Nothing another nude encounter with him wouldn't fix. He could even be furious with me and want to beat me up, and I'd still sleep with him. Oh, God, I had it bad. And now I was about to jump into the cage of the tiger who, if she ever found out, would surely have me gangraped, tape it, and send it to him.

Or worse, have it played on one of those celebrity smut shows for everyone I ever cared about to see.

I bounced to attention, nearly biting my own tongue I was so hot for Marco, when she cooed at me, "Welcome, Shannon. I'm so glad you could make it!"

I walked behind her into her den, the torture chamber of my imagination. I was looking for the gangster guys who would be standing by with whips and chains and bungee cords. My life would come to a horrible screaming end. And Marco would never see me again as a person. I'd be a corpse he would identify by picture as, "Yes, I slept with her in Boston."

Such an ignoble way to go. She could even get away with it. Or, perhaps she'd shove me off the balcony. With my fear of heights, it would be the worst way for me to go, turning my lungs inside out with my screams, wetting and pooping in my pants as I made myself deaf just before I splattered my everything all over the concrete edges of that blue glorious pool I'd seen pictures of. I wouldn't even make it to the beach one more time. I'd be surrounded by lawn chairs, wet towels, and empty beer cans.

Rebecca had her hands on her hips and was smiling at me. Could she read my mind? This was worse than I imagined, and I could imagine a lot.

"I've seen your work, Shannon. You're very good with your arms, and you have graceful hands," she said as she winked. Her stare into my soul was way too long for comfort.

"Th-thank you." It was all I could think of.

Come. On. Shannon. You're. Not. Twelve.

It was like the day I saw a boy's penis for the first time because his friends at school had pantsed him. Even his butt cheeks blushed.

Really, Shannon? This the way you're going to start your big girl career?

Rebecca Gambini picked up a tumbler already prepared with a single ice cube, handing it to me with the brown liquid glistening inside the crystal, calling my name and laughing that I couldn't handle any hard liquor.

She shoved it into my chest, so I grabbed it.

"Come on, Shannon. Let's get shit-faced and tell dirty stories," she said. I perked back to life when she loudly clinked my glass with hers like it was the clash of the titans.

Well, it was, sort of.

We both drank, and I was good at not spitting it back into her face, though I wanted to. For lots of reasons, I wanted to.

She added the warning I knew was coming. "And if you print a word of this, I'll sue your ass to the next century—I'll sue your parents, your siblings, and your children. Then I'll sleep with your husband and make him fall in love with me so I won't sue him."

She really said that. She. Did.

Rebecca was magnificent if she was anything. Except she was a total witch, not a bitch like I heard Marco said she was. She was red meat to a vegetarian. A cat with claw extensions to a tiny helpless mouse.

I was that mouse.

I knew I wouldn't survive the night.

CHAPTER 9

Marco

THERE WERE TIMES when it was necessary to keep my wits about me, and there were times when it was necessary to get drunk. I was even more dangerous when I got drunk, so I wanted to do it alone.

I ordered up some of Ollie's best Scotch and warded off his suggestion for the grape juice, orange liqueur, and cherries or whatever the hell it was that turned the drink into a Midnight in Manhattan. I was going to have the zombie apocalypse Manhattan with dried fruit and fish skeletons as stir sticks. I was having my own midnight in the garden of Marco Gambini's future, and it sucked big time. I didn't want anything diluting the drunk I was determined to accomplish tonight.

By drink number two, I was on my way.

Then I had a hankering for steak. And all of a sudden I wanted a new car, new clothes. I even wanted to set fire to my apartment at the Towers I hadn't even gotten properly dirty in yet. I shaved every day, trimmed my beard carefully with my expensive beard shaver, took a shower at least twice daily, carefully put away my dirty clothes, and laid out the clothes I was going to wear the next day.

I felt the need for the *Old* Marco Gambini to come out and play, that old crusty guy who didn't mind letting his beard grow wild and wore the same sweats and t-shirt for more than three days. I was hungry for lots of things, but steak would be first. Then

I'd like to settle in and finish Ollie's bottle and watch porn. Maybe stumble into a bar at six in the morning or throw croissants at runners passing by while I sat outside on a park bench and tell them they were at least an hour late or ran too slow. I'd run if challenged. Even in my wingtips, I'd beat them. In my suit and tie, I'd beat them. I might hurdle park benches and sit with the bums and drink out of brown paper bags.

What good was it to be so razor-sharp ready for anything, prepared and regimented with my life if it was all turning to shit anyway?

It was *that* kind of a night, and it wouldn't be over until the sun came up and I could make the next day a shitty one too.

But first, that steak. Then I got a great idea. Fuck the bank who turned me down. Fuck the woman who screwed half of SEAL Team 3 in the old days, even though everyone told me she didn't. Fuck the flabby banker at East Coast who was probably screwing his secretary in the broom closet. Maybe I should go rescue her from that flabby fuck. I'd love to ring her chimes and bring her with me to Barbados where we'd lay naked on the beach and screw all day long.

But first I had to have steak. And my idea needed birthing. I dialed my Bentley dealer.

"Tony?"

"Holy crap, Marco, don't you know it's past midnight? Shit, it's one A.M."

"I know it. You have any Bentleys you haven't sold yet, a convertible?"

"Yeah," he yawned and mumbled into the phone.

"Can't hear you, Tony. I gotta have a Bentley."

"Sure. Sure, I got a red one, real pretty. Palomino interior, a real—"

"Wrap it up, put on your clothes and drive it to Boston."

"When? You mean now?"

"Yup. I'll give you an extra twenty-five thousand dollars if you get it here before the sun comes up."

"Oh God, Marco. Is this going to be one of those conversations you won't remember?"

"I'm writing it down. One. Red. Bentley. Convertible."

"Comes with a warning."

"What's that?"

"You gotta drive it sober, Marco. You'll love that thing but you'll wrap it around the first telephone pole you come across if you don't do it sober. And it's a babe magnet. You better hope not to go monogamous for at least two years. About the time it needs new tires, then you can trade it in, like all the others."

"Sold! I'll take it."

"Don't you want to know what it costs?"

"You think I'm worried you'll overcharge me and lose a good customer?"

"No, but don't you—"

"I'm using a credit card. Bring your machine when you come."

"No, I can't do that, Marco. You know it doesn't work like that. I'll take a check. Even an IOU will do, coming from you."

"Fine. Have it your way. Am I convincing you to sell me that red convertible?"

"Yes. You made the sale, Marco. I'll get it there as fast as is humanly possible. Will you be awake?"

"I will. I promise. If not, you can wake me."

"No harem, Marco. I'm not waking you up in a middle of little pink asses."

"Have I ever asked you to do that?"

"No, but just hearing your state of mind, I'm wondering…"

"Shut up. You're wasting time. You know where I live because you got me into this prison."

"So now it's my fault, is it?"

"Sort of."

"You're in a rather self-destructive mode. Are you sure you can afford this machine of mine?"

"I can. My credit is at least *that* good. Ask me to buy another 747 and the answer will be no."

"You need a woman, Marco, not a car."

"Nope. Already tried that."

"I mean a real woman, not a banshee."

I poured my fourth tumbler and remembered the smooth ass of the lady I pleasured a week ago. I wanted more of that, wanted to feel more of that. I wanted to stay in bed with her or in the back seat of the Bentley for a couple of lost days. I so needed just a couple of lost days…

And the lady lived in the Tampa area, which gave me another booze-filled brilliant idea. I was liking the images coming at me fast and furious…

"Are you still there, Marco?"

"Which would be faster, bringing the car to Tampa or to Boston?"

"Shit, Tampa's a thirteen-hour drive. I could make it to Boston in about six if I break the speed limit the whole way."

"Change of plans. Have the car delivered to the Oceanis Resort in Belleair Beach. That's right outside of Tampa. Can you have it there tomorrow? I'll wire the funds in the morning."

"If you wake up, you mean."

"I'll be awake. I'm going to fly to Tampa tonight if I can."

"Why Tampa?"

"Something I forgot to do."

"Okay. I'll email all the information to Frank, as usual."

"Nope. We go direct on this one. Just have the car in Tampa tomorrow, earlier the better."

"Probably won't leave until the morning, but I think we can have it there tomorrow night before it's too late. What's so special about it?"

"I have plans for that back seat at sunset. So, make it before sunset."

"Then I'll have to start tonight. Fuck, Marco, are you sure you're okay?"

"Tony, I've never been worse, and I've never been better. I'm going to grab hold of something good, and if it isn't good, I'm going to hold it until it *is* good. But I don't have a lot of time. I have to be in D.C. by Tuesday."

"I hope you know what you're doing."

"One thing is for sure. It's either the dumbest thing in the world I could do or the best thing in the world. I've already done some pretty good things, and I've just come off of doing a really dumb thing, so the odds are good I'll hit one of those extremes again. I feel it in my bones and some other places, too."

"Somehow I get the impression *there is* a woman involved."

"You could be correct."

"A reconciliation with Rebecca perhaps?"

"You just lost your twenty-five-thousand-dollar bonus, Tony."

"I don't want to take your money, Marco. I just want you to be safe."

"This is not only safe, it's a life-saver. It's going to change my life forever. Trust me."

"Well, if the president and the vice president and the secretary of state do, then I do as well. I'll get working on the papers now. And I better brew some coffee."

After he hung up I thought about the Tampa weather girl as I scanned the clouds lit up by the lights of the harbor district. I remembered she'd cried, for some strange reason, and it wasn't because I'd hurt her. It was because some kind of connection was made. I knew that connection was going to be just the lifeline I needed.

Maybe the thought of screwing—no, *making love*—in the back seat of that convertible with that beautiful, gentle, and intriguing woman was all a fantasy. But I willingly walked head-on into that fantasy, welcoming the images of her lips, her breasts, and the way it felt to make her shatter with her hips hugging mine and her arms holding me pressed against her. Her combination of softness, sweet female pheromones I hadn't experienced for years going back to before Rebecca, was something I'd missed and somehow overlooked.

I dared to peek under the carpet and examine that part of my life that belonged to Emily. I forced myself to feel the pain of her loss, staring right at the reality of how my life would have been different if she hadn't been killed in that accident. It was something I'd not had the courage to look for years. Somehow, Shannon brought back those days like a spirit from the past.

Maybe the old Marco hadn't been such a dumb fuck after all. Maybe that's where my mojo, my secret of success lay. It was a shame I'd laid it down with tuber roses and lilies at that little grave in Santa Rosa. Maybe, contrary to what I'd told myself these past fifteen years, that was the day all this craziness started and, maybe, just maybe it had nothing to do with Rebecca.

Well, I was going to find out. And if I didn't get all my answers, at least I'd have some new memories of sunsets and leather seats, soft arms and lips that craved to be pleasured. Maybe she was someone who needed me just as much as I needed her. In a few minutes I'd phone her, and make sure the welcome I'd felt was still present. I wanted her to anticipate my coming, to ready herself for someone to rock her world. It was better that she was fully ready to receive me rather than being surprised. Give her a chance to get out all the nice stuff and try to make an impression, because that's what I was going to do. I was going to woo her in a way she'd never been wooed before. She'd never forget this weekend.

Maybe we could need each other into oblivion, stop all the pain and hurt, and begin to heal in each other's arms.

There were crazier ways to find out, but I liked that it would start with an impulsive private flight to Tampa tonight, as soon as I got confirmation my pilot was ready, and I finished packing. It would continue with a fast drive to the gulf in an even faster red convertible. And maybe it would end with a sunset to all the darkness in my life, a bon voyage to all the misery and pain, and the start of a new day.

CHAPTER 10

Shannon

A<small>S A DRINKING</small> buddy, Rebecca made a fine one. I was actually having a great time, stumbling around, playing music, mostly oldies for her. Her favorites were all Em's favorite tunes too: Fleetwood Mac, Van Halen, even some Steely Dan thrown in. All these albums we found on her cell phone. We danced together like two long-lost friends. Except for her cutting wit and nasty language, it was almost like dancing with Em herself.

"Truth or Dare, Shannon!" Rebecca shouted, holding her glass high above her head. She turned down the music. "Best night *ever* when you were a teen?"

The oddness of the question made my insides flinch. I saw Marco, a much younger version of him, bending on his knee, presenting me with one of the flowers he'd plucked from the bouquet he'd laid at Em's coffin. His eyes were red, and his cheeks were streaked with shiny rivulets of tears. He couldn't talk, but I saw in his eyes the tremendous loss my sister caused him. How I wanted to ease that pain. He'd always been so kind to me, even defending me to Em sometimes. He was the bright spot in my Mother's Day whenever he showed up.

I was the invisible preteen.

"Remember her this way, kid," he'd said as he handed me the scented flower.

I would have preferred a hug or an itty bitty, teeny-weeny innocent peck on the cheek. He probably thought I was dumbstruck, my grief overwhelming me, which of course it did. But my small fingers shook as I took the flower, just to be in proximity to the man who had brought my big sister so much joy. I knew it would be the last time I'd see him, the last time our fingers would touch. I wanted to make it better by telling him how wonderful he made her feel, but I froze up. My knees locked. My insides shredded like an old curtain flapping in a glassless window frame.

"Yessss!" Rebecca hissed. "*That* one. What was *that* one about?"

I really had no idea why it would have been the best day of my life. It was certainly the most impactful. As the years went by, I saw that tiny flower not as a plant or once-living thing, but a torch given from one sister to another. Like the movie when the actress tells him to come back for her in time. Was he saying he'd see me later?

Of course not, and I was nearing the edge of sanity to think so. My head spun. I blamed it on the alcohol, which was also partially true.

"I think the Scotch has gotten to me. All that dancing. I'm dizzy. I need to sit down."

She was all over me like a mother, just like Em had, darn it. I couldn't get the thought of how similar and yet so dissimilar they were. I really wanted her to scrape her hands and arms from my body, but she clung to me because she was drunk too. She sat me down, carefully, on the couch, sat right next to me, and pushed my hair from my forehead.

"You're burning up, Shan."

Oh God! Not the name Em used to call me too!

I groaned and leaned into the couch back, which distanced my body somewhat from hers. She was on her feet, and nearly slipping and upturning the coffee table, she made her way to the fully stocked Penthouse kitchen, picked up a tea towel, and turned on the faucett so hard it splashed all over the counter, tile back, and her face and front. She screamed, then threw her head back and laughed. I recognized the reaction.

I resigned myself not to be surprised anymore. She acted so much like Em. Somewhere in my alcohol-sloshed brain, I understood that perhaps that's how he'd picked her. But the comparisons were driving me into a moroseness I didn't desire.

"I'm so sorry, pumpkin," she cooed, patting my face and forehead with the wet towel.

At last a name Em hadn't used!

"Thank you," I mumbled into the towel, helpless to do anything else and wishing I could get that day out of my head. But with Rebecca, I wouldn't be so lucky.

"I'm sorry I brought up something painful, Shannon. What was it? You can tell me."

"I-I really don't want to talk about it."

She lowered her chin, stuck out her lower lip, and gave me the puppy dog look I hated, which won me over all the time with Judie. "Please?"

Danger! Danger! Pitfall ahead!

Something inside me was trying to warn me off some course of action I'd regret forever. She laced her fingers through my hair, placing it neatly behind my shoulders. She took my hand in hers and squeezed.

"Talking about it might make it better."

"Believe me—" I started to say.

Her hand was up, taking no prisoners, shaking her head. Did she know she was really being cruel?

I pulled my paw from her grip and righted myself, cleared my throat, and asked for a glass of ice water.

"Gas or no gas?"

"What?"

"Sparkling or no?"

"Sparkling, if you have it."

"Lime, lemon, or orange flavored?"

All the choices right now I really didn't want to make.

"Lime."

"Good choice. My favorite too," she said breathlessly as she popped two bottle tops and returned with two tumblers full of ice to pour the sparkling water into. It was the needed delay I was seeking, but I knew I wouldn't escape.

Why *had* I thought of that moment when she asked about my best day ever as a teen? Again, I blamed it on the Scotch.

"Now. Spill the beans, Shannon. I promise nurse Rebecca will make it all better."

If she only knew.

"What you don't know is that I had an older sister. I'm not sure why, but I was reminded of the day of her funeral."

Rebecca clearly wasn't understanding my words. Her nose scrunched up. Her cheeks puckered to cover half of her eyes.

"I'm so sorry, pumpkin."

That name again…I was starting to hate it.

"But why? I mean, how come you thought about *that* day?"

I searched for something desperately to say. At last I came out with words I immediately regretted.

"You kind of remind me of her."

Rebecca moved away a couple of inches on the couch as if I was made of molten lava. Still watching me, she considered something. Then her shoulders dropped, and she sighed.

"I'm so sorry, Shannon. She sounds like a *wonderful person.*"

That comment sobered me up all of a sudden. Of all the selfish, wrong things to say to someone who was missing her sister, that was about one of the most heartless things she could have said. I was back on top, ready to complete the mission I'd set out to do. I'd have to be just as good a liar as she was. I could do that now.

"I think the reason I wanted to interview you partially was because of that. You do remind me of my sister. And, well, I thought I could do an interview that would do you justice, do her justice too, I guess." I shrugged. "In a way?" I raised my eyebrows into my hairline, opened my palms up on my lap, and waited for whatever was due me. I was such a sneak, such a bad person.

"I'm touched, Shannon," she said in her breathy, sexy tone, her expression brightening, almost becoming flirtatious. But I didn't get any sexual vibes, thank goodness. No, this woman was made of something else, and it was dark and deep. She was damaged goods, clear through. I reminded myself she was dangerous.

"I hope you didn't take offense, Rebecca."

"On the contrary. If I'd had a little sister, I could only hope that she would have been one half as sweet and cute as you, honey. But you've touched me. I want to help."

Uh-oh. She. Said. Help.

"Tell me about her."

"She was pretty." I looked up at Rebecca's eager face and the wild expression in her eyes and added, "Like you."

"Ah, that's nice of you to say. I'm not as pretty as I was once, but then, my next new boyfriend is going to be a plastic surgeon."

"New boyfriend?"

"My last boyfriend was an attorney who helped me with the divorce. I am eternally grateful, too. But my next one will be a gifted surgeon who loves to travel."

I tried to giggle, but it came out more like the lament of a pained cat. I coughed and took another long sip of mineral water.

"Go on. Tell me more about her. I'm fascinated."

"She was fun loving. She loved people and was always the life of the party."

"And you always felt mousy instead, am I right?"

That was not information she was entitled to. It was only half of it, anyhow. I didn't feel mousy. I felt ignored because Em was such the favorite of my parents. I'd even told my mom one day when we argued years later that I wish I'd been the one killed so they could have continued living instead of the life they had with me. I'd gotten a slap for that comment and then a hug. Then we both burst into tears. My mother did the best she could but her heart was irreparably broken. Our mother-daughter bond was there because we had that pain in common.

"You're perceptive," I lied, trying to shed the sorrow that was being stubborn.

"How did she die?"

"It was an auto accident."

"Oh, so sad. You never got to say good-bye." Her lower lip was protruding, but it almost looked like she was mocking me. I began to see more difference between her and my sister. She didn't really have an ounce of compassion in her body.

"No. I didn't."

"Did she die right away, at the scene?"

The hairs at the back of my neck began to stand up. Did she have some morbid desire to dig into my pain, my past?

"Yes, we think so. My parents were devastated."

Rebecca stood and stared off into the dark bay, the lights of the pool and landscaped grounds reflecting back into her face, giving it a chilling light from beneath her chin like in some horror movie.

"What was her name?" she said absent-mindedly.

Did she suspect who I was? Even Marco didn't know who I was. I scrambled, but my tongue was thick, and my brain didn't function like it normally did.

"C-Connie," I blurted out. "Like Connie Stevens, the singer. Mom named her after her."

Rebecca nodded and opened the sliding glass door slowly, with cat-like movements.

"Come see the beautiful lights and the early morning air. It will be sunrise soon, Shannon."

"I-I'm afraid of heights, Rebecca. I'm so sorry, but I think maybe I should be getting home. I do go in early tomorrow. I have to set up my—"

Then I thought about the interview. I had neglected to ask her any questions. I had nothing to go work on. I could do background, but I'd already done some of that previously while researching Marco. I had to get something to show for the evening's meeting.

"Can I ask you some quick questions for the interview? I'd really rather talk about something else, if you don't mind. This was supposed to be all about you and the project, not me. And if I stand out there on the balcony, I'll unload all my dinner over the good people out there." I gave a sickly whinny.

She was the one being morose and very, very odd. She looked down. "Lovers. There are only lovers out tonight, walking around the pathways, stealing kisses amongst the large palm fronds, watching the koi, and listening to the cicadas."

"Sounds beautiful, but I'm still staying put right here. If you don't want to do it tonight, how about you come into the station tomorrow? It's only a half-hour drive. Would you agree to that?"

"I can do that," she said as she closed the glass door, locked it, and floated over to sit at a forty-five-degree angle to me. She studied me. "Ask some of your questions now so I know the approach you'll take and I'll be prepared."

I fumbled for my cell phone, where I'd stored several questions. There was a call I'd missed from Boston, since I'd turned off my ringer. I scrolled to my notepad.

"Um, we already know you like to dance and sing. Tell me about the project and why this is so important to you?"

"Because Navy SEALs deserve a home. They fight. They leave their whole lives out there on the battlefield. Sometimes, they come back empty. They lose their families often, everyone but their brothers. So many of them die lonely, misunderstood, and without the support of those who loved them or could help them. They prefer the company of their teammates. And it's hard for a family to understand how lonely they are."

"That's so wonderful that you do. Having been through it, of course," I added, thinking it was a safe comment.

But her eyes morphed into slits. "You don't know anything about my relationship. It was completely different. But that's another interview for another day."

"Of course." I nearly dropped my phone, scrambled for my notes and read off another question. "So tell me how the idea came to you, and how do you imagine it going forward?"

"It didn't come to me. It was Marco—that's my husband—my ex-husband, I should say—it was Marco's idea from the get-go. I actually fought him on it. But after I saw what a mess he was making of his businesses, I decided to resurrect his mission, since he didn't have the money or the time."

"How good of you." I gulped down more water, taking some of my bile with it.

"I admit, at first I did it to make him mad, but you won't put that in the interview, will you?"

"Of course not."

"That's a good girl," she said with a strong dose of condescension. I was starting to hate her now. Again, I thought it might be the alcohol talking/feeling/confusing me.

She began again. "I thought it might be a good idea to hang around some of those hunky silver foxes. SEALs are an odd lot. Strong yet so weak in the relationship cajones, if you know what I mean. They fall for women easily and then don't know what to do with them once they've gotten them. They certainly know how to use their equipment—"

I blushed. She noticed.

"Shannon, you're holding out on me…" She was smiling, but I still felt under her thumb.

"Your comment, well, I was thinking about—what I'd heard—about SEALs. I mean, they're supposed to be great lovers, and all." I quickly added, "*Not* speaking from experience, of course."

She chuckled. "My husband was an expert at everything. He qualified expert in his diving, firearms, demolition, languages. He was the fastest runner on his team, even the day he disengaged. And he could make me wet just by looking at me. He could make me wet with his little finger, with his tongue…"

I stepped on my own tongue and quickly closed my mouth. My blush was obvious.

"It turns you on just to hear me talk about it, doesn't it, Shannon?"

I knew I had to be very careful. While I was foggy-brained from the alcohol, Rebecca's wits were becoming sharper, more honed. I realized that it was where she lived as a woman. She was a competitor, a pure driver who liked to be in control even when she was drunk. I could see that competing against Marco would make her feel stronger, not weaker. She lived for it, in fact. Em was competitive in that she never gave up, especially hope.

"Well, I've never had this kind of conversation, and this certainly won't go into the interview."

"Oh, I know it won't. Because it will reflect badly on you. But come to the interview tomorrow with those thoughts in mind, and then we'll have a real girl chat, on camera. Let's not tape it. Let's go live and bare."

I was dumfounded, sure my program manager would never approve of this. I was thinking about how I was going to tell him. It was on impulse that I answered her, with more guts than brains, as if someone else were talking through me. "Okay, Rebecca, let's do it. Don't know if it will get approved, but I'll try to make that happen. Let's fly off into the history books—together, like real sisters."

She threw her head back and laughed so hard I thought she and the chair would flip over backwards.

Then my phone rang. I really should have checked who had called me. I knew better. But I didn't. I was so worried about what I was going to do tomorrow and how I'd pull this off without ruining the station's or my reputation, it didn't occur to me that things were about to heat up even hotter.

"Hello, Shannon."

It. Was. Marco. The sound of his sexy voice slithered down my spine and ignited my sweet spot. I felt the pulsing wetness between my legs.

"Oh, hello." I sounded and felt like I was twelve, my voice cracking. "It-it's kinda late. Could I call you back?" I whispered.

"Are you with someone I have to come over and strangle? Want me to?"

"Well, you're not here—I'm in Clearwater."

"I'm getting ready to fly to Tampa as we speak. I thought perhaps we could have breakfast when I arrive, and then I could book you for dinner at sunset, if you'd be agreeable."

I was so agreeable I was nearly wetting my pants. And then I saw the smirk of the woman across the coffee table from me. She had a Cheshire cat grin.

"That would be nice. But can I call you back?"

"You *are* with someone."

"It's not what you think, M—Mike."

"Mike? You're a nasty little girl, Shannon. I want to know more. I want to hear you whisper it to me when I pump you full of everything I've got."

Oh dear God! My face, my chest, my boobs were fiery red, engorged and tingling. My pounding heart was making it difficult to breathe. And my panties were so wet I could even smell them.

Rebecca was trying to listen, her eyebrows raised. I made sure to press the phone to my ear and wished I'd brought my earpiece.

"Listen, call me when you get here, please" I tried not to make it sound like a beg. "I'm with a girlfriend and your comments, well, they're embarrassing me." I gave a wide-eyed sweet smile to his ex, and that made everything worse.

"But are you looking forward to my visit? Just tell me because I won't come if you have to rearrange your whole schedule…"

Marco, you could rearrange my whole life! My brain was shouting, my inner angel was beating up the lonely witch inside me.

"Of course I am. Very much so. A pleasant surprise. Tomorrow, then?"

"I can't wait."

"Neither can I," I said, staring right into the eyes of his ex-wife.

I DON'T REMEMBER how I got home, but I did. I don't know how she believed that my boyfriend was coming to Tampa for a surprise visit. If she only knew.

I took a shower, washing my hair so I didn't smell anything like Rebecca or her motel room. I laid out something I hoped I'd look spectacular in and tried to sleep the two or three hours until morning.

But it was impossible. My body needed rest, but it was all fired up, wide awake and unrelenting. My eyes were going to look so red. My heart was pounding in my chest so loud I felt like I was shaking the windows. And I had to do that interview with Rebecca at ten A.M. Right after my breakfast with Marco. And if he got here late, well, I'd have to cancel it.

I toyed with the idea of having someone else do the interview and thought, as I walked on the beach at sunrise, that that would save my bacon. There was only so much a girl could do. He was hot on my trail. He wanted me. There was no question I'd be sleeping with him and partaking of that elixir he so deliciously gave out. I was helpless, talking to him while she was watching. It was like the question she asked me, "What was the best day ever..." Well this was the worst and the best day ever.

And I knew it would get worse before it would get better. I hadn't been wrong about his attraction for me. It *was* mutual, after all, not some figment of my imagination.

As I walked the beach in my bare feet, I clutched the phone in my right hand, waiting for the call that would change my life forever.

If I didn't screw the whole thing up.

Now I really had to start going back to church.

CHAPTER 11

Marco

I WAS CUTTING it close to get to Tampa by breakfast, since the flight itself would take three-plus hours. My pilot was ready, but the jet wasn't quite. That gave me time to shower and shave again, finish packing and take a car to the airport. We were wheels up less than fifteen minutes after I arrived.

The attendant my pilot brought along mixed me a mimosa and handed me an assortment of vitamins and lots of Vitamin B, probably understanding the condition I'd been in when I booked the flight. I passed on any further alcohol, took my pills, and promptly fell asleep.

I landed just as it turned seven A.M. The bright sun was scalding my pupils. It had been a few very grey days in Boston, with light drizzle occasionally, so coming into the moist warmth of Florida's Gulf Coast was very welcome indeed, but an adjustment, nonetheless.

I tried to remember the conversation I'd had with Shannon just a few hours ago, but I did remember she agreed to meet me for breakfast and dinner later on, and she wanted me to call when I landed. I did so now.

"I'm in Tampa. Just landed."

She hesitated, sounding a little nervous. Well, I was a little nervous too. It felt like prom night all of a sudden.

"I'm sorry about last night. I had a few too many, and..." she began.

"You too? I hope you didn't have the kind of day I had."

"I'm not sure you could have. It wasn't one of my finer moments. I don't think you'd believe me if I told you."

"All forgiven. I'm here now. I can't remember what I said last night, but I believe I did invite you to breakfast and you agreed. And dinner too, is that right?"

"Yes." She giggled. "That part I remember."

"I hope I wasn't too—well, I was pretty wasted."

"So you want to reconsider the whole thing then?" she said sharply.

"Not at all. As a matter of fact I was looking forward to it, dreaming about it."

She didn't say a thing, and I got worried.

"Marco, I have an appointment at the office at ten this morning, unless I can get out of it, and I'm going to try but can't reach anyone there. So if you're not up to it, we can skip breakfast. What I'm trying to say is that it wouldn't be a problem."

"Are you telling me you'd just rather meet me in my motel room?" Before she could answer I abruptly cut in. "I'm sorry. That wasn't very respectful of me. You seem to bring out both the best and the worst in me, Shannon. I promise to be on my best behavior."

I began to exit the plane as she replied.

Her raspy voice instantly got me even harder. "I don't mind your bad behavior. Was sort of looking forward to it, but I was just saying that I don't mind if we skip breakfast and just have dinner, if you're too busy."

I decided to tell her the truth. "I came here to see *you*. This is not a business trip for me."

"But your project—?"

"Will still be there after breakfast and probably after dinner as well. I want to see you." I hoped I didn't sound too desperate, but I was beginning to feel some hesitation on her part. I meant it when I told Tony that I was going to hang on until she'd let me rock her world, and I meant every word of it.

"I want to see you too."

It was music to my ears.

"Where should I meet you?"

"I could fix some eggs if you're not too picky, Marco."

"Your place. You're inviting me to your place?"

"It's not fancy. Just a little bungalow at the beach about a half mile from your project."

"Ah, so you've checked up on me?"

"Of course I have. You wouldn't expect anything less, right?"

"I'm flattered."

"So how do we do this, Marco? You tell me."

"Text me your address and I'll be over there in about a half hour, depending on traffic."

"It's Saturday. No traffic. I'll see you then."

My driver took me to a local florist shop inside one of the supermarkets, the only place open, and I selected a bright bouquet of flowers, which I thought safer than roses. I'd bring her roses at dinner, but for this morning these would have to do. The clerk wrapped them in green tissue and placed a pink bow on them.

She lived off the main Gulf Blvd. on a side street that served houses that fronted the beach itself at Indian Rocks. Her house was one of the more modest structures, but it was surrounded by McMansions.

I heard music coming from her frosted glass front door. I knocked and found her fresh face even more beautiful than I'd remembered, and I'd remembered a lot. I extended the flowers to her, but before she could take them, I slipped my arm around her waist and pulled her into me. She arched backwards, slid her arms up over my shoulders, and pulled my head down to hers where we ignited the flame of our past encounter. The long lingering kiss could have easily lead to something more, right there in the doorway to her little house, in front of the eyes of my driver. It was the welcome I had hoped I'd receive.

I turned my head and nodded, indicating he could go, and he did so after giving me a salute.

She welcomed me into her living room and this time, took the flowers from me, burying her nose in them.

I was fascinated with her collection of artwork. She had a variety of acrylic paintings of some of the beach bungalows I'd seen previously on my visits here. There were a few watercolors and several beach plaques with beachy sayings on them. Perhaps she made some of these, but they were locally produced.

Her small living room was dwarfed by the enormous butter yellow leather couch that had been well worn and sun-bleached, as it faced the ocean and beach beyond behind a huge glass window. Something about the whole scene was oddly familiar to me. It felt very safe.

I turned to face her, and she erupted.

"Oh my gosh, I'd better get these in some water."

She dashed off into her bedroom, closing the door behind her. A few seconds later, she came out.

"Wrong room," she said as she blushed and headed for the kitchen. "Would you like coffee?"

"I'd love some."

She arranged the flowers and then poured me coffee. "Cream?"

"Of course."

"There you go."

I couldn't choose between the steaming mug of delicious-smelling coffee and the vision in front of me. I set it down, and held my arms out wide.

"Come here, Shannon. I don't want you to be nervous with me. You know by now I'm a man who knows what he likes, and I want more of what we had. There was something…"

She held her fingers over my lips and kissed me.

My hands moved over her ass, then up under her shirt, seeking her nipples as we kissed. Her fingers unbuttoned my shirt, and soon her lips were tasting my wartime badges, the ink I had placed on my body to remember everything, the good and the bad of it all.

She undid my fly, and I hissed, inhaling as her fingers found me.

We separated, breathing hard, looking into each other's eyes, and then she took my hand and led me to the bedroom.

I sat down, removing my shoes and socks while I watched her undress in front of me. She laid my shirt on a side chair, folded, and placed my jeans underneath. I slipped off my briefs, revealing the hard-on I'd been sporting for several hours now.

She was still in her bra and panties as she took a condom from her nightstand, kneeled in front of me and pressed it over my shaft. She rubbed my balls and ran her forefinger up the underside over the condom.

I released her bra and slipped her panties down to her ankles and then parted her knees. I watched her eyes as I fingered her carefully, feeling how ready she was and watching her arousal fuel my own. Then I crawled back up onto the bed, leaning against the cloth headboard, waiting for her to come to me.

Her knees slid over my hips to straddle my lap, and I slid inside her slowly at first, then deeper, and at last fully seated as she writhed above me. I wanted to feel every ripple, every moan coming from her body. Her soft mouth and tongue tempted me to go deep, so after several minutes of soft sex play, I flipped her onto her stomach, held her belly up with one hand, and smoothed over her butt cheeks with the other as I took her from behind. Hard. Her body resisted me at first, and I worried she was so tight the condom would break as I pumped her furiously.

It all changed when her orgasm started. Her spasms began, slamming against me, pulling me deeper inside her channel. I was filled with lust at her moaning and loss of control. I pulled out to taste her. She screamed in frustration, but I wouldn't relent. My tongue was already lapping her juices. I spread her knees wider to gain more access, and she tried to reach back to touch the top of my head. She gripped her own buttocks, spreading them wider still for me, dug her knees into the bed, and pressed herself up into my face. I played with her, lapping and sucking until she begged me to go deep again.

Slipping my thighs between hers, I gently lifted her by the waist, seating her on my lap as I buried my cock deep to the hilt. She gasped as I held her in place. It felt so perfect, so good to pleasure her and feel the turmoil going on inside her.

She leaned back against me, and we tried to kiss. I bit her earlobe, and whispered, "I love fucking you. Your sweet body was made for me. I should never have let you go that morning. What. Was. I. Thinking?" I said as I pumped to her screams.

Her fingers laced with mine as I pinched her nipples, and made her squeal.

"Come for me, Shannon. Let me feel it while I fill you."

She groaned, ground down on my lap as I pushed up and pressed against her sweet spot, ardently knocking on the door of her womanhood as my shaft swelled against her pulsing muscles. I burst up inside her as she came totally apart.

I held her tight so she wouldn't career over the side of the bed, she was so limp. She clung to me like a rag doll. I kissed the sides of her neck, probed and pressed her little hot nub with my forefinger, making her bounce against me as I completed my mission. I pulled her hair up from her neck and kissed her sweaty skin until I was nearly spent.

We crashed into the bed, a tangle of sheets, legs, and arms, her orgasm coaxing and prolonging mine until we were both completely wrung out.

She clutched my hand in hers, drew it to her chest, curled like she'd done before at the Towers, and fell asleep tucked into my arms.

This time, she didn't cry.

CHAPTER 12

Shannon

W E MUST HAVE slept for an hour or more. My cell phone rang, but there wasn't any possibility I'd be able to extricate myself from Marco's arms and legs to answer it in time. His hand lightly rubbed my shoulder as I looked up and into his face and gave him a kiss.

"So much for breakfast," I yawned. "But I might have time to whip something together," I whispered.

"If you do it naked and I can watch."

"I think I can arrange that." I started to move, sliding off the bed, but he grabbed me and had me pressed against his chest again.

"I changed my mind. I'll have you for breakfast."

"But I have an appointment at the office."

"Cancel it."

I knew I had to tell him. Now was as good a time as ever, or he'd never understand why I had to rush off. He'd go digging, and I didn't want him showing up at the station while in the middle of the interview. I searched his face just in case it was the last time I'd see how lovingly he smiled at me. I sat up, looking down on him as he settled his arms beneath his head on the pillow.

"What's up, Shannon?"

"I have to tell you something. You might not like it."

"Oh? I doubt you could ever say or do anything I wouldn't like. So why do you think that?"

"Trust me. I've gotten to know a little about you."

He remained relaxed on the outside, but I could sense he was very alert on the inside. He drew the back of his hand across my cheek and brushed against my lips as I kissed his lingering fingers. "Yes you have. And I believe it goes both ways."

He waited.

"I have taken on an interview this morning. It was arranged before I knew you were coming, or I certainly wouldn't have done it. But it's a human-interest story."

In my silence, he whispered, "What, Shannon?"

"It's a story on your housing project for Navy SEALs. And I'm interviewing Rebecca today at ten. That's who I'm meeting."

At first he didn't believe me. Then his eyes got dangerous and he began to breathe deeply. He stared at the ceiling and stopped touching me. I knew telling him was the right thing to do because he'd find out anyway. But I so regretted having to tell him at that moment. Out of the side of my vision I could see he'd focused on me again with something deep and penetrating. I slowly returned his gaze and started to explain further. I was even prepared to give an apology, but he put a finger to my lips.

"Does she know?" he asked.

"Does she know what, Marco?"

"About this. Us. Boston." His voice was a little louder, anxious and scratchy.

"No. Never in a million years."

His eyes didn't wander from mine. I knew he was serious. "I want you to tell her after the interview. Tell her you love sucking my cock. Tell her we're gonna screw all day and all night."

While I was mildly pleased he didn't toss me from the bed and leave, I could see that I had hurt him, and he was reacting like I knew he would. A wounded bear. As he began to say something in anger, it was my turn to stop him with my fingers to his lips.

"No, Marco. She has nothing to do with us. Nothing about us has anything to do with her, unless you bring her in."

His eyes sparkled, new light brightening the darkness at the centers. He cocked his head to the side to listen.

"I'm going to just go in and do my job. She'll find out or not, but not from me and not this morning before or during the interview. You have my permission to tell her if you want, because that's not my call. It's yours."

"Really? You'd let me do that?"

I couldn't tell if he was being sarcastic because his mood was still stormy, but I relied on the color in his eyes and those tiny smile lines at the sides of his lips. And his voice. He was soft, if not raspy. He was patient, staging himself in case he had to control an outburst. I could tell all this just because I'd seen it years ago when he argued with Em about getting married. He'd held her off, and although she cried into his arms, he promised to return to her after that first deployment. And he did.

She was the one who didn't return. They never had counted on that.

"Why spoil our chances with each other, Marco? This is all new, exciting, and exactly what I want. Don't let her spoil it, like she's spoiling the rest of your life. Don't give her that much power."

He reached out to touch my arm, and then changed his mind and covered his eyes with his forearm. I wasn't going to let him know his emotions were showing no matter how much he tried to hide them up. That was part of the Marco I wanted to be with.

"So don't bring that woman into our bedroom," I said as I peeled his arm from his face, took his hand in mine and kissed his palm. He watched. Then his powerful fingers slid up my neck, into my hair, where he took fistfuls and pulled me down so he could ravage me with kisses.

"I need to fuck you, Shannon. Hard," he whispered in my ear, flipping my body over onto my back.

"Oh God, yes!" I said, relieved, my arms pulling him down on top of me. It was the only answer I was capable of giving him. My body wasn't nearly enough, but I didn't mind sharing my complete surrender to him. He took a chance on me, and I wanted him to feel like he could take me any time.

I was his vessel. I didn't stop him to put on a condom he never asked for because it didn't matter what the outcome was. Judie would tan my hide if she ever found out how risky it was, but I just didn't care how un-modern and stupid I was being. There were some things more important than being appropriate.

My tears were hot but silent as he thrust into me and wildly pumped. He slipped his arms beneath me and pulled my shoulders down so we could mate as tight as possible, picking up the intensity. I thought the bed would rock off the frame, or we'd break it. I felt the bulging muscles in his back as he worked feverishly to his peak.

"Can you come for me?" he whispered in my ear.

I didn't answer him. His pause was brief. Then he resumed his earlier frenzy. At last I felt him pulsing inside me, and then he started to pull out. I held his buttocks with both hands, pressing him deeper and telling him not to stop. I accepted every drop unconditionally.

Afterward, he collapsed onto my chest, and we caught our breaths together. He finally looked up at me and brushed my eyebrows with his thumb, nibbling on my lips. "You should have stopped me, Shannon."

I shook my head, brave to let him see my tears. "I wanted it too, just this way. Because what I think I have here with you is real, and I've thought a lot about it. Marco, for however long it lasts, we belong together right now. Here. I'm not going to let her take any of that away. It's just us."

He turned his head as if carefully considering my words. Heck, I didn't even believe it myself. Evaluation and calculation were ruminating inside his brain. I knew he was trying to figure out if he could trust what I said.

He frowned. "It's still not how I want to treat you. You deserve more."

"I would have stopped you, and you would have honored my request. For me, Marco, you were never out of control, and I trust you. As crazy as it feels, I do trust you."

I was looking for another word that wasn't appropriate, and I stuck to my guns and reverted to the safe Shannon who wasn't going to press him, even though I was his completely.

Then he asked me, "How did all this come about?" He was still nibbling on my neck, putting his tongue in my ear, biting my earlobe, making me ticklish. I loved the intimacy between us, as if we'd been lovers for decades.

"I saw her interviewed on another program yesterday. I had no idea you were going to call, to come here. I asked my program manager if I could also do an interview because I did want to do one on your project anyway. And I guess I was also a little bit curious about her."

"Did you satisfy your curiosity?" he whispered.

"I have no right to say it, but she's not good for you."

He stared back down at me without moving a muscle.

He was beginning to make me nervous, so I continued explaining, hoping he was as calm about it as he seemed.

"But I did it so I could begin to do a piece on your work, this project. Did I hope that somehow it would lead to you? I'd have to answer that question with a yes. But if I'd have known about you coming here, that you did want to see me again, I never would have set this up. And now I'm very sorry. But trust me, Marco. She is not part of our relationship. She belonged to the man you no longer are. I have this one," I said as I pressed my hand against the tat of the sun on his chest over his heart. "For however long you'll grant me access, I want this. I want us."

He watched me and, after a brief few seconds, placed his hand over mine.

"You be careful, Shannon. She's dangerous."

"Yes, I already know that."

He angled his head. "So, you've met her already?"

I didn't want to answer.

"She was the person you were with last night when I called?"

I wasn't proud of my answer but this wasn't the time to start lying to him. "Unfortunately, yes."

"And you don't think she knows?" His voice was beginning to raise. "If she could hear my voice—"

"No, Marco. She didn't. It was one of the most awkward moments of my entire life. I promise you I kept that phone tight to my ear."

"Because she'll hurt you if she can. You know that, right?"

I nodded.

"She knows I'm out to get her. She'll hurt you to get to me, Shannon."

"I'm not a part of that war, and like I said, she has no standing, no place in this relationship. Tell me you agree and understand that. I need to hear it. Or, am I wasting my time?"

It was one of the hardest things I'd ever had to ask.

"What do you think?"

I couldn't tell him that I'd known him for over fifteen years, followed his career and how he lived because I'd studied it. And I knew he wouldn't just use me and walk away, but he didn't know that. I knew I'd have to do the reveal about Em some day and probably soon before we got too involved, but today wasn't that day. But if we became a couple, a real couple, it would have to be done. Right now, I wasn't sure what we were except a bright new beginning of something magic.

"I'm right where I want to be, Marco. I think you feel the same."

"I want this too," he whispered. "No more secrets, Shannon, okay?"

He must have felt my body flinch, but I softened it with a lazy smile. God, I was being such a good actress, or I hoped I was anyway. Because I really did want this to work, and I prayed that he'd forgive me somehow when it came to Em.

His face broke into a smile. "I guess you like to live a little on the dangerous side of life, maybe a little like me, then. You're an adrenaline junkie too. Not a drama queen. Is that what you're saying?"

"I'm responsible for all this, yes. But did I plan it that way? Hell no. I'm not going to try to cover up what I've done. I can't do that to you, Marco. If you can't trust me, what do we have?"

"It still would have been worth it, honey," he said, lovingly adjusting my hair over my shoulder so he could look at my breasts again. I was relieved when he kissed my nipples one by one, and added, "But I like the idea of a sunset dinner somewhere special and, who knows? Maybe there will be more."

"I want more, Marco."

"Don't I scare you? You should be scared, you know?"

Not being able to be with him was the scary part. Maybe I did like to live dangerously because if I ever had to get over him, I knew I never could.

"I want the way I feel when I'm with you. I want the man I think I'm beginning to know. That man, who's gentle, who protects and keeps me safe. I'll do battle with anyone because my biggest fear is losing this."

That got him chuckling. "I'm supposed to be thinking about a big meeting I have in D.C, on Tuesday and a trip I have to take halfway around the world. Also, a job I will probably have to oversee in Africa. I have to look for a new CFO. And I have to deal with a loan called against my assets and show up in court to produce documents."

His hand fished down under the covers until he touched my wet, throbbing sex. Then, as he delicately fingered my opening and pressed a thumb into my clit, he spoke very seriously, directly to my face.

"But, all I can think about is a weather girl in Tampa with the softest skin and the sweetest kisses. I can't stop fucking her in my dreams, in my bed, in your bed. Anywhere. I can't stop, Shannon. I don't want to lose this, either."

My tears flowed. I just couldn't help them. Part of it was relief, but part of it was knowing that the other secret I'd been holding onto might be the end of us. I knew my life would be a lot easier, but duller, if I'd never gone to Boston, met him, and fell in love that first time.

There was that word I couldn't speak of.

But it was too late for that. I was in deep. And there was a world war ahead for me to win first.

CHAPTER 13

Marco

IT WAS HARD to let her go. We nearly didn't make it out of the shower. I quickly dressed, and she dropped me off at the Oceanis, which was on her way to the radio station.

"Come check out the room I've got, Shannon," I begged, knowing it would do no good.

"No, Marco," she said, shedding my hand as I tried to pull her inside the lobby.

I grabbed my leather bag, gave her one more kiss, and waved as she drove away.

"Checking in, sir?" the bellman asked.

I was directed to the front desk.

After signing the registration card, I was handed a small sheaf of papers, messages from the office in D.C., the old office in Manhattan, and from the Towers in Boston. I knew, of the three, the one from the Towers would be the most innocuous so dialed them on my way to the elevator.

Jerrold Hoffstedler from the accounting office sounded like he was still in high school, complete with the croak in his voice that made me think it had just changed. His nasal tone was a little off-putting. Perhaps he had a sinus infection.

"We're having trouble processing the balance of your lease deposit, Mr. Gambini. It seems the bank says you're overdrawn."

"That can't be. I have millions. Used to have billions. I've not been overdrawn for nearly twenty years."

"I know it's probably some glitch in your accounting system. You were approved without any problem, which means they checked your assets. These things happen all the time when we have guests relocating from other metropolitan areas. I once had a Saudi prince who bounced a three-hundred-thousand-dollar check to us. He was quite embarrassed."

"I should hope so."

"I'm sure it's a condition of moving and something just didn't get flagged properly. If you could call us back tomorrow or Tuesday, there won't be any further action needing to be taken."

I was hoping that my CFO wasn't giving me a good-bye headache. He left because he was scared he'd not have a job if he didn't. But I doubted he'd do anything vindictive. In fact, I was sure of it.

But Rebecca, on the other hand, was another story entirely.

The suite I'd hired was spectacular. The views spanned nearly fifty miles of white sand beach coastline. I felt like the King of Atlantis, above the gulf, even above the gulls and pelicans flying through the blue sky containing billowy clouds the largest I'd ever seen. It would be a spectacular sunset. I threw my leather bag on the bed, and began to plan out what I was going to order for dinner.

The concierge helped me coordinate the delicacies I was seeking. She reminded me that there were monogrammed towels, robes, and blankets in the bedroom closet and let me know if I needed any more, she'd send them right up. I felt confident handing over all those details, including the most fragrant long-stemmed red roses she could find.

"Is this a marriage proposal, Mr. Gambini?"

"No. Just someone very special. And if tonight goes well, then anything is possible."

"Oh I'm so excited to help you with this. Clients like you are why I have this job. I'll put on my thinking cap and call you back with some ideas after I've made some calls. You shouldn't worry about a thing."

I laughed. If only.

It was out of the question I would call the East Coast Bank & Trust, in either Manhattan or Boston, but I had to get the loan covered or this alligator would have a bunch of babies. And then I'd be asking for a job at the front desk, or selling Bentleys with Tony.

And that reminded me! I had a Bentley coming soon. I called the pretty concierge and told her to let me know when it arrived and to have several blankets placed into the trunk and figure out how I could keep a bottle of champagne chilled when I drove the beast. She squealed and promised it was a task she'd lovingly carry out.

But it was time to face my financial woes. I'd let the bank stew long enough. I believed there was another way to handle my predicament and remembered Frank's comment. I didn't have the answer yet, though.

My attorney was the call from D.C. and I called him next.

"Marco, not getting much cooperation from Frank. Is he on an extended vacation? Seems like he took his whole office staff with him."

Great. So much for simply fading into the woodwork.

"He's on a temporary assignment," I lied. "What can I help you with?"

"I'm being pressured for financials for the Trident Towers. You remember, we had that subpoena we had to produce documents? I've asked three times for a Performa P&L from his office and I get crickets. You wouldn't have that kind of information with you, I take it?"

"You know I don't."

"Well, they shut down the office in Belleair because there was a shortfall for payroll. Looks really bad when that happens. I thought you were tending to that with the transfers so this didn't have to happen. It's bad press."

"Have Celia in the HR department issue a memo about bonuses coming before Halloween, just in time for the holidays. An extra bonus for all their hard work and to thank them for their patience. And get them back to work."

"Yes, yes, we can do that, but we don't want to run afoul with Florida or Federal employment law. They'll have to be paid first."

"That's going to be my next call. Don't worry about it. All but on its way."

"Never mind the damage control. What I want to know is how did it happen?"

"I had a loan called."

"How much are we talking?"

"Ninety million."

His whistle was long and loud. "Are we solvent?"

"Of course we are, Bob. I could sell a couple of airplanes and raise the cash, given enough time."

"So where's the hole in the piggybank?"

"Guess. Where is it always? She got to somebody, and it started a domino effect."

Rebecca had intimidated the staff at the interior design group's office so much that one time she had overspent funds to redecorate our new build-out in Manhattan, a state-of-the-art center with an interactive display showing all the hot spots in the world today, and how one thing always leads to another. It was a brilliant idea, showing how something that happens in Africa could affect the price of water in the San Joaquin Valley for pear and prune farmers. Nothing was ever as simple as it was laid out in the large metropolitan newspapers. Stuff was always brewing just below the surface—stuff the general public and half our government didn't know about. But I did. I tracked these every day.

But even though it was a brilliant success and widely acclaimed as a masterpiece lobby, she spent twice as much as she was authorized. She had them all shaking in their boots, intimidated to the point of trying to hide that big goose egg under fear of being fired, until one of the junior clerks manned up and came to me, spilling the beans. He was the only one in that design department to keep his job.

That was the beginning of my seeing what she was doing. It

was like Chinese torture—holding my eyes open with toothpicks. We had the longest and loudest argument of our marriage. In the process, she destroyed a whole package of carefully wrapped paintings I'd just purchased to add to my extensive collection. I retaliated by grabbing her box of jewelry and throwing it off the balcony where it fell into the pool and marble surround at the Ritz in Paris, the place we were staying.

She became caustic and bitter, and we never made up. We fucked like dogs in heat, occasionally and rarely, but we never made up.

We never would.

Her new tactic of tying up my assets and putting holds on funds already approved for different projects, which, at the front end anyway, usually meant paying the visionaries to get the ball rolling on a new project, was what she had done since the divorce. I couldn't figure out why she still would have such a hard-on for me. She got nearly everything she'd wanted in the settlement.

But there was one thing she didn't like hearing, and my attorney rammed it hard into her and was unrelenting. She had the special clause he'd designed stricken from the settlement agreement. The language required that she distance herself from me, my companies, and my employees for the rest of her natural life. If there ever was any doubt, I was severing all ties to her, that clause was living proof I was as serious as a heart attack. She was to go away and never grace my doorway again. I'd paid a lot of money to make sure she would do that.

It took months, and even though she refused to sign it, we still left it in the agreement because I wanted it there, lined it out in red, and both of us eventually initialed it so we could be done.

But that's exactly what she was refusing to do. She was determined to continue to ruin me further by these antics and little surprises I had to juggle to fix. She would never give me my freedom as long as she was alive. And since I wasn't flush with cash like I was used to be and wasn't the jerk I could have been, she remained alive and able to walk the planet nearly unimpeded, spending *my* money to take away even more of mine. The lock-downs were having a debilitating effect on doing just every day, routine stuff.

"I know you've thought about putting a bullet into her brain, so don't quote me on it. But some how we have to get rid of her, and I don't mean physically, either, just so we're clear. Doesn't she have something else she likes to do besides make your life Hell?"

"I think if something were to happen to her, everyone in the world would blame me. But honestly, she'd probably rise from the grave and haunt me as well. She has no scruples. None whatsoever. If you ever get some good ideas, shoot them my way, please. Until then, we just have to do it straight up, because if we make a wrong move, she'll pounce on me."

"Just so surprising she would turn on you that way."

"Bob, I did nothing except ask her to leave. Maybe she thought I'd one day come crawling back to her. Ain't ever gonna happen."

"Yeah, and all of us have to keep our distance too."

I thought about Shannon. Maybe I'd have to adjust my standards if she tried to go after her. But hopefully, not.

"So call me tomorrow after you get this banking thing set. Let me know who can give me those records, or I'll have to ask for an extension."

"Get the extension. I've got to go to D.C. Tuesday. Then I'm off to the Indian Ocean for a few days, including travel time."

"The sultan?"

"Yup."

"You should ask his advice. How many wives does he have?"

"I think he's going on thirteen. And yes, I've admired how he can seem to keep his household in shape."

"Well, unlike Rebecca, they don't have much of an alternative."

"I think you're right, Bob. Rebecca has lots of options now that she's gotten the settlement. I'm going to try to get it all back, and then some. But I'm going to do it legally."

"Music to my ears, Marco. You did it once. You can do it

again. I'm keeping my ear to the pavement for wind of anything, and I'll let you know. You just go out there trying to patch everything up and I'll fight your battles in court."

I was glad I'd never taken anything out on him personally and still felt bad for how I'd treated Frank. I had deserved that one big time, and I really missed having him at my side.

My cell rang. Harry's familiar voice tried to charm me. He wanted to put the sultan on the line.

I was okay with that.

I was going to ask his advice. I embraced the inevitable that my future was somehow linked with his purely because he was probably the only person on the planet Rebecca couldn't get to.

Maybe that was his secret.

CHAPTER 14

Shannon

I FOUND JARED as soon as I walked into the station.

"I have a problem with the Rebecca Gambini interview."

He was crisply dressed in a white shirt, tie askew. His sleeves were rolled up. He'd been writing something, and as usual, he'd been dunking wads of discarded drafts, mostly hitting the garbage can in the corner.

He sat forward, elbows on the desk, checking his cell phone.

"The interview that's supposed to start in twenty minutes? That what you're talking about?" He eyed me closely, squinting, as if he suspected some change had come over me. Or maybe I was just feeling like I had a big sign on my back that said "I slept with Marco Gambini."

"She's already here, Shannon. She brought you a coffee. She told me she'd promised it to you."

"Oh God." I mashed my face with my palm.

"That bad? She have a disease of some kind, Shannon?" He wasn't getting any of what I was feeling.

Of course he isn't!

I looked down on him. "I slept with her husband, Jared."

He scratched his chin and fingered his lips, checking down the hallway to make sure no one was listening.

"Tell me why you thought that was a good idea?"

"I *didn't* think. I'm not sorry, but I didn't think."

"Let me see if I have this straight. You're the young lady who wants a career in broadcasting, is that right?"

I nodded.

"You ask for special favors, which I give you. Did you do this *after* or before I helped you get the interview all set up?"

"Both."

He cocked his head to the side as if he was going to knock water out of his ears. "I don't believe I'm hearing this. I once worked for an editor of a small-town newspaper who told me *never* to hire women. Work only with men. I'm beginning to understand why he told me that."

"Jared, I can't interview her. It would be unethical of me."

Jared stood up, walked behind me, and closed his door. He stood no more than a foot away. "No, Shannon, that would be *what you already did!*" He calmed himself and whispered, "I don't give a flying fuck how you manage to justify this little viper's nest of sex, lies, and video tape, but I won't be a part of it. And I'll not save your bacon, either. You're on your own. Get your little buns down to makeup so she can remove that disgusting peachy glow off your face and paint your lips red. Bright red. You Jezebel!"

Him raising his voice knocked some sense into me. He was right. It was all my problem. Why had I even told him? With my back still turned to him, I mumbled an apology and opened his door. As I was leaving I heard his stinging rebuke, controlled and softly spoken.

"You should have had the drink with me. That was the choice you should have made."

I carefully closed the door behind me and heard the crash of something hitting the wall in his tiny office.

Sandy, our makeup gal, took a look at my hair, still wet from the very steamy and soap-lathering love licking and kissing tickle fest in the shower and rolled her eyes. Her Cuban accent was always stronger when she was annoyed.

"Why didn't you just come in soaking? You got parts here that stick straight up and parts here that are limp, see? I cannot do curling iron on you because it will burn your hair. And it's no good to see that on camera, either. So, we leave it?" she said, with her wide, fake smile challenging me in the mirror.

"Yes, I think so. Where is…"

"Ah," she leaned over and whispered in my ear. "That beech I'd like to slap across the face. I do her makeup, all pretty. You know, for the taping? She stares at me and wipes it all off with tissue, smudges her lipstick halfway up to her nose. They gonna think I gave her a bloody lip. You watch out for dat beech."

"I already know about her. Just get some powder and lipstick on me so I don't look like I'm sweating through my clothes, which I am."

"Ya. I do a good job for you. I got a whole two minutes to do a good job for you. You know it takes much longer to do professional makeup."

"Stop it, Sandy, and just get it done. And, say a prayer for me."

She said something in Spanish I didn't understand and crossed herself.

"What did you do to get hooked up with this chica? You musta been a bery, bery bad girl."

"You don't know the half of it."

"So you gonna get your butt spanked today? It going to be a regular catfight with dat one."

"Sandy, this isn't helping. Please, I have to get to the set.

"Oh, the set! You should see the roses got delivered for the set. Making half the older folks around here sneezing their butts off, too. Roses is too strong I tell you."

"Who are they from? For me?" I was blushing through all the powder she was applying.

"No card. Nothing. I think they were for *her*." Sandy lowered her voice and whispered in my ear, "She musta got one of them gangsta boys or a Don. Someone who's all sorry he got nasty with her. Yea, dat's what I think."

But I knew otherwise. Marco was inserting himself into an already complicated and dangerous situation.

Bunny Copperfield poked her head into the room. "We gotta

go, Shannon. Everything's set." Her headsets were falling off the back of her head. She hugged her clipboard to her enormous chest. That was the way she always ran around here, covering herself up.

"She was askin' about the flowers, Bunny. You know anything?" asked Sandy.

"A secret admirer. We teased Rebecca about that."

Except no one else knew she was coming in except the staff here and Marco.

"Come on, Shannon. They're playing the weekend show credits."

"This is live?" My knuckles clutched the metal handles on the black makeup chair.

"Yes. Didn't Jared tell you? She requested it. He said he tried to call you." Bunny pulled my arm and extricated me from the chair. I ran quickly behind her to keep from falling.

The set was different than the normal routine. Hanging in the background was a huge American flag. On the raised dais were two light blue easy chairs, halfway facing one another on either side of a low coffee table with two paper coffee cups. On the table was an enormous glass vase filled with heady deep red roses. I didn't check for a card or note, because if there had been one, I was going to sit on it.

Rebecca came onto the set from the other side. She pointed to my coffee. "I brought you a cappuccino, just like I promised, Shannon."

I was frozen in place. This wasn't happening to me right now because I was somewhere else—anywhere else, floating up to the moon or someplace never to be heard from again.

Bunny whispered, "Sit, ladies! We have to start now."

I collapsed, kinda awkwardly onto one hip, then adjusted myself, pulled my hair behind my ears and over my shoulders, and smiled at the camera after I licked my lips.

They had a teleprompter all ready with my introduction, which I was grateful for and hadn't even thought about. As I focused on the letters, I heard Rebecca clear her throat and then gargle a tiny bit.

It was distracting. I was sure I looked like a cat about to be hit with a broom.

"Good morning, Tampa Bay!"

The canned applause had me looking off into the blackness to see where the audience was.

"We have a very special treat in store for you today. As many of you know, this station supports veterans causes, and when we heard that headway was being made on the new Trident Towers building for disabled Navy SEALs, as well as other at-risk and deserving veterans, we knew you, the viewers, would love to hear more about it. As luck would have it, we have our very own celebrity with us today, Rebecca Gambini, wife to former SEAL Marco Gambini..." My stomach lurched and almost tripped over the fact that they hadn't mentioned they were divorced.

When my introduction was complete and the canned clapping died down, I turned to Rebecca, who smiled back eagerly. I could see a little of the lipstick Sandy was talking about but doubted it would show. She was dressed in red, white and blue. I was in all blue.

"Welcome, Rebecca."

"Thank you, Shannon, for having me. I'm delighted to be here. Did you sleep well?" She followed it up with a wink.

I froze again. Did she know?

I studied my fingers twisting around themselves in my lap, brushed the hair that had fallen into my eyes, tossing it behind me, and then turned to the camera.

"What Rebecca is referring to is a very pleasant evening we spent together, listening to oldies music and drinking entirely too much wine."

Rebecca beamed. The canned audience laughter was a little late on cue.

"It wasn't wine. We were drinking Scotch," she said, nodding in my direction. To the camera, she announced. "It was one of the funniest girl's night outs I've ever had!"

I quickly jumped in, whispering, "Don't tell my mother. She thinks I only drink wine."

Again, more canned laughter.

"So, Rebecca here is working on the Trident Towers. Tell me about it and what are your plans? How can we help you as a station?"

"Well, thank you. I appreciate that so much. The Trident Towers is part of the mission statement of my husband," she raised her eyebrow and spoke lower, "my *ex*-husband, that is. And don't worry. It was an amicable divorce. In fact, I think he sent these, unless your boyfriend did, Shannon."

My pulse quickened. Either she was living in a fantasy world or she was tooling me. I couldn't tell which one it was, and what complicated it more was that she was right about some of it.

"No, I'm sure they were meant for you, Rebecca," I lied.

"I still enjoy working closely with him on his various philanthropic projects. As wives and family of Navy SEALs, it is often our calling to help heal these heroes when they come home. As I started to tell you, they have a saying, "Leave no man behind," which is throughout all our military as a code of conduct. Some who come home can't take the first step to becoming whole, to healing. They leave it all out on the battlefield and come home empty. We want to show them we love them. That they are not forgotten."

She delivered it well. I put myself in the place I would have been if I hadn't felt Marco pulsing inside me as he held me close— if I had never met him, tasted his kisses, or seen the way he looked at me when we made love with our eyes open.

"Such an honorable and noble plan, Rebecca. And how unselfish of you to carry on your husband's vision, too."

"I think if you really loved someone once, you always do," she answered timidly.

I imagined if Marco were watching the interview he'd throw something at the set right about now. She was exquisite with the lying and the play acting. Far better than I.

"So when does construction begin, and will all the designs be the same as previously proposed?"

"That's the part I love the best. I should have been an interior decorator. We're picking out colors right now, placing holds on fabric and carpeting. The construction will begin just as soon as the modified plans come out of design review. We have the financing all ready to go. I'd say, by next April? And occupancy on some of the earliest units in the back a year from now. Just in time for Thanksgiving and Christmas."

"Really?"

She nodded, proud of herself.

"What kind of changes are you making to the plans?"

"Well, we've created some group living spaces where several bachelors can live together, share duties. They will be offered at a reduced rental rate. We have small condominium-style apartment homes for purchase, which will of course qualify for VA so the vets can come in with no money down. We've got a scale model prepared for the hearings, and I've brought in a whole new team of sales agents and representatives of the non-profit to help these men and women find the right home for them, based on what they can qualify for. We'll have some that are handicap accessible for some of our disabled veterans."

She made it sound like Shangri-la. I was genuinely impressed at how well thought out the project was. "I'm sure our viewers will be anxious to hear more about it. When you have the interior renderings and color schemes, would you come back and share it again with us all?"

"I'd be happy to, Shannon."

"And how can veterans get in touch with the non-profit group that is helping to spearhead this?"

"Well, when I took over, I naturally had to make some staffing changes. I have a brilliant general manager working under me and he has charity background, so he's going to handle the sales. Perhaps we can have him come on and share as well. He's smart.

He's about your age, Shannon, and he's very cute!"

I couldn't help but blush. I immediately sensed he was her new boyfriend, her new toy. Someone she could torture and make run away.

"I'll leave the contact information so anyone can call the station and get that given to them," she added.

"That would be great!" My voice broke so I grabbed my water.

The ending music began, and I was surprised how quickly the ten minutes had gone by. After I thanked her for her time, we talked out of earshot of the audience. She became fixated on the roses and touched them.

"You are sure your boyfriend didn't…because this looks like…" she started.

"No, ma'am. If he had sent these, there would have been a card. Trust me on that." A nervous giggle erupted from my throat, and then I had a hiccup.

"May I take them with me?"

"Of course. They're yours, Rebecca."

She eagerly grabbed the huge vase, peeked around the bouquet and asked, "Care to join me for a bite to eat?"

"No, thanks. I have some things here I have to work on for the weather report later on."

"Dinner?"

"My boyfriend, remember?"

"Oh yes. Well, maybe tomorrow then. If you're free."

"I'm going to play it by ear. He has to leave on—" I hesitated giving too much detail. "I think he'll be here until Thursday, and I want as much time with him as possible. Thank you so much for doing this, Rebecca."

"I enjoyed it."

CHAPTER 15

Marco

THE BENTLEY WAS to arrive soon, so I quickly showered. I thought about the phone call I had with sultan Bonin earlier today. It went well, which is to say I gave him everything he wanted. In return, he got *me*. He didn't want anyone else. He wanted me. And he would have paid double what he offered me. It was an insane amount of money.

So I light-heartedly asked him for his advice on the woman front.

"My biggest problem, son."

"Oh really? Because everyone looks pretty happy to me."

"You are not family. With family, they fight like cats and dogs."

"So how do you keep the peace, then?"

"By never expecting it to change. Now, when my affairs of the heart get in the way of my duties as administrator of our tiny kingdom, my ministers' step in, and that's when it can get ugly."

"You love them all?"

He chuckled, then fell into a coughing fit that concerned me. "If they are blowing on my balls and sucking my staff, yes, I fall in love. I like to fall in love several times a day. But you, Marco, you are at a very great disadvantage. You should have been raised in our part of the world. You could have—"

"I never wanted more than one woman at a time. That's where we're different."

"Ah, so you have been bitten hard by the snake of love. Then it is simple. You will feel much pain and be miserable until the day you die."

It was my time to laugh. I nearly spit out my coffee.

"Haven't you learned by now how to ignore them? I've seen pictures of you guys running on the beach. You don't grab the pretty ladies who like to show themselves to you and take them in the waves, do you? You focus on your mission, and that is why what you offer is a gift greater than happiness, than all the wealth of the world. Me? I don't have that. I learned my lesson. I fell in love with Harry's mother. I could never make her my wife, but she was the wife of my heart. It was her face I saw when I was bedding my wives. I saw little Harry's tiny face when I greeted my other children and grandchildren into the world. And because of that, I had to move her away from the palace, or both their lives could be at risk."

"You see her?"

"It was a long time ago, Marco. I don't want to see her now. She was the sweetest flower of all the land. I want to remember her that way. My seeing her would be dangerous for her. I had to cut out those feelings with a sharp knife, because it was my love that would cause her death."

"Fascinating. We are polar opposites."

"So why all this talk of managing harems you will never have? Sounds like perhaps you are in love with two women at the same time?"

"No, not really. I thought I was in love when I was married. But now I don't know what it was. It was like I was running away from something. I needed something from her for a time, and then when I stopped needing it, somehow, we just ended. The fun and excitement were gone. She's probably right. I was the one who walked away, even though she was the one who was unfaithful."

"Women are complicated. You ignore them. You let them go. You bury your happy memories if you have to, but you let them go find someone else. And then you pretend to be happy for them.

You see? That's how it works."

"So I shouldn't have gotten angry when she sued me for divorce and took away half my fortune—or more?"

"Mmmm. I see, young Marco. You didn't fix this soon enough. What were you doing, this running away?"

"I was driven to become a success. And the woman I loved, I made her wait too long."

"Go back and get her, Marco. And tell these two other women who are fighting over you to—how do they say it, 'put your big panties on?' The sultan laughed until he began the coughing spell again.

"Are you sure you are well?"

"Who cares? I am in pain, and I know there are things inside me that are not right. But as long as I can still fuck, I'm alive. In my mind, I go someplace else, and I cavort with all the nubile virgins who I haven't tried yet."

Maybe the sultan was right. I was running from Rebecca, who wouldn't let go. I was running into the arms of someone new. Perhaps I'd been running away from the one I should have married, my dear, sweet Emily. And I couldn't go get her because she was gone forever.

"You are too pensive. I don't like you pensive, Marco. I wish my sons had as much honor and commitment as you have in your little finger. I wish they thought more about their choices and the consequences of those choices. You're too hard on yourself."

"You're probably right. But my problem is that the first one I loved is no longer walking this planet."

"Yes, I think Harry told me about this. I am so sorry for you. So you cannot repair things with your wife, or is the new girlfriend too much of a temptation to walk away from?"

"Neither. Rebecca, my ex-wife, won't leave me alone, even though I left years ago. And now she's bitter, spiteful, and making my life miserable."

"You will really have a problem when she learns about the new one."

"She won't."

He laughed again, this time surviving without the coughs. "Women always find out. You be careful. Your new one is tough?"

"She's strong, not tough. I don't need tough. I need to feel like I did when I had Emily. She's very much like her, in certain ways. In other ways, no. Emily was simple. She wouldn't have cared about all the money I made or what kind of a house we lived in. In a way, I don't think she would have loved the man I became when I was married to Rebecca. And all Rebecca wants to do is take everything away from me."

"Ask the favor you are afraid to ask, my son. I see no easy doorways open to you."

"No, I'll think of something."

"Marco, you need a loyal friend who can play in your sandbox. You are going to help me with these kids of mine and their project in Africa. I don't care if they lose money. I just don't want them killed in the process. They don't see danger all around them. They still think they're in Disneyland. I send them to schools. They are indulged, fancy boys who make horrible decisions and even father children from low caste women. And why? They could have all the beauties they want. But no, they want the common girls, the street urchins. Why, I'll never know."

"Well, I understand that a little, I guess. They want to do it on their own. I hope that they don't realize too late what a gift having you for a father is to them. You are their greatest fan, their silent ally."

"Ally! That's the word I was looking for. So. Marco. How can I help you? I want to be your ally."

I wasn't proud of it, but he was offering his hand. "I need a miracle, sultan."

"Done. You tell Harry how much."

"How did you know I wasn't going to ask you to get rid of my wife?"

"Because, Marco, you would never do that. You'd die first. And that's why you are going to protect my sons. I won't murder for you, but money? I can do money."

THE STATION WAS just about to air Shannon's interview when I got the call that the car had arrived. I slipped on some shorts and flip flops and dashed downstairs shirtless, doing a skidding stop on the smooth marble floor of the Oceanis grand lobby. I felt I was playing Poseidon in a movie or something, with all the colorful larger-than-life mermaids and sea creatures suspended from the multi-storied ceiling and depicted in beautiful stained-glass windows that gave the feeling of being under water. I was hoping I could get back upstairs and watch the news in time to see Shannon's program.

When my forward movement stopped, I noticed I'd attracted quite a bit of attention. A couple of ladies sitting in the bar gave me a loud whistle and a toast, already smashed at ten in the morning.

I took my bow, and ran outside to behold my new toy. It was cherry apple red—the most brilliant red I'd ever seen, that lipstick "I'm in trouble" kind of red, or the red a naughty girl would wear to church. The ivory and caramel leather interior was stunning. No one would ever mistake this beast for the cockpit of an airplane, and that was why I loved it so. Light Ash dash, heavily grained, made a gorgeous contrast to the sleek lines and tan colored top, which was down, of course. She looked dripping wet for me. I was going to have so much fun in this baby.

"Mr. Gambini?" A tall, handsome twenty-something kid came toward me wearing one of Tony's white polo shirts with the Bentley logo on it, extending his hand to give me the keys.

"You won't really need these, but you might have to valet park. Come on and let's get your thumbprint recorded, shall we?"

He looked like he was having as much fun as I was. I pressed my thumb against a tiny square piece of what looked like glass embedded in the shiny chrome of the driver's handle. His fingers pressed tightly on top until the few seconds passed and a discrete beep came from somewhere on the dash, indicating my fingerprint had been stored.

"So if someone wanted to steal this car, they'd have to bring me with them, right?" I barked, turning heads in the entrance.

The kid had a healthy laugh, showing perfectly straight and brilliant white teeth. "Well, your thumb, at least. And if it's detached, before it gets too wrinkly."

It was funny. The kid was okay. I immediately wondered if he needed a job, since everyone was quitting these days.

I focused back on my new ride. "Can I take it for a spin?"

"Of course, sir. She's all yours. You want me to show you all the bells and whistles?"

"I guess I can be patient. How long will this take?"

"Seriously? About forty-five minutes." He didn't flinch, so I knew he was telling me the truth.

About halfway through the demonstration, Corrine, the pretty concierge, came running out with her arms full of beautiful camel-colored blankets with the distinctive *swimming O* that was the logo for the hotel embroidered in blue at one corner.

"Pop the trunk, and I'll place these inside," she said with a confident grin.

I hit the wrong toggle and started the windshield wipers, getting water on the leather front seats. She handed the stack of blankets to me and quickly rubbed the seats down with one of the monogrammed towels she had also brought.

"I'll just get you another, Mr. Gambini," she gushed, covering up my misstep.

"I'm so sorry. I guess I should have paid more attention."

The delivery salesman pressed a button on the key fob, and the trunk popped open slowly without making a sound. Inside was a matching set of his and hers luggage pieces, made from the same darker accent leather on the interior, so it tastefully matched the car. He found a space between the two pieces and laid the blankets down.

Corrine was running off to the lobby area and as an afterthought, turned and waved at me. "Don't go away. I have something else to show you. Wait right there!" She was jumping like an oversized piece of popcorn.

The salesman completed his instruction, showed me the compartment where the leather-bound car manual was located. Tony had provided him with my insurance information, so that was tucked inside. The booklet holding everything was embossed with my initials, MG.

Corrine came clickety clacking down the entrance steps, taking what sounded like little bird hops, carrying a wicker basket with a bottle of champagne nestled inside, surrounded by fresh towels.

"It has no ice, just gel packs, which you can re-freeze and re-use."

"Or, you can store them in your little cooler in your trunk, Mr. Gambini," Tony's guy said.

"You have to be kidding me?" she gasped. "You have a refrigerator in your car? That's amazing. You could drive from here to San Francisco and never have to stop for cold beer!"

Under her arm, she held another folded fluffy white towel to replace the one she'd used on the seats. They had my initials on them as well.

"I guess you can steal the towels here, Marco," said the kid.

I knew I'd already missed Shannon's show and figured she might have saved me a clip. I really didn't want to think about Rebecca, anyway. I hadn't brought my license so Paul, the young salesman, accompanied me on the test run.

When I pushed the button, the thing growled and idled like the racehorse she was. I commanded her with both hands on the steering wheel, released the brake, and away we went. The car's pedal was going to take some getting used to, featherly light and so sensitive. I was getting turned on by how little I had to do to get such a complete monster reaction out of her. We drove down Gulf Blvd., turning heads everywhere. She wanted the freeway, but I wanted to treat her to a nice tree-lined pasture for her maiden voyage. She cornered perfectly.

She was going to be my second love.

I couldn't wait to show her off at sunset.

I left the keys with the concierge, who squealed with delight. "I want roses tucked in two bouquets on the rear seat floor, the champagne in the middle."

"Oh, and I've found some to-die-for grouper bites, too, and some blackened shrimp. I'll put some grapes in there as well. I didn't have time to get the flutes monogrammed, sorry to say."

I kissed her on her cute little forehead. "Go make me proud, Corrine!"

"What time will you arrive?"

I checked my cell. "She is supposed to meet me at six. I've got the right spot picked out for our little picnic."

"Leave it to me, Mr. Gambini. And you'll want roses in the suite as well? Some midnight snacks in the refrigerator? More champagne chilled in a bucket?"

"Perfect. I'm hiring a car to go pick her up, so you can get the red-head ready. We should be here no later than six-thirty, but I'll text you."

"Oh, Mr. Gambini," she said, her hand clasped under her chin, "You are such a romantic. She's a lucky girl."

"I'm the lucky one."

I WAS AT her house when she arrived home, using the key she left for me in a flower pot. I'd taken the time to study every piece of her artwork carefully. I didn't want to pry, but something about this woman was a mystery, as if we'd been connected in another life.

And I never believed in such things.

"Is that your car outside?" she asked as she ran to me.

"Of course it is. He's waiting to take you to your surprise." We kissed. She smelled so good, and with the good news I had with the sultan, I felt free to just enjoy her lovely body, her happy spirit. It was one of the things I did need from her. And I'd always been a man who didn't need anything from anyone.

"So how did it go?"

"You didn't watch?" She wrinkled her forehead, disappointed.

"I'm sorry, but I had something that I had to do. But you'll get a copy of it, won't you?"

"Yes. I just hope that you're not upset when you watch it."

"Why would that be?" I said as she folded into my arms.

"At first, I thought she was just going after this project because it was something you felt strongly about. Now? I actually think she wants to do it. She's hard to figure out. Could you ever see your way to letting her take it over?"

"Never."

"But if she left you alone?"

"I don't know what it would take to have her leave me alone."

She laced a forefinger over my lips. "I think she needs a job in life. Maybe she just wants to prove to you that she can do big projects."

"She can't." I separated us, walking over toward the kitchen, rubbing the back of my neck. "And I'm done talking about her."

My words must have been too strong because Shannon looked like she was about to burst into tears. I crossed the room like a flash, took her into my arms and rocked her. "I'm sorry. That came out wrong."

She broke away from me this time. "Give her a chance, Marco."

"Maybe I better see the video before I answer that."

"Fair enough. I can live with that."

SHE QUICKLY SHOWERED and changed into a very low-cut black cocktail dress and some sparkly sandals that highlighted her slender ankles and beautiful, long legs. She wore a brightly colored scarf for a wrap, and as the car drove up the ten miles of beach homes, I could see that we were nearly out of time to watch the sunset, but we'd make it.

When we pulled into the Oceanis entrance, we scattered a flock of flamingos who were crossing the approach. We stopped just behind the beautiful cherry red Bentley convertible. I pulled her from the back seat, and sent the driver off. The bellman came running, bringing me the keys.

"Sir, we were afraid you weren't coming. You didn't text."

"I was so happy seeing my girl I completely forgot." Shannon smiled back at both of us.

"Ready to take her for a spin?"

"This? This is yours?"

"Yes, ma'am, and you're going to drive us. Can you do that?"

Shannon curled down her lower lip. "Is it a stick shift?"

"Nope. Automatic. Twelve cylinders of pure cherry-flavored pussy."

I loved seeing her blush. I helped her into the driver's seat and strapped her in.

"Marco, it has champagne. I don't want to spill it, and flowers. OMG, there are dozens of roses here. Did—"

I stopped her with a kiss. "Yes, I sent them. Did you like them?"

She didn't answer.

We headed up Gulf Blvd. until I found the beach access road I was looking for. She carefully drove the lush green jungle trail until we came to the clearing on a vacant lot I owned. I instructed her to face the car toward the street and aim the rear at the beach and ocean.

"Come on," I said, running to her side. I unlocked the trunk and pulled out the blankets, handing them to her, then brought the wicker basket with the treats and the champagne. I pulled her up over the dunes, and we lay the blankets on the white sand, sat and watched the orange globe of the sun begin to set. Everywhere we looked the sky was orange and purple. A warm breeze blew off the bay as I sat behind her, holding her in my arms.

"I never get tired of this view. It's the best thing about my little bungalow."

"Agreed. You have one of the best views. Tiny house but big view."

"No one's here."

"I know. That's why I chose it."

The sun hung so low it nearly touched the water as I poured her glass and watched the bright orange glow in her face and shoulders, the way her eyes sparkled, the way she smiled at me.

"To us, Shannon. I made this sunset for us."

"To us."

She touched her glass to mine, took a sip, and watched the sun disappear.

I parted the towels and found some still-warm cheese biscuits and grouper bites, which were amazing. They'd put grapes and strawberries in there, along with cheeses and some crackers. She fed me, and I sucked her fingers if she wasn't quick enough.

It was beginning to chill with the sun having set, but the air was still streaked with color. The waves washed the beach clean as birds ran over the smooth sand foraging for food.

"Wanna try something with me?" I asked.

"Now you have me intrigued. I could sit here all night. It's so beautiful."

"You can see it a little better from the car, Shannon. And I can turn the heater on, if you like. And it will smell like roses."

Her dancing eyes told me she was game.

We gathered everything up and walked the tiny dunes trail to the car. I removed one of the vases of roses and the holder that was keeping them balanced and placed it on the ground. I pushed the seat forward, spread two blankets on the floor and the seat and directed her to kneel so she could see the view.

I poured us each another glass of champagne and joined her. Bringing another blanket up to her shoulders, I whispered between nibbling kisses, "Take your panties off, Shannon."

She set her finished glass on the floor and blew back to me, "I'm not wearing any, Marco." I let her remove my glass and then work on my pants buckle, unbuttoning my shirt as she did so. Her cool fingers slipped down the front where she gently squeezed my package. Her eyes didn't divert from mine. Her tongue touched my lips, then my extended tongue until the kiss deepened and that glorious rush of adrenaline came over me.

I palmed her bare ass, rubbing her up and down, then let one hand press between her thighs in front to touch her where she wanted to be touched.

Holding her by the waist, I sat her sweet little bottom on the folded canvas top, and parted her knees. I could still see her lips, swollen, abused, and about to be used some more. Two fingers slipped inside her as she moaned and leaned back, resting her torso on the canvas. I removed her sandals one at a time, kissing her up the inside of her legs until my tongue found the warm, pulsing folds of succulent flesh. She pressed one foot against the headrest of the driver side and slid back farther, spreading her knees wider.

Her dress slipped off in my hands. Then I slowly suckled, kissed, and penetrated her with my tongue.

"Oh, God, Marco! I'm going to come in your mouth already."

"Yes, Shannon. Give it to me."

Her sweet juices covered my lips, my chin and my nose. I nipped her clit with my teeth and she went wild with need. I savored and watched her squeeze her breasts, then sit up and hold my fingers as I entered her over and over again until she drew my face up to hers and took from me a long, lingering kiss.

I carefully turned her over, her glowing ass making me hard just looking at it. Her elbows rested on the top. I rubbed her sex and then gave her space to think about what was coming next while I removed my shirt. I plucked one of the roses and let it tickle her from her neck to her anus. I crushed the flower and allowed the petals to fall all over her nude body now being illuminated by moonlight. My pants fell to my knees as I stood on the seat, kneeled slightly and pressed her body against the car. I positioned my cock so she could feel how engorged I was. I rubbed my tip over the crease in her ass, probing, sliding and then finally entering between her fluttering labia. Holding her hips, I pulled her back and onto me, rocked her with my thighs, allowing her to straddle my lap, and then rammed inside deep as if I could split her in two.

Our tongues played as we kissed from the side. I spread her cheeks, and moved deeper still. Her behind pressed against me for full penetration, her feet at my sides as I pumped her, picking up the pace until her long rolling orgasm completely overtook her. I grabbed her hips, pulling her to me as I spilled. And then we paused, listening to the sounds of the ocean and the birds who came out to feed.

With the sky turning gray and the ocean chill invading the bluff, we gathered our things, put the top up, and returned to my motel.

I knew I was going to remember this night forever. I was hoping that she would too, when she turned her head and whispered, "Marco, I never want this to end."

I was going to do everything I could to make sure it wouldn't.

CHAPTER 16

Shannon

I WOKE UP with a headache and briefly calculated how much champagne I'd consumed—we'd consumed—and took in a deep breath. I was alone in the bed, covered in rose petals. Some of them were caught in the strands of my hair splayed all over the pillow.

I took stock of what the night had been like, both of us unable to sleep because just about every flesh on flesh turn of our bodies created another sensual experience, if not a full-on intense love-making session. Overwhelmed was the word that described me perfectly. My stomach churned. My heartbeat was still racing because my libido had been amped up so often it was stuck on full tilt.

I brushed his pillow where his head had been then grabbed it and pushed it against my face, inhaling his strong, masculine scent laced with an exotic cologne I'd gotten so used to. I couldn't get enough of him.

I was lost.

We'd whispered many things to each other in the early morning hours, and yet I was careful not to sound too smitten. But the truth was I was drowning in pheromones for this man, and it would be a mistake to be the first one to utter the words "I love you." But that's how my heart sang no matter how much I tried to stuff it down.

My experience with men was seriously lacking, but I knew that he was volatile enough to go through heavy mood swings, and because of his current financial situation, he'd be more vulnerable to this now. I didn't want to be one more problem he had to deal with. I could be patient if I wanted that chance for the brass ring.

With the interview with Rebecca, I'd already caused problems enough.

I wanted to be his calm before the storm, the someone he could reach out to and trust, even while I harbored that deep secret of my past and how it intermingled with his from so many years ago. I guess I was lucky he didn't remember. No chance I'd ever forget it, and no chance I would ever be able to recover from all this, either.

Somehow, I'd find a way to tell him. He was a man who deserved as well as needed the truth. I. Would. Do. This.

I heard him talking on the phone in the living room, so I slipped on an Oceanis white cotton robe, cinched up my waist, passed on the logo slippers, and padded out to the living room barefoot to find him. I grabbed my phone on the way and, as I approached, took pictures of his back as he sat on the arm of the couch, legs crossed, looking out at the ocean.

I walked around him to block his view, still taking pictures. He frowned until I opened the sash of my robe and let my body do the talking. I began filming his expression as more of my body was revealed. He uncrossed his legs, lost his place, and stumbled to finish a sentence.

His eyes were filled with lust as I moved slowly towards him, slipped my robe off my shoulders, and then kneeled in front of him.

He was desperately trying to end his conversation, which made my ministrations all the more exciting for me. I discreetly turned off and placed my phone at my side and let my fingers walk up from his knees to his hardening cock, spreading the robe over his knees to look at what I'd created.

With his eyes closed, he tried to concentrate. "So you've got it all set up, then? And he'll—*argh*." He gasped as my lips and tongue played with the tip of him. I looked up, watching his eyes as I took one long lap of my tongue from his stem to his tip.

He suddenly gasped.

I could hear whomever was on the other end of the line ask him if everything was okay.

"Yes. Yesss," he hissed as I took him into my mouth all the way until my lips were pressed against his lower belly. He tried to continue. "I'm just so taken with the view from up here. It's incredible." He leaned over and let his hand slip down my spine, traveling clear to my butt crack and then smooth over my buttocks, giving me a silent paddle. "It's so fine," he whispered. And then he sat up and signed off the call.

He threw his phone on the couch. "I hope you didn't tape any of that?"

"Just the part before I slipped off my robe," I said, licking his tip and running it over my lips. "I hope I didn't embarrass you too much."

"You are soooo bad, Shannon," he howled, standing, picking me up and throwing me over his shoulder. He spanked my ass several times on the way to the bedroom.

He spanked deliciously hard.

"Ouch!" I howled.

He threw me on the bed and shook his head as well as his right forefinger.

"You deserved every one of those, and you know you did. You are a naughty. Little. Girl," he enunciated as he climbed up to join me, brushing rose petals to the side.

I stubbornly kept my legs tight together as he tried to separate my thighs. I watched him struggle, my hands above my head, fiddling with my hair. My stomach undulated and teased him, as I acted absent-minded. I pretended to fight him off, all the while needing him to consume me one more time. His cock was red and huge this morning, engorged since our last encounter.

He finally got my knees to separate and I arched up, feet planted on the bed, giving him full access.

"Oh, baby. You are so swollen. Did I do that to you?" He mocked concern, frowning.

"You did, and I liked it."

"Poor thing. Look at how pink and"—he dipped his head and lapped my sex—"hot you are. I'd say feverish."

I felt the jolt from his touch all the way up my spine. Something in my stomach lurched.

"Fix it," I whispered. I let him see the desperation in my face.

His eyes sparkled with the birth of an idea. He held up one finger and ran to the kitchen and pulled something out of the freezer. When he returned, he had the gel pack in one hand and a leftover champagne bottle in the other.

"Hold still. Doctor Marco is going to fix it for you, sweetheart." He held the frozen but still soft gel pack against my flaming lips and pressed. At first, I felt nothing, due to the swelling, but all of a sudden my insides began to spasm and react to the cold.

Discarding the gel pack on the floor, he opened the champagne, took a swig, and then tipped it over, and poured it all over my lips. He lapped and poured, poured and lapped, letting the champagne also drip down his chin onto his chest.

"You want some?" he asked, his eyes wide and dangerous.

I nodded, raising my head to accept the cool bubbly liquid. My ass was sitting in champagne-soaked sheets. My boobs glistened as he did a pour-over and sucked my nipples. The pulsing inside me continued. He drank the rest of the bottle, letting it roll off the bed and onto the carpet.

I was insane for him to be inside me. "Marco, please," I begged.

He fingered my folds again, gently pinching my clit. "You want this, don't you?"

I nodded again, breathing hard and licking my lips, loving how he rimmed and penetrated my opening.

His motions were gentle as he adjusted his upper torso forward, taking hold of my wrists high above my head with one hand and pressing his warm cock at my cool entrance with the other.

Slowly, he pushed his way inside, watching me, watching how wide my eyes got, watching my breasts rise and fall as he stretched and massaged my throbbing parts. He rubbed my nub gently and breached my entry, violating me so lovingly. I felt my muscles immediately close down around him. I arched, pressing my breasts to his chest. He kept my hands immobilized but lifted my left knee to above his shoulder, angled to the side and pressed deeper and then deeper until he was knocking on the door of my sweet spot.

His slow hip movements, expertly riding me and playing my body like an instrument replaced the throbbing pain with pure pleasure. His back and forth was slow, deliberate. There was no urgency to any of it, as his gentle rhythm grew my arousal slowly.

This was all about me, and he made no mystery of it as he watched my face and my body react to him. I writhed against the constraint of his fingers gripping my wrists, so I could fully enjoy the capture.

Several minutes later, my internal muscles suddenly clamped down on him, causing me to suck in a deep breath. I exhaled and sank into the wonderful rolling orgasm, leaving my body shaking.

"Oh, baby. You are so beautiful. Look at that," he whispered.

He plunged in and then held himself as I continued to spasm, falling over the edge of my quick little orgasm like a leaf over a waterfall. And then I felt the familiar pulsing as we both stopped moving and experienced the full impact of our union.

I had never felt so loved. I would never recover from what he'd done to me, both to my body and to my heart.

I was lost forever.

WE ATE BREAKFAST in the fern and palm tree courtyard dining area filled with filtered morning sunlight. I was still reeling from the emotional love-making session that preceded our dangerous shower. I couldn't stop smiling, looking down at my lap, almost embarrassed at how intimate and persistent Marco was with me.

I felt cherished.

I also felt a twinge of sadness that I was having an experience that perhaps should have belonged to my sister. And yet, I wondered if their relationship was somehow different from what I was feeling now.

I could tell he was studying me from across the table.

"You're awfully quiet, Shannon." He took my hand across the table and smiled.

"I have no words. I'm a reporter, well, a weather girl," I said as I tossed my head from side to side, "and I have no words. That's kind of funny, don't you think?"

"You mean like me not doing something because I'd be afraid it would be dangerous?" he tried.

"Yes." I leaned forward, putting both elbows on the table. "I never expected this. To—" I was going to say, "to feel this way" but stopped myself.

He was showing his confusion, his brow furrowed.

I understood now why Emily was so upset when Marco postponed their marriage until his next deployment was over. Almost as if she knew she didn't have much time left. I did have time. I just didn't want him to go. I continued.

"I guess I'm regretting how I'll feel when you've left our sunny state."

He paused, still holding my hand. "Then come with me to Boston, Shannon. You could even find work there if you wanted."

I didn't want to go to Boston as his extra piece of luggage. I wanted what I had here, and I never expected to feel so torn.

"No, Marco, I can't do that."

"You visited me once. You could come again. You have friends there, right? Some other reason you came to Boston?"

This was the question I didn't want to address. I wasn't ready.

"I just felt like it."

He angled his head. "Did you come to see me?"

I had to lie. "Not entirely. My friend told me about this Bachelor Towers place where women weren't supposed to own apartments. I had to see for myself because it sounded so backward. But when I read an article about who lived at the Towers, and saw that you were one of them, well, with your project here in my little sleepy town in Florida, I had to see who this man was."

I didn't want to look him in the eyes because I was afraid he'd see the truth. I'd just dug my hole a little deeper. Would there ever be a way I could extricate myself out of this and keep us together?

"I hate the press. They can be so cruel. And you know, you can't trust much of what you read."

"I'm with you there, Marco."

"So about my leaving, I have to go early tomorrow morning. I've got some business things to attend to and fix a wire transfer that I found out this morning didn't happen. I can't do that from here. And then Tuesday I go to D.C. If Boston is too soon, why don't you meet me there, then?"

"Washington, D.C.?"

He nodded. He wasn't pushing. I was flattered with his persistence.

Relieved we'd gotten off the subject of my first trip to Boston, I smiled. "You know the answer to that. I have to work, but thank you, Marco."

"Then quit."

"I don't *want* to quit. I like my job, most days. And I like the warmth of Florida. The beach, the tropical breezes. It's sort of exotic to me, a mixture of Mexico and the Caribbean. I feel at peace and at home here."

He nodded. "Someone asked me yesterday if you were tough, and I told him no. But I was wrong. You are very tough."

Ask me a different question, Marco. Tell me something I can count on.

I was proud of myself, until he asked me another question.

"Okay. I'm going to try one more time. Come with me to India, to the sultan's palace. That's exotic. You can smell the spices in the air. Beautiful beaches, blue water. His Pink Pasha actually sits on an atoll with coral pink sand. They import flamingos so you'll feel right at home. Imagine wandering around the palace at midnight. The stars never looking brighter. Torches flaring. Beautiful silks and tapestries blowing in the breeze. Opulence you wouldn't believe. You could use it as background for a news story about traveling to exotic lands."

"And when are you going?"

"I have to be there in five days. I'll be done in three, maybe four days, to meet with his sons and their team, but he'll want me to stay longer. Why don't you fly to Boston first and we'll fly out together? It's a long flight, but on a private jet, it's way more fun." He wiggled his eyebrows.

I found it hard not to blush. My heart was fluttering at his beautiful descriptions of a place I knew nothing about. I agreed it would be an interesting trip, to learn about those lands and cultures, since my cultural exposure was so limited. It was very tempting.

I decided to split the difference, keep the door open but make sure I wasn't something he intended to drape across his arm. I didn't want to be a harem princess. The train had already left the station and I wanted to see where it went. I hoped to contribute somehow. I never wanted to be a restricted bird in a golden cage.

Marco would have never liked that, either. Why did he expect that I would?

"I'll ask for time off. I'll ask for a week, ten days, and I'll try to give you an answer today. But I don't want you to be angry at me if I won't quit my job to do it."

"I understand."

He held out his hand, and we left to attend his project meeting. Our plan was that he was going to take me home and then pick me up again for dinner. He'd already told me he wanted to retire early. So that gave me an idea.

"About dinner, Marco. Why don't I make you something at my place? If you're comfortable, you can spend the night, or come back here. But it's up to you."

"What would *you* like?"

I waved my hands out above my head. "This is beautiful. It really is. But I like my little place better. I like hearing the ocean. I like to cook. You've shown me how you live. Let me show you how I live, what I like to do in that little space. I don't need all this. I'd like you to stay with me before you go."

It took a few seconds for it to thoroughly sink in. "Okay, we'll do that. If that's what you want, that's what we'll do."

"Thank you."

"For what?"

"For listening to me, for understanding what's important to me. Not everything in my world is about money."

He was silent for a moment, and then he said something that brought tears to my eyes.

"You remind me of someone I used to love a long time ago. She passed away way too soon, unfortunately. But I suddenly miss her."

"I understand."

And I did.

CHAPTER 17

Marco

THE OFFICIAL BONE Frog Development group sat on mismatched office chairs we'd secured from thrift stores, along with several desks and some file cabinets in beige and sand colors. Our rented office was one block from the construction site, in a repurposed gas station. It wasn't fancy, but it was cheap space, and the group had shown their creative genius by fixing it up with a great sound system, bright colors, and eclectic artwork. I found some of my old things I lent to them as well.

My loosely labeled manager, Rhea, and her partner had designated themselves as leaders of this little conclave, the "mother hens" so to speak. They were fiercely loyal, and I liked that they were invested in the project and loved bossing people around. But they were effective at it, not abusive. The team we'd hired together loved them both. Each of them had a different style, which worked well. I couldn't have made it with just one without the other. Between their talent and their management style, it was a winning combination. I also felt they had my back.

Between the two, Rhea was the one who didn't have a problem speaking her mind, whereas Dax, her partner, was the soft touch and the person who smoothed over ruffled feathers. Rhea had been born into a military family and had lived all over the world, and she'd served as a communications officer in the Marines for ten years. The only person she reported to was me, but she didn't mind co-managing the group with her lifelong girlfriend.

"It isn't about the money, Marco. It's that you backed out on your promise, man," Rhea barked. "I never thought we'd have to face this, Boss."

I could see we had more of a problem than I'd calculated. I knew I should have been on it sooner. "But I didn't do it. Rebecca did."

Rhea had a small contracting company doing remodels. She hired mostly women carpenters, plumbers, and electricians. It made it so much easier that I didn't have to worry about little construction defects or issues at the space, because Rhea and her ladies could fix anything. I was counting on some grant money for having such a large female staff and hoped I could award the buildout to them. Rhea could also do material takeoffs faster than anyone I'd ever met since she knew how to read plans.

"I'm not abandoning the project. I can't battle everything at once, guys. I've made a promise. It isn't going back on my word. I have to do this strategically."

She didn't like it, but she seemed to accept it. I caught her eyeing Shannon several times and knew I'd have to make a private, formal introduction or there would be gossiping going on all over the place.

One of the new hires I didn't recognize, who was wheelchair bound, added, "We do appreciate the extra, but I gotta get a job. I can't wait around to find out if I got a permanent job."

Rhea pointed over her shoulder with her thumb. "He's reception."

"I may not have legs, but I'll bet I can climb a ladder faster than you!"

The group laughed and I was grateful for the lightheartedness. I hadn't seen him do that, but with my experience in several foreign countries, I'd seen people do amazing things without the use of their legs, and climbing ladders was one of them.

"Look, guys, I got it." I was truly sorry for having brought them together, gotten them so excited about what we could do, even with the divorce raging, without it occurring to me that my personal life would affect theirs. I fully intended to make it up to them, and told them so. I asked for their patience and to trust me.

Almost no one believed me. The groans and whispered swear words were frequent and disturbing.

"I thought you had the financing all set up, Marco," someone asked.

"It got pulled. I had a note called, part of my divorce attorney battle, and it caught me completely off guard. But I've secured the replacement, so all will be good."

"Except she's going around town telling everyone she's in charge. So what does that make us?" someone else commented.

"We're the barnyard animals," countered Rhea.

It bothered me that these people, who had so little, had shown their loyalty to me and I was in danger of letting them down. Somehow, I'd get this thing back on track and turn it into the flagship I knew it could be.

"And that's the problem. I can't stop that as fast as I can make sure you get paid," I added.

"For how long?" one of the big guys asked. I knew he'd also been a Marine. "I got a kid and a wife. I gotta get a job, Marco. Unlike you, this isn't a hobby."

I did understand, but they obviously felt like the little guys, the ones who always got the shaft. I was going to make sure that didn't happen.

"I'll promise you'll get paid for at least two months, maybe three. We still have work to do. We collected a pretty sizeable list of possible donors. Those people have to be contacted. And we have the suggested recipients. Rhea, you said you wanted to work on the standards. Everybody's needs will be different, depending on their situation. Most of the project will be guys, but we had a family unit set up. I don't know what she's doing about that, since she's having some changes done. But our work isn't done."

More groans erupted from my group.

"Someone is going to have to go over to the Design Review office and find out what changes they are proposing. I understand they aren't approved yet, and I guess I'll be forced to speak with Rebecca, through her attorney, of course."

I didn't see much hope in their eyes.

"Why doesn't *she* ask her?" Kevin, a twenty-something with full sleeves asked, pointing to Shannon. "They're buddy-buddy. She's the weather girl, Shannon Marr."

"Not really," corrected Shannon. "It was just an interview and probably a one-off at that."

"But you could ask," suggested Rhea, giving her a respectful wink. I could see Shannon wasn't entirely comfortable with her.

Shannon looked at me, and I gently shook my head. It was a bad idea.

"I'm not sure she's still in town, anyway," she answered. "But I'd be willing to try, if you think it would help, Marco."

God dammit. This is the last thing I need.

"I don't want you anywhere around her." I stopped all the crosstalk that had erupted with my voice rising over their chattering. "The checks will be couriered here tomorrow—for all of you. You'll get checks every Monday for at least two months. You can count on that."

I asked Rhea and her partner to meet me in the back, out of earshot of the rest of the group. Shannon joined us.

Rhea looked her up and down. "Hey Boss, do I have to train my replacement?"

"I couldn't replace you, Rhea." I pulled Shannon over to my side, wrapping my arm around her waist. "This is personal. Very personal. And none of your goddamned business, either."

Rhea chuckled, and Dax looked relieved. "Nice to meet you, Shannon," she said.

"You ladies are in a perfect position to try to get yourselves hired over on Rebecca's crew. If you do, and you report back to me, you'll still get your salary here, too. But I want just the two of you to go first. I need to know if she's really serious about the buildout."

"Boss, I don't understand why you don't just talk to her. Work something out," said Rhea.

"So she can screw me again? I wouldn't give her the satisfaction. I'm going to be gone for about two weeks. During that period of time, divide everyone who's staying into groups and put someone in charge of each one. One group can contact donors. Another can interview the vets who responded to the interest post card. I want the team leader of that one to interview every single one of them. Go to their houses. Get a sense of what they really need. We'll start with this group, make a list of their needs, and then adjust from there. I need to know what handicaps we're building for."

"Did you have the trees cut down?" Rhea asked.

"I did not."

"So she's started spending her own money, then. Or has a loan in place?"

"Yes, unfortunately, she has a lot of money, and all of it was mine."

"What if she really wants to help, Marco?" asked Shannon.

"She's uncontrollable. She wants to be in charge, and she has no experience with building things."

Shannon spoke up again, objecting. "She told me in the interview she had a new project manager helping her run things."

"Yeah, I feel sorry for the guy," I added with a chuckle.

"What if her plan is a better one, Marco?" Rhea's partner asked.

"It's expensive getting a subdivision re-drawn. I can't imagine anything we missed. That's about thirty thousand dollars right down the drain. But you're right, we need to see what she's got up her sleeve."

"I'll go see what's been turned in, and then I'll look her up from the City file. I can send the redraw to Boston, if there is one?" Rhea asked.

"If you can get a set of plans, that would be awesome," I answered. As an afterthought, I added, "You guys get in there and dig around. I think you'll make the best spies. If it works out, I might be able to use you somewhere else."

"Where?" they both said in unison.

"Either of you ever been to Africa?"

WE DROVE BACK to Shannon's place, where I dropped her off. Before she went inside, she stopped and asked, "While you're gone, can I have a set of your old plans to look over, just for giggles?"

"Sure, I can get a set sent to you."

"Would you mind if I hang around the office in my spare time? I'm good with the phones, and a lot of people know who I am."

"I can't see that it would hurt. Let's talk about it tonight at dinner. What time, and do you need anything?"

"Just you. I even have more wine than I know what to do with. See you about five-thirty or six?"

"Or before."

"I'd like that too. You can pick up something sinful and chocolaty for dessert, if you like."

I had some great fantasies about chocolate syrup and whipped cream but decided I'd leave that for another time. This was going to be our good-bye dinner for now. I was grateful I'd have a few hours to myself to make some calls and check out of the hotel. I might even need a nap!

I needed to think about where we were going as a couple. She was being very good about not bringing it up, but I could tell it was on her mind.

The sex was great. We had fun. I loved surprising her. But all that would not hold up forever, if there was no future.

It was kind of dangerous to be jumping head-first into a relationship again. I hadn't exactly been the poster boy of success in that arena. But I knew deep down that if I walked away from this one, maybe there wouldn't be another.

Emily had taught me that.

"You gotta grab what happiness you can and hold onto it with all your heart. No regrets, Marco. We jump in without hesitation. If you need to do your deployment, go do it this one time, and I'll be here for you. But after that, I get the white dress, the flowers, the party and the honeymoon, and you're gonna wear your dress blues. Because when you come back, your ass is mine."

Those were the last words she'd told me. I wore my dress uniform at her funeral for the first time. I'd wear it a lot during the years as I lost people. Funerals, always funerals. So many men and women who didn't come home.

I'm still here. Maybe so I could get it right this time.

CHAPTER 18

Shannon

JUDIE POPPED IN unexpectedly. Looking over the mess in the kitchen, she knew something big was happening.

"*Fresh* pasta? Boy, I must have missed a whole lifetime. What in the world have you been up to?"

"It's too much to explain."

"Try me."

I pulled my hair off my forehead with the back of my hand. I could feel the flour trickling into my scalp, which meant now I had to make time for a shower and shampoo. I nearly burst into tears, which really surprised me. But the change between where I'd been when Judie and I last talked and where I was floating around now was so dramatic, it was just a bridge too far.

"Uh-oh, Shannon. Now you've got me worried," she gasped. "Your lower lip is protruding. What have you done?"

I didn't try holding back the tears. I placed my hands on the floured countertop and looked directly into her eyes. "I've gone and fallen in love with Marco Gambini."

"No! Say it isn't so!"

"I'm afraid it's true."

Judie gave me a puzzled look. "But, most people, when they fall in love, they're like dancing around the room, hugging babies and old men. They're whistling in the grocery store. Life is suddenly beautiful." She carefully delivered her kill shot. "You don't look that way."

"It's complicated."

"How could it be complicated? He's gorgeous. He's got a ton of money." She frowned and tilted her head slightly. "Unless…he's not in love with you. Tell me that isn't so."

"We haven't talked about it. But I think so."

"Ouch! Boy, he'd be off my list."

"He's worth it."

"Ew. I don't like the sounds of that. Shannon, it's not that complicated. Of course, I'm the one who never takes her own advice and has sex before there's a commitment. Like the Love Vixen lady says, get a ring and date first."

"I don't think she's ever fallen in love with her older sister's fiancé, who was a billionaire, and is now struggling to survive. He's got a lot on his plate."

"So you won't be the focus of his world, then. I'll bet right now all he wants to do is screw, am I right? He probably doesn't go calling his board meetings and signing contracts when you guys are working on the birds and the bees, fulfilling yourselves to your highest climax."

I felt a little guilty. She was right, or at least from what she knew she was right. I'd had more sex in the last three days than I'd had in three years.

I checked my timing. I needed to clean up the mess and start making the seafood alfredo topping for the fresh pasta, and mix the green salad. And I needed a shower.

I began wiping down the countertops.

"Oh, Shannon, here. Let me do that. You get yourself into the shower."

"No, I have to make the sauce!"

"Okay, but let me do the clean up here. You take that side of the kitchen while I clean up this one."

"You got it."

I was ruminating about all her questions. I hadn't even gotten to the part where I was going to accompany him to a real sultan's palace in five days. That I was taking a whole ten days off work, and I had to promise I'd do all kinds of things to get that favor, too. I hadn't told her I'd gotten drunk with his ex, either.

The tears were threatening to spill over my lower lids again as I added the butter and flour into one pan while sauteing the salmon and fresh scallops in another. I added some coriander and then some cheese until it melted into the butter mixture, then added the cream and stirred.

Judie put her arms around me. "What a problem to have, right?"

I chuckled, adding the fish mixture to the pan. I handed her the wooden spoon to stir since she'd cleaned up everything. I began rinsing vegetables for the green salad.

We worked in silence for about five minutes. Her mixture had begun to thicken, and I was done with the salad fixings, placing them in the refrigerator to chill.

I poured two huge glasses of red wine and handed her one. "We need to talk."

"You want to go out to the beach?"

"Not today, Judie. Maybe you can help me figure out something."

We sat in the living room, across from each other.

"Shoot," she said.

"I'm going with him to an island in the Indian Ocean, some sultan's pink palace. Supposed to be a really beautiful place. We're flying by private jet and then helicopter. This sultan has like thirteen wives, maybe more, he doesn't know. I'm to meet him in Boston in five days and we leave from there." I gulped down the whole glass of wine and gasped. Judie watched me with eyes as big as saucers. "And he still doesn't know who I am."

There. I'd told her everything.

She had barely touched her wine, which wasn't like her. Her gaze was focused on something on the floor because she was thinking about something. I diverted my focus to the side before she could make eye contact.

She took a sip and whispered, "I can't fix this."

I BARELY HAD my clothes on when Marco was at the front door, bringing me some of the roses from his room. He had something in a bright pink box tied with candy-striped string. I could smell it was going to taste divine.

"Here, take these, and I'll get my things from the car."

I added the roses to another vase, placing them at the table, and moved the spring bouquet onto the countertop. He entered with his leather bag, leaving it by the door instead of putting it in the bedroom. I began to get nervous.

He came to me, and I melted into his arms, feeling safe and loved. I inhaled the heady scent I never wanted to be without, and steeled my heart for whatever was to come next. His fingers laced through my hair.

"You want some wine?" I asked.

"Sure."

He was watching me carefully as I poured from another bottle. I was a little tipsy. Maybe that's what he was noticing.

He toasted my glass and remarked how good it was. I already knew that. I wanted to hear what was on his mind because his mood had changed.

"You want to eat?" I asked. "It's all ready."

"Smells wonderful. I'm starved." But neither of us moved.

If I wasn't careful, I'd be bursting out in tears, and nothing had really happened. I was just so sad all of a sudden. I had no basis for coming to that conclusion, but I felt like I'd blown the opportunity of a lifetime.

"Let's sit down," he said.

My knees stiffened. My stomach began to clench. It wouldn't be cool if I threw up in front of him, but I was headed there. I left my wine glass on the counter and took a seat across from him, just where I was when I talked to Judie this afternoon. I liked looking at Marco better.

"I have to tell you something, Shannon."

Oh, here it comes.

"I think I've taken advantage of you, and I'm so sorry I did that."

"I don't feel that way."

"But I do, and that's important to me. I just burst into your life, upsetting everything. I asked a lot from you."

"Nothing I wasn't willing to do. I'm a grownup. I didn't feel put upon. I've enjoyed being with you."

"But like you said, this world of mine? It isn't your world, and I wasn't being sensitive to that."

"It's a lot to get used to, don't you think?"

"I totally agree. And that's not my point."

"Okay." My heartbeat was still racing from the dark wolf in the forest.

"Remember when I talked about the woman I'd been in love with all those years ago? My first love?"

My veins turned to ice water. This was becoming a horror film. They found Emily, dug her up, and she was now a vampire She'd bit him and taken him back. Something like that.

"Her name was Emily. She was a lot like you. And it's got me thinking…"

He's figured it out! OMG he thinks I've lied to him!

"Marco, I know what you're going to say. I'm so very sorry. I shouldn't have done it. Can you forgive me?"

He suddenly looked confused. "Nonsense. You haven't done anything."

"I should have told you sooner is what I meant."

"But Shannon, we never spoke about it before today."

"I know, Marco. And that is all my fault."

"That's impossible. You could never do anything I wouldn't love. That's what I'm trying to tell you. I'm in love with you, Shannon."

I couldn't speak. He slowly stood, came over to the couch, and knelt down in front of me, holding out a huge diamond ring. "I think I knew the first time I saw you. Everything fit into place so perfectly. Like we were long-lost friends, soulmates from another time and place."

"But…"

"Shannon, marry me. I waited too long before. She didn't want to wait. This doesn't have anything to do with her, but she taught me something. And I felt her come to me this afternoon, and it was like she was telling me I should stop waiting to join her, that I should find someone just like her, and do what I should have done before."

"But…"

"Don't you see? I never believe in these kinds of things. But it was like we were predestined for each other. You're the girl I've been looking for, waiting for my whole life."

I was in shock. I let him lift my left hand and slide the beautiful ring on my fourth finger. It was so heavy I felt like I'd fallen into the ocean, and that ring pulled me right down to the bottom of the sea, where I'd be forever.

CHAPTER 19

Marco

S HANNON DIDN'T REACT how I expected. I knew she didn't suspect that I would impulsively propose, but I didn't plan on her shivering, distance, and the look of pain on her face.

"What is this, Shannon? What's happened?"

"Nothing *happened*, but it's—"

I got to my feet, then sat next to her, my arm around her shoulder. She'd been playing with the ring, which was a little too loose. She was twisting it around and around her finger, staring down at her lap, gently rocking back and forth.

"I'm sorry about the size. I guessed. It will be easy to adjust." Was that the real problem going on with her?

She stopped rocking.

"Are you ill?" I persisted.

She carefully shook her head from side to side, her eyes still focused downward.

I decided to just wait for her to tell me. Maybe she couldn't get the days off she hoped she could and was somehow upset about that. Maybe Rebecca paid her a visit. But something was definitely different, and I was worried, getting more so by the minute.

Then she turned toward me, our knees touching. She wrapped her arms around my neck brushed her cheek against mine. I felt her whole body shaking. When we parted, I could see she'd been crying.

Had I missed something? If she was averse to getting married,

I'd try not to pressure her, but this wasn't the Shannon I had gotten to know. At last, she wiped her tears off her cheeks, removed the ring, and placed it in my palm, curling her fingers over mine and began to sob.

Through her tears, she said, "I can't accept this until you know the truth, Marco. I've been lying to you, and I feel horrible. I'm not the woman you think I am."

"I don't understand. What big dark secret do you have? I swear to you it won't matter."

"You don't know that," she mumbled, again wiping the tears from her cheeks. "I've been so dishonest with you."

Anger was beginning to boil in my belly. I'd been certain she would be thrilled at the prospect of spending the rest of her life with me. I felt punched in the gut. I was beginning to wonder if I knew anything about women because obviously something had happened and she was locking me out. I wanted answers and I wanted them fast.

I got up, shoved the ring in my pants pocket and started to pace. "This is complete bullshit, Shannon. I expect the truth from you. You better tell me the score or I'm walking right out of here and I'm not ever coming back."

Even that didn't make her spring to action. I felt a twinge of regret that I'd spoken to her harshly. Whatever it was, it was serious. I'd never seen her this way before.

I started guessing. "You're married."

She shook her head.

"You have five kids."

"God no."

"You have an incurable disease?"

"No, not that either."

"Does this have to do with Rebecca?"

"No." She inhaled deeply and then stared into my eyes. "The reason you thought everything was so familiar between us was that we *have* met before. We met over fifteen years ago."

She was waiting, searching my face to see if that helped me

figure it out, but I still didn't have a clue.

"How did we meet? Fifteen years ago, you were what? Ten?" I asked.

"Emily was my older sister. I'm Melanie Shannon Mabry. When I moved to Florida and began at TMBC, I picked a stage name. I used my middle name, Shannon. But—"

"Em always called you Shan," I said from memory, pictures of those days flooding my mind. The horrible pain and loss came back, and I felt like a terrible trick had been played on me by God.

"Marco, I was a preteen. Braces, bushy eyebrows, and skinny. I wore glasses in those days, and they were thick and huge. I got Lasix. I grew up, and when I shed all those things, I was a different person. Like a butterfly breaking out of its cocoon."

"So, you planned all this?" I demanded. I couldn't help but tighten my fingers into fists, trying to destress, but it wasn't helping.

"I didn't plan for all this, no. But I came to Boston to see you, to meet you, because I'd dreamed about you all those years. I just wanted to see—"

She began to tear up again.

"I never had what Em had, Marco. I wanted to see what that would feel like. I didn't intend to come insert myself into your life. I just wanted a taste, maybe just to experience something *she* had, maybe in some small way to bring her back. And that's stupid, I know."

I ground my teeth. I really thought I had experienced Emily talking to me, telling me to move on today. But it must have all been a figment of my imagination, because deep down inside, I must have sensed little Shan was just like her older sister. My mind had figured it out when my heart wasn't paying attention.

Here was yet again one more heartless betrayal. One other instance where I hadn't been paying attention. I was so intent on deepening this relationship out of pure fantasy, I was blindsided and I fell into the trap I'd fallen into before. Twice before.

The fact that she'd lied to me was so painful, I couldn't look at her any longer. I felt so completely ridiculous spending so much money on that diamond. Buying the red Bentley. What was I thinking? I didn't even know her. Heck, we never even talked. I hadn't asked her what it was like growing up. I didn't have a clue what I almost had gotten myself into.

"I do appreciate one thing, Shannon. I'm glad you told me now, not when we were halfway around the world, and thank God you told me before I entered into some sham marriage based on lies. It takes guts to tell the truth."

"No, I wasn't that noble. I thought you'd caught me. I knew I'd tell you eventually, but things got so hot and heavy, and then I never wanted it to end. I kept pushing it off into the distance, looking for a way, a time to tell you. But yes, that ring forced the truth out of me."

"So you basically *stalked* me?" I couldn't believe how vulnerable I was. "Am I that dumb?"

"No, it was chemistry. All that was real. I just came on stage under false pretenses. Don't beat yourself up, Marco. And because I used to watch the two of you, and when she was home on weekends from college, she used to tell me about you. I used to think about what it would feel like to kiss you. I didn't mean to take what was not mine."

I suddenly was transported back to that time. I leaned over, scrambled her hair on the top of her head, and said what I used to say all the time, "It's okay, kid. Things will turn out."

She broke down, hugging her knees. When she looked up at me at last, I saw those strong, unflinching eyes that I could get lost in. "I am so sorry. So very sorry. I never meant to hurt you. I know you'll never forgive me, but I want you to know, because I probably won't ever get the chance to say it again—I do love you, Marco. That part was real."

THE UNIVERSE HAD tilted, and I was in free fall. This was going to force me to re-think and re-evaluate every decision I'd recently made. My businesses were falling apart, and Rebecca hadn't done that. I did it. I was the one responsible for causing all this. I'd lost my focus, and now it suddenly had gotten worse.

Ten years ago I would have completely lost it with Shannon. But now, I was just numb. I could even understand why she did it, and that really surprised me. What I had the most difficulty with was that I didn't catch on. I pieced together the clues, and instead of coming up with a pink flamingo, I'd created a pelican. It was close. She was right. The chemistry was indeed there. But I was ill from knowing my firewall had been breached and my judgment was flawed. I acted with my heart instead of my head.

I vowed never to do that again.

I said good-bye and thanked her for our time together. I told her I needed to get somewhere all by myself and get my head on straight. I promised I'd let her know when I got back from D.C., and maybe we could talk. She told me she wanted to help out with the Trident Towers, asked my permission to see if she could get Rebecca to cooperate. She silently accepted my leaving without further drama, which I was grateful for.

I walked away knowing that she was wrong. She wasn't anything like Emily. If anything, Emily was the younger sister. Shannon was a complicated, confident woman who was even stronger than Rebecca, just in a softer way. She could move mountains with her smile. She charmed me, and that was because I wanted to believe in love again. I *wanted* to be charmed.

It would be hard to watch her on the TV, thinking of all the things we'd done. I tried to fill in the blanks, because we never talked about it. How she grew up. How her poor parents were. They'd been so devastated with Em's passing. I didn't have any of that information. And maybe it was better that way.

I asked the Oceanis to store my convertible and to wash it every day, even park it out front if they wanted. I wasn't sure what I was going to do with the car.

I arranged for my pilot to come over early, and within three hours of my botched proposal of marriage, I was wheels up and headed back to Boston.

My pilot didn't ask too many questions and focused on his job, of course. He hadn't bothered hiring an attendant. I nestled down in the wool blankets and fluffy pillows and slept all the way until we landed. I vowed I'd stop being so indulgent with the alcohol, the desserts, the exquisite foods, and go back to my "Go-To" diet, and I'd start working out again. I had to get through these next few days. If I could get my body into action, focus on re-connecting with all the D.C. allies I lost touch with as I fought off the attorneys, and when I got back out into the field, covered in dust and jumping from airplanes again, I would start to heal. Hiding, rescuing, defending people and leading escape missions would bring me back to life. That's the only item on my agenda, while I cleaned up the pieces of my broken fortune.

Alone.

Maybe Em had taken that happy family and the true love por-tion of my life to the grave with her. It was only now, fifteen years later, that I finally caught on.

But at least I caught on.

Shannon would land on her feet, because that's what she de-served. It wouldn't be useful to be bitter about it. That never was her intention. We both got caught up in that fantasy and were equally at fault. I didn't want to expend the energy blaming her, because it wasn't true.

As my driver pulled up to the Bachelor Towers, I handled my own bags, stopped by to pick up a Midnight in Manhattan from Ollie and went right to my floor without answering any questions.

The sterile place felt like a shiny gilded cage as I walked in all alone once more. I had to get more paintings on the wall, some color in there.

I removed my tie, brought my drink into the bedroom, ex-hausted, and began to get ready for bed early. The sun was still up.

In the shower, I thought about Shannon. As I tucked myself into the sheets naked, I thought about Shannon.

Yeah, I had been bitten by the snake of love, just like the sultan had advised. A tiny regret tugged at my heart. It was unfair, but it was definitely there. I'd looked forward to bringing her back here, remembering our beautiful first night together. I wanted her in every part of my life. How in the world would I ever forget how I felt with her? Even as determined as I was, there would always be that hole, that place where I felt safe in her love.

I thought about all the lovely things we would have done in this bed, in this apartment, had looked forward to.

If she were here.

I fell asleep with a smile on my face.

CHAPTER 20

Shannon

I'D NEVER CALLED in sick before, but I did today. I needed a day of sleep and walks on the beach. I needed to face the reality of what I'd done, look inside my heart, and try to figure out why it all went so wrong. Why did I think that not telling him would make things any easier later on? It was a stupid, foolish idea. It was important to get it settled in my own head first. Then I'd meet the world and embrace the rest of my life.

But I did prove one thing. I devised a plan, executed it, and went for broke. And I nearly made it. Never again would I use a lie, even a white lie, as a coverup for being real. My choice was real. It was how I did it that doomed the mission. I should have told him that day when he said, "No more secrets, Shannon." That would have been the perfect time.

So many of the wonderful qualities Marco had were complementary to my own. We made a good pair. I resigned myself to the fact that if there was one man I could run off with in reckless abandon, there had to be another. I didn't need five or six. Just one more. When the right time came along. I completely pushed out of my mind the worry that perhaps there would never be another. That there was only one man for me. That I'd met him, fallen in love with him honestly and with my full heart, and that my methods were completely wrong. But I had to believe that, one day, there would come another.

On Tuesday, I went back to work and told Jared that I wasn't flying off to a pink palace in the Indian Ocean. He almost looked disappointed for me. If he studied my face any closer, he'd see my puffy eyes—the result from an all-day crying jag.

It had taken Marco several days before he called me again after our first encounter in Boston, but I didn't expect he'd really call me this time, even though he said he would. I braced for that. Accepted it as the consequence of my actions. I respected his boundaries now, unlike before. I wasn't going to delude myself or pick weeds in his garden, because it wasn't my garden.

But it sort of felt like making amends to show up as a volunteer at his center. It made me a better person, and I needed that. Nobody expected it, and I even asked permission, just to keep it clean. I intended on doing this in and around my work schedule, since I had no social life now.

I didn't expect any resumption of our former relationship, so I concentrated on doing more meditation and stretching. I started eating less and drinking more water. I knew in time it would stop hurting so much. Time and the beach.

The beach heals everything. It was my favorite plaque on my wall. I would live by that motto every day until I was whole again.

I even accepted Jared's invitation to have a drink later in the week. I thought he was going to fall off his chair when I said yes.

I stopped by the project after work on Wednesday and helped Dax's group make calls to donors from our curated list. I used my real name, since anonymity was what I was going for. I was just doing the pure work and not getting celebrity status out of it. It was the least I could do after creating such an upset.

Judie and I planned to go to the movies on the weekend. We both had a lot to catch up on together. She loved hearing about Marco and how he lived his life in the old days before either of us knew very much about him. We made up stories about what we'd do if we inherited hundreds of millions of dollars. And now I realized how shallow that had been. It was Marco I had fallen in love with, not his lifestyle, his handsome body, or his warrior mentality. I loved the part of him that reached out to me and trusted me, before I shattered it. I would try to think of him that way. Always.

Rhea got a set of plans from the County, and before she sent them to Marco, I looked them over. Rebecca had submitted extensive changes, she pointed out.

"The cost of concrete for these foundations will be at least double what it was before."

"How so?'"

"Well see, she's used the full forty-two-foot height, adding additional units for a third floor, complete with balconies. Many of the exterior windows had been changed to sliding glass doors for access to those outdoor places. That also means there will be new engineering costs and calculations. We don't have earthquakes, but we have tropical storms and hurricanes to consider. More stories, more windows. More balconies, more weight."

I could see, as she pointed out all the details, Rhea understood that this project wasn't anything like the original proposed plan.

"She's going to have to go before the design review, but maybe the planning commission too," sighed Rhea. "I wonder if she knew that."

"So that would delay the project, then."

"Yes, I think we're looking at maybe six months, a year additional, maybe longer."

"I don't get it. Why do you think she's doing this?"

"Well, it is a much nicer design. I mean it's really pretty, but it's going to require a lot more money. I hope she's got unlimited funds."

I wondered if she'd gotten a wealthy backer.

"Did you try to get hired on?"

"That was a no-go. She recognized me right away. Dax too. And she has some guy who used to work for Marco there too. I've met him a time or two."

"Who was that?"

"He's an accountant, I think. Calls him her project manager."

I decided I should speak to Rebecca, see if she would open up about her plans. Maybe I could still be useful for Marco.

Judie was against it when I told her later on.

"That's not a good sign, Shannon. You need space. You need to distance yourself from all this. Time to move on. Didn't you get the memo?"

"I am moving on. This is how I move on. By doing something important for someone I care about."

"No you're not." She sighed, getting ready to give me the lecture I probably deserved. "This is what got you into trouble before. Face the facts. Move on so you can make the clean break. It will continue to cause pain if you even have the possibility of running into him again."

"I don't think that will bother me."

"Would you listen to yourself? You must be joking, Shannon. You're setting yourself up for a huge fall. What happens when he brings his new love into the office, or you see his picture in the society column on the arm of a beautiful heiress or something? You'll be looking for him everywhere."

"Am I that obsessed, still?"

"Yes! Finally something smart out of your mouth. It's unhealthy to hang on."

"Okay, then. I'll speak to Rebecca, communicate to Rhea what I've learned, if anything, and then move on."

"Unbelievable. You are the most stubborn woman I know, and I know a lot of stubborn women too! That's what you said when you went to Boston—'just to get a glimpse, have a drink with him.' That's what got you into trouble in the first place. Now do you get it?"

"Thanks for your advice."

"Which you're not going to take."

"I can't. I want to do something good for him, and then I'll exit the stage and go home."

I left her shaking her head, mumbling things loud enough for me to hear as I walked to my car.

I didn't pay any attention.

REBECCA'S SYRUPY SWEET demeanor was as overpowering as her perfume. She was packing, returning back to New York, but agreed to meet with me.

"All my friends loved the interview, Shannon. I should hire you as my press secretary. Want a job?"

Of all the things she could offer me, that one made me laugh.

"What's so funny?"

I knew I couldn't be honest with her. And here I went again, making things up. I probably should look into becoming a private investigator, the way I snuck around, spying under false pretenses.

I decided to keep it as clean as I could. "Nothing. Just hit me oddly, for some reason."

"You have quite an interest in our project here. Would you consider working on it?"

She was actually serious! That gave me the segue to ask some of the questions I needed answered.

"Let me ask you this first, if you don't mind."

"Go right ahead." She placed a cosmetic bag, bulging with tubes of creams and makeup, on top of her folded clothes, with a towel separating it. She saw me eyeing the towel. "Yes, I steal towels all the time, if they're good ones."

"I—I wasn't going there. I just noticed it. That's all. No judgment."

She continued packing but was nearly done, so I had to think of something quick.

"Can I buy you lunch? Or do you have a plane to catch?"

She checked her watch. "I have forty minutes before the car comes to take me to the airport. If we can order and finish in forty minutes, I'm all yours."

Rebecca made a big point of telling the waitress we were in a hurry and ordered her lunch without using the menu. I just agreed to the same thing to make things easier.

"What do you want to know? And you're not recording this, right?"

"No, ma'am." I thanked the waitress for our waters. "How did you meet Marco?"

She sat up straighter, her eyebrows rising under her bangs. "At a party in Coronado. A buddy of his was getting married. I knew the bride. The groom was a SEAL. We danced. We drank too much, and the rest is history."

"No big romantic date, then? The stars didn't fall from the sky the night you met?"

"He was in a mood. He'd just lost someone. He wanted to forget." Her eyes sparkled with deep dark undertones. "I liked the way he screwed. I was hooked." She followed it up with a pert smile.

I knew the feeling well.

"But in time, you fell in love, right?"

"I think he did. We got busy. He was all fire, going out to play on those ridiculous missions of his. I loved that he was so happy to see me. I enjoyed it when he was gone. I loved it when he came back." She smiled again, like she was withholding a secret. "I became indispensable. He has a real blind spot for people he tells himself he cares about."

"*Tells* himself? I'm sure you loved each other."

"Oh, I never loved him. I loved being around him. I don't think I'm capable of love."

I must have looked shocked because she continued.

"The only thing he truly loves is his job, his missions, his brothers. They are an old school of guys who leave a trail of ex-wives and kids behind them. They usually don't manage their money well. Marco was the exception to that. But still, when it came down to it, he'd rather go do something dangerous, make money for others, than enjoy being a husband, a father."

"Is that why you never had kids?"

"I couldn't have any. I don't think he's the fatherly type."

"I'm so sorry."

"Don't be. I was raped when I was sixteen, had a complication of a pregnancy I never should have had, and just like that, no babies for me. One of my father's friends. He should have been charged and sent to prison for what he did to me. I decided that day that I wasn't going to let any man do that to me again. I made what I could out of it. Hated my father for the rest of my life. It actually became a blessing in disguise because I could do things other girls couldn't. I expressed myself through sex. It opened up a whole new world for me, so I grabbed it and ran. I don't spend any time on regrets. What about you?"

"It has to mean something for me. I am very guilty of wanting to be alone a lot. My books are my best friends, my boyfriends too."

"You'll have to meet my new manager, Frank. He used to work for Marco. He's married, but he's not a bad lay."

I was repulsed.

"Oh! I didn't steal him away from Marco," she said, holding up her hand, "if that's what you're thinking. I do have some scruples."

Except you made him cheat on his wife.

"He's not permanent. I'm still looking. And who knows? This project takes a year or two longer to complete? You never know. Marco might get lonely and come walking back through my door. I'll take him with welcome arms. We were a great team. I miss all those sweaty nights."

I suddenly saw what she was doing. She was never going to let go of him. He had way underestimated her. His only option was to quit the project, and be done with her.

But I knew he couldn't do that.

I asked her a few more questions, and we agreed to talk again after she got settled in New York. I told her I'd do a follow-up piece for TMBC later, and she was delighted.

"Think about what I offered you. I could teach you a lot, Shannon."

If she only knew what a sneak and a cheat I had been as well, I think she would have been impressed. But I didn't want any more of that. The bitter taste in my mouth was hard to get rid of.

I missed the fresh kisses and whispers. I missed the soft, trusting intimacy we had. I wanted what was real. My heart told me my love for him was real, but I knew I had to carefully bury it. I still loved Emily, too, and always would. Loving her wasn't predicated on me being around her every day or even visiting her grave.

Just like it would be okay to love Marco still, and never see him again.

CHAPTER 21

Marco

M Y MEETINGS IN D.C. went well. I got a track on a couple of projects the State Department was orchestrating, selling protective gear for IEDs in several third-world countries. I would be the middleman, and because it wasn't arms, it came under our foreign aid categories and didn't need congressional approval.

My company in Vietnam made these blue "ponchos." They could stop anything but a .50 caliber round and were very effective for roadside bombs.

We were also selling these to other contractors, and I was given the lead to a large award I didn't get because I was indisposed. But I could sell them the goods, and that was almost as valuable. I knew there were some Chinese firms who were trying to duplicate my product. I was scrambling to move my factory to the Midwest so I could say it was one hundred percent American made. And I had to be realistic, my designs and fabric would be copied. It was only a matter of time.

I interviewed a couple of candidates for the CFO position, two in person and one via video conference. Bob had done a great job working with the HR Department, finding candidates. He was also pleased to learn I was headed to India.

"Rebecca's attorney has quit. He called me yesterday to tell me he thought things would be quieter."

"He can say that?"

"Professional courtesy. He's resigning his firm, going into the

Peace Corps, if you can believe such a thing. I think he's lost his taste for blood."

"That's what she does. Uses people and spits them out," I added.

Bob was watching me.

"You look tired, Marco. I think the trip will do you good. The sultan really stepped up to the plate this time for you. You're the luckiest guy I know."

"Spoken by a man who only feels comfortable in three-piece suits."

"Okay, I didn't like that, but it was justified. But I'm bringing this up because you've been driving so hard and fighting so long. Time to come home from deployment. At some point in your life, you have to learn to enjoy it."

"I do enjoy it. I enjoy the hunt. Exceeding capacity. Winning in court occasionally is actually fun, now. Except for the cost."

"I'm not reducing my fees."

"Wasn't asking."

"You're forty-five?"

"Watch it. Forty-three."

"Time to start raising a family, or raising someone else's family. You know lots of good men who never came back. Their wives are good women, Marco. Doing the best they can. Go pick one, get married, and fulfill someone else's dreams who you respect. Raise the kids to love their father. And learn to be one. I'm going to personally go out on a limb and say all these things, because after all the wars are over, you know what we have?"

"Not sure what you're saying."

"We have a country to come home to. Some people don't have that."

"Tell me about it. I'm headed to one soon."

"I can't even imagine what that will be like, taking care of those boys who have been raised in a pink palace. Kids who spend more money on their shoes than some of those people they will be working with earn their whole lifetime. Do you think what they're doing will make a difference?"

"Oh, hell yes. They need housing."

"If they can keep it privately held. Until some new warlord comes into power and takes everything away or blows it up."

"You've been reading too much, Bob," I said as I stood and shook his hand. "And in answer to your question, it's just like the graffiti problem."

He angled his head and furrowed his brow. "I don't understand."

"The secret to getting rid of it is to keep painting over it over and over again. They put it up. You take it down. You know when you're taking it down that they'll tag it again, but you keep doing it. Someday, they grow up, or move, or go elsewhere, and it starts to change. Some day. We got to keep thinking about someday. The sultan will build these houses, and yes, some of them will get destroyed. But someday, someone else will build houses, and then maybe another, and eventually, they will be allowed to stand. There will be houses to pass down to their kids and grandkids. And the people won't live in fear anymore."

"God dammit, Marco. You're a fuckin' optimist."

That was funny. I laughed. I'd never thought that about myself. And then it hit me, I believed in the Happily Ever After, like those books Emily used to read. I knew that someday everything would turn out.

'It will be okay, kid.'

CHAPTER 22

Shannon

I WAS RUSHING to get to makeup in time for my first afternoon report. There was a big storm coming, and people would be tuning in to find out where it was going to land.

Sandy commented on how tanned I'd been. "You are spending a lotta time outdoors. It's good for you, Shannon. Your skin is lovely today."

"I've been watching what I'm eating and, yes, been taking more walks on the beach."

"I used to do that when I was younger, too. You get older, and you just don't do those things any longer."

"I plan never to stop."

I had started to feel better with each passing hour. Day by day, I found meaning in Marco's project. I enjoyed the crazy people at the station more, even that bastard Clarence Thompson. We, openly pretend-flirted on the air, since we both knew if he tried anything, he'd get fired, and at his age, he was probably unemployable. And I saw him with new eyes. I saw the vacant part of his life. The guy was lonely.

'I guess it takes one to know one.' My mother used to say that all the time. Emily used to tease me with that when I called her a rat or a cheater or when I tried to take the biggest piece of cake. Funny, I had forgotten how much we actually did fight over little things. In the wash that was necessary to heal my heart, what also was lost were those little details. I tended to think of her as perfect,

of our childhood as perfect. But she could be a little shit, too. I took it as a good sign that a lot of things were healing inside me. My internal housekeeping was redecorating, freshening up the curtains, recovering couches, and painting the walls a different color.

I stepped onto the set, adjusted my microphone, and squinted at the teleprompter. I hoped that this didn't mean my eye surgery was failing. I blinked several times, and the letters got clearer and larger.

"Well, now we come to my favorite part of the day. We have Shannon Marr here to tell us what's coming up along the Gulf. You have any fun plans for this weekend?" Clarence asked, winking at me, daring me to say something racy.

"Just some good beach time, Clarence," I answered.

"Oh darn," he said as he clicked his fingers. With his hand up to his mouth, as an aside to the audience, he whispered, "At my age, the only way I get my thrills is by listening to her talk about her boyfriends."

Someone had turned the canned laughter off. Clarence looked up above him, as if he'd been suddenly covered with bugs.

"Hey, I thought that was funny! Oh, well, give us the weather, Shannon."

"Thanks so much. Well..." And then I began moving my hands in front of the green screen, watching the monitor to make sure I didn't worry all our Tampa Bay people by misplacing the eye of the next storm smack on their town, instead of well out in the middle of the Gulf of Mexico. I did that once, and the newsroom was flooded with panicked calls.

"And that about wraps it up. Oh, and we have a special programming note I'm supposed to read."

The screen went white for a couple of seconds and then letters began appearing. I inhaled and began.

"Shannon, will you—" I stopped because it wasn't any special programming message. I heard laughing around the set. Out of the darkness, behind one of the camera operators, walked Marco, dressed in a stunning royal blue suit with a red tie, holding a bouquet of red roses. And he was smiling, headed right for me.

I looked around the stage. Even Clarence was grinning at his podium. Everyone must have been in on it, because they kept me live. Marco knelt before me, held out the beautiful diamond ring I'd seen all too briefly the other night, and asked, "Shannon Marr, I've been a complete fool. Will you forgive me, and will you agree to be my wife?"

They didn't even wait for my answer before the canned cheering and clapping was played. I looked into his face, the handsome face of my one true warrior, the love of my life, the man who was so right for me in too many ways to count.

And I said yes, even though everyone else was already celebrating.

Marco slipped the ring on my left hand fourth finger, and it fit perfectly. Of course it did.

I kissed him, as he stood and properly showed me, live, like a hurricane headed for the Gulf, that he loved me and would never leave me again.

I touched the sparkling jewel and whispered, "What does all this mean, Marco? What are we going to do with Rebecca?"

"I'm not marrying Rebecca again. Did that. Didn't work out so well. And for the record, I'm not asking you to either."

"I'm serious."

"So am I." He winked at me. "Waiting for Rebecca to start playing nice and not being a thorn in my side would be like waiting until there were no more wars overseas before we get married. I don't have that much time. Even you don't either."

"But doesn't it bother you?"

"It has nothing to do with my decision."

I don't want to quit my job. You live in Boston. How is this going to work?"

"Well, since I won't be a bachelor, I should probably move out of the Bachelor Towers. I thought maybe you'd be able to put me up at your place until I could get that house built."

"House?"

"The lot on the bluffs? I own it. I want to build a house there. For us."

"But what about my bungalow?"

It took him a couple of seconds. His eyes blinked fast while he thought of something to say. "You always manage to throw curve balls, don't you?"

"Well, I was just thinking—"

He turned to the camera man. "Is this all being recorded?"

"No, we're off the air."

"Could you turn off the lights, please?" he asked.

It was dark, with a deep blueish reflection on the equipment, the desks and the metal surfaces of the studio to keep people from tripping.

Marco cleared his throat. "Let me try this again. Shannon," he said, his patience being tested to the max. "Would you like to live in your house or the new one I'll be building? It would be big enough for your parents to come visit. If we have children, they can each have their own bedroom. But, my dear, if you say no, then we'll live at your sweet little home. And I'll pay rent."

He said it with a completely straight face. With tears streaming down mine, I crushed the roses he was holding between us, hugged him, and whispered, "I'd like to do both. I don't want to sell the house I lived in when I met and fell in love with you. We can take vacations there, just down the street."

He smiled as we parted. "Anything you want, sweetheart."

I reached up to touch his face. "Then I want you to kiss me."

UNLEASHED

Bone Frog Bachelor Series
Book One

SHARON HAMILTON

CHAPTER 1

MY DRIVER DROPPED me off at her Tampa television station, TMBC, so we could head to the airport after Shannon's last airing. I was a few minutes early. The original plan, which had been changed so many times I was having a hard time keeping track, had been to have a quick meet and greet with her parents before the two of us flew off to the Maldives. From there, we'd take a helicopter flight to the Sultan of Bonin's posh little island. Legendary for its pink sand beaches and pink exterior architecture, it was rare anyone from the West or even Europe would stay there. But my contract with the sultan to provide a security team for his sons during their African housing development project opened doors everywhere, including Washington.

At the last minute, I'd had to rush off to New York to settle affairs and to begin the shutdown of my Manhattan offices. I had initiated staff changes after the resignation of half my financial team and hired a new CFO. I planned a relocation to the Tampa area to be closer to Shannon's job at the television station, the Trident Towers project, and the construction of our new home on the Gulf Coast. Manhattan didn't suit me any longer. I was ready to make new memories, with Shannon.

My advanced security team were already on their way to meet us in the Maldives, which would be our base of operation. But Shannon and I would be the guests of the sultan, not far away.

I'd missed the lunch reservations with her parents due to the last-minute shuffle. Today, I considered it to be the most important meeting of my life. Better late than never.

Mr. and Mrs. Mabry sat in the Green Room. The large, noisy concrete-floored warehouse-type space resembled a cafeteria led to the main sound stage. Several make-up rooms adjoined, a few in use. I knew a more intimate studio existed for special interviews.

The two of them looked smaller now, grey-haired and seated side by side. They had not aged well and, seeing their profile from the rear, appeared frailer than I remembered them years ago when I'd been engaged to their oldest daughter, Emily. While I had been off being a Boy Scout on my first of many SEAL Team missions fifteen years ago, she'd tragically died in a car accident. Shannon had been a teen. This was going to be a difficult meeting for them.

Several large screens played live feeds from Tampa, as well as a couple of their affiliate stations in other locations in Florida. One wall was covered in vending machines—the only source of food or drink at the station. The chairs were old, and the couches were lumpy. Rolling set backgrounds had been stored there as well, which could be used to change the stage quickly for TMBC's various programs.

I approached the old leather couch from behind as they studied the screen with Shannon's beautiful face plastered five feet wide above them.

I placed my hands on their shoulders softly, careful not to scare them, and then slipped around and sat down next to them.

"I am the one to blame for not being here when you arrived. But we're delighted you could come. It's been a long time. And now you live in Florida. How wonderful." I spoke carefully, examining the lines on their faces and watching for reaction.

I held my hand out to Mrs. Mabry first, who was closest to me. Then to Shannon's father. Shannon was the spitting image of her dad, and I'd forgotten that. His piercing blue eyes evaluated me quickly, and I wasn't sure I'd passed the test. But her mother gushed, even blushing and touching my leg with affection, completely nervous, like her daughter would have been in this situation. Way back then, I never felt they blamed me for Em's death, but there was no doubt that my presence reminded them of those horrible years right after they'd lost her.

Shannon's mother spoke first.

"Delighted to see you again. Oh, Marco, it was such a long time ago. Even back then, we heard so many wonderful things about you. We've followed your career, all the amazing things you've done. What a busy man you are! Last we saw you was when you went off to become a decorated Navy SEAL. Em was so proud of you. We were too. *Are* proud of you." Her smile was genuine, although awkward, but I still didn't want to take advantage of it. I wasn't going to slick over or whitewash their feelings. Loss hurt, and pain wasn't going to disappear just because we re-connected or even because I was going to marry their other daughter. It would take time, perhaps lots of time.

"Truly, I am sorry." I nodded to both of them, individually. "All this was very last minute, as I'm sure Shannon's told you, and we couldn't put off the trip any longer."

"Is it safe where you're going?"

Her father asked the question I would have asked. He'd already lost one daughter, and I'm sure it was top on his list of things to worry about.

I nodded, not breaking eye contact. "Well, sir, there really isn't any place on this planet that's safe any longer." I shrugged. "Probably never was. But people hire me to protect them, so I think she's in good hands—as long as she follows the rules. But you know Shannon."

I gave them a half smile. Mrs. Mabry reacted immediately. "Oh, indeed! Headstrong—"

"Bull-headed," her father added.

"Definitely has a mind of her own," her mother continued. "She loves adventure, though. I'll give her that. You'll have your hands full, I'm sure."

"I love her independent streak, rather like me. I love everything, even the stubborn parts. It will be pure pleasure to show her some of my world. I promise it will be an adventure, but we'll make it as safe as we can."

"So this is India?" her father asked.

"Not quite. Bonin is an independent island nation. Many of the other older kingdoms have been brought into the Maldives proper or rejoined with India over the centuries. Other countries, as well. But there are only six independent kingdoms left. Used to be hundreds dotting islands all over the Indian Ocean. Most of them eventually went bankrupt and sold to huge hotel chains or wealthy corporations. The sultan is a good manager of his assets and has taken care of his little kingdom well." I added, "And he knows how to keep good friends."

Mr. Mabry scowled and shook his head. "And now he seeks to expand to Africa? Nigeria, is it? That's sure not a place I'd go to set up business."

"Not exactly. He's doing a housing development, sort of a joint project with the U.N. and with a little underwriting from Uncle Sam. But it's a legitimate development investment for profit. I'm private security."

"Because it's so dangerous." He nailed me with the truth. I wasn't going to lie to him.

"North Africa is one of the most dangerous places on the planet. And there's much work to be done to help its people progress into the twenty-first century. But not to worry, sir, Shannon won't be going with me there."

He shot back a blank stare which gave me a chill, some kind of premonition, but I shook it off. Mrs. Mabry laughed, wringing her hands and straightening her skirt.

"Would you like anything?" I stood and motioned to the machines.

"We already ate. If I drink anything now, I'll be up all night long," her father said, rather glumly.

I was concerned he didn't approve of me. I knew I'd have to be patient and hope that he'd eventually come around. But that obviously wasn't going to be this evening.

"How was the Oceanis?"

"Big," he answered. "It must have cost a fortune."

"Well, as you've seen, you'd have been sleeping on an air mattress and sleeping bags at Shannon's."

He shrugged his shoulders. "We didn't mean to put you out. It was just for an overnight."

"And you deserved to be comfortable."

I was trying. Shannon had warned me about being on my best behavior, to get rid of the fangs and claws I sometimes showed when being challenged. But this was different. Everyone grieves in their own way, and I had mine.

Standing in front of them, I felt like I was giving a lecture, but the words had to be said. I pressed my palms together. "I just want you both to know how happy Shannon has made me. I had hoped that we could spend a lot more time together. And I should have asked your permission before I proposed, but I guess I was a little stubborn too. I didn't want her to get away."

Mrs. Mabry abruptly looked down at her lap. I'd made her cry, and it pained me. I knelt in front of her on one knee, placing my hand gently on her shoulder.

"I'm so sorry. Truly, I am."

When she looked up at me, her tears spilled over her cheeks. "Just take care of our little girl. She's all we have left, Marco. Life is fragile. Sometimes too short."

I carefully leaned forward, asking permission, and hugged the frail woman tightly. She resisted at first, and then I felt her muscles soften, and she allowed me to support her as I tried to show her how much love I had for her daughter. It was one of the most uncomfortable things I'd ever done.

Mr. Mabry stood with his back to me. I knew he'd been affected too.

As I drew away and rose, I wondered if this was just one thing too many we had tried to jam into our lives before leaving. I scored it as a mistake or wishful thinking on Shannon's part, and I wished I hadn't let her talk me into it.

Shannon entered the room, abruptly stopping when she saw the three of us standing like tongue-tied cows watching a train go by.

"Oh my gosh. What's happened?" she asked.

I let her see my worry over the conversation I'd just had with her parents.

"Did we have an argument?" she asked.

"Shannon, you were wonderful!" her mother said, completely ignoring the comment. Her father stoically hugged his daughter a second.

Shannon put her hands on her mother's shoulders and stared. "Mom. What's the matter?" Then she scowled at me.

Well, I guess I deserved it.

"It was rather more emotional for your mother than she expected," said Mr. Mabry, but his voice broke in the process.

"I see. Well, all that's over now." She tipped her mother's chin in the air as if Mrs. Mabry was the five-year-old and Shannon was the mother. She spoke directly to her face. "Mom, this is supposed to be a happy time. We don't have to live in the shadows of the past. We've done that. This is a new chapter in this family's life. Like I said, a happy time. I don't much care for the other one. I think we've done that enough."

"Well said." Her dad put his arm around his wife's shoulder. "Marina, you're raining on the happy couple's news. We should celebrate that."

Mrs. Mabry shot him a coarse look.

"I've got just the thing," I said, remembering he'd battled with alcohol all his adult life. There were several mineral waters in an undercounter refrigerator. I brought out four frosty bottles and opened them one by one, handing them to everyone. "To the love I share with Shannon and the many years of marriage we'll have together."

I held mine up, and we all toasted. Mrs. Mabry gave me a grateful smile. Shannon was at my side and whispered so softly only I could hear, "Thank you."

CHAPTER 2

WE FLEW FIRST class to JFK and then boarded a non-stop charter to the airport at Male in the Maldives. It was going to be a twenty-one-hour flight. By the time I got there, I would be so confused about the time of day it would take me several days to catch up.

We'd been escorted by a handsome uniformed attendant, who carried our on-board luggage, while a cargo crew brought several containers and stowed them in the baggage compartment. We mounted the stairs, and Marco introduced me to the cockpit crew, readying to take off. They were cheerful and appeared to be friends.

"Nice to meet you, Shannon. Glad to see someone finally grabbed hold of this guy before he gets too old to move. He's been rather elusive," the older of the two said.

"He surely is," I agreed. "But I think I got him just in time. I like silver foxes."

They both laughed. The younger pilot saluted Marco and put on his headgear.

"How does it look?" Marco asked the other pilot.

"I think we should have a fairly smooth flight. No big storms in the Atlantic, a little turbulence off the East coast of Africa, but nothing we can't avoid," came the answer.

The attendant asked us to do a quick tour to make sure everything was as Marco had ordered. "As soon as you're ready, we'll take off," he said.

I'd never been on a private jet before, and I never expected to be on such a big one, either.

The plane was leased by one of Marco's companies, a converted and upgraded Airbus for private commercial use. No expense was spared, with all-leather massage recliners and marble topped tables clustered here and there between them. A large table sat just in front of the galley, which was well stocked with enough meals and snacks to support a team of ten. A small bathroom was located there as well.

"We share this with the crew, but we also have our own. You'll see," he said as he wiggled his eyebrows.

Behind the kitchen was a large entertainment suite where we could watch or listen to anything we wanted on several big screens at once.

"We've got movies, internet—anything you want," he said.

In the rear, he showed me a private bedroom suite with a bathroom completed by a shower and a soaking tub decorated in white marble. The large king-sized bed was covered in brightly colored silk pillows.

He shrugged. "I had them add some, like you have at home. Just thought you'd like it."

Draped over an easy chair in the corner were two matching terrycloth robes and slippers.

"It's beautiful, Marco. You've thought of everything." I was truly stunned.

"I told you private jet travel wasn't like anything else in the world. You'll be so spoiled; you'll never take a commercial flight again."

"Are we ready?" the attendant asked from the doorway.

We took our seats, side by side, strapped in and held hands.

"A little champagne perhaps?" the attendant asked, handing us two flutes.

"Why not?" I said as I grabbed mine and passed one to Marco.

I leaned back and put my feet up on the leather ottoman while the attendant strapped in. As we sipped our champagne, we heard the engines roar to life, and soon we were taxying down the runway and then up into the night's sky.

After we leveled off, our attendant brought the bottle of champagne over in an iced stand. "What else can I get you?" he asked.

Marco waited for me to answer.

"I'm not very hungry. Maybe some fruit, some cheese, and crackers? Nothing heavy," I answered.

"Did you bring that seafood chowder I like?" Marco asked.

"Of course we did, Marco. You want me to heat some up? Shannon?"

"That would be great."

As he exited to the kitchen, I turned to Marco. "Never in my whole life did I expect to be doing this."

He finished his champagne and poured us both another one.

"You haven't seen anything yet, Shannon. Wait until you see the sultan's palace. It will blow your mind."

The attendant placed two steaming bowls of chowder on the table he moved to our chairs, along with a platter of fresh fruit, crackers, and cheese.

"Thank you." I hardly knew where to begin. "Everything is so lovely. Do you travel like this all the time?"

Marco shook his head. "Absolutely not. Sometimes it's a real bare bones deal, a red eye out of some place in a hurry. I occasionally have to stay twenty-four hours in the same set of clothes, even soaking wet. Depends on what I've been doing and how fast I have to get out of Dodge. But I thought tonight would be special. It was important to me."

How could I have ever doubted him? The more time I spent around him, the more I became convinced that his ex, Rebecca, was a complete whacko. How in the world would anyone discard him, even for millions? She'd had it all, I thought. And she blew it.

"You're awfully serious," he said, feeding me a strawberry.

"I know. It's just that I know you've had some setbacks recently, and you are juggling a lot. Are you sure you can afford all this?"

"I got a sizeable retainer. I'm good for a while. I have new projects in the pipeline. We're simplifying the office, so I'll save money there being in Tampa instead of Manhattan. The belt tightening is all good, Shannon. I'm not taking risks I don't think I can overcome."

"But with all the things Rebecca is pulling…"

"I think she's still shopping for another attorney after the last one quit. I just have to work a little harder, Shannon. In a way, it's a good thing. I've had to pay attention to more things now, because I can't afford to make mistakes. But I don't mind. I'm used to the pressure. It was a mistake to be so angry all the time. It dulled my sword for a bit. No more."

"But she really screwed you."

"She hasn't won yet. Sure, she got some things, but I think I might get them back and then some. That's the plan anyway. And, if not, it's not going to stop my forward momentum. That has nothing to do with her. It has everything to do with us. All she got was money. Stuff I can earn back. I got you. That's what I really wanted."

We kissed, and boy, did he light the flame! Maybe it was the champagne, but I wanted him so badly I was about to climb onto his lap in front of our attendant.

He leaned back and eyed me suspiciously, forming that little smile that drove me wild.

"Whatever are you thinking, Shannon?"

"Guess," I whispered.

"You didn't finish your chowder and only nibbled a bit on your fruit." His eyes were dark, serious. His aftershave clung to me. My chest was heaving. I was unabashedly totally turned on by him and wasn't in the least bit afraid to show him.

"Say something, Shannon," he said as his lips brushed against mine.

"Guess. And it has nothing to do with food."

He drove his eyebrows up into his forehead. "Ah, I see. I was going to pretend I am being slow to catch on, but I don't think I could hold myself back either."

"I'd see right through it, Marco." My forefinger caught on the top button of his crisp white shirt. I flipped it open.

At the second button, he sighed, giving our attendant a sheepish smile. "I think we'll go in the back and watch TV for a bit," he said.

"Of course. I'll clean up. Just buzz if you need anything."

I was working on the fourth button and hadn't looked at anything else but his tanned, muscular chest and the silver chain with the old Spanish coin attached to it.

He picked me up, and I waved good-bye to our attendant as he carried me to the bedroom, closing the door behind him.

I was tossed on the bed. While he undressed, I removed my dress and everything else except the very expensive lace panties and enhancing bra I'd purchased for the trip. He noticed. They were specially designed to make my chest look double, almost obscenely larger my normal size, which wasn't small. I loved his reaction.

He slipped a finger under my panties at my hip and pulled them to my ankles, but he left the bra in place. His thumbs smoothed over the white lace material as he bent down and kissed me. Moving a pillow under my hips, he took my hand and pressed it against his erection while he carefully teased the moist petals of my sex until I was wild with need. I tried to push down onto his fingers. He kept moving away, teasing me.

I squeezed his package, stroking him, begging him to enter me, but he continued to wait, watching my eyes, drinking in the lust rippling through my body. My libido spiked when I saw him dip his head, looking at me one last time before he dove into me, filling me with his tongue and fingers. His thumb found my nub. He brought his head up to watch as he pressed it, and I began to shatter beneath him.

I was already on the verge of an orgasm, but when he lifted my knee over his shoulder, angled his hips, and plunged inside, I was completely undone. I gasped for air as he nibbled my neck, kissed my ear, and bit my earlobe. He whispered my name as his fingers laced through my hair, pulling me up to his mouth. He kissed me then let me down gently and rode me harder. He was so deep. He grabbed my buttocks, forcing himself deeper still, rocking his hips as I pushed back, embracing his charge and giving him resistance. My internal muscles gripped him and would not let go as he moved back and forth, picking up speed.

I could no longer control the movements of my own body. My brain exploded into a thousand points of light as he held me tight against him, lifting me up by slipping a knee beneath my rear as we peaked together.

I stared into his eyes, unashamed that I needed him so much. We held this embrace until our breathing returned to normal.

He pushed the pillows off the bed, pulled back the silk coverlet, and wrapped us both in it. With my head buried in his chest in the warm cocoon we'd made, at over thirty-five thousand feet in the air, I was completely spent.

And I was completely his.

CHAPTER 3

I AWOKE AS rays of sunshine poured in one of the bedroom windows I'd forgotten to shutter last night. I slipped on some pajama bottoms, wrapped myself in the robe, and slid into the slippers provided. Leaning across the bed, I pulled down the shade so Shannon could continue to rest.

We'd nuzzled around off and on during the night but finally turned in under the covers to go to bed proper. I knew she was tired, and I wanted to make sure she kept her strength since we'd be in a much warmer climate than Florida's. Along with the foods and dust from the land, she'd get exposed to lots of new things. I exited the bedroom, leaving the door closed behind me, bringing my laptop. I wanted to work on some reports I was expecting from my new CFO.

I set everything up at the conference table, connecting a dedicated printer/scanner/fax I had stored in the upper compartment just in case I needed to send, receive, or obtain a paper copy.

Our attendant slept soundly, but he awoke when the pilot, Ron Hansen, entered the cabin from the cockpit. I'd previously worked with Ron when we both were in the Navy. He was part of a crack SEAL delivery team. He and his men had gotten us out of a lot of close calls back in the day, and I always relaxed when I was able to book him for these trips.

"Marco, everything to your liking?"

"I can't complain, Ron."

We shook hands. He used the head, and I went back to examining my reports.

When he returned, he asked, "You want some juice or a coffee?"

"I'll take an espresso. You making one for yourself?"

"Yup. I need a little caffeine right now. I can't nap for another four hours."

The espresso machine was loud, and I was concerned the high-pitched squeal might wake up Shannon. I watched the bedroom door for signs, but it remained closed.

Ron brought me the dark, frothy goodness in a little ceramic cup. Even on the plane, I insisted on using the Murder and Hate Espresso blend from my favorite veteran-owned coffee company.

He smacked his lips. "Wow, that's good. I gotta hand it to you. You don't scrimp on the details," he said as he toasted me and sipped his coffee again.

"Details, details. Very important, as you know."

"Roger that."

"She's in good shape?" I asked him, referring to the plane.

"You've got an engine running borderline hot. I'm watching it. I've got your crew meeting us when we land to check it out. Hope that was okay."

"Safety first. No problem here. I trust my guys."

"That said, I don't think it's anything to worry about. She's an older gal, but she purrs real good."

I smiled. "You let me know."

"Will do." He returned to the galley. "Another?"

"I'm good. I want to get back to bed if I can. Unless something snags me here," I said, pointing to my computer screen.

"You don't take these trips very often anymore. Been what, three years since we've been in the Maldives together?" he asked me.

"I've been doing mostly domestic things or government contracts, and hey, they pay for the plane, so yeah, it's been a while."

"What brings you back here? Understand you're doing work for the sultan?"

"He's an old friend, and I'm helping his boys out. Never say never. You know how it is."

"I truly do. What's he up to?"

"This is preplanning. The boys are off to Africa for a housing development project. I guess that makes me bait."

Ron chuckled.

"How are the wife and kids?" I asked. He'd met his wife while in the Navy, and I recalled they had a whole handful of kids.

"Had a bit of bad luck there. She's out finding herself, but unfortunately, she took the kids with her. I'm working as much as I can. I'm going to be paying for braces, college, and then weddings all within the next five years. So I'm saving up."

"I'm sorry to hear that. But you didn't get divorced?"

"We wrapped it up. It's final, but it was clean. You know how it is when you were on the Teams. They want someone at home more. Kids don't grow up by themselves."

"I hear you."

"How about you?"

"You didn't hear about Rebecca?"

"I was being polite, Marco, letting you tell me what you wanted to and no more."

I chuckled. Score one for Ron. "I'm glad you don't read the papers."

"Your Shannon's nice. A future Mrs. Gambini?"

"She has a ring to prove it. Did you ever meet Em back in Coronado?"

"Don't think so."

"I dated Shannon's older sister. When I went off on my first mission, Em was killed in an auto accident. A drunk driver hit the girls. It was pure luck we ran into each other," I lied. "I met Shannon again after fifteen years."

"What are the odds of that? Did you know when you met her?"

"Didn't have a clue. I'm kinda glad it worked out that way too. I don't think I could have touched her if I'd known. Back then, she was all braces and huge glasses, a skinny little thing but very sweet.

She grew up well."

"I'd say. When's the date?"

"Just happened, so we're working all that through. Just got re-acquainted with the parents again before we took off. I'm locked and loaded, Ron. Hopelessly snagged. And you?"

"I think I'm going to just focus on being single, trying to get in my dad time, whatever I'm allowed. But I'm looking."

We smiled. I'd always found him to be very easy to be around. He had his world of expertise, and I had mine. He'd saved my life on more than one occasion, and I owed him my undying loyalty and friendship.

"If I find someone exceptional, I'll be sure to let you know, Ron."

"You're alright, Marco. I'm happy for you." He stood, setting his cup into the galley sink. "Well, I better get back." He held up a mineral water. "Pete's thirsty. Oh, and I wanted to verify, we got it scheduled for seven days downtime. Is that firm?"

"For now. Once I get to the palace and see what's involved, I'll know more. We'll make sure you get plenty of notice. Are you traveling off the island at all?"

"No, I don't usually do that. And with this engine thing, I'm going to hang around tight. Probably catch up on my reading and some rest. Might try the beaches. Been awhile on that score too."

"You never know. Shannon always says 'The Beach Heals Everything.' I believe her."

"I like that. See ya."

The tall, lanky former Navy man meandered back through the cockpit door, after greeting our cabin steward.

"You need anything, Marco?" he asked.

"I'm good. Just going to work here for a bit. Then I might turn back in."

"You let me know what time you want breakfast, okay?"

"Thanks. I appreciate that."

I dug into several emails my new CFO had sent last night. I was pleased that he was able to get me so many detailed reports.

I'd asked him to do a forensic analysis of some of our cash flow leaks and large transactions in and out of the company. He'd identified several unusual line items and then given me more detail.

Someone had been undercutting my equipment pricing, selling my own goods to a third party and then keeping the profits. He identified a small team of salespeople who lived down in Virginia doing contract work. I wasn't sure which one of them was the leader, but I suspected all five of them were involved.

I wrote a memo freezing their purchasing ability, unless they got my permission first, and when I recognized who the customer was, I fired off an email asking them to call me. I suspected that the procurement officer for Homeland Security, who I knew quite well, didn't realize anything about this. It was an easy pickup for these guys. I'd allow the discounting to continue, but I wanted to keep the funds, not let it wash out. If the officer was not guilty, he'd call me. If he didn't, well, he just lost his good deal permanently and our friendship.

We'd had offers already on the office building in Manhattan, which relieved me greatly. My ex had way overspent when we did the building re-design. I'd had a hard time keeping architects and engineers on the project because she was so volatile. That was about the time I realized she had been slutting herself around, preparing for her cash infusion via the divorce. So good riddance to it and everything in it, including the huge interactive display of hot spots in the world, her pet project, in the lobby.

I had incurred a big loan on the building while buying her out, but the equity would be useful and, post-divorce, wasn't anything I had to share. I instructed my agent to accept the offer they thought was most promising, verify the qualifications of the corporation purchasing it, and then enter into an exchange escrow so I could start looking in Tampa. But I warned her, if anything looked out of the normal in any way, to get in contact with me. I didn't want to be tied up in a lengthy escrow with someone who couldn't perform.

My bottom line was improving but still not where it needed to be. When the job was finished with the sultan, which wouldn't be for another six months at least, I'd be in good shape and then some. But Rebecca had tied me up everywhere. I couldn't refinance anything.

I had to sell off two of my planes and enter into a partnership with another shipping company to take some of the heavy carry off my back. Maintaining the ships and crew was not something I had the time to monitor closely and required someone who could step in and do that job. My new partner had been in the merchant marine business for nearly thirty years, forced out with a nice cash buy-out of his contract when the owner he worked for retired and sold to a Chinese concern who brought in their own team. He drooled at the opportunity to work with me, especially since he didn't have to buy anything, just keep it working, floating, and manned.

Rebecca had managed to muck up the Trident Towers project to such a degree she was getting pushback from the neighborhood now with her re-design. Her approach was attractive but unnecessary, and I felt like she'd be looking to back out of it. She'd made herself a money pit, just trying to keep me from having something I believed in: housing for disabled Navy SEALs, right on the beach. Rhea, my manager at Bone Frog Development Group, gave me all the skinny, all the juicy gossip, including a very public firing of my former CFO who she'd stolen away from my company, Frank Goodman.

He'd lasted all of about three months. That wouldn't look good on his resume.

Frank's father had been one of my first early backers and was a smart man who taught me a lot about investing. His son had worked for the IRS for twenty years before I encouraged him to go private with me. Turned out, the old man was indeed the smarter of the two, and I was glad he hadn't lived to see what a mess his son had made of his career.

I scanned the other profit and loss statements and the indexes attached and was generally pleased with what I saw. He made some good suggestions on ways I could trim the fat but not have to endure a total haircut that would block my expansion. One of his first suggestions I even received as a bonus the day he interviewed with me. He advised me to sell the Manhattan building, and that was turning out to be the best thing I'd done all year so far.

Well, other than asking Shannon to marry me, of course.

I also sent an email to Harry, the sultan's social secretary and illegitimate son who had been raised in the U.S. with his mother, informing him when we expected to land and requesting several reports on the Africa project I hadn't received yet from the "boys," as I called them—the sultan's legitimate sons and his half-brothers.

I received a nice invitation to a grand opening of a new Eastern Bank & Trust building in Boston, with a personal note from my old nemesis, Mr. Rory Cullen himself. Something was clearly up there, but I'd let him stew and get back to him when I returned to the states.

Next, I reviewed three new proposals for security services in areas I had no interest in serving in the Middle East. Although technically safer than Africa would be for the next twenty years, based on the number of U.S. deaths, I wasn't as familiar with the arena as I'd been when I was an active SEAL. The intel was so critical. Even when it was accurate, things could go all to hell. And it was difficult if you got into trouble, due to the language, and the fact that you were working for leaders the public hated, and arguably might even be criminals.

And with the age of electronic warfare and surveillance with drones, it was hard, unless you had a big backer, like Uncle Sam, to affect any safety measures. Missiles could go stealth and farther. Drones could pack lethal doses of firepower enough to blow up an apartment building or shoot an airplane out of the sky. Electronics were tricky when without a dedicated satellite net. It was an easy way for bad guys to come raid your bank account just by making a telephone call home. It was scary stuff, and not what I had been trained in.

Africa, as dangerous as it was, still required all the old school knowledge we used to use when we were first in the Middle East. It was all about luck, and nothing to do with sophistication. Whomever had the biggest surgical strike team and the best intel, with the possibility of escalating troop numbers for backup, won. I was going to try to do that without the huge backup numbers. And I relied on locals to give me the intel, which I'd learned how to read and who to trust.

I asked my assistant to send my standard rejection letter to each, and to indicate that I'd be able to entertain future work in the next eighteen to twenty-four months.

I also emailed Senator Campbell, letting him know when I'd be arriving, and reminding him of his generous offer for Naval support, should I need it, from Diego Garcia. I was traveling with a letter on his letterhead indicating I was a top-level friend of Uncle Sam, and that no reasonable ask for assistance should be refused. It wasn't on Naval letterhead, from the Commander at DG, which would have made it official, but as Chairman of the Senate Armed Services Committee, he had even more clout, in a strange twist of fate. Besides, his wife, Beth, was the First Lady's younger sister.

I closed my laptop and stared out at the clouds in the bright blue sky. We were flying above the dark green lands of the continent of Africa now, nearly halfway to the Indian Ocean. I felt pretty good about all the planning, albeit last-minute, for this trip.

But I knew, it never really worked out that way. Something always went wrong and went to hell.

And I was trained for the unexpected. That was how I survived.

CHAPTER 4

MARCO WOKE ME up, and if he hadn't, I probably would have slept all day. The drum of the engines seemed to lull me to sleep with their white noise.

I eyed the tub and frowned.

"Maybe on the way back," he said, prying me out of the bed. "The shower is nice. I'll even join you, if you want. But breakfast will be ready in a half hour. Brunch, really."

"First, you tease me with a little shower fun, and then you tell me we only have thirty minutes? That's so unfair, Marco."

"So sorry, sweetheart," he said, grinning. He lifted my nightie up over my head and spanked my bottom, so I'd head to the shower.

We made the most of our few minutes' escapade with the lemon shower gel. I loved letting him shampoo my hair. His hands were so strong, and he transformed it into a great back and shoulder massage that turned my bones to rubber.

The bathroom even had an expensive hair dryer and a full complement of my cosmetics and creams. "You did this?" I asked as I showed him the contents of the vanity drawer.

"Guilty as charged. All I did was take a cell photo of it at your place and give it to my assistant. Check out the closet."

He'd stocked the tiny space with several beautiful dresses, hanging in padded bags so I could wear them without a wrinkle. I had slacks and tops and a ratty pair of jeans I knew I'd love.

"Even shoes?" I asked, looking down at my favorite brand of

running shoes, walking shoes, and a pair of flats for evening wear. "You are incredible."

"I had a lot of help, Shannon. All I did was document it. I can't claim anything special here. Let's just say I hire and pay well."

"I can see that." But I silently worried if we could afford it.

I wore a casual pair of slacks and my pumps, along with one of my favorite embroidered tops from my suitcase. It was slightly wrinkled, but for breakfast and arriving for the first time in an island nation, I thought I was good to go.

Connor brought us a delicious crab and cheese omelet, coffee, and orange juice that looked fresh squeezed. Marco was examining my shirt.

"I'm going to have Connor iron that for you," he said.

"What's wrong with it? It's not too bad."

"You are expected to look and dress like the soon-to-be wife of a billionaire."

"But—"

"It's all impression. And nobody knows out here I don't have the billion any longer. We're working on it, right?"

I nodded.

"The point is, we never know who will meet us at the airport, sweetheart. They still have a royal family, although the country is run as a republic and the monarchy has no power, just tradition."

"They are independent, is that right?"

"Yes, a republic, but they did just re-join the British Commonwealth and have lots of ties to Great Britain. They have a duly-elected president. Since any of them or their representatives could meet us, we have to be prepared. It's a great honor to be greeted by any member of the royal family, who are also closely aligned with our employer, the Sultan of Bonin."

Our attendant brought me the robe to wear while he took my shirt to the bedroom and ironed it. Marco kissed the side of my cheek.

"Thank you. There's a lot to learn, but you're a fast study."

"So where do I get to wear the shabby jeans? Those are actually my favorite of all the clothes you brought for me," I asked him.

"I'd say long walks on the beach at night." He winked at me. "I'm sure we'll manage to use them."

Several hours later, we landed in the middle of a turquoise paradise surrounded by the Indian Ocean. I could see the string of islands going both north and south. But surrounding every single one of them were concentric rings of turquoise waters bordered by white sandy beaches.

Connor helped me select some of the clothing I'd bring, including all the dresses in padded plastic carriers. I hefted my computer case over my shoulder and grabbed my carry-on items while he organized our heavier luggage.

A blast of warm wind hit me as soon as the cabin opened, and we descended the gangway. Marco thanked the pilots first and then followed behind. On the tarmac, a bevy of crew scurried around in orange jumpsuits, tending to the large bins in the storage hold, as well as securing the shutdown. I'd never heard their language, and even the lorries put-putted their tiny two-cycle motors, honking and hustling.

Marco grabbed hold of my arm and urged me toward a waiting black SUV with black tinted windows the crew was beginning to load up from the back. I checked behind me, and Connor was not more than three feet behind.

"No entourage?" I asked Marco.

"Apparently not. Boy, did they miss the boat. Now everyone here will be talking about that American movie star they missed."

"What gave me away?" I continued the ruse, raising my voice a bit to reach over the sound of the plane's engines.

"Why, your two handsome escorts and those big sunglasses, of course!"

Checking his physique from behind, he did kind of look like any woman's wet dream of a security detail with his huge shoulders, slim waist and hips, thick neck, and enormous corded forearms that held the bags as easily as carrying a piece of cardboard.

We bid farewell to Connor. I gave him a hug, not sure if that was appropriate, and he blushed. Marco handed him an envelope.

"Thanks, man. See you in seven days, or before. I'll stay in touch with Ron, and he'll let you know, okay?"

"You got it, Mr. G. Have fun you two." He gave me a wholesome wink and made my heart skip a beat.

Marco turned and headed for the vehicle in long strides, and I barely could keep up with him.

"Why don't you think they'd guess you as the VIP guest?" I asked, after we jumped into the blissfully cool second row of the SUV. I noted that the doors were nearly six inches thick, even the windows.

"Because I'm the old guy. It's never the old guy, sweetheart." His eyes danced in the darkness of the car's interior, continuing the tease. He checked me out from my head to my shoes and winked again, adding an appreciative nod.

If his age and the gap between us bothered him at all, he didn't show it. He leaned forward and directed the driver in an Indian dialect. The driver nodded, pointing to a piece of paper he held in his right hand.

"You know Arabic?" I asked him.

"Some, but that was Maldivian."

All I could do is stare at him. He finally turned his head and feigned surprise. He was definitely messing with me, and I was falling for every single one of his little jokes.

"What?" he asked. "I know a little bit of a lot of languages. Helps to know if they're talking about you or they're impressed with something."

"How many do you know?"

He rolled his shoulder. "I think about a dozen, give or take. You lose it if you don't speak it every day. I'm rusty on a bunch of them."

"You're kidding!"

He leaned over, grabbed me by the waist, and pulled me into him. "Oh, I'd kid about a lot of things but never about languages or sex, sweetheart." His raspy whisper made my toes curl. I was so ready for his kiss I was breathless.

"You okay?" he asked when we parted.

"It's the heat."

His eyes twinkled. "It is. It is that all right."

As we traveled, I watched the luxurious foliage with large hotels behind ornately carved gates as we passed down the gulf road to where we'd be staying tonight and meeting the rest of the team. Marco pointed out one enormous conch-colored Victorian hotel with a pair of guards in crisp white uniforms standing outside an enormous gate.

"The royal family stays there when they come. Several of the kids spent their honeymoons here."

"Really?"

"There's another one around the other side that is actually built on an island itself. Very private."

"These are all privately owned?"

"Oh, sure. The government is poor compared to its citizens. Some of the palaces and temples date all the way back to the 1100s. We'll try to tour a couple of them, where you can wear your shabby jeans, if you like."

"And if it's hot, can I go without a bra?"

He leaned over and whispered in my ear, "You better not. I'd be upset if you did."

Finally, we drove up a small hill, paved in exquisite inlay designs. A large gate automatically opened for us when we approached the outer grounds. Beyond the green foliage, I saw an enormous three-story building that was brand new, with balconies, verandas, and colorful canvas awnings everywhere. We drove through an avenue of flags from several dozen countries flying in the breeze. The driver pulled up to a spacious granite lobby area and opened the door for me first.

"Mum," he said in his Indian dialect.

Marco slid out next to me, slipped his arm around my waist, and tipped the driver, who bowed and said something back.

"Wait until you see this, Shannon," Marco said, pulling me up the rose-colored granite steps into a grand foyer lit by an enormous stained-glass ceiling depicting a jungle theme with flowers, birds, and turquoise water lapping on a white sand beach. It was the largest stained-glass window or ceiling detail I'd ever seen.

"We're staying here?"

"Not quite here. We have a cluster of bungalows built out into the bay on a jetty. Ours has its own swimming pool. But I have a special surprise for you.

I was actually somewhat exhausted from just hauling my computer and carry-on case. It was a relief when a young man in a red uniform took them from me and placed them on a cart. He offered to take Marco's, but he declined.

He picked up two key cards and retrieved some messages while the rest of the luggage arrived. I didn't see the large trunks.

Taking my hand, we crossed the lobby area, lined with jewelry shops and very high-end clothiers. At last, we came to an outdoor covered walkway that appeared to stretch out into the calm Indian Ocean for a mile or more. Branching off in several places were clusters of mini houses, some with pools and some without. Marco unlocked the gate with his key card and then held it open for the baggage cart and the handler.

All five bungalows fed into a large pavilion in the middle. It wasn't yet dusk, but already a huge fire was burning in the firepit, encircled with silk pillows and ottomans. A gentle spicy mist infused the whole area with an Oriental-Arabic scent.

We had one last gate to pass through, and we were finally at our front door. He pushed it open and stepped aside so I could walk in first.

The view of the calm, light blue waters and white puffy clouds in the sky was stunning. Looking straight out, no land was visible. It was just ocean and sky. Our private swimming pool waited just outside a wide patio door to the left. Colorful futons and umbrellas were staged at angles all around the pool. The oversized living room also had a firepit in the center and an open kitchen, with a bedroom I mistook for the master.

"Come, I want to show you something," he said, motioning for me to join him down a tile-lined curved staircase to the level below.

Which was *below* the level of the sea! Soon, I began to realize what he wanted to show me. The large king-sized bed of this master suite faced one glass wall, and on the other side of that wall was the private pool.

"Talk about a room with a view," I gasped.

"Maybe you could put on a show for me. I wouldn't mind."

I shook my head and laughed. "I wouldn't even attempt it. I'm not graceful in water."

"Baby steps, my love. We'll take it slow and do one wonderful thing at a time."

I was in his arms in a flash, grateful, happy, and so much in love.

"Thank you, Marco. I didn't even know any of this existed."

We kissed. "Truth is, Shannon, before you, it didn't really. Or if it did, I never saw it. It's fun because I love watching the expression on your face."

"Well, I'm just wondering how you could ever be happy lounging around my little house in Florida. After what you've seen and how you've lived? It's just incredible. That's all I can say."

He drew me to him again. "We're just getting started, Shannon."

CHAPTER 5

W E MET AT what I called the "common room," where a light dinner, consisting of local seafood delicacies and fruits, was set out for the team. We also had an open bar and refrigerated non-alcoholic fruit juices they used at the world-famous spa located on premises.

It was a job, but all three of the equipment trunks were brought in as well. We'd learned our lesson once, leaving those items on the plane on a past mission. We not only lost the equipment, but the hijackers took the plane as well.

One of the trunks had already been off-loaded and sent by ship to the sultan, chock full of his favorite wines from California, jeans and gifts for his wives and children, some electronic toys he didn't have access to for the grandchildren, two smoked turkeys, and half a dozen smoked hams. He wasn't allowed to have pork, but his obsession with the taste trumped his religious convictions. I was only too happy to feed his addiction.

The rest of the equipment I intended to have delivered to the boys once the paperwork was signed and the scope of the job was agreed to. But I had already been paid twenty-five percent of the overall fee, which I could keep if we didn't come to terms. I wasn't worried about that.

In the meantime, these trunks would stay with my team until we made arrangements for the sons to have them delivered. Since the importation of guns in regular luggage was forbidden, I had some weapons designated for my team in one trunk, signed off by

Senator Campbell and agreed to by the sultan. I hadn't even carried my Sig, and I was feeling mighty naked without it. It was one of the first things I retrieved.

I introduced the three staff who I'd hand-picked for this preliminary mission.

"Shannon, this is Karin Atkin. She's got State Department experience but also is fluent in Arabic, several other African dialects, and a little Mandarin. Right, Karin?" I asked her.

She blushed and nodded her head. She had married an American, a Marine sniper, who was killed on a mission in Afghanistan several years ago, but she still kept her Canadian citizenship and passport. How she managed to get top security clearance without being a U.S. citizen was still legendary, and my attempts to find out were always rebuffed.

I noticed Shannon kept a close eye on her, since she was an extremely intelligent and beautiful blonde. They shook hands.

"Congratulations. I think you've got a wonderful guy here, if you can keep him out of harm's way."

Everyone but Shannon laughed.

I had gotten the hard one out of the way first so went on to introduce the other two. "My coms guy, Nigel Macron, builds drones in his spare time. I think he has an AI wife somewhere, but we don't know for sure."

Nigel shook her hand. "He lies through his teeth. Don't ever trust him," Nigel said as he gave her a wide smile.

"Nice to meet you, Nigel. You're from the U.K.?"

"Actually, the border country. Scots by birth. Most of my ancestors were inventing weaving machines when Marco's were herding cows."

"Watch it. You can't eat wool," I said. "What's the use of staying warm if you starve to death, Nigel?"

"You're terrible," Shannon scolded me.

"Smack talk. You start hanging around my people and you'll swear like a sailor in time. Doesn't take me long to get right back in the groove."

"And here you were talking about ironing my clothes. What a snob!" she reminded me.

All three of my guys howled at the gotcha. I knew I'd get even later on tonight.

"And finally, Forest Davis, who still holds the record at Florida State for the mile, or has that been shattered yet?"

"Almost. They're a couple of ticks behind but catching up." He stepped forward and shook Shannon's hand. "Very nice to meet you."

"Likewise."

During our meal, Shannon asked what other things the team was specialized in.

Karin began. "Asking permissions to go into foreign countries as an NGO takes a little skill at times, especially when governments are experiencing various degrees of instability. I try to stay in touch with the players. They know who I work for, and sometimes that's easier than if I was with Uncle Sam, looking to butt into some country's internal affairs."

"I can see that." Shannon asked another question. "Can you get denied in the middle of a mission?"

"Oh, we've been close but not yet. Most of these things, while sometimes surprises, can be worked out. And cash talks, too, when everything else fails."

"Karin is also an ultra-marathoner, and she's been on two Everest trips."

I'd embarrassed her, and she shrugged. "Sort of my life. No family, so I push myself," she said.

"Karin was one of my first hires."

I recognized great talent, and I had seen she was going to spin out of control after the death of her husband. Rebecca never liked her, but then Rebecca didn't ever like anyone who could potentially be held as a rival.

"I can see why. I'm very impressed. I can't do all of that, but I do like to jog a bit, and I'm good at floating on a blowup pink dragon on a pool somewhere warm, sipping on an umbrella drink."

"Now you're talking my style," said Forest.

"Shannon's the weather girl for TMBC television in Tampa. And I'm still trying to find those films she had parts in."

"Oh, don't!" said Shannon. To the group, she stopped suddenly. "It's not how he makes it sound. A couple of Indies, not porn films. Marco, where are your manners tonight?"

"I'd still like to see them. With or without your clothes on."

"It doesn't take much talent to get covered with blood and scream in a corn field. My part was not memorable, and the other one got cut out." She paused before looking at the next person. "And, Forest, what's your specialty?"

The handsome black former Marine Recon searched the ceiling before he answered in his most angelic tone. "Death."

Shannon did a double take.

"Explosives, firepower, poisons, knives—whatever I can use in the field to help break in or out of something quick. I help with the drones, too, and the communication equipment in general."

"He's also had a career in Mixed Martial Arts," I added.

Shannon commented, "I feel safer already."

We had a brief meeting, just like we used to do it on the Teams. I apologized for the lack of material coming from the brothers.

"Yeah, and that's not a very good sign. You have to make them understand, Marco. We can't protect them if they take a lazy attitude toward this," said Nigel.

Both Karin and Forest agreed.

"It's my biggest problem with this deal so far. And that's what I'll be evaluating when we meet."

"You going over tomorrow?" asked Karin.

"That's the plan. I've got Paul on standby to fire up Little Bird. He's been here for a month doing the safety checks, and he's told me we're good to go. Just waiting for the final okay, which I should get tonight. If not, we'll hang here a day with your guys."

"I researched the two towns in Nigeria and a bit of the region you said the project was going to be located. You're starting right at the beginning of rainy season. Was that intentional?" Karin asked.

"Not my choice."

She nodded. "Well, we've got roaming bands of militia running from Chad and Benin, going back and forth across the border. It's a red zone, Marco. A U.N. certified red zone, the whole prefecture. You said they had permission from their regional minister?"

"That's what Harry told me."

"I'd sure like to see that chit, if you can get your hands on it."

"Got it," I said as I pulled out my little vest pocket notebook and wrote it down. "Any actions recently?"

"It's been pretty quiet the past six months," she said. "Sort of like an earthquake, though, the longer the time from the last one, the more likely the next one is right around the corner."

"Great. You're the queen of good news."

She smiled. "That's me. Keeping it real for all of us."

I appreciated that about her. The two men admired the comment as well.

"I got your sidearms and extra stuff in trunk number two, so help yourself," I said to the group in general. "What you ordered should be there. And, Nigel, I have your C4 and other shit in there too. In trunk number one, I've got Kevlar, Invisios, and the phone grabber. I brought the two drones you ordered, too, and a backup radio in case the SAT phone doesn't work."

"Santa has been good to me this year. Thanks, Marco. I know exactly what I'll be doing tomorrow."

"Watch out for that stuff, though. I don't want you bugging the tourists or interfering with air traffic with those things. Do it carefully."

"No worries." Nigel was rubbing his hands together eagerly.

"Karin, I'd like an assessment of how many men you think we'll need for the Africa trip, just preliminarily. I'll get more of the details to you after my first meeting on the island."

"I can get started, yup."

"Okay, gang. Rule here is they come in and leave your meals and supplies in the great room. So keep the trunks locked. Your rooms are all off-limits, but they'll leave your sheets and towels for you in here. If you need a cleanup, you have to request it. But no one is to bother you in the room. Oh, and breakfast is at eight-thirty. That was the best I could do."

I looked around at my little team, all different in builds and expertise, but all first class in their fields. We were to keep our room keys on us at all times, in the lanyard provided by the hotel. I knew by the time we were ready to leave, everyone would be good and fed up with having to swipe the gates so many times just to get access to their private spaces, but it was for their own safety. Unless there was a sea invasion, we'd be safe here, and the management was doing flip-flops to keep my business.

We said goodnight, and I took Shannon's hand, walking to our room. I needed a few minutes to check my emails for those things I'd demanded and not yet received. I halfway suggested she take a skinny dip in the pool while I was doing that. She wrinkled up her nose at the suggestion and retreated to the bathroom.

I opened my laptop and started reading over a report from Harry about the location of the project and the permits and approvals pending, which I forwarded to Karin's computer. He also confirmed the time we had permission to land, so I sent another email to Paul asking for him to deliver my Sikorsky and got quick confirmation he would.

I was studying a new report from my CFO when something caught my eye. When I looked up, Shannon was putting on a show for me in the pool.

I slammed shut my laptop and had my clothes off in about thirty seconds.

CHAPTER 6

THE BLACK SUBURBAN met us just outside the lobby of the hotel at ten o'clock, and three hotel staff assisted in loading up our suitcases and the long garment bag filled with my evening wear and a tux for Marco.

I was still glowing from the night we spent under the stars, both in and out of the pool. There had been jokes at our expense as the rest of the team chided us over breakfast, asking if we'd heard the pirates who had managed to break into our pool and patio area.

And here I thought we were being so quiet.

Marco had a perpetual smile on his face and didn't say a word, but he managed to slide against me, touching me in private ways several times during breakfast and afterward. I was finding him to be an even more affectionate man than I thought as I learned to read his little expressions and carefully crafted whispers and growls.

The tough, unflinching exterior worked well for him in his business dealings, but his intimate tenderness with me left my ears ringing, leaving me in a heightened state of sexual need for him constantly, day or night. The addiction I felt for his touch, his kisses, and mere presence of his powerful body had grown from the first time we were re-acquainted back in Boston only a few weeks ago. Our romance was stuck on one speed: fast and intense. My life before I met him faded into a pale background.

Vaguely aware that Marco's world completely overshadowed

my own, I nonetheless welcomed all of it with reckless abandon. The more we were together, the more I wanted to be by his side. If there were any warning signs, they were completely shut down.

Karin slipped a printed report into his hands before we left, and he tucked it into his computer case as the Suburban took off down a crowded single lane freeway of sorts, toward the airport.

"Will all these bags fit?" I asked.

"Fit? You mean in my Little Bird?" His eyes nearly glowed every time he mentioned his special helicopter, a lighter version of the one the President of the United States had, he'd told me.

"Exactly."

"In a pinch, we can seat more than a dozen with gear. So no problem."

I couldn't imagine a machine so large, but as soon as we arrived, I saw the red and white two-toned bird with the BFI logo utilizing the frog skeleton discretely placed on the side. The pilot came out to greet us with a co-pilot left inside, which surprised me. Marco was right, the cab could easily hold a dozen or more passengers.

He held us back until the rotors began to turn, eyeing me carefully. He was of Indian descent, very handsome with dark skin and jet-black straight hair, making his white teeth look nearly fluorescent. In his jumpsuit and military-looking Aviators, he was the picture of a swashbuckling pirate most my friends would fall for, like one of the heroes from my romance novels.

He addressed Marco first. "Nice to see you again, Marco. Got all your messages," the pilot shouted over the sound of the twin engines.

"Good. Paul, I want to introduce you to my fiancée, Shannon Marr."

His eyes grew as the recognition of our engagement settled in.

"Shannon, this is Paul Vijay."

His handshake was warm, and firm. "Very, very nice to meet you, Miss Marr. Is this your first visit to the Indian Ocean?" he asked.

I could barely hear him, but I got enough of it to answer one word. "Yes."

"Well, shall we get started then?" He motioned toward the helicopter.

"You had everything checked out?" Marco asked while we ducked under the rotors.

"Yes, yes. I have the report you can read inside. Very little trouble considering how long it's been since she's been used. It passed certification no problem."

"Excellent," Marco mumbled as he helped me up the step and pointed to a wide leather seat behind the pilot. The co-pilot gave me a brief nod and salute. Marco reached over his shoulder and shook his hand.

"Kenny. Thought they had you in the Caribbean this week."

"Someone else got it. That's okay. I wanted to spend some time in the Maldives with Paul, here. When I heard it was you, well, I had to come."

I was struck by the fact that, everywhere Marco went, his crew respected him and treated him warmly, whether they were his hire or contracted out by others. Everyone surrounding him were like brothers and sisters of the same family, and not a dysfunctional one.

I was probably being naive.

Marco placed a headset over my ears. An epic movie score type theme song was playing in the background, perfectly matched to my sense of adventure.

"Everybody ready?" Paul's voice asked over the com.

Marco gave a thumbs-up, and I nodded.

We rose straight up thirty feet, and then the front of the helicopter dipped as we accelerated and launched out over the ocean. The island's turquoise reef and white beaches were striking as we flew under a blue, cloudless sky.

"Music okay?" Paul asked.

I nodded.

"I'm going to turn on a little more air. Going to be hot today," he said.

Turning to Marco, I mouthed, "How long?"

He held up one hand with a four and the other with five fingers splayed. Forty-five minutes.

Slicing the deep blue of the ocean was a huge cruise ship headed for the Maldives. Other container ships and a large old-fashioned sailing vessel dotted the areas between a string of islands, all with the same turquoise rings, looking like a giant squash blossom necklace from the Navajo. As we traveled what I assumed was farther north, the shipping lanes disappeared and many of the islands we flew over appeared uninhabited.

He grabbed my hand in both of his, kissed my palm, and placed it on his thigh.

Paul turned slightly. "Did you see the Eagle?"

I wasn't sure what he meant.

"The three-masted cutter we passed earlier?"

I nodded.

"It belongs to the U.S. Coast Guard. They're doing trainings here, getting ready for a big international race next month. She's hoping to win this year, but there will be about fifty others—lots of competition. Beautiful craft."

I tried to talk, but it was useless.

About a half hour later, Paul pointed forward as an island with a wide bay and deep, pinkish-toned sand came into view. We must have been several miles still out to sea, but there was no mistaking the huge light bisque-colored palace with turrets and spires looming up from the lush jungle foliage in front of us. I felt like I was flying to Disneyland.

The pilots chattered to someone on the ground, who responded in heavily-accented English and signed off.

"Shall I do a three-sixty around, Marco?" Paul asked over the com.

He shook his head no.

An airstrip appeared suddenly as we descended between forests of palm trees just past the massive bay. The palace was completely obscured from view by the foliage. A pair of black SUVs waited next to the heliport hangar as Paul soft landed and shut the motors down.

Marco removed my headset and hung it on a hook at my side, securing it with a strap.

"Did you see the palace?" he asked me.

"How could I miss it?" I asked as the door opened and I was helped down to the concrete pad. "I looked it up, but the pictures I saw didn't look anything like that. The place is huge."

"I'm surprised you even saw a picture. You probably saw an old dummy photo of another palace. He's a very private man, for being so wealthy. I doubt he has more than a handful of real close friends."

I was counting my bags as Marco noticed something and straightened up tall.

"Here he is, Shannon."

I turned and watched a rather rotund older man appear through a line of uniformed and armed men, wearing golden robes that flowed in the breeze over white pajamas. His headdress material matched the robes and wound like a cloth crown about his enormous head. His wide, almost pure white handlebar moustache made him look like the perfect postcard picture of a sultan. With his arms outstretched, he greeted Marco warmly, kissing him on both cheeks.

His deep guttural voice cut right across the other noises of the airport.

"It's been too long, my friend. You traveled well?" he asked Marco.

With his arm over my shoulder, Marco proceeded to introduce me. "Very well, thank you. We were in the Maldives last night, so we're rested and ready to get to work. Your Highness, may I present my fiancée, Miss Shannon Marr?"

The sultan fixed his gaze on me, his smile wide, enlarging the size of his moustache and revealing several missing teeth.

"Welcome to Bonin, my child." He opened his arms, and I was

suddenly pulled towards him, smothered in a tight embrace. Knowing I wasn't used to the protocol, he turned my body by clutching my shoulders and kissing first one cheek and then the other. Just as fast as he grabbed me, he let go as I rocked back on my heels to keep from toppling.

"Oh, Marco," he said, winking to me with an obvious flirt. "You have such a pretty one. Beautiful."

"Thank you, Your Highness."

"My dear, you will make my wives jealous!" And then he gave a big belly laugh, turned, and gestured to the second SUV.

"Are your sons here?" Marco asked.

"Tomorrow. They went to Mumbai last week on business. But they return tomorrow morning. So we dine and celebrate until their return. It is good, *n'est pas*?"

His eyes twinkled as he twiddled his fingers in the air, showing off quite an assortment of jeweled fingers.

He didn't wait for Marco's response.

We sat in a seat facing the sultan, right behind the driver and another uniformed guard holding a small semi-automatic.

"Now, tell me all about your life since we last talked on the phone, Marco." Before Marco could begin talking, he interrupted. "You know, Miss—I'm sorry—"

"Marr. Shannon Marr. You may call me Shannon."

He cackled and cocked his head. "No, I will call you Miss Marr, or I will have trouble at the palace. Marco here is very, very smart and does not have fourteen wives. He marries for love and chooses with his heart. He is bitten by this snake, I think, yes?"

I hoped I'd not started an incident I'd be scolded for later.

"So you've told me," Marco softly responded, squeezing my hand.

"So what I was going to say is that this man is very special to me. He is like a son."

"Thank you, Your Highness."

"You are. And you are well trained and disciplined. The money part and all that stuff with Rebecca—I assume you know about

Rebecca, yes?"

Before I could answer, he continued, "I remember you once told me this. That which doesn't kill you makes you stronger. Am I right?"

"You are correct, Your Highness."

"In a way, this little kerfuffle with her is a good thing. Otherwise, I have it on good authority you wouldn't have accepted my job offer. Am I correct?"

I could feel Marco's insides churning, even though he was doing a good job of masking it. I expected what he said next.

"For you, Your Highness, I would always clear the decks to work on a project. Sometimes, it's not possible. Depends on the contract I've signed, but yes, the timing was good and I'm available. That part was fortuitous."

"Fortuitous indeed, Marco. Good for both of us."

"Thank you. I agree," Marco said with a slight bow of his head.

"And good for you, my dear. What an adventure," he said with mirth, pressing his palms together.

I had wanted to watch the beautiful gardens and lush wild forests we drove through, but the sultan was an all-consuming figure who demanded our full attention. I picked up right away that he was used to getting his own way—not frequently but always.

"So come on, tell me," the sultan demanded.

"The most important part is that we are now officially engaged, and—"

The sultan held up his right hand, moving his fingers back and forth, demanding a look at my ring. I placed my hand there.

"Very nice," he said as he gently kissed my knuckles and released my hand.

I couldn't make out the look the two of them shared. In fact, I was sure I was missing half the nuances between the two men.

"And what else?"

"I have successfully sold the Manhattan building, or at least we're about to enter into escrow. Then I'm going to start looking in Tampa."

"You are moving from New York to Florida? Will you walk around in shorts and sandals now? Do you think this is wise?" At first, his stern look alarmed me. Then he burst out laughing. I presumed it was his way of telling us our lives were little and his was big.

He would be a dangerous enemy.

"I'd actually like that. Mostly, my business is done over the phone anyway, so what does it matter if I wore my red, white, and blue boxers?" Marco added with a smile, happy to play along.

"I don't blame you there. I used to spend long hours at the beach. Not so much now. I might get mistaken for a whale, and one of the fishermen would haul my carcass in with his net!"

I noted Marco lightly chuckled but was careful not to be anywhere close to the sultan's casual and overemphasized demeanor.

"Your office in Manhattan, I'm sorry to say, was a horrible fiasco. I never liked that place. Too cold and drafty. Sterile. Looked like it was designed by a German." His honest evaluation was duly noted. Marco agreed.

I would ask Marco later about the German comment but guessed it had to do with past history.

"So now you are about to start your new life. And babies. You'll want to have babies right away. We'll make sure while you're here that you drink our love potions that help a woman's belly to conceive."

I was shocked at the liberty he took with me, someone he didn't know, and my body. Marco squeezed my hand before I could blurt out something I would regret.

We arrived. Two guards on white horses and in red uniforms outlined in more gold braid than I'd seen anywhere stood on either side of the enormous palace's carved archway and doors. Above us, the many spires and towers of the palace looked down. I heard birds calling and smelled the delicate sandalwood scent of incense. Marco helped me out of the van as several aids scurried to take all our things inside. Marco kept his computer slung over his shoulder, but I gave them everything.

We stepped through the archway into a room that was nearly three stories high, lined in blue and green tiles with colorful designs. There was a row of a dozen heavy columns several feet wide, all tiled, creating corkscrew patterns as they ascended up to the golden domed ceiling above. Tiny windows at the top allowed shards of light to pour over the inlaid marble floor. The colors, the detail, and the glistening gold of the great room were unlike anything I'd seen in any of the greatest cathedrals in Mexico or pictures of European churches.

"You like, my dear?" the sultan asked me.

"I'm speechless," I whispered back. It was the total truth.

The last couple of days had been more than I could have imagined. But this, this eclipsed even my wildest dreams and fantasies.

I felt like I'd stepped back in time by hundreds of years.

CHAPTER 7

T HE SULTAN WAS a good study of human nature. He put Shannon and I up in the turquoise room, instead of the pink one he'd given Rebecca and I some years ago.

Attention to detail.

That's why I was hired, I reminded myself.

As Shannon stared aghast at the opulence of the wide stairways of marble and semi-precious stone, I had to grab her several times to avoid her knocking over a priceless urn or statue. The balcony-feel hallways leading to the guest rooms upstairs, overlooking the grand room entrance, were illuminated by the golden stained glass ceiling hovering above us all, as if Heaven itself was keeping a special, watchful eye on us mere mortals.

While she tried to take in everything, I watched her, enjoying the sense of wonder and awe I'd bet she had as a child. Nothing made me happier than seeing her in this state, far away from all the pressures of her life in Florida. At least, she thought she had pressures. In reality, she had no idea what the world was really like, and that this was all an illusion.

But I had too much love for her to take it away now, and so I observed how she absorbed the centuries of wealth and tradition, just like I had done some ten years ago when I first met the man who was more generous than any other I'd met and would treat me like a son, if I let him.

I actually thought of him more like an older brother—someone whose help he needed to keep his progeny alive as they put on their little water wings and tried to explore, to compete in the outside world. He and I both knew, as they approached their late twenties, they were both in danger of becoming hot house plants—raised in the stifling world of the sultan and his wealth and power, where work was not required. If they got in a jam with their studies in school, a first-class tutor could be flown over to bail them out. He wanted them to make their mark but not die trying. It wasn't important if they failed, as long as they came home alive.

My secret mission was not only to help them come home in one piece but have them come home in triumph. For that, prayers to the sultan's elephant god in my honor would be required every day by his entire kingdom.

He'd watched us climb the stairs, bidding us farewell with a wave as I turned around and smiled. He'd asked permission for Shannon to attend a party put on by his wives and their attendants.

"I promise they will transform her, pamper her in luxury, and turn her into a harem princess fit for a king. You'll thank me, Marco," he'd said.

Shannon had frowned, not sure if she was going to accept, but I bowed and thanked him for his kindness. There wasn't a chance in the world I would let her pass up this opportunity, and it was as much for my benefit as hers.

Shannon's expression wasn't lost on the sultan as he gave a faint belly laugh and then motioned to the grand stairway, which was wider than Shannon's house, saying to our backs, "One hour then. They will collect her at your room in one hour."

I pulled Shannon behind me and gave her no room to turn around to give him the attitude I knew brewed inside her. One thing I had learned about Western women was that they were in such a hurry to achieve what their male colleagues had, even to surpass it, that they forgot sometimes the enormous power they had as a female. I'd told my men many times out in the field to watch out for the mothers and girlfriends, even the school-age girls, because they were the stronger ones in some of the cultures we fought in. They'd honed their strength by being oppressed for centuries. It wasn't fair, but it made them extraordinarily strong and difficult to challenge.

Shannon wasn't one who knew her strength yet. She was unblemished, relatively unscarred, except for the loss of Emily, which would forever be a basement emotionally for her. What I enjoyed was her light, her softness, and her ability to experience wonder and be happy. As she grew to learn the nature of her womanly power, I never wanted her to lose that quality. It would always be her secret weapon, bringing light to a dark world. Perhaps, she was my safety net, as well, if I ever got there.

She was the only woman I'd ever met that I would consider having a family with.

But all that would be hopefully coming at some future date. Right now, I had to explain the gift that was given her and convince her to embrace it, allow it to be something she enjoyed. Even if she was unsure or a tiny bit uncomfortable, she needed to keep her claws inside.

I closed the heavy door painted with scenes and designs from their culture. She marched up to the bed, because it was on a pedestal requiring three steps to reach the top, tossed her computer bag down on the satin tufted coverlet, and peered down at me.

With the backdrop of the carved four poster sandalwood frame wrapped in long, shimmering drapes, she was magnificent in her stubbornness and anger. I think the smile I couldn't help breaking out added to her emotional meltdown.

"Who does he think he is? Marco, there's nothing wrong with me. What is this, a Mary Kay meeting or something?"

I shrugged. "They just want to fix you up."

"Did I express to anyone that I needed fixing?"

"No, sweetheart, you did not."

"Then why didn't you let me refuse? I'm humiliated."

While she stood there with her hands on her hips, I made imaginary designs with my right foot, tracing the inlaid patterns of stone. "Because I think you'll enjoy it. It's a routine they do. They take great pleasure making each other look more beautiful."

"That's an awful custom. They're just objects of his desire. I want to be more than an object."

"Oh, they are far more than objects of his desire. They inspire him to be a great man, Shannon. He enjoys how they honor him by pleasuring him."

She abruptly looked away and sat on the bed, thinking. Perhaps I'd cracked a tiny part of her shell.

I added more, hoping she'd understand. "If you won't do it for fun—"

"Fun? That's not fun. It feels like a slumber party when I was a teen, where we'd talk about boys and—"

I knew what was going to come next. Em had told me. I wouldn't break the confidence, even though she was long gone. I remembered how she used to talk about dressing Shannon up, putting makeup on her, brushing her hair out, and making her look exotic at twelve, braces and all.

I mounted the steps slowly, watching her deal with thoughts I had no right to invade. But Em had told me so much about her, almost as if she had prepared me for the bride I would have, not the one I expected. My eyes filled with water as I watched hers overflow.

You are so like your sister, and yet you are so different.

Finally, she inhaled, wiping the tears off her cheeks with the back of her hand. "Go ahead," she said without looking at me. "You were going to say something about this being fun." Then she chanced a glance up at me. I sat next to her and took her hand.

Her hand gripped mine, knuckles white. I brushed the hair from her neck and whispered to her ear. "Shannon, become my harem girl, for just a night. Pretend what it would feel like to be a queen of an exotic and strange land where you are waiting for you prince to come claim you." I paused, feeling her tension disappear. "It's in your novels, Shannon. Go play a character in one of those stories. Pure fantasy, sweetheart. Let me be the hero to your heroine tonight." I kissed her as a follow-up and waited.

Her breathing was ragged as her emotions welled up.

"Say you'll do it for me, Shannon."

She nodded then returned my gaze. "Just when I think I know and understand everything about you, Marco, you come up with something like this that just blows me away."

"It's because I love you."

I lifted her chin, and we kissed. Her cheek pressed against mine, her hands around my neck, and the way she kissed had me in great anticipation of what was to follow. I knew the world for what it is, but for today, we'd make of it what we wanted.

Nobody in the universe would ever be able to take it away from us, either.

She leapt to action, escaping from my embrace, suddenly. She was at the bottom of the platform before I could stop her. "Marco, what do I wear? I should change my underwear."

I fell back on the bed, laughing.

"No, I mean it. Are they going to dress me in some saris and such? I should have my clean, newer things on. I just wanted to be comfortable today so wore my cotton—"

Tears streamed down the sides of my eyes, soaking into the satin coverlet. I could hear her unzipping her suitcase and ransacking her neatly folded things inside.

I came up on one elbow, watching the spectacle of her nervousness. "You are dressed fine, just the way you are, sweetheart. They'll do everything for you. I'm sure they'll dress you—everything. All you have to do is enjoy it."

"But you said I shouldn't be wrinkled, that I—"

I shook my head. She had misunderstood everything I'd told her. "That's different. That was on making a good impression to a head of state, someone who has a staff of more than two dozen to make sure he shows up impeccably dressed. It's a form of respect. This is different. The rules are different for the harem."

I got the look I deserved. With her hands back on her hips, she scowled. "And how do you know?"

I didn't want to tell her Rebecca hadn't enjoyed the encounter and had asked them to stop after the first few minutes. But she had good reason to not like stranger's hands on her body, with her past. That wasn't my secret to share with Shannon.

"Because I've had conversations with his sons, mostly Harry, his favorite, Shannon. But you—" I said, as I got up, descended the stairs and held her by the shoulders. "You'll have the first-hand experience, and you can tell me all about it. I want to learn about every detail."

She grabbed me and pressed her face into my chest. She mumbled into the fabric. "I'm such a klutz. You must think I'm the most clueless girl in the universe."

It made me sad to hear this. I gripped her tight, my fingers massaging her neck and shoulders and sorting through her long hair. I kissed the top of her head.

"Nothing could be further from the truth."

We heard a timid knock on the door, and I held her hand as I opened it to a bevy of lovelies, dressed in silks and jewels. The older woman in front bowed with her hands together. "If you would please do us the honor of lending us your wife, sir, we would be grateful."

"Of course."

Shannon's wide eyes studied the stunning ladies in front of her. I transferred Shannon's hand to the older woman and observed as they closed ranks around her, whisking her down the marble hallway with only the gentle swishing sounds of saris and tiny metal bells tinkling as they took her.

With another wife on her other side holding that hand, Shannon looked up at me from the top of the stairs, paused, and meekly smiled.

I blew her an air-kiss and watched them take her away from me.

CHAPTER 8

W HATEVER I WAS in for, I promised myself I'd try to enjoy the pampering. Searching from face to face, all I saw were beautiful women, from barely twenty up to Marco's age. They were stunning creatures, their shiny black hair worn in braids while jewelry dripped from their earlobes, wrapped around their necks, wove into their hair, and dangled down onto their foreheads. Their dark eyes were lined in heavy black charcoal.

Their saris sparkled in the light as we descended the grand stairway, walked down the marbled corridor decorated with granite, alabaster, and dark-veined marble statues of women in various states of undress. In between, every ten feet or so, another pair of carved columns supported a carved ornate Arabic arch decorated with paint and tile relief in varying designs. The ceiling above was blue, like a summer day in Florida, complete with clouds and occasionally a bird. Tiny windows let in beams of light through the hallway walls just above shoulder height, made with interconnecting filigree, ceramic tiled blocks.

My two monitors did not let go of my hands nor did they say anything to me. Others behind me whispered. I felt hands on my long hair, which I had secured with a clip. Someone made a remark, and another hand removed my clip. My hair fell to my shoulders.

Two young women opened a metal gate that had turned light green with a patina from centuries of use. I stood in the middle of a dome inlaid with tile, semi-precious stones, and gold. In the center, with three shallow steps down, was a turquoise pool covered by flower petals floating on top. Steam rose from the water, indicating it was warm.

All around the pool were settees and lounge chairs covered in long, brightly colored silk pillows. Several alcoves at the sides led to closed doors or revealed specialized workstations for massage. A tall, frosty refrigerator carried an assortment of fruit juices and a large bowl of fruit at the bottom.

Hands removed my shoes, storing them out of sight. Then my shirt came off. Someone else reached for the back of my bra to undo the fastener.

My spine stiffened as I scanned the circle of women that had formed around me.

"It's quite all right, mum," said one of the younger wives, a pretty thing near to my own age. Her English was flawless. "You need to relax and just allow us to wait on you. We do everything for you."

My bra loosened, and my arms instinctively crossed over my breasts to hide them. Two women took hold of my palms, beginning a finger massage on them, applying oil and rubbing it into my skin as they lowered my hands to my sides while another woman unzipped my slacks and slipped them down over my hips.

Again, my reaction was to draw my arms back up to my chest, but my attendants continued my massage, holding my hands firmly in place at my sides.

Next, my panties fell to my ankles. The group moved away from me a step and called out things I couldn't understand, as they circled around me. I knew they were making plans, evaluating me, perhaps deciding what kind of treatment they would provide. They rubbed my elbows, felt the texture of my hair, examined my eyes, and no doubt found hairs on my upper lip I'd neglected to pluck recently. One woman held up my hand, studying my nails. Someone must have remarked that I had pierced ears because there was a light rumble of agreement to the discovery.

"You have a beautiful body, mum. We are going to make you

look like a princess."

"Thank you." I didn't know of anything else to say.

"Your skin is dry, mum, so it needs a good exfoliation and then a yogurt masque. Your muscles are tight, especially around here…" She touched my lower neck and traveled along the top of my shoulder. "Your nails need painting. Your hair should be conditioned, and excess hair will be removed."

I was used to getting facials, so this didn't sound half bad. Nothing on that list bothered me.

"But first, you must relax and meditate. We must get your body ready to become the vessel it was created to be, so let us begin with a warm perfume flower bath while we prepare the other tables."

My clip miraculously appeared again, securing my hair up on the top of my head. Three of the wives dropped their clothes and led me naked down the steps into the pool and sat with me at the edges. A bucket was brought, filled with scented water. With large natural sponges, they sluiced the warm liquid over my shoulders, my neck, and both my front and back. Warm oil was poured over my skin as the sponges brushed and rinsed the oil evenly all over my body above my waist.

One of the three women was pregnant and just beginning to show. I pointed to her belly. The English-speaking woman answered my query.

"She is five months along. We will all celebrate the sultan's new child before the end of the year."

I smiled at her, but she turned her face away, covered her mouth with her hand, and giggled.

"You are outside the family. It isn't customary to speak of it if you are a stranger. But you come with Marco, who is like a son to our sultan. You do not know our customs, so all is forgiven."

I was directed to sit up at the lip of the tub as the oil and sponge routine was performed on my legs. One of them scrubbed the bottoms of my feet and between my toes, which tickled, and I jumped. She used a pumice stone on my heels, scrubbing with a coarse salt mixture made with yogurt and honey. The same treatment was given to my elbows, and then I jumped back in, and they sponged me off.

Next, I was directed to lie down on a cloth-covered massage table. A cool face mask was applied, allowed to soak for a bit, and then wiped off. Four hands carefully lathered and shaved my underarms and legs while a woman at my head waxed my upper lip and chin then wove tiny hairs into my brows.

At last, a warm face masque was applied, and my eyes were covered with a folded ice-cold washcloth. "You will try to sleep now, if you can. Just one little procedure first."

When I felt fingers down in my pubic area, I sat up, tossing the washcloth to the floor.

"Wait. What are you doing?"

"Have you not had this done?" she asked me, her large brown eyes showing concern.

"Once. I had it done once. But—"

"Mum," she started, laying a gentle palm on my shoulder, speaking in a soft lilting tone. "We endeavor to deliver you as hairless as possible. It will bring you both a great deal of pleasure. We have found that often it increases the man's ardor."

I wasn't worried about Marco's ardor at all. I was worried about the pain I knew was to come. I deemed it unnecessary, and I told her so.

"Mum, if you will just allow us to try. We have herbs that make the experience more pleasurable."

I doubted that. It was the reason I'd vowed to never do it again. It had been a dare in college.

"Just lay back and try to think about how smooth you will feel, like a baby's bottom, when we are finished."

The washcloth was replaced. More masque was applied as I lay back and felt a cold kind of gel being applied to the hair around my sex. Before too long, I realized it was a numbing cream. My knees were bent slightly and then spread wide as they applied the cooling gel up and down both sides of my labia. Within seconds, I felt like my female parts had been partially frozen, not to mention thoroughly examined. The gel was wiped away, and warm wax was drizzled over my skin as the layers of silk were pressed into place and then suddenly ripped loose. I was prepared for the worst.

I hardly felt a thing.

Greatly relieved, I could finally relax as they worked to make sure every hair was gone. They even held my knees to my shoulders and denuded my anal area.

The masque was peeled away, and a yogurt and honey mixture was painted all over my face and front, including my ankles and toes. Warm sandalwood oil was poured onto my scalp as strong fingers worked it into my hair and temples, giving me the best scalp and head massages I'd ever experienced. At the same time, my feet were drizzled in warm wax and placed into plastic baggies. They gently pushed them inside insulated cloth sacks smelling of lavender. They repeated the same thing with my hands.

"Time for a nap, mum."

"Okay," I mumbled, not daring to move.

I had no idea how long I slept, but when I started to feel the spray of warm water over my body, I remembered where I was.

Everything was repeated on my backside. The plastic bags were removed. Warm oil was poured over my back and legs and then a sheet applied to soak up the excess.

Someone's strong hands found every muscle pull, every place I held tension in my upper back, neck, and shoulder area and lovingly working it out of me while two or three others massaged the long muscles of my calves, thighs, lower back, and arms. The pressure was too firm for me to doze off, but when they were done, I could hardly sit up. I felt like a cloth doll.

My neck and shoulders were worked on from the front in the same process, pouring oil, soaking it up, and then working it into my skin. Even the soles of my feet were attended to.

I was moved to another station where I sat in a recliner, my feet propped up and given a thick juice drink, like a smoothie, with the most unusual color of rose red. It tasted delicious.

My English translator rubbed her belly and pointed to the pregnant woman. "Very good for welcoming a child."

The young wife nodded her head in respectful shyness.

"What is it?"

"Mother's milk from water buffalo, sweet beets, yogurt, and passionflower petals."

I sniffed the glass and could finally smell the gamey milk scent. Figuring it would be polite not to, I finished it off and asked for a glass of water to rinse my mouth with.

I was given a sparkling water with a lime in it, which tasted delicious.

She helped me lie back at the edge of the chair, lowering it over a deep sink and pouring more oil onto my scalp before wrapping my head in a hot towel. She placed sliced cucumbers over my eyes and waited several minutes before adding shampoo and carefully rubbing in circular motions until the mixture was lathered into a stiff peak.

I would never be able to tell him, but they gave me an even stronger, more thorough shampoo than Marco did. An herbal conditioner was applied, and again, a warm towel was wrapped around my head. I was moved to another station.

This time, I was directed to lie on my back on top of moist strips of silk. They had been soaked in chamomile, she told me. Gently, they wrapped me in these strips, my arms bent over my stomach, fully encased like a mummy. And then they wrapped me in a light-weight metallic blanket and strapped me to the table in four places.

"Time for another drink and another nap, mum," she whispered, holding up a glass with what smelled like apricot juice mixed with white tea and sprinkled with pomegranate seeds. I used a supersized fat straw and consumed every drop.

I fell asleep to the sounds of water splashing and playful laughing.

Yup. I could get used to this all right. And just when I thought

I'd floated off to Heaven, she placed a headset over my ears, and I listened to sounds of the waves at the ocean.

That's when I thought about Indian Rocks Beach and how the surf and the sounds of the sea birds had lulled me to sleep every night since I'd arrived and began to call it home. I couldn't help it, but I felt Marco's hand in mine as we walked the beach, watching the bright orange and yellow clouds turn purple and grey, as I allowed tears to drip down onto the table.

I missed my little place and the simple people there. I missed the decorated golf carts at Halloween and Christmas. I missed the firepits and the stolen kisses. I missed the way his body protected and warmed mine when we spent the night under the stars.

Did I have to come all the way over here just to find out I belonged somewhere else?

Maybe that was the point of it all—to experience something totally different and mind-numbingly beautiful only to find what I would come back to was even better.

CHAPTER 9

I REVIEWED SOME of the files Karin had printed out for me, studying maps from my SOF days back in Coronado. The Navy had never asked me if I'd turned off the software, so I continued to use it and figured I'd get the axe one of these days. Or maybe, someone purposely left it on for me.

But for now, it was a portal to some of the most accurate information I could get about our deployment schedules and, more importantly, why. It didn't tell me all the strategy or high-level decisions the senior chiefs would have with the president or his Washington team, but by watching what they were moving and when, I could put it together fairly accurately.

And there was a lot of concern about Nigeria, neighboring Chad, Mali, and others. While we focused on the Middle East, our friends in China had developed partnerships with many of the central African countries. And when I say partnerships, that meant an infusion of capital. We'd gotten stingy with our cash, demanding some of the leaders clean up their act, especially after Benghazi. Our public didn't have the stomach for things like killing ambassadors and troops who really couldn't do anything anyway but were getting murdered.

The bold strokes we made with our catch and grab routines in Afghanistan had worked for a time. What we'd lacked was the will to help those countries transition to a peaceful civilian-run government, based on good science, not voodoo economics. Wishful thinking got a lot of guys killed, and most of them were patriots like me. It was a sad story, Vietnam all over again. The only people who were saved were the ones who got airlifted out. The country was going to do what the country would do, and we could only destabilize it by inserting ourselves without concrete plans.

Oh, we did a good job, and we learned quick after Vietnam. A lot of our military leaders grew up cutting their teeth on these things and learned the hard way. Right after World War II and again twenty years after Vietnam, none of our Joint Chiefs had ever seen combat. There was a vacuum. They were learning in the war colleges from men who had never seen the hell of combat. Some of our boys paid the price until we got to take the training wheels off.

I didn't have the luxury of second-guessing all that, and I didn't hold a grudge. I cared about it, and I cared about the guys we lost. But it wasn't my rodeo. I was punching tickets at the tollbooth, granting admission to the arena of war and training these boys so they could live to see another Christmas or get lucky in the back of their pickup truck when they got home.

But what made my project, the Trident Towers, so important wasn't that I was making these injured guys whole. I was giving them a chance at a somewhat normal life. I'd been damned lucky. I was paying it back for the ones who weren't.

It dovetailed nicely with what I did on the security front. Sure, I knew guys who liked to swagger around, telling everyone they were badass Navy SEALs so they could pick up chicks and be the kind of kid their parents would be proud of, especially after 9-11. They'd become personal trainers to the Hollywood crowd and fly on corporate jets with politicians and captains of industry. Every day before I got out, I heard those stories. And it made me sick. It was one of the reasons I couldn't do it any longer.

I wanted to be a captain of industry too. I'd earned my stripes and paid a heavy price for it, as well. I wasn't about to go take cushy jobs that looked more dangerous than they were. I wanted to do more than get those looks from boardrooms and Ted Talks.

My ego didn't require that. I wanted to help the non-professionals cope with and see the real world for what it was: a dirty, evil place filled with people who would take away what wasn't defended, managed by desk jockeys and politicians who didn't have a clue. The empty shirts made good speeches and kissed babies. I wanted to teach *regular* citizens how to deal with these groups, how to help out the sorely needed populations of these war-torn countries.

Anybody could be a big guy when they're HALO jumping with thirty other lethal warriors at midnight who would die to keep you safe. I was dealing with the detritus, the part of the world who had to handle the aftermath when all the soldiers were gone, when they were fighting with rakes and shovels and slingshots. When their whole lives were consumed with protecting their kids as they went to school or their wives and daughters from traffickers when they tried to go to the store or hold a job. Dynasties like the sultan's could be overthrown in a heartbeat. He knew it, too. And when it came right down to it, for all his wealth, he was still a father and husband trying to protect his little brood.

No, I wasn't one of those who came crashing in with a new administration, cocky as hell, and not smelling my own shit. Because I knew the real truth of it.

Nobody *ever* got it right more than a small percentage of the time.

Nobody.

A gentle knock on my opened door caused me to look up.

"You are working? I thought you would come downstairs and we could wait together, have a little chat, Marco."

"I'm sorry. I was just taking advantage of a little quiet time. But you're right. I should have kept you company."

The sultan sat down in the overstuffed chair adjacent the table I was seated at. It was painful to watch him. Life was slipping away, right through his fingers. He wasn't able to buy himself another one.

"You work too hard, Marco," he said as he turned his bloodshot eyes on me. We studied each other silently before I answered him.

"Not sure I can do it any other way, Your Highness. I'm like you. I have a lot to do, a lot to live for."

He slowly nodded his agreement. I noticed his fingers were swollen, and there were purple patches around his ankles from lack of circulation. It wouldn't do any good to recommend he lose weight or start walking or riding a bike. Or avoid eating that magnificent honey-baked ham I brought him.

"I always thought it was Rebecca who drove you."

"Never. She was the sidecar, but in the end, she didn't inspire me. I don't think she ever did. She was a user." I pointed through the doorway. "Shannon inspires me."

"Ah, I do understand inspiration." He smiled. "Some people get it going to their Christian church, worshiping a virgin, unspoiled woman or a bloody corpse on a cross. My ancestors? They would have me worship an elephant with four arms, so fat, like me, he's pulled on a cart by his great friend, the rat. When I was a little boy and first began to read and watch television, I discovered the beautiful buildings in Rome and wondered why I had to worship an elephant and not some golden God in the sky above. That might have brought inspiration to me."

His story was funny, and I chuckled. I enjoyed seeing the world, or little glimpses of it, through his unique perspective. I would miss him when he left us. He would leave an irreparable vacuum behind. I appreciated the confidence he had in me to be able to show me his tender, mortal side.

"Highness?" a timid house attendant spoke from the doorway. "You wish anything to drink, perhaps?" I knew his English was for my benefit.

"You brought some of that California wine, didn't you?" the sultan asked me.

I got up and handed him the Cabernet he loved. It was from the winery founded by a famous director, and I'd described the tasting room that held so many famous movie props from the man's movie career to the sultan many times.

He held the bottle up, admiring it. "Someday, you will introduce me to this director, yes?"

"Definitely. You come to California, and I'll set it up. I think the two of you would get along. He runs a powerful kingdom too."

The sultan handed the bottle to the attendant, who quickly disappeared.

"Do you have any questions you wish to ask?"

"One thing I didn't see in the material they sent was copies of their permissions with the heads of state. I'm told there's a process and has to be sorted. I wanted to know how far they've gotten."

He wrinkled his brow. "We'll have to wait until tomorrow. I was told everything was in place. But they don't always tell me the truth. That's why I've hired you, to ask the right questions."

I suspected as much.

We were brought two wine glasses on a silver tray, along with the corked bottle. The attendant set it on the table. I moved my things out of the way, stowed my laptop, and tucked the confidential reports next to it.

He held his glass up when we were again alone. "To youth. Nubile, beautiful women and the inspiration they bring to our lives."

I could easily drink to that, and we clinked glasses.

"Hmm. That's so good. You know they tell me in Delhi they grow wine, but I don't believe it. Too rocky and dry."

"They made wine in Egypt, even found some in the great pyramids."

"Ah, those wizards of the heavens. They made wine out of anything. I mean *good* wine."

"Australia has a huge wine growing region. The Greeks did. And there are even wineries in Alaska."

"Not the same climate."

"True."

The looming thought between us was the women, who would be joining us in another hour or two. As if I'd pushed that into his head, he asked me about it. "You think she is enjoying this?" he said as he took another sip of wine.

"It's been over two hours, and she hasn't bailed yet." I smiled. "Thank you for that, by the way."

"Oh, I am curious too. I haven't had so much fun anticipating this for a long time. I didn't want to tell you what they had planned until you got here so you couldn't back out."

"She's a pretty good sport. But I think she'll enjoy it, if she lets herself."

"Isn't that the truth? We only enjoy what we let ourselves enjoy." He pulled a gold pocket watch on a chain from the folds of his clothes and flipped open the case. "Well, at this point, I'm going to need a nap. We will have dinner at five o'clock sharp. We'll have some entertainment, some dancing, and a feast to celebrate your arrival."

"I'm sure Shannon will love it."

"Oh, it will be just you and me. The ladies will entertain us."

My glass was halfway to my mouth as he said that. "Excuse me?"

"They will feed her today, take care of all of that. They'll do a ritual juice cleanse meant to honor you. She'll come to you refreshed, pampered, decorated, and maybe a little bit hungry—for you!"

He chuckled.

"I have no doubt you'll be pleased, Marco."

CHAPTER 10

I WAS DIPPED, washed again, drizzled with scented oil worked into my skin, soaked in a soothing chamomile cocoon, and then gently washed and rinsed again. My hair felt silky from the hot oil conditioner. Every pore of my body was wide open and alive, rejuvenated with the oils and masques.

I was given a spice-scented deodorant and helped into a fluffy terrycloth robe. While my hair was blow-dried and curled, my nails and toes were painted a delicious rose color. Once again, oil was sprayed onto my forearms and calves and massaged into my skin. My feet were encrusted in warm cotton slippers while I sat in a chair and watched the hairdresser work her magic.

She was a true master at design. Delicately, she wove strands ribbons of gold into my hair, braiding them, twisting them into patterns coiled around the top of my head. The bulk of my hair was curled and allowed to flow in ringlets then carefully pinned up and adorned with tiny tuberoses and miniature buds that looked like roses. More gold ribbon was used. Several long strands were tightly curled and allowed to hang down my back.

A tiny gold chain with a single ruby was pinned at my crown and allowed to dangle on my forehead. She placed long golden bangles adorned with rubies and other stones on my ears with a matching ring on my right hand.

They applied foundation and began drawing dark black outlines around my eyes, similar to how the other wives wore it. It made my eyes look enormous. My eyelids were garnished in turquoise powder, and my lips were smoothed in a tingling red lipstick.

When she showed me with a hand-held mirror what my profile and back of my head looked like, I nearly didn't recognize that it was me. The bright colors on my face and the glistening jewels dangling at the sides of my neck and on my forehead did make me look like one of them.

A princess.

The robe was removed, and several women brought in armloads of saris. I'd read about how sari fitting could sometimes take hours, that there was an art to it. The older woman's critical eye picked out several, holding them up to my face and neck, bunched them to drape at my hips, and finally selected a half dozen to work with, sending the others back.

She stepped close to me, her finger dipping in a little pot of some kind of pink salve that smelled exotic, infused with flower and spice scents, even a hint of cinnamon. She smiled as she rubbed a small dot into my skin just under my earlobes. Then she pasted over both my nipples with the salve, which stimulated and tickled them. And finally, she came to her knees and applied the mixture to my nether lips, rubbing it into my now-hairless mound, even placing a small dab at my anus, which caused me to jump. Several of the ladies giggled.

As the women started drying off and getting dressed, the woman worked her magic, wrapping the white silk under wrap around my chest, under my arms, and about my waist. With a deep turquoise sari sprinkled with tiny silver threads, she wrapped the fabric over one shoulder and around my chest again, leaving the ends loose, while she used another slightly lighter shade of turquoise sari with a gold border around my waist, bunching it at my left hip and securing it by tying it off with the undergarment. Another paper-thin transparent fabric draped over them all, which she tied in a loose knot at my other hip. She pulled ends of the large panels of fabric, tucked yardage in various places until she was satisfied they wouldn't move.

She asked me to walk a few steps forward, turn, and come back to her, which I did. With her hands together, she bowed her head, adding several strands of delicate gold chain around my neck that hung to below my waist.

Jeweled sandals were carefully placed on my feet. Someone also snapped in place an ankle bracelet of tiny tinkling bells I'd heard earlier and added one at each of my wrists. Bending her forearms at the elbow, she asked me to flash my hands back and forth to make the bracelets come alive.

The enchanting sound was laced with the infusion of the exotic spices.

The women formed a circle, and I was encouraged to follow their movements as they dipped their arms and hands below and then above their heads, twirled, and shook their wrists to make the bells tinkle. They showed me how to cover my face with the light veil, to bow my head, cast my eyes down, and concentrate on the motion of my fingers as we moved gracefully in the circle.

At the end of my little rehearsal, we all bowed to each other with our hands together.

The room exploded into spontaneous chatter as the women piled up all the used towels and repositioned the lounge chairs and pillows. I was handed another smoothie, a yogurt mixture with pomegranate and other blended fruits and given a slice of fresh coconut. Handing me a toothbrush, I brushed my teeth, drank some mint tea, and they applied more red lipstick.

We were ready for the show.

I felt like one of the wives as we made our way down the hallway of statues, our bells tingling, filling the air with wonderful scents. I wasn't the tallest, but one of them. We followed behind the oldest wife, two-by-two. The English-speaking woman whispered in my ear.

"Do not look at him. Make him watch you, but don't make eye contact until you are alone. It is most good for the time later on, if you understand."

Oh, I understood. I knew it would drive Marco crazy. I knew

everything about this little caper would send him right over the edge. Way under my skirts, my flesh quivered at the thought.

I couldn't wait to see how hard he'd have to restrain himself.

We entered the great reception area, which contained several couples I presumed to be loyal subjects of the sultan. They followed behind us as we made our way to the banquet hall and throne room. An enormous golden statue of a sitting elephant with four arms sat on a raised dais on the far side of the room. Dwarfed in comparison, an ornate pair of golden chairs sat on a one-step pedestal just below the statue. I saw to my left a large banquet table had been prepared that served only two people. The sultan was on the left, and Marco sat in a black tux on his right. True to my promise, I lowered my eyes and did not look at him.

I followed the other pairs of wives as we circled in front of the giant statue, and one by one, we each bowed our heads, our hands together in prayer and adoration.

I could hear the sultan's deep voice, and his belly laughs. I didn't hear a sound from Marco. Perhaps he hadn't noticed me?

We formed the circle we'd practiced in the bathing room, each of us following along behind the other, making the sweeping hand movements and dips. We shook our wrists and twirled. I pulled the veil across my face, bowed when I was closest to the sultan, like the others did. He whispered something guttural to Marco, and I heard the word enchanting, but I wasn't watching either of their faces. I demurely allowed the veil to cover my face again as the circle turned, and I was presented once more.

Our movement stopped, and we formed one long line, all dozen of us. Out of the corner of my eye, I could see Marco with his legs crossed, elbows on the armchair he was sitting in, with the fingers of his right hand drawn across his face below the nose. There was no question he was breathing heavily, and I took great pleasure in that thought.

But I remained with my eyes averted. I even made eye contact with the young wife who had given me directions and the pregnant one, who both gave me a slight bow and smiled. I was caught off guard as the whole line of women kneeled on one knee, their heads low and palms held together in front of them. I was the last to make the formation, but I waited, just like they did.

The sultan walked down the line, touching each one of his wives, placing a hand under their jaw and raising their eyes to see him. He stopped for a moment in front of me but didn't touch me. Several times, he said something private to the woman. He chose three, including his oldest wife, whom he took by the hand and led down the hallway, through the entrance, and off down another long corridor. I presumed it was the royal chamber, but it was just a guess.

Nobody else moved. I heard Marco approach, and then I saw his black trousers and his polished black shoes. I felt his fingers encircle my right wrist, the tiny bells calling to us, as he commanded me to stand, and I did so. I wasn't sure what to do next, so I kept my eyes cast down until he delicately pushed up my chin, and I could no longer avoid the searing heat from his eyes.

As he led me across the marble floor and up the wide staircase to the room upstairs, I turned and smiled to the nine other wives who had watched, lovingly bathed, and coached me. They now smiled back.

It was a scene right out of one of my storybooks when I was a child. It was all about the handsome prince choosing his princess above all others, in an unbelievably beautiful old palace on an island kingdom in the middle of the Indian Ocean.

CHAPTER 11

WHEN I WAS a kid, I remembered reading a cowboy story—in hindsight, it probably was a romance novel I found of my mom's—about a guy who mail ordered his bride from China. When she arrived on the stagecoach, she was dressed in her traditional Chinese garments and his hands were shaking as he had to peel away her silky top with the funny buttons made out of knots.

I probably shouldn't have been reading that book, since I was about ten or twelve, but I couldn't put it down. I'd known exactly how he felt because I'd never held a girl, let alone undressed one with callused hands, nervous and ill-equipped to know what to do. I'd imagined her exotic scent, her mannerisms, and the way she averted her gaze downward. Plus, she was so tiny the cowboy was worried he'd offend her or, worse still, somehow break her brittle bones.

Leading Shannon up the stairs in her flowing robes with her brightly painted face and the music of her little bells at her ankle and wrists made me feel the same way. I was right back to being a young boy with no experience. I had never been shy before, but her beauty overwhelmed me.

Yes, it *overwhelmed* me.

It had been sort of a lark that I put her in the sultan's harem's hands. I didn't think of it as too significant, just a new experience, something she might find fun. But seeing her dressed in the silks, watching her dance and copy the other traditional women who had been trained their whole lives to be what they were today, touched me some place deep. I was delighted with the outcome, but I was ashamed I'd put her through it.

No denying it. I did force her to play this game. I never allowed her to object. I forced my way on her, and for that, I was not proud.

I never wanted to make her do anything like this again, and my shame only grew with the lust I felt for her. This was not the man I truly was. This was not the honorable man I'd become. I was play acting a role that put women as second-class—put Shannon as subservient to me. And she did it. She followed along with something she never would have chosen on her own.

I could feel her eyes on me, wondering why I wasn't saying anything. But I didn't want to further embarrass her in front of a household of people where this was the custom. But it wasn't Shannon's custom. It wasn't the way I wanted to treat the woman I planned to spend the rest of my life with. This discussion had to be done in private where I wouldn't cause her shame nor bring shame on the palace and my very dear friend.

I closed the door behind us as we entered our room. Someone had brought champagne on ice and a huge bouquet of large, colorful wild jungle flowers set in a Chinese urn. The whole room was filled with the heady, flowery aroma.

Shannon stood in front of one of the carved wooden posters on the bed, pulling the sheer silk material from the canopy between her fingers. She knew something was wrong. Her downcast eyes were not due to the part she played. She thought I was displeased with her.

Nothing could be further from the truth.

I walked to her, tipped her chin up, searched her dark eyes, felt the soft porcelain texture of her skin under my thumb, and tasted her ripe red lips. She melted into me, her arms traveling up to my neck, her lips breathless, ravenous, and hungry. I folded her into my chest like the precious doll she was and gently swayed while she squirmed in my arms.

At last, we parted, and she stepped back.

"What is it?"

"I am ashamed, Shannon. That's the truth."

Her scowl was quick, her spine rigid, and her chest heaving, making the tiny golden and silver strands of her clothing twinkle with the rise and fall of her full bosom. "What's happened, Marco? What's changed?"

I was in deep, unchartered waters. I'd been trained to do all kinds of indescribable things, but I suddenly felt myself unable to speak, and the longer it took to respond, the bigger problem I had.

"I had no right to ask you to do this," I whispered, studying my idle fingers.

"*This*? Explain." Her face was hard to read, but it certainly wasn't friendly.

"They've turned you—I made them turn you into a slave girl, a harem girl, someone who is my property, and for that, I am ashamed."

Her anger was quick to flash. With her hands on her hips, she shouted at me, "You son of a bitch." She didn't care if the rest of the palace heard her, either.

Now I was confused. "Shannon, I'm sorry, but let me explain."

"No. Are you so uptight that you don't want to do a little dress up? Did you ever do that when you were little?"

"Yes, but—"

"I'll bet you even tried to get little girls to play doctor with you, too. It's disgusting but kind of normal."

I recalled trying to get some free feels in junior high school under the guise of bumping into one of the early-development girls in my class. I was just as scared in front of them then as I was right now.

"A Halloween costume? Did you ever buy Em or Rebecca some really kinky underwear? Come on, Marco, I know you, goddammit."

"Shannon, please lower your voice. I don't want—"

"Well, at this point, I don't care what you want. I care about what *I* want. I've been pampered in more ways than you can imagine—oiled, shaved, massaged, and other stuff too. I've been fed elixirs to make my womb receptive to your seed. I've even had my butthole waxed and oiled. And all the time this was going on, I was thinking about you, doing it for you. To bring you pleasure. And you're ashamed? You're ashamed I want to be your fantasy princess?"

I'd gotten it all wrong.

Fuck!

"So you tell me? Are you going to participate or are you going to watch me pleasure myself?" She stepped close, her hot nipples brushing against my shirt, her hand with the little bells sliding down to my enormous cock, which swelled as she squeezed me. She looked at my lips as she whispered, "Do you have what it takes to fuck me, Marco? Use me? Hard? To make my whole afternoon worth it? I want you to touch me all over. But mostly, I want you to touch me. Here." She grabbed my hand and placed it against her left breast, right over her beating heart.

And then she kissed me, ramming her tongue down my throat.

I sprang to action. I slipped the sari over her shoulder, exposing her left breast and bit down on her knotted nipple as she moaned. Putting one hand between her legs and the other over her shoulder, I lifted her up and tossed her back on the bed. I watched her writhe in front of me, exposing her leg and her luscious thigh as she undulated her hips forward and backward while I threw off my tux, quickly unzipped my pants, and discarded my shoes, leaving everything in a pile at the foot of the bed. I started to unbutton my shirt but was fumbling so I rolled up my sleeves instead and presented to her my throbbing member as my knees walked their way up to her hips so she could touch me.

One of her hands cupped and squeezed my package while the other unbuttoned my shirt. Her hot tongue was at my belly button as she yanked the shirt back over my shoulders and threw it across the room.

Her curls were falling, becoming unpinned. The little ruby

necklace on her forehead was crooked, but she slid underneath me and took me into her mouth, pressing me way down into her throat all the way to my stem.

Her saris were wrapped and tied. I couldn't find a zipper or button anywhere but began to pull at her folds, releasing the material slowly until the turquoise silk unpeeled at her sides. She put my cock between her breasts and squeezed. I picked her up, hands beneath her rib cage, and moved us both back up into the middle of the bed. She tried to keep her knees together, and my fingers soon found out why. Up and down her moist slit, my forefinger felt her velvety petals, completely hairless, until I slipped over her stiff little bud and entered her.

She arched back, giving me access. I spread her knees apart and saw her glistening mound, covered in some exotic salve as I dipped my head and tasted her. She rocked her hips and moaned, pulling at my hair and throwing her knee over my shoulder as she reached for me.

I flicked my tongue back and forth over her petals, sucking their juices, inhaling her sweet womanly goodness. Her fingers stroked and pulled me until I gave in to her need, touching the head against her opening and scooting herself down as I thrust up slowly, but eventually deep.

Back and forth in long strokes, my member glided in and out of her, fully visible, fully open so I could see it all.

I turned her slightly to the side, with her leg and bent knee still over my shoulder, and fucked her at an angle. I kissed her neck, her ears. I dug deep, holding her tummy and stroking her from below while arching up into her. My thumb pressed her nub again as I felt her muscles begin to milk me. She turned onto her belly, holding my fingers in place as her leg slipped over my shoulder. On her front, her fingers buried between her legs.

Coming to my knees, I plunged my tongue into her hot, juicy sex, gently curved her rear up by placing my hand under her belly, and pulled her back and onto my shaft.

Shannon shattered as I lazily stroked and kissed her from behind, my hands roaming over the smooth contours of her butt cheeks, my fingers exploring all the nude parts of her. After a succession of deep, quick lunges, I held myself deep inside her, and then we released together, collapsing on the bed.

Her makeup was smeared, her hair in a wild tangle all over the bed and her shoulders. The ruby necklace was gone, discarded somewhere on the bed. The well of flesh at the top of her shoulder smelled like cinnamon, as did the spot just beneath her ears. Her nipples tasted like ripe berries.

I was still catching my breath as I pulled her up on top of me and reveled in the smooth swale of her back and how it felt to rub her wet sex over my package. I could feel her heart beating urgently. I lifted her head, pulled her up by the waist, and kissed her.

"Did you feel it there?" I whispered as my hands squeezed and massaged her left breast.

"I did. And you?"

"Everywhere. You were made for me, Shannon. Every little thing about your body belongs right here, in my arms."

She traced my eyebrows and the arch of my ear and my lips, planting tiny kisses there and under my jaw. "What was it like when you saw me? Did you like that I didn't look at you?"

"I didn't like it at all. I wanted to strip you down and fuck your brains out right there in front of everyone. But that wouldn't have honored you or me. It made me insane. I was so filled with lust and couldn't say anything about it, couldn't even show it to you in my eyes. I wanted you to see how you made me feel, watching you dance, watching you shake your little wrist things."

Our fingers mated, resting on the turquoise silk. Her dark eyes searched mine, her hair slung to the side as one of her earrings dangled like ripe fruit.

"What was it like?" I asked, wondering.

She placed her palms on my chest and rested her chin there. I held the rest of her long body between my thighs, stroking her backside and hip as she spoke.

"They do this for fun. It's just like dress-up when we were little."

"God, I wish I'd grown up with you and played dress-up. I would have played doctor, too."

"See, I told you. I don't understand why you felt—"

"I misunderstood. I really did. I worried that you felt forced, like I'd forced you into something non-consensual, because I remembered you hesitated."

"I did," she nodded. "When they took all my clothes off, I was shy. I covered my chest, but after a while, I got used to their hands on me. I pretended they were your hands. I felt myself becoming softer, more beautiful. I *wanted* to be your gift."

"You are my gift."

"But it's special when someone *wants* to be your gift, your vessel. That's what they call it, becoming a more perfect vessel. For you, Marco."

"Gosh, I got it so wrong."

"I like the play." Her fingers slipped up my neck into my hairline as she arched her way up until our lips touched. She wrapped her legs around my waist and moved her sex against my navel. "Play is fun."

She sat up then slid down to find me, and our eyes locked as we were joined again. I felt every little quarter inch of her channel until I could go no farther, and then she pressed down, inhaled, and I moved another inch inside her.

Her hands against my shoulders, she lifted her torso up and down on me. She looked at me with eyes of need, and as her lids closed in slow motion, she shuddered. "Don't stop. Don't ever stop."

CHAPTER 12

MARCO WANTED TO give me a tour of the palace grounds after breakfast, so we came downstairs and helped ourselves to a lavish platter of cut fresh fruits artfully arranged. Assorted bowls contained foods I'd never eaten before, like a green mint porridge with herbs and coconut milk, black rice pudding, kneer with quinoa, garnished with cinnamon and chickpea crepes with sautéed vegetables, peanuts, and sweet-hot chutney. Everything was colorful and tasty, and I suspected healthy.

Marco went wild for the chutney, covering his fruit generously. We sat down at a large table set for twelve as one of the servants brought us both a chai latte.

"It's past nine, and no one's up," I whispered.

Marco stopped shoveling the fruit and hot mixture down to check the surrounding area, but all we could hear were the sounds of staff working in the kitchen and gardeners outside chattering.

"He's not an early riser." Marco leaned into me and planted a soft kiss on my lips. "I'm kinda surprised you're up so early for the tour. I'm a bit worn out myself." His dreamy eyes set my panties on fire. I blushed. "Lovely," he said and kissed me again.

I realized he wanted to tell me something else but apparently decided against it.

Several loud blue parrots cackled outside in the side garden, making a mess, splashing water everywhere, screeching in and out of the large fountain, and chasing after each other. They left as quickly as they'd arrived. Tall spires of torch ginger and fragrant yellow bush flowers bloomed, sending a sweet floral scent our way, reminding me of jasmine or gardenia. I could almost forget that there was another world out there.

"He lives here alone with the wives?" I whispered. The eeriness of the empty rooms sent a chill up my spine.

"And his children and grandchildren. I believe they are traveling in India at the present time. It can be quite a crowd when they're all home. But you should see it when they do these pilgrimages. They used to book whole floors of hotels wherever they'd go. I remember, some years ago, he went shopping in Paris for some rings and bracelets for some of his favorites, and he walked into Cartier's with a bag of jewels the size of a croquet ball. He gave them a list of what he wanted but let the artisans at Cartier's design everything. He had it delivered by armored courier protected by a small army some months later."

"But there's nobody here. Doesn't he have security?"

"They're here. You saw some of them in front. The compound is fenced and monitored by state-of-the-art stuff. He doesn't want to feel like he lives in a prison, but he takes it seriously. Trust me, he's well-guarded, or I wouldn't have brought you here."

"I would think so. Where does the family live?"

"There's a gated compound on the north shore where some of the grown children and their families live, and it is heavily guarded by palace guards, like the uniformed ones out front, who have served the family going back several generations. They and their families live here as well, which is part of the perks of the job."

"So he cares for everyone, supports everyone?"

"Family who want to stay can stay. Most of the adults leave and go on to do other things. Once that happens, they cannot return. It's his natural attrition, or this island kingdom would be overrun."

It reminded me of an old man I knew once who ran a hotel at the ocean in Oregon. Constant turnover and nobody stayed full time, he'd complained to me. And none of his kids wanted to take over the business, so he just continued on well into his eighties. It filled me with a bit of melancholy.

"If they need surgery or something specialized, where do they go?"

"He has a medical staff who work at a small clinic he built. For anything major, they go to the Maldives, India, or even Europe. As you saw, the island is only forty-five minutes from the Maldives, two hours to the southern coast of India. The world has gotten to be a much smaller place since the days of his grandfather. For many generations, the family was isolated. It was a long trip by boat, before air travel. Now he can reach any big city almost as fast as we can in Florida."

"He must be one of the richest men in the world to be able to support this household."

"It helps when you have claim to an enormous oil field. His grandfather actually went to school in Texas around the turn of the century and made friends in the oil business. He came back, did his homework, and invested in making claims offshore just north of us before anyone else was even exploring there. The area now is known as the third largest oil field in the Indian Ocean. He secured his family's legacy—forever. Arjun's father was a playboy sultan killed in a plane crash during World War II, so he was raised by his grandfather, who forbade his sons from moving off the island or spending too much time being absent landlords, unless they relinquished their inheritance."

"He was a smart man."

"Very. But in many ways, a lonely one. He knows his children—many of them—would rather set up businesses of their own, not just live here, as beautiful as it is. So he's encouraged several to attend college in the U.S. and elsewhere. Several have married and settled outside the tiny kingdom. The two I'm going to be watching over want to be builders. I'm here to protect them."

"He's like the fairy tale, except in reverse. He's the princess who is walled up in her golden kingdom and longs to live outside the beautiful palace. And everyone else wants to get in.

"I actually think he's okay with it. When not with his wives, he spends his time in solitude mostly. He has an enormous library. I'll show it to you sometime."

"Please. Now, with a dozen or more wives, will he take on more?"

"I doubt it. He doesn't travel much any longer, and finding a wife is complicated in the culture here. There are week-long family meetings, events that have to be catered for hundreds of people. The bride price has to be fixed. The parents of the bride pretend the groom is not good enough and hold their daughter for ransom. For a good girl from a good family with no health issues, the whole process can be exhausting, I've been told. And with a stable of beauties at his beck and call, I don't think he feels the need any longer to search for a new one."

We finished our breakfast and a second cup of the delicious chai. "Well, doesn't appear we'll have company. I'm ready for my tour."

Marco took my hand, and we slipped out a side door from the main pavilion, following a lush garden path. I had brought the sheer sari that I wore last night, using it was a loose shawl over my shoulders since the air was still chilly and not at all humid yet. We came to a huge pool complex—a shallow one next to a much deeper lap pool. In the shallow pool, there were slides for children and water features that popped up at random to spray the whole area and then disappeared. There were tables and lounge chairs scattered about the patio overlooking the blue water. A small dollhouse was decorated with bright inlay tilework and sat in a small forest of ceramic mushrooms of various sizes children could sit on.

Seeing this deserted area where children should be laughing and playing made me a bit sad.

The wet areas were fully gated off, but we pushed through a metal entrance door opening to an area outside the complex. The gate clicked, locking behind us and startling me. Marco held up a key card for re-entry.

We walked past several bungalows tucked in a cluster in the

dark foliage. Several of them had golf carts outside the front door or parked in the driveway. We passed a tennis court and an intricately carved open-sided wooden pavilion. Through another gate, we followed a narrow garden trail that turned sandy, spilling out onto a peach bisque-colored sand beach. The color contrasted nicely with light turquoise waves rolling and slamming on the wet sand, as the ocean showed its petticoats in the hissing surf.

Ahead of the waves was the horizon, with no obstruction, the water a slightly darker shade of aqua. Billowy white clouds rose high in the sky, churning and rolling, slowly heading our direction.

I knew India was just beyond that horizon, but as we stood there, hand in hand, I felt like we were in the middle of some undiscovered and abandoned island.

"Are there a lot of these, islands with palaces?"

"Most of them are in ruins today. Mostly uninhabited islands, atolls really. He once told me not all of them were mapped, if you can believe such a thing."

"So who owns them?"

"They mostly align with the country closest to them— Maldives, India, or Sri Lanka. Like everything else in the world, it's shifted as the world-wide balance of power shifts."

I inhaled the moist air, now warming up. It reminded me of a really good day at the Gulf back home. But as far as I could see, there was only ocean, clouds, and sky. "Why would anyone want to leave?" I asked.

"It's because of what's out there, the opportunities we cannot see, the feel and taste of the unknown. Adventure," he whispered, slipping his arm around my waist and kissing the top of my head.

CHAPTER 13

WE WERE WAITING for the house to get up, so I used the time to go online, using my SAT hotspot. I determined that our plane had been diagnosed with an engine problem that would require a new one be installed. It would delay our trip home for nearly a month, so I approved the work order but contracted for another plane to arrive as soon as was possible. They promised it within three days. I thanked Ron for his quick work and for lining up our Plan B checklist.

That new engine was going to leave a fifteen-million-dollar hole in my budget for the year, so I asked for and got terms. Everyone was doing that nowadays, even governments.

Next, I called Harry.

"Hold on, hold on. I'm sorry I wasn't there to meet you at the airport. I'm close, should be there in about an hour."

"Just wondering. I'm not usually the first one to arrive. Nobody's here, Harry. What the hell's happening?"

"He's in a rather crabby mood these days. Rather anti-social, if you ask me."

"He seemed perfectly fine to me," I objected. "But I mean, nobody's here. Where are the kids? Usually, those bungalows are overflowing with relatives. Is there some plague I haven't been told about?"

"No, Marco. Just the luck of the timing. Are you managing to have a good time? Kind of nice to have more access to him, isn't it?"

"Yes, we've had quite an adventure already. I'll tell you about it later." I hesitated discussing business over the phone, but I wanted him thinking about some of the answers I needed. "Harry, the stuff you sent me from the kids is very light. I mean, there are more gaps than swiss cheese. They are taking this seriously, I hope. It's not like I'm helping them put up a condo complex in Florida, right?"

Harry said something I didn't understand and sighed heavily into the phone.

"Okay, since you're going to find out about it anyhow, Khalil had a little problem with a casino in Macao and wound up blowing a big advance the sultan gave him for the mission. I've actually been working with the casino today, getting a loan for him to get some of it back. Of course, he insists he'll win it back. Considers it a temporary setback."

"How much money did he lose?"

"It—it was a lot. But I managed to get about three quarters of it back, at a competitive interest rate, too. But my dad is not to know about it."

"Don't tell me things like that. If he asks me, I have to tell him. I don't like being put in that position. If he can't know, then don't tell me, okay?"

"Okay, I see your point. No problem. His trust fund can handle the payments. But I've got to let him know tonight his gambling days are over until this project is finished. He's not going to be happy, not that he'll complain to the sultan."

"I should hope not. He really wants to believe in these kids."

"You are wrong there, Marco. He doesn't want them to get killed. He already knows they'll be making mistakes. You're hired to make sure they don't make lethal ones."

"Well, getting in bed with the Macao tribe is not very smart."

"I agree. The Triads are in it for the money, and as long as the money comes, we're all good. Don't worry about this. I think I got it all under control."

I wasn't so sure, and this bothered me more than I would be

able to show. Shannon was already listening to my conversation, even though she tried to look like she was reading. I'd piqued her interest.

"So when do they arrive today? The sultan said this afternoon. Do you have any details on this?"

"I think they're en route. Haven't talked to them today. They know you're coming, so they'll be there."

"If they're not rotting in some prison somewhere penniless."

"Look, it's not that bad. You're getting worked up over nothing, Marco. You'll see."

"How's the writing coming?" I decided I'd beaten that dead horse enough and wanted to switch the subject.

"Slow. My time will come. The public isn't ready for a gay Westside Story or Romeo and Jules. See you in a few."

"Ciao." I shook my head in disbelief.

Shannon was studying me. "Is there a problem?"

I wasn't going to lie, but I couldn't tell her everything. "I'm dealing with a couple of young pups fresh out of graduate school. The usual problem is raising capital for this kind of project. Here, we don't have a lack of funds. We have an issue on the budget and line items we're spending it on."

"Do you do that too?"

"When one of the principals is gambling his stake money away? Yes, then it becomes my problem. It's a behavioral issue. They're going to have to become disciplined if this is going to work. I'm going to lay it all out there tonight, or I'm not going to Africa."

"I'm sure you will. I'm sure they'll listen."

I liked her faith in me. I was starting to doubt I'd made a good decision to get involved. But part of me wanted to protect the sultan, too, since there were any number of outfits he could hire who would rip him off and not do a very good job of protecting his kids.

"Thanks. Okay, gotta make a couple more calls."

Karin Atkin picked up the call before it rang on my end.

"We're expecting the boys here this afternoon, and I have some questions I'm going to press them on. What else should I add to my laundry list—and thanks for all the reports. Very helpful."

"Thanks, Boss. Not sure if you saw it online, but they've appointed a new Minister of Culture, and he's a missionary-trained Christian. I'm not sure how much influence he has with President Mtoto, but the fact that he's a new hire tells me your president has had some kind of religious conversion or a shakeup in his cabinet, perhaps."

I was trying to think about how that would be a problem.

"Your boys are Hindu, right?"

"They are."

"I'd buy them a couple of gold crosses to wear when they're swaggering around the project and definitely when meeting with any of the political leaders. I know if they were Muslim this would be a sacrilege. Do you think they'll mind?"

"Well, that's a good thing to discuss with them, then."

"And I wouldn't mention the sultan's wives. They generally don't like that, either."

"They probably wouldn't like gambling then," I added, suddenly seeing a path forward in my discussions with the boys tonight.

"Definitely not. Now, if it was in the neighboring valley, then you'd all be wearing prayer beads and covering your head."

"Me? You mean the boys."

"Right. We'll make sure you bring a nice bible with you when you go, just in case."

"A good plan. What else?"

"Well, Forest will probably tell you, but they caught a bunch of Somali pirates who tried to take over a Chinese cargo ship yesterday. He was headed into port here. As expected, nobody lived to tell the tale, but the point is that there are apparently several groups out there trolling the waterways, and we want to be careful. Watch everything. Even check your security at the palace. These guys are getting bold."

I'd seen little crafts rigged with an outboard motor barely the size of the lifeboats on these huge merchant marine ships go after these ships in a pure stupid David and Goliath move. Consequently, the ships started installing water cannons, since they weren't allowed to arm their crew and everyone knew it.

The cargo ships weren't very maneuverable or fast, but they could cut right across a little skiff or blast everyone out of their seats with their hoses. It was a fool's game played by desperate men who were trying to save their loved ones at home being held hostage.

"Thanks for the tip. We'll keep an eye out, and I'll mention it to the sultan."

She handed the phone to Nigel.

"Hey, Boss, tried to get some drone footage when the story first broke, but the air was locked down."

"No, that's not a hill you want to die on. Good thinking. But there are others?"

"Tis the season. Been practicing take-off and landing. Night vision is super defined. These lot have me dancin' a jig."

"Good. Anything else?"

"When are you going to work an invitation to the palace for us? We'd even do dishes for you."

"Maybe when it's all over. I've got some fierce conversations happening tonight, and then I'll drill down on what we need to get us up to par, because this isn't it."

"Righto."

"But Shannon and I are having a good time, managing to stay out of too much trouble."

I found her over near my side of the bed. She'd taken her top off and had wrapped her upper torso and head in the veil that showed everything. She slowly turned, taking the little steps she'd been taught. She'd put her ankle and wrist bracelets back on, and the sounds of the tinkling bells brought back extremely erotic memories.

I lifted the phone back up to my ear. "I'm going to sign off.

There's something I have to take care of, and it won't wait."

I hung up and ran to her side, peeled back the veil from her face, and kissed her while my hands slid down to her perfect ass. I whispered in her ear, "So we're playing dress-up, are we?"

"I thought you wouldn't mind. Looks like you brought yourself a stash." She pointed to the open drawer beside the bed. I didn't know what she was talking about, but I'd put her ruby headband and the bells in there this morning when I was cleaning up, just to get them out of the way.

"Oh? I wasn't aware there was anything—" My fingers pawed through various items. Gels and stimulating creams, textured condoms, and several sex toys were lying in the bottom of the drawer with her necklace and the other two bracelets. I put my finger to my lips. "Oh my."

"I didn't know you were into that stuff," she said.

"Well, *I* didn't bring them. I think they were provided."

She picked up a metal tube and read, "Ruby red cherry excitement jelly. Looks like it's even written in Arabic as well."

"It doesn't surprise me." I took the gel from her fingers, unscrewed the top, and sniffed it. "It does smell like cherries."

Her big eyes watched me squeeze a tiny bit out and taste it. Then I fed her some. My lips started to tingle, so I pressed more from the tube onto her lips and kissed her.

"Mmm. Very nice, Shannon."

"Is it for me or for you?"

I took a step forward, our thighs rubbing against each other in a casual movement. I was so hot for her and hoped we'd have enough time to get the party started.

"Here," I said, guiding her to sit on the edge of the bed. "I want to try something."

Her eyes were half-lidded as she leaned back on her elbows, the turquoise silk still wrapped around her perfect skin. I grabbed the zipper at her hip, peeling her pants down to the floor. My hand traveled the full length from her knee, up the side of her thigh, then dipped into the top of her black lace panties. She spread her knees. I slipped the elastic at the inside of her upper leg to the left, exposing her deep pink lips, all puckered, plump and moist already.

I took a long time to squeeze a line of gel on my forefinger about two inches long, set the gel down on the table, and let my forefinger apply the pink goodness up and down, running inside and outside her delicate lips, ending with a gentle press on her clit.

She moaned, her head arching backwards, so I applied two fingers to her channel, pressing her clit again with my thumb. Her flesh was on fire. Her chest grew blotchy with red; her nipples became tight knots.

Her arms reached out to me, whispering, "I want you inside me, Marco. Please."

Taking one of her hands, I placed it on the front of my pants. She worked the buttons until she could take hold of my throbbing member, collected gel from her own sex, rubbed it all over me, and then stroked, fondled, and squeezed.

Stepping out of my pants, I pulled her body closer to the edge of the bed, rubbed my shaft over her needy lips. The tingling sensation grew as the gel began to warm. I watched her guide me and, when she moved her hands to my rear, pulled me inside her. I held her legs up to my chest so I could enter deep.

"Is this what you had in mind as far as dress-up?"

CHAPTER 14

WE WERE INTERRUPTED by a voice coming from downstairs. Our bedroom door was closed, but whomever it was began running up the marble steps—an unmistakable tap-tap-tap of shoes on stone. Marco was riding me from behind, and I was just about to come.

"Oh no!" I moaned into the pillow, knowing he was going to pull out and waste a perfectly good heavily ribbed condom. I scrambled to get decent.

Marco swore under his breath and bent over, holding his package to stop an enormous explosion I was going to sadly miss. We ran into each other naked, looking for our clothes buried in the silk sheets, coverlet, and pillows. He managed to get his boxers on. I was still in my black panties and bra when the bedroom door burst open.

"*Hola! ¿Cómo estás?*" the twenty-something young man said in his blue championship Warriors warmup as he ran straight to the middle, covered his eyes, turned around, and left.

"I'm sorry," apologized the muted voice on the other side of the heavy door. "I thought you were alone, Marco."

"You fuckin' moron. I told you I was bringing Shannon."

He opened the door, the back of his head facing us as I continued to find my clothes. "No. You. Didn't. But it doesn't matter. I should have given you privacy."

I was completely confused. "Who is that guy?"

"That's Harry, the sultan's son and social secretary."

"He's allowed to barge in on you like that?"

He rolled his eyes and shrugged. "It's a long story."

Marco slipped on his slacks and motioned for me to take my clothes into the bathroom to finish. I left the door open so I could hear their conversation.

"Okay, Harry. The coast is clear."

"Hubba-hubba, Marco. You've been working out."

"I *always* work out, and you're an asshole. That's never okay."

"Guilty as charged, but man, look at those pecs."

"I mean it, Harry, you're testing my patience. This was not cool. You violated her space."

I peeked through the crack in the doorway and watched Harry walk over to the bed and examine our little experiments—the little hand-held buzzer, the cherry gel, and two opened packages of pleasure palace extra-large condoms, because we'd used the other one already.

Harry crossed his arms. "No, Marco. You violated *her* space, and from the looks of it, you did it more than once!"

"Shut the fuck up!" Marco erupted.

I thought they were going to come to blows, so without the benefit of a brush, I slipped out the doorway into the room barefoot, disheveled, lipstick smeared, but fully clothed.

"Well, hello, gorgeous," Harry said to me, coming over to take my hand and kiss my knuckles. He toyed with the little bells on my wrist. "Cute."

"Unbelievable," Marco muttered, turning his back to us.

"So this is the lovely Shannon. I totally approve."

I didn't warm to his overly flirtatious expressions, nor did I like the fact that when he talked to Marco, he looked as much at his chest as his eyes. I found Marco's zipper pullover and tossed it over to him, and he immediately slipped it over his head, covering the beautiful abs he'd worked so hard to develop. "Thanks."

Both Harry and I sighed, and then I stopped myself and started picking up the wrappers and straightening the bed.

"I really am sorry, guys. It's been three years since I saw Marco last. He is the favorite of all my sultan's friends. And I'm so happy he's come here to help us out. And if you are a friend of Marco's, we're going to get along just fine."

I wasn't too sure. I just continued straightening the pillows and putting the toys back in the drawer discretely. I sat on the stairs leading to the bed platform and waited until I turned invisible.

Harry sat down where Marco had his computer open, moved his briefcase onto his lap, and pulled out a sheaf of papers. "I brought these things you asked for, copies of agreements and some permissions. The boys have other things, which I hope they'll bring today. Have you seen them yet?"

"No," said Marco, absent-mindedly reviewing the paperwork. "I don't see any permit issued by the Minister of Culture or a declaratory letter, either. Do you know anything about this new hire by the president, a new minister?" He looked up, noticed my sitting in the shadows, and motioned for me to come over to him. He sat, and I climbed onto his lap.

What our visitor couldn't see was that Marco had slipped his fingers down the back of my pants, harmlessly swishing the top of my butt without paying any attention or addressing me. He was listening to Harry prattle on about his half-brothers and how difficult they were being.

"You're making me think perhaps I made a mistake coming here," Marco said. Then he leaned forward and kissed my back, through the fabric of my top, of course.

I was balancing on his thigh, alternating my weight so that it gave me delicious pressure against my nub. He whispered in my ear, "I know what you're doing, and you won't get away with it."

"What?" Harry asked, thinking the comment had been addressed to him.

"Shannon and I were having a conversation earlier about getting dressed up for dinner. Is there someplace we can go for a private dinner one of these evenings?"

"Actually, there's a very good Indian restaurant over by the control tower at the airport. It's in that little strip mall?"

I continued undulating so slowly that Harry wouldn't be able to see it. It didn't take much to register my need against his thigh. I turned to speak to Marco, enabling me to adjust my hot sex, moving it back and forth against him.

"I'm starved," I said.

I looked down at his lips while I licked mine. I grazed my fingers backwards over his cheek and let my forefinger trace his bottom lip while I drilled him with an expression I was glad Harry wouldn't be able to see.

"Me too," he said, his fingers slipping back down the gap in my waistband until he reached the crack and stopped. I planted a long, languid kiss on him.

Harry jumped up. "Okay, I get it. I interrupted something, didn't I?" he said, slipping his briefcase strap over his shoulder, scratching the back of his head. He headed straight for the door, but then I didn't see, I only heard, it open and close, because Marco had started searching for my nipples, his hands sliding up my ribcage.

He picked me up as I straddled him, walking me over to the bed. "You're gonna make me an old man, Shannon. I haven't had this much sex since—" His eyes smiled at me before his lips did. "Since the last time at your place. I'll never forget that night."

"Nor will I."

I shed my clothes, and he removed his pants. I waited for him on my belly while he made some choices from the drawer. "We're out of the condoms, but we have a few other things here we've not tried yet." He held up a brown jar and unscrewed the top and smelled it. "Nice. Cinnamon?"

"They used some wonderful cinnamon massage oil on me yesterday. Let me see." I held my hand out, and he placed the open jar on my palm. "Yes, that's it."

He took it back, dipped his finger in it, sliding his hand beneath me and traveling from the circular massage of my clit back up all the way past my anus.

"It's a healing salve, I think. It feels wonderful, cool and stimulating."

"I see," he whispered.

He was up to something, so I turned my head. He was twirling something small, a little navy-blue plastic object that looked like a baby's pacifier with a bulb on the end of it.

"What's that?" I asked. My radar began to flash, but my pulse quickened.

"An experiment. A little something new, if you've never seen one."

"What is it?" I asked again.

"Can I show you? If I'm very gentle?" His devilish smile made my insides twist in knots. Without him touching me, I could feel the pulse of my sex, full of anticipation.

I nodded.

He dipped the little bulb end into the jar, twirled it a turn or two, leaned over me as he slid the object from my gaping sex back up towards my anus, and then very slowly pressed the bulb end inside me.

I inhaled at the sensation, the forbidden feeling of something I'd never done before. He was breathing in my ear, asking me if I liked it.

I nodded again, gasping, having a hard time catching my breath. Marco turned the little object, refreshing the salve and sparking the sensations again inside me. He drew a soft green silk pillow underneath my belly, kissed both sides of my butt cheeks, tenderly touched my flesh, and made me shudder, and then he lifted my pelvis up with his hand bracing my belly and inserted himself into my dripping sex.

Very slowly, he stroked me in and out as I nearly exploded with need. He carefully crouched over me, moving his hips back and forth, fondling my lips with his hand beneath me. I felt the spasms beginning, the long, rolling orgasm stronger than I'd ever felt before when he thrust deep, held me firm, and pressed down, sending the plug deeper still.

I moaned my pleasure, and he asked me if I was in any pain, and I answered, "God no!"

He increased the pressure, sliding deeper inside my channel as the little object delivered the dull ache I was beyond grateful to receive. I inhaled, my muscles clamping down on him as he spilled deep and hard.

Several minutes later, he stroked my hair, kissed my cheeks, and whispered again in my ear, "I think we're going to have to go to that little purple shop off Gulf Boulevard when we get home. I can see you're beginning to develop some latent talents and appetites I had no idea you had. I don't intend to let you leave me behind."

"I look forward to the instruction, my love."

I knew the very first night we slept together in Boston during that little gift to myself of one perfect, anonymous evening with him that he was going to be my addiction. I had no idea where it would go or how strong it would become. I knew I'd jump into the fire with him anytime, anyplace. I needed him to teach me how to keep him satisfied and how to explore my own boundaries of pleasure and satisfaction.

And I knew it might consume me.

That's exactly what I wanted.

CHAPTER 15

W E'D BEEN SUMMONED downstairs for drinks before dinner. The servant told me the sultan's two sons were arriving any minute, and there would be a few extra guests for dinner.

"Perfect. May I ask, is this a formal dinner? Should I wear my tux, evening wear?"

"I don't believe so. The brothers have traveled far today. They arrived by boat."

"Really? I didn't know the sultan owned a boat—you mean a yacht, right?"

"Yessir," the young servant said. "But the boat belongs to the brothers."

"I see. Well then, we'll be down in about thirty minutes. Tell the sultan I'm looking forward to it."

"Thank you, sir. I certainly will."

Shannon put the long dress my assistant had picked out back into the padded garment bag and zipped it back up, placing it in the closet. "Makes it simple," she said with a shrug.

I didn't put on a tie, but I liked the look of blue jeans with a long-sleeved button-down shirt as crisp, not too formal, and slightly hip. I wasn't old enough to be their father, but these were mid-twenty-year-olds who had lived a wealthy, spoiled lifestyle and were very experienced travelers. I anticipated our conversation was going to get slightly intense, and I needed their respect, in all ways possible.

Shannon was loving the silk sari and the jewelry. She'd lined her eyes with black. Her cheeks were rosy, and her lips lusciously red. Her hair was pinned up with little rhinestone clips, allowing some strands to drop to her back. She also had on her bells. Every time I heard her walk across the room, I had very naughty thoughts.

"What's so funny?"

I placed a palm at her cheek. "I like this new you."

"It isn't too much?" she asked.

Her dark hair and flawless skin contrasted with the shimmery turquoise material wrapped over her head and around her neck. I pulled one corner away so I could kiss her without interference. "You're so beautiful, Shannon."

She blushed, averting her eyes, and then finally returned my breathless gaze. "Thank you."

We descended the steps to join a small crowd in the grand room. The sultan wore green robes tonight with a matching headwrap garnished in the front with an enormous emerald. A small white feather extended out of the top. His first wife was on his arm.

I was surprised to see him wearing makeup consisting of heavy eyeliner, face powder, and a touch of lip gloss. His dark eyes greeted me warmly and then studied Shannon before he quickly glanced back to me.

"She is becoming an Indian princess, no?" he whispered.

She was speaking with Harry as he admired her sari and was oblivious of the attention she was getting.

"You have no idea," I said and bowed.

"She is adventurous?" His eyebrows elevated, waiting for my answer.

"More than I thought possible."

"And you've only been here one night. Very exciting. Her spirit embraces the palace with grace and dignity."

"I think if you came to Florida you'd be wearing flip-flops and shorts and a floppy hat, Your Highness."

"You'd transform me into a beach bum?"

"It could be done." I looked around me at the opulence, the beautiful colors of the inlay work and golden trim. It was his cocoon. His safe place. "Shannon tells me the beach heals everything. What would it be like if you walked the surf, ate king crab, and drank beer at sunset, my sultan? Who would you be then? Would your costume make you a different person?"

"Interesting discussion, my friend. Perhaps in another lifetime," he said and winked.

We heard Harry laugh at something Shannon told him. I noticed the sultan's eyes were sad. "Did he bring you the items you requested?"

"I haven't had time to review them thoroughly. I need to have a conversation with your boys this evening. A rather frank one."

"Good. Very good."

"I understand they own a vessel?"

The sultan rolled his eyes. "I made many mistakes as a father, but my biggest one was indulging them too much. You will have to evaluate whether or not they are ready for this project, Marco. It gives me no pleasure in saying this. I am disappointed in their behavior of late."

"Harry—"

"Should keep his mouth shut. We will not speak of it, because I don't know about the gambling debt in Macao."

"I understand."

The sultan's wife approached and slipped her arm inside her husband's. "I see your Shannon is enjoying the saris we fitted her for."

"She does. Hardly takes it off. Almost wants to sleep in it."

She pulled her hand up to her mouth and giggled, partially hiding it from me. "I am glad you were pleased."

I couldn't look her in the eye. Being pleased didn't even begin to describe how I felt when I first saw her walk into the room yesterday evening.

Asrid, the sultan's wife, was adorned in the same colors as the sultan. Her sari was golden yellow and forest green, covering a deep green silk undergarment. She also wore an intricate gold and emerald necklace and clusters of dangling emeralds for earrings.

A servant appeared, holding a silver tray of glasses of some fruit and a light purple yogurt drink. I was going to drink it in one gulp, but the sultan held his glass out in a toast.

"To a successful business venture."

I could drink to that. The mixture was delicious.

I caught sight of Absalom entering the great room, followed by two other young men about the same age with longer hair. They were craning their necks as they looked up at the dome the columns and stained-glass ceiling above. Absalom stood next to his brother and whispered something.

Studying the two friends of the boys, I didn't like what I saw. It wasn't specific, just some internal radar I had when it came to sizing people up. It was obvious they weren't used to being around such wealth, which meant they traveled in different circles. It could also mean they were aiming to take advantage of the boys. The sultan, if he was concerned, didn't show it.

"Your Highness, I'm going to go re-introduce myself and make sure they leave time to discuss some questions I have."

"Please," he said, gesturing for me to cross in front of him.

I broke up the little foursome, extending my hand to Khalil. "Marco Gambini. Nice to see you both again." I shook Absalom's hand as well. The friends faded back a step and allowed us to talk.

"Hey there, coach," said Khalil, who addressed the two friends. "This guy, Marco Gambini, he's a decorated Navy SEAL. Did all sorts of shit—jumps out of airplanes at night and crap. Really cool stuff."

He didn't sound like the engineering student I was expecting to meet. He'd gotten taller than the last time I saw him. He'd almost lost his Indian accent entirely.

"Navy SEAL, huh? You guys fight in Afghanistan or Pakistan?"

I was aware that people who were from India, regardless of their birthplace or family nationality, were sensitive to the location of our deployments and with whom we were embedded. So I gave a big whiffle ball answer to that one.

"Mostly South America and Africa, man." I made sure my handshake hurt just a little. If there was going to be a man contest, I wanted to win the first round.

"I'm Yassir."

My brain calculated several things and came up with the probability that he was Iranian. Names in this part of the world were very important and were not made up or chosen because they sounded nice.

The other friend didn't come forward.

"Yassir and Hamid found this great catamaran for us. Did Harry tell you?"

"He did not," I lied. "Where did you get it?"

"Male."

"Shannon and I were just there. We could have met up with you, but your father said you were in Mumbai."

"Yes. We had some business things to handle. There is a Nigerian Department of Trade in Mumbai. We went there to get our permits. They said it would take about five days to get all the signatures. So we did some traveling," said Khalil. "Went back and they still weren't ready, so we flew to Male on our way home and met these two gentlemen. It was pure luck. They were helping a British couple sell their boat, so we bought it."

"You bought it from the couple from the U.K?"

"They were very ill and had to sell their boat. They had to go home, but their agent sold it to us. Very good price."

I was afraid to ask.

"Does your dad know?"

"Yes, yes, I believe Harry told him about it tonight. We are going to take the family out tomorrow for a little demonstration. It's really cool, even sleeps fourteen, and we have a crew we've contracted with. Now we will be traveling in style."

"Where?"

"I beg your pardon?"

"Where will you be traveling to?"

"Oh, all around here, the Maldives, Sri Lanka, maybe take it up along the East Coast of India."

"He doesn't like our idea, man," muttered Absalom, who had been pretty quiet.

"Oh stop. You don't know that." To me, Khalil said, "Wait till you see her. She purrs like a kitten. A big, white kitten."

The waters in the Indian Ocean were well known for piracy. The thought of two twenty-somethings worth several billion between them cruising around pirate-infested waters would give me nightmares if I was their father. And their use of this boat was dependent on the crew they'd hired, so everything was out of their control. Literally everything.

But I had to deal with first things first.

"Khalil, you've managed to do a lot since I first agreed to sign on to work your security in Nigeria. I have to ask you, is that still a priority for you?"

"Oh absolutely." He turned to Absalom, who nodded enthusiastically.

"What about all your permits?"

"Still waiting. We paid an extra tax to get it pushed up the line. Nigeria is very, very busy. Very prosperous. People coming from all over the world to help them build sustainable infrastructure."

"Housing. You're building housing."

"Sure, sure. We build it the green way."

"Did you have to promise it would be green? I'm just not sure you can get all the materials there. You'll have to look into what it all will cost."

"Well, we have you, right? How much does it cost to build a house then, Marco? A two-bedroom house, small size. Green. You tell me."

"First of all, it depends on where."

"Of course. Different building standards for flood zones, etc. Like here. Monsoon windows. Danger of flooding here in really bad storms since our elevation is only four."

"Four what?"

"Four feet. From sea level."

"Oh, now I understand. Yes, those things factor into your building costs. But before we go there, I want to make sure it's feasible, and they'll actually let you build. You have to get the permissions, Khalil."

"I told you, Khalil," Absalom interrupted. "Mr. Gambini, we appreciate everything you're doing for us. Maybe you could get the permits for us. Rattle their cages a bit?"

"In Mumbai?"

"Yes, exactly."

My patience was waning. The whole project was beginning to look like someone's wet dream, and not the kinds of dreams I'd been having lately, either.

"You need a project manager. Someone to do those types of errands. But that person has to know what the rules are, first. I'm hired to do something else. I'm supposed to create your security plan. To keep you safe. And—" I was beginning to see boogie men behind every column. I also didn't want to appear too negative. "We can talk about all that tomorrow. Tonight, I need to go over with you exactly what you do have, who you've talked to. We may have to make some calls tomorrow."

"Sure, we can do that."

I exhaled, relieved. They were going to let me look at all of their files—I didn't pick up any resistance. But there were some huge blind spots we had to shed light on first.

The timing of our talk had been perfect. We were called to take a seat at the table. As we made our way to the dining alcove, I was going to break away and follow Shannon to the dinner. But Yassir mumbled to the side of Absalom's face, "Hey, can you get me a seat next to that Indian chick over there? The pretty one."

My forward movement stopped all of a sudden, and someone behind me ran into my back. I grabbed an arm off both Absalom and Yassir, yanking them out of line and over to the corner.

"Shannon's with me. She is engaged to me, and if you value your life, you'll be polite, and stay away. Do you understand?"

Yassir's forehead wrinkled as his eyes widened. With new appreciation for who I was, he said, "Oh, my bad. My bad."

I was going to forgive him for just being a clueless dickwad until he added, "But way to go, Gramps."

CHAPTER 16

M ARCO SAID VERY little during dinner. I did small things to entice him, which didn't warrant a smile, nod, or any reaction. I began to feel he might be annoyed with me. Harry and I had become great friends during the evening, and I invited him to come down to Florida and visit since his permanent address was Brooklyn with his mother.

Perhaps something happened when he spoke to the boys.

Or when he spoke with the sultan?

I didn't have the room for any of the items presented on silver trays loaded with sweets and delicacies brought out for dessert. I did take a chai latte.

Even the touch of my thigh against his didn't elicit a reaction. With my elbow on the table, I balanced my head on the palm of my hand, turned, and spoke to him, trying to keep it just between us, barely moving my lips.

"Everything alright?"

"Um hum," he answered, nodding.

"Are you sure?"

That's when he looked at me, smiled, and whispered back, "You worry too much. I've got a lot on my mind. That's all."

So it did have to do with the brothers!

I noticed he'd been focusing on the two strangers sitting at the end of the table next to Khalil and Absalom's mother. She was relaxed when speaking with her sons and reserved when speaking to the others. But that was the custom.

A couple we had met during one of our walks sat near us. They had come to ask the sultan permission to marry, since she was one of his daughters. They were young, barely in their twenties, and had met in their first year of college in New York. He was of Indian descent, also a Hindu, but had been raised in the states.

"Did you get permission?" I whispered the question.

"He has to offer the bride price to my parents first, which signifies his acceptance. If they approve, then we can wed," the young man said.

"Will they negotiate much?"

She answered back, bobbing her head from side to side, "This is just a formality. We've already decided we'll be married. But we're attempting to satisfy the traditional values of our parents."

They still looked so young. When I was her age, I hadn't yet let a man, boy, anyone touch me or even kiss me. That door was closed, and I wasn't even motivated to explore what I might be missing.

Because I was so much younger than Marco, I wondered if he saw me as being young, like the sultan's daughter appeared to me. I thought about all the beautiful women he must have slept with during his years after Em and before Rebecca. All the women who had tried to throw themselves at him when he was a SEAL. With his dark hair and onyx eyes, ripped body trained to perfection, I bet he was beating women away every day.

But I did have one advantage. I had fallen in love with him, maybe not as I loved him now as a full-grown woman, but to the fullest capacity of my twelve-year-old heart, because he was kind to me, and Em had told me all the stories. I felt as though I was with them on all their dates, even felt the tension between them when they decided to wait to marry until after he came back from his first deployment. Em returned to college after the break, and I didn't even get to go shopping for her wedding dress. He was overseas, and Em was hit by that drunk driver, killing her and her sorority sisters.

He'd looked so handsome in his white uniform. I pretended he came back to town not for my sister's funeral but to see me. I had a hard time forgiving myself for those thoughts because I achingly missed my sister, my confidant, the one who should have had the happily ever after I was now going to have.

I heard the sultan's daughter whisper to her fiancé, "I don't think she's listening."

"I'm sorry. You reminded me of someone. I sort of had a daydream there for a second."

"That's okay. It's getting late. I think we're going to turn in," she said. "If you feel like it, come to the baths tonight. I promised I'd meet my mother there and spend a little time. You're welcome to join us. It will be very low-key. A good soak in the scented pool will help you sleep better."

"You know, that sanctuary is how I imagined Heaven to look and feel like," I answered.

Her fiancé leaned across the table and whispered, with his finger crossing his lips, "Shhh. I'm not supposed to know anything about that room, since we are not married."

"Someday, after they take hold of your fiancée to prepare her for your wedding night, you'll hear all about it. It's really quite miraculous. I know it's not fair, but I promise you the wait is worth it."

I caught the sultan watching me. His smile was gentle. I genuinely liked the man.

"Let me see what Marco will be up to, and if he's tied up, maybe I'll take you up on your offer."

They got up, said their good-byes, and left. Several others left as well, leaving the sultan alone at the end of the table, so I rose, asking him if I could keep him company.

"Of course, my dear. Here, finish my pear. I can't eat it."

"I have no place to put it, but thanks," I said as I sat perpendicular to him.

"Things are going okay with your handsome Marco?"

"Yes. And thank you for all of this. I'm not sure what I was expecting, but your generosity in sharing your family and your beautiful house with us is most appreciated."

He smiled, placed his hand on mine. "Tell me about your father. He must love you very much."

A sharp jolt of sadness rippled over me. I took a deep breath and began.

"He was closer to my sister, and when she passed, he never quite got over it. So my relationship was a bit fractured, but we tried. We've gotten as close as we can be at this point. He really drilled Marco about bringing me here, worried that it might be dangerous. Having adventures and taking risks are scary to him. And I'm all he's got left."

"He should be very relieved to know that you are marrying someone who knows how to take care of you and keep you safe. I wish I could have Marco stay here with me and protect my family. But your father is very lucky. To have a man, a true warrior, to love and care for his daughter, it must make him feel very grateful and relieved."

"I never thought about that. I'm going to tell him what you said."

"Don't tell Marco. His head will get—big!" He stretched his arms to show how large his head could swell.

"I meant my dad. You put it so beautifully.

"Let me ask you something. When your wedding day comes, would you consider perhaps having it here in the palace?"

"I couldn't ask you to do that."

"Of course not. That would be rude. But I'm offering."

"Let me discuss it with Marco first, and if he says yes, then I'd be delighted." But concerns and thoughts of the expense it would cause my friends was a factor, too.

"Your parents, of course, would be my guests here, as well."

"They'd be pinching themselves for a week."

"Ah, here is your handsome fiancé now."

Marco placed his hand on my shoulder and spoke to the sultan. "I'm going to go see if we can iron some things out tonight, so we're going to meet over at Khalil's bungalow."

"Very well. Good."

Marco leaned down and kissed me on the cheek. "Not sure how late I'll be, so don't wait up for me, okay?"

"No problem. I've been invited to wander over to the baths for a soak. I don't think after that I could wait up for you, so take your time."

Marco shook the sultan's hand and once again kissed me on the check.

I WALKED ALONE down the tiled passageway with the golden domes and carved archways. I had just come from a room with a roaring fireplace in the center, heading to another warm and moist room full of scent, steam, and relaxation. But the breezeway between where I was walking, with its little openings in patterns above the intricate tilework, was chilly. I wrapped the sari around my shoulders tight, lifted the delicate fabric at the back of my neck, and pulled it up over my head while continuing on toward the scented chamber.

I pushed open the metal gate and found several of his wives there, some lounging on chairs and several others in the pool, which is where I was headed.

I slipped my clothes off, folding them with the beautiful sari on top, placed my shoes under the padded lounge chair, readjusted several pins in my hair to keep more of my hair from falling into the water, approached the lip of the pool, and then stepped in.

Today, white petals floated in the turquoise blue water. A wooden bucket with natural sponges floating in a scented mixture was placed next to me. I took to washing off my arms, then sat on the edge, washed my legs, and slipped back into the pool.

The warm water was soothing, and as I sat down on the ledge under water, I still felt the swelling of some of my delicate body parts, reminding me of my all-too brief last encounter with Marco this afternoon. I heard his whisper in my ear, his hot breath making my pulse quicken, the way his big hand gently held my belly against him, my back feeling the solid wall of his chest.

The sultan was right. I was lucky to have him in my life. If I could give back a fraction of what he was giving me, I'd risk it all to do so.

CHAPTER 17

"**K**HALIL, I CAN'T authorize your new friends to come with us to Africa. I don't know them. They're not properly vetted."

He shrugged, not upset by my refusal of his request.

"All I said was that I'd ask. He probably knows this."

Absalom was checking his cell phone, finally tossing it on the table in front of him. I knew he wouldn't have any service.

"We gotta get Dad to install a tower. Someone would pay for it," he mumbled to his brother.

I couldn't believe I was seeing this. I concentrated on being clear, calm. I put my hands together, resting my forearms on my knees, and began.

"I'm not sure we're ready for this project right now, guys. I'm not sensing there is the focus, the discipline we need to pull this off."

Absalom frowned. Khalil's eyes flashed anger.

"What do you mean? Marco, you've been paid a lot of money, brought here, and—"

"And I'm doing my job, Khalil. He's hired me to protect you both, not build houses and get you both killed. You're out there running off to Macao, buying boats, and partying like you were in college. That just isn't going to cut it, nor will it instill any confidence in my team or the team we want to hire. Maybe you better think about it and get back with me tomorrow, okay?"

"Yeah, but at this point, we're the ones who have done all the work," Khalil shot back at me.

"Not true. I've flown a team over here, three of them doing research as we speak from the Maldives. We don't have a valid set of permissions—don't get me wrong, we have a ton of paperwork, but not the kind of paperwork that will get you the green light you need. You bring new people into the mix and bring them *here* to your father's house. You've just spent—what?—a million dollars on a boat?"

"Nine hundred and eighty-six," Absalom corrected me. "It was a bargain."

I could see I wasn't getting anywhere with them. "Are you sure this couple from the U.K. were the real owners? Did you do a title check and have the hull numbers verified? Could this boat be stolen? Ask yourselves, who are these people? You're smart; you've both done incredibly well in school. You earned that. But what's happening here?"

Khalil's eyes were cloudy. I read defiance in them. "Can't you allow us a little leash to celebrate? In the scheme of things, the cost of the boat isn't that much. A fraction of what we'll spend. But this, this will be fun for the whole family. We can take the whole family out—well, some of the family out. We can go fishing, take Dad fishing. He hasn't ever done that."

I was thinking that there were some abandoned piers in Florida he could go fish at for a lot less than a million dollars. "Fishing is free in Florida."

I knew right away it was a mistake to say that. This time, Absalom reacted, standing in front of me and pointing down with such disrespect, I decided right then and there this was not for me. I'd even decided to try to return the money, all of it, to the sultan before the kid started flapping his gums.

"You don't understand what it's like. This is *our* project, not *yours*, and not our dad's. We bought the boat with our *own* money—"

"You could have hired a first-class project manager to fly over and get your permits. You could have spread that money around and got you some cooperation. You had lots of choices. I'm telling you straight. By the way,"—I stood up too—"don't ever point your finger at me like that again, because I'm not on your payroll. I'm not one of your subjects. You're not the sultan yet. I've just contracted to buy a fourteen-million-dollar engine for my plane, and I have to pay a guy his full salary to wait a month here while it's being replaced. For fourteen million, I could have bought a boat, a brand new pretty nice one and gone gambling. But I didn't do that. I waited here for you guys to show up. And now you're not giving me the time of day."

I began to leave the house.

"Marco, don't!" Khalil shouted after me.

I inhaled, worked on calming myself down so I wouldn't say anything else I'd regret. I was already worried about the report the sultan was going to get. I tried one more time. "What I'm saying is that there isn't anything wrong with streaking off on your own, having a little fun, or having a life adventure. I get it. I did that too. But your choices are all f—messed up. You're making poor decisions. You're not using the talent brought here for you, the full opportunity your father has provided. You're not questioning yourself enough. Anyone can go out there and make a splash and be able to afford to pay for your mistakes. It isn't about that. If you're going to build an empire—again, that's if you really want to do it—and if you want to build something that will last like your grandfather and father have done to preserve your family's legacy, you have to be smart about it and use the advice and knowledge available to you. Otherwise, this beautiful kingdom, this island dating back to the 1100s? You can destroy it in one generation if you're not smart."

I turned on my heel, hoping I'd remembered to give it to them straight, and took off. I ran through the garden. Torches had been lit along the path. The exotic flower aroma annoyed me. Even the casual way the sultan treated his wives and children, giving them free reign to walk all over him and spend ungodly sums of money while knowing they were ill-equipped to handle the project he'd asked me to watch over annoyed me. Was I part of his expendable world too?

Had I fallen this far when I had all the warning signs that this was a trap? Perhaps. Flypaper, something shiny and exciting to share with Shannon. In truth, I'd dumbed down my normally very good radar system, made allowances I shouldn't have made. The spiral of my own bad decisions was eating me alive. Had I mistakenly placed Shannon in harm's way because my own fucking ego was too overly confident this could be my ticket out of my other horrible decisions?

It was Rebecca times ten. I hated that thought. I'd just allowed my own blindness—the very thing I lectured the boys about. I didn't heed the warning signs and ask for help, real help—too proud that I might lose half of my own kingdom. Now I could lose it all.

Instinct told me I should get Paul on the phone and have him bring Little Bird over here and take Shannon home to Florida right away. Like tomorrow morning. I could live with all the talk, let Senator Campbell think I'd lost my nerve, that all my best days were behind me. Had I squandered my good creds? My opportunities?

Maybe that was what made me so angry.

And I hadn't done anything as stupid as fly off to some casino kingdom and lose a couple planes worth of cash. Or buy a boat I couldn't operate by myself. My idea of a real boat was something low and fast. No fucking cupholders and fancy radar. Something built for streaking across the Gulf of Mexico so fast it might propel me forever into the stratosphere all the way to the moon. Something that gave me some serious G's and pulled my cheeks up over my teeth like dropping from thirteen thousand feet.

I had some of those demons. That's why I was so good at finding them in others. Maybe even attracting those types to me.

The hallways were quiet and totally abandoned. The great room was put back together—pillows readjusted and the feast cleared. Gentle trade winds blew the silks covering opened windows around like the ghosts of the sultan's ancestors. I traveled through and around them, climbed the marble stairway, and stopped at our bedroom door.

I had a big problem. I was suddenly re-thinking everything. I was pushing Shannon to do things perhaps she wasn't ready for. Her soft, gentle nature was pleasing and so enjoyable, but she was dressing up. We were play acting about something. She was doing these things to please me, and I had no right to watch her supplicate herself to me. Maybe it was more honest with Rebecca, a bitch I could never fully relax around, someone I could fuck but be worried she'd have a knife to my neck the next minute. I saw all that when I married her, didn't I? She was the opposite of Em.

I placed my forehead against the door.

I've been unfaithful to you, Em. I was tempted, and I caved. I'm so sorry.

I sat on the tiled floor, my back against the door. Bringing my knees to my chest, I lowered my head and let the tears fall.

Tears I should have shed long ago.

CHAPTER 18

I WOKE UP with a headache then discovered the drapes had been left open all night long, so the bright morning sun was pouring into the room.

And Marco wasn't there.

I listened for sounds of the shower running, but all was quiet. Slipping on my silk robe, I slowly opened the heavy wooden door, checking the hallway in both directions and then moving over to the railing overlooking the downstairs.

I heard noises coming from the kitchen, but there was no one seated at the long table we used last night. No one used the pillows and chairs in the great hall. Through a window next to the front entrance, I saw one red-suited guard standing against one of the massive carved wooden columns with another seated on a settee next to him.

I turned, leading the way to the throne room, since I didn't think I'd find Marco in the women's wing. Incense had been lit. A set of bowls of fruit were arranged on a wooden table in front of the massive golden elephant statue, along with several red votive candles. But no one was anywhere.

My stomach began to turn into knots as my apprehension grew, and my mouth became parched. I re-cinched up my robe, turned, and was about to leave the tall room when I heard something. Someone was snoring.

I walked back to the host table and then peered behind it. On the floor were Marco's shoes, next to his bare feet. He was asleep on several cushions he'd removed from the great hall, his jacket over his shoulders for warmth. I knelt beside him, placing my hand on his shoulder.

He flinched, quickly opened his eyes, and sat up, shaking his head. I saw a nearly empty whiskey bottle tucked under a short stool.

"What are you doing?" I asked.

As I leaned over to extend my hand, he got up, slipped on his jacket, straightened his hair, and adjusted his pants. Finally, he looked down on me as he helped me to stand. His normally sparkling eyes were dull and filled with worry and pain.

I could see he wanted to say something, but I was suddenly afraid of hearing whatever he was going to utter.

"What is it, Marco? What's wrong?"

"I'm going to take you back to Florida. We're leaving this morning."

"What?"

He was avoiding eye contact again.

"That's it? You're not going to explain to me why you're here, sleeping in the throne room, still drunk from a bender? This isn't you, Marco. What's going on?"

"I've been doing a lot of thinking. I told the boys last night I wasn't going to take the job. I'm going to give the money back. This isn't for me. A lot of things are going to have to change, Shannon. I've been just going in the wrong direction with both my business and my life, and I have to fix it. I've probably ruined an old friendship, but I won't be responsible for this thing in Africa under these circumstances. I can't take his money. I have to get back to my real life. Not this—this fairytale with you."

He didn't even try to give me any softness, an ounce of kindness or consideration. His cold eyes showed me a calculating focus that scared me. I never thought I could stare back into his face and not feel any love coming from him. No affection. It was like he was looking at wallpaper.

I wasn't going to let him see me cry, but the hurt and pain I felt was nearly too much to bear. But my iron will took over, and I wanted to reflect back to him what he was giving me. Things were sorting in my head as I began to question our last interactions, wondering if I'd crossed some line, offended him some way.

And then anger began to boil up inside me.

How dare you?

Had he used me all this time and finally had enough? Was this the real Marco, the one Em didn't live long enough to discover? I was so glad she didn't. If he could flip that switch inside his head so quickly like this, perhaps he was even dangerous.

I stepped back. Then I took another step and a third, looking at the full length of his body, from his shoes all the way up to the top of his head. He was a statue. A marble, inanimate statue set in some alcove in a Pink Palace somewhere off in this fairytale kingdom.

That's the part that hurt the most. He actually said that. "Fairytale." It had been the place I'd been dreaming and dancing in for the past two days, imagining all the possibilities, all the adventures we could share. But it was fiction. Pure fiction.

I was just the tragic heroine in some play that was over. The costumes were put away, the sets removed. The audience was gone. Lights were out.

It was over.

I turned around and ran down the beautiful, tiled floor, past the shiny turquoise-and-gold infused columns, underneath the carved wooden arabesque-styled pointed archways, under the bright flowers of the most beautiful stained-glass ceiling I'd ever seen. I ran up the white marble steps, pushed through the door that was ajar, and threw myself on the bed.

Here, I could finally cry.

But my eyes were dry. I couldn't shed a tear. The pain was still there. I'd been betrayed, used, and discarded. I'd been dumb enough to fall for all of it. Who was I to expect that this magic and fantasy world had anything to do with me or anything I'd ever wanted? I hated all of it. I sat up, scanning the room. I hated it all.

I quickly dressed and packed my bag. I even left the turquoise sari neatly folded on the bed. I moved the jewelry I'd been wearing last night into the drawer on Marco's side, the drawer that had all those ridiculous toys. The bells. The buzzer. That awful navy blue thing I would never tell anyone about! I was ashamed of how blind I had been.

I didn't want to look at it so slammed the drawer closed.

Then I heard the door open behind me.

"Shannon, I'm sorry. I should explain. That was very unthinking of me."

I whirled around and faced him. "Unthinking? Is that it? How about unfeeling? How about trying at least to let me down gracefully? You used me, Marco. You used my body, which is one thing, but you used my heart."

I ran to him, about to slap him across the face. But I did add, with all the anger I could muster, in a deep, growling, ugly voice. "You even used my memories of Emily."

He saw my hand flinch.

"Go ahead. I deserve it."

"I won't give you the pleasure."

I really hated him now. He was a complete monster. So selfish, dancing around the world like he owned it, like he was the sultan of his own fictional kingdom, pulling strings, using his connections to make people dance around him like puppets. Master manipulator. He pretended to be concerned about making me perform for him.

Oh. My. God.

"So you've packed."

"You said we were leaving today. I'll just wait right here until you tell me we're ready to go. And no, I don't need anything, thanks for not asking."

I pretended to be interested in the book I'd been reading, opening it and crossing my legs in my favorite pair of sloppy jeans. When I got to Florida, I'd cut them up and maybe send them to him. I didn't want to have anything that belonged or reminded me of him.

He knelt in front of my chair. "I am truly sorry. I didn't do this right. I didn't think it through. Shannon, I'm in survival mode here."

"*You're* in survival mode? Think of how I feel. I'll bet those conversations with the sultan were interesting when I was getting all plucked and pampered for you. You two must have had a big laugh. And then you tried to tell me how you were so concerned about how I felt, when all the time you were crafting a creative time to—to—do things to me. Make me wear a butt plug. Abase myself."

He snickered, and this time I did slap him. His head fell to the side. I could see he was totally caught off guard. I was going to do it again when he grabbed my wrist in midair.

"Don't."

I gave him my nastiest stare, reaching all the way down to the soles of my feet I had to dig so hard.

"I understand how you feel. I am truly sorry. But it was not like that for me. I thought—I thought that…" He let go of my wrist.

"You honestly thought you loved me?"

He looked up at me and nodded. "I'm not the man you thought I was."

"I got the message, Marco. No worries there."

"But what I mean to say is that I'm sorry for leading you on with all this. You're right. I think I did take advantage of you. I was trying to—to reconcile the two parts of me. I thought I'd found that part of me that died when Emily did."

His eyes were moist. Mine were bone dry. I wanted to feel sorry for him. I tried to feel sorry for him. But I repeated over and over again in my head that he was just setting me up to use me again.

"Well, I chalk it up to my lack of experience on all levels."

His eyebrow rose.

"If I'd had more experience with men, I might have recognized more red flags. But no, you picked a girl who fell with reckless abandon for you. For everything. I believed all your bullshit, Marco. You picked someone who wouldn't know she was being had. That's the part that hurts the most. Because I don't think I'll ever love anyone as much as I thought I loved you. No other man in the world will ever have that, because my heart just cannot afford it."

My lower lip quivered, and I looked away as tears spilled down my cheeks. His hand cupped my chin, and a finger smoothed away my tears.

"So what was that ruse in Boston? When you dressed up and picked me up in the bar downstairs, for the express purpose of seducing me? Don't you think you used me as well?"

"It's not the same."

"But you started it. You wanted a piece of me. You went after it. You grabbed the brass ring, Shannon. You went bold. You played for keeps. At first, when you told me, I was angry. All the old voices screamed at me about not being able to trust women— and I questioned my judgement. But then the more I thought about it, you gave me exactly what I'd been looking for. You gave me that little piece of you that jumps in with both feet. I wanted some of that. You helped me throw caution to the winds. And maybe I didn't think about the consequences."

"You're actually quite charming. In fact, you're the most charming man I've ever met. Afterall, I fell in love with you when I was twelve and thought about you—"

"You stalked me. Admit it, Shannon."

"I don't see it that way."

"Of course you don't. This might surprise you. I think you're stronger than I am. You're fearless."

"More of your jeweled tongue elixir." I did feel a softening in my belly. I was a hopeless moth to the flame.

"I owe you this much honesty. I love everything about you, Shannon. I even loved that you seduced me. You nailed me. You really did. You hit the bull's-eye. I love how excited you get, and I forget that life isn't a fairytale, because around you I start believing in fantasies and happily ever after, and then I make stupid decisions. I start making decisions from here," he touched his chest, "instead of here." He pointed to his temple.

"I don't want to live with a man who doesn't make his decisions about love from his heart, Marco. A man who only thinks and doesn't feel, doesn't trust himself to let love take over his whole life, is not someone I want to spend a life with. I thought you were that man, that incredible combination of heart and action. You even calculated that picnic at the beach, had it all planned out like your missions. I like that kind of thinking and planning. Because it's what keeps us alive. Gives us something to live for. It's not all about bank accounts after successful missions. It's about what everything else is *after* that's important, Marco. We work hard so we can love harder. It has to be that way for me. And, regardless of whatever else I said, I'm not ashamed of that. I embrace it. The funny thing is you *taught* me that."

"I did?" His fingers played with the hair on the top of my head.

I looked up at him. "I saw it in *you*, Marco. You *are* that man, if you want to be. You're brave and honorable. You'd rather suffer than cause someone else to pay the price, and you knock yourself out at the knees. You really do. You have to trust your heart, because I honestly believe it is the *best* part of you."

"I am a complete fool."

"You told me that already. You even did it on camera, remember?"

He nodded.

"Did I lose you, Shannon?"

I shrugged. "I don't know. You tried to send me away. I packed my bags, but I'm still here."

"What do I need to do to get you to stay?"

"I think you know."

"I have to trust my heart."

"Yes. And?"

He knelt down and took my hands in his. "I want you to stay.

You're the best thing in my life. Can you trust *me*?

"It's a practice, Marco. We train, we practice, right? We get better. We get stronger. We build. We don't tear down. And we never, ever run away."

He kissed my fingers. I drew strength from his handsome face, leaned forward, and kissed him.

"No more wrecking balls to my fairytale castle."

"Yes, ma'am."

"So are we leaving?"

"I didn't call anyone yet. But I do have to tell the sultan they're not ready. It would be a huge danger to themselves and everyone else if they went forward."

"Maybe in time then?"

"I'm going to return the money he gave me."

"He'll be disappointed. What are you going to do if he tries to talk you into it?"

"It doesn't change the facts. When they're ready, I'll be there for them and for him."

"I think he'll like that honesty, Marco."

"I'm going to talk to him now. You stay here for a few minutes?"

"Take as much time as you need. He's been a good friend. I understand that."

But before he could open the bedroom door, the sultan burst in. All the color had drained from his face.

"Marco! I'm sorry, but they have taken them. They have taken my boys."

CHAPTER 19

T HE SULTAN GAVE me the ransom note he was delivered.

"Who brought this to you?"

"Korem, one of the palace guards. He said a young boy delivered it on a bicycle."

Shannon was at my elbow, reading over my shoulder. "Ten million dollars. Wow."

"The money is not a problem. I have dollars. Curious that they would know that."

"Do your boys know that?"

"Yes, but they do not know how much I have here. And how do I know my boys are safe? How will they return them? They tell us where to leave the money, but they don't say where the boys will be."

The sultan looked small and helpless. His normally confident demeanor was completely shattered. I wanted to tell him the truth, but I didn't think I needed to put him through that much pain. I'd learned that, in most places in this part of the world, the hostages were often killed right after pictures were taken or a message was recorded. They would just bog them down, since, as slaves, the boys would be useless. And that was the best part of it. They wouldn't be trafficked. But their chances of survival were slim, if I was playing the odds.

"You need to sit down." I helped him to the chair Shannon had been sitting in. "Did you know those men who came with your sons last night?" I was kicking myself for not insisting I talk with him before he retired.

"No, but I knew what they were doing with the boat and everything. People tell me things."

"I understand. But have you ever seen these two men before? Or does anyone in the islands know them by chance?"

"No. I don't think they knew them until recently. But I'm sure, and it sounds like you agree, they are involved."

"Absolutely sure. No doubt in my mind. I wish I'd said something to you last night."

"They normally are not so foolish."

I couldn't believe he was telling me this. "You're making excuses. Now I want you to think about this. Is there anyone in your household here you don't completely trust? Anybody new to the staff?"

"I don't think so, no."

"They were going to take everyone out on the boat today. Do you know where it is?"

"There's a long pier and a deep-water port northwest from here. We use it for receiving things by ship from the islands, India, and Sri Lanka. Absalom told me we would leave from there." He put his head in his hands. "Oh, my god. I'm being punished for all my past deeds."

"No, Your Highness. It does no good to say that. It's not true."

"I should have been more careful."

"Now you're beginning to sound like me."

Harry flew in the door, skidding on the smooth tiled floor as he tried to stop.

"Papa! I just heard. They have left you a note?"

"Here." I gave it to Harry.

"But this is written in English. Why did they not write in Hindi? And they misspelled ransom. You see? They wrote it with an e at the end. Your sons would not make that mistake, my sultan. They are very well educated."

I hadn't noticed that. But then, my spelling wasn't known for being perfect.

Harry went back to keeping up the ruse about not being the sultan's son, probably for Shannon's benefit.

I was concerned about the sultan's blood pressure, and in light of what I knew of his current state of health, he couldn't handle too much stress.

"Can I borrow your car and go look?"

"I'll get a landscaper's truck," Harry said. "That way we can cut across the gardens instead of taking the road. I'll meet you outside the front door." He dashed off to find the vehicle.

"I think you'd be more comfortable if you sat in the grand room and put your feet up."

"I want to retire to my bedroom. I am useless. But I can get you the money. I keep it there."

There were two attendants waiting for him outside our door. They helped him downstairs to accompany him to his chambers. As I dialed Paul's number, I noticed Shannon was in shock. "I'm going to see if I can get the helicopter over here. Maybe have the team come help us find them."

"That's right. You have drones."

I nodded.

"Paul? Say, Paul, we've had an emergency here. The sultan's two sons have been kidnapped and are being held for ransom. I need you to bring Little Bird over, if you can."

"That's most distressing news. You know they caught a group of pirates, the Navy did just two days ago. It was all over the news today. Just found out about it. They were smuggling in arms from Iran."

"Well, the Navy might be interested in these guys too. There's a boat involved. I'm going to go see if it's still here. They may be using it to run something."

"You have the numbers? I can have one of your guys look it up."

"Unfortunately not. But I'm calling them next."

"I'm going to top her off, and then I'll be there in an hour or less."

"I'll have them meet you at the strip."

Next call was to the team. Karin said she'd search for reports of missing boats to see if we could get a hull number or registration I.D. She said she'd also give our contact at Diego Garcia a heads-up. They were dropping everything to head to the airport.

I heard a tiny engine outside.

"It's him. What do you need, Marco?" Shannon asked.

"Maybe you could get the keys for the first bungalow, see if anything they left behind tells us something. You know where it is?"

"Yes, but how do I get a key?"

"Let's go downstairs and talk to Harry about it."

We flew down the marble steps and outside. Harry was waiting in a green three-wheeled truck with a dump bed on the back covered by a rounded corrugated metal roof.

"Harry, do you have a SAT phone?"

He held his up.

"Let me dial my number. I want to leave mine with Shannon."

I coded in my phone number, and it rang. I handed it to Shannon.

"Do you have keys to the boys' room at the bungalows?"

Harry dug into his pockets and produced a single key. "Don't tell anyone, but it opens all of them."

I transferred it to her palm. "Thanks, sweetie."

I gave her a kiss and hopped in the little truck. Harry called out for one of the guards to climb in the back, which was a good idea, since I didn't bring my Sig. Harry floored the pedal, but the thing was about as responsive as a bumper car, especially with the three of us on board.

We barreled down the main path in front of the entrance, followed the curve to the right, through a small intersection of connecting paths, and then crossed a fragrant garden with several cascading water fountains competing for attention in the middle. I had yet to see this part of the palace grounds. A team of gardeners was trimming a flowered hedge. Harry waved to them as he cruised by at top speed.

"Is this the fountain they talk about in the note?"

"That one, Ganesh, in the middle."

We quickly zipped passed it.

"We're almost there," Harry barked over the sound of the die-sel motor.

I was concerned about losing the element of surprise with the noisy truck, but speed was also important. I could feel the mois-ture and taste the salty air, so expected to see the blue waters of the Indian Ocean any second. The foliage separated, revealing a long boathouse on stilts and concrete blocks. Like everything else on the island, it was adorned with carved wooden beams along the roof line, extending over the double-door entrance where the beam curved up and was adorned with a carved creature like that of a figurehead on a ship.

Harry pointed to the odd building. "The goddess of the island lives here."

"Isn't it for boats?"

"It's for her boat. We store it inside. Sometimes offerings are left there by the wives."

"So she is special to only them?"

"She is the goddess of the island. Every island has one. They pray to her. And to Ganesh."

Harry abruptly stopped. A long wooden pier extended easily fifty feet or more out into a perfectly flat and lapis blue ocean. There were no clouds in the sky today. There was no sign of land.

And there was no boat.

CHAPTER 20

I WAS CLOSE to the entrance to the baths as I continued down the corridor, heading towards the bungalows. I could hear wailing and the quick urgent chatter of women who were in duress. Their voices and sad sobbing echoed off the walls.

My heart ached for the mother of the two sons.

Unlike my family when there was a crisis, they were isolated and had only themselves to console. My family huddled together. Stayed tight. Maybe it was too tight because, after a while, I couldn't breathe. My parent's grief was so huge I carried it for years as my silent cross. Maybe this was a better way.

But it was still sad.

I assumed the women would be the last to get any news and resigned themselves to helping the mother relieve her stress in an attempt to help deal with their own. I also knew that those mothers of children who were on the pilgrimage were probably just as worried. With no real power, all they had was their community.

The early afternoon air was getting hot and sticky. Within a couple of hours, the Tradewinds would start blowing across the island from the east, and things had a chance of cooling down.

Marco told me the brothers were staying in the first house, so I inserted the key and turned the front doorknob but found the door unlocked. I stepped inside to a scene of total chaos.

Cushions were ripped apart, sliced with a sharp knife, and stuffing removed. They'd destroyed every single one, including the tops of several silk-covered ottomans. All the sheets had been removed from the bedrooms and piled up on the floor. The foam mattresses were sliced, hanging over their box springs. Clothes were thrown from the hanging closet, and all the drawers in each bedroom's dresser were upended, the contents spread everywhere.

I searched through the discarded items but was at a loss as to what I was looking for. Anything of written material was prepared in Hindi character fonts, so notes, tickets, and wrappers were useless to me.

But I did find a brochure of a yacht sales office in Mumbai with several boats circled. The prices didn't correlate to anything I could understand, but when I was reviewing the pages inside the brochure, a business card fell at my feet.

Kenny Singh.

He sounded like a salesman. Perhaps Harry or Marco would be able to get information from him that would help. It did give us an idea what they had been looking at in Mumbai, at least.

I carefully gathered papers spread close to the brochure, including several meal and lodging receipts, placing everything in a plastic bag from the kitchen.

As I scanned the mess, I wondered what the thieves had been looking for. It was odd that the pillows would be sliced up if they were looking for cash.

As I opened the front door, I almost missed a pile of papers that had been in a side table drawer, now upended on the floor. Poking out from the bottom of the pile was a cell phone. I used a dishtowel from the kitchen and, without touching it with my hands, wrapped the phone in it and added it to the contents of the plastic bag.

I turned and scanned the living room one more time and then locked the door behind me. I beat myself up about not using a piece of towel before touching the doorknob. But what was done was done, and I was at least bringing something to the group that hopefully would lead to some clues.

On the way back, I hesitated at the hallway, hearing the women's voices on the other side of the doors at the end of their wing.

Should I go see them? Would I make it worse?

Deciding being helpful was the better choice, I opened the gate, traveled the short distance to the entrance of the bath area, and walked inside.

Their mother was on a settee, surrounded by several other wives. She looked exhausted. But others were actively sobbing, wringing their hands and pulling their hair. The older wife searched my face for some sort of news I, unfortunately, didn't have to give her.

She looked at the plastic bag, so I showed her the brochure, and I unwrapped the cell phone, which she quickly grabbed.

So much for preserving prints.

She lit the screen, pressed buttons, and read characters and texts I couldn't decipher.

"Is this your son's?" I asked.

She nodded. The young wife who spoke English approached. "Can I help?"

"Ask her if she can look at the last calls and if she recognizes any of them."

I waited for my answer, and unfortunately, it was no.

"Whose phone is it?"

I heard Absalom's name quite distinctly.

"Can she make the last pictures come up?"

The mother was having a hard time getting pictures to display. One of the other wives helped her out. So now we had two extra sets of prints to deal with.

All of a sudden, the women got excited, pointing to the pictures. She held the screen up to me and displayed a beautifully clear picture of a sparkling white craft with the two boys standing in front of it. I also noticed that numbers on the hull of the ship were easy to read. I knew Marco would be pleased.

"One more favor, please," I asked the woman who spoke English. "The password. She knows the password for this phone. Can I have it?"

The answer was, "July seventh. But spell out the numbers."

I put my hands together as they handed the phone back. "Thank you," I said as I bowed and ran with my plastic bag of goodies, anxious to show them what I'd found.

When the SAT phone rang, it surprised me. I'd stuck it in my back jeans pocket and totally forgot I had it. "Hello?"

"We're back. The boat is gone. Did you find anything or are you still looking?"

"I did better than that. The place was trashed, but I found Absalom's phone, and he'd taken a picture of the boat. You can read the numbers on the front, just like you talked about."

"Super. Where are you now?"

"Almost to the great room."

"I'll meet you there. Harry's gone to pick up my team from the heliport. I was going to go, but I think I'll stay behind and look over those pictures. Good job, Shannon."

"See you in five."

As I entered the great hall again, I heard a vehicle leave the driveway in front. Marco greeted me before I made it to the large dining table. I handed him my bag of booty.

"What's all this?"

"The phone's in there, but I found a brochure from Mumbai. They were looking at boats there, too, and there's a card. And I just picked up everything around it, in case I got anything else of value. I can't read most of this stuff."

He picked up the cell phone and tried to get the screen to light up.

"You have to hit oh seven, oh seven. I got it from his mother."

He dialed as directed and called up the picture of the boat. "I'll be damned. Where did you find this?"

"On the floor. They'd made so much of a mess it got covered up."

"Look at this, Shannon." He enlarged the picture, and I recognized one of the men they'd brought to the house standing at a distance in profile, talking on his cell phone. He was completely unaware he'd been caught on camera.

"Wow. I didn't see that."

"And we have a timestamp when the picture was taken, depending on the setting. But we know when that call was made, and we know who made it. That's some good forensic evidence."

Within minutes of the team arriving, the entire table was taken up with laptops, phone chargers, a fax/printer, and several other electronic boxes I didn't have a clue what they were used for.

The big drone case with the sleek, white beauty and its parts took over several colorful silk pillows of two ottomans pushed together. Nigel was sitting nearby, admiring it like it was his new baby. And I guessed it was.

"Pretty bird."

"She is," Nigel said, running his hand down her body as if he was caressing a woman's thigh.

Karin shouted out, "Marco, we have a hit on the boat. Our friendlies know all about it. A couple from Florida owned it, and it was reported missing a week ago."

"Where are they now, back in Florida?" he asked.

She shook her head. "Presumed dead."

Marco looked at Paul. "Can we find them? They can't be too far away. How fast does this thing go?" he asked his pilot.

"About thirty, thirty-five miles an hour. They've been gone an hour plus, so they could be 40 plus miles away. I don't think there's anything within that range they could moor. My guess is they're headed to Male. That's about eighty miles." He lowered his voice considerably, almost whispering, "Little Bird is faster."

"Karin, let the Navy know where we think they're headed. And see if you can get hold of that yacht salesman. Paul, let's go see if we can get eyes on them."

Forest stopped him. "Hold on there. These guys are hostages, if they're still alive. You go flying overhead, and you've just tipped them off. They have the boat. They'd want the money. I'm guessing ten million is worth the risk to come back. But they won't come back for it with this boat if they think they're being tracked. My guess? They'll dump the kids in the ocean and get a bird to bring them back here for the pickup tomorrow."

Paul let out a string of choice words. Marco was thinking. He finally added, "I know we'll catch that boat. I want to get the kids alive."

"So maybe we take Little Bird. If we think we see them, I'll send out the drone," said Nigel. "We'll get pictures and send them along to the friendlies. But at least we'll know if they're still alive."

"If they're on deck," said Marco.

"Yup, if they're on deck."

It was a sobering thought for everyone.

I had an idea. "Well then, we just have to get lucky. No other way to be sure. And, if we don't try, we'll never know. You lose one hundred percent of the at-bats you don't take. Didn't Joe DiMaggio say that or something?" I scrunched up my nose, not sure if I'd added anything or not.

"Marco, if you don't marry that girl, I'm going to," said Nigel. He wrapped his arm around my shoulder.

As if Marco could get jealous.

But he was back. Marco was back. He looked at me the way he did when I was all dressed up, dancing in front of him with the other wives. It wasn't his eyes I noticed, because I was only seeing him out of the sides of mine. It was the way he cocked his head, the way his chest rose and fell, his fingers rubbing against each other.

It made me love being the object of his desire. I stretched my arms longer, tilted my head in a graceful angle, shook the little bells at my wrists, and let him hear the swoosh of my thighs against the silk layers of fabric.

I was turning his night into magic. It was *real* magic.

For both of us.

CHAPTER 21

I INVITED SHANNON to come along, after checking with Karin and Forest to make sure they didn't need additional help. Harry wanted to stay behind and check on his dad, so we borrowed his van for the short trip to the heliport.

She was more familiar with the routine this time, even managed to get herself strapped in and was the first one other than Paul to get her headset on. I sat up front next to Paul. Shannon sat behind the pilot and Nigel behind me. I asked him to check her seatbelt, and she stuck her tongue out at me.

"She's locked and loaded," Nigel told me with a wink.

Behind them, the drone case had been placed and then opened for quick use. Nigel kept the controller box on his lap the whole time.

"Everyone ready?" Paul asked.

I gave my thumbs-up, as did Shannon. Nigel nodded, and Paul directed Little Bird to climb straight up and then lowered the nose, and we took off in a large arc over the ocean. He flipped a switch, and we had some Star Wars theme songs to fly by. I settled back, since there wasn't much but ocean to look at. A handful of small islands no larger than my car back home popped up here and there. Nigel used his binoculars and called it for no evidence of the catamaran.

I knew the lighter the water the shallower it was, so I figured it would be easy to spot the boat if they'd sunk it. The more we encountered these shallow spots, the more relieved I became.

"Do you want to swing back and forth here, check everything out, or do you want the pictures for the Navy?" Paul asked.

"I want to find the boat first. I want to give the frogs as much information as possible so they can nab these guys in time."

Several bright white sailboat masts were scattered all over the area, but our big boat hadn't been spotted yet.

"Should I turn my drone on? It will register the other boats and store the data. But we won't get pictures until she's in the air."

"I don't have room up here in the cockpit. Any way you can go into the rear seat and turn it on there?"

"No, Marco. Just the nose. I got it right here." He handed me the black plastic cone no bigger than a bar of soap. "It's registering, so just point it straight ahead and try not to move too much."

"Easy for you to say."

"It will keep us from getting false flags."

"Gotcha. Is this okay?"

Nigel leaned toward Shannon, trying to get a visual of my arm. "Just a second. Let me get out my slide rule."

Paul cackled.

"So you come up here and hold your arm out for an hour, thank you very much."

My SAT phone rang.

"Oh shit. Can you reach it?" I leaned forward to allow Shannon or Nigel space to get the phone from my rear pocket.

There was no mistaking the feel of Shannon's hand pulling the phone out but also giving me a nice little rub. She held it to her ear.

"Okay, just a sec," she said. "Karin wanted to tell you the salesman in Mumbai tried to sell the boys a new yacht, but they wanted to keep looking for a used one. Coincidentally, he just got a call today from a party who thinks he wants to sell his. He was asking about prices and things. He doesn't think it's a real seller call. He's kicking the tires."

"Okay, good. Tell her to have him let us know if he hears from that seller again or if he gets wind of a used 44 Cat Aquila, especially if it has Florida registration numbers."

"She said she would do. Should I hold the phone?"

"Yes, please."

I heard a beeping noise. I focused on the horizon to see if I could find anything and couldn't.

"Yup, that's a sighting all right. It's bigger than a sailboat," Nigel said.

"Hand me the binoculars." I spotted her right away. There were more than two people on the deck, but I couldn't tell who they were.

"I think I'd better cool it. The wind is going towards them, so they'll hear us long before they'll see us. But I can call in coordinates, rough ones. If you want."

"Let's get the bird out there first, Paul," Nigel requested. I nodded agreement and handed the nosecone back to him. He handed the comm to Shannon and scrambled to the rear. A short time later, I heard several clicking sounds. Paul banked Little Bird, retreated a few hundred feet, and began to hover low over the water so we would have a lesser chance of being heard.

Nigel sat back down, strapped in, reached behind him to retrieve the drone, holding it in his left hand, and flipped the on-switch. We heard a low, purring whir of the motor kicking in to gear. With his right hand, he slid open the cabin door, transferred the bird over, extended his arm outside the cabin so the wings wouldn't get caught on the doorway, and just dropped it. He didn't bother closing the door until he was able to take back the controller and start to direct its flight.

Then he closed the door and clicked it shut.

"Paul, you're gonna want to get some elevation or I'll lose signal. We're stretching the boundaries here."

Little Bird did a slow spiral upwards, and after a couple hundred feet, he leveled out.

"That's fine. We're getting some good picture quality. Hold on. There!"

I turned around and saw the white deck of the fat little boat, but when Nigel magnified the picture, we could practically see what kind of beer they were drinking. There were three people on the deck, and as we all studied the pictures, none of them looked like either of the two sons. We did recognize one of the house-guests, though. That was welcome information.

Nigel directed the drone to come back toward us and then take another pass. He skillfully got a good shot of the below-decks, where an open door showed one of three bedrooms on the boat. Someone was hog-tied, wrists and ankles together, lying on their side on the bed. There was just one.

Only one.

But there could be more in the other two bedrooms.

Nigel took about twenty still photos, which would be uploaded to his computer back at the island. All of them would have their coordinates, as well as the date and time recorded on each of the frames.

"You have enough?"

"Can we get Karin to get into your computer to forward them on?" I asked.

"Sure thing. I have no secrets," said Nigel. "Why don't you dial Karin and hold the phone up to me. I don't want to put this thing away if I have to re-photograph anything."

Nigel gave Karin access to his computer, and about a minute later, she got confirmation that the photos arrived intact. "Karin, make sure to tell them their direction, and that they're traveling about thirty to thirty-five miles per hour, okay?"

I heard her answer back that a cutter was on its way over, and there would be an intercept within the hour.

"Music to my ears, Karin. Looks like we got them just in time. Tell them thanks. I'm out."

She confirmed.

"Hot damn. That was close, but I think we got it done. Now up to the Navy. Thank God for Uncle Sam."

"Good deal," said Nigel. "I'm putting her to bed."

"Does she follow us home?" Shannon asked.

"Nope, you'll see." He handed the comm to Shannon temporarily. "Don't touch that," he said, pointing to the stick.

Unstrapping, he lifted the black memory foam that held the drone parts and pulled out a folded one-foot square piece of netting, attached to a metal arm which telescoped to make it longer. Nigel opened the door again, shouting Paul instructions.

"I don't want the drone to hit Little Bird, and it's dangerous, this part. So I want you to just try to pull up, walk alongside of her on your right. Try to get as close as you can but be the higher bird. This arm expands to about ten feet. But the net is what will catch her."

Paul trailed behind the drone, and above, then slowly lowered us and got us closer. I was praying for no turbulence. That drone could foul our blades, and we'd be dropping to the sea in no time.

But his skillful maneuvering got us so close that Nigel plucked the drone right out of the sky like fishing for salmon. He barked to Shannon to cut the power on the comm. We all breathed a sigh of relief when he carefully maneuvered the netting and drone inside and set it behind us.

"Let's take her home, Paul. I think we got a mission accomplished here. I got a date with a shower. I'm soaking wet."

I chanced a backward glance at Shannon's face and saw her downcast eyes. But then she raised them and smiled at me.

I was going to enjoy that shower.

CHAPTER 22

J UST BEFORE WE arrived back at the palace, Karin called us to say that five hijackers had been captured, with no significant injury, and both the brothers had been rescued. We were all in a buoyant mood when we landed.

Harry was waiting for us at the front door. His face was downcast.

Marco grabbed me around the waist and gave him the good news about the boys.

"Couldn't come at a better time. The sultan's having a rough afternoon. He's been coughing non-stop. I saw a little blood on his Kleenex, and then he denied it. Is he sick, Marco?"

"I can't answer that. But it's hard to diagnose when he won't go to the doctor. You get him in for some tests."

"I will. I'm going to stay over a bit until he's feeling better. He worked himself up pretty good."

"That's the way he is. You should know that by now."

"I certainly do."

"I need to talk to him about his plans for Africa. I don't want to bring up too many things at once, so you tell me if he's well enough to perhaps receive some bad news."

"Oh dear. Someone got hurt. They cut off one of the boy's ears?"

I had a hard time keeping a straight face. "Should we go see him and give him the good news ourselves?" I added, "Maybe then we could assess how he's feeling, and Marco could talk to him but just a little bit. Would that work?"

"He won't really tell me. Maybe he'll be more honest with you. I know he has a good heart and just wants to protect me. But, at the same time, this is a complicated family unit. There are a lot of people to consider here."

"Let me see what I can do," Marco said. "Oh, and do I have permission to put the team up here tonight?"

"I don't see why not. They've earned it. I have three vacant bungalows so, if they double up, should be enough private space for them. We'll have a feast tonight to celebrate the return of my brothers. I'll have to get more staff in, but it's easy to do."

"And you promise to get everyone to hold over?"

"Yes, Boss."

"Why, Harry, are you angling for a job?" I asked him.

"I have one, as you know. But I plan parties and events all the time in Brooklyn. For something like tonight, I'm all over it."

"I'm counting on you," Marco said.

On our way to the front door, I posed an idea. "Marco, you should consider hiring Harry. Seriously."

"I have an assistant. But maybe going forward. For our grand opening, whenever that will be."

"You'll get there. I like his energy."

"I do too. In fact, I have another idea as well."

"Tell me."

"I don't want to spoil it. But come with me to speak with him."

We received a warm welcome from Karin and Forest.

"How did you know you'd need the drone?" Forest asked.

"It was just the strength of the team. I don't think we'll do any project without them now."

We headed off toward the sultan's rooms when I remembered the party tonight. "Marco, you didn't tell them about the dinner."

"Thank you. Going to fix that right now." He turned around and shouted out to the two of them. "And everyone stays over tonight. We have a big dinner, debriefing. Mini board meeting with alcohol."

"I'm up with that," said Karin.

"Tomorrow, we'll get you guys back to the Maldives."

"Cool, Boss! Thanks," said Forest.

I was struck with how the palace was beginning to feel like a fancy office building. The whole place was transforming.

We entered the sultan's chambers, passing by the throne room with his elephant god dominating everything in there. I recognized his younger, pregnant wife waiting by the door.

"How is he?" Marco asked.

"He just seems to want to rest."

"That's probably what he needs," I offered.

"Harry thought I could—"

We heard the sultan's voice from across the room. "Marco, is that you? Please come in."

She moved aside, whispering, "Not too long. He's very weak."

"I bring good news, Your Highness," Marco started off. "The boys have been found, and the U.S. Navy gets all the credit. They might be home in time for dinner. They're going to have to give statements first, and then they'll be home."

"I'm delighted with this. I've been dreading the outcome. I'll have to get up and make more of an effort—"

But the sultan fell back, disoriented and confused. "The mind is willing, but the body tells me I have to rest. I was looking forward to fishing with both of you."

"We'll do that. We'll do that soon."

"Shannon, you come over here to the other side and sit with me a while."

I did as instructed.

"You sit, too, Marco. Now tell me, Surya says you slept in the throne room last night, Marco. And you brought alcohol in there. Was there something that went on between the two of you?"

"I wanted to talk to you about it."

"Oh, dear. Something else has happened?"

"I'm just going to be brutally honest with you, Your Highness. They aren't ready. Your sons are young in their business years.

They understand business theory, but not how to go about getting things done. It's a lack of maturity. It's not a character flaw; they just haven't had to, well, work. They don't understand the concept."

"But they both went to—"

"Yes, very gifted students. That's *theory*. They have no street smarts."

"So what does this mean?"

"We should do the project when they get some experience. I suggest give them something to build here, not this African complex. And here's another thing. West Africa is having problems right now. It's even more dangerous than before. That alone was almost enough for me to recommend we not do this."

"Right now or are you turning me down forever, Marco? Just be honest with me. I consider you—you're a son to me. Please be honest."

"No, I'm not turning you down. But I don't want to be responsible if something happened to them. This whole thing today—it's mostly their fault. They invited those men into your house, Your Highness. You don't have nearly enough security here. You trust everyone and have a big heart. You are extremely vulnerable. They are the same way. They learned it from you."

"So this is also about me? You don't think I've raised my sons to be worthy citizens?"

Marco leaned over and grabbed the sultan's hand. "No, my friend. Hear what I'm saying. Nothing could be further from the truth. They're naïve. They buy a boat without checking the title and spent nearly a million dollars on it, too. That's a lot of money."

"Well, to me, I'd just rather they be happy. If they waste it on things like this boat, it won't really hurt me or them."

"But a million dollars is a lot of money to a lot of bad guys. People do bad things for far less. It bothers me that you are so exposed."

"I do not want to live in a prison."

"You have to protect your legacy. I told them the same last night. If they're not careful, they could undo what ten centuries of your ancestors created here. This little jewel, someone could try to grab it. And they could do it in one generation."

"What's the point of having wealth if you have to be locked up with it?"

Marco looked over to me. I could see he was asking for my help.

"I think what Marco is trying to tell you is that the world is changing. This little kingdom was well insulated from all the rest of the world's problems. Now, you're less than three hours from active wars, concentration camps, and food shortages. There's instability. You can't ignore this any longer. You used to be able to. And it isn't anything you did. It's what's going on out there. Outside."

"I never made demands of the outside. And my family, if they wanted to stay, they could stay forever. I'm seeing that the younger generation want to go live their lives away from this island. I used to think my grandfather was too harsh to not allow us to travel abroad to go to school. Now I understand why. Is my little kingdom dying? Is this what you mean?"

"It will die if you don't change. Who in this family can run this household like you can?" Marco asked.

"I see your point. So if you're not leaving me and not turning down the job, then what are you saying?"

"I'm saying they aren't ready *now*. I said I'd do it, but not when the odds are stacked against us. Maybe in a few years. They're not ready today."

"Well, that's a problem, then, isn't it? I don't have a few years. I have a year at best, Marco. And not a word of this to Harry, either. You do not have my permission to tell anyone."

"Understood."

"Marco, how did you do it? What special quality made you so successful? Was it your training? You were one of a handful. What made you so different?"

"I was tested, you're right. And some of my colleagues in class expected to and didn't make it. Eighty-seven percent didn't. But the honest truth is that I just didn't quit. I had no options. I didn't grow up in a hothouse where everything was provided for me. I got to experience the value of my own work. In giving them everything they want with no consequences, you not only endanger you and your wives but you endanger them."

"So teach them. Mentor them."

"I made it because I had a huge advantage."

"What was that?"

"I started from zero, and I wanted it with my whole heart. I was constantly on the lookout for something that would derail me, send me back to the dorms, or make me drop out. After a while, I knew they couldn't get rid of me."

"So what can we do, then?"

"We hire lots of mentors. We exhaust them with information. We make them study things they didn't learn in their programs. We hire project managers and financial managers. We take on less ambitious projects, like drilling wells for villages. Things that don't pay well. We do it because we want to learn and change. They have to study to live in the world, while doing good things that we are proud of."

"Like build houses."

"Yes, that's a good goal. But we don't do this in such dangerous places, not when they're learning. I still think your Africa project has merit. But it's not something we can just do overnight."

"Where will these mentors teach them? Do they go back to school?"

"Well, I'm just now thinking about this, and I'm not sure why I didn't come up with it before. Maybe, Your Highness, they start by working for me first. I have a project on the Gulf. They could help me get that one off the ground. But I warn you, they'll work hard. Otherwise, they'll be fired."

The sultan started laughing and then coughing. "That would be something, wouldn't it? You? Ordering my sons around?"

"It's not about ordering them around. It's about teaching them to work. Because it's worth it to preserve your legacy. Their legacy. If they care about that, they'll learn everything they need. They'll be unstoppable. A force for good, not some ornament hanging on a fence or in a museum somewhere. Your kingdom will not only survive. It will thrive."

"Let's do it. Let's get this started."

I was proud of Marco for telling him not what he wanted to hear but what he needed to hear.

"There are two conditions, Your Highness," Marco added.

"Go on."

"First, they have to say they want it. I'll work out a plan and schedule, a long-term plan for the Africa project too."

"Otherwise, they don't get to participate. They get fired," the sultan guessed.

"Exactly."

"And the other condition?"

"You give me a couple of weeks, and we'll live in my house. You'll wear shorts and flip flops. We'll go fishing every day. Nobody will know who you are. You'll learn how to cook, bake bread, and go shopping. You become curious about how average people live and cope with their daily lives. You can only bring one wife, because those are our laws. But you come and learn what it is like to live outside your cocoon, in my world. I want to take your training wheels off. If you do it, just for two weeks, I think they will too."

"What do you think, Shannon?" the sultan asked.

"It's the chance of a lifetime, Your Highness. I'd take it."

"The question is what do you think, Your Highness? Do *you* want it?"

"I think I'd like to try when I feel stronger. Not too long, but I should get to the doctor, don't you think?"

"An excellent start. Now you have a short-term goal. Your goal is to get as healthy as you can so you can do well at boot camp."

He fell back in the pillows, laughing and mumbling, "Boot Camp." He coughed. "I'm going to be a fuckin' Navy SEAL."

CHAPTER 23

S HANNON WASN'T ABLE to keep up with me as I took the marble steps two at a time.

"We're going to work on that too."

Her eyes got as big as saucers. "Not me. I'm not a marathoner. I run on the beach a little bit, but no, I don't do running up and down stairs."

"We'll see about that." I finished the steps, looking forward to the shower, and heard her mumbling. And yes, she also picked up a little swearing, placing it in there nicely, just like the sultan did.

She entered the room and sat down, breathing heavy. "Are you going to be one of those?" she asked.

"Our first board meeting is tonight. I'm going to introduce the boys and you as well. Let's see what happens."

"Did you just offer me a job?"

"I did."

"They call it a presumptive close. You just used a sales skill on me. Your fiancée."

I knew she was going to continue on with the lecture about sales closes. I could name just about every one, including some of the more obscure ones. I conducted a little experiment, trying out another close. I ripped off my shirt and kicked off my shoes.

She stopped talking. Lesson learned. She wasn't gasping for air any longer, either. "Oh? Did you want to go before me? I can wait."

"This is so not fair," she mumbled.

I approached, hesitating to take the final step. "You're not going to slap me, are you? Because—"

"Would you please shut up?" And then softer, she said, "And kiss me."

I reached for her head, my fingers deep in her hair, messing it all up as I preferred it. My mouth covered hers, and I pressed her lips open with my tongue, a full-scale frontal assault. I even felt her knees cave a bit. She leaned against me slightly. I wouldn't let up until I transferred my attentions to nibble her earlobe and then kissed around her neck and down between her breasts.

She was still leaning against me when I was done.

I could see she was puzzled. She was evaluating my performance, perhaps? I decided to wait until she was ready to tell me.

"What's gotten into you?"

"I've kissed you before, Shannon. So what*ever* do you mean?"

"This, this way you're being. That look on your face."

I turned around and looked at myself in the bathroom mirror.

"I don't see it. May I undress you so we can discuss this in the shower?"

She squinted, but I recognized some play acting there. Fake anger.

"Well?" I slid my pants down to my ankles. My particular body part was very happy to see her, bobbing up and down and trying to get her attention.

I unbuttoned her jeans, and they dropped to the floor. She stepped out of them. I removed her panties and top. She wasn't wearing a bra.

"Come, my dear." I tugged at her hand, and she followed me into the shower enclosure.

"What I meant was you're in a strange mood. Not that I mind."

She leaned her back against me and placed her arms up behind my neck, and I soaped off her front, making sure to be very thorough. I still had plenty of soap on the fluffy sponge, so I brushed it against her neck, pressing her head forward. Still with her back to me, I bent her over slightly, washing her with long strokes from her hips to underneath her arms and from the tops of her thighs all the way over her perfect ass and up her spine. I was thorough about washing her behind but even more thorough about rinsing. I had plans for that pulsing opening between her legs.

Bending my knees, I prodded until I easily slipped into her wet channel I was so fond of violating.

"Love you, Shannon," I whispered.

She moaned. "That's how I like it."

"You're the romantic, aren't you?"

"I am. Marco, you feel so good."

We had a slightly longer board meeting in the shower. But she wasn't bored. In fact, by the time we finished, I was ready to discuss more topics. I had a whole drawer full of them, just waiting for me to choose one.

I STOOD AT the end of the dinner table. We'd packed up all the electronics but kept them nearby in case we needed them.

Absalom and Khalil were picked up at the airport just before we were about to begin, but they wanted to go shower after their ordeal. I'd already gotten the report that they'd not been harmed physically, but the expression on their faces told me they'd gotten very seriously shaken up mentally. I'd seen it with hostages many times before, when they'd reach the point that they'd just give up and die.

The boys had only been gone a few hours, but they'd never experienced anything like this, and it horrified them. It was the first lesson of their mentorship. Don't put yourself in a compromising situation with someone you don't know—especially anywhere close to Africa.

So I told them no.

Khalil did a double take. He'd turned and was already heading down the corridor.

"I was tied up all day. I'd like to take a shower."

"I was looking for you all day. We all were, Khalil. Please sit down. We're having a board meeting, and then we'll eat, and then you can take your shower."

He looked at his brother, who didn't react.

"First, a couple announcements. We have three new hires. We have Khalil and Absalom from the Kingdom of Bonin. They are CEOs-in-training. And we have Shannon Marr, weather girl at TMBC in Tampa, who is being hired for strategic planning."

Everyone clapped.

"You boys are being sent by your sultan to learn how to become a successful businessman. Since your particular interest is in housing, we're going to have you work on the Trident Towers, a multifamily housing project on the Gulf of Mexico for disabled and retired Navy SEALs and their dependents. Your father has told me I can put you up in adequate housing of my choosing."

The boys were both stunned. Shannon knew what I was doing but kept a straight face.

I went over some of the ground rules. Forest told the one about swearing double on Fridays. Karin told everyone not to ever bring me a coffee without a lot of cream in it. Paul told the group that Little Bird was my favorite toy and had been responsible for saving many lives over the three years I'd had her. Nigel reminded everyone that football meant soccer and that Americans were getting better, but they really didn't know how to play.

I mentioned that we'd decided to do the project in Florida first before we did Africa. But we were working on obtaining all the permits needed anyway. The ground-breaking would be a way off, though.

Shannon was the troublemaker already. She raised her hand, and I called on her.

"You forgot to give me one."

"Okay, shoot."

"The beach heals everything."

"And that would be correct. You get a gold star today, Shannon. I'll present it to you in private, later."

Everyone laughed.

Absalom raised his hand. "Did Dad really give us to you for a year?"

"You're not slaves. You're going to learn how to work. You'll be required to run errands, like shopping, and keep your apartments straight. And there will be regular physical fitness things, like swimming and running. You will find that living in Florida won't be anything like living here, but it's not too bad. The weather is a little cooler, but usually less rain."

I told them I was looking for an office building in Tampa, so I would not have anything left in New York or Boston areas. I was going to maintain the leased condo in D.C. That I was divorced from Rebecca and marrying Shannon.

I went over the next few projects and indicated that most of them would center around Florida.

Lastly, I asked everyone to give a high-five to the brothers, who were going to be far from home and living in conditions they were unfamiliar with.

"Someone a long time ago told me that if you wanted to learn something, teach someone. Please help them out as best as you can."

I explained that we would be sending them back to the States on Thursday, but that Shannon and I were staying the full week.

AFTERWARDS, SHANNON AND I went to the sultan's bedroom and were granted an audience. His coloring had improved. I reported that the boys did extremely well, but I knew they'd probably want to talk to him.

"One more item I discussed with Shannon the other night. I wish you two would consider having your wedding here. It would be a week of celebrations, one party after the next. I can honestly say my house puts on the best receptions anywhere on the globe."

"You discussed this?" I asked her, surprised.

"I did. We were busy for a bit, and then I forgot to ask you. I'd be in favor of it, if you are. It would save my folks a lot of money, and it would be spectacular, unlike any wedding either of us have ever attended from pictures I saw.

"Thank you, sir. We'll look at some dates so we can start planning that."

He asked permission to let the boys stay an extra week to spend more time with their mom, in light of the circumstances, and I agreed.

"Now go. I must sleep, but you two go do something fun. And thank you again for bringing my sons home to me. I will forever be in your debt."

"Maybe that was something they had to go through to get their attention. But it's an opportunity, and if they cultivate it and learn from it, some day they may save someone else's life, or possibly their own."

He was going to schedule his doctor visit and would let me know when he was coming for his Boot Camp. I kind of had a logo all picked out for it. I couldn't wait to see him in shorts and flip flops.

WE WERE ENJOYING the warm night. The Tradewinds had shown up, but they were warm tonight.

"My mom and dad used to play this game with Em and I called Best Of. We did it on every vacation, talking about the best of the whole trip," Shannon said.

"I like that idea. What would yours be for this vacation?" I asked.

"Well, it's not over, but I'd have to say the first night, when they made me up in traditional dress, pampered me, and showed me what it was like to live here. They showed me their community and culture and taught me about the power of becoming irresistible."

"That's exactly what you were. What you are."

"What about you?" she asked.

I knew it wasn't going to be as beautiful as the moment Shannon shared with me, but it was my favorite part. And, after all, I was a guy.

"It was all the things in that drawer and what I learned about the power of your love. I hope that, in time, I can make you as happy as you've made me."

RESTORED

Bone Frog Bachelor Series
Book Two

SHARON HAMILTON

CHAPTER 1

I, THE SOON-TO-BE Mrs. Marco Gambini, had a lot to think about this morning as I did my routine run down the sugar-sand beach of Belleair Beach. Marco had left late the night before, taking a flight to D.C. to meet with some senators who could run interference for his Trident Towers project on the Florida Gulf Coast. They were having issues with local building officials concerning their redesign, and he needed powerful allies to help smooth the kinks.

Plans for our wedding in the new year were going well, although most of it was outside my control since we'd accepted the Sultan of Bonin's invitation to host the entire event, including any guests we wished to invite, at his private island in the Indian Ocean. He would house most guests in his Pink Palace and others at various other hotel-like properties on the pink coral beaches. The sultan's wives and servants were preparing everything, and all I had to do was pick out my dress, write my vows, and show up for the party.

Meanwhile, Marco designed a dream home for the two of us to live in on property he'd owned for several years, near his veterans' housing project. I was learning to make decisions: figuring room sizes, placement of windows, overall layout of the house footprint and future gardens surrounding a large pool right on the beach. The house was so overwhelming in size and scope I was having a hard time sleeping. Colors, numbers, building materials, and decorating samples floated around in her brain.

But as complicated as all these decisions and plans were, that wasn't what had me preoccupied. *Worried* wasn't really the right word. How could someone so incredibly lucky worry about a thing, I wondered. Yet something bothered me, and it made no sense.

Marco had asked me to quit my job at TMBC, the TV station in Tampa where I had worked as a part-time weather girl before my recent promotion to reporter. I was rumored to be on the fast track for an anchor position. It was what I'd dreamt of being since I applied at the station—ever since she got my acting and deportment coach after my brief experience acting in a couple of indie films and nearly being cast in a TV series.

And yet, he asked me to give all that up. It wasn't a career like his years in the Navy as an elite SEAL or as CEO of several multi-billion-dollar companies. I was technically part-time, could be fired at any minute and made very little money. I had to get up incredibly early, which meant getting in a dark run on the beach and shower, driving into work just before sunrise when I'd rather be in bed snuggling with my fiancé—the strongest, most gentle and patient man on the planet with a body twice as hard and sculpted in the flesh as he looked in interviews.

I found myself dreamily longing for my days off when he could show me the passion he felt for me as he extracted that same ardor from me in return. Their all-consuming multi-hour love-making sessions made me weak at the knees whenever I thought of them.

But...

I'd acquiesced to moving into the big, beautiful home we were building, even considering letting go of my little beach bungalow when the time came. But quitting my job—that was going to take some special courage.

I wondered why.

And this morning, even though the crisp saltwater sprays, the calls of the sea birds, and the dark purple sky turning pink with dark grey clouds appearing out of nowhere reminded me of all that was good and perfect about my life, I was afraid to cut off the old ties to the sleepy little beach town that helped me heal after the death of my sister—the woman Marco Gambini had been engaged to until her fatal accident. My sister should have been the one to enjoy this abundance and joy, even the excitement and danger that came with Marco and his lifestyle.

I needed to hold something back, something private and all my own, something more precious than my little bungalow. My work gave me a career to fall back on if the unthinkable were to happen—if suddenly Marco were taken from me or left for some reason.

Maybe it was an insurance policy. It wouldn't support the life I was living now, but I could throw myself into it, if I needed to.

I asked myself repeatedly whether I was indeed happy living this life my older sister, Emily, had intended on having with Marco. Or was I playacting? Was it just something I told myself was a dream come true? Was this really a dream I ought to be head over heels about or did I want it because it was something Em would have loved? Again, was I living in Em's place when it came right down to it?

Although I loved Marco more than anyone else in the whole world and knew I'd feel that way forever, the thought of cutting off my past and all my ties to the girl I used to be terrified me. It made me dream about running away, bolting from the idyllic life as a billionaire's fiancée and exchanging it for something common, something I was used to, could trust. I would never be able to return. I didn't want to give up what I'd worked so hard to attain at the station. I'd built it all by myself, too. And I liked my job.

Back and forth, I tossed these ideas as my feet turned down the beach access bridge to Beach Trail Drive, then across an alleyway to Gulf Boulevard, and into the small three-block subdivision of more modest homes. I headed toward the marshes of the dog park and the inlet of Tampa Bay beyond. The gentle tap, tap, tap of my running shoes on the sandy path at the park was in tandem with my breathing, also keeping track with the swishing of my ponytail under my Rays baseball cap. Using my earbuds connected to my trusty old wristband player, I listened as voices sang a sad dirge for a slow king's coronation march. The instruments underneath enhanced the emotions of the singers.

I wound around the outside of the gated doggie play area and heard occasional traffic noises on the wet pavement of Gulf Boulevard and the distinctive rumble of a large diesel truck pulling into the parking lot. The motor stopped, which caused me to stare at it. The windows were blackened, and I could see the glow of a cigarette being lit inside the cab but had no visibility of the driver's face.

Instinct told me to slip on over to the marsh trail between mangos, sea grapes, and scrub oaks with moss dangling precariously in the light of the full moon like on a Disney ride. Cicadas and other insects chirped and formed their own chorus, creating an almost pulsing sound filled with thousands of tiny reedy voices. I was exploring a back way out that I'd heard about but never seen before, so I kept my running pace.

The truck door slammed.

I felt a spike in my awareness that I might be in some danger, and I silenced my earbuds. My deep thoughts had made me blind to the possibility that perhaps this driver had followed me here to the park, intending on God knew what. I was struck with the ridiculous thought about how quickly my choices were now limited to living or perhaps not living or being harmed. Forget the regret at the TV station, everything—the good and the bad— might be taken away in a flash.

I felt vibration through the wooden planks as a heavy man's footsteps shook the boards beneath my feet. I dared not to turn to look for fear he'd seen the terror now resident in my face.

As I rounded a slight curve to the left, I examined my choices. Both sides of the walkway were filled with thick greenery, oversized Elephant Ear plants, mangroves, and wild Bird of Paradise trees going up forty feet or more. But the water was of unknown depth. Between the right side and the left, I couldn't tell which was deeper or which would be more hazardous if I leapt over the railing and attempted to escape through the jungle of foliage.

I chose the right without hesitating. I grabbed the railing and used it to pole vault, swinging my legs up over the wood. Landing mid-calve in the cool water, I winced as the splash was a little too loud. Ripples disrupted the glassy surface of the marsh. The telltale sign revealed something big had landed there: me. I quickly took a step behind a large mangrove and squatted, feeling the coolish water through the seat of my pants, and breathed shallowly. My pulse raced.

A pair of white cranes flew off into the early morning air, their warning cry further revealing my location. But I still waited and hoped the stories were true that crocs didn't like the saltwater marshes and would only invade those areas to feast.

And that could mean…

Suddenly, a flash of light crossed the sky, briefly lighting up the dark grey clouds and the tops of the water-slogged greenery. The crack left my ears pinging, certain that it had landed not far away. I was stranded in a huge marsh of water, with lightning all around me as the second and third flashes and cracks developed, making me jump. Various other birds flew up each time the crack and resulting boom hit the area. I could see the wooden handrail bouncing in the pressure of the early morning storm.

I tried to still myself, but my heart bounced all around in my chest, my shallow breathing making me lightheaded. I was grateful for the commotion, even though it drowned out the footsteps of the approaching man. And when it was at last quiet, as the rain began to trickle down, I heard nothing at all. Just the drizzle—the water washing over everything, as if wiping away whatever had lurked there.

Something grazed past my leg just above my ankle, and I inhaled sharply, about to scream before I remembered the presence of the stranger. So, as I listened for more signs of him, I looked down at my legs in the water, hoping against hope that I wouldn't see a slithering snake or sea worm. It was just black, mucky water.

And now I noticed it smelled of old decay and rotting wood. I nearly gagged.

Squinting through the greenery and without making any sound in the water, I attempted to view the path from which I'd just come and found it completely empty.

Stretching my arms out behind me, I carefully rose, felt a large boulder big and solid enough to sit on, and leaned back to make a perch of it. My knees and calves rewarded me with a thank you. My heart rate began to die down. My breathing extended into long, deep takes as I realized, with the feel of daylight approaching sometime in the next hour, I would soon be fully exposed.

Almost as if reassuring me, I heard the diesel engine kick in. The truck shifted gears and then shifted again and sounded like it pulled off onto Gulf Boulevard. Then it was gone.

I waited about a minute longer and then, slowly and without a sound, slid ~~her~~ my shoes over the lumpy rocks and mud in the marsh, reached the walkway, placed ~~her~~ my hands on the path, and hoisted ~~herself~~ myself up to seated position with ~~her~~ legs dangling. As I examined my wet shoes, socks, and ankles, I realized wild, rotting grasses wound around my lower leg, at first looking like tiny snakes. The harmless dead reeds were easily brushed away. The mud was scraped off my shoes and ankles with my forefinger.

And then I stood.

I had two choices, walk along the path through the unknown area of the neighbor's yard somewhere off in the distance based on information that may or may not be accurate or go back the way I came where I could call someone—except that I hadn't brought my cell because Marco was unreachable, still enroute, and probably sleeping in the back of a black limo.

But going back the same way I'd arrived seemed safest, so I started home with a brisk walk, gradually advancing it into a jog. My shoes shed bubbles of grey water and squeaked as if I was running on baby mice.

Except this time, I wasn't thinking about the sadness of giving up my job. I was grateful no truck lingered in the empty parking lot, nor was there a truck along Gulf Boulevard, the hundred steps until I made it to the Beach Access trail and Beach Trail Drive, or to my own front door.

Once inside, I locked and deadbolted the ten-light glass-paned door, vowing to replace it with something more difficult to breach as soon as I could arrange it.

I'd gotten so used to the feel of Marco beside me nearly twenty-four seven, I'd allowed my mind to wander into the ridiculous depths, nitpicking and finding fault with something that had come to me like a miracle—a Navy Blue dream of a man who loved me so hard I might not have to worry about anything ever again.

Except someone, somewhere might be wanting to take all that away from me. I wouldn't make that mistake again. This could all be taken away just like that flash of lightning, just like what had befallen my sister, dying in the car accident along with her friends from school. How quickly things could change if I didn't protect this gift of life.

I vowed never to complain about any of my feckless reasoning about all the choices I was making. I would embrace those choices so hard they could never be torn even from my cold, lifeless fingers at the very end. I'd hang on and never, ever give up hope or take for granted my perfect life.

This isn't for you, Em. It's for me.

CHAPTER 2

I FELT SHANNON'S warm body purring next to me, spiking my libido and turning on all my senses. Even my fingertips craved the touch of her flesh as I reached over to gently crawl up the inside of her thigh—caressing the perfectly baby smooth of her body—as her hand gripped my wrist. She rolled over on her back, bent her knees, and pressed my palm and those wandering fingers against her sex, moaning as she helped me violate her.

"Tell me how it feels," I whispered. I kissed the side of her neck and squeezed her nether lips, causing her to arch up and present those perfectly formed breasts as my gift. "Give them to me, Shannon," I begged hoarsely.

She did as she was told, as she always did when I commanded she do something in bed. It wasn't me being overbearing; it was me showing her how much I needed the friction of my flesh against her soft pink parts, her long smooth parts, and the hairless parts of her belly, her rear, her forearms, and those long silky legs.

Her eyes were open as she arched farther. She placed her warm and slightly sweaty chest against mine, wrapping one leg up and over my hip.

She looked straight at me as I inserted my thumb again into her channel.

"Give it to me, Marco." She smiled and let her little pink tongue dart around her lips. I sighed at the perfect view of my lover in full arousal, longing for the salty taste of her sweet juices.

I inserted my thumb again, playing with her, mocking her

erotic impatience. She rubbed my fingers over her clit and forced my thumb and forefinger to squeeze the tiny nub, which made her squeal, throw her head to the side, and arch her pelvis up to rub against my belly button. Then she climbed over my hip and rubbed herself back and forth over my protruding hip bone.

With her arms pressed together, her blonde hair all a mess like I liked it, her breasts protruding seductively while she ground away on me, she whispered, "Make me come, Marco. I want you inside me."

I flipped her quickly on her back and impaled her, throwing her knee up over my shoulder as I rammed my cock deep, moaning with her. Her wet channel vibrated all around me and drew me in even deeper.

"Oh my God!"

"Yes?" My half smile was intended as a joke, but she was serious.

"You can't ever leave me. I want to walk around all day with you inside me. I want to stay in bed until the sun comes up tomorrow, and I still want you to be fucking me, making me sore, taking me any way you want while I still want more. Make me a rag doll, Marcos. I want to be exhausted, used, pleasured, and lit on fire."

"No problem, baby. Hang on so we can fly together. Give me just—"

And then I began to spill, which nearly set me in tears because I'd wanted to fuck her senseless, and now that dream was gone.

"I like it when you come fast. You know I do," she whispered.

And indeed, I did. She loved making me lose control. She loved showing me that there was no way in Holy Hell that I could ever resist her or wouldn't want to ravish her to oblivion. I'd fuck her while she laughed at my expense because I loved seeing her face as I did it. For, no matter how hard I tried to exert control, she was my better. She was the spark that lit me on fire every time. I would never get enough.

And in five minutes, with enough breathing exercises and

mental meditation, I'd be bigger and harder again, ever bigger and harder than the first time. And then I'd love that look on her face as I pierced her veil and surprised her.

IN THE SHOWER, I told her about my trip. Yes, I'd gotten the support I was looking for from Senator Campbell and two of his colleagues. I was guaranteed a quick review of the final plan by the Veterans Housing Board without a senate hearing, which would be a huge waste of time and cause months of delay. I was promised that they would intercede, if necessary, with county and city building officials who might make problems for me or who owed an allegiance to my ex, who had originally sent in her design that I fixed.

She was soaping off my back when she brought up the subject of her safety when I was gone.

"Something happen?"

She rubbed my back with the lavender gel she used on her body, which would not make my skin as smooth and smell as nice as hers, but I was okay with it. And then she rubbed more gel, her fingers barely smoothing over my back. Her non-verbal communication told me something was brewing, and I wouldn't like it. She was unhappy she'd made me aware of it too.

"No, silly. But I was just thinking, you know how I take those morning runs along the beach? I was wondering if perhaps I should get a permit to carry a gun. Or carry mace or something. Cat's claws, you know, for defense."

I turned, and her eyes were downturned, avoiding mine.

"What is it, Shannon?"

"I said it's nothing. My imagination, I guess. This time when you went away, I just got jumpy. I started seeing things or imagining—wondering how I would defend myself if someone came up behind me or jumped from the bushes. I've had so much on my mind with the summer plans and the wedding—"

"Which you don't have to do anything for. You are remembering that, right?"

"Yes. Yes. But there is the guest list, gathering everyone's addresses, picking out my dress, and writing our vows... unless you're going to use something you've found in a Navy manual somewhere."

That's when she finally looked up at me, her long lashes dripping with wet goodness, the innocence of her face a sweet mask over the powerful woman I knew lived inside. Her tempting little comment, needling me, making fun of my uniform code of conduct even as she reveled in breaking me down.

I pressed her against the tile of her little shower, suddenly grateful for the tight spot. "Tell me that again, but look at me this time," I whispered, glancing my hungry lips across hers as if I was breathing life into her soul.

When she smiled, hesitating to answer me back, I placed my hands under her jaw, tilted her head back, and kissed her long and hard. I wanted her wet and slippery. When we parted, her eyes were filled with tears.

"You overwhelm me, Marco," she said before I could ask. "Sometimes, I fear not having you." She looked at my biceps, palming my upper arm from shoulder to elbow joint and back again. The smooth and hairless mound of her sex slipped by my thigh, and its proximity to the root of my soul made my pecker vibrate.

"The same goes for me, sweetheart. I must go to sleep with cold towels wrapped around my waist. I run into walls and wake up with the biggest boner—even bigger than when I was in my twenties. I am a distracted, mess of a man who's without his mate—"

"The solution is easy, then. We'll never be apart. I mean it, Marco."

"Is that healthy?"

"You mean you couldn't carry on your business with your fat dick inside me?"

"Shannon, that's not nice..."

"I have a serious craving."

"Then let's fix it right now."

I whipped her around, bent her over, went to my knees. Before she could object, I had my tongue deep inside her cave, the water crashing down upon us both. I nibbled and sucked, ran her delicate lips through my canines, and accessorized her moans with some of my own. I sucked her bud by spreading her cheeks wide, searching for her most intimate bright pink pretty parts. I inserted my tongue, rolling it in and out, and added a thumb. Then I got to my feet and slid my cock deep inside her, one hand on her belly to hold her tight against me, the other keeping her bent over for optimum penetration.

With my thighs, I made a seat for her while she wrapped her lower legs and ankles around mine and forced herself against me, pushing against the tiled wall with her palms. The crescendo built, the water was going cold, and it mattered not one bit as she squealed, inhaled, then shattered all over me. I pumped furiously. She resisted and then began to shake, demanding, clutching around to my buttocks with one hand, at last holding firm against me until they both felt the delicious spurt of my seed.

It had begun to occur to me during these especially deep penetrations that we'd stopped using protection. I didn't think it was possible that I couldn't fill her belly with a thousand babies. And I'd love them all.

Her face was pressed against the now-cold tile as she started to giggle, like she'd been drinking. I cupped cold water and washed her sex with careful fingers.

"It's not going to work," she said.

"What?"

"I can't be fixed." She turned, her face flushed and rosy, red lips mesmerizing me. My heart hung on her every word, and that's exactly how attentive I intended to be.

"I don't want you to be fixed. I want you afflicted, craving me, so I know what you mean, Shannon. I can't be fixed either. I never want this to change."

"Then let's try not to be separated."

Oh, this again.

I was sure something had happened. I turned off the cold water, grabbed a white fluffy towel, wrapped it around her, and then carried her to the bedroom without allowing her to dry her hair. I dropped her onto the tussled sheets and pulled them up to her chin, unwrapping them from her legs. I sat, peering over her, still dripping wet, wanting to make her tell me what had happened.

"You brought up the safety issue, Shannon. Not me. If it will make you feel more secure, I'll have you apply for the CCW permit and enroll you in the course, and I'll weapons train you. We'll pick out your personal sidearm together. I'll make suggestions and you tell me what feels the most comfortable."

She smiled. "Thank you, Marco. That would mean a lot."

"So what brought all this on, Shannon?" I asked, hoping the sugar of her possible new weapon and training would sufficiently assuage her from keeping her barrier up.

She gulped air then began her story—a story I wasn't looking forward to hearing, but one I must hear, nonetheless.

"Two days ago, the day you left for D.C., I was imagining things like crazy. A big truck rumbled suddenly into the dog park where I was finishing up and parked. I saw the flare of a lighter behind the tint, but the windows were too dark for me to see the person. And when I came back and looked around, there was no evidence of the truck anywhere. I think it was just my mind playing tricks on me. Maybe with a conceal permit I'd not have those kinds of disturbing thoughts."

I was more concerned than I let on. "But think, Shannon. Was there a truck following you or not?"

"I thought so. But whoever it was drove off before I could see them."

"I meant, did he follow you along Gulf Boulevard or just when you got to the dog park?"

She shrugged. "I don't know the answer to that."

"So what made you *think* he was following you?"

"Because I hadn't been paying attention. I realized when I

heard and then saw him that he could have been following me earlier, but I never noticed it until the park. I'm sorry, Marco, but it's the truth."

I had to acknowledge her courage to admit her distraction. Anger boiled up inside my belly, but I knew it would completely end the conversation, or worse, end it with an argument. "What happened next?"

Her voice was quiet, timid like a little girl's at first. Then she spoke up, seeing me lean over and bend an ear.

"I thought I heard his footsteps on the wooden planks of the path."

Fucking pervert! Now I wasn't regretting the facts. I craved them so I could skin this moron alive and drag his carcass behind my Hummer all up and down the Florida coastline as a lesson to anyone else who would mess with my woman.

I did two silent box breathings and then spoke to her calmly. "So, Shannon, he *was* following you then, wasn't he?" I was irritated with Shannon's lack of specificity. She said she didn't see his face but that he smoked. The windows in the truck had all been blackened, a common occurrence in Florida. "Did anyone else see him?"

"I don't think so. This was like five-thirty in the morning, before sunrise."

"And you were off the beach and the beach trail."

"Yes."

"Why the hell would you go over to the dog park? There aren't lights there. No one should be there at that time of the day. It's asking for trouble, Shannon."

"I have no clue, Marco. It was just the place that came up next. As I already stated, I was thinking about the wedding, and the— the other stuff we talked about. I was going to come right home afterwards, before the sun rose, and get to the station near sunrise. That's always what I do."

"What other stuff?"

"It's not important now."

"Fuck's sake, it is." I saw her eyes flash wide. "Sorry. I want to know everything you were thinking and why."

"That's another conversation, Marco. And yes, we'll have it. But it doesn't have anything to do with the situation. It would be off track to go there."

She was hiding something, and I didn't like it. But I'd already gotten way more out of her than I'd expected. I breathed another couple of reps and felt my blood pressure calm, but my heart still pounded, my fists needing to punch and fight.

"Promise me you'll change your routine. No more running before sunrise." I knew she would be lying if she said yes.

"That's why I wanted to talk to you about personal carry or mace or something for protection."

"But why become someone's bait in the first place? Why tempt someone who might be looking for an opportunity thrill. Evil does exist, Shannon. That's just not smart."

She nodded, and because she was lying down, I could see the tears spill over her cheekbones into the pillow. I gently spread them over her beautiful face, sending the liquid into her hair with my thumbs, bent down, and kissed her.

"You are the most valuable thing in my life, Shannon. But I don't own you. That means you must make the kinds of choices that keep you safe, not do stupid things." I gripped her shoulders as she objected to my description.

"Remember that you prove by your actions whether or not you want to spend the rest of your life with me. You do what you do best. And trust me to do what I do. I promise to keep you safe, but you must promise to always use your head. That means when you're busy, you always have eyes at the back of your head, your ears must hear things you didn't before hear as patterns, things that we've seen and heard on the Teams. You must notice how people look at you and when they don't. You always check for multiple ways to get out of a situation, whether it's a meadow, a street, or a room. You have to determine what you have to break, who you have to punch or kick, and always understand that, if you're prepared, you will have the greatest advantage a woman can have."

"What's that?"

"They will underestimate you. You be prepared to deliver them a message they either will never forget or they'll never recover from. You do it without hesitation. You feel good when you do it. You use everything at your disposal, and you win."

CHAPTER 3

MY CONSTRUCTION CREW was delighted with the news that Senator Campbell and his committee were going to help troubleshoot some of the roadblocks we'd been having with the Pinellas County Planning Department concerning the Trident Towers. We went over the improved, final plans—or at least we hoped it would be the final version.

I explained to the group that I'd decided to scale back the size of the fitness center and instead open a PT office, especially for the permanently disabled veterans who were going to constantly need PT work with competent therapists in order to progress in their fitness and health goals. Many of these vets would not have the benefits to cover all the expenses of prosthetic and orthotic work, so the corporation was going to hire a staff orthotist at no charge to the residents. In this way, the gym and ancillary offices would serve as an in-home outpatient clinic for chronic bone and joint injuries, also enabling the vets to take training while remaining in their homes.

I could see that Shannon was in awe how much I cared about my former teammates and other servicemen and women who had sacrificed so much and received so little. She completely understood the community would help heal itself with the concept that we were all still on the same team, and always would be.

"Our ethos is, 'No man or woman left behind,'" I explained at the meeting. "I hope that this will be a model for future vet centers. I wish I had the money to build a hundred of them, and even that wouldn't be enough. These are not throwaway men and women. They are those who answered their highest calling—to serve their country. They serve regardless of religion or race, although the hours are long and dangerous and the pay not commensurate to what they gave up. These men and women are our heroes."

Every time I talked about the project, Shannon saw how straight I stood, how my chest expanded, and how tall I had become. Even with all the problems we'd encountered, my zeal and passion for it only increased.

"Can I ask you a question, Boss?" Rhea, now my newly titled Vice President and Construction Manager at Bone Frog Development, asked me. I'd lured the former president of an all-female construction crew in the Gulf Coast away with my grand ideas and ability to see them through.

"Shoot. What do you need to know?" I replied.

"Just where did you get the idea for this project? I mean, is this a charity, or are we going to make money here?"

"We're going to do both, to answer your second question first. I can't afford to do this as a charity, and I don't dare give it to some non-profit or government agency who will drain the cash as well as the inspiration for it. We're not managing people here. We're transforming people's lives. Veterans' lives."

"But she wants to know why," reminded Dax, Rhea's life partner and second in charge.

"Because it's my calling. Because I'm the one who can get it done. And by done, I don't mean 'check the boxes.' I mean, do it right. Create something that no one else has done before. I'm hoping that if people see what's possible—because people have no imagination for things—once they see it can be done, they'll help organize and back others. I want this idea to catch fire and expand beyond what I could ever do with my companies alone. Think of it as a pilot for a new series."

Watching Shannon study the faces of the group of Bone Frog Development employees, I could tell she was struck with the realization that I had created the most coveted and rare emotion possible: awe. Every face reflected their complete amazement at what had been proposed. Not one person had crossed arms, slouched shoulders, or a skeptical expression. I'd mesmerized the room into silence.

Admitting it to myself, I chuckled. "Well, don't everyone speak at once. You must have bigger questions than that." I shrugged, and in unison, the group politely laughed.

"Now here's where some of my concerns lie," I began again. "Part of this plan incorporates my mission to train the Sultan of Bonin's two sons in managing a large project like this, as a precursor to their African project, which we are helping them run."

Several people shifted uneasily in their chairs.

"Now, I don't know if I can ever whip them into shape. They've spent years being coddled, almost treated as the sultan's pets. And I don't want a word of this to get outside this room, either. Grounds for immediate termination, understood?"

The group followed my playful attitude, some smiling and shaking their heads while others only shaking their heads, "no". But everyone agreed to my rules.

"They are to be treated with respect. They are students of mine. Not my sons, not pampered princelings, they'll be normal twenty-year-old boys learning how to run a business. Their idea of buying and selling is using a credit card to get anything they wanted in life. But they've both done very well in school, have college degrees, and want to learn. This isn't being forced on them by anyone but me."

Again, the room erupted into chuckles and smiles.

"If they treat you without respect, you come straight to me. And yes, you can tell them they did so. Don't be afraid of them. They can't get you fired. Is that understood?"

Again, the team nodded agreement and mumbled to themselves.

"When do they start?" someone asked.

"They'll be here in two days. I'm waiting confirmation on their timing this afternoon." I took two long steps across the front of the room. "Here's another thing, assume they don't know anything. You show them everything you do. Pretend they are your replacements—and *once again!*—they are not your replacements but pretend that they are. You train them with everything you do. I'm going to hope that some of it sticks."

Rhea chuckled loudest. "Oh boy, it's going to be a long hot summer, Boss. I sure do hope you know what you're doing."

"You're allowed to swear, Rhea. This is our culture here, our country. They won't like it, so keep it at a minimum, if you can. Dax, you help her with that."

"Roger that, Boss Man!" Dax said, jumping to her feet. "I'll need help washing her mouth out with soap, but I'm game to try."

"Let's hope it doesn't come to that. Now. For your homework. I want you to give me a full assessment of where you feel the project's biggest problems are, in your opinion. What is going to be the most difficult hurdle to get over or take the longest to accomplish. I want these reports on my desk tomorrow morning. Nothing is more important today. This also means that if you think I need to hire another key person or you've observed someone on our team can't handle the workload without additional help, you state that. I want to eliminate as many obstacles and issues as possible. I want to train to be prepared for the unexpected."

"So, Top Dog, we get to make suggestions about you, too?" Forest Davis asked. Forest was an expert drone developer and explosives expert. He also knew everything there was to know about poisons and knives, as well as customizing some of their firepower for missions in hostile locations. He had been embarrassed to tell the team that he'd posed for the cover of a romance novel. Shannon had thought that was pretty cool, but he got a lot of ribbing for it.

"Absolutely, you can give me some of your black sarcasm. Go ahead and see how far you can get kicking my butt. But be damned sure, I'll listen," I answered. "I might veto it, but I promise you I'll listen."

Everyone laughed at that one.

"Well, all right then. Here's one for you. You need to give this little lady here some work. I mean, I can guess you guys work pretty hard at home, if you know what I mean."

Everyone chuckled. Shannon blushed, and I adopted a scowl.

"Watch it, Forest…"

"No worries, my man. I was just thinking she looks good here, and I'd like to see her give us some good publicity, maybe sweet talk her way into an interview about what we're doing and drum up some community support, like she did when Rebecca tried to highjack this little opera."

Most everyone agreed. I could see Shannon was delighted.

"Marco, I could write a series of press releases, since I know the look and feel of them, how to do them. I could perhaps get you some interviews with other stations outside Tampa, so it wouldn't interfere with my bosses here. Station affiliates. It would expand our brand and perhaps cull more support."

"I like that, Shannon," I said, giving her a wink. I swung my head over to focus on Forest. "You're way smarter than I sometimes give you for, Forest. Thanks!"

"I love to be underestimated."

Nigel, who was from Edinburgh, suggested they could even get an interview through his sister's connections there. "She'd love to interview you lot. Always pestering me about the famous Marco Gambini and what he's up to," he said, with the brogue Shannon loved.

Nigel stuttered a bit and added, "And of course, the mysterious woman who bagged that famous playboy. Well, Shannon, she'd love to interview you too!"

I saw Shannon blushing for the second time today.

"We'll set that up, Nigel, thanks."

"Oh, I think it would be so romantic to do a piece about the new house you're building, don't you?" Karin Atkin asked Shannon. "We could put her up in one of Marco's properties and give her the tour. I'll bet she'd consider it an experience of a lifetime!"

"She would at that, dearie," Nigel agreed. "Her nickers would be in a bunch for weeks afterward. I keep telling her about this place. She might never go home, and me mum would have my tail for that. But it happens." He shrugged while the team laughed.

"I'll get you my list of things I'd need and personnel, Marco, by the morning," Shannon smiled up at me, which caused my bushy greying eyebrows to raise.

"You do that, my love, and you'll get a gold star," I whispered and then winked again, while running my finger along Shannon's spine, sending a pleasurable zing of electricity from the base of Shannon's neck to her toes.

The meeting was adjourned. Dax and Rhea came up to speak to me in private, so Shannon stepped discretely away.

"Hey, Shannon, don't go slinking off. You can hear this too," barked Rhea.

"What gives? Hope this isn't a resignation, because…"

"Relax, Boss," Rhea said as she spread her hands to the sides and let her shoulders raise. "We have a delicate matter to discuss. And, well," she looked at Dax, "we want your blessing."

"What the hell have you two cooked up?" I sounded angry, but I was playing with them.

"Dax and I want to get married. All legal-like. You've been very good to us. We've made good money, and we're ready to buy a house, and, well, we just wanted to be legit." Rhea searched Shannon's face as well as mine.

"You already are legit," I said to them. "You love each other, and everyone knows it. You don't have to get married to…"

"Then why are you doing it, Marco?" asked Dax.

I stepped back, clearly blindsided by the question. I examined my hands and then looked up. "Touché, Dax. You're right." And then to Shannon, I instructed, "Cancel the wedding. We don't need any paperwork or wedding to show the world we love each other."

Shannon froze in place but then saw the twinkle in my eye.

"You know, Boss, you're a fuckin' asshole," shouted Rhea so loud some of the other team turned around to watch. But then she grabbed me and gave me a hug. "I'm not taking no for an answer. We want you to be the one to give Dax away. And I'd like to walk down the aisle with the lovely Shannon!"

"But that's reserved for your dad," Shannon objected, but I could tell, inside she was dancing.

"Fuck that bastard. That sonofabitch doesn't deserve that honor. He's completely out of my rolodex. But I have some nieces and a few nephews who might come, and we'd like to make it a simple, elegant party. Nothing fancy. And could we use the Towers building site? Just make it a beach party. Invite some of the would-be owners and tenants?"

"Sounds like a lovely idea, Rhea. I'd be honored." I had extricated myself from Rhea's strong body slam and bowed to her respectfully as if she were Queen for a Day. Dax stood to the side, her hands clasped, tears running down her face.

"Awesome!" Rhea hugged her partner. "We're doing this, Dax. I told you he'd be good about it."

I added one more condition.

"But let's get the final permits, okay? I don't want to count our chickens before they roost. I sure as hell wouldn't want you to be disappointed to have to cancel your big day just based on some bureaucrat's say so. We need to remove that hurdle first. Then it's all out, okay?"

CHAPTER 4

I TOLD SHANNON I had plans for us for dinner.

"Oh really? Where to?"

"You'll see. Something special."

"I should go home and change. Is it fancy, a fancy restaurant?"

I loved surprising her. "*Very* fancy. But you're dressed fine."

Shannon looked over the sundress and sandals she was wearing and frowned. "I wish I could wash my hair and put on clean undies. I've been sweating all day."

"It makes no difference to me."

"Well, it might make some difference to the other guests. I smell like a road crew member."

I pulled her to me. "Stop it, Shannon. I get some say here. And I say you're perfect. Besides," I checked my watch, "we don't have a lot of time left."

"What time is the reservation?"

I checked my watch again. "7:21."

Shannon wrested free. "Stop making fun of this, Marco. No one makes a reservation for 7:21. Come on. Quit pulling my leg."

"I do. I do a lot of things other people don't. Just humor me, go freshen up in the bathroom if you want, but we need to be outta here in like ten."

"It's going to take us that long to get there? Tell me we're not flying or something."

"No, but that gives me a good idea for next time." I placed my hands on her shoulders, turned her around, and demanded,

"March!" directing her to the ladies' room, which was stocked with towels and deodorants. I knew Shannon stored a couple of lipsticks and some perfume in the cabinet for occasions as this.

While she was occupied, I chose a tube from my office and slipped it into the back of my Hummer. Folded next to it were three large Turkish muslin beach towels. Shannon stepped out, and we were on our way.

"At least tell me where."

"You'll see."

She leaned back into the seat, resigned that her inquiries would yield the same result as the previous ones: nothing.

"I got you registered for Wyatt's permit class. And if you're interested, his daughter does a women's self-defense class. Just let me know, and I'll get you registered for that one too."

"Thanks, Marco. You know this guy, Wyatt?"

"Very well. Marine sharpshooter, even tried out for the Olympics. He was one of their best instructors and, later, joined the Tampa police force where he's taught classes nearly his whole career. Now he's retired, so it's his full-time gig. Wyatt's a smart fellow who teaches you all the things you need to know and all the things you don't know to ask. You'll have a healthy respect for firearms when you're done."

"So next is picking out one. Is that it?"

"Yup, I was thinking we could go look tomorrow if we get done in time. Your classes don't start for three weeks, plenty of time to get your ammunition if it's not in stock. We'll want to get you something that won't be too difficult to arm or expensive, like a 9mm. Some sidearms are great, but the rounds are scarce or overly popular right now."

I turned down Gulf Boulevard, passing the dog park where Shannon had the encounter with the man in the pickup. I noticed that she searched the parking lot.

"Does it still scare you?" I asked.

"Not really. Like you said, it wasn't a very good idea. I'm not going there in the dark and by myself again."

"Do you think you could recognize the truck if you saw it again?"

She shook her head. "Maybe the sound, but then, diesel trucks always sound the same. It had a deep, heavy idle."

"Did you see the grill? Could you tell if it was a Chevy or Ford? Or was it something like this?"

"Not a Hummer. I would have recognized the shape. Even the pickups are different. No, it was a big heavy-duty truck with big tires. And I think it was a four-door model. But that's it."

I turned down one of the avenues to Beach Trail Drive.

"Where are you going? Are we…?"

"Yup. Going to the lot."

"For dinner?"

"I hope so. I paid a boatload for it. We'll see."

Beach Trail ended, and then a dirt road wound around the sand dunes, at last coming through the green foliage to the flat graded plateau prepared for their new home on the five private acres.

I scanned the horizon, now turning purple and orange with golden clouds crossing the horizon and slowly changing shape. In the center of the leveled pad was a table and two benches. The table had a white tablecloth on it, adorned with a bouquet of red roses and a silver champagne bucket with a bottle chilling inside. Surrounding the table was a circle of hurricane lamps, lighted, which showed us the way. I was pleased to notice the red cube food transport box, keeping my special order both warm and chilled.

"This is just beautiful," Shannon gasped as I turned off the engine and we looked at the display in front of us. "How did you do this?"

"Well, obviously, I didn't do this. I hired someone else to do it, because I was with you, right?"

"Oh, Marco, you amaze me how you think of these things."

"Good. Mission accomplished then. Let's get out before it gets cold."

One thing that I loved about the Gulf area was that, even near sunset, the air was still warm, and even if there was a breeze, it was a warm one. Waves crashing in the background infused excitement and unpredictability.

I opened the door for Shannon and led her to the table. Then I went back and brought the blankets and the tube, placing them beside the table. Shannon stood facing the dying sun, her hair blowing in ringlets behind her. She turned.

"I don't think I'll ever tire of this view. I love it from my little place, but from here, with all the privacy around us, it's spectacular."

I uncorked the champagne and brought her a glass. We touched, kissed, then sipped the light pink liquid.

"To happily ever afters. To new beginnings. To imagining and then creating miracles. That's our life now, Shannon. This is what every day will be like from now on."

Her face was lined with tears. She sipped her champagne and leaned into me. "I think this is going to be my best day. We used to play that game when I was little."

"I remember Em telling me that."

"Best company. Best sunset. Best dream come true. Best everything."

"Yes. I'm marrying the girl of my dreams. I will forever be grateful for Em bringing us together. I hope that's something you can embrace."

"I'm getting there," she said.

I pulled my arm around her waist. "Are you hungry?"

"Starved."

I led the way back to the table in the middle of the circle of fire. Pulling out the red insulated box, I unzipped the top layer and placed a chilled platter with a dozen oysters swimming in lemon slices. I handed one shell to her and took one for myself.

"Lemon?" I asked as I held a slice over her oyster.

"Of course."

Having properly garnished the half shells, we both slurped

them down. Shannon took another sip of champagne and then reached for another.

The tabletop was still lighted with the lamps all around them. Next on the menu was lobster bisque. The main course was a perfectly poached salmon, still warm, with fresh buttered green beans, and a long grain rice pilaf with pine nuts. Two delicate green salads with a lemony dressing were individually chilled and wrapped as an accompaniment.

For dessert, we had chocolate mousse garnished with golden raspberries.

I was pleased with the presentation and made a note to ask the team to use this caterer again for any of our special events coming up.

I picked up a hurricane lamp and one of the blankets and the tube. "Shall we sit in the living room?"

"Where is it?"

"Here, see for yourself. See if you can tell me where it is." I held the tube to her, and she stretched out the house plans in front of me. With the aid of the lamp, she walked several paces and then pointed to an area. I spread the blanket there and invited her to sit down.

"You approve? You like the living room here?"

"I'd like to study the plans better, but yes, it matches what we talked about. I wanted the living room to be open to the coastline, to watch the sunsets. This is perfect!"

We sat side by side, arms wrapped around each other, continuing to watch the sky turn darker and darker, and then the stars began to come out. Remnants of huge puffy clouds still glowed pink in the afterglow of the sunset against the new night sky.

"Ready for more?"

"Absolutely."

I stood, helped her up, then took the lamp and pointed to the plans. "How about the master bedroom now? We'll have to pretend we're on the second floor."

"So it's back here, because there's a deck off the master suite, which is over the living room. I think the bedroom would start here." She pointed back about twenty feet.

"And where would be the bed?" I asked.

"I'd say against the back wall, so it would have a perfect view of the ocean in the morning and the sunset at night."

"Where?" I asked again.

"Right here." She pointed to one spot, and I lay the blanket down then placed two hurricane lamps on either side. I added another blanket to the corner and then invited her to sit.

"How's the bed?" I asked.

"A little firm, but nice." She linked fingers with mine and leaned into me, placing a kiss on my mouth that lingered. "I can still taste the oysters and the lemon."

"And I think I tasted a little bit of mousse as well."

"Yes."

"Shall we try out the bed?" I asked.

"You mean?"

"Of course. I want to remember this evening for the rest of my life."

"So do I. I see you've brought another blanket."

"So when you're naked you won't be cold. I want to see you naked on my new bed, Shannon. I want to make love to you in our new bedroom. I want to start the memories before the house is built. What do you think of my plan?"

"I think,"—she crawled over my lap and began pulling her dress over the top of her head—"if you don't get me out of these clothes, I'm going to burn up."

I knew I'd never forget this night nor the way she needed me under the twinkling stars, and as she shattered beneath me, I whispered, "I love you more every day, Shannon. You bring the magic. You're the talisman. You're the one who's saved me—you've saved us both."

CHAPTER 5

I WAS TROUBLED again as I drove to the station in Tampa. Marco had never asked me, but I still hadn't done what I'd promised him I'd do, and that was to quit. Even with the suggestion of my helping the team out with interviews and promo features like engaging other stations, producing podcasts, reaching out to my friends in the industry, all of which I'd mentioned in my report on Marco's desk, he didn't ask me about it.

I knew he'd eventually find out. All the mention of my PR work didn't trigger in him a second opinion that maybe I should hold off quitting until sometime in the future. No, on the contrary, he made notations about what he wanted me to do in the upcoming weeks and even mentioned I would be spending more time with him in this process, which of course thrilled me. But it still left me that black hole. I had to face the fact that he was expecting me to quit. I'd given him my word, and that meant I needed to either do it or come clean about my avoidance and have a damned good reason why.

I hated all these back-and-forth things bouncing around my brain. I wished I had the focus and deliberative skills Marco had. "Life would be so much easier," I whispered to myself while driving across the Causeway that led from the beach communities on the island and the mainland of Florida—Tampa my destination.

My lesson of the other morning still gurgled in my stomach, with how close I might have been to a negative situation. My attempts to downplay it were a no-go with Mr. Super-mind-reader-and-all-round-God-Marco. He could see through my little ruse as if I wrote it on six-foot posters in front of him.

He told me it was because of his training, his practice. It had been drilled into him. He practiced mind control, box breathing, meditating every morning (when I didn't interrupt him) and every night. He told me he was gaining back the strength he had when he was in his peak.

"You are at your peak, Marco. Just look at you," I'd said when he explained this to me.

"Nope. Not even close. My awareness isn't what it used to be. There's a big difference too. You must feel the danger, and trust me, it's all around you all the time. There's always evil. We want to think everything is good and happy, fairies and such. But those are brief glimpses of a world that could be but isn't for very long. We grab it and enjoy it when we can. Other times, we embrace the suck. We adapt, train for the unexpected, so we aren't caught off guard with no solutions."

And that's exactly what had happened the other morning.

I was so unlike him in so many ways, stubborn just like Em, but neither of us ever dwelled in a place of expecting evil and danger. We both had lived in a bubble, that HEA bubble where if the two of us obeyed the rules, were good to people, our lives would turn out to be picture perfect.

But Em's accident and death was a perfect example of an HEA gone horribly wrong. And that day at her funeral, when Marco bent down and handed me that flower from Em's grave, looking right into my 12-year-old eyes, I knew he would forever be my warrior, my savior, and the man I was destined to be with. If that meant learning how to shoot a gun, box breathing, meditating, and mind control, so be it. I'd do whatever it took, give up whatever I had to, to be with this man.

Even my job at the station.

I pulled into the parking lot, already flooded with vehicles. It was going to be another Florida scorcher, something I still had difficulty adjusting to. The island was usually a bit cooler, with the breezes we got there sometimes, like a gentle mother whispering that the oppressive heat wouldn't last long. In California, I could leave my windows open at night and the whole house would be cool by early morning. But many summer days in Florida, the temperature needle, even in a rainstorm or hurricane, sometimes never moved.

Though I heard birds barking back and forth at each other from the forty-foot palm trees lining the station entrance, the pavement I walked across seemed to hiss.

Once inside the lobby, which had recently installed a waterfall feature that gave the main floor a chlorine odor, I passed security, nodding to the two female guards manning the reception desk. I took the elevator to the fifth floor, where the programming and accounting offices were located, and inquired about setting an appointment with Jared Newsome. They promised some time with him after my broadcast. I knew he wouldn't arrive until well after seven, just as I was about to go on the air. Today, they were giving me a feature to read, hooking up with a local reporter giving updates on the red tide affecting sea life on the island, as well as the all-important tourist trade.

I took the elevator up a floor and came to the production level where the studio was located. I walked toward the Green Room, stopping by Sandy's makeup station to have my face painted. A new script had been left there on the counter for me to review before I went live.

"OK, I gonna make you look real pretty so you can tell that story about all those poor dead fish."

"Yes." I sighed. "You've been reading my mail?"

"Well, God yes. Gotta have some perks of working here. Those pictures are disgusting. I'm gonna give your fans something pretty to look at."

Sandy began spraying my hair with dry shampoo and doing a quick curl with the iron.

"Bear in mind there are going to be live shots from the scene.

We only use these when the feed doesn't work. You do know that."

"Like I said, those poor dead fish. Nobody cares about the fish lying on the beach stinking up things. It gives the little one's nightmares, not very romantic for couples strolling hand in hand by moonlight."

"I agree with you there," I added.

"And where's Greenpeace? But no, you kill a couple of whales or a dolphin or if a Croc takes a toddler and, OMG, you'd think the world came to an end. It's like those salamanders in California. Tiger something. My sister said they practically shut down all housing developments in Bakersfield over those little things nobody would ever see. Must look at them with special lights at night. They threw themselves at police cars and chained themselves in front of the EPA in Sacramento, yet these fishes?" She shrugged. "Nobody cares. They just want them outta here."

"Good summer job for some."

"Are you kidding? You know the guy who picks up dog poop in all the Pinellas County dog parks makes about sixty grand a year! Can you believe that?"

"What are you going to do? Can't have that stuff everywhere."

"They want dogs to be able to poop all over places, let fish die on the beaches because someone kills all the sea grass by dumping phosphates into the gulf, but oh boy, you kill those salamanders, and you lose your right to have a house. I think this place is hella mixed up."

"You know, Sandy, one day I'm going to interview you, and then you can tell them what's truth. *Life of Sandy* and all your past adventures."

"Oh God, no! I don't want any of my old boyfriends coming back. They'd paddle from Cuba and show up at my doorstep if you do that. Very embarrassing for the kiddos, you know?"

"Well, I think you're a treasure. It's the world's loss. We should be hearing from people who have lived outside the U.S., people who appreciate freedom."

"Oh, they do in Cuba. They just can't tell anyone." She smiled, her mind lost in thought as she hummed a little lullaby in Spanish, moving her hips and remembering something pleasant.

"You miss it sometimes?"

"Yes and no. I miss the fictionalized version I came away with as a young girl. I don't know what it's really like, but each year, I remember the rolling parties when we used to roll the tobacco with our mothers, swat flies, and man the fans, while our overseer read stories to us. Julio Ortega. He'd been a famous fighter back in the days before the big war. Came home with one eye, and he still read to us. He was very handsome with his dark moustache, his white Fedora hat, and his cigar. We sang together. Some of us little girls danced and made our mothers laugh. The purge and the revolution were not good for our family. But before then, it was paradise. Maybe it will be again."

I always loved talking to Sandy. I also wondered what her real name was, suspecting the name was related more to a beach term than an American girl call sign.

Sandy pulled my plastic smock off and then nearly jumped. "I forgot. Your lipstick. I'm feeling orange today. How about you?"

"I could go for orange. Deep orange, though."

"Perfect with your blue."

During the broadcast, Clarence Thompson, the evening anchor, was filling in for the new morning anchor, Sylvia Torres, who announced she was pregnant with her first child about two months after she was hired. Several of my colleagues argued the spot should be given to me, since most at the station believed that Sylvia knew about her pregnancy when she was hired and was using them all.

But I had been grateful I might be given a morning time slot, which would enable me to be home with Marco at night. Until now.

Clarence's face went from a sour disposition to outright disgust, appearing to nearly vomit as the pictures of the hundreds, if not thousands, of dead fish bloating in the hot Florida sun came up. Their eyes were hollowed out by sea birds, tiny crabs, and flies, which were everywhere. Even some stingrays and unusual sting-ray-like prehistoric fish with long rat tails washed up that I had never seen before.

The area reporter explained matter-of-factly that the fish ate the red algae or didn't have sea glass to hide in or devour, depending on their species, due to a release of approved chemicals that were supposed to be safe for human swimmers but killed the grass.

Clarence went through two glasses of water, the last one shaking in his gnarled hand as he raised it up to his face, studded with age spots and hair plugs. He took several deep breaths and was caught on camera doing one, which would cause a scene after the show was over. Clarence would no doubt try to get the camera-man fired for having "shit for brains," which was the most common adjective he used.

"Well, Rob," I began, "thanks for that detailed report. I guess I won't be eating in any fish restaurants anytime soon, although—"

A noise on the other side of the podium caught my attention. Even the cameraman heard it and focused in for a headshot of Clarence Thompson throwing up all over his desk with white chunks of whatever he had for breakfast—probably oatmeal—sticking and dripping from his red tie.

I LOOKED FOR Jared Newsome, TMBC's Program Director, as I was taking off my equipment and handing it to the tech on duty. I expected him to be waiting in the dark wings, stoically watching me perform with his arms crossed and his glasses shining in the dim light, not revealing his expression.

But he wasn't anywhere on the production level, so I went downstairs to Floor Five, turned the corner, and nearly crashed into Bunny Copperfield, the evening anchor gunning for Clar-ence's job. In fact, I had recently heard that Bunny was starting the rumors again about the older man's hands and suggestions. Clarence was stupid, especially in this day of sexual harassment, but I didn't think he was that stupid. One of these days—and it would take something more than a vomit on air—he would do something, and his career would be over. It was the price he would pay for not paying attention to the fact that while the world had moved on, he hadn't. Now his behavior, once deployed in poor taste, was something an attorney could extract a huge sum from. He didn't see it, and I wondered if he did if he wouldn't care anyway.

I bounced right off Bunny's enormous chest, which left me covered in a cloud of perfume that made my nostrils itch. Instead of reacting, all I could do was sneeze.

"So sorry, Bunny. I wasn't paying attention. That sneeze was a whopper," I lied.

"Hmph. You could hurt someone. Try paying attention, or perhaps walking more like a lady than a pirate's second in command?"

The veiled reference to Marco was kind of funny, even though her voice was laced with venom. Of all the people at the station, I trusted Bunny least of all.

Jared's door was still open, and he was standing, no doubt having just said goodbye to Bunny.

"Hey, Shannon. Sorry I didn't get up there this morning. I heard we had quite a Red Cross moment."

I rolled my eyes. "I was just glad we had socially distanced the desks, or I would be going home to change."

Jared pointed over his shoulder to the door that led to his private bathroom. "You could always use my shower. Anytime, Shannon. Anytime."

"Oh, please. Haven't you gotten tired of that, Jared? It never worked on me; it never works on anybody."

"I guess that's why you're safe to just play around with. Nothing meant by it. Don't be so prickly."

Checking my insides, I admitted my nerves for what I had to tell him were mixing things up, but I easily reeled it all in, took a deep breath, and began.

"May I sit down?"

"Absolutely." He pointed to a chair in front of his desk. He slung his right hip and thigh on the edge of the desk and leaned against it, rather than taking his rightful place behind. "What's on your mind?"

"I've decided to leave the station."

Jared stood up, hands on his hips. "What did you say?"

"I'm quitting."

"But you can't—"

"Yes, I can, and I'm going to."

"But you have a contract to fulfill. Have you forgotten that?"

"No, but that doesn't matter. I'll buy it out. And if you get nasty with this, I can always throw some dirt on Clarence. Then you can get rid of both of us."

"But I don't want to get rid of you. I was just thinking of giving you Sylvia's job during her leave. You've been wanting an anchor position. Shannon, your timing sucks."

"Marco is so busy with the Trident Towers, and we'll be going to Africa next year to start that project for the sultan. It's going to require I be available to lend a hand. And I want to do it, Jared. My priorities have changed."

"What if I doubled your salary and, say, let you go in six months? Can we arrange that?"

"Why are you so interested in giving me a shot suddenly? And do you really think money is the way to get me to stay? That was never my goal, even before I met Marco."

"I just don't want to lose you. Getting hard to find good talent. All the interns we've hired have quit, either because of Clarence or Bunny. And Bunny just gave me an ultimatum to get rid of Clarence. I'm going to do it, or I'll have to let Bunny go. Either one is going to be very sticky. You're like the one I can count on. I need you, Shannon. I really do."

"But this isn't my life any longer. I mean, don't get me wrong, it was my life. I was so looking forward to having years here, but compared to what Marco has planned, I just couldn't pass up that chance to work on these things with him. And we'll be married."

"Well, I wasn't going to ask you to give that up. I'm not totally insane. Aren't you afraid you're not doing what you want to do? It's all for him. You're getting sucked into his world. It never was yours."

I smiled. He was good but not that good.

"You're right. When I first discussed it with Marco, I reacted a bit to the idea of quitting. Yes, I wanted my piece of the pie all my own. But look what I'd be giving up doing that. Don't you think, after years of hard work, I'd look back and say, 'You should have gone for the brass ring. You settled for second.'"

"But it's your ring. Your idea. Your vision, not Marco's. And working at this TV station is far from second. It's a huge market and a real chance to advance in the industry. You know this. Surely that has to count for something."

"But I have found a place for me inside his organization. Do you know how come I know?"

"Go ahead. I can see I'm losing this argument."

"It's because I've found a place in his heart. I love the idea of being in his shadow, having him protect and cherish me. I don't see that as anything lesser than running my own timeslot on a TV station in Tampa. It might be the world to you, but it's not for me. There's more out there. I just didn't realize it until I fell in love with him. And, yes, I thought I could do both. But I can't, Jared. Not really."

Jared stood, walked around to the back of the desk, and took his chair. "How about just giving me time to find a replacement?"

"I don't think so."

He was good at changing the subject. "I'll bet that wedding is going to cost more than you'd earn in ten years here. Hard to compete with that kind of firepower."

"This isn't a competition. It's a choice. A chance at a glorious, adventurous life with the man I love. And, by the way, you're getting invited to the wedding."

"Oh my. I have nothing to wear."

"Do you have swim trunks and flip-flops?"

"You know I do. Not used much these days, but—"

"And your expenses will be paid—you'll get to stay in a real palace and bathe on a pink sand beach. Imagine that."

He shrugged. "Doesn't thrill me if I don't have a job to come home to."

"They'd fire you over taking a few days to go celebrate in a sultan's palace on a pink sand beach, all expenses paid?"

"Spite and envy are dangerous when you work for a female owner of your TV station."

"Nonsense. Besides, that's not just a female trait. Everyone has a little bit of that in them. We're the ones who get blamed for it, that's all. So don't come then. See how that sets with you. Tell that to your grandkids. Tell them what you passed up. See how interesting that will sound to them."

"You gotta allow me a little wallowing. The two people I don't want are fighting over everything. The one I do want is leaving. Let's face it, I'm screwed."

"It's not that bad, Jared, and you know it. Are you really trying?"

"Trying? I'm trying harder to keep out the fruits and nuts. You wouldn't imagine the whack jobs I have coming in here. They say such stupid things. 'Oh, my grandmother thinks I'm so photogenic and she always pictures me on TV or the movies!'" he said in a starlet tone of voice. "Or guys with facelifts, blonde hair, and horrible teeth implants who are beyond their years, making me wear my sunglasses all the time their teeth are so bright. I'm wondering where all the normal people are."

"You forget, this is Tampa."

"So?"

"I think Florida attracts 'whatever goes' type of people right now. Probably won't be that way forever. You just must dig a little harder. I'd lay down the law with Clarence about the interns. And Bunny, Jared, she's not that talented. You know this, right?"

"If I fire her, would you stay on?"

It was a tempting proposal. But I had made up my mind. Before I could answer, Jared came up with another proposal.

"How about you give me just six months? I'll double your salary for six months, and during that time, I'll fire Bunny. But we can't tell anyone, okay? That will give me time to get a replacement and a good HR attorney. This was your big break, Shannon. Couldn't you find it in your heart to have a little compassion for me, the one who gave you that break? I've always treated you fairly. I just don't have the billions behind me or the body of a Greek god."

"Those aren't the reasons, and you know it."

"Find me a Wonder Woman, Shannon. I want a life like yours."

I giggled at that. "You're being silly."

"I need someone like that in my life."

I sat up straight then leaned over on the desk and stared into his eyes. "She's out there, Jared. And while you're being all miserable and envious or whatever else, she might be overlooking you, because she's looking for the same thing. People who are special don't just fly in the office window one day. You must work to attract them. Focus on what you do have, not what you don't. You'll have more takers than you can handle."

Jared wiggled his eyebrows. "I can handle a lot. So that's all I must do, make myself attractive? I thought you went after Marco. At least that's the story I was told."

I stopped at that. He was right. "Yes, I did. But there was a backstory, and that backstory was solid. Besides, I wasn't going after him to 'get' him. I wanted to see the man Emily fell in love with. I wanted to see if it was real or if I was just imagining it all. You forget, I heard lots of stories growing up. I felt like I knew him first."

He stared at me, nodding his head, perhaps afraid to say something I'd object to, so he kept quiet. It was a smart move.

I continued. "Make this place, this environment an attractive, visionary place to work. Get rid of the dead wood, the people who step on dreams."

"Clarence."

"No, Bunny."

"She's aggressive, I'll give her that."

"She's a witch, Jared. And Clarence is wounded. He's a bird with a broken wing. He's not a bad person. He's just forgotten that he has value and worth. Make him Superman. You'll find your Wonder Woman in due time, Jared. Maybe you already know her."

"I'm never going to be able to explain this conversation to a soul. I'm embarrassed to say I had this conversation with you. But thank you, Shannon. So we have a deal?"

At the risk of getting some flack at home with Marco, I agreed to three months only. Besides, there were two golden coins in the basket Jared was offering me. First, I could finally be around to see Bunny fired, like she deserved. And second, maybe I could give enough counseling to Clarence Thompson to save his career. Neither one of them were about money nor my career, really.

It was about justice and seeing justice done. And people getting what they deserved. Maybe Marco would understand.

Just maybe.

CHAPTER 6

"**H**EY, BOSS, WE got someone from the Planning Department who says he wants to see you," Rhea said as she opened the glass door to my office.

I hoped it was good news, since I usually had to chase down officials when I needed signoffs on projects. Him coming over to the Trident office was going to save me a boatload of time.

A handsome man with a Hollywood smile entered. He was about forty, trim, with dark hair and piercing blue eyes. His smile disturbed me. I could smell a shark a mile away. It wasn't just the cologne, the pinky ring, and the custom-tailored suit that set off alarms; it was the icy cold smile trying to disguise itself as "friendly." The man had the tenacity and deliberate movements of a well-trained serial killer. Nails buffed, shoes polished, no wrinkles or creases out of place on his white shirt under the shiny navy-blue suit.

And then his voice cinched it.

"Sorry to come barging in here, Mr. Gambini," he said in a slightly Eastern European accent, but I wasn't sure.

I extended my hand for the shake, which also confirmed my suspicions since the man nearly liberated me from his fingers until I twisted his wrist at an awkward angle, as if examining the expensive watch at the base of the man's hand, which caused a slight crack in one of the little bones and caused the man some pain. I was sure of that.

"I'm a great admirer of a man who wears the finest watches,

Mr.—"

"Sivic. This is Theopolis Sivic." Rhea stared down at the card and frowned but continued, "Independent Regional Planning Director."

"Ah, private contractor. You are not a county employee then?"

"No, I have more authority," Sivic said coolly as he withdrew his hand and tried not to show the pain he was experiencing.

I knew I'd won round one, but a wounded bear was always twice as dangerous.

The gentleman straightened his spine, pressed his shoulders back, and shook his arms to allow the fine fabric of his suit to readjust unwrinkled. He pulled on his cuffs, one at a time, as if he was trimming fat on a good steak, inhaled, and stared back at me.

Challenge accepted, asshole.

I counted five for his box breathing and let the gentleman make the first move. I'd be ready.

"I have been retained by the City of Belleair Beach on behalf of her citizens."

Yeah, I'll bet you're careful with the ladies. You're still an asshole.

"I've been asked to look into the allegations that certain liberties have been taken with the change in plans for your Trident Towers project—contracts that involved local workers that will not now be honored in favor of construction crews from out of the area. Your approval and contract with the city states—"

"Excuse me, how do you know what my contract and development agreement states? That information is supposed to be confidential."

"Ah, yes, but that doesn't apply in the case of fraud or misuse of public funds. You've been given a density bonus, allowing you to build an additional twenty-three units added on your latest plan. But it's a conditional approval. It provides for the provision that you do your best to hire local contractors—"

"They are local. You're mistaken."

"But we have it—"

"I don't care where you have it or how you carry it. You're simply wrong."

"Would you please demonstrate to me why?"

"I don't have to. This doesn't concern me, and you've illegally obtained copies of my development plan. I don't even know if this card," I tossed it on the desk, "is legitimate."

"I see. So you are going to make this a fight." His eyes searched mine dangerously. The man was not only slimy and cunning, but he was also mean. I saw one telltale scar on the bridge of his nose, which looked like an injury not quite repaired seamlessly. His blue orbs begged for a physical confrontation. They twinkled, almost iridescent, anxious for action.

"I have no reason to fight you. I have no reason to pay any attention to you. Get out of my office immediately, or I'll do my cop buddies a favor and toss you out myself."

Rhea was no stranger to yelling and anger, but her eyes were wide, her mouth dropping to her chest as she looked between the two men both itching to prove themselves. Behind her, a room full of my team had stopped whatever they were doing mid-motion and looked equally disturbed.

I wanted to smile at her to give her some confidence but didn't want to take his eyes off Mr. Sivic. But he saw the room out of the corner of his eye and noticed the lack of motion, the phones going unanswered, as if some God had stopped all time in its tracks while Sivic and I were still breathing.

Sivic was going to speak when something happened I did not expect. Rebecca sauntered in through the office, looking right and left with casual distain at workers who, if they knew her, hated every cell in her body. She wore a bright orange ruffled dress knee-high, with little multicolored abstract shapes dotting all over the fabric, as it swayed easily with the movement of her hips. Her very long legs were fully exposed to her mid-thigh when she stepped forward due to a large slit on either side of the front panel. Her fingernails and toes were orange this time and matched her new hair color: Lucille Ball red.

She slipped her lithe body next to Sivic's, delicately pushed her arm through the crook of his right elbow, and leaned into him so I could see Sivic's upper arm remained buried in her breasts. She even gave a little shameless moan.

How in the world could I have ever latched on to this vampire? What was I thinking? Oh yes, I wasn't thinking. I was looking for intensity, something to obliterate the pain.

She was repulsive to me, and I didn't mind showing it.

"I've been waiting to talk to you again. Have you not gotten my messages?" she asked, coyly, turning, nearly engulfing Sivic's hand in her crotch. I enjoyed the little parade because I finally saw Sivic's breaking point, that twitch in his left eye and the pulsing vein in his forehead. He was uncomfortable with the display.

I pulled my eyes off the struggling Sivic, who was now suddenly less bold in the presence of the emasculator, *Rebecca the Terrible.* I nodded to Rhea.

"We're fine here. Let's bring in an extra chair, and we'll have our meeting in my office." I sat, looked up at the two standing before me, and asked, "Would anyone like coffee, tea, or some wine?" I blinked a couple of times to keep myself from stifling a giggle, even though I knew I was going to be handed a pile of shit.

"I-I'll have coffee," said Sivic. "Just black, please." He turned to Rhea, whose eyes expanded nearly to her ears.

"Thanks, Rhea. Rebecca?" I craned his neck up.

"I like pink champagne. *Sophia*, was it that? Our anniversary champagne." She smiled, but it was cut short by my comment.

"Sorry, I don't remember any of that. But I think we might have some. Right, Rhea?"

"I think so, Boss. You want some Sparkle?"

"Love some."

When Rhea closed the door in front of her and turned to the rest of the office, everyone scampered like mice, not wanting to admit they'd been glued to the action inside my office like a good series on TV.

I checked my phone for messages and silently waited for Rebecca and Sivic to take a seat and begin their no-doubt rehearsed presentation.

Rhea mercifully didn't take long to bring the drinks. I avoided direct eye contact with Rebecca, something I knew would drive her crazy. She whispered things to Sivic, at one point, making him chuckle. I found it easy to ignore them. I sipped my sparkling lemon drink, folded my hands on my desk, and sighed.

"I'm sure we all are busy, so can we get down to it?" I directed my gaze to the space between Rebecca and Sivic, making the younger man turn and check behind him. "Everything you have to say could have been said through an attorney or with an email or letter. I don't understand the need for the meeting in person. I have nothing against you, Theopolis—if I may call you that?"

"Of course. Most people call me Theo. That's fine as well, Mr. Gambini."

"Then it has to be Marco."

"And Marco it is."

I deduced Rebecca was annoyed that the two men were building rapport and she was being left out. Her flowery dress with the plunging neckline was in constant motion, and she crossed and uncrossed her legs several times, showing off her orange toe polish and jeweled sandals. I found I had no emotion when it came to her. No regrets, no images of happy days in the past. It was a fifteen-year blur, a prison sentence from which I'd been liberated.

"I'm going to say it one more time. I'm busy. I'm sure, with your important job, Theo, you are as well. What seems to be the issue at hand?"

Sivic began explaining that formal approval of the Trident Towers did not have legal authority. It was going to require he bring the project before the planning commission, which was booked up for nearly four months. He said that continued work on the development could create fines for every one of the violations. He promised that there were many of them.

"Well, that's going to be a disappointment to my partners," I stated calmly. I took another sip of my Sparkle and watched

Rebecca's shaky hand deliver the champagne to her gut at the same time.

"Partners?" she asked, frowning.

"The Department of Veterans Affairs. They have a stake in this, and I understand they have jurisdiction over local laws. I also don't understand how you could determine I'm in violation of the labor clauses of our development agreement since we have not yet begun work."

"We understand you are employing labor from India. We have it on good authority these individuals are being smuggled into the country without passports," Sivic neatly laid out.

"So you are under contract with the State Department as well? Impressive, if I do say so myself," I said, raising my eyebrows. "If what you say is true, I will contact Senator Campbell and ask for his assistance to this oversight. You know he is married to the First Lady's sister?"

Sivic briefly glanced at Rebecca and then remembered himself. "We are going by sworn affidavits."

"Which are not worth the paper they're written on, even if they do exist. Look, I'm growing tired of doing this waltz. You aren't going to win."

"But we can make it very expensive, Marco," Rebecca hissed.

"Why? So you can take away a chance for a normal life with vets that have served their country well and have been forgotten? You want to take away their pride, their future? The comfort of a home over their heads to share with their children while they crawl their way back into society with dignity? Everyone else sees them as heroes. What's gotten into you that you can't see this is a losing proposition?"

"I'm not fond of losing, or have you forgotten?"

I drilled her a look that was deep and dark. "Don't fuck with me, Rebecca. I didn't like it when you pretended to be in love with me. I like it less now that we are sworn enemies. You have no right to do this."

She set her stemware on my desk, admiring it, her fingers running up and down the graceful stem with the etched pattern near the top. "I see you still have our crystal. Does it bring back memories?"

"No." I hadn't remembered they were. I was going to throw them all away, these at the office and the two I had at home. "Why, Rebecca?"

"Because I can."

"I can do a lot of things, but I don't do them. For one, it would send me to jail, but for another, I don't go chasing windmills or ghosts from my past. I can't help it if you were raped at your father's horse ranch or that you cannot have children. Perhaps therapy would be a more agreeable solution, and I can recommend any number of therapists to help you with that troubled mind of yours. I'll even pay for it."

"Just a minute, Marco—Mr. Gambini," Sivic blurted out, placing his arm across Rebecca as if protecting her from the onslaught of Marco's words. "This is a civil discussion."

"Is it? You can't give me a reason all this is befalling me and my organization? You call that civil? Messing with me? I've done nothing wrong. You might consider your own options, Mr. Sivic. This is what happens when you end a relationship with Rebecca. Ask yourself: Is this what I want? There are several gentlemen of good reputation who bailed. Just something to think about."

"You're taking this too personal, Mr. Gambini."

"Am I? Then ask her why she's doing this. See if you can get a straight answer from her. I could shout it from the rooftops. I'll go to the tabloids if I must. I've got more information on her cold, perverted world than anyone else out there." I drilled another hateful stare into her. "I'm the one who deserves revenge. You're the one who left and took everything. You got what you wanted, so get out and leave me alone. You can't have what isn't yours."

Sivic was blathering about getting a cease-and-desist order when Rebecca cut him off.

"I need to talk to Marco alone."

"I don't think that's a good—"

"Get out, and I won't ask you again."

I knew I'd rattled her cage, and if I wasn't careful, I'd allow myself too much pleasure at her expense, part of the dark sexual games she liked to play. And it would sully me, not her. So I reeled my emotions back inside.

My tone was soothing, like I was reassuring a favorite dog. "Theo, give us just a moment. I'm sure it will be all right. Just a minute." I watched as Sivic left the office, but he took up a chair outside and watched through the window. Team workers stared at each other, confused and worried. They kept their distance from the strange, obsessed man.

I began. "I'm not going to play along with this. Tell me what you want. Is it more money? What will it take for you to get out of my life altogether and never come back?"

"I made a mistake walking out. I'd like the opportunity to make it up to you."

I was stunned.

"I do tend to bite the hand that feeds me. I'm sorry for that. I've recently come to the realization that I need you, Marco. I need your strength. I miss your fucks worse than you can imagine. I'm baring my soul to you. I'm a wreck without you."

The words sounded hollow. I knew it was all lies, part of the game. Catch the mouse, injure it a bit, let it go free, and then capture it again, each time doing more and more damage, even licking its wounds, before the final crunch or a "natural" death. The term "Cat and Mouse" was only a partial description. It was more like something from Dante's Inferno.

I inhaled carefully and continued. "This, this is how you ask for sympathy?"

"Because I know you won't give it. I'm not asking. I'm demanding."

"You're insane, Rebecca. I should have you arrested and—" I was seeing another side of her entirely. A very unbalanced and dangerous side. I knew she could smell my fear too. She was a predator. I was a protector. It was going to be a fight to the death.

Her mind had completely unwound.

"Rebecca, don't destroy the last ounce of respect I once had for you with this. Get some help. This is a suicide mission. You'll take a lot of innocents down with you. And you'll still lose. Are you there, still there, Rebecca?"

I wasn't going to allow myself to feel sorry for her, but I was a fair man, a man of compassion, which made me feel proud. Rebecca had become an animal and probably was well on her way to full insanity.

I asked again, "Are you taking anything? Is there an underlying problem I don't know about?"

"You see the shame in admitting all this? I was counting on you having something left for me."

I shook my head. "I care about you as a person. But you've done some horrible things, things that have cost people jobs, cost me millions. You delayed a project that was near and dear to my heart. Even if I had anything left, I have a new life now. I've moved on. There is no place for you here."

"I could make one."

A cold chill slithered down my spine.

"What did you say?"

"I thought you needed me as much as I needed you. I thought you needed that intensity we had together. I wanted the biggest make up fuck of my lifetime. But it didn't work out that way."

I saw the imbalance taking over her. I leaned slightly to the left and made eye contact with Sivic, who stood, waiting to be invited in.

"What's your freedom worth to you?" she asked.

I could almost see a snake's tongue protruding from her mouth—all my imagination.

"I'm sorry, Rebecca. I'm not following you." I looked at her hands, her purse, her pockets, suddenly fearful she might be carrying a small caliber revolver. "Are you using something because you're not making any sense. There is absolutely nothing you could do—"

I hated myself for this slip of the tongue. That's the last thing I should have said, because Rebecca stood up and ended their conversation with—

"Think about it. Is your freedom worth the life of someone very dear to you?"

"Rebecca, you can't mean that—"

"Can lightning strike twice?"

CHAPTER 7

I GOT HOME early and was preparing one of Marco's favorite meals: lean steak, garlic mashed potatoes, and string beans, heavy with butter. For dessert, I made fresh custard with half the sugar, just as Marco liked it. It was simple, reflecting the man and his modest tastes beneath his complicated body armor, but it was the basis on which my love found safety, a firm foundation built on rock and concrete, like his buildings. Not built on sand.

I'd had an exhausting day at the office, especially avoiding anyone who had reason to interact with me, except Sandy, of course. Clarence was on his good behavior, and I asked him if he'd like to have a late lunch after my weather report at noon tomorrow. He delightedly accepted.

With twinkling eyes, like a kid at Christmas, he asked, "To what do I owe this kind gesture?"

"I want us to have a talk and understand something," I answered.

He quickly looked down at his feet. "Oh."

Apparently, he'd had lots of these types of conversations, I guessed.

"It's not what you think, Clarence. I want us to work together, but I first want to set up the ground rules. I want you to be perfectly clear where I'm coming from. If you pay attention, you'll avoid something that's coming your way that you're unprepared for."

He turned his head to the side as if he could hear better from his left ear. "Sounds serious. Dark and delicious."

The waving of his eyebrows was unnecessary and annoyed me. *Are you really that clueless?*

"I'll drive and drop you back here well in time for your evening preparation," I said.

"I don't mind the distraction. It would be my honor—" He reached out to grab my hand for a Victorian kiss, and I stepped back.

"No. That's partly what I'm going to talk to you about. Part of the rules."

He adjusted his body and looked up to the sky as his fingers mimicked rain. "Okay, okay, no touchy, no touchy."

I thought about that as I sliced the green beans and set the water to boil on the stove. Marco would be home any minute, or he'd call.

I dashed to our tiny bedroom, removed the robe I'd worn after taking my second shower of the day, and added some fancy underwear. The new crotchless panties and a matching bra that exposed my nipples made my privates pulse in anticipation. I used a slight spray of Audrey Hepburn's favorite recipe perfume, directing it mostly at the back of my neck and beneath my ears, and then spread a thin layer of cherry gel over my nipples and my private parts.

I didn't consider it to be manipulation but was going to need all the help I could get as I tried to explain to him about the fact that I'd disobeyed his command. If I let him take it out on me sexually, it might remove some of the sting. But I wasn't sure. All this was new territory. I wanted to be compliant but not a victim begging for mercy. A planned supplicant, showing my need for him to be master of my life because I'd done a course correction he might not agree with. I wanted to sweeten my indiscretion with a little sugar, a little salt, and a whole lot of passion.

I placed the silk robe back on and cinched the tie with a bow. Candles were lit. A bottle of red wine was opened and waiting on the table, along with two beautiful pieces of stemware he'd commandeered from the office. The water was hot, covered, waiting. The broiler was not yet on, but the steaks were marinating on a platter, properly peppered and lightly salted. The mashed potatoes were already done and sitting with a dollop of butter melting sensually into the peaks and valleys of the white and red-skinned fluffiness.

The ocean was a bit angry with white caps and a sky that was turning dark grey, meaning it would rain tonight or sooner. The sunset would still be later, depending on how many of the monstrous clouds joined them in the next hour.

Marco's Hummer pulled into the Beach Trail Drive parking spot next to my car, and I heard the door open.

Something strange was in his expression, almost like regret as he quickly scanned my outfit, the table set for him, and then looked away.

I knew better than to press things but did it anyway.

"You look like a whole lot of good news walking in here like that."

"Sorry I don't meet your standards," he whispered, setting down a sheaf of papers. He looked over at the table again and sighed. "I guess my timing sucks."

"There's nothing at all wrong with your timing. You're going to have to work harder if you think you can brush me off like that. Stop hiding. What is it?"

His shoulders dropped as he exhaled. "Shannon, I can't. I have to think about a few things first."

I walked over to him, and he did begin to smile then. I figured he smelled my perfume and knew I'd made myself extra pleasing for his behalf. I acknowledged that he liked it, or normally liked it.

"You don't have to do a thing, Marco. Just sit down, and I'll take your shoes off. Your feet must be hurting. Can I rub them?"

He angled his head and then looked deep into my eyes and let me know his intention was there, even if his will was lacking. I got the message.

"Let's see what I can do."

He started to say something, and I placed my palm over his lips, bending over so he could see the gap in my robe. Then I knelt and began to slip off his shoes and socks, only worn today because he had meetings with bankers, he'd told me.

"Those poor little toes," I said as I manipulated them back and forth, gently rubbing the underside of both his feet. I leaned forward, knees to the area rug beside his toes. One shoulder became exposed as the rob slipped slightly.

I massaged his calves through his slacks, then used my knuckles to trace the ribbons of sinew on his thighs. I reached for his shirt and began to unbutton them one at a time while he watched me carefully. I noticed his breathing was getting deeper. My forearm brushed against the bulge growing in his pants and I ignored it.

I spread his shirt open but didn't remove it from his arms. Next, I lifted his tee shirt to expose his chest and the bulging abs and pecs moving up and down with his slow breathing.

Coming to my feet, I relaxed onto the leather couch, placing my knees at the sides of his waist and unbuckled his belt, releasing him to my deft fingers.

Marco sat up straight, inhaled, and overcame my mouth, sending his tongue down my throat, making my sex drip with desire. He pulled my hair aside and bit my earlobe then kissed my neck. With his other hand, he worked with mine to slide his pants down off his hips just enough so he was fully free.

His fingers went to slide the panties to the side for a quick, urgent entry, but he soon discovered it wasn't needed. With both hands on my hips, he watched as my body covered his lap and he held me down, deep, then moved my frame up and down his shaft. I untied my robe and showed him my rosy, red nipples knotted and begging to be kissed, pressing above the black lace of the bra, engorging them dangerously.

He lifted my leg up over the armrest of the couch to widen his access to me. I locked my hands behind his neck, squeezed my breasts together as he buried his head there. He sucked, grunting his pleasure, stopping his hip action several times to cool his arousal. But I would not be stopped. I moaned and begged for him, trying to come down on him again, but he seemed to enjoy restraining me.

At last, he pulled me down and urgently stroked my insides, building up to a hot crescendo with such ferocity he flipped me on my back, tore off his shirt and pants, and rammed inside me again, making me squeal with delight. He rolled and pinched my nipples and then sucked them back to softness. He pulled my bra straps down to my elbows, unhooked the back and freed my breasts as he arched, pumping with quick little hip motions while my insides flamed and started to pulse.

I arched up to receive him, but he lost traction in my lumpy couch when one knee slipped to the floor. He slipped his arm beneath my back and flipped me over again, bringing me on all fours and mounting me from the backside, pulling my hips tight against him as he squeezed my butt cheeks apart, which sent me into orbit. After just a few more strokes, my orgasm began to roll through me, shaking my body as my internal muscles held and stroked him in return.

"Never. Want. This. To. End," he whispered in my ear, as I pressed against him, rose with him to my knees, gripping the backrest of the couch until I felt him begin to spill. He held my shaking body as he poured into me, taking me deep, nearly lifting me with an arm around my belly, drilling inside, demanding to stay, holding me still so we could both feel the friction of flesh against flesh until we melted into the miracle of our combined union.

It was over too soon for me. My heart was still roaring as he slowed his pace, placing grateful kisses up and down my spine, splaying his fingers through my hair, and finding parts he'd missed kissing earlier at the back of my ears, at the nape of my neck, and down every vertebra.

We collapsed, sitting side by side, my robe halfway under me and halfway on the ground beneath our feet, breathing in tandem until I could inhale without gasping. I leaned my head against his shoulder, my hand gently stroking his chest, then kissed him under his chin. He wrapped his arms around me and let me just breathe in the warmth of his embrace. Leaning my cheek against him, I listened to the steady beat of his heart.

I was satisfied that whatever had been troubling Marco when he walked in through my door was now safely forgotten. Or at least I hoped it was.

He cleared the hair from my forehead, pressing strands behind my ear to look into my eyes. A tiny dark cloud remained there.

"What is it, Marco?"

"I am the happiest man alive, Shannon. I'm just grateful."

There was something else, but he wasn't going to reveal it, and I didn't want to spoil the glow I felt all over. "Me too," I said and placed my forehead against his. "Can I suggest some dinner perhaps?"

"You think my heart could stand it?"

"It's steak. Good for your libido. Not oysters, mind you, but nearly as effective. Garlic mashed potatoes, string beans, and dessert too. Are you ready?"

He gazed down at his shirt and pants. "I think I ruined my shirt."

"Oh dear. I liked how you got carried away. So sorry about the shirt, though."

"I'm not." He smiled. "Come on. I'm starved. I'll grab some pajama bottoms, but you can stay just the way you are."

I smiled, disobeying him again by wrapping the robe around me and cinching the waist while he retrieved his pajamas from the bedroom. We walked to the table I'd set, the candles still lit, the flowers I'd bought still standing, waiting for attention.

While I fixed the beans and put the steaks in the broiler, he replaced the wine glasses with two juice tumblers for some strange reason and handed me a glass.

"To endless nights of good food, good wine, wonderful stories to think back upon and remember how perfect we are together.

The perfect pairing," he said.

"I agree." I clinked my glass against his. "What did you do with the wine glasses?"

"I like these better." He sipped, closing his eyes. "The wine tastes better in these."

I took a sip, closed my eyes, and let the taste roll over my tongue and call to me. "Yes, I think you're right." I was going to say more, but he'd covered my mouth with his, his hand squeezing my right breast.

The smell of our steaks cooking refocused our attention to plating our food and sitting down, finally.

Toward the end of the meal, he asked me about my day at the station, which immediately put me on the defensive. His questions were answered with vague or one-word answers, until he finally put down his knife and fork and sat back in his chair with his hands folded in his lap.

His face was serious. "Tell me," he said.

I knew better than to try to hide something from him. But the evening had been so wonderful I didn't want to spoil it. I trusted him with the truth, hoping I'd not miscalculated.

"I met with Jared today to put in my resignation."

"And?" He watched me, not resuming his eating.

"And I didn't quit."

"But that wasn't the plan, Shannon. You promised you would quit. I haven't asked you about it until today. And today you chickened out?"

"No, I decided to give him three months to find a replacement."

There. I'd said it. I continued eating.

"Impossible. There is no possibility he could replace you in a year or even two."

"Not just me. He's going to fire Bunny."

"And keep Clarence."

"Yes, I told him to."

"That's another bad decision. Who cares if he must replace all three of you? In my opinion, neither Bunny nor Clarence is doing anything for the station. In fact, they're hurting it. You're the only bright spot there."

"They have a new hire who's going on maternity leave. Sylvia. She'll be good."

"This manager of yours hires a new anchorperson who's pregnant, leaves an aging beauty queen in the position to boss everyone around and scare half the crew, and coddles an aging Casanova who drools and vomits over himself at the sight of dead fish. Have I got that right?"

I wanted to laugh because Marco was spot on and making very funny sense, too. "You make it sound like it's the Little Shop of Horrors or something."

"That's an apt description," he said brightly, holding up his fork and stabbing another slice of steak. "You're needed here, beside me, to help me with our plans. Our plans, Shannon. They're not my plans. They're ours."

"Yes, I understand that. But, Marco, I told him I'd give him three months *and* we agreed I'd cut back my hours. It's what I thought was the right thing to do. He's been good to me, Marco. I can't just leave him in the lurch. I'm sorry if you're angry with me." I placed a hand on his. "Please understand."

"Oh, I understand all right. This postpones everything I'm doing then. Am I to believe you're okay with that?"

"No. Like I said, I'm cutting back my hours. No evening or afternoon anchor fill-ins. Just weather and an occasional story in the morning, working with Sylvia, not Clarence. He and Bunny can duke it out in the evenings. I'm out of that scene. I'll be with you more. I'll be home or back at the office three, four hours earlier, and if you have a trip, I'll take off from the station, no problem. He agreed to that. All of that."

His face got dark again.

"Marco, what is troubling you so?"

He put down his fork again and pushed away from the table but remained seated. "I've spoken to our new Security Chief. He's worried about your stalker."

"I'm not going to jog in the morning. Not alone, anyway."

"That's a start. But in addition to the classes, we're going to beef up our security in general—everywhere. Our office is too open. We need to run it like the station does. And I need to keep you protected."

"You think there's a threat to me?"

"We do believe there's a credible threat. Yes."

His eyes were cloudy again. They quickly diverted from my questioning gaze and didn't connect.

"What else?"

Marco threw his napkin on the table. "Dammit, Shannon. Can't you see I'm trying to take good care of you? It's my job to do that, but it's just something that I couldn't live with if—"

"If what?"

"If someone were to try something."

"As in harm me?"

He stood, walking to the large slider overlooking the beach. The moon danced amongst the large puffy white clouds in the night sky. I followed the trail of a string of cotton balls as they blew past us both. He knew I loved this house. Was he saying I'd need a posted armed guard at my back patio? Front door?

"I get the concern and the need to get all the information, but why does this make you angry? I don't understand your reaction. I'm asking normal questions, Marco. And if there's a plot against me, why should I be left in the dark? Shouldn't I be told these things?"

He turned around and nodded. "Yes, you're right."

He retook his seat, held my hand, and began again to say something he did not want to tell me, and that made me fearful.

"We've analyzed it, Shannon. We think Rebecca might try to harm you. We have no proof, just theory. Promise me you'll alter what you do, and perhaps we'll assign a guard for you as well. If I can't be there around you twenty-four seven, someone else has to be."

"Did you run into Rebecca today?"

He rubbed the knuckles on my hand, and nodded.

"And she admitted it, that she might harm me?"

"It was an indirect implication. I've already done some of the research, and it isn't enough to get a restraining order against her."

"So she isn't on some island with her future Mr. Ex-Rebecca like you told me."

"She means to delay our project. No, she's not given up. Now do you understand why I need you where I can watch over you? Don't you see how important it is?"

I couldn't believe Rebecca would rise to that level, but if Marco did, that would be proof enough. He was the expert.

No wonder he was in such a dour mood when he arrived home.

"So what do we do?"

"We can go into all that tomorrow, Shannon. I'm still working on it. And frankly, I'm tired."

So much for romance, I thought. Just when it all was feeling so perfect, limitless, with so much to live for, to work for, so much good that we could do together, someone would try to dash those dreams and get to him in the worst possible way. Rebecca had figured out his Achilles heel.

And was crazy enough to try to use it.

"But why, Marco? What's she about?"

"I think she's mentally unbalanced. I'm not sure how, but I'm going to get her exposed and try to take care of it that way. Clinically. But I won't lie to you. It's a slippery slope, and we must be very careful, or it could cause a lawsuit. She's still got a lot of my money to throw back at my face with attorneys. We've been duped, I'm afraid. She's been summoning her troops."

I was crestfallen. I picked up the dishes, rinsing them in the sink, and began putting them in the dishwasher. He came up behind me, encircling me in his arms, and whispered, "I'll figure out a way. I promise to love and protect you, and I'll spare no expense figuring this thing out. I don't want you to worry. I just need you to play smart and keep your eyes and ears open. Remember what I told you about evil? Well, evil doesn't sleep. Crazy people don't sleep, either."

I remembered what we'd talked about many times, that love was stronger than hate. And the enemy would always think that I was the weakest link.

I wasn't going to let that happen. And I wasn't going to take anything for granted, either. It was ridiculous to allow it to ruin a beautiful evening with the man I'd love forever. And if I had to, I'd fight to make it last forever.

But I had to get ready for it first.

Marco interrupted my thoughts.

"Come on. It's time for bed. We can finish the rest of this in the morning." He took my hand and walked me to the bedroom.

"Shower?"

I nodded.

He smoothed the lavender gel all over my body, washing every part of me diligently. He took great pains to hose me off, again smoothing his scarred and massive fingers over my flesh, making my arousal flash in waves. Everywhere he touched me, even if he violated me, I glowed. Wanted more.

I threw my arms around his neck, allowed him to hold me under the warm spray, and sobbed into his chest.

He was my lifeline. I would do or say anything to protect him as he would for me. He was like a drug, and I became more and more addicted to him with every passing day, every time our bodies touched, fondled, and made love.

When I was done, he spoke softly. "We'll figure it out one step at a time. I'm going to remain calm, logical. I need you to keep your head about you too. There must be an answer to all this. It's just not coming to me right away, but it's there."

"I know you will. I want to help. And I'll follow your lead and instructions."

"Thank you, Shannon. Thank you for trusting me."

I winced, tried to engage his attention, and then put my palms on his cheeks. "Except for the station. I need those three months partly to help us with the social media and press we're going to need, Marco. I know what I'm doing."

"You're even more stubborn than Em—I'm sorry, it just slipped out."

"It's okay. I don't mind that I remind you of her. I'm actually quite honored, flattered."

"For being stubborn?" He gave me back a puzzled look.

I kissed him again under the water. "Thank you for letting me be me. Thank you for telling me the truth."

But something was at the tip of his tongue, and he wouldn't let it out. I finally asked him as the water turned cold.

While drying my head under the towel, I told him, "You know you can confide in me anything. Anything at all, Marco."

He stopped for a minute. "All in due time. I have some things I must sort out, but yes, after I organize my thoughts and create a plan, I'll share it with you. All of it. I won't leave anything out. I'm going to get the very best people on it, and we'll come up with a plan that will work."

"Then nothing can stop us. No problem too great that we cannot handle when we're together. Make me believe that we'll live this way for the next hundred years and that it will keep getting better and better."

"It will, Shannon. I promise it will. Love is stronger than evil. It always wins in the end."

"No matter what."

"No matter what. There is nothing that can separate us. I will never let that happen."

CHAPTER 8

I DROVE SHANNON to the station myself because her car wouldn't start. I had a repairman stop by the house, to see if he could get it jumped and fixed by tonight. I never minded being her chauffeur, and it was part of the plan anyway.

"I just had it serviced a month ago. It has less than ten thousand miles on it," she complained as we headed for the station. "I was supposed to have lunch with Clarence."

"I can't make it for lunch. Ask him to reschedule. I don't want you driving with anyone else."

"Aren't we being a little too dramatic?" she asked.

"Shannon, we talked all about this last night. I thought I made it perfectly clear that we're beefing up security. This isn't a joke, you know."

"I've never had any trouble with this car."

"You probably left your lights on or the radio," I answered.

"They aren't like that now. Even my cheap little car shuts off the lights or anything electronic when the engine has been turned off."

I reassured her that it was probably something very simple as we sped down the highway to the bridge over the bay, headed to downtown Tampa.

We arrived. I kissed her goodbye, and after she went upstairs to get her makeup done, I slipped into Jared's office. I knocked with my knuckles on the open door's frame. Jared had so much paperwork covering his desk, his two guest chairs, and the upturned wastepaper basket he looked like a hamster making a nest. Even the floor was littered with files I carefully wandered around.

"Ah, the man himself. The maid's got the day off," Jared said, peering through glasses perched at the tip of his nose. He stood, and the we shook.

"Shannon told me about your little arrangement."

"You put her up to it. Don't blame this on her," barked Jared. His phone rang and he couldn't find it under all the papers. When he did, the ringing stopped. Checking the number first, he tossed it on top of one of his piles.

"I don't think you need a maid. You need a bulldozer. We used to have a liaison in the SEALs with a desk that looked like yours. He was always complaining that he never got the memos everyone else did when, in fact, he'd buried them. Until, of course, they were no longer pertinent. We thought it was his strategy all along, that way he only had to do half the work for the same amount of pay."

"I take it he didn't advance."

"Secret is, you have to stay in long enough so you can coast. You can't pull these things off while you're essential. When you get kicked upstairs, that sometimes means you're not needed. The Navy doesn't fire people; they promote them. All the branches are the same. The brass at the top depend on the grunts to get the work done, under pain of detachment. But once you've ridden up the food chain a bit, you never had to worry about that. He started slowing down too soon, and yes, he got sent to Alaska to run a supply warehouse that supported the SEALs training up there."

"Not exactly Coronado."

"Nope. No coeds, no warm ocean breezes, palm trees, or beach volleyball."

"That's a fuckin' sad story, Marco. What was the point of it?"

"Hell if I know."

We both laughed as worthy sometimes-adversaries.

"What can I do to convince you to let her go early, like in a week or two, maybe tonight?" I asked.

"Funny. I was just going to ask you the same thing."

I picked up a sheaf of papers on a chair and set them on the floor beside me as I sat in front of Jared. "But there is something you can do, and you never know how deep my gratitude can go. What do you know about my ex?"

"Rebecca? Shannon's the one who interviewed her, not me."

"A tall, handsome Program Manager who decides what leads and what goes and the butterfly from hell attracted to publicity like her life depended on it. That sounds like a perfect match made in Heaven, Jared."

"That's a blood sport. I don't have the stomach."

"She can wear on you. She can be charming if she wants to."

"Now you've just about explained every woman on the planet. Oh—I forgot. You're still in the 'honeymoon' phase," he said, emphasizing it with his fingers making quote marks. "Blinded by love."

"I am hopelessly in love. And I have my own ideas what I'd like to do with Shannon, which means anyone who gets in the way is a problem for me. You wouldn't have it in you to play a little cat and mouse?"

"You must be fuckin' nuts, Marco. She's like this wild two-hundred-pound mountain lion, and I'm one of those little pink feeder mice with his eyes still shut. That would be no contest. One gulp and Jared would be no more. Can't you find one of your former SEAL buddies who might be just a little bent in the bed-room, if you know what I mean? I understand she has tastes that are difficult to satisfy."

I stared him down.

Jared stood, holding his hands out in front of him. "Just a ru-mor, Marco. I have no first-hand experience."

"I'm looking for a favor here, Jared."

"No, to be quite frank, you're wanting to send me on a suicide mission."

"Then find a way to get some information on her. I want to know why she won't leave me alone. She's beginning to worry me."

"Now you're worried? After all you've been through?"

"I need to know what she's planning."

"Marco, she's not going to tell me."

Jared did look like a skinny mouse, I thought. Shannon had told me how many times he'd asked her out, even after it was discovered she was with me. It was a "feel sorry for me date" I had been trying to set up, on the chance that an opportunity might present itself.

But then I had an idea.

"What if she thought she could get inside information from you about me, through your working relationship with Shannon? If she thought you were useful, she'd let you live for a bit."

"You instill such confidence, Marco. I'm not interested in living for a bit. I'd like to live to an old age and die comfortably in my bed. No. The answer is no. This would be too rich for me. I'm not smart enough, I don't have the cunning or the stealth you have, and I'll get nervous and blow it. I'm the last person in the world you'd want to use."

"I think you're wrong."

Jared fell back into his chair again, staring off to the right, not making eye contact. "This is the part where you threaten to kill my mother and my sisters. Then you'll firebomb the station, and I'd be spectacularly out of a job. The whole thing caught on camera and presented to the Tampa market by *someone else's* TV station."

"We could help you make some improvements. Get you in on the ground floor of the Trident Towers, interviewing happy vets being given what they deserve. You'd have exclusive interviews, and then imagine the talent who would come calling? Bone Frog Development could become one of your best advertisers. Your owner would love that."

Jared suddenly looked very small, tucked into his enormous chocolate brown high-backed office swivel chair. "Might even get you a real secretary to have this place looking like Fox in no time at all. If we were going to interview Tom Brady, you'd have to do a substantial remodel, and of course, you'd need season tickets for ten in your box seats."

"None of this would be remotely important to me if I was roadkill, Marco. You know I'm no match for her. You could give me the sun and the moon. I don't even know what the hell I'd do with them. You do see, the answer is still no."

I continued nodding as I stood, leaned over, and shook Jared's hand again. "Well, it was nice having a little fantasy with you. But you think it over. If you come across something you just can't live without, you let me know. Ever been on a safari? We're taking some people over there in the spring."

"Just my kind of place. I've always wanted to vacation in West Africa with all those exciting macho Jeep jockeys running around cutting the heads off people who look like me. That's you're style, not mine."

I chuckled. "You're funny, Jared. I think you could have done standup comedy."

"Let's add that to the list then, shall we? Just another missed opportunity."

The standoff was beginning to annoy me. I wasn't used to being told, "No". But I knew that if Shannon and I spent enough time on it, we'd discover Jared's weakness.

And then we'd be home free.

But we had to come up with something he'd risk his life for to get.

ON MY WAY over to the office, I got a call from Harry, the Sultan of Bonin's youngest son, from Brooklyn Heights. Harry had become the trusted social secretary to the sultan, his father. He lived with his mother, the beautiful Salima, the sultan's favorite companion. Since she was from a servant family and not nobility, he could not make her his wife. She was sent away along with her illegitimate son, for their own safety. The sultan gave her a stipend and purchased a brownstone for her as long as she lived. The rest of the harem wives and children pretended not to know this or openly admit that Harry was their relative.

"Marco, are you ready for the princes?" Harry barked over the phone.

"Are they here?"

"They land in New York in about an hour. Then there's the plane to Charlotte and finally Tampa. They will arrive this evening around ten if everything goes well. But we might have some issues. Do you want me to arrange a car?"

"That would be nice, Harry. Thanks. What issues? Plus, I've got to make sure the condo is ready for them. I thought they'd be here tomorrow. Isn't that what you said?"

"It was, but you're going to love this story. Absalom gets to Delhi a few days early. He's looking for a beautiful girl to bring with him now that he is away from his mother and her sister wives. Those boys should not be traveling without a guard or secretary, Marco. They just don't know anything about the world. So he finds this beautiful girl, a dancer. She performs in one of the supper clubs in the Chennai District for wealthy men who keep her safe and pay her enough to send home to her parents."

With Harry, I'd learned long ago to just let him talk. Besides, I was driving and had the phone on speaker.

"Okay."

"Absalom convinces her that he will bring her to the United States, where she can learn to surf. Imagine that? Absalom wants to learn how to surf, Marco!"

"It doesn't surprise me."

"He's kept her longer than he was supposed to, and she misses her shift at the supper club, and it causes an uproar. My father himself got angry messages from the Provincial Director, who is a very close confident of the Prime Minister. He calls me in a panic. They're threatening to put Absalom in jail if he doesn't return the girl. So they hire a driver to take them to the airport a day early. They want to tell the airline company they've changed their minds and want to leave now, not wait for the next day. I had to explain to them that wasn't the case, that you don't just tell the pilot to take off because of the other passengers. They've only flown private charter, you see."

"Um, Harry, am I going to hear the punch line today or to-morrow?" I asked.

"Uncle Marco, no worries. I'm almost finished. They show up at the airport and argue with security, and finally, the airline company allows them to purchase a ticket for the girl and re-book their flights to come a day early. But she has no passport, which could be a big problem."

"That's *always* a problem, Harry."

"Don't you know it. She's never had one. Again, accommodations must be made. Both my father and I are calling all the officials we can think of for favors. We get it all worked out, which does delay the plane by nearly an hour. Khalil says the passengers want to lynch them for making them late for their connections, but now they are all set. Just as they board the plane and it begins to take off, the Provincial Director drives out on the tarmac with his cruiser, lights flashing, very dramatic, and tries to shoot the pilots with his pistol."

"Oh God. I hope—"

"No, no. They were fine. The Director was so upset he was shooting all over the place, and airport crews were running for cover. But the plane couldn't stop. I saw it on the news, and it was hilarious. If he hadn't jumped out of the way, they would have run him over."

"Jeez, Harry. Maybe this wasn't such a good idea after all."

"You have no idea what you're in for, Marco. You have to teach them everything."

"I knew that. But no common sense. Is this true?"

"Oh, yes. They are royal people, and royal people don't have to do what the common folk do. Rules are made for the little people, they'll tell you. You better get ready to babysit them twenty-four seven."

"Just what I need." I could see I would have to speak to the sultan, who was also coming over in two weeks, or these boys would be totally out of control.

"In hindsight, we should have brought an escort for them. They're like six-year-old children, Marco."

"What about this girl? We've got to send her back," I stressed.

"Good luck with that. I'm calling you to ask you to get someone to intercede for them when they get to New York. She won't be able to get through customs because of her passport status. Any irregularities, especially now, they'll deport her back to Delhi."

"So she goes back. Simple as that," I said.

"But Absalom can't escort her there, which is what he'll demand, because the Provincial Director will see to it he's locked up. He may never be able to fly into Delhi again. Or out of it, for that matter."

"That's just great. Okay, I better get on the phone with one of my senators. Can you text me the flight number and the arrival time, please?"

"Yes, yes, I will. No problem."

"How long is their layover?"

"This is another problem, Marco. The transfer time is very short, so they may miss their connection. That means getting them a hotel for the night."

"There's one in the airport."

"Yes, I'll set something up just in case. Other than that, things are pretty smooth."

"Uh huh. I better call Senator Campbell to see if we can head off this impending disaster. They have passports, right?"

"Yes, they do."

"How's the Westside Story coming along?"

"Did you tell my father about that? Man was he pissed at me."

"Oh, no. I didn't go there. It didn't come from me."

"He was screaming on the phone. My mother was crying in the background. I couldn't hear a thing, thank goodness. I just handed the phone to her, and they talked it out. I'm never to tell anyone I wrote a gay Westside Story. She had to promise him that she'd burn the manuscript."

"I admit, your family dynamics are a bit out there, Harry. I'd love to talk, but I better get the senator on this."

"Yes, I understand. I'll let you know if they aren't going to make their next connection, Marco."

It took the rest of the way to the office to reach Senator Campbell's aide, and as I arrived in the parking lot, I was still finalizing the details. But at last, I could relax, knowing that even if the girl wouldn't be admitted to the U.S., the princes would be allowed to continue to Tampa. I hoped the senator had his magic gloves on today and wasn't out golfing with the president.

Just in case, I had my pilot ready my jet in Tampa and hold on stand-by.

CHAPTER 9

I DID A short follow-up to the red tide story from yesterday, and this time, Sylvia was with me on the podium, without a live reporter.

"Thank you, Shannon," Sylvia said, with her wide smile, bright white teeth, and blood red lipstick. In the short time she'd been with the station, she'd been very popular, especially with the Cuban population in the greater Tampa area.

"I take it you did not go out for fish last night?" The anchor tilted her head, her eyes flashing, waiting for an answer.

My first instinct was to blush. The question was unexpected.

"Why no," I stuttered, looking down at my script that would be of no use to me now. "I prepared a nice dinner at home. We had steak." I felt my chest go blotchy, my heart racing and my stomach gurgling. My friend Judie would know exactly what I was thinking about. It was impossible to look at the cameraman.

"Come on, Shannon. Look up so we can see that pretty face," the assistant director whispered in my earpiece. His growly voice turned buttery and sexy, which made everything worse. He had a fantastic voice but was not fit for the camera due to his three-hundred-pound size and his pink puffy cheeks.

I obeyed, giving direction to the right, and then noticing the light was on the camera left side, so switched, turning on my stool to give an over-the-shoulder view. I felt ridiculous, but it was what was required of me.

"Atta girl. Perfect. Sylvia? Go top that one."

Sylvia leaned forward with her chin in her hand, something they were repeatedly told not to do, but in this instance, the gesture gave an air of mystery to the set.

"Gee, inquiring minds want to know. What did you and that handsome soon-to-be-husband of yours have for dessert?"

"Back to you, Shannon. Make it sexy."

Caught between the assistant director and my competition, or what was to have been my competition at one time, I flatly refused to play along.

"Custard. Homemade." I stared right into the camera and then gave a slight smirk.

The camera light went out, and Sylvia went on to other news. There was a new art gallery opening in Tampa, and auditions for the children's ballet company production of Nutcracker were starting next week. Several outdoor concerts were sponsored by various banks and investment firms, most of them Grammy-winning performers who would play a weekend spot and then move on to another town. There were hatchling turtle sightings at the beaches, and volunteers were out combing the low tides to help protect their journey into the ocean and keep the children of locals and tourists from helping themselves to a baby turtle for the drive back home. Residents were asked to keep their patio lights out so as not to confuse them or their mothers who, once they laid their eggs, went back out to sea to welcome them to the family.

I was mesmerized with my good fortune to have found this place after my sister's passing. I remembered the days when our parents took us to Indian Rocks and we built complexes out of sand and buckets and sea water, driftwood, shells, and discarded bird feathers. It suddenly struck me that now, with Marco, I was sort of doing the same. And the ghost of Emily was ever present between us, but as a welcome visitor. At least for me, it was. I hoped that Emily was watching us now and enjoying our adventurous life together as she sat in the back seat. She wouldn't cry, I thought, but she would have a bowl of popcorn.

The set had gone dark when I looked up. Had I missed the

weather portion? Everyone was gone, and the place was deadly silent. I heard monitors playing in the adjoining room where a crowd of station employees were glued to the screen.

Something's happened!

I ran to watch on the screen as half a dozen ambulances and fire rescue vehicles were combing through debris of a collapsed building. I knew before I saw the altered sign hanging from the third floor what it was. The red, white, and blue letters were partly shattered and sparking, swinging by one bolt holding the whole thing in place. It was missing the first letter, and read:

one Frog Development Group.

Sandy was by my side in a flash. "Oh my gosh, Shannon. Is he okay?"

I ran to my desk, looking for my phone, but it wasn't there. I searched the tops of all the other desks, all my drawers, and underneath the desk. I ran back into the set to see if I had left it in the studio but couldn't find it.

"Sandy, where is my phone? Did I leave it in your dressing room?"

"No, I usually check right after I finish, just in case. People leave all kind of things there sometimes when they're nervous. But no. Where is your purse?"

That's when I realized it was no accident my phone was missing, because my purse was gone as well. The deep bottom drawer in my desk was unlocked with the key still inside the lock, but it was empty.

"I think someone's stolen my purse, Sandy."

Someone from the crowd turned and asked me to be quiet. Jared came up behind me and placed a palm on my shoulder.

"Shannon, the police are looking for you, honey."

I turned and tried to find some sort of hope in his face but was disappointed. His eyes were blinking rapidly. He gripped my shoulder.

"Come into my office. I have Emergency Services on the line there."

"My God, Jared. It can't be Marco."

"I'm afraid it is, Shannon. But I don't know anything more."

One of the college interns turned and announced to the crowd, "They have three dead so far. Not releasing names."

With her clinical tone, I wanted to run up to her and slap her face. But that would be another conversation for a much later time. Holding on to Jared, I made it back to the elevator, and once alone, Jared folded me in his arms.

"Hey, kid. I'm praying for you. For you both."

I got a bit prickly but accepted his comfort anyway. I briefly laid my head against his chest, discovering my knees were shaking. In fact, I was shaking all over.

"You need to sit down," he said as soon as the doors opened. He barely got me to a chair before I collapsed. When I awoke, I remembered him holding me, keeping me from slipping onto the floor. I remembered him shouting for someone to call 9-1-1.

"Thank you, but where is the phone?"

"It's an old-fashioned landline. FCC requirement. Come. I'll help you."

His office was a complete disaster, worse than I'd ever seen it. And he'd been ripping awards and plaques off the wall, tossing them, and missing into a metal garbage can.

"Look, don't pay any attention to any of this. I was having a temper tantrum. Come. Sit here. Here's the phone." He helped me sit in his big brown leather swivel chair and handed me the phone.

"H-hello?"

"Is this Shannon Marr?"

"Yes, it is. Is it Marco?"

"This is Sergeant Ben Healy of the Pinellas County Search and Rescue. There's been an explosion at Bone Frog Development Group building, and we have your fiancé here, getting ready to send him to Bay View Hospital Emergency."

"He's alive?"

"Yes, he is, but he's not conscious. Several members of his staff have been identified as deceased. Can you come down to the hospital?"

"Of course, I'll be right there. Who?"

"We haven't completed the identification. They're all young. All women. But we haven't started the notification process. You can probably help us with the identification."

"Certainly. How bad is he? Where are his injuries?"

"I don't know, ma'am, I'm not a doctor, but he's pretty badly hurt."

"Of course. I'll be right there."

I dropped the phone on the desk, pressed my forearms on a pile of papers, buried my head on top of them, and began to sob.

JARED WAITED WITH me in the Emergency Room, which was on overflow capacity since several other businesses had sustained damage to structures and had injuries as well. I noticed a TMBC camera crew trying to make their way over to me, and Jared pushed them away, screaming. Of course, that was caught on camera and would likely show up somewhere, if not at TMBC itself.

"Assholes."

"They're just doing their job, Jared. The news must go on, even when we're in it. Sucks, but that's the way it is."

"Miss, do you want some water?" a young aide in a light blue uniform asked me.

"That would be heavenly. Thank you."

"I'll have one too," Jared said but was already talking to her backside. "So much for being a big shot."

Slightly relieved that Marco had been confirmed as not critical when I arrived, part of my spirit began to come back. "Relax. I'd be happy to share mine."

"I don't want yours. You're going to need it. What I really need is a drink."

I watched a cluster of family members praying in a circle. A baby was crying, and another ambulance siren could be heard as the whooshing sound of the large automatic doors opened and another gurney was rolled inside with someone grey and lifeless, covered to his neck in a bloody sheet. They were immediately admitted to the surgery wing.

I closed her eyes and asked for healing, white light, strength. I told Emily to help Marco out.

Go rub on his chest, wiggle his toes—he likes that. Tell him he must wake up and that you'll see him eventually, but not now. Please do this for me, Em.

I waited for a reply, with my back straight against the wall for support, my hand entangled in Jared's, resting on my thigh. No one answered. But I kept asking for my sister's help.

I must have fallen asleep, because out of the fog came the sound, "Mrs. Gambini?"

I opened my eyes and saw that Rebecca was being spoken to by the doctor. Jared was just awakening and jumped to his feet at the same time.

"Hey, I'm Mrs. Gambini. I'm the *new* Mrs. Gambini. She has no business being here." I pointed right at Rebecca, who looked ten years older and very stressed.

"Oh, sweetheart. We both love him, don't we?" Rebecca threw her arms around me, and I pushed her off.

"Get your hands off me. Jared—" I looked around to see if he could help. "Get the police. I want her out of here."

The young Emergency Room doctor was confused. "Just a minute, ladies. I need permission for a procedure. I need the legal spouse of Mr. Marco Gambini."

"Well, it's not her," I blurted out. "Jared, get her out of here. Throw her out if you have to."

Jared was quick to act but a hospital guard, part of the police force, came between them. "Hey, wait a minute, bud. We don't want to cause a scene, and we're delaying the emergency treatment for Mr.—what's his name?"

"Gambini," all four of the arguing parties shouted back.

"Doctor, I'm his fiancé," I said. "We're getting married in the spring. I can prove it, just not here. But I have this," I held up my left hand and demonstrated my huge diamond. Rebecca rolled her eyes.

"She's a little gold digger after my husband's money."

"Ex-husband. You dumped him, remember?"

"Stop it!" the guard called out. "You're divorced, ma'am?"

Rebecca took her time in answering but finally did. "Yes."

"You have any power over his health care?"

"I still have a piece of paper he signed."

"When you were legally married."

"Of course. And I didn't write it. He did."

"You can go, ma'am. Doctor, please proceed." The guard took Rebecca by the elbow and began nearly dragging her out the emergency entrance.

"I'm sorry about all this," I said.

"Now, who's he? If you tell me he's your ex-husband, I'm not going to talk to you either," the doctor said. He was lashing down his patience, but it was about to come unraveled.

"He's my boss and a dear friend."

"Okay, here's the story. We must go in and remove a large piece of metal—we think it was from part of the construction— metal studs or something. It very nearly severed his femoral artery, and if that had happened, well, we wouldn't be having this conversation."

My tongue was stuck to the roof of my mouth. I felt black circles encroach around both eyes, obscuring more and more of my sight as the seconds ticked by.

"I have to sit down."

"Please." The doctor sat beside me. "He might lose his leg. We may have to take the leg to save his life. He's lost an awful lot of blood. He has a very weakened pulse, and for the time being, he's unconscious, which is the body's way of trying to heal itself. But the damage to that leg is significant. If we cannot get the blood flow back, the leg will atrophy. He has a shattered thigh bone, his knee's screwed up because all his weight came down on his twisted leg from the blast. He was apparently very near where the bomb was planted."

"A bomb? You said a bomb?"

"Yes, ma'am, that's what I'm told, and from the extent of his injuries and the burn marks, well, it's consistent with war injuries I treated in Afghanistan. But I need permission to take the leg. If he doesn't wake up, I may not be able to ask him. I will save his life, one way or the other. But his chances are greatly improved if I don't have to worry about the leg."

"Do what you have to do to save him!" Jared inserted.

The doctor looked at him with full-throttled distain.

"Miss? I need your permission."

I thought about it. I knew what he would choose for me if the roles were reversed. He'd tell them to save my life and take the leg. But that decision may not be the right one for Marco. As a fighter, he'd want to try. He'd want to be on his feet for the next battle. He was strong and healthy with an enormous will to live, especially if it meant there was some form of retribution coming against the perpetrator of this crime. He certainly wouldn't want to do it from a wheelchair, even though I would love him either way. If he was a complete vegetable, I'd love him.

But I was certain he would not make the same choice for himself he'd make for me. He'd want to first fight to see if his leg could be saved. It didn't matter if he had a limp or if the process was painful or required multiple surgeries. He'd want to remain with both legs, even if one was held together with baling wire and metal rods. He'd find some way to use it as a weapon. He wouldn't even think twice about it.

But there was one problem with that possible solution. If that decision meant that he lost his life, then he'd lose the ability to protect me, and I knew that was his primary goal. And he'd never agree to that.

I inhaled, leaned back, and pressed my spine into the wall, asking for Em's help again. "I can't give you a straight answer." I opened my eyes and investigated the doctor's. "If it costs him his life, then no, take the leg. If that's the only way to save him. If you can save him and not take the leg, even if it's high risk, do not take the leg. I know this man. I know what he'll do to recover. I know the discipline that is such a part of him that will not let him quit. He'd want to make this decision himself, and I'll get flack for making it for him if it comes to that. But if he has a chance to live without taking the leg, then that's the choice I make for him."

The doctor nodded. "You're a very courageous woman. He's going to need that."

"I'm fully on board. Do your best, doctor. This man is still an elite warrior. He is one of those guys who do it all. They are the ones who keep us all safe. You must get him back up on his feet to continue his fight, because he's not done being a warrior. He doesn't want to die off somewhere forgotten, gracefully pass into Heaven. He's going to fight with everything he has left. Don't take away any of his tools. He'll need them. We all need them."

"Very well. Consider it done. I understand the type, ma'am. I saw the tats. Those guys are special, and I haven't lost one yet." He patted my leg and smiled. "I hope you know what a lucky woman you are."

"With every ounce of my being, doctor."

I WAITED TEN hours, sleeping in the waiting room. Finally, they made up a bed for me, and Jared finally went home. Since Marco wasn't in ICU, they allowed me to sleep in his room after his five-hour surgery. The doctor told me there would be many more. He told me Marco should never attempt to jump out of a plane again. We both had a laugh over that one.

But the good news, delivered on a beautiful pink and orange sunlit morning in Tampa, overlooking the blue water and all the little white boats zooming back and forth, the glistening city in the background standing proud, was that he was going to be okay.

"He must have some angel looking after him. For the life of me, I don't understand why that piece of metal didn't completely sever the artery. It was like someone was holding it until we could get in there and see it was going to tear away any second. We got it in time. His blood flow is good already. And he will heal. He won't like the way the leg feels at first. But he'll adapt."

"Thank you, doctor. May I give you a hug?"

"My pleasure."

I returned to Marco's room and climbed in the bed beside him. I looked outside our window at the clouds and the day full of promise and hope. It wasn't a view of the ocean, but it was a wonderful view just the same. If I could stick with the positive, somehow, the evil things coming our way would shed off like an old skin.

I turned on my side, watching his deep rhythmic breathing. His stubble was growing fast. His lips were full and dark pink. His forearms were covered in bands of tats chronicling all that he'd been through—all the men he knew who didn't come home, the people he saved, the ones he couldn't, and the wars he fought. His flesh was like a patchwork quilt stitched together with scars and scratches, holidays here and there where the dark hair didn't grow back at all.

He was like one of the old quilts my grandmother had made, telling stories about the materials she used, the dresses her mother used to wear, all connected with stitches—the sinews of the heart.

I was still the luckiest girl alive.

CHAPTER 10

I AWOKE TO the sounds of snoring nearby and discovered Shannon was asleep in a bed next to me. My head was woozy with a lot of pain coming from my left leg, but the leg itself felt like it had swollen up to the size of a large oblong balloon about to burst. I couldn't wiggle my toes, and I had no feeling on the other side from my waist down.

I tried to raise my head, even to speak, but all I could manage was a small squeak from my throat. I didn't have the strength to try making words or sentences so dropped back into the pillow, exhausted.

My right forearm was taped to a flat plastic brace that looked like a small tray, where a smorgasbord of tubing fed into my system. The insertion of a catheter down below did catch my attention, however, and with very little movement of my right hip, my urethra burned. I howled, which managed to wake Shannon from her slumber.

She sprang to action, hopped off the bed, and gave me a kiss. "How are you doing?" she asked brightly. I could even say she was perky, dammit. I did not feel perky.

"I feel like I've been made into a human punching bag," I mumbled. "This your idea of some sort of sexual domination game? Because I'm not liking it one bit." The pain in my right leg was shooting up the back of my thigh into my butt cheek, where it constricted a muscle there and produced a world-class cramp. "Argh. Oh man, I've got a cramp in the back of my thigh."

"Let me rub it—"

I stopped her from slipping her hand under the covers. Lord knew what she'd find, and the thought of her fingers sliming through my shit made me sick to my stomach. To say I was feeling vulnerable was an understatement.

"Don't touch me!" I wanted it to sound definitive, in control, but I sounded like a scared teenager as my normally deep baritone voice wailed like a wounded female cat in heat.

Her face was filled with tears, but she was smiling.

"Sorry," I mumbled.

"I'm so glad to see you awake, Marco. It was very touch and go. But you have a great doctor. The worst part is over. Now we can concentrate on healing."

"How bad is it? Give it to me straight. I can tell they didn't cut off my dick so whoop-de-doo! Am I going to be one of those guys who sets off all the alarms at the airport screening now?"

"You'll definitely raise attention. But then, you always do get the looks wherever you go, especially if there are ladies nearby."

"I'm not talking about ladies. What did they do to me? Will I be shitting out into a bag from now on? Am I wheelchair-bound?"

"Well, they considered removing your left leg, but I wouldn't let them."

"Atta girl." I was still confused. I closed my eyes to try to remember what had happened and how I got here to the hospital. "What else?"

"You'll have a lot of pins and plates, and a rod or two in your left leg for a time. Not sure about what stays and what gets to come out."

"You put it so delicately, 'Gets to come out!' Like it is a privilege I get to be wired and plastered back together."

"Your back and neck aren't broken, so no wheelchair at this point."

"What else?" I closed my eyes, tried to adjust my hip again, and stopped, crying out.

"You need me to ask the nurses for something for pain?"

"I don't know. I can't think straight. You tell me. Am I in pain?"

"Sounded like it. Why don't we wait a bit and see if you can begin to feel things? Dr. Patel told me they needed to know what you could move and what caused you pain. Your left leg is the one most damaged. He said you'll have to have more surgeries. All they were able to do was stabilize your broken bones and repair the blood vessels, but your knee is still messed up and will have to be replaced."

"Ouch, not looking forward to that."

"I was told to push the call button when you awoke. Let's do that now." She leaned over, took the small device no bigger than a Vienna sausage, and pushed a white button on the end of it.

"I could have done that, Shannon."

"But I nicely did it for you, Marco. Say 'thank you, Shannon.'"

"Thank you, Shannon."

The loudspeaker above my bed squawked unintelligibly, but Shannon answered, "He's awake, and I think he needs something for pain."

The speaker cracked and then shut off. About five minutes later, a young pretty nurse entered the room with a vial and a needle.

"So where are you having pain, Mr. Gambini?"

I pointed with my forehead to the middle of my groin. "I'm not joking. My dick hurts, at least I think it's my dick." I adjusted my hip again and the hot searing pain returned twice as strong as the first time.

"I'm sorry, Mr. Gambini. I'll give you a little something, but that's from the catheter in your penis."

"What did they do, fuckin' put it in sideways?"

Shannon covered her mouth, snickering.

"I'm going to look and see if it's infected. Sometimes they do these pretty quickly and they can scrape the insides."

When the nurse lifted the covers, Shannon looked away. I tried to raise myself up to examine the pulsing body part, but it was no use.

"Oh, I can see it now. Looks like there is a little blood, and some bruising. I can place some numbing cream there, which will help. You're already on a whole regimen of antibiotics, so that's not necessary, but you're going to have to live with this for a few days. They'll take it out as soon as they can, and that means we're getting you up to use the toilet. But until then, I'm afraid we're leaving this in and monitoring the output. Don't expect a miracle."

I laid back, staring at the ceiling while the nurse left then returned with a small jar of salve, which she applied around the opening where my penis accepted the plastic tubing. She followed the path of the tube where it was depositing urine into a small jar on the floor.

"Your color looks good, and you're peeing up a storm, so I'd say, compared to how you could have looked, you're doing very well."

"Gee thanks. When do I get to eat?"

"Going to be just jello and broth for lunch and dinner. I'm sorry we can't offer you the gourmet menu, but you'll get there soon. Not to worry."

"They said if I wanted to, I could take a shower," Shannon asked the nurse. "I've been up all night in the ER, and I feel dirty."

"Yes, you can use the guest shower at the end of the hall. I'll get you some scrubs and a towel. You need shampoo?"

"Yes, please," answered Shannon.

After the nurse left, I saw her eyes were red and puffy. Little flashes of activity popped up in my brain, and I began to remember things slowly.

"This happened at Bone Frog Development, right?" I asked her.

"Yes. They said it was a bomb."

"I didn't see any bomb. But I do remember looking out the window when something hit me from the side—my left side. It felt like someone slapped my left hip with a spiked baseball bat, and I lost my footing. I smelled sulfur, and I almost puked."

Then I remembered I was talking to two new hires Celia was introducing to me, and as she was talking, her chest erupted when a piece of metal stud nearly cut her in half.

"Celia, the gal from HR. She was badly injured," I said. "I saw it. How bad?"

"There are four fatalities. She was one of them," Shannon told him. "I'm so sorry, Marco."

I couldn't get the vision of the explosion out of my head. "I couldn't move. I tried, and then I just passed out."

Suddenly, I remembered Harry and the arrangements for the two princes to arrive in Tampa. I attempted to get up as if I was going to change my clothes and drive myself to the office. But immediately, my limitations sent me back into the mattress and pillow. "Did Harry get the two boys to Tampa?"

"Yes. Rhea told me to tell you they're arriving—" she checked her watch. "No, I think they should be here now. Apparently, there was something that held them up in New York. She said to tell you Pete and Ron picked them up in the jet and are bringing them to the condo. They know about the bomb, and so does the sultan."

"Okay. I'm sure Rhea and the crew will watch over those boys."

"She said to tell you, '*Like glue*' so you needn't worry."

"Who else?"

"Jennifer, Connie, and Maggie. I only remember meeting Jennifer. I think the other two were new interns or new hires getting their paperwork straightened out. Those were the pictures of people they said were killed. I'm so sorry, Marco."

I was getting sleepy, probably from the drug the nurse had injected into my tubing. Just then, she arrived with a folded towel and some blue-grey hospital sweats, along with a plastic bag filled with personal items for Shannon's shower.

"Here you go. Be quick about it because I believe Dr. Patel is going to stop by very soon." Shannon took the pile and promised me she'd be right back.

"So how bad is it?" I asked the nurse, hoping to get more technical information about my condition.

"I haven't seen Dr. Patel's work on you, but apparently, they came close to removing your left leg. You have pins holding everything together until some of the soft tissue heals."

"Shannon said they still have to repair my knee?"

"You're going to be in and out of here quite a bit, yes."

"Any other damage elsewhere?"

"I don't think so from your chart. But he'll go over that with you, Mr. Gambini. You're very lucky he was on call yesterday. You got one of the best orthopedic surgeons in Florida."

"That's where we are! Finally, someone tells me."

"Where did you think you were?"

I shrugged.

"All this happened at your office. You should see that building."

"I can only imagine. Will I be able to walk soon?"

"Finally, something I know. They might have you up tonight. Depends on whether he lets you out of bed to put any weight bearing on this leg, but I highly doubt it. I think they'll have to do the knee fairly soon."

"How many injured?"

"The news is reporting twenty-three injured with four fatalities."

"I guess it was a big deal then. Where are the police?"

"Right outside your door. They want to talk to you when you feel up to it. You should get it over with as soon as you're able."

"Why spoil the party? Send them in."

The nurse next shuttled the pair of investigators into my room and asked if they needed her to stay.

"No, ma'am. We'll keep it short."

"Please do. His fiancé is showering down the hall and his doctor is due in to speak to him. I'm going to do my best to make sure he has a long, restful night's asleep as much as possible. You can come back tomorrow if you have more questions, understood?"

"Yes, ma'am," the younger of the two investigators answered. The two of them stood on either side of the bed, studying my face, and following a bulge under the covers where all the action was.

"Mr. Gambini, did you have any warning this was about to occur? Did anyone threaten you or make disparaging comments to your face or anyone else on the team, that you know of?"

"It was my ex-wife, Rebecca Gambini. She's the one behind this. She practically told me so."

"Um, we met with her downstairs, and she definitely appeared to be most distraught. She appeared to us to look like a woman in pain, that she cares that you were caught up in it," said the younger investigator.

"Still, I think she's responsible. She might not have wanted to hurt me, but I'm sure she's at least partially responsible for the bomb that injured and killed others."

"How did you know it was a bomb, sir?"

"Because everyone's been talking about it. And I felt some sort of impact, something big hit me."

"Explain why you think Rebecca is behind this attack."

"She made a comment about my first fiancé, who just happens to be Shannon's sister. Emily died in an auto accident fifteen years ago. We had a heated discussion regarding the Trident Towers, which she wants to be part of, and she has no right. But she won't leave me alone. At the end, she asked me if I thought lightning could strike twice."

"And you took this to mean, what? That you could lose your new fiancé, or that she might have had something to do with your first one?"

I noticed Shannon standing in the doorway, her palm covering her mouth. I knew it was a mistake that she'd heard the investigator's question. It was the one detail I'd left out of my discussion with Shannon, and I knew this was going to be a huge problem for her. The look that I shared with her in that long moment broke my heart. Her expression was the same as if she'd walked in on me in bed with another woman. I could tell she felt betrayed.

And in fact, she was. I hadn't been completely honest with her. Now I was about to pay the price for it.

I called out to her, but she quickly disappeared.

"Shit." I muttered under my breath. "You have to help me protect her, officers. I didn't tell her about the veiled threat and—"

"Sounded pretty overt to me," said the younger investigator.

"What I mean is that she may have been the intended target. The blast or whatever it was that hit me like a ton of bricks came from her office. You need to keep her away from Rebecca. I don't have any of my security detail around me. You've got to help me get her some protection."

The two men shared a quick glance and then excused themselves.

I punched the button again. When the radio squawked, I screamed, "Get in here and get me a goddamned telephone!"

CHAPTER 11

I GRABBED MY extra gym bag stuffing my clothes inside the large satchel and flew to the elevator. I pushed the button down from the 4th floor surgery center to the lobby. I was still stuffing the remainder of my dress I'd worn this morning into my bag, not watching where I was going, when I ran into Rebecca Gambini.

"Oh my God, I'm so glad I found you. Listen, you're not safe," Rebecca whispered. Her disheveled look did alarm me. She was normally so put together, but right now, her hair was tied in a knot and held with, of all things, a clip—something I never thought I'd see her wear. Her eye makeup was streaked. Lipstick had worn out hours ago. A mustache of perspiration had formed on her upper lip.

I jumped back as Marco's ex tried to grab me. "Don't you dare touch me. I'll scream. I'll have you arrested. You know, Marco has already told the police investigators you're the cause of the whole bombing. You killed innocent people, Rebecca. A small child was injured and twenty others hurt, some seriously. Have you no shame, no conscience?"

It felt good to let it all out full tilt. My hours of waiting and then carefully stepping on eggshells while Marco awakened and took stock of what had happened had only built up the pressure to act, to strike out, to right the wrong done by the bomb and by the betrayal of my own fiancé with information about my sister's death and the possible involvement *with his ex-wife!*

Rebecca came after me, pulling on my top and grabbing the bag's handle. I called out to the guards at the hospital entrance. "Help! This woman is trying to steal my purse!"

Both uniformed officers, a man, and a woman, ran to me immediately, the woman speaking into a shoulder mic, asking for backup. Two bystanders, both hospital staffers, came to my aid, and the group of them held Rebecca back while I flew through the automatic glass doors of the front of the building and out into the freedom of the street.

But, without a purse, without a cell phone, I was completely stuck with no means of transportation, no way to call to anyone for help. I cursed myself for not thinking about all this while I was sleeping next to Marco, waiting for him to open his eyes. I wasn't ready. I should have been five steps ahead of all that, because now I had to act with only scant tools to fight the fight.

A cab pulled up and asked me if I needed a ride.

"I'm so sorry, but my purse has been stolen in the bomb blast," I lied, "and I was just trying to get home to get some things before I come back to be with my friend."

"How far do you live?"

"I'm on the island."

"Ah, never mind. I'll take you there. Come on, get in."

"Thank you so much. You don't know how much this means to me."

"Hey, if that had happened to me, I'd be doing the same thing. You gotta come first for your friends and family. You worry about who the thief is later. He'll get his due."

I watched the scenery flash by and noticed how gaunt and unhealthy I looked in the glass reflection. "He sure will," I whispered back, thinking about Marco.

"So where are we going, Miss?" the cab driver asked, stopping behind a line of cars, holding his hands off the steering wheel. "I'm pretty handy with a hammer, but I'm not a mind reader."

I smiled. "I'm so sorry. I'm not myself. It's in Indian Rocks Beach, 2245 Beach Trail. Near the Kooky Coconut."

"I know right where that is. My kids love it there. They love the ice cream better than the beach. We'll give you a flat rate, forty bucks. If you can find some cash, good. If not, well, do a favor for someone else some day in return. Are we square?"

"Yes, thank you. I think I might have money in my other purse. Not sure, but if you give me your name and address, I'll mail you a generous check. Thanks again, so much."

"No problem." He drove for five minutes, glanced back at me in the rearview mirror, and then again, several times later. "Hey, you're that weathergirl, Shannon Marr. Isn't that right?"

"Yes, yes, that's me."

"You got a rich boyfriend. Is he the one who is at the hospital?"

Now I didn't know what to do. Our relationship was all over the Tampa area, since the proposal was even done on-air. I'd interviewed him, done stories about the Trident Towers. There was no skulking around Tampa without being recognized. So how should I answer that question? If I started telling too many lies, my credibility would go right out the window. But at the present time, I didn't know who my ally was and who were the people who had deceived me.

"He is. They're going to prep him for further surgery. He was badly banged up. I'm supposed to get him some papers at the house and bring them down to the hospital. I totally spaced out that I didn't have a car, no purse, wallet, no cell phone, and the clothes the hospital gave me."

He cackled, throwing his head back. "Well, no worries there. You make any pair of scrubs look good, Shannon. Don't you worry your little head about it. Uncle Andy's going to get you home, and I'll take you right back to the hospital afterward. I can't wait to tell the missus and the kids that I took Shannon Marr on an errand, twice in one day!"

I smiled and tried to play along but needed to be alone. I needed time to think. The last place I needed to be back at the hospital with the nurses, the investigators, and Rebecca! Hopefully, they had her under control by now. I remembered Marco's expression when he saw me standing in the doorway while he told them Rebecca had confessed to being involved in Emily's death.

How could he hide that from me? Emily was the most important person in my life before she met Marco, and with his betrayal, despite my feelings for him I couldn't deny, my trust had been broken. I wondered how he could think that kind of stab in the back would be okay with me.

"I appreciate your kindness, but I'm going to quickly go through things, and then I'll call some people from his office to help me find what I need if I can't locate them. So, thank you, but I think I'm covered for the return."

"Okay, we'll be there in about ten then."

I thanked him profusely again.

Rather than reveal which house we lived in, I had him drop me off at the root of the access trail to the beach. "The driveway is non-existent, and I don't want you scraping the car in the alleyway made for scooters."

As he pulled to a stop, he handed me his card. "Please, Shannon, it's been a pleasure, and if you ever need a good driver—you know I drive limos too. I'm your guy. My P.O. Box is on the back, and my personal cell I never give out except to good clients. Give me a try, and if you never send the check, it's just been a pleasure to help you out."

"Thanks so much," I looked at the card. "Andy. How much is the fare?"

"Like I said, forty bucks flat rate. You send it when you can, but it's been nice meeting you!"

He sped off as I ran in the opposite direction to my house then hit the beach, doubling back, climbing up on the access bridge and then walking up one block to my bungalow. I picked up the key under the doormat, another thing I was going to change, and let myself inside, locking the door behind me.

I'd hardly had time to get my breath when I heard a banging on the door. It made me jump. I slipped into the bedroom and peeked through the corner of the drapes on the window perpendicular to the front door. My car was right behind the man in a mechanics jumpsuit.

So now I'd have wheels! Opening the door, I stared at his face.

"Geez, what's the matter with you?" he asked.

"The bombing—Marco's in the hospital."

"Oh, that was his office? I'm so sorry. How bad is he?"

"Major broken leg, knee's banged up. But at least he's alive. Four others didn't make it out."

"Was it a gas leak?"

"No, it was a bomb."

"Yeah, I had intuition about that. You know, your car was tampered with. First, they disconnected the battery on one side, but they punched holes in one of your hoses, and your engine would have overheated if you'd gotten it to start. Now you're talk about this bombing, and to me, and I'm no cop, but it looks like someone didn't want you to go anywhere."

"Or wanted Marco to drive me. I think that was the goal."

"Well, you guys have enough on your plate. But I'll send the bill by email, and Marco can take care of it when he's out of the hospital. In the meantime, you be careful. Watch for little things because even though I went through the car, looking for other stuff—checked the tires, made sure nothing was put in the water or drained the coolant, gas tank, etc., you never know. No driving at night alone in case something I didn't catch pops up, okay?"

"That's fair."

"Here are your keys," he handed them over. I could have hugged him I was so happy to have wheels. As he was turning away, I called out to him.

"In the commotion with the explosion, somehow, I lost my purse and phone. Where can I get one of those 'temporary' ones, cheap?"

"Any of the liquor stores would have burner phones for sale. Some of the stereo stores too. Walmart has some with instant prepaid service. There's a Walmart just down the road about two miles. Big one too."

"Thanks so much." I hesitated but decided to ask another question of the friendly mechanic. "By the way, do you work on anyone else's cars at Marco's company?"

"You mean on his dime?"

"Yes."

"Well, he's got a truck for Rhea or maybe Dax. Not sure who drives it the most. Company truck."

I nodded.

"He's got the delivery van for hauling things to and from here and the airports, picking up supplies, things they need. And then there's Rebecca's Mercedes. He still services it."

"How long has that been going on?"

"Oh hell, they first came out here in, well, it would be about seven or eight years ago. She lives in Manhattan, of course, but when she drives it down, it always needs servicing, detailing, and little things fixed."

"That never changed after the divorce?"

"Well, he kept paying the bill. So I guess nothing changed, did it? At first, I wondered, about a year ago when I did some work for her, when the divorce had been finalized, and I figured he'd object if he didn't intend on paying for it, and he didn't squawk at all. Pays in full and quick. Wish I had a hundred customers just like him."

After the mechanic left, I went in search of any cash I'd left in a purse or favorite jacket or drawer, finding only a few bills and some coins. I searched Marco's things and then pawed through his little secret drawer by the bed where he kept his special creams and lubes—his little surprises for me in bed. But despite some interesting toys he'd yet to show me, there was no evidence of a second secret life he might be living outside our relationship, and there certainly was no cash there, either. But on the top of our dresser, I'd forgotten about a bowl that contained spare change he'd deposit there before taking his evening shower. I picked out all the quarters and even a couple silver dollars, which added up to nearly twenty-five dollars. I hoped it was enough to buy a phone.

I placed the coins in a baggie and drove to the local drug store, finding a prepaid phone on special for just under fifteen dollars, and after tax, I had a few quarters to spare. The packaging touted that it would accept collect calls but no messages, which was perfect. The young man behind the counter inserted the activation chip and turned the phone on to make sure it worked, handing it back to me with a few simple instructions for use.

Sitting in the parking lot outside, I dialed Judie but got no answer. Then I dialed Jared, almost hanging up before he answered.

"Jared Newsome."

"Jared. It's Shannon. Listen, I'm in some trouble."

"Already? I just left you—what?—a few hours ago at the hospital. How's Marco and how the heck did you manage to get into trouble at a hospital?"

"Marco did well in surgery, but it's going to be a long road for him. Remember when last night I couldn't find my purse and cell phone?"

"Yeah. From the look of this number, my guess is you bought another?"

"Yes. Just got it. Still haven't found my purse, which I think was deliberately taken with all my contacts in that phone."

"Okay, so where's the trouble part and why are you so stressed and buying phones? I figured I would have heard it on the news if he—anyway, what the heck's going on?"

"I overheard a conversation I wasn't supposed to hear. He admitted to the investigators Rebecca might have been responsible for my older sister's death. He told them Rebecca was probably the bomb procurer, the one who set it up. Everyone in the world wants to talk to me, and I need to disappear somewhere. Marco even told me I'm not safe. I don't feel safe, even with all the bodyguards he's proposing. I don't know who to believe anymore and who I can trust."

"I'm honored you called me."

"Don't get any ideas."

"One can hope."

"There is no hope, Jared. But I need your help."

"Why don't you feel you can trust Marco?"

"Because he lied to me. Or he omitted this information. Why would he do that, Jared?"

"Well, he did just wake up in a hospital with injuries from a bombing. Maybe he didn't have time. Are you sure you're thinking clearly?"

"That's why I need to get away. I need somewhere I can think, piece things together."

"Where are you calling from?"

"I'm outside the drug store where I bought the phone. But I don't have any credit cards or money right now. I can go to the bank tomorrow and get all that straightened out, but could you spot me a few hundred dollars just for a couple of days so I can buy gas and food, a motel room—whatever I need, until I figure out what's going on?"

"I could go by the ATM, pick up some cash for you, but not too much, you know. I have a limit."

"Yes, I do too. Could you bring it by—wait, even better, can we meet at the Crab Shack? I'm not sure it's safe at home."

"Why not meet here at my office?"

"No, even worse. Too many people asking questions. I need time to do some research."

"You're welcome to stay with me. You'd be safe there. No one would bother you."

"That's a bad idea. Listen, if you can help me out, I'll really owe you one. Big exclusive, breaking news type event I'll give you when I got it. Okay?"

"What are you working on?"

"I don't think I should talk about it."

"Okay, then don't promise something you can't deliver, Shannon. I'm just happy to help, although I have a bone to pick with your boyfriend for putting you in this situation. Rather inconvenient him being in the hospital and all."

"Funny. He told the investigators he thought I was the target, not him."

"And how did he come to that?"

"Because the bomb was planted in my office, next to his. If I'd been there, I'd be dead, Jared."

"Now this is the part where you tell me you're so grateful to have a job, that I saved your life today, and waited with you until I couldn't see straight while he was in surgery that you've reconsidered your leaving, because you discovered he's lying to you and you've suddenly gotten the urge to become an investigative reporter and will give up traveling all over the world in private jets. Please tell me you were going to say all that."

"Hardly. Just come. We'll sort it all out later. For right now, I need funds, and I need to disappear. And I promise, with your help, I'm going to research this whole thing and Rebecca's involvement in Emily's accident. I want you to bring all the files you can find on it, the interview notes, police reports, everything. I want to know what happened to the guy who got the DUI."

"Whoa, whoa! All that happened in California, Shannon. How do I get those records?"

"You do someone a favor. Cold case. Bombshell exclusive you'll share. You must have some contacts in the San Francisco Bay area you can lean on."

"Where was the accident?"

"Up in Sonoma County. The girls were supposedly up for a weekend in wine country."

"So, name some towns, Shannon."

"Santa Rosa, Petaluma. Sonoma—Sebastopol."

"Sebastopol! That's it. I had a buddy in college who inherited his parents apple farm, and he later became a cop. I think he was chief of police in Sebastopol for a spell. I'll try to look him up."

"And you'll need newspaper contacts."

"Kind of discouraging there. We don't really share. But give a cop a chance to solve a cold case or right a wrong, he's all over it. I'll bring over what I can find right away, and then I'll do more later. And not a word of this to anyone, Shannon. You're not to tell the police, Marco, no one. I gotta protect my sources, and I won't give them up. I don't want to get an old friend in trouble."

"I understand. And you're helping a newer friend stay out of trouble. I need to know why Marco would hide all this from me. Don't give me any names. I want to see the records. We could say someone wanted justice and left the files in the mailbox for you."

"It happens. Not to me, but it happens."

"Jared, we have to be careful. If the wrong person went to prison over this, if it was someone else's order, that makes it murder, not manslaughter. It's a whole new ball game. That's why I'm going to have to disappear for a bit. I'm going to need your help on that."

"Well, hell's bells, I may be the Program Director, but I can do a quick Witness Protection caper at the drop of a hat. I'm flexible, good looking, willing to save your life, and I adore you. Explain to me why you want this guy, who's practically old enough to be your father? The guy who doesn't tell you the truth?"

I inhaled, reset my nerves, closed my eyes, and thought about everything for a minute, and then I said, "Because, in spite of everything, I love him."

CHAPTER 12

I WAS ON the telephone when Dr. Patel came in to see me. I motioned that I was almost done with my call. Without expression, the doctor waited nearly a minute before checking his watch again and then forcibly removed the phone from my hand, turning it off, and placing it in the large pocket of his lab coat.

"I was just finishing up, as I showed you," I said defensively.

Dr. Patel cut me off. "You don't get to do that. This is my hospital. You don't work for me. You hired me to do a job, and I'm going to do it, or I will send you someplace else where they don't care what kind of quality care you get. Am I making myself perfectly understood, Mr. Gambini?"

"Yes. Are you going to give me my phone back? I have important—"

"Oh, we are so important. I understand you have yet to thank the woman who saved your leg."

"I thought you did that."

"No, Mr. Gambini, I'm talking about the woman who made the decision that I should take your balls rather than take your leg."

"What?" I was ready to throw myself at Patel.

"You need to listen to me carefully, Mr. Gambini. We have a few more things left to do. Or, if you like, I can stop doing anything, and then we can watch you heal into a cripple. It will be funny to see this former, big strong man hobbling around, chasing women, and pushing people around with his cane. People will laugh at him, and they should. Because he's a very, very stupid man who has an enormous ego and hasn't yet learned his lesson."

"What lesson?" I asked.

"First, we crawl. Then we walk. Then we run. Do you ever remember hearing that during your SEALs training? Do you know that there are people who break records and win marathons who crawl or walk during part of the race? Figure that one out. Do you know why that is?"

"Because that's how they've trained."

"No, Mr. Gambini. It's because they are not idiots. They are true champions. They do what they can do, but they do *all* they can do. They put their whole heart into it, to the last drop of their blood. Those people are winners. You used to be a winner when you were a SEAL—"

"When called, I could be again," I interrupted.

"I don't think so. You're going to look like Mr. Toad walking down the road because your ego is so attached to that cauliflower next to your ear you call a cell phone that you're not paying attention to getting your body ready to be able to be all you can be. If you don't pay attention to it, it will in turn kick you in the ass."

"You have a crappy bedside manner, doctor."

"I have a horse's ass for a patient. You might think you're special with your millions, your tats, and the fun things you get to do. Meanwhile, I'm fixing people's frames so their plumbing works, so their head doesn't roll to one side. I'm a simple car mechanic. And you want to take that car out and run it on three wheels, telling yourself you're the best driver on the planet. But you can't win any races with three wheels. And your mechanic is screaming to you to let him fix the tire. But of course, you have much more important things going on. World-class things. Have you ever wondered why someone might want to blow up this wonderful body of yours? Think about it. Someone may want you dead, Mr. Gambini."

Dr. Patel started to walk out when I said, "I'm sorry. You're right. I've been a jerk."

"That's not the word I would have used. I understand that you let that woman walk out of here who stayed with you all night long so she could see you first thing when you woke up, who slept in a damned plastic chair in the waiting area for six hours, hoping for some good news that I might bring her. She told me to take the risk, save the leg, and—hopefully—also save your life. She had courage. And yet, you let her just walk away from this place without even a 'thank you.' What kind of a man are you? A big man or a little scared one?"

"I'm better than that. I had reasons for not telling her everything I knew. I just found out. I was trying to keep her from danger."

"That's between the two of you. But remember what I said in the beginning. This is my hospital, not your office. We do things my way here, not your way. Here, we respect people not for who they are but for what they can do. Right now, all you can do is get well. That's it."

"But I have to find her. And I must find out about her older sister's accident, because it might not have been an accident."

"Well, have it your way, Mr. Gambini. It will certainly be no accident when your big toe rubs flush against the arch in your other foot. When you pee and shit out of the same hole. When getting up to put your underwear on is so painful you have to go back to bed for an hour. These things could happen. Do I have your attention now?"

"You do. And I apologize."

"Okay." Dr. Patel sat on the edge of the bed, leaning into me. "I am going to need to operate tomorrow on that left knee. I was worried about your hip, since the full force of your body landed on that leg, and it apparently was bent back at a very unnatural angle. Hips come before knees. Since the hip checks out fine, now we can focus on the knee."

"How long will I be here, then, recuperating?"

"If your femur is beginning to heal and accepts the pins and rods we've placed there to stabilize it and the knee operation goes as planned, you'll be out in two, maybe three days."

"What about this damned catheter?"

"I might just keep that in for spite, Mr. Gambini."

I didn't detect any change in the doctor's expression. He looked deadly serious.

"That's not funny."

"We can remove it when you can go pee in a toilet, even if you have to have help doing so. Once that begins, then we no longer need the catheter. Until then, we advise against wetting the bed. Patients who do so have to mop the hallway afterwards and frequently get spanked with a stiff boar bristle hairbrush."

The doctor was funny as hell but at my expense. I had to convince him that there was danger all around him, and that if Shannon was on her own, her life was in jeopardy.

"Allow me to assemble my team for a meeting, a brief meeting. We'll put into motion a plan, and we will stick to the plan. But I must lead them. That's the way it works in my world. Someone in my group has been compromised, and until I find out who, everyone is suspect and no one is safe, least of all Shannon. And time is of the essence."

Dr. Patel stood. "I will return your phone provided you limit your calls to one hour a day."

"But that's not nearly enough—"

"Is this your hospital, Mr. Gambini?"

"No, but—"

"And you will be allowed one meeting, today if you prefer. Tomorrow is surgery day, so no meetings. You must get a good night's sleep. Your minions can serve you very well, I suspect, if you let them. Your job is to let your body heal. Stress, especially undue stress, emotional agitation, is not your friend. I personally think they dissolve stitches."

"But I can work, right? I can text and give directions, and I can send emails from my phone."

"Yes, I believe so."

"Then I'll be the model patient. You won't have to worry about me."

"Remember what I said to you initially. This is my hospital. It's not going to be transformed into your office." Before he left the room, he turned, reached into his pocket, and tossed me my cell.

"Thanks, Doc. When will I see you next?" I asked.

"I'll stop by tonight between eight and ten, depending. I'm going to make sure my assessment still holds, so don't do anything stupid like try to walk or fall out of bed. We had a Pacific Islander family here one time visiting, and our guy was a huge man. I think he topped three-fifty. Naturally, he had to have both knees done at once because, well—"

"He is a lineage from a warrior class."

"Exactly. I mean, my cousins are still digging archeological sites, brewing chai, and doing telemarketing on their stationary bicycles generating electricity for his home—you know that little Indian guy who always calls you with the name of Chad or Kevin to tell you your car or computer is nearly out of warranty? I'm probably related to him."

"Don't beat yourself up. My great grandfather made a small fortune selling wine to Garibaldi during the great unification war."

"I'm not familiar with that one."

"Half Italian," I said pointing to my chest. "It's a different kind of bravado, but wine can be very important to a successful campaign."

"Oh, indeed. I agree with you there. Well, despite me telling him to wait for the orderlies to take him to the toilet, he had several of his family members help him go, and of course, he fell. So that night, I didn't get any sleep. I had to replace his hip, which was now fractured, and then we went in a couple of days later and re-did the knee that I'd done so well the first time."

"Did he stay down?"

"I hated to do it, but it was a necessity. Told the family they'd be arrested if they tried it again, and we tied the poor fellow to the bed. He's back out there playing Rugby again. I'm sure our paths will cross another time or two."

"That's a great story. The moral is do not slip in the bathroom."

"No, don't get your friends to try to take you there. First, you have a catheter, and I can make it so you are constantly reminded of it, Marco, so don't test me. But second, your femur is weaker than an eighty-year-old woman's right now. I'm not sure I can put it all back together again. It's a very bad idea, Marco. Be patient. Like I said, let your minions do the work for you. Have your meeting, but try to be done by eight or I'll embarrass you in front of them."

"You remind me of a couple of my drill instructors at Coronado, Dr. Patel. I think you might have missed your calling."

"No, I'll let the Navy train them. I'll let their wives and girlfriends love the hair off their bodies, and I'll patch them up when I can. I know my place in the world, Mr. Gambini. I'm not going to try to be anything I'm not. But I know a thing or two about people. I know when I meet a hero. And I know when I see the woman he should go after. If you don't get her back, it will be the worst decision you will ever make in your life."

"Coming from experience?"

"That information is private. I'm a happily married man with two small children. My life is just as exciting as I want it to be. I go to sleep at night knowing I've made the world a better place."

"So do I, doctor. So do I."

I was sorry to see him go. But I was getting texts already from my team with information on Shannon and other things concerning the bombing. I hoped I had time to talk to the doctor at length about his life, what he'd lived through, and how he came to be such an incredible human being.

I stuffed the room with nearly twenty people. I was grateful, even though there were a couple of them with patches and splints, that everyone who could come did. For most, it was the first time they'd been in contact with each other.

"First, we want to remember our teammates who did not survive. Jennifer, Connie, Celia, and Maggie. Celia was doing a great job with the new hires, and many of you have your jobs because of her."

Someone sniffled. Half the group watched me, and the other half looked down, fidgeting with their shoes.

"Nobody comes to work and expects to die. Unfortunately, I've seen too much of it. It's especially heinous when innocents are caught in the fray. Death is indiscriminate, can happen at any time, and it devastates those who are left behind. What I'm asking of you, and you're all civilians, is that you reach inside your heart and make what you do from now on count. Let's find out what happened and make sure we can bring them to justice. Nobody is to go streaking out on their own. We're a team. Lone wolfs die in the wild. The ones who survive stay with the pack, blend in, and find a place there. It's a crazy, fucked up world out there. But we're in this together. We're building a project I've wanted to do since I first got out of service. I bought the property on an option before I had any idea how I was going to pay for it. But we're the kid who throws his hat over the fence, which means that now somehow, he must get over that fence or his mother will kill him if he comes home without his only hat. He tosses it because it kills off his options."

I tried to make eye contact with every person in the room. I knew some would have to let the events percolate before they could come out of their shell. For others, it would spur them to action. Many, it would add to their fear of living every day. Some would help others on the team deal with it. Others would become the comic relief, and even make fun of the leadership from time to time. They were a ragtag squad of mostly kids who could have made more money packing books at Amazon, but they were there to help me bring my idea into fruition. They were one unit. One powerful force for good.

"I'm proud of you all. Hang in there. It's not going to be easy, but we're going to get this project built, and we're going to bring the evil to justice. We rely on each other, help each other, hold up each other, just like we did on the Teams. This isn't just one of those incidents that will languish on for years and no one ever finds out what or why it happened."

I sat back because my back was hurting me now. I reached for a pair of readers I'd had brought up from the hospital store and read over some notes I'd made.

"We're going to replace those we've lost. I need a good HR person, and I need them pronto."

"I got that covered, Boss. We know a lady who is out of work because her contractor retired. She's terrific. I've tried to hire her for years."

"Okay, you and Dax go after her. Offer her what's a little above good. And, by the way, all of you get a ten percent raise for staying on board. If you must leave, go with my blessing. Anyone in that category?"

I looked over the little crowd, and nobody raised a hand.

"Okay, that's taken care of. Rhea, did you find out anything about this boyfriend of Rebecca's?"

"Working on it, Boss. He's all bark, no bite. Knows zip about construction. She got to someone on the Planning Commission. I'm heading that one off at the pass."

"Are we going to have to go through a third re-design?"

"Not if you can get your senator to help out."

"I'll call him next." I checked off a couple of items and crossed out something I changed my mind on.

"Karin, I need you to see if there is any chatter in the sultan's orbit. Reach out to him and reassure him that we have support in Washington and that his sons will be safe on my life."

"Absolutely. I also am putting out feelers to see how deep Rebecca, or whomever is responsible for this, got, whether there is a faction that is resistant to the project for some reason."

"Excellent idea."

"Kevin, you're on surveillance. Any idea where Shannon went off to?"

"She's not at your house, Boss. I asked at the station, but everyone is in limbo, scattered and covering stories, helping affiliates get information. But Jared left early, about four o'clock. He usually waits until the ten o'clock news is over before he leaves. No one seems to know where he is, so I'm guessing she might have reached out to him."

"I think that's a good assumption. Keep working on that. She has a friend named Judie who works there too. See what she has to say, or see if she's perhaps covering something up, lying."

"There's also some tension with Shannon and this Bunny evening anchor person. But she doesn't look the type."

"Hard to see Dolly Parton become a Unabomber," said Dax.

Everyone laughed.

"Find Judie. Find Jared too."

"Art, you're former FBI. What are they looking at now? And do we know where Rebecca is?"

Art had been standing in the back row and made his way up front. "She was going to be detained, but she got that Criminal Defense attorney, Hernandez, who got her released. He's agreed to bring her in for questioning tomorrow."

He stumbled on his words a bit, then stopped, and scratched his head.

"What's going on, Art?"

"Well, in my line of work, you get a pretty good read on people very quickly. And I'm not feeling it for Rebecca. I just don't get that she'd want to murder innocent people. I don't see the bomb as being her idea. I just don't see how she would get access to a pro like the person who planted it. If I may say so myself, I think you should have Forest look into it. I think that bomber had military background, from the placement of the bomb to making one strong enough to collapse the building but not blow up everyone. That takes skill."

"I thought the same thing," said Forest. "To me, it looked like you and Shannon, or maybe just Shannon, was the target."

I added my opinion. "Because I wasn't killed, I'm thinking I wasn't the target. That's why it pointed me to Rebecca. She hates Shannon, she clearly is angry, but in our private conversation, she practically begged me to come back."

"You want me and Art to work together, go over what the police have as far as evidence?" asked Forest. "I think both of us have some skills in getting some things out that aren't released to the public."

"Yes. Excellent. And see if you can get a freelance profiler. We need a read on who Rebecca has been spending time with. Maybe she's being coerced."

I went over other job assignments, putting people in charge of finding another location to set up the offices. A team volunteered to help with cleanup after the police were done with their investigations.

"I can see we're also short on surveillance work, too. Nigel, we might have to deploy some cameras. I want to see who is interested in the site other than the police or ATF."

"I can have those rigged tonight. Already started thinking about that. We also have footage inside the lobby area that was saved. All that goes off-site to another server. When the cameras were destroyed, their feed was not."

"Good. I want you combing over those. If you need to hire a couple of helpers, go ahead. And, Kevin, get a couple of your buddies to help with the tracking. Let's find out where Rebecca is and who she's talking to. We have to find Jared and Judie."

"What about Shannon's friend Sandy, Boss? She talks about her all the time. The Cuban makeup artist at the station," reminded Rhea.

"Yes. Kevin, get on that right away."

"Will do."

I surveyed the room. "Where the hell are Ron and Pete? Didn't they get back from their trip to get the princes in New York?"

"Oh, they already have some stories," said Kenny. "I'm pretty sure they are at a couple of strip clubs downtown. The girl they brought with them is a real handful and, I guess, a pretty good lap dancer herself. They asked me, and I agreed probably best to keep them busy, away from their cell phones, and not able to watch the news. Pete didn't want to get the ultimatum from the sultan himself to bring the boys home. They wanted to talk to you."

"Okay, you let Pete and Ron know that they are to not let Khalil and Absalom out of their sight. I'm going to call the sultan tonight, and I'm having surgery in the morning, but as soon as I'm myself again, I want to have a conversation about what we're doing and why, especially now that the project has changed."

I left the last few minutes for questions. Then I told them to go home, get to bed early, and start work at eight, or earlier if they needed to. I wanted them to take notes, so that when I was able, I'd get a status update.

"Before we knew we had some hurdles to go through. Now we know we have an enemy. Believe it or not, that makes it easier. The solution will present itself as soon as we can figure out who that enemy is."

I dismissed the group and called the sultan, who had been in touch with Senator Campbell, been reassured that the princes were safe, and knew I was going to recover.

"I'm rethinking my visit later on," the sultan said.

"Don't do that. You promised."

"Yes, but I didn't expect this."

"Well, let me find out who we are battling first. Then I'll give you the chance to rethink your decision. But don't pull out on me now. Once I get healthy, you know I will protect them with my life."

"You are a man of your word, Marco."

I greeted Dr. Patel one last time before retiring. The night nurse gave me a sedative to help with my sleep. With my pain meds refilled, a new fresh pillow placed on the bed, I began to doze off, dreaming of the warm sand, the beaches, and the sunsets I missed so. Shannon walked beside me, her hair blowing in the gentle moist wind that billowed her skirts and puffed out her blouse. How I wanted endless days of forever with her, just like that. No jets, no bombs, no last-minute rescues. Just building sandcastles on the beach, watching the warm glow of the dying day fall into another bright morning.

My cell was charging by my head, and my screen lit up. I turned and tried to pick up the case, nearly dropping it. The text message was from Shannon's phone number, and at first, my heart was elated.

But then I read the message.

You will never see Shannon again.

Attached to the text message was a picture of her sitting across a table from Jared Newsome.

CHAPTER 13

I SIPPED MY margarita, even though this wasn't a social meeting, as much as Jared would like to think otherwise. It was annoying to me that he kept bringing it up. My filter was getting clogged with all the detritus I'd accumulated—things I learned about people I thought I could trust completely—and now I wasn't sure that filter was even able to function. A clean break from everything, staying away from Marco and the team, staying away from the station and the police, from everybody, seemed the right thing to do until I got my head on straight.

But I did know he was having surgery tomorrow morning. Part of me still wanted to be there at his side. But something was wrong with the whole situation. The fact that he was still paying for Rebecca's bills, which he should have told me, and even suspected Rebecca as being responsible for Em's death chilled my heart. I didn't hate him. I was confused. His empire seemed to be crumbling all around everyone, and I was no longer sure who was the enemy.

That meant I had to get into my journalist research mode—my personal safe space. I needed data. When all else failed, investigating the situation, analyzing the evidence, and looking at the pattern with all the facts at my disposal was the only way I would know for sure. In the meantime, if something didn't add up, that person had to be eliminated from my rolodex for now. Facts don't lie. Emotions do. And there was no doubt in my mind that I still loved Marco and couldn't quite think of him as evil, but somehow,

I wasn't sure that he didn't contribute to Emily's accident through his associations with others, namely Rebecca. And how could he be married to someone who would do such a thing? What did that say about him, his judgment, his ability to keep me safe?

As I swirled the strawberry drink around to pick up some of the salt on the rim, I thought about how ironic it was. I had just gotten to the point where I felt I could fully trust him. I'd begun to relax to where I saw that as not only a pleasurable option but a reality. He was the only one who could teach me, set up the framework to keep me safe, and create a position for me at his side.

But when it came right down to it, he didn't trust me with a truth—a deadly and dangerous truth—that changed the whole picture for me. It was my right to know if he suspected someone else was involved in Em's death. It wasn't his secret to keep.

That experience with the man in the pickup was like a burst of reality that my safe bubble was an illusion. Marco even said it was. He was so right. I had to take things under control, learn how to defend myself, and never rely on anyone else one hundred percent to keep me safe. Without my own active involvement, safety was always going to be a fantasy.

Jared had been watching me, and he was now beginning to make me nervous.

"Aren't you even going to look at the information I printed out for you?" he asked.

"I will, when I'm alone. Not here."

"Well, this was your choice, Shannon. Look—" he reached out to touch my hand and I pulled back. "It's not like that."

"Then stop doing it. You freak me out every time you touch me."

"But I'm not the enemy. I'm not the one you should be afraid of."

"Oh, so now you're going to be my security, like Marco thought he could?"

"Shannon, I started to uncover some irregularities with your sister's death. Who else has brought you this kind of information? If you couldn't trust me, why bring me something to do that might endanger me or my position? I care about you, deeply."

"There you go again."

"Now you're being spoiled. Can you afford to select nobody to trust? Really? You ready to carry that load?"

"Clearly I'm not." I sighed, dropped my hands to my lap. "Jared, we're friends. You helping me with this doesn't mean we'll ever be anything but friends. I gotta know you're doing this because you are my friend, not someone who wants a relationship afterwards. When you continually bring up how much you care, you assume I don't see that you want more. But you don't stop telling me, so of course I do. And that bothers me. I'm okay that you want more. Are you okay if there never is any?"

"Maybe you misunderstand me," he whispered.

"Oh, come on. How could I?"

"We are headed into very dangerous territory. You're launching a campaign that might expose you to people who want things kept quiet—not for any nefarious reason, just not to open old wounds or something. I don't know. But I do know this: I agree with what everyone has told you, Marco, Rebecca and probably others. I think you're in danger. If you were the target of the bomb or the fiancé of the person who was, it makes no difference. Your proximity to the source of that danger and the fact that you're pushing away everyone who wants to help you just because you don't trust them is concerning. You have to trust someone."

I smiled. "That's exactly what Marco said."

"He's right. Look, I'm jealous as hell about the guy—"

I drilled him a look that stopped him mid-sentence.

"Okay, I guess I'm trying to convince you like you were a guy or something, because clearly, I'm not getting through. The point is, and this is the only way I can say it, if I'm so jealous of him and I still don't think he's your enemy, maybe you should reconsider that as well. I know I told you earlier not to get him involved, but what if that's a huge miscalculation? You could be setting yourself up for disaster. I don't have to be in love with you to care about whether you wind up in a dump site somewhere with your throat cut."

My first reaction was anger at the suggestion. I couldn't think of anything to say back to him or to refute the logic of his argument.

"There has to be an explanation. You're doing your own research, but you're not involving the one person who is very close to the center of it all. How smart is that, Shannon?"

I was getting tired, and the alcohol was beginning to wear on me with what little I'd eaten today. I needed a good night's sleep to catch up, to be able to think. I knew Marco was probably sending out people to find me, so I might not have a lot of time to do it.

"Okay, I'll take your information, I'll review it tonight. I'll get to bed—get a motel—and crash. I'll call you in the morning. I'll talk to you first before I talk to anyone else."

"Fair enough. I'm still worried. But I won't launch anything until morning. And if you don't call me, I'm going to make a huge noise, so don't do that, okay?"

"I promise."

"One other thing. I think you should leave your car here, in case someone's tracking you, and let me drop you off at a motel that's safe. Please let me do that, Shannon. I will rest better tonight if I know you're checked in safely for the night."

I worried my lack of wheels would make it more difficult to get everything done tomorrow. I had to go to the bank to get a new credit card and some cash, and I had to get some clothes, as I needed to avoid my little house by the beach. But that was where I really wanted to be. But the alternative wasn't much of a problem. I could always get a taxi back here, pick up my car in the morning.

It was a weak moment, I knew. But I was getting tired of fighting all the worry inside my head.

"Okay. I'll do that. I made a reservation without a credit card at the Wyndham in Clearwater. I've been there before."

Jared settled our tab. I picked up the manilla inner-office folder filled with items he'd copied for me, my briefcase with my laptop in it, and the satchel with a change of underwear and some toiletries. I'd left the scrubs at my place, in favor of a fresh pair of jeans and a long-sleeved tee shirt.

The two of us pulled out of the parking lot, which was jammed with people arriving for the evening entertainment and headed north on Gulf Boulevard toward Clearwater.

I LEFT JARED sitting in his car at the lobby entrance. After confirming and checking in, I came back out and waved him off. Then I headed straight for the elevator to the tenth floor, locked the deadbolt, and pulled over the security bar. As I sat in the dark, my emotions welled up, until I began to sob.

It was not exactly the way I expected these few days to go. I was alone, in the dark, and left without resources in a sterile room overlooking the breathtakingly beautiful glistening waters of the Gulf of Mexico. Even at night, it was stunning.

How could I have come this low?

I wet a washrag with cool water and wiped my face and neck, examining myself in the mirror. It was a frightful sight. I looked into the face of someone totally out of control.

What have I done?

I tried calling Judie again, and this time, my friend answered. She sounded like she'd just pounded down a good bottle of Scotch, which was her drug of choice.

"Judie, you sound terrible. Are you sick?" I asked.

"Oh God, Shannon, I came down with a migraine and went to bed. I woke up today to a dozen angry calls from Jared. I'm so sorry I worried everyone. And you, you've been through a lot, Shannon. What the hell is going on?"

"You heard about the bomb."

"Yes. Marco's in the hospital. Is he okay? Nobody at the station knows anything. Everyone's running around trying to chase leads, and the whole place is just a mess. Police in and out, some of Marco's guys there—"

"Marco's guys? Who?"

"I think two of his military buddies interviewed me just a half hour ago at the office. They were looking for you. Where have you disappeared to? And why?"

"I'm not sure myself, except I discovered Marco thinks Rebecca might have something to do with Emily's death, as well as the bomb."

"That bitch? No way."

"Well, he thinks so."

"She's a piece of work. But I just think her world's falling apart, and she's lost the war. I mean, Marco belongs to you now. She was up at the station today looking for Jared, like everyone else. She got into a huge argument with a couple of the techs who had her removed. It was bizarre to say the least. I guess she tried to go see Marco but no one would give her entry."

"I was there, I know. So, Judie, I may need your help."

"You got it. But wait, why aren't you at the hospital?"

"I have to check some things out. I'm trying to stay out of sight, looking into the theory that Em's death wasn't a DUI case after all. If I ask you to, would you run some errands for me?"

"Of course. You need anything tonight? I can run out to the beach, no problem."

"I'm not at my house. I took a place up in Clearwater. I needed the space to think and do a little online research." I didn't like lying to my best friend, but I didn't want to reveal too much.

"Okay. Well, I hope you know what you're doing. I mean, Shannon, there's a bomber out there, and it's not safe."

"Tell me about it."

"I don't like the idea you're out there all alone, Shannon. Are you sure you're doing what's smart?"

"I'm just trying to be safe."

I heard a knock on my door, which jolted my senses.

"What was that?" asked Judie.

"Someone's at the door. But only Jared knows I'm here."

"Hotel security, ma'am. We need to speak to you for a second." The muffled message came through.

"Don't open that door, Shannon. Call the police. Better yet, let me call them."

"They say they're hotel security."

"No. Do. Not. Open. That. Door," Judie insisted.

A small explosive charge blew the handle off the door. In my shock, I dropped the phone to the floor. As it swung inside through a small cloud of white smoke, a man dressed in all black entered, charging straight at me. I had nowhere to run, but I tried to protect myself with the TV stand and desk at the foot of my bed. He crashed through, sending the lamp and the monitor to the floor in pieces.

I could still hear Judie screaming on the phone. The man lunged for me, caught me around the waist, and pulled me like a rag doll toward him.

I was keenly aware of the fact that I had no idea what to do to fend this attacker off. He applied pressure with his hand at the side of my neck and the room began to spin, blackness creeping into my vision until there was only a spark left.

My last thoughts were the realization that if I survived this night, I'd never let this happen to me again. I'd learn how to treat my body as a weapon. There was only one person in the world I trusted to teach me how to do that.

And he was lying in a hospital bed trying to find me.

CHAPTER 14

I WAS FRUSTRATED, trying to think and work with my team even though my mind and senses were dulled. Several nurses requested my visitors removed with no luck. Finally, they reached Dr. Patel, who showed up at the door like the Grim Reaper.

"Stop. Stop all this." He surged across the room and stood over the bed, his face about to explode in a flurry of bitter words.

I interrupted his fury. "It's a life-or-death thing. Shannon is in danger." I showed Dr. Patel the picture on my cell. "Even if I wanted to, I won't be able to relax, Doc." My head fell back into the pillow.

"I don't understand how come you're still awake, Marco. You're threatening the surgery and, in a way, threatening your own health and safety. I cannot be responsible for this."

Art stepped forward, introducing himself. "Dr. Patel, this person," he said, pointing to Marco's cell, "texted that picture from Shannon's cell, the same one stolen from the television station yesterday when the bomb went off. That makes a direct connection. We have to find her before he makes good on his promise."

Patel looked at the faces of the five team members who were conferring, taking notes, talking on the phone, or standing at the ready, waiting for instructions.

"Then, if it's that important, we must figure out a quick solution, because this man needs surgery tomorrow morning. If it's postponed, I'm not sure we'll get the same result, and with a full calendar, they may not be able to accommodate him. Just so you understand, you have to wrap this up." He looked at his watch. "I give you twenty minutes only. Then I'm going to make everyone leave, and I'm going to personally confiscate his cell phone."

The room was quiet. Several nurses stood in the doorway awaiting instructions from the doctor. It was a brief standoff.

"That's what we're going to do then," I said. "Get everyone up who can help out. We must find Shannon. I want all of you to re-contact everyone you've been in touch with and check for updates on her sighting. And has anyone reached Jared?"

"I just did," said Rhea. "You want to talk to him, Marco? I got him on speaker."

"Yes." I was feeling fully awake now. I grabbed her cell.

"What the hell's going on there?" Jared shouted.

I ignored him. "Where's Shannon?"

"Well, um..."

"Shut the fuck up and tell me. I have your picture sitting with her at a restaurant. The text underneath said I'd never see her again. So where the fuck is she? If something happens to her, I'm going to personally hold you responsible."

"Oh, geez. That means—"

"Means what?"

Someone from the background shouted out, "I have Judie. She says someone broke into her room."

I screamed across the room, nearly ripping myself out of the bed, "Where?"

"She doesn't know," came the answer.

"Did you hear that? Judie says someone broke into her room." I was ready to launch into another tirade, but Jared blurted out,

"Wyndham Clearwater."

"We're on it. Have the cops meet us there, Rhea," said Forest. Art and Kevin left with him.

"I'll meet them there as well. I didn't anticipate all this," Jared said before he signed off.

I was already giving him a piece of my mind when I discovered Jared was no longer on the line. I felt like I was about to explode. I drew my arm back, the drugs pulling back the veil of my control, intending to throw the phone into the wall.

"Wait!" shouted Rhea. "That's my phone." She yanked it back and handed it to Dax. "Marco, you have to get right in the head. You're not thinking."

Dax looked up at Dr. Patel. "He's not going to hear back in time. You gotta let him stay up until they locate her. Please."

Patel paced the room then turned to Marco. "Give your phone to your crew, Marco. If there is news, I will instruct them to come in and disturb you, let you know."

I shook my head. "No. We have to postpone this surgery. I gotta get out of here. I can't have—"

"Even if you weren't having surgery, the answer is no. You're in a semi-sterile environment here, one I can manage. Even if you could navigate outside, and you can't, you'll move that leg around. You could disturb all the alignments. I'd have to go in and operate again. You run the risk of losing your leg. You were that close," he said, using his fingers to show. "We're building up your blood supply, cutting it close as it is, so no, it's out of the question, what you're thinking. I know what you're going through—"

"Do you?" I barked back.

"Boss, I'll stay right here all night if I have to. The doc's right. Try to get some rest," pleaded Rhea.

Dax was checking Rhea's phone. "Forest has already contacted hotel security, and the surveillance footage from the lobby area will be available to the team when they get there. They're restricting all movement out of the hotel. Police are five minutes away."

"All right. We've done all we can. I want the two of you out. Marco, your phone…" Dr. Patel held his hand out. I reluctantly gave it up. Dax and Rhea were ushered out, Rhea whispering assurances as she was literally forced from the room.

I was in full-on combat mode but without the weapons and physical ability to get into the fight. Instead of using my brain to strategize and help plan, I was trying to figure out a way to get out of the hospital, which I realized could cost me dearly. I knew this was counterproductive thinking, but with the drugs in my system, I was fighting a losing battle over my consciousness. Patel instructed I be given another sleep aid, which at first only intensified my mental wanderings.

Every single one of my mistakes came flaring to the surface. Yes, I should have told Shannon about the full conversation with Rebecca. I should have demanded someone go follow her. I should have demanded answers from Rebecca that afternoon when they visited her. There were so many things I should have followed up on and didn't.

But the biggest regret, as I fell into a deep sleep, was that I hadn't assigned someone to Shannon's security team immediately. That was a fatal flaw and had the possibility of causing—I didn't want to think about it. I'd been a dumbass, worrying about the project first, when someone was already two steps ahead of me.

And I had no clear idea who or what I was fighting.

CHAPTER 15

I WOKE UP with a skull-splitting headache. I was also sick to my stomach and dizzy. I tried to roll to my side but found I was fully restrained. My panic only escalated when I discovered my mouth had been taped over with duct tape. That meant I could suffocate on my own vomit!

My legs were also bound with duct tape at the ankles, and my hands done the same way behind my back. I tried to push my feet against some surface to right myself since I couldn't use my arms, but when I did, I felt pieces of equipment moving rather than a hard structure to boost from. My ears buzzed with the sound of a heavy-duty diesel motor. I was in the camper shell of a diesel pickup, just like the one I'd seen at the dog park that day!

Another wave of nausea came over me. I inhaled and exhaled deeply, hoping to clear my head while telling myself I was not sick, trying to coax my stomach into submission. I did not have the ability to put my head between my knees, but the deep breathing calmed me, and soon I became distracted by all sorts of ideas and visions.

I took an assessment of my environment. I could hear traffic, like on a freeway. The road was smooth. The equipment my feet had encountered was small enough to slide and it rattled with the rhythm of the truck's bouncing over occasional uneven pavement. I checked all my extremities. Nothing hurt, but the lack of blood circulation to my wrists was painful, making my hands feel warm and swollen. But as I tried, the tape didn't budge.

When I checked my ankle restraints, there was more movement. But after several minutes trying to pry myself free, I couldn't make enough space to get one leg released. So I went back to my hands and, this time, felt something sharp against my fingers. Then I smelled oil or some solvent. From the shape of the sharp metal piece, I identified it as a propeller blade, perhaps a small boat motor. Trying to push it back and forth, I confirmed that it was heavy and began to rub the tape against the edge of the blade until I was able to slice through the tape to free myself.

Next, I removed the tape from my mouth and gasped, inhaling in gulps and becoming sicker, my stomach gurgling in protest as I smelled and almost tasted the thick fumes from the motor in the stifling hot compartment. I didn't have much in my stomach, so when I involuntarily vomited, all I gave up was a sickening, bitter bile.

I was able to sit up at last, leaning over to unbind my ankles, rubbing them to increase circulation.

I became aware that lights flashed occasionally through tiny windows in the side of the camper shell, figuring out they were streetlamps as we drove by. As the light illuminated the contents of the camper, I recognized pieces of camera equipment that looked vaguely familiar. Several heavy black electrical cords were in the corner, wrapped in coils and strapped with Velcro ties. On the side of the body of the camera was a decal. Upside down, I read the letters: TMBC.

I instantly recognized the camera and the operator from my last broadcast. The assistant producer had made some creepy point about having me smile and look pretty for the viewers. Was this the person who had been stalking me? And could he be the bomber? Was he hired by someone else?

Scanning the area, I looked for a weapon. The cords were too thick to use for anything. The camera was too bulky, and I doubted I could even lift it. But beneath my feet I noticed two metal rods, part of a boom assembly to hold up a microphone from a ceiling location. They had been unscrewed and laying side by side, and when I picked one up, it felt light enough to wield and heavy enough to do damage.

The truck was pulling off the freeway, but instead of stopping, it exited onto a paved surface with potholes, and the driver slowed down.

Who was he? I had worked at the station for some time but never saw his face. Perhaps he was new, but in the environment I was in, the surrounding area was mostly dark when we filmed, all the lights being directed at the podium. I never had occasion to speak with the crew except Sandy, my makeup artist. In fact, I couldn't recall any of their faces and probably wouldn't recognize them in public.

When the truck tires thumped off pavement and onto a gravel road, my pulse spiked. Now, if I managed escape, I'd be in a more remote area, probably some area the driver was familiar with. On a freeway or main road with streetlamps, I had more of a chance of stopping a passer-by or witness. Listening for other signs of life, I heard no other vehicles running.

Off in the distance, I heard a siren, which quickly passed by without slowing down or stopping, but that gave me a directional signal back to a traveled main road of some kind. If I could somehow get away, that's where I would head to.

Thunder clapped suddenly, and I almost screamed. It was followed by the sounds of heavy droplets falling on the top of the shell. The smell of the rain hitting hot, humid soil was the only thing familiar about my surroundings. But then, that's what all of Florida felt like in the middle of rainy season.

I felt the speed of the truck begin to slow, so I picked up the metal pole and fiddled with the back window, latched from the outside. If I launched the pole and broke the glass, the driver would know I'd gotten myself untied and would be forewarned. And the glass would be tricky to maneuver through without getting seriously cut. So I waited.

I wondered if Marco's team was even aware that I'd been taken, since they didn't know I went to the hotel in the first place. I remembered dropping the burner phone during my conversation with Judie, but the only person who knew where I'd gone was Jared.

No, I thought, I was on my own. It was by my own design. Again, another bad decision made of haste. My lack of trust in Marco had caused this whole problem, just like his lack of trust in me exacerbated things when he didn't divulge information he was withholding from me about Em's death.

Playing back all the elements of today, I remembered Rebecca trying to restrain me at the hospital, desperate, clutching, and saying over and over, "You're in danger."

Did Rebecca hire this person, who now was going rogue? And was it even possible the two of them could be involved in Emily's death? And what did that say about Marco, being married to a murderess for fifteen years? Wouldn't he know she had a secret blood sport?

The truck brakes squealed, and then the truck's forward momentum stopped. It was time to get ready. I lifted the pole gingerly, readying myself to strike given the opportunity. I heard footsteps crunching on the gravel surface, heard the latch on the shell being turned, and finally felt the cool, moist air as the lid to my dungeon was raised.

One quick jab to the man's upper sternum sent him reeling backward, but he scrambled to right himself, howling in pain. I slipped my legs through the opening and dropped to the ground. My feet were covered in mud all the way to my ankles.

Then I ran.

By the light of the moon, I sifted through dense foliage, stepping into little tidepools filled with who knew what. I didn't even want to think about predators in the area: coyotes, crocs, snakes, and other animals that could be deadly. But I held onto my pole and used it to poke areas I was afraid to step in.

The sound of rustling leaves and branches told me he was following right after me. I knew I would not be able to outrun him, that this area was probably some familiar place for him, putting me at a disadvantage. If I were captured again, I likely wouldn't survive the second ordeal, so I crept behind bushes and through ponds to avoid capture. I hoped to at least get closer to the roadway to seek help. If I found somewhere, I could hunker down until morning, where light would be my friend.

When I no longer heard the brush moving in the distance, I stopped to take stock of where I might be. That's when I recognized the sound of rushing water but not like from a river or stream. It was coming from a spillway of some sort at my feet, and I sensed a steep gorge below. Using the pole for balance, I slid down the bank beside the metal culvert, not sure how far it would drop, until I found an area below it that was dry and formed a sort of cave.

Wind started blowing rain into the opening. I moved as far back as I could, still clutching the pole in my now muddy hands, hugging my legs together to make a small ball, and leaned back as far against the back of the opening as possible. I was rewarded with the wonderful feeling of warmth and the smell of moist loamy soil falling all around me and giving me partial shelter from the cold air. Though the rain was heavy, the surface of the terrain remained warm from the hot sun of that afternoon. I leaned into the wall of mother nature's womb and felt safe for the first time in hours.

CHAPTER 16

S UNLIGHT POURED THROUGH the hospital window, covering my upper forehead and scalp. I blinked then tried to cover my eyes, but I realized my right hand was already hooked up to an I.V. I was confused and startled for a few seconds until I remembered this was my surgery day. I turned my head away, searching for anyone else in the room, and found it empty. After a brief search, I pushed the buzzer.

Several minutes later, one of the floor nurses came in with Rhea right behind her. Both were smiling. I was starved for some good news.

"They found her, Marco. Early this morning, Kevin and Forest located her hiding in a water culvert."

"Is she all right? Did they hurt her?"

"She's fine. Scared and a little scraped up. She apparently ran through a tule lake and got some enormous bug bites, but nothing that won't heal quickly. Kevin says she actually looked pretty good for what she's been through."

"Thank God." I took in a deep breath and blew it out, as if that was the end to a very long and painful chapter. "I suppose she's still angry at me?"

"Not on your life, Boss. She's grateful they found her. And she knew you'd send out the dogs after her. We caught the guy too. Art and his buddies located his truck, which had gotten stuck in the mud. We had one hell of a rainstorm last night. He was trying to make his way back to the highway on foot when the Coast

Guard chopper located him, and Art and the guys picked him up."

"Who the hell was he?"

"He's the lead cameraman at TMBC for the evening news. Turns out, he has some history. I'll let the boys tell you about it."

"But what about Rebecca?"

"She tried several times to come back here and talk to you. I managed to convince her to tell me what was so important. She knew this guy was a whacko, had run into him on the street when he told her he was working on some breaking news regarding your project. He told her he was a reporter there. She spilled the beans on all kinds of stuff about you and Shannon, what she knew anyway, and that's how he figured out how to get to her. Technically, Rebecca is an accessory, but I think she didn't realize she was being used until she ran into him at the station, looking for Jared."

"I'm not holding my breath. I don't think her claws retract. She's still committed to ruining me for some reason."

"Woman spurned."

"Except she did the turning away. I don't buy that for a minute."

"Well, just forget about it. You've got to get ready for your big day and then, after that, a reunion with Shannon. So I just wanted to let you know. Decided since it was good news, I'd let you sleep. Doctor's orders."

"Thanks. Where's Dax?"

"She went over to be with Shannon. I mean, the cops must take pictures and process everything. She's in for an ordeal before she can get cleaned up and get some rest. I guess Shannon's friend Judie is meeting them at the station to help as well. She's got good support. She'll be fine. You worry about you."

I looked at the nurse who was injecting something through my I.V. "This is to help with the surgery, so just relax. Dr. Patel will be in shortly. We'll get you down to surgery right after. How do you feel?"

"Hungry."

"Any pain?"

I looked between my legs. Rhea scrunched up her nose and upper lip. "Ouch," she said.

"Well, I'm sorry. Can't do anything about that unless you want me to look. I can pull the curtain," the nurse said with a smirk.

"No, thank you. I'll have the doc do it." My irritation was rising. I wanted my life back.

"How are the princes?" I asked Rhea just before Dr. Patel entered.

"Sleeping off a bender. You owe Pete and Ron a nice, quiet vacation after this. With the girl, I guess it was quite a scene."

"But no trouble, right?"

"Reckless but no trouble. Honestly, for being bright guys, they sure don't seem to act like it. We're to call over there when you're out of surgery. I think they've been instructed to pay their respects."

"Just what I need."

"Except you're gonna have Shannon back, Boss. That makes a difference, doesn't it?"

"If she'll have me."

Dr. Patel, who had been writing in my chart, moved closer to the bed. "Okay, Marco. We're ready. I understand the team had success last night. So, all's well with your future?"

"I hope so."

"Looks like you're going to owe some pretty big thank yous. I'm glad it worked out. So now we must focus on the next big hurdle. There is always the chance that the knee repair will result later in a total knee replacement, but we'll see how well I can get you fixed up. And there is always the possibility this new surgery will exacerbate the femur stabilization. So let's keep our fingers crossed. You think about all the good things in your life you have to look forward to, except perhaps running marathons, and ask your little healing angel to give you a hand."

"Angel?"

"The one who held your femoral artery together until I could get in there and repair it."

"Oh, that one. Will do." I didn't have a clue what he was talking about. I began to feel sleepy and noticed, late, the nurse had added something else to my drip.

"I'm going to get prepared, and I'll meet you downstairs. Wave to all your fans along the way. It will take your mind off the procedure."

I was getting confused. Rhea looked like she had two heads, and then my eyes got very sleepy. A warm feeling overcame my body as the pain in my leg and knee drifted off into space. Just as I was told, as they wheeled me through the doorway and down the hall to the elevator, I waved to all the imaginary fans in the wings.

"You got this, Boss. We'll all be here when you come back!" Rhea's voice got smaller and smaller until I couldn't hear anything but the squeaking of the wheels on the gurney.

The two male orderlies working the head and foot of the gurney were whispering.

"You got plans for lunch?" one asked the other.

"The burger basket was all I planned. You can come," the other one answered.

I barked, "That is so unfair," just before I fell asleep.

MY FIRST SENSE that I was still alive was I heard laughing. Of course, they'd be laughing. I only hired people with a good sense of humor, and the boss was always the brunt of all the jokes. I tried to count the laughs, since there were no words being spoken and people were trying desperately *not* to laugh.

I must have moved, because someone shushed everyone to silence. I expected them to say something like, "Let the king speak," but of course, that was ridiculous.

At last, the mystery was killing me, so I opened my eyes and let the smiles in the room come fall all around me. God, it was great to be alive, I thought. That was something to smile for.

Just as promised, Khalil and Absalom were right there, without their normal silk pajama attire. No jewelry either. Each of them wore a pair of Hawaiian print golfing shorts in solid blue and green and bright matching Aloha shirts with pineapples, flamingos, and old 1950's vintage convertible cars with surfboards coming out of the back seat. They looked like they were having a good time. Each sported a big grin.

"Boss!" said Khalil, who reached over and grabbed my hand in a grip, not a shake. Absalom was a bit shyer to adopt the custom, but his warm, eager expression told me everything.

"Father sends his respects for a smooth and easy recovery, Marco. He wishes that you reschedule his boot camp," Absalom stated in a formal, clipped Indian dialect.

I began to feel hot pain coming from my upper leg and twisted a bit to try to elevate my knee, but my entire leg had been immobilized. I closed my eyes. "Just a minute. I'm having a hard time getting the right position."

Dr. Patel introduced himself, and the two boys dialogued with him in Hindi. Then he gave his attention to me. "It's normal to start to feel pain right now. I've ordered you something for it, which should be here soon."

"I forgot that part, Doc," I whispered.

"Maybe I have something better for the pain," Patel said softly.

Shannon appeared at my bedside. Her pink cheeks and soft red lips looked so fresh and inviting. Her timid smile made even my toes, which hadn't recovered from the anesthetic yet, tingle.

"Hey there, sweetheart," I said, my eyes filling up with water. "God, I owe you a lifetime of apologies. I misjudged everything. I almost lost you."

"But you didn't. I'm here, and I have much to apologize for as well. But I like the lifetime of saying whatever it is you want to say to me. I promise I'll listen. I'll hang on every word, as long as you get back to your perfect, ornery self and start chasing me around with your cane."

"A cane is it, Doctor? You didn't tell me about that," I said as Shannon bent down and kissed me gently on the lips. "Ah, paradise. I've been to paradise."

I watched Shannon blush and waited for the doctor's response.

"We'll see. I wouldn't bet against you, Marco. But let's be patient. Your body has been through a lot of stress. No ordinary person would be expected to get up and start dancing. But somehow, for you, it will be different. I'm sure you'll be breaking records, my man."

I held Shannon's hand while Rhea and Dax greeted me next. Then Forest and Kevin entered with Art right behind.

"I understand you guys found this little worm in a storm drain?"

"Not quite, Marco. She was hiding in a cave underneath it. Very smart little lady," said Art.

Shannon squeezed my hand. "Lucky for me, it happened in Florida, where the ground is warm, even in the rain. It kept me toasty until morning. I fell asleep. Of course," she showed me the several dozen bites on her forearms and neck, "I think I slept with some other creatures, too, who extracted their bounty on me."

"So who was this guy? Rhea told me he was a cameraman at TMBC?"

Art nodded. "I have a former profiler friend who now does something safer, and she told me it sounded like a fan gone crazy. That didn't make sense, because at the time, we were thinking Rebecca, and she wasn't a fan."

"That's for sure," Kevin mumbled.

"A fan of who, me or Shannon?" I wanted to know.

"A fan of Shannon's. And it turns out, my friend was right, although it didn't help us solve the case. We got him from the surveillance tapes at the hotel, and, well, let's just say he chose the wrong place to show up. Gulf Boulevard has more security cameras than New York," he said.

"Yup, and we were able to track him all the way north until he came to the entrance to Honeymoon Island State Park. Parts of it are rural. The park was closed, but he must have known the terrain, because we think he was headed to an abandoned Ranger Station there. It's dotted with little trails and picnic pavilions all over the place, amongst the virgin slash pine stands, which is what got her all cut up. If she'd have kept running, she'd have made it to the beach," added Kevin.

"We owe the Coast Guard a thank you for finding his pickup, or it would have taken us a day or two to comb through the area on foot," Art continued. "We thought we'd find her or him with the night vision the chopper has, but no luck with that. She was safe and sound in that cave."

"So what was his story?"

"He's from California and did work in Santa Rosa. Fancied himself a director of sorts, but his specialty was gory car wrecks. Worked for the newspaper up there, mostly freelance work. When Emily's accident occurred, he covered the funeral, everything. He hounded the drunk driver for years, even getting arrested for confronting him after he got out. The driver only served about five years."

I squeezed Shannon's hand. She was looking down at the bed.

Art continued, "And we think he became obsessed with Shannon. Like he thought he was her protector. He followed her to Florida, knew about her modeling and acting career, and even tried to get hired on as an extra. He'd been planning this for a long, long time, Marco. He was one mixed-up dude."

"So how did he get the position at TMBC?" I asked.

"He had a fairly decent resume, lots of crime footage, courtroom drama. He tried his hand working with starlets, mostly encouraging them to do skin flicks, but he was not really making money, so when Shannon got the part-time position at the station, he went in and got hired. I guess he had talent and lots of experience. But he was more of a tabloid guy. Probably missed his calling."

"We think that's where his obsession blossomed," added Kevin. "He sort of had her all to himself right under everybody's noses."

"And I never noticed him."

Art nodded her way. "He sure knew a lot about you. We found all kinds of photos and notes. He'd probably been stalking you for some time. Got some racy bedroom scenes, Marco. I'm sure they'll come up at trial."

I tried to smile but felt my blood pressure start to shoot up as the pain level rose to an alarming level. "Doc, I need those meds now."

I was given something in my drip line, which didn't take more than a few seconds to calm me down, and all was right with the world again.

Art added, "We're still looking for the bomber. So far, this guy is not saying a word. We have to be prepared it could be two separate people."

"So the investigation continues, then."

"We'll get him, Boss," added Rhea. "So far, the police don't think Rebecca had anything to do with it either. But they're combing through lots of evidence. I think your stalker fellow is an opportunity player. One down, one to go."

I had so much to feel grateful for, I didn't want this new worry to spoil my joy. But the team wouldn't let me down, and they wouldn't stop, either, until it was solved. I had to trust them, for now. My job was to keep Shannon safe.

Nigel stepped forward. "I got some beautiful surveillance photos with the drone. Of course, I was following the wrong girl for half a day. You didn't tell me Rebecca was now a red head."

"Oops."

"Well, sir, we'll be more than ready next time. My drone worked like a charm. I've got some features I can't wait to show you. I'm hoping to be able to use it when we lift off for Africa."

I was nodding my head, noticing the enthusiasm from the brothers. "Our father says perhaps the trip has been moved up to spring?"

"I don't know. We have work to do here, obviously. I have a bit of a bone to pick with you two about your behavior."

The princes wiped the smiles off their faces.

"Just because we are living in the United States right now doesn't mean you forget your noble birthright. Remember, you are an example of your father's kingdom, and as such, you can wear bright clothes and go out dancing and drinking if he allows it, but you must always think of your mothers. Consider that they are sitting to the side watching you."

The news wasn't greeted warmly, so I decided to do one more rub.

"If that doesn't work, we could always bring them over and do it real-time. Understood?"

"Yes, sir," they both said in unison.

"Where is—" I spotted Pete and Ron, who had become their babysitters for two days, leaning against the hospital room wall. They quietly shuffled over to the bed. Pete pointed a finger at me.

"You owe us big time."

"So I've been told."

"I haven't had so much alcohol since I was a freshman in high school," said Ron. "I'm off the clock for at least seventy-two hours, man."

"Duly noted. And where's the young lady?"

The tiny dancer was beautiful, with dark skin, long black hair, and bright blue eyes. She was barely five feet tall. She took my hand and bowed. Her gold bangles and anklets tinkled delicately. "Sir."

I looked at Ron and Pete. "You sure about her?"

"What? Her age? She's twenty-five," said Ron. "She has a passport now, but it was verified with her mother."

"Somebody's looking for her. That's what I meant. No more of this," I barked. "We don't—"

"I am of the age of consent. I was already a widow at sixteen years of age, sir," she said in perfect English.

Ron and Pete shrugged. Ron added, "They're here, they're legal now, permissions secured where necessary, and everyone's happy. They're ready to work, Marco. Pete and I talked about the jobs they'll be doing, helped them get things for their condo, the one their father bought. We showed them the beaches, some of the places we ate and drank, what was left of the office, and bought them both a computer and a new cell phone. Their dad paid the bills. They're set. I think they're ready."

"And so are we," added Pete.

The room laughed.

I smiled back at the young girl, Selima. "Welcome to Florida. We hope you like our paradise."

"Thank you, sir." She gave a slight nod and retreated to the back of the crowd with her two companions.

I thanked everyone. Shannon had tried several times to give me the use of my hands by letting go, but I grabbed her back each time. This time I winked at her and threw her an imaginary kiss, mouthing *I love you.*

"Okay, I'm afraid showtime is over, ladies and gentlemen. Marco needs rest, and he can't do that with an audience." Dr. Patel turned to me. "I've been told that Shannon now has your cell phone."

"That's fine by me."

"If you would like to stay, my dear, you can sit over there while we do a little dressing change and check out his vitals."

The crowd disbursed into the hallway. I still had so many questions to ask, but I lay back, staring at Shannon's shining face before me. I was going to set things in motion to make sure, if anything like this happened again, no matter how unexpected it may be, that there was a protocol to follow that neither of us deviated from. This time, we'd been lucky, and due to the skill of my team and her quick thinking, the outcome was a happy one.

But next time, we'd be prepared. I had a lot of making up to do, and I couldn't wait to get started.

CHAPTER 17

Four Months Later

I ARRANGED THE table with fresh frangipani blossoms floating in shallow bowls and lit candles creating a cascade of warm light nearly as bright as the sunset at the horizon, which tonight was flaming a deep rose and purple.

The first floor of the house was built, raised on concrete stilts to withstand hurricane force tides and winds. The structure would be concrete block but covered in a warm light green stucco we'd picked out. Framed in white painted pine, with plantation-type shutters, and Hawaiian gingerbread trim along the upstairs decking, it was indeed going to be the house of my dreams. But right now, it was just a floor on stilts, with partial walls on one side overlooking the perfect sunset and beach at Indian Rocks.

I still loved coming home to my little bungalow and never planned to do a thing with it, except clean it up after storms and occasionally rent it out. I planned to keep it as a reminder of where I started, the simple life I adopted when I first came to Florida after the death of Emily.

At the top of the walls, iron bars extended another fifteen feet up into the air, looking like antenna on a spaceship. They were wrapped and tied off to hold them in place until the concrete blocks were set around them. The upstairs platform was to be the huge master bedroom suite with views nearly one hundred and eighty degrees wide and a gingerbread deck as wide as the entire house to sit by candlelight and watch whatever the gulf gave them.

But tonight, we were in the living room, getting ready for the gourmet meal prepared by a private chef downstairs in the dunes. Marco was talking to the gentleman about all the places in the world he'd traveled and what brought him to Florida, always interested in people and their pasts. Beyond the two men were a team of guards, well-hidden in the dunes and along the beach here and there. It was a necessity that had to be, our admission price to living the lifestyle we wanted here.

He looked up at me and raised his wine glass. His tanned face and neck contrasted with the white muslin shirt he wore, his dark and silvery hair blowing in the breeze. If there ever was a picture of a Greek god in the flesh, Marco was him. His body had healed. He stood straight, his massive shoulders wide and firm with just a slight limp and only occasionally using his cane. I had never seen him happier, loving the project we were both working on and making the most of our new life together.

He'd hired several specialists to help me with my training, both weapons as well as self-defense and defensive driving courses. We'd sparred against each other one-on-one when he got strong enough and after I'd been working with the trainers. On occasion, I'd been able to land a good blow to my handsome hero, which delighted me to no end. I began to love the physical conditioning and getting my body into shape. I'd even teased him about rescuing him some day.

My first question, when the subject of Rebecca came up and the police cleared her, was why he paid for her car maintenance.

"I never knew I was. It was set up on an automatic billing. We all missed it. She wasn't going to tell, of course. But I've stopped that and put your little car on the account instead."

Marco and David, our chef, looked like long-lost friends. Their conversation was animated. They kidded with each other and probably told war stories of their different lives. It was fun to watch Marco throw his head back and laugh. He was no longer the troubled, tense former anything—whether it be a SEAL or billionaire. He was just the Marco I loved, working on things he loved in a place he loved.

The chef insisted he bring the platter of grilled vegetables and seafood up the steps himself. Marco was still careful about walking up and down stairs without his cane, but tonight, he used it for balance, since these stairs did not yet have handrails.

David laid the platter down amongst the flowers and candles, explained the variety of fish and shellfish he'd grilled, pointed out the vegetables, and motioned to several dipping sauces he had prepared, some with yogurt and others with spicy oiled mixtures, tamponades, and sauces. Beneath the table, he'd brought some of his signature whole wheat French bread in a large, unsliced loaf. He held it up over the dinner feast and broke it in two, handing one to Marco and the other to me.

"You have butter here as well. But it's excellent for soaking up all these lovely juices. Have fun!"

With that, he bowed, left down the stairs, and drove away slowly.

"Wow!" I squealed. "I have never seen anything so beautiful. Even crab, small pieces of corn on the cob, and sausage."

"He said the sausage is very hot," Marco reminded me.

"I think I'll try some crab and butter, with some bread." I broke a piece off, used a pair of tongs to place the crab meat on the butter-soaked bread, and tasted the orgasmic flavor of the grilled meat enhanced by the ocean salt air and the gentle wind flowing onshore.

Marco watched me, his chin in the palm of his hand, not interested in doing anything but observing me enjoy my food.

I stopped. "What? Is something wrong?"

"Absolutely nothing's wrong. What could possibly be wrong?"

"Don't you want to just dive in?" I asked him.

"No. I want to watch you do it first. I will, trust me. I will."

He took my hand across the table and kissed my palm. Tracing the lifelines coursing back and forth there, he said, "Tell me about the angel. Dr. Patel said there was an angel who helped him fix me. Did you see anything like that?"

He looked up and directly into my eyes. His gaze could not be denied. He wanted an answer.

I stopped chewing, swallowing hard. Staring back, I took a deep breath and whispered, "It was Em, Marco. I could feel her when I asked that she help you. I told her it was too soon for you to join her again. I asked her to send you back. And she did."

Marco stopped tracing my lines but, other than that, didn't react. "Not exactly. I came back of my own choice. I didn't sense her at all, but I don't doubt that you did. And I think she knew I wanted to stay, to stay with you."

I watched his face illuminated by the orange and red sky, soaking it all in. My eyes filled with grateful tears. I could hardly express what I was feeling.

"You came back for me?" I felt ridiculous for asking but wanted to hear it one more time.

"You are the light of my life. We were made to be together, Shannon. I came back because you are the only one I have ever truly loved. It will always be that way."

I was speechless. So he added, "It's where I belong, where I've always belonged."

I didn't want to break the magic of the moment, but I needed to tell him what was in my heart. "I knew this, what we have now, would be my destiny right from that day you gave me the flower from her grave. I felt it, not like a twelve-year-old, but as the full-grown woman I am today. I saw this day, felt it in my heart, deep inside my bones. I never forgot that feeling growing up, even as I was grieving Emily's passing. I held onto it in that special place reserved for only you. It sustained me, Marco. And it drew me back to you. I had to see if it was real. And it was."

He turned to face the gulf, tears streaming down his cheeks.

I sat back, both hands now folded in my lap, unsure how to proceed. He was searching the horizon, and then finally, he spoke. "I think what makes life so special is that it doesn't last forever. It's rare. And so beautiful. And love is worth all the risk. It's worth protecting. I'm going to make an artform out of it, Shannon."

We picked at our food then placed the tray back in the zipper case provided by the chef. Otherwise, we'd be sharing it with the sea birds later. Hot lemon-scented towels had been provided, which I felt I needed all over, but it did the job on my hands, forearms, and face.

Marco came around the table and took my hand, walking us both down the stairs of our new dream home, to the dunes and the surf beyond. There was just enough light to make out the outlines of the clouds and still see some stars beginning to pop out of the deep turquoise of the sky.

The surf was warm on our bare feet. No one else was on the beach, yet we knew there were protectors in the dunes. Two tall white egrets and a battered old sea gull studied the waves, perhaps waiting for someone to come for a visit from the ocean.

His tender embrace and kiss lingered a lifetime. My knees were weak. Water splashed up to my knees, and I didn't care. My arms wrapped around his body. "I'm never letting you go," I whispered.

"You couldn't push me away. Not possible."

We'd worked hard these past four months. Diligent with his exercises, his bones had healed, and the terrible gashes that were stitched up completely covered over. All the scarring remained, but he could walk straight. His hip and knee no longer bothered him, and he continued with his PT work to such an extent he was cleared to do some weighted squats and possibly some running eventually. But slowly, day by day, he was recovering even better than before.

The Trident Towers was filling up fast with reservations. Some vet groups came to help with the construction, sometimes for a day or two, sometimes for a week. Our development group had helped train other construction companies and developers to copy our plan and facilitate having towers built in their communities. It was the best kind of giving back I could think of. Khalil and Absalom became used to giving interviews, even drumming up support for the upcoming project in Africa, which they were proud to be made construction managers of.

I thought about all these things as we ascended the stairs again and sat on the top step.

"Who knew Khalil and Absalom would turn out to be great team members? What a rocky start they had," I whispered. "I think of all the arguments they had with our team to begin with."

"They had to learn that respect is something you earn, not what you're born into. That was a hard lesson for them. I could have easily sent them back for attempting to fire trusted members of our group. And I let them know, if they made me choose between them and my team, I'd chose my team any day. They had to hear and confront that."

"You think they really learned it?" I asked.

"We taught that too. Fake it until you make it. That lesson was easier for them." Marco chuckled. "Easier than staying out of strip clubs and being too forward with the ladies, at least."

"They love to surf."

"I think that kept them here when nothing else could. Yup, they manned up real good. I'm proud of them."

The wedding had been planned for January, only two months away. All the invitations were mailed out, and all the details of the wedding were worked out by the sultan's wives. I knew there would be some surprises and new adventures waiting for us when we arrived at the Pink Palace.

"I can't wait for the wedding. Are you nervous?" I asked him.

"It's a big step, isn't it? But no, this is how to do it right. Make a big festival out of it. Celebrate with all those you love. I think I learned that from the sultan himself."

As a gesture of good will, I had even consulted with Rebecca on some of the lobby decorations, but Rebecca was not given a credit card nor a checkbook or authorization to spend. I enjoyed working with her. Knowing Marco like I did, I knew it would be impossible for Rebecca not to still be in love with him, and I made my peace with it. Rebecca's ticket of admission was that she behaved, never got in the way, and never exerted her will over any member of the team. And Marco insisted that she not be paid for any of her work, either. The truce had held.

"I'm ready to turn in. How about you?"

I nodded.

They left the candles to blow out on their own and walked to the back of the platform where a large pillow bed had been placed this afternoon. Inside the bed was a layer of lavender infused in the foam.

I searched for evidence of their guards as Marco began removing my dress over the top of my head.

"I told them not to look."

"But I'm"—and as he pulled the dress away, I finished— "naked!"

He wrapped his arms around me and helped me into the soft sheets and lavender scent. "Only to my eyes. You are soft and naked," he said as he stroked me, "and a pleasure to touch, to kiss, and to love." His fingers laced through my hair as he kissed my neck and down between my breasts.

It was a warm night. I watched the stars above him as he slowly worked his magic, brought me bliss, and set us both on fire.

His hands, mouth, and tongue showed me the need I filled for him. He demanded all of me. I needed him deep, setting me ablaze and then letting me float through the clouds with my fingers and legs entangled in his, holding on to forever with all the intensity of a forever dream.

We were and always would be made for each other.

CHAPTER 18

THE SULTAN OF Bonin had done everything he could do to avoid coming for the promised visit to Florida. I wasn't going to let him forget that promise, and knew that once made, it was a life-or-death thing for the sultan.

He'd been instructed not to bring more than one or two wives, but as Shannon and I waited for them to deplane, I could see the sultan had violated the first rule in the style to which he was accustomed. He brought six wives, each with their own servants plus servants for the servants to carry all the clothing and equipment they required.

The sultan stood in the doorway of the private jet entrance and held his hands out to the side with a frown. He was asking for forgiveness already. I thought to myself, I should have known better, but this meant another eight-bedroom house would have to be procured just to lodge everyone.

I approached him and hesitated to give him a hug in public. But the sultan initiated it, grabbing me by the upper arms and examining me from head to toe.

"You are strong and well, Marco. I can't believe it. You are bigger and stronger than before."

"Good to see you, sir. I can see you followed my instructions," I replied, noticing the bevy of women congregated in the doorway, waiting for permission to enter the lobby area.

"You know women, Marco. I tried to choose the oldest wives first and the younger ones objected. I tried to figure a lottery system where it was random, and they refused. Luckily, several didn't want to come and told me they would never in their lives wear a bathing suit and expose themselves to strangers. But that didn't solve the whole problem."

I knew he didn't try very hard to cull the entourage.

"I expected this to happen. I just didn't think there would be so many. We'll make it work somehow."

"They don't all need separate bedrooms, you know. They are used to sleeping all together. The servants too."

"I understand. Do you want to ask them to enter? It's hot in the breezeway."

I presented Shannon, who was greeted by the sultan warmly, as well as the wives.

As we walked through the small concourse, private jet passengers stared as the crowd passed by as if they were watching the U.S. President and his staff arriving.

My earpiece squawked. "You think six more Suburbans will do?" Kevin asked.

"Hopefully. How fast can you get them?" I asked.

"We had them on standby, so they're here."

"Thanks. That earns you a bonus, Kevin."

The sultan looked puzzled.

"I have an earpiece so I can talk to my team. This is a large group. I wanted to be sure we had enough transportation."

"They can wait. That is no problem."

"I've arranged it. It's all done."

"Excellent."

Shannon and I rode in the car with the sultan, who elected not to have part of his group with him. I knew it was because he needed to discuss something that he didn't want known. I braced for another surprise.

"My health is not very good right now. I had a physician who specializes in cancer research come in and take a battery of tests and evaluate me. There is some alternative treatment available, but he fears I'm too far past that point."

"You have lung cancer?"

"Confirmed."

"Then have surgery."

"I don't want surgery. I don't like the recovery time."

"But if you don't, they'll just watch you fade away. It could be a long process and more painful than the surgery. I wish you'd reconsider."

"I think I've made my decision to do nothing. I want to see my sons go to Africa and come back successful businessmen before I go. Perhaps see them marry too?"

"But why cut your life short?" I was stunned at his decision.

The sultan watched the Florida landscape through the window as they zoomed past beaches, palm trees, and stopped for beach-goers in wagons with little children in tow.

"So this is Florida. Much different than I thought. I was expecting Miami Vice. Corvettes and bright pink and turquoise buildings and lots of neon lights."

"No, that's a bit south, and we can visit there, but not with a group this size and not with you wearing your fine clothes," I pointed to his gold pajamas studded on the chest with jewels which he wore like medals.

"The world is changing, Marco. There are fewer and fewer kingdoms like Bonin every year. Some of them perish because of bad decisions in business or changes in global politics, shipping rules, and governments. Friends die, policies change. And all the while, there are bad women out there who sometimes cause kingdoms to fall as well."

He looked up at me as if judging my reaction. "But you're rock solid." And then he gave a belly laugh. "But we're only as good as our healthy family. Family is everything. But they are all leaving. They can see the writing on the wall. The ones who want to stay don't work. I find myself supporting more and more of them every year. It is not a sustainable situation."

"I'm sorry to hear that."

"Don't be. It's what I choose. I want to go out on top! I don't need to watch it all fall into the ocean. I don't want to know who will inherit my throne. I will be the last Sultan of Bonin. And then, I'd like my family to do something good with it, in memory of me."

I was touched with his kindness and the fact that I'd been entrusted with an important secret I had to keep.

"Shannon and I will not say a word to anyone. But thank you for honoring your promise. Considering the circumstance, you didn't have to do it. You could have told me."

"Nonsense! I'm not dead yet." He stared at a road worker holding an orange sign that read STOP. "Does he do that all day. Doesn't he get hot?"

"They have rest breaks, and they drink a lot of water."

"Stop, stop please," he shouted to the driver, who had been given the go-ahead to proceed.

"Pardon?" asked the driver.

Before I could intervene, the sultan asked, "Do we have any bottled water with us?"

"Yes, there are several in the chest at your feet."

"Excellent. You wait right here."

The sultan cracked the lid, picked up four bottles of water, opened the door to the Suburban, nearly tripping on his gold pajamas, ran to the man with the orange sign, and presented them to him. The road worker looked at the sultan as if he was a green man from Mars. Shannon and I couldn't tell what he was telling the worker, but he waved and came back to the car. A long line of cars behind him started honking.

"Sir, you must be strapped in before I can go," said the driver.

"Marco, help me with this."

I attached the belt, and the entourage was allowed to proceed.

WE PULLED UP to a massive pink stucco home on a triple lot facing the beach and gulf beyond. One by one, the passengers were dropped off. I helped the sultan up the steps, which he had difficulty with. At the top, he wheezed and took a moment to catch his breath.

"I'm not sure this house will work for me," he said.

I kicked myself for forgetting about the elevator on the back-side and informed him of it. "It goes between all three floors. There's a beautiful pool out this way too. And…"

The two front doors swung open, and Khalil and Absalom were standing in their bare feet inside on the marble tile floor. They both wore their favorite Jams shorts and Florida-themed tee shirts. Absalom's orange shirt had a big green alligator on it with the word "SNAP" on the front.

"My boys!"

Both came to him and took turns giving him a hug.

"Father, we have shorts for you too."

"Oh, this doesn't have to happen. Let me get my breath and look at this place first. We can talk about beach attire later."

"But you must. It's tradition. You're in Florida now."

"Not in front of the women," he whispered.

Everyone could hear squealing as the ladies were let out of their cars, chattering with each other and with their servants. The drivers stood at attention, stoically attending to their needs. Luggage was pulled out of a large white van filled to the top with various bags belonging to the different wives and their party.

The sultan walked to the living room and examined the beach and bay below. "This is fantastic. And the pool is beautiful, such a lovely color! I wish I'd brought the grandchildren!"

I rolled my eyes and looked at Shannon.

"I think you'll be happy here. We have provided a cook for you."

"Oh no, we cook our own food—"

"Well then, you will show her how you cook. We have ar-ranged for a couple of catered dinners, and our chef has two helpers who will go to the store for you to get anything you like, within reason. Bear in mind, we don't have a large Indian popula-tion, so you might not have all the things you had at home."

"Then I will eat like a person from Florida."

"We call them Floridians."

"Yes, Floridians. I will eat like one of those."

I smiled and had him shown to his bedroom, explaining I had some logistics to attend to.

"Well, that went well," Shannon said as our driver brought us back to our new offices.

"He does this to me every time, always springing things on me. But we're used to it."

Inside the new building, Rhea approached me with a grim look on her face.

"Sorry, Boss, to bring up some bad news. But the Nigerian government is refusing to allow Karin Atkin's plane to land. She was to have an appointment with the Minister of Culture tomorrow morning."

"What's going on?"

"Shall I get Senator Campbell on the line, sir?"

"Please."

Shannon stopped to grab a notebook from her office, checking in with her assistant before following me into my office. I could hear her listening to her messages, but couldn't tell what was being said. Shannon ran to my office alarmed, and we listened to the last message from Paul Vijay together.

"Shannon, Marco has to get the senator involved in this. The control tower is demanding that I land. We are to be escorted by military police and have been notified that the plane will be confiscated. I am not allowed to leave Nigerian airspace without involving their military, and you know what that means."

I was on speaker phone with Senator Campbell.

"What do you mean they've changed their minds, Senator?"

"If you ask me, it's a shakedown. Karin will have funds, right? You usually send her carrying millions."

"She does. But only to pay for advance work, contractors to begin the bidding and ordering process, underground and road crew, and all the planning staff, who, I might add, have already approved this development."

"My guess is they'll take a few million. Your cost of doing business has just gone up."

"But normally, this is negotiated by a State Department rep, someone from the government. I've never been told I'm not allowed to land a plane previously approved for a meeting with a public official without that official making contact. I need more authority than an air traffic controller!"

"Hold on, Senator, you need to listen to this from the pilot, which just came in," I said and played the message.

"Shit," was all Senator Campbell said. "Sounds to me like they've had a coup. I'll have to get with State and find out. And you better get prepared for a rescue mission in case our government gets gutless. You understand?"

"Only too well. Please let me know. I've just greeted the sultan and his wives here in Florida. Got the kids here meeting him. The whole kingdom came, it seems."

"He's probably safer there than in his own palace, Marco. Things are blowing up everywhere."

"Yeah. Have a nice day and get some intel I can rely on."

I hung up the phone and hit my desk with my fist.

"Dammit! I'm going to have to go over there."

"No. Not yet, Marco. You don't know what you're getting into."

I knew she was scared, but I didn't have much faith in the intelligence gathering from the State Department these days. Policy was more important than truth or accuracy. Success was measured in how not to respond rather than cause confrontations, even if those were going to happen anyway. If we could get into the country, I had assets I could use and even people I could pay to get the information I needed. I knew Karin was in danger. And with all that cash, someone might think this was going to be as good as it gets. Then her usefulness would be devalued.

Her life was on the line.

"I'm the only person to lead this mission, Shannon."

"I'm coming too."

"No, you're not. It's one thing working with me in the office, even working with me on the project there. Even with all your training, it's not enough. This may turn out to be a hostage rescue situation, a full-out combat mission. You have no training in that, sweetheart. Bless you for wanting to help, but now I must get ready to mount this mission. There's a lot at stake."

"Send someone else first. Then you can go."

"Why would I ask someone to risk their life and not risk my own? This is my gig. We don't operate that way, sweetheart."

"But no one would think ill of you sitting this one out. You've just healed from a horrible injury!"

"But you and I know I'm healthy and ready to do it. I couldn't live with myself if I didn't try to save one of my own. They'd do and have done the same for me."

NEARLY TEN HOURS passed until the report came back that the plane had landed and all on board—a small group of six, including Paul—were taken to quarters in a police station outside of the capital, run by one of the warring warlords. Somehow, he was apprised that Karin carried lots of cash, and he didn't want a piece of it.

He wanted all of it.

He didn't need a plane. He already had three others he'd taken in the past week. He was promised troops and equipment from a Russian go-between businessman who had offices in Washington, D.C.

He was on a path he couldn't turn back from now. So he took the money, blew up the plane, and held the hostages, threatening to kill them all if he didn't get a face-to-face meeting with the man who sent the plane.

He wanted a "friendly" sit-down with Marco Gambini.

And I was going to give it to him.

REVENGE

Bone Frog Bachelor Series
Book Three

SHARON HAMILTON

CHAPTER 1

Marco

T HIS WAS GOING to be the most difficult day of my life—at least my recent life, post-Shannon. I had to pack, strategize, and get ready to depart for Africa, leaving her behind. We'd been fantasizing and dancing and loving our time at the beach, with everything going as smoothly as any big house project or construction project at the Towers could be, and now that fantasy of our wedding at the Pink Palace, and the honeymoon afterward, seemed to be dashed. Or at least dashed for now. And that's what I told her over and over again.

She knew I was holding something back. And I was.

The odds of rescuing Karin and my two pilots were long. It was dangerous, and the intel I was getting from my friends at state, and through Senator Campbell's office, was sketchy at best, flawed in truth.

I was beside myself with concerns for my staff and my team's safety, which was so important to my whole operation, as I was a security expert. How could I claim that title if I couldn't keep my own people safe? On the other hand, I had a pretty good life here with Shannon. If someone were to ask me, I don't know that I'd be able to make the decision which side was more important to me, which part I needed to defend. My competitive nature and my training logically told me I needed to stick with what I knew, and that was security and safety.

My training as a Navy SEAL, although more than a decade

ago, had prepared me for the difficult ops we had during my time of service. My new experience running security plus operating an airline and shipping company also gave me knowledge that would be invaluable. The problem was I didn't know who the enemy was. And that was always the most important factor we tried to identify when we were on the Teams. We didn't just go in when we knew something bad was happening. We had it all laid out before us, strategized, with pictures of who we were looking for and why.

This mission would not be like that. This mission had the very real possibility that I would be running into a hornet's nest or a snake pit, filled with more than just vipers. I'd be battling forces both within and outside the community. Even foreign and powerful sources were afoot here. It wasn't just trying to take out one particular warlord who had requested I meet him. It was how to get in and out safely with my team, under the military support and heavy firepower of a foreign entity perhaps.

But I didn't know for sure. And that bothered me.

There was also the issue of the sultan's presence with all of his entourage. I had planned to spend time with him, give him a tour of the Florida I loved, and show off some of the things his sons had begun learning. I knew he already wanted to go home. I wasn't going to let him make that decision. My way of dealing with it was not to call him until I had arrived in Africa. It wasn't very slick or honorable, but it was what I needed to do. Everything had to be focused on finding my staff. And, if I was lucky, it would just be a negotiation, not a rescue at all.

As I packed my duffle bag and two hard cases with medical supplies and items I could use for protection, I hesitated. Even with my State Department clearance, it would be risky for me to bring in firepower, but I was going to anyhow. In case my weaponry got confiscated, I arranged to have someone meet me on land when I arrived in Cape Verde. While technically against the law, there would be no chance of the mission going forward without defensive weapons. I called on some old friends from Europe, knowing I couldn't jeopardize any active-duty Navy

SEALs to come to my aid. I also had some choices to make about others who might be able to help me with the rescue.

But the only way to get it done was for me to show up myself, take a full inventory of what the problem was, as best I could, and then assemble the team. That was not the way I liked to do it. But this situation required it.

I was confident I could carry out the mission, but it was a good thing to be scared, because a SEAL going into harm's way without being fully afraid to meet Dr. Death in person was not a fully trained SEAL. You had to know that the odds were against you and never let it stop your forward momentum. If you weren't prepared for that, then you wouldn't be prepared if some huge obstacle fell in your way. And that's what I was confident of overcoming.

My biggest difficulty was with Shannon. I wanted to convince her everything would be okay, not because I liked lying to her, but so she wouldn't worry. It was my way of trying to let her live in that sweet pink bubble of our wedding and honeymoon, and I'd told her so many, many times to keep focusing on the good stuff, the future that we had. Every time I brought it up, she let me know she just wanted me to come home safely and her entire life was going to be put on hold until that happened.

I wanted her to go on. In fact, if something did happen to me, I wanted her to be able to embrace life to move on and find somebody like me, or maybe the opposite of me. Maybe she'd marry an accountant or a librarian or something, a pencil pusher. Whoever it was, I wanted her to go on with her life even if I wasn't there.

Every single time I brought it up, she refused. She fought me, and she asked me not to tell her that again.

So, as hard as it was, in spite of the fact that I wanted to ease her pain, I agreed for this last day to not remind her of the dangers or that I wanted her to spend her life doing productive work, whether or not I was around.

"So your driver's coming at 10. Is that still your ETD?" Shannon asked, using my abbreviated term for departure.

"Yes, sweetheart. I'll be just finishing up here, and then maybe we can sit, talk, and say our goodbyes for now."

I didn't add anything more to it other than the "for now" because I wanted to show her that I was trying very hard to do what she asked.

"Well, there's not much to say, because you've already made your choice. And I *understand* that choice. I just don't like it. I wish you would wait until you get a proper team put together. This is not how you normally like to do things. Marco, you must understand I know this. Don't hide it from me."

"It has to be this way, Shannon. This is a different kind of operation. It's a rescue mission, and first, I have to identify who has taken them and where. I have guesses, but I'm going to have to nail that down. Trust me, I put all my assets on alert, and I will get the team. It's just safer if I don't insert with a whole group, but come in by myself, alone."

I hoped she would buy that! It did seem to calm her a bit.

"There's one other thing I need to ask of you. Don't let the sultan leave Florida. I'll call him when I arrive, but I'm not going to tell him I'm going. Please put up a good front and make happy contact, even though he'll know the truth soon. Can you do that for me, sweetheart?"

"Of course. Anything else?" She was sad, resigned. Her shoulders drooped.

"It's going to be okay. Please have faith in me."

I turned to finishing my packing. She left the room.

We didn't get much of a chance to talk, because I got several calls at the last minute, and I instructed certain key people, including Shannon, on the new sat phone that I had purchased, so that my digital imprint could not be traced. It would be underestimating the enemy if I assumed they wouldn't try to do that, or if they didn't guess that I would come to the aid of my staff. Underestimating an opponent usually meant death when we were involved in things during the Teams, and I certainly wasn't going to repeat the mistakes others had made.

"I love you more than life itself, Shannon. I owe it to these people who have put themselves in harm's way, and although they are not fellow SEALs, they are part of my brotherhood. Part of our life, and I say 'our' because I do this also for you. Unless I can satisfactorily extricate these people, there will be problems with not only the sultan's project but our future project and credibility as a whole. You know this. You're smart. You've watched me. I don't like it, either, but this has to be. So think of it as the right choice, not the sad one. And like everything worthy in life, it comes with risks."

She nodded her head stoically. She was thinking of something as she examined her lap. "I don't have experience like you do, and you know this. But I do remember the night I decided to meet up with you in person at the bar at the Bachelor Towers in Boston. I just knew it was something I had to do, even though it might dash my dreams or my idea of who you were—find out if my dead sister's fiancé was really a hero, like Em and everyone else said. I'd always thought of you that way, and I was prepared, after your years of marriage to Rebecca and the way you healed after Emily's death, to walk in and find a monster. I didn't think I would, but I was prepared for it. Now, I believe you when you say this is the only way. And I hope that you're right. I have no experience to tell you otherwise, Marco. But I will tell you, my life will be forever altered if I have to grieve for you as well as for my sister. I don't say this to burden you, but—"

"Ssh." I put my fingers up to her mouth. "Please don't waste your beautiful lips on those words. Kiss me, Shannon. Give me a kiss that we'll both remember for the next several weeks, maybe forever. Kiss me like you'll love me no matter what, completely unconditionally, danger and all, everything about my life that goes with it."

We sunk into a deep erotic kiss that ended with some clothing malfunctions and a very quick lovemaking session, all urgent and leaving us breathless and begging for just five or ten more minutes. I had to quickly man up, get my clothes on, help her with hers, walk with her to the doorway lugging my duffle bag behind me, and hand it off to the driver.

The kiss I gave Shannon this time was short, but she knew what was in my heart. And I could feel the same thing was in hers.

CHAPTER 2

Shannon

M Y WHOLE BODY went numb as I watched the black suburban clear the streets. My little bungalow on the beach was so lonely, darker than it felt before, and cold for some reason. I adjusted the air conditioner but realized that wasn't the real problem. I was stone cold with fear. This time, I had a terrible premonition, like that was the last lovemaking, that was the last kiss. That was the last goodbye.

I stood at the sliding glass door facing the ocean, tears filling my eyes and running down my cheeks. I knew what I must do, and I knew what kind of routine I needed to adopt immediately, keeping my mind off the incessant worry flooding my body.

I slipped on my swimsuit and padded out over the sand dunes onto the fluffy white sand until it became firm, dark gray, just to the edge of the surf. I walked for nearly an hour down the beach. It was a nice day, and people had gathered in various groups all along the shore as I walked past. The condos were filled with snowbirds returning after the hot summer, family members gathering in groups, anticipating the holidays to come.

We had planned a nice holiday, a pre-Thanksgiving celebration with the sultan and his entourage, and now even that was on hold. It might have to go on without Marco, if there were complications overseas. I wasn't looking forward to my conversation with the man who had been one of Marco's best friends and benefactors. It wasn't right treating him this way, but I was just playing the hand I was dealt. That's the way I had to think of it all.

I felt lonely and distant from the crowd. I was glad for their happiness, the joyful laughter and scamper of kids playing in the surf, digging sand castles or pits, and curious onlookers examining the roped-off sections for where sea turtles had buried their eggs. It was the time of year when these little hatchlings would come out at night, begging for a new chance at life, headed for the gentle waves.

I wished them all well. I hoped the families' children would never see violence or drugs or human trafficking or anything negative in their lives. I knew the world was an evil place at times, and I hoped for all these wonderful people who gathered together at the beach to be spared from some of the things that I'd heard and seen in my short life. Marco had helped me see the world the way it really was.

I had been so naive. Em and I both had.

This was why I was super afraid for where he was going and why.

I came back into the house, showered, and decided to get an early start in the office. They didn't expect me today, knowing Marco was leaving. It just seemed like the right thing to do to begin immediately. I didn't need any gaps in my day. I wanted to fill it with work, productive work. And that's what Marco wanted me to do too.

For now, it would be too painful to investigate the wedding plans further, but I was prepared to do that in a few days, after I got adjusted to the routine of being alone. Marco had posted security at my house at night, but I'd requested he not hire a driver for me during the day or to patrol my house. However, occasionally I saw someone walking on the beach who seemed to be more than a little interested in what was going on at my bungalow and would quickly turn away if I appeared on the deck. I suspected he still had people following and protecting me, and I knew it was just like him to keep that reveal from me.

The office was buzzing. Dax came up to me and seemed

stressed out, but genuinely happy to see me here.

"So the old man went and did it, did he?" she said. She had her hands on her hips as her partner, Rhea, slowly creeped in behind her.

"Yes, I'm afraid so. But it looks like you guys are not in for any downtime. While the boss is away—"

"You should see the list he left for us. Shannon, I don't think I could get this done in two months, and he expects us to give him a report in a week. It's just not possible. But I know what he's asking for. He's asking for the impossible. So we're going to try to give it to him."

I was so happy Dax and her partner were Marco's stealth hires. They were the backbone, the spine of the organization when he left. And the rest of the team respected them and their judgment since Marco did. They'd earned the creds, honestly.

"So give me a job, Dax."

She blew her bangs off of her forehead and re-positioned her Rays baseball cap. "We got some feedback from the County Planning Department, and they've asked for engineering figures on a few of the changes. I thought we'd given them that already, but now they're asking for more based on a reported public concern."

Her forehead was creased and unusually wrinkled. Dax had always used huge doses of humor to tackle anything, but today, she looked like she was walking around in lead weights.

"Do we have an idea where this public input came from?" I asked.

"Well, I could guess and say something like 'Rebecca.' No offense, Shannon, I think it's stupid to have her involved in this. But I still think she's doing her voodoo stuff behind the scenes. Things keep coming up. When we think we've handled it all, something else happens. And it could be things she did weeks or even months ago that are now surfacing."

"I have not nearly the experience that you have, Dax. But isn't that pretty much what happens every time? I mean, isn't that the nature of any large project? Especially a high-profile project?"

"Yes. I think you're right. But I need to check on it. I've got a planner here who made the inquiry by email. It's not anybody I've heard of before. And he's not an independent. I mean, he really works for the county, not like the other asshole we had to deal with." She handed me a copy of the email, and I read it through.

"Okay, so Tyler Mason. I'll phone the office and see if I can get myself an appointment with Mr. Mason. And I'll let you know. Anything else?"

"What about the sultan?" she asked.

"I'll deal with that. Just don't want to do it today. Wait until I get into the routine."

"The boys told me you have an invitation—well, both of you have, but…"

"When?" I sighed.

"Friday night. They're cooking for you."

"Okay, then I'll start dieting now. Thanks. Let's try to hold back the news until I get over there and can speak to them face-to-face. And the boys?"

"We haven't seen them. I think they're with their father. I didn't think you'd object. Saves us having to babysit."

"Okay, anything else?"

"I think that's it for now. And I would just advise you not to say anything to Rebecca, in case she is involved in it. I just still don't trust the woman. I'm all for your wanting to give her a second chance, but I know Marco doesn't trust her, either. He defers to you. He's my boss. I work for him. I work for you, and that's the way it's going to be. I play straight. Even though I'm—"

"Gay. I get it. And you're not straight. I love you just the way you are." I gave her a hug, grabbed the email, and took it to my new office.

The building had been renovated to suit our needs, although it was much smaller than the original building we had, which had been blown up in the bombing. The police investigation of the bomber was still ongoing, which was another thing that put my nerves on edge. But there hadn't been any threats or recent incidents, and we all knew to look out for something in case whoever it was knew Marco was out of the country.

I straightened my desk and went through several boxes of files I'd requested from the move out of the stuff we were able to salvage after the explosion. I placed them in my locked file drawer as I wanted to have them so I could access things quickly. I had my own sort of filing system with urgent things in the top drawer and the other three drawers for support material. The bottom one was usually reserved for copies of plans rolled up and not filed in any particular manner since they were in tubes.

I headed down to the Pinellas County Planning Department with a set of plans under my arm. The office of Mr. Mason was chock-full of wicker baskets. There were at least ten of them, all stuffed with rolled plans. He had a zoning map on the wall behind his enormous desk, which was also completely cluttered with files and bits of paperwork. His bookshelf contained all of the current Florida building codes and copies of local ordinances. They looked like they'd never been touched, appeared brand new.

I waited while the receptionist went to find Mr. Mason.

I immediately understood why the books seemed so new when I saw Mr. Mason's appearance. He looked like he belonged in high school still. While I took that to mean I could reason with him, I wasn't sure. New graduates of environmental studies schools often were problematic for builders, unless they had some kind of a building background either themselves or in their families.

He leaned over and gave me a firm handshake. His fresh face and quick smile was instantly disarming.

"Hello there. You must be Marco's fiancé, Shannon? Is that right?"

"Yes. I see you study your customers carefully." I smiled and noted he matched mine.

"Well, as the non-serving member of my extensive military family, I have to say I hold a soft spot for his Trident Towers project. Or rather, I should say your Trident Towers project. I have a funny dance that I have to make." He sat on the edge of his desk.

I liked the fact that he was less formal with me than some of the other planners had been in the past, and he exuded a great deal of confidence. But I knew there was going to be something I hadn't found or counted on, which of course was the purpose of my meeting.

"I appreciate that, Mr. Mason."

"No, please call me Tyler."

"Tyler, thank you so much for agreeing to see me on such short notice. I'm curious what kind of a dance you're talking about?"

"Well, while I'm sympathetic to your project, we are under certain pressures here... all of them created by the general public, of course. And I have to say there have been some complaints. And those are troublesome. I've had to make inquiries about your plan and the security of not only the building itself but the job site."

I was stunned. I had no idea this was coming. Again, I had to remind myself this was why I was here.

"Okay, so tell me what you received and give me a chance to assuage your fears. Our goal is to do something that not only is good for veterans, but good for the community. Good for the county, even. We want this to be something all of us can be proud of. And, of course, the bottom line also is that we need to make some kind of profit, or at least pay for all the expenses. This isn't a charity project, much as I think Marco would like it to be. He has donated the land, but he will not be able to pay for all of the construction one hundred percent. But it will be built at a more reduced rate than normal. And again, we want this to be a win for everybody."

He stood and made his way around the desk to sit behind it. "I understand all that. And I trust what you're telling me is the truth. We have a unique situation here, Shannon. Due to the recent bomb blast of your building, we seem to have an active terrorist on our hands. We have no idea whether it's something personally directed at you or Marco or the project, and because of that high profile nature of Marco's past and his existing clientele, some of our public is concerned that perhaps he's the wrong person to be building this project. I have to say, personally, I don't agree with that view. But I'm getting some pressure from people upstairs."

"How can they object to who builds it when he's the one most likely to do so because he's the most passionate about it? Are we talking about somebody within our ranks of friends or are we talking about somebody on the outside?" It was my tactical way of fishing to see if Rebecca was involved in this.

"We believe it's somebody outside, who perhaps has had experience with you before. Or Marco. Or has something against the project itself. That's the profile we seem to get from the police. However, the public thinks that perhaps due to the previous bomb blast that everything should be put on hold for now, until the investigation is completed or until cause of the bomb blast has been solved. And I can see their point. The planning staff and our head building official agree that if they give the green light to something and then it turns out they've just inherited a huge terrorist plot of some kind, or revenge plot, the public's not going to look on that as being a very favorable outcome."

"But that could happen to anyone anywhere at any time. I mean, we're talking about housing for vets. It's not as controversial as, say, a pipeline or laws that affect social values or voting rights or, you know, other issues. This is something that's pretty specific, and I don't think there's much disagreement about the value of it nor the fact that we're helping disabled veterans. I would think everyone would want to jump on board with that."

"You would think so, Shannon, but I'm afraid that's not the case."

"What are you telling me then? That these changes you're asking, even if I address them, there'll be more and then more and then more? Is this your staff's way of bleeding us dry with changes? With delays?" I was beginning to feel that rumbling in my tummy and was getting a headache. This whole meeting wasn't making headway. I was dealing with someone across the desk who didn't have the power to fix the problem. So I had another idea.

"Well—" he started.

"Let me interrupt you here. I get it. You perhaps can't do anything about the situation. Who is it I need to talk to?"

"I think you need to talk to the head planner, and I think you need to ask him who's giving him the pushback. Because he very clearly is scared about this possible danger. And he once was very enthusiastic. I mean, we talked about how this was so good for the community for hours. Now if you tell him I told you that I will lose my job. My being in this job is one of your greatest assets right now, Shannon. You need to keep me employed here. But you can perhaps ask him questions I cannot. And I think you need to find out from him who's pressuring him. Because whoever it is, they're strong. They're very strong. And he's got something he's worried about losing. I've never seen the man so spooked before. Shannon, I almost feel like it's a matter of life and death."

CHAPTER 3

Marco

I TOOK MY private jet to JFK, where I had a critical meeting with a member of a UN security team. He had a recommendation for me to use a certain translator who had family in the region where my staff had last reported from. I thought it would be important to try to get a local person involved in the hostage negotiation, someone who knew the history of the factions—to tell me, perhaps, who the good guys and bad guys were.

It could mean the difference between life and death.

The interpreter had worked with UN forces as well as some of our Special Ops teams in Africa over the past decade, but he had adopted a safer life working for the UN. He was an invaluable asset to the peacekeeping mission as a whole and was on a fast track toward someday becoming an important figure in the UN, he was so well respected.

We landed, and it wasn't until I was met at the gate by the UN representative that I heard Mr. Carson Odingo, the interpreter, wasn't going to be able to meet me until the next day. It wasn't the type of layover in New York City I had anticipated, and I scrambled to find a luxury hotel for the evening. I didn't want to be seen and start rumors afoot that perhaps I was coming back to New York to re-establish my office in Manhattan or that anything at all was happening negatively for me in Florida. I really didn't want that kind of added scrutiny.

And I hadn't told Shannon I was going be staying overnight in

New York. I gave her a call, indicating we'd had a little delay and had to stopover for fueling, but I didn't let her know I'd be spending the night. It was just easier that way.

Instead, I called Harry, the sultan's youngest son, and we agreed to have dinner some place in his Brooklyn neighborhood.

The restaurant Harry chose was Italian, which suited me fine. In the background, several operatic tenors were singing, and a waterfall flowed in the middle of the restaurant, lined with torsos of naked men draped in colorful kaftans, no doubt to cover up their parts. Harry was gay all the way from his cowlick to the hair on his big toe, and of course, he would pick some place super romantic and over the top. I only had to wait about ten minutes before he showed up. But he didn't come alone.

He brought his beautiful mother, the sultan's favorite non-wife, with him. Salima was as gorgeous as I remembered her. Her nut-brown complexion and statuesque physique would turn heads just about anywhere she went. She could have had a huge career as a model with her stately good looks and slim body, but although a "common" girl and thus a "non-wife" to the sultan, she adopted the culture just the same and did not do anything that would put her in the public eye nor expose any large portion of her lovely body.

Harry was extremely protective of her, and she doted on her son to the extreme. They made quite the impressive pair, equally devoted to each other.

"Ah, there is the famous Gambini. I knew eventually I would see you again!" said Salima.

I stood and kissed her on both cheeks. "You are just as beautiful as the day I first saw you. Life has treated you well here in Brooklyn?"

"Yes. Harry keeps me very busy. And thanks to my great love, he provides very lavishly for me. I'm not sure how much of this you are supposed to know," she said as she lowered her eyes.

"Oh, he knows all about it, Momma. He's an expert on all things sultan. We have no secrets between us. He even knows about my production."

Salima took one of the menus and fanned her face, her eyes rolling in mock disgust. "Honestly, Harry, you push the limits so far I am just not sure you are my child. First of all, he would never approve of your lifestyle here, even under my watchful eye, but do you honestly think you have a chance in hell of ever producing that play?"

"Musical, Mother."

I was delighted to see their repartee and the affection they both showed for each other.

"So what brings you here, Marco?" Harry asked me. Salima was ordering for us in the background. I knew better than to ask what was good on the menu. They would just order what they liked to eat, and I would, of course, eat whatever they chose.

"I am waiting for an interpreter who I understand might be available for my little emergency mission. I wish I could get him over there tonight, but apparently, he's not available until tomorrow. So there is only one person in New York left for me to talk to. Only one person that I trust and like, and only one person who I consider a friend. I left all the rest of my friends back in Florida."

"And I hear my Arjun has paid you a visit in Florida?" Salima asked.

Her dark eyes and intel didn't miss a thing.

"Yes. The timing is horrible, but I'm hoping I can wrap this up and be back before he gets too antsy and tries to go back home."

"Oh, that's just like him. He talks tough, but he's really just a great big pussy cat."

I could see the love still burning inside her heart for him. I knew how he felt about her as well. But these would have to remain secrets. I couldn't betray the sultan's confidence.

"And he brought the tribe? The waggy tongues, as Harry calls them?"

"Mother, that wasn't supposed to go outside our household."

She was less than enthusiastic about apologizing for her misstep.

"Yes, he brought nearly half of them, with servants and two cooks. Does he ever do anything uncomplicated?"

She smiled and paused before continuing. "And you now have a new love? So I missed out, are you telling me that, Marco?" Salima asked, her lips turning up at the edges and stifling a grin as she batted her big brown eyes. Unlike the sultan's other wives, she wore eyelash extensions that were nearly a half-inch long. I knew he wouldn't approve of it, but the chances of them seeing each other again were slim to none.

"Salima, you realize I am a smart man. It would not do well for me to become attached to the former wife of a client. Surely you know this."

"One can always dream, Marco." Her smile was warm, extremely flirtatious, and as she intended, I felt extremely flattered.

"Your loss Marco," said Harry. "I have it on good authority that my mother is good at all womanly things." He leaned into me and whispered, "My father says she was the most innovating and exciting woman he has ever met."

Salima had heard every word, though whispered, and she slapped his arm, crossed her legs, and looked in the opposite direction, searching for our meals and pretending to be miffed at the comment.

"This is probably the point where I tell you who it is I have decided to spend my life with then." I began by pulling out a picture of Shannon, the one taken for the TV station. "This is Shannon, and she is the younger sister of Emily, the woman I was engaged to before I married Rebecca."

"That viper," Salima said. "I could never understand that, unless it is that you have certain sexual proclivities, which I also find sort of exciting." At first, she didn't reveal any expression at all, a trick she'd learned to trap men into revealing themselves, but then her eyes danced. She broke out in a hearty laugh, her large white teeth glistening as she wiggled her tongue and played with my insides.

I was shaken and stirred, deciding to take the bait. "No comment here. I like what I like. Sometimes I don't know until I try it."

Harry jumped up. "Now that's about it. I'm going to stop you two right there. Otherwise there's going to be some kind of a family malfunction, and I'm going to be right in the middle of it."

"Sit down, Harry. Nothing to worry about here. I'm as attached to Shannon as I could possibly be. I think this is the last big job for me, and I'm hoping to God I do it properly so I can live to have many years with her and raise many children, just like you Harry."

"So she works as an anchor person then at the TV station?" Salima wanted to know.

"No, only part-time. I'm working on having her quit. For right now, she just does special assignments. But she is my right-hand person, and she very much wants to be involved in the building business. As you know, I've been hired to make sure the sultan's other sons don't do something that might be unfortunate."

Harry butted in. "He doesn't care about making money. He just wants to make sure they don't get themselves killed. Isn't that it?" Harry asked.

"Precisely."

"Ah, I see. So how are all the other lovely ladies there? You have seen them, I assume? Does the sultan look well?"

"I have, and he's not well." I didn't want to go any further, so as they both peppered me with questions, I held up both my hands.

"This is not a conversation we can have. You can read all you want into it, but just hear me out. He's not doing well, and I don't want to cause any extra stress on him. I even tried to talk him out of doing the project, but it's something he feels is a crowning glory for him, like how the Trident Towers is for me. So you didn't hear it from me, and if I hear that you told him, I'm going to deny I said anything about it. But just understand, I'm not fooling around. This is serious, and I think you should firm up your ties one way or the other."

Salima looked visibly shaken. "Is he—?"

I knew the answer to her question before she asked it, but it wasn't something that was for me to answer. "I'm not at liberty to tell you about it, mostly because I don't know everything that's involved, but that's a conversation that you need to have with him yourself. He may or may not want to hear from you, I don't know."

She was hesitant but slowly leaned forward, placing one palm on the marble-top table, and asked me, "Do you think he still loves me?"

"I do. How could he not?"

We finished our dinner and then made small chit-chat. She told me about the organizations she was involved with, doing good for neighborhoods, especially immigrant African families, single mothers in the New York and New Jersey areas. She enjoyed her work, she said, and she was considering even getting a college degree so she could do some counseling. I knew she didn't need the money, but I was glad she had a vocation she was excited about.

Harry was getting antsy. And I knew his time being the sultan's social secretary was coming to an end. I didn't think the sultan would be taking as many trips as he used to, so Harry's job was likely to be lost through attrition as his father worsened.

We said our goodbyes, and I retreated to the luxury suite at the Waldorf Astoria.

I'd heard that the Chinese government had taken over a large share in this hotel, so I was careful not to use the internet, and I didn't activate my sat phone anywhere close to the hotel building itself. I was going to keep that relegated to the confines of my private jet, where we had sufficient jamming capabilities.

The hotel was just as lovely as I'd remembered it, and the suite had been redecorated, but I recognized it as being one of the many I used to frequent when I was an eligible billionaire bachelor.

Feeling bad about lying to her, I gave Shannon a call before retiring.

"Twice in one night. That's a first," she said. "So you arrived already?"

"No, sweetheart, I'm sorry, but we are still in New York. I was delayed for a refueling, and I have one member that I hope to be able to bring with me, and he's not available until tomorrow. But I had dinner tonight with Harry and his mother. They were both very delightful."

Shannon was a little silent on the phone, quieter than normal. I could tell she was nervous. I wondered if she caught on I'd told her a little fib earlier. I was prepared to apologize.

"How was your day, sweetheart?" I inquired.

"I spent part of the afternoon talking to a planner at Pinellas County, and I have some further work to do with him. I need to find out what information has gotten to the head of the building department. He was apparently all for our project until some kind of public pressure came to light. I don't know what that is, but I have an appointment to meet him tomorrow for lunch. He refused to meet me in the office."

"Which means he has something he wants to tell you he doesn't want any of his cohorts to know about. That's probably a good sign, Shannon. That means you're going to get the straight scoop."

"Have you ever heard of him—William Warren?"

"Never heard of him. Is he new?"

"I don't think so. I met with his underling, Tyler Mason, and he told me after hedging around a bit that he didn't have all my answers. I knew that. So he told me that this gentleman had been scared off by something someone had told him, and it had to do with the fact they were concerned for safety for the citizens and construction workers and the overall public as we built this project. They didn't like the bombing incident. It had spooked them or spooked somebody pretty important."

"Well, that kind of makes sense. Be careful what you promise and run it by me before you agree to anything. He probably knows you don't have the authority to do everything, but if you think something's super important, give him assurances we will work with him, and let's see what we can do when I get back. I should be arriving tomorrow sometime, but I wouldn't wait up in case it's late. Just know, unless you hear otherwise, I'm safe. Okay?"

"It doesn't work that way, Marco. I worry about you until you call. You know that. You'd be the same way. I don't worry about you having dinner with a beautiful African or Indian queen or a gay playwright from Brooklyn or even a whole harem full of women. I worry about the people you don't see who want to damage or harm you."

Then I made the big mistake of adding on to her sentence. "Or you."

As soon as I said it, I regretted it. "I didn't mean that, really. I just think you should keep your eyes open and understand that, while I may be a big target, you have to remember you are as well. Shannon, not just because you're with me, but because of who you are in your own right. Please be careful, sweetheart."

"I will. You have my word. Now go to bed, Marco. Thank you for both your calls. Tomorrow is a big day for both of us. I will dream about you all night."

"And that will send me to sleep quite nicely, my dear. Love you more than life itself."

CHAPTER 4

Shannon

I HAD NIGHTMARES. They were ugly, bloody, and when I woke up in the morning, I was sweating. I felt like I'd encountered a malevolent stranger like I did months ago at the animal preserve. I relived that early morning with that terrible man in the pickup truck who had followed and harassed me. I knew he was sitting behind bars, but for some reason, I still felt I was in danger. Or, as I mused while taking my shower, perhaps I was thinking of Marco.

I had planned on really getting into my holiday festivities this year, since we were going to be married in just a couple of months. But now as invoices became due and deposits had to be turned into full payments prior to the wedding and the reception, I was faced with bills and decisions. More than one time in twenty-four hours, our caterer asked me if I was sure everything was going to be on time with Marco's trip to Africa. My answer was always the same.

"Absolutely. We go as planned. Nothing has changed."

But of course, everything was changing. And it was difficult to work and make decisions when I didn't have him right next to me to consult. I thought perhaps I would be more help at the office than I actually was. And that bothered me a lot. I needed a distraction, a day or two at the beach to just sleep in, laze around in my pajamas, and do nothing. Of course, I couldn't do that, because Marco wasn't doing that, and it would be unfair. I needed Marco in order to relax. I needed Marco to finalize things. I was capable of making all of those decisions, but I needed Marco to be sure.

I'd always been very independent, and I loved how Marco allowed me the room to do anything I decided to do. But there were some things, especially when we were talking about hundreds of thousands of dollars, I just didn't feel comfortable deciding on without him being here. He was so far out of my league as far as planning, financial compilations, and payment of resources I was simply a poor substitute.

I knew it was wrong to feel this way. He would laugh at me if he heard me talk about it. He would disagree vehemently that I didn't have the chops to keep up with his lifestyle. But I didn't have the intuition nor the killer instinct. I wasn't my sister, Emily, who never had anything to do with any of Marco's business ventures, and I also wasn't anything like Rebecca, who would ride over people in her Porsche if she could. Neither one of those women were available to me; one because she was gone and the other, well, I still didn't trust Rebecca.

Being perfectly honest with myself, though, Rebecca was better suited for all these decisions than I was. Maybe this was the opportunity for me to prove I had what it took. Because if I screwed this up or screwed up something horribly here at the Towers in Florida or anywhere, Marco would not think the same of me again. He might be forced to keep me on the sidelines or tell me he'd rather have me take care of a home and a family than help him run his business. I desperately needed to show him I could do it. He hadn't even been gone two days, and already, I was feeling the pressure.

That meant I had to stop making excuses. I had to stop telling myself these negative things.

I decided I needed to start meditating, maybe do some regular exercise. It had been weeks since I'd done any running, instead devoting myself to Marco's recovery after the bombing. The beach was right outside my door so I had no leg to stand on, and I was not using my normal methods to de-stress. So I vowed to take it one step at a time. I had to make a plan.

What would Marco do?

First, he would create his morning routine. He would get up at the same time every morning, meditate, stretch, and go for a workout at the gym or walk the beach, if we weren't making love in the early morning hours before the day started. Whatever it was, he would do it intensely, shower, and still get into the office an hour before anyone else, ready to seize the day. Maybe I needed to adopt the same attitude. Maybe creating my own morning routine, a sacred time to get myself focused and ready for anything, would help me set a foundation.

And then what would Marco do?

Well, he'd make a list of all the people he needed to talk to, catalog the allies and the obstacles. He would record all the decisions he had to make. I think he called it the *Ben Franklin* list—weighing the pros and the cons of every decision he had to make. I would list all the good reasons to do something on the left and all the potential drawbacks on the right. And then I would look at those decisions as a whole and pick one.

And then what would he do?

He'd execute! He'd go forward and never look back. And that was a problem for me, because I was second-guessing everything I was doing. They threw stuff at me yesterday I had never done before. I had never signed payroll checks amounting to well over a hundred thousand dollars, like I was doing now. It was all Marco's money, which didn't lessen the burden. It piled it on even more! I had never signed my name to anything that cost more than the price of a car, and here I was signing change orders to the tune of one, two, three hundred thousand dollars. There was even a change order for over a million dollars from an underground construction company that was substituting for a company that had to back out due to scheduling. After I signed that, I practically spent the next hour in the bathroom sick to my stomach.

Time to get my brain in motion by putting my body in motion!

I went for a run on the beach, sprinting for a good thirty minutes and then loping along in the surf for another half hour. As the sun came up, I spent a few minutes stretching and cooling down.

Today, I was conducting an interview at the station and would be heading to the office later. It was a jam-packed day already, and that was before I even looked at my emails. True to my word, I didn't do so until I stopped driving. I scrolled through, making sure none were from Marco, and then closed them.

"You're compartmentalizing, taking this one step at a time, Shannon," I said to myself.

When I pulled into the parking lot in Tampa, I was shouting affirmations in the car at the top of my lungs. I was listening to some inspirational music I'd found on a channel and warming myself to the idea of battle. I wasn't just walking into the station and covering a story; I was doing battle, fighting for and promoting this project and everything else that Marco's company stood for. I was going to do what he would do if he were standing here.

Most importantly, I would do it *my* way.

And what was *my way* going to be? Well, I'd been raised a proper young lady, even though the death of my older sister had pretty much gutted our family unit big time. I'd be respectful of our parties and would speak up if I really objected to something, but if I didn't, I would let the game play for a bit and then make the course correction. That seemed like the logical and natural way for me to be. I didn't want to take charge, because I could be sending everybody down a rabbit hole. I wanted to rely on and listen to the advice first, then choose the decision I thought best fit the situation. No matter what I decided to do, if I thought carefully about it and tried to consider all the aspects of that decision, Marco would forgive me if I made a mistake.

I was more worried that I'd *disappoint* him.

On Floor Five, the set was darkly lit, except for the anchor consoles. I approached the dais and looked for Jared, the station manager, and interacted with a few of the new PAs who had shown up for their internships in the fall. We always had a bevy of five to ten interns from the local broadcasting school, and these young, fresh faces brought new life to the station. I met several as I grabbed my coffee on the way to the set.

Ever since we'd had the incident with the stalking cameraman who fixated on me, I made it a point to go up to the cameramen and greet them, look at their faces, and shake their hands. I think they understood they were being assessed. But I could never walk onto a darkened soundstage again without knowing who was zooming in on me. I felt more vulnerable on stage than I ever had before.

Clarence was his usual self, humming, practicing his vowels, popping vitamins, and giving himself a breath mint and spray of mouthwash at the last minute.

"Hello there, Miss Sparkly Face. I've missed you, Shannon," he said.

"Well, I'd have thought you'd be pretty busy meeting all the new interns. I do hope you're behaving yourself, Clarence."

"No, I tease them a little bit, but I learned my lesson. I want to thank you for how you helped me survive this war with Bunny."

Bunny's quick departure from the station was a relief for most everyone who was there, and Clarence really upped his game afterwards. He took on a fatherly role at the station, since there was no one there to challenge him, and more of a leadership position. He was even able to settle Jared down from time to time when my station manager was apt to go off on a rant if things didn't go his way. Already elderly, Clarence had grown up. I was happy to see it.

"I understand Marco is overseas on a quick visit?" he asked me.

"Yes, but I do expect him back soon."

I thought about elaborating further, but rumors were rumors. I decided to just let them take their course rather than trying to correct public perception. If people thought he was having problems with the business, they'd be right. But there was no reason to let them know that. I'd just as soon let them all guess.

"Do you have any idea what we're going to be doing this afternoon, Clarence, other than the Towers update?" I said as I took my seat at the desk.

"Sweetheart, first, you get your makeup done. Or did you decide to go *au naturel*?"

I blushed. I had completely forgotten to make my run through the makeup studio. It was too late. My friend came running with her blush and tools, quickly swabbing me with a little makeup spray, some powder, and adding bright red lips. We were ready to go in less than two minutes, and I studied the teleprompter.

The story I was going to do was on the Towers, but it had been written by Jared with the approval of Marco before he left. That was contained in a little note Jared left for me to read first. I was okay with that, since all I was going to be doing was reciting what had already been discussed. But I hadn't reviewed the material yet.

I was surprised to see Rebecca walk into the room and take a chair in the near dark like a stealth ops guy. She gave me a warm smile and a slight wave, her movements cat-like and efficient. I would have to say predatory, dammit.

I must have reacted negatively in some way. "You didn't know she was coming?" whispered Clarence off camera.

"No, I'm just seeing this for the first time," I said as I pointed to the teleprompter. It was obvious I was going to be doing an interview with her. I noticed she had clutched a sheet of paper in her right hand. Apparently, she had been given the questions in advance. She was armed, locked, and loaded, and I was blindsided, dammit.

"Where would you like me to sit?" she asked me after the makeup artist dabbed her face with the brush. I turned to my left and saw two red leather chairs sitting on either side of a stubby coffee table with two mugs on it.

"Looks like I have a little preview, then we cut to a short commercial break, and we'll sit over here on the red chairs for the interview. How about that?"

"Perfect," she purred.

Clarence gave the rundown on several news stories before my feature, and I watched him intently as the camera was also on me. I remember Jared telling me once that how the two anchors interacted toward one another was how signals would be conveyed to the audience as far as their credibility. If I paid attention and nodded and agreed with him, the audience would do the same. I tried to remember that as I listened to Clarence bungle a couple of words, stumble, then restart himself. He recovered well. He was professional, and it was obvious he was trying very hard at his craft.

I decided to give him an on-air compliment, something he wasn't expecting.

As the camera swung over to my closeup when Clarence addressed me, I smiled and spoke back to him.

"Thank you, Clarence. I'm sure our audience knows this already, but I have to say, Clarence does a wonderful job here at the station. I've learned so much under his tutelage. And I just want to add that it's a real honor to be able to spend time with you on air, Clarence. I admire how polished and professional you are and how you just seem to get better and better."

He was clearly taken aback and blushed. Flustered, not knowing what to say, he finally just thanked me and gave a weak smile to the camera.

If I could have, I would have winced, because that wasn't very smart of me. But I felt he was due a compliment, and I wanted to give him something the whole community would see.

"Now we have our continuing story on the Trident Towers project, the brainchild of Marco Gambini." I read ahead to the next line on the teleprompter and saw how Jared had woven in Rebecca to the scene. "As many of you know, when this project began, Marco Gambini had the help of his wife at the time, Rebecca Gambini. She has always been a champion for this project and has spent countless hours trying to grease the skids to help it to fruition. It's my distinct pleasure to interview her and ask her about some of the early days of the project. We will come back to her interview right after this commercial break."

As the lights went off, Rebecca joined me on the little platform and sat across from me in one of the red chairs. She'd worn a skirt that was slightly longer than her normal knee-high length, conscious of the camera's angle and her wanting to give her legs a shapely and flattering look. I, on the other hand, had worn a pantsuit and crossed my legs, studying the script. Before the cameras began to roll, I looked up at her and asked, "So you've read over the questions?"

"Of course." She was a little distracted, but very direct and courteous. She didn't appear to be nervous, not nearly like I was.

The bright lights flooded over both of us.

"Welcome back to our interview of Rebecca Gambini and the Trident Towers Project. Rebecca is with me in person today, and I just want to say what a pleasure it is to have you here, to give us some perspective on how all this got started. Where did the inspiration come from and how did it develop?"

She had tucked the questions beneath her rear and, without need of any notes, confidently started.

"Well, as you know, my husband at the time, Marco Gambini, always wanted to give something back to the community, especially military veterans and Navy SEALs, men who had honorably served with him over the years. He felt there wasn't enough being done by the Veterans Administration or the government, and he tasked me with looking for something to do to give back to that community. I scoured all over Boston, even Manhattan, looking for a suitable project."

"After searching in the upper-Atlantic and the mid-Atlantic, you finally began looking in Florida, is that right?" I asked. I knew it had been Marco's desire to locate there since it was as far away from Manhattan as he could get and still be on the east coast.

"About that time, we sort of went our separate ways, but I stayed involved in the project to a certain degree. One thing led to another, and even though other things had changed," she gave a brittle smile and I knew why, "I was still needed here, and I began helping where I could to see the project along. At one point, it looked like perhaps the scope and size was going to be too much for him to handle on his own, with all of Marco's other business ventures. But, of course, Marco is extremely resourceful, as you know." She nodded to me, clearly lobbing the ball in my lap. I knew what I had to do. I had to step forward without flinching or skipping a beat, even though what I'd just heard and allowed to put out on the air was a complete lie.

I inhaled and volleyed back. "And I'm sure when everything is finished, everyone is going to owe you a great deal of gratitude, Rebecca. Tell me, how did you guys decide on the plan, what the rooms would look like, who you might want to design the project? How did that work out and what kinds of consultants did you use?"

I had surprised her, but far from throwing in the towel, she'd been emboldened.

"Well, we chose the architect right away, even before we had the site developed. He had worked on a couple of other rehab developments in the past and had done some work for several groups building modified homes for handicapped police, fire, and first responders. His designs were innovative, creative, and really gave the recipient of the home a feeling that he had finally returned to his roots, that he was in a home made specifically for him or her."

I nodded. "That sounds very smart."

"And then it became a question of whether these units would be for sale or for rent, or would they be subsidized. We weren't quite sure what the investors would stand for. We knew they, of course, wanted their money back and at a decent return, but we weren't sure how much outside funding we would be able to get or what kind of grant money we could rely on to lessen the burden. We were quite pleased when the public really kicked in and the partnership took off without any government underwriting or help, really. We were promised we would get some consideration as far as getting permits through, but nothing out of the ordinary, nothing that any large project wouldn't normally receive. This was going to be important for the community, but we wanted to make sure the community accepted us, and they have."

I could see an opening here I wanted to explore, even though it wasn't on the teleprompter. It was going to be important for my meeting with the planning director this afternoon.

I launched my new campaign. "That's very important, what you just said, Rebecca. You wanted to build something the community could really stand behind. And that's really been what's the best part about this project, isn't it?"

She nodded with a coy smile.

"The community really wants this for veterans who have given, in many cases, limbs or been so badly injured that they would have to be on assisted living the rest of their life. This way they get to have dignity in life and be independent. Isn't that correct?"

"Exactly. That was what we were hoping for, and the Tampa Bay area and all the beach communities here have really jumped in and helped make this a reality. It's one thing to try to build a development like this; it's another when it just sort of catches fire and takes on a life of its own. I wish I could claim credit for that, but as you know, Marco can be quite charming." She winked at me.

I couldn't take offense at this, because Rebecca was actually helping me.

She continued, "But even Marco with his charm couldn't have pulled this out of the bag if the public wasn't behind it one hundred percent. It feels so good to be able to do something good for people and something the taxpayers love. They also love the fact it doesn't cost them anything in government funds. It's all being privately run and managed. And that's what's so unique about this project—everybody who works on it believes in it."

I could have kissed her on the spot. She just gave me a little sound clip of something I could use when I talked to the head planning director. I needed this ammunition. In fact, I intended to ask Rebecca, after the interview, if she'd accompany me. I was going out on the skinny branches a bit, but this was the kind of innovative decision-making I wanted to try. And I really thought it would work.

I couldn't wait to ask for her help.

CHAPTER 5

Marco

IN THE MORNING, I was informed Carson Odingo would not be available until nearly one o'clock. This news didn't make me happy, but other than blindly take off and head into the country looking for my pilots and Karin, I really had no choice. They sent a car for me, and I was transported to the private jet hanger at JFK, where I could use my sat phone and work in a secure location. That part I was grateful for.

I checked in with the office, and Dax informed me Shannon was in Tampa, finishing up a pre-scheduled story on the Towers. She also caught me up to date on some of the changes that had gone on with the project, the fact that Shannon was helping out with the planning director sometime today, and informed me about the new underground contractor. The big elephant in the room, of course, was that no one had heard from Karin or the pilots or anybody from the Nigerian government.

"She's managed to dig right in. I'm impressed, Dax."

"She's your lady, boss. You should know. I wouldn't want to cross her any way. Very sweet, but tough as nails," Dax said lightheartedly. "She aims to impress you, in case you didn't know."

I chuckled. "That's what I like about her the best." I knew Dax would be blushing right now since she took all my meanings as being sexual, unless directed at her or Rhea. I appreciated the levity at this most stressful time. I didn't do waiting well.

She cleared her throat. "Have we heard from Senator Campbell's office at all?" she asked me.

"I was about to ask you the same question. I'm calling him next. I know he would've called me if there was some important news. I'll text you or let you know if I hear anything, and you do the same."

"Roger that, boss." Dax followed it up with her best, chipper repartee. She told me not to worry, that everyone was working full speed, very focused and very "frog-like." I chuckled at that, a new moniker she began using to describe our little band, and it oddly fit.

Senator Campbell's office was difficult to get through, but I finally reached his personal assistant, Shelly. He was always having new hires, and he worked them hard.

"I'm so sorry, Marco, but the senator is on a floor vote right now, and I'm not able to disturb him. I will let him know you're still in New York and you're meeting with the interpreter soon. At this point, I think we're all hoping and praying this fellow can be your key. The senator may have heard something on the senate floor, but we've not received any news or gotten any ransom demands, and he's been on the horn with State all morning before he left. Hang in there. We'll get it done somehow."

While I appreciated Shelly's positive attitude, I was getting tired of finding doors closed. I needed to get into action to get my people out of that country before it was too late. God knew what they were living with, if they were still alive. It was like they just disappeared, prompting me to go look for them, which was, I suppose, what the design was.

Or maybe I was overthinking things a bit, giving too much importance to my value to the world. Yet, it was a tactic used very successfully by those who were pros at kidnap and ransom or kidnap and then capture the rescuers to increase the size of their treasure trove. I didn't have to be a rocket scientist to know that was always the chance.

I also suspected that whomever was holding them would bleed

them for every dollar we could give, so I didn't think they would be dumb enough to just eliminate them and put their heads on pikes like what was happening in other villages in the area. Some of the poor contractors sending temporary housing containers and equipment to the remote places met very unkind ends. Although being Marco Gambini might save me from an unceremonious death in front of the site of a massacre, that would only grant me for a few hours or days.

After they got what they wanted, I was expendable just like all the others. Contractors I worked with often recruited employees from France or the Netherlands, even Ireland, choosing men and women who had either worked in UN peacekeeping forces or knew the terrain from their years trying to train the local armies in order to keep their projects safe. But the sobering fact was this work was even more dangerous than when they served in uniform.

I knew this was going to be a dangerous mission, but I thought we had enough allies who were motivated by money that we'd be safe.

I was mistaken.

I left a message for Shannon and let her know that my ETA was somewhat delayed, but we were more or less on track. I probably would only be able to let her know I'd landed safely in Nigeria and wouldn't be able to give her much in the way of details. I told her I loved her and that the office had given her glowing marks. I knew she'd be happy with that.

Carson Odingo sauntered into the little cubicle I was using in the lobby like he'd stepped out of a GQ magazine. He was tall and extremely fit, very handsome, with a stature that demanded respect. He carried a suit bag on a strap over his shoulder. I stood and reached out to shake his hand.

"I'm sorry you had to wait, Mr. Gambini."

His soft African dialect was pleasant, but his English grammar was perfect.

"Marco. Just call me Marco."

"Okay then. And I'm Carson, like in Johnny Carson?" He removed his hand from my grip and smiled, setting down his bag. He was waiting for me to ask.

"It's an unusual name for an African boy. I assume you were raised there?" I knew that to be the case before I asked him. I also knew he spoke and wrote fluently in several African tongues, even mastered a little Russian and Mandarin.

"Yes. I was a schoolboy in a little village just near the Benin border. I took music lessons from a priest who ran a mission school there until I was ten. He owned a black and white television, and my mother used to watch Johnny Carson. I think she had somewhat of a crush on him."

I found that funny, but he wasn't laughing. "Did your mother ever travel to the states?" I asked.

"Never got to. Never left Nigeria. She's still there."

As my eyebrows rose, he added, "In the ground, Marco. With the rest of my family, the ones we could find."

It was going to be redundant, but I said it again. "So sorry. I can see that your work at the UN then is a hard-fought war you're waging against such atrocities."

He nodded. "Precisely."

"So you left when you were ten? After the death of your parents?"

"Not exactly. That happened about five years later. That day, when I was ten, this group came through and killed everybody they could grab. A bunch of us children ran off into the brush. Lucky for us, our parents had been in town selling chickens at the market during the raid, so the only casualties were the elderly, some children who could not run, teachers, and the priest who taught music."

I chose silence. Nothing I could have said would have been appropriate.

"You see, it was what my childhood was all about. I grew up with these things happening every few years, sometimes months. My father didn't come home one evening. We never did find out what happened to him. My mother stayed home more, to watch over me and my three sisters. Unfortunately for them, they were all pretty. Even my mother. And about five years later, a band of militants came through and took them all. I escaped and wondered about their fate for several years, even after I was smuggled out of the country and sent to England to finish my schooling."

I didn't want to push for an answer, but I could see he had one. I was going to wait for him to offer it up.

"So I am very familiar with this area, if familiar is the proper term. I'd like to ask you one question, Marco. Why the hell are you building in this particular province?"

"Well, I'm not sure if you are aware, but I am doing this for the Sultan of Bonin, a close personal friend and business associate of mine."

"Yes, yes. I understand. But why there? There are so many other countries that could really use the projects. I just don't understand why Nigeria. Why the central west coast?"

"He has some connection there. I don't know, maybe it's just a piece of land that he bought. He's a rather stubborn man, sometimes unrealistic."

"But my understanding is you are going to be protecting his two sons and your company is going to run security for the operation, as well as help build it?" he asked me.

"Yes, that's correct."

"Then I think it would be wise on your part, after we rescue your staff, to tell the sultan he has to make another choice. This is not a tenable situation. And if someone had asked me before you started this whole caper what I thought of it, I would've said they were absolutely crazy. You cannot force animals who are used to living in cages to live in buildings and do the laundry and clean the dishes. You understand what I mean?"

"I do understand, and I think the sultan's position is that he would like to construct buildings that common people could live in. He wants to do something for the people, not for the government. He wants to give them a chance to have shelter, roof over their heads, something safe they can defend."

"With broomsticks and pieces of scrap metal?" Carson stared at me and then shook his head slowly from side to side. "You people who are so altruistic, rich people with everything in the world to live for, why would you want to risk your lives for this?"

I had an answer for this. It probably wasn't what he was expecting, but at least it was an answer. "I've heard him talk about it before. And he's told me, 'We build this, and somebody will come in and burn it.' He knows this."

"But why?"

"I'm getting there. He says then someone else will come in and rebuild it. And perhaps then someone will tear it down again. And he said one time, eventually, somebody will build something there and it will stay. He said he wants to make a statement. He's not worried about the money. He wants to make a statement, a stand against evil. Now I'm just thinking out loud here, but it's far enough away from his island kingdom that I suppose he doesn't think it'll come back to haunt him."

"Except if he loses one or both his sons or perhaps his friendship. I understand losing money, even though I've never had much, but I don't understand if someone has the chance to live free from the violence why they would run in and have to try to intervene. It's more than any one construction project or any wealthy sultan can do. There are a dozen countries trying to stop these militant groups in North Africa and all over the whole continent. The UN has tried everything they can, and it's almost hopeless. We hope it will be solved, but there is so much greed and corruption and just pure evil, I'm not sure it's worth it."

I was surprised to hear how pessimistic Carson was. I didn't expect this. I expected some kind of inspiring speech about what a good thing we were trying to do, even against all the odds I knew were there. Some sort of thanks, not someone who would request we quit.

"Do I surprise you then?" Carson Odingo asked me.

"I guess I didn't mask my feelings very well, did I? Yes, you have. And I'm wondering why."

"There are wars that you can win, things you can change, and things you cannot change. Isn't it like that twelve-step prayer they do? The courage to understand the truth of it and the wisdom to know the difference between what can be saved and what cannot be saved? I'll grant you, the intended outcome is to have peace, and I would love nothing more than to have peace especially in my homeland. But I'm not chasing windmills, Marco. I'm going to try to keep some expats and Americans from getting murdered at the behest of Senator Campbell and with the blessing of the organization I work for. It is what I do. I negotiate. I want to have peace, but we have to pick our battles, don't we? We really do need to be smart about our resources. And even if we win, and this place gets built, and everyone cheers and has a big celebration, how long do you think it'll be before it'll all be pulled down again?"

"That's not for me to say, Carson. It's really not what I'm sent to do. I understand your concern. I've been there too. When I was a SEAL, I did ops all throughout north and central Africa, you know this."

He nodded.

"We weren't in the business, at that time, of making a permanent change. We were in the business of identifying and extracting the bad actors. It's what we were told to do. Our job wasn't to build; it was to eliminate some of the threats."

"That I understand, Marco. It takes a smart and a brave man to confront pure evil, run in and try to put the fire out while the building is collapsing around you. It's admirable, and I wish the world were made up of millions and millions of people who would willingly do that every day. It's just that there's so many innocent people that get hurt in the meantime."

He was completely right, of course. It was the stuff of nightmares and sessions on a couch in a lonely office, the reason sometimes meds were overprescribed because no one really knew how to get rid of those nightmares, especially the unintended ones we all caused.

Those were the worst.

The only thing I'd learned was not to ever give up. So I wasn't going to today.

"Well, we have agreement then, Carson. Because I think it can eventually be wiped out. I think good is stronger than evil. I think if we're prepared and trained and have good intel, there's practically no limit to what a small force can do, even up against much larger odds. I've seen it happen in my time on the Teams. I've trained people to do it in countries that needed their own support system. I do believe in eradicating evil. And if we get to do that while we build some housing for some people, I think that's a worthwhile cause. It may not be the kind of thing my fiancée wants me to do, but it is a worthwhile cause."

He watched me just to see if I blinked or showed some sign I was blowing smoke up his ass. I knew he was an extremely good judge of character. He changed his stance, clapped his hands together, and then rubbed his palms.

"Okay, then. I think we better get started."

We discussed some of the logistics. He understood we were taking a charter flight to Cape Verde, where I had some equipment and some friends I wanted to pick up. He told me that he had three key men who had spent many years working for the UN forces and Afrika Korps and were well-versed in the terrain, as well as the language and the population in general. We could pick them up in Benin near the airport. We would travel to the Nigerian border, get as far inland as we could, and then do the rest on foot.

"At least that's the plan, Marco. If you agree. I'm also in favor of just swooping in, landing, and not doing the land excursion. And you would probably save a day or a day and a half if we did it that way. But it's a lot more problematic. I'm not sure I can get my three guys to meet us in Nigeria. But I could try."

"Is it possible to do? My concern is these are not people who are used to being captive in the jungle somewhere, with God knows who doing what to them. We've not received any ransom demands. Other than the money they confiscated from the plane, we don't believe they're in it for that. At least whoever is running the show isn't. They already blew up my plane, so they don't care about the resource. Only thing I've been told is that someone wants to have a meet and greet. But where and when, I haven't a clue."

Mr. Odinga let out a huge sigh, drowning out my mumbling narrative as he spewed out, "His name is John Okubo. He was in prison in Portugal for several years, after being caught doing some smuggling in Benin. He and a band of several others escaped and made their way back to Nigeria, which is their homeland too. He has a special hatred for Westerners, for people who like to come in and do good, like aid workers and UN peacekeepers. He likes to sacrifice villagers. His favorite method is beheading. He leaves examples everywhere he goes." He shook his head before continuing.

"I have heard enough from the reports we've received to be able to positively identify him as the culprit. Johnny cannot be stopped. He has to be killed. But I didn't tell you that. I think the number of people he has murdered with his own hands is approaching a thousand by now. And there would be a very loud round of applause in the whole African community here if he were put down like the dog he is. I don't know if we can do that. But we should consider that as part of our plan. Because trust me, he probably already knows you're coming even though you've had no contact. And he's looking for someone high profile he can make an example of. So, Marco, on top of everything else, you have to try not to get captured. You want to run and get shot. But you don't want to get captured. Unless you want your entrails splashed all over the Internet. Am I making myself clear?"

I saw what he was describing, and it wasn't my body with my guts coming out. It was somebody else's. I knew in my heart I could do this. If I had the right people and the right tools.

I swallowed hard and set those images aside for a minute.

"I say we fly in, pick up your guys in Cape Verde, hop over to

Nigeria, we get the job done, we rescue them, and we get out. I don't want to be marching through jungle for a day and a half hoping that we'll find them alive when we get there. So let's get our butts in gear, and go get them."

"Easy day, right?" he said, fist bumping my left hand with his.

"No, that's what the JV team says. The varsity team says 'let's go spill some blood.'"

CHAPTER 6

Shannon

AFTER THE FILMING, I headed to the ladies' room, right behind Rebecca. I pulled out my face wash, dabbed a little in my palm, and handed my bottle to her.

"Thanks. I should have thought to bring something, but—" she started.

"I have everything you might need here. I've done this so many times, and I hate going home all painted up, if you know what I mean."

"You're the natural type, Shannon. Beautiful without makeup. I, on the other hand, well, I'm a little older, and I like the dragon lady look a bit, probably too much." She rocked her head from side to side and pouted her lower lip as if she was accepting something about herself or admitting she had a flaw.

"I just think you like wearing makeup. Some women do. I never learned to."

"What did you want to talk to me about?" she asked as she brushed water on her face and began to scrub with the cleanser.

"I thought you did a wonderful job of explaining the history of the Towers and especially the part about how it was so important to the community. We're having a little bit of trouble with the Pinellas County Planning Director, who was once in favor of the project but now seems to be a little hesitant. Have you ever run across him before?"

I watched for signs she was somehow complicit in the planning director's change of heart. But as she looked at me, her face dripping with fresh water, I didn't see a thing to indicate that. I was struck by how beautiful she was without makeup and wondered why she felt she had to wear so much. I had lost myself examining the lines and the graceful contours of her face when, all of a sudden, I remembered she needed a towel, which I promptly found for her in the cupboard.

"I'm sorry about this."

"No worries," she mumbled into the towel. "You are welcome to use that clip as much as you like, for advertising or promotional purposes. If that's what you were going to ask me, I give you permission."

"Thank you. I appreciate that. But I wanted to talk to you about something else. I just wondered if you would agree to help me with the planning director. You spoke so eloquently about the project, and you were involved in it early on, unlike I've been. I admit that. It's not a problem for me. But I just think it would be good for the project if you could come with me and speak to him."

"All right. I suppose I can do that. When?"

"In about—" I checked my watch and then looked up at her. "About forty-five minutes from now, if you're free."

"Is he in Tampa?" she asked.

"No, Clearwater. The county offices are in Clearwater. I was to meet him at a local restaurant, but now he wants to meet in his office. I'm taking that as a sign the relationship is going south."

"Well, I don't think we're going to be there on time, unless we leave right now."

"Then you're saying yes?" I couldn't believe she was that easy to convince.

"Yes, absolutely. Whatever will help this project go forward, I'm all in."

It was the second time today I could have leaned over, grabbed her, and hugged her. But, of course, I didn't. There was still a little bit of hesitation on my part, that little piece of me that still didn't completely trust her, but I was going to take her at her word and give her the chance I thought she deserved. She had not been playing games with me after all. She probably had some misgivings about working with me as well. I thought perhaps we might be a good team, coming at this particular problem from two different positions.

We quickly gathered our things, and I offered to drive, but Rebecca insisted on following me in her car. "I have an old friend coming to town who's taken a house out at the beach, so I just think it'll be better if I follow you."

We arrived approximately five minutes before our allotted time and found parking in the city lot next to each other. We hurried up the steps into the large foyer of the planning department annex, announced ourselves, and were shown to the hallway that led to the planning director's office at the end. As we click clacked down the concrete floor to the glass office door with his name painted on the front, there wasn't anything about the office, the hallway, or the building that was warm and friendly. In fact, it reminded me of a prison or a tomb.

"Boy, a little paint, some color, some—"

"Plants?" she interrupted me.

"Exactly!"

"I could never work in a place like this. That's why I love Manhattan, with all the beautiful art deco exteriors and Rococo. I love the wood paneling and the tall ceilings, how ornate things are, or how simple and streamlined. I love architecture. This is just a box. It's just an ugly box, and it's even painted an ugly... what is that color?"

"I think they call it puce."

We both giggled, reached the door, and pushed it open.

Inside, the office wasn't as bad as the hallway, but it was plain, containing six gray desks that were probably vintage by now, at least forty years old. Every single desk was covered in stacks of legal-sized manilla files. In the back left-hand corner was another frosted glass door, and this door also had the planning director's name stenciled on the outside. We were greeted by a secretary who promptly took us through that door and introduced us to the planning director, William Warren.

"Mr. Warren, this is Shannon Marr and her companion—I'm sorry, I didn't catch your name?"

"I'm Rebecca Gambini."

"Yes, yes, that's fine," Warren dismissed his secretary with a bark.

He was rotund, at least wider than he should have been at his small five-foot-four-inch stature. He was standing, pulling his trousers up around his rather large waist and repositioning his belt buckle. He peered around both of us and addressed his secretary again, who had not left the office.

"I said we're fine here, Cora. If you would please hold my calls, and I've got an appointment in about a half an hour, so if we're not quite finished just have Mr. Woodward wait a few minutes if he doesn't mind. Okay?"

"You got it, sir."

Cora left the room and closed the door behind her.

We had not been invited to sit, so Rebecca and I glanced at each other and remained standing in front of his desk. Mr. Warren sat, first looking up at us and then ordering us to take a seat. I pulled a folding chair from around the side of his desk, and Rebecca took the one chair that was directly in front of Mr. Warren.

"I understand we're to be discussing the Trident Towers today, is that correct?" he asked, fluttering his eyelids as if he was thinking of what to say. I found it terribly distracting that he didn't look me in the eyes.

"Yes, Mr. Warren. It seems there has been some kind of a delay in the processing of our permits. I have submitted everything that's been requested of us, and now we understand there's some additional engineering that's required. I think we're getting a letter in the mail, so maybe you could help me there."

"The letter went out yesterday morning," Warren said tersely.

"Perhaps, to save time, you could illuminate some of the issues for me. Until I get the paperwork, of course. We just thought we'd come here, discuss it with you, and see what you or your staff's concerns are."

Warren's forehead wrinkled up, and he had an expression making me think he was experiencing a belly ache. But it passed. He leaned over the desk with his tiny hands clasped and folded on each other, inhaled, and began telling us about how understaffed and overworked they were. He reminded us there had been a literal explosion of building projects in the area, and it was taking all of their time trying to keep up with the workload. Yet each day that went by, they were getting further and further behind.

"I'm limited on my budget, so I am not able to hire more plan checkers, so I'm going to try farming it out to independent firms who do that. I'll have to pass the costs on to the builders, of course—"

"Of course," I agreed and let him explain further.

"I've already blown through thousands of dollars worth of discretionary funds that I was holding for part of our hurricane relief fund. We always have to hold something in reserve for approving emergency projects that come up after our season, as you know."

"It makes perfect sense. Budgets are important. So is time, Mr. Warren. I'm trying to expedite things a bit, if you will allow me to ask some questions."

"Of course, go right ahead and ask." He waited but checked his watch first.

"We've not made any changes to the plans since the end of March, other than what you or your staff have suggested. It seems to me six months is an adequate amount of time to get all your questions and concerns answered, but we're finding things coming in dribs and drabs. We solve one problem, and then we are faced with another. It probably isn't, but it feels like an intentional delay."

He didn't like that, and I wondered if I'd overstepped my boundaries or came across as a threat. I needed to soften the blow.

Rebecca beat me to it.

"You will remember early on how excited everyone was to be working on this development. Even the news media and the neighborhood were on board," she said straight to his face.

He paused, tapping his fingertips on his desktop without making a sound. "That was before the bombing. I've gotten some feedback from the public about concerns about the safety of people living near the Towers."

"Complaints from neighbors? We've heard of nothing, only encouraging remarks," I added. "I have to say I've not even heard one person make a complaint. You are talking about people living in the neighborhood of the proposed Towers?" I asked.

"Yes, in the general area."

"And can you tell me about the nature of their concerns for their safety?"

"Well, as you are very aware, the building where you housed your construction company was completely obliterated. It was a bomb, like a terrorist bomb. We don't want that kind of element here in Florida, and we don't want the type of businesses that are going to elicit this kind of negative reaction. There are some that wonder if this is what the Towers is going to bring us and if we really need such activity!"

"Of course not," I agreed with him. "No one wants that. We don't think that's what we're bringing you here, Mr. Warren."

I turned to the side and could see Rebecca's wheels were turning. She smiled and addressed him. "I think perhaps you might have misunderstood something about that incident," Rebecca started. "The police don't think this is an attack on the Towers as much as it was an attack on perhaps Marco and his construction company. And when I talked to the officers myself, they told me it wasn't a sophisticated bomb, but something homemade, something kind of slapped together at the last minute. That to me doesn't sound like an organized crime issue or anything other than a personal grudge by some deranged person. Someone who perhaps hates billionaires, possibly high-rise development. We don't think it's something that has to do with our veterans."

"But we don't really know, do we?" he answered her.

"Mr. Warren, please, we all know that we can't protect against every single eventuality, since there are crazies out there we can't control."

I thought she made perfect sense.

Warren scrunched up his chin, his lips, and then lastly his nose and forehead. It was as if someone had laid a piece of stinky cheese in front of him. "That's not the impression I got."

"So you talked to the police then?" I asked.

"No. I just talked to a few individuals."

I could see he was hedging, holding something tight to the vest.

"Well, if that's the case, I think the best thing to do—" Rebecca said, "would be to meet with these people directly. And we'd like to do that. We have absolutely nothing to hide. It's not fair to make you have to convince them this project will be run safely and securely and will turn out to be the wonderful project we all know it will be. The community really wants this. Maybe there are a handful of people who are concerned, but I'm sure we could convince them here's really nothing for them to be concerned about. And due to this prior event, we'll be even more diligent than we would've been otherwise. We plan to fully fence the area, have security guards twenty-four seven, and anything else that's required."

Warren was beginning to get squirrely. He was afraid of something. I followed Rebecca's lead.

"We want to respect the neighborhood, so we aren't going to ask for football lights or anything invasive to keep intruders away, but it will be very complete and secure. We want that, we want to protect our employees and our subcontractors, and we want to get this built for our veteran community members ASAP. This is a win for everybody. You know how exciting this will be. This will put us on the map here in Indian Rocks."

Mr. Warren reluctantly nodded his head. "Well, why don't we do this then? I'll call a meeting with some of the planners and a few of the individuals who represent the business community who expressed their concerns to me, and we'll have a meeting in the next few weeks or so. Let's see where we go from there."

I looked at him in disbelief. "The next several weeks?"

"Well, I think it will take that long to assemble everyone."

Rebecca leaned forward. "I think we could do it much quicker than that," she said. "What we could do is use the television station to advertise a town hall discussion. That way any interested parties could come to the town hall and give their opinions. Let Shannon and me and the staff respond to those questions or opinions. Now, we wouldn't suggest that if we expected to be run out of town, would we? I think the public's curious and excited about what we're trying to do. Once they see the plans and hear what's going on, they're going to be fully assuaged."

Rebecca was brilliant. I was learning. I added, "This takes it off your shoulders, Mr. Warren, and makes us give the presentation to the people who are the most concerned. What we have right now is that nobody is approving anything, and we can't even start. We have contractors already having to pull out because of the delays. Any good contractor has lots of business, lots of work on their schedule, and they can't just sit around and wait forever. So we think it's in everybody's best interest to get this taken care of right away. And if it's as big a problem as you say it is, then at least we'll know where we have to start. But right now, we're completely in the dark. And that's not a solution we can do anything about. But you can."

Both Rebecca and I smiled at him. Rebecca was nodding her head. I started to do the same.

He searched our faces, back and forth between Rebecca and myself.

"All right. If we can get an announcement out there on the TV station, as you say, we might be able to do something within the next ten days. Something like that. Two weeks?"

Both Rebecca and I said in unison, "That's too long."

"How about a week from today?" I finished.

"All right then, a week from today."

CHAPTER 7

Marco

T HE NEARLY EIGHT-HOUR flight from JFK to Cape Verde didn't happen on the type of jet I was accustomed to. It was a stripped-down version of a charter flight taking tourists from New York to Paris or London for less than the cost of a good meal in Manhattan. I didn't comment about it, due to Carson's background and some of his expressed disgust for people with money. I knew it wasn't really about the money or the people who owned it, but what they did with their money.

And I agreed with him.

The flight got bumpy as we began our approach to the airport at Sal. After a couple of tense moments rattling around in the bucket of bolts, we finally took a hard landing and then stopped abruptly on a runway that appeared dangerously too short. Either that or the brakes needed adjustment. We nearly scraped a twenty-foot-high concrete fence with our right wing as we turned to taxi to the hangar. The fence was sculpted with deep horizontal slices where other jets had not been as lucky. I knew Carson would not hire pilots who weren't experienced with this sort of thing, and I was grateful for that.

We had discussed very little on the flight over, more background material on the Johnny Okubo mercenary and his men. We talked about the weather, terrain, and what life was like growing up in-between the raids.

But we remained focused on the mission.

I had several boxes and duty bags loaded with some specialized equipment, including a drone. Baggage handlers unloaded us quickly, and Carson commandeered a large cart. He was going to get a baggage handler as well, but I declined.

"No, I think I want to handle this equipment myself. I don't want any eyes on it."

"We do have customs to go through. They're going to want to look at your bags, Marco."

"Yeah, and that's why I've got a special badge for that. I also have a letter from Senator Campbell."

"I understand."

Just as planned, the check-in with the local immigration official was completed without a hitch.

We brought our things to a waiting black Suburban with tinted windows. When I opened one of the doors, the thickness of it told me it was enhanced with extra security and would take rounds, keeping all inside safe. It wouldn't however save us from a grenade launcher.

Carson tipped the driver and gave him an address. We headed toward the downtown area of Espargos, about twelve miles away from the airport. We followed along a ridgeline down the middle of the island. At a distance, we could see several large cruise ships and yachts perched in the blue waters of the Atlantic. The horizon was bright blue and the sky so clear I thought I might catch a glimpse of the coast of Africa to the east. But not today.

Carson had arranged for an overnight at a large western-styled hotel until our early flight out tomorrow at just before dawn. I had arranged for three members of my team to meet us there. Carson's men would have to make their way to meet up with us in Nigeria later. It was what it was.

"Who is this guy, this Norwegian guy you are meeting?" Carson asked me.

"I've used him on occasion. He's been an aid worker in Nigeria and Mali and Benin. He's traveled quite a bit throughout Morocco, even into the Congo. He's former FSB. You know who those guys are, don't you?"

"I've never met one. But I understand they're as tough as your SEALs."

"You're right about that. We train with them sometimes, and I don't think there's a better fighter in cold weather than that group of guys. I mean, they're lethal anywhere, any temperature, but they could stage a war from the north or south pole. Polar bears, we call them."

I had nothing but respect for Sven Tolar, and prior to that, I'd heard so much about him for years that, when I had the opportunity to use him, I didn't even have to do the normal vetting. He was always willing to jump into the fray, even though he was trying to settle down. He just couldn't find someone to settle down with.

"How long have you worked with him?"

"About three years off and on. I've used him for intel from time to time. Had a rough trip my last tour to Africa, before working for the sultan. He saved my bacon big time. I swore I'd never go back."

"And why was that?"

"I think you know. It's so unsettled. Just like you said earlier, it might take a hundred years before the right kind of changes occur that will bring peace to the continent. I hope I'm wrong, but I think it's the most dangerous place on the planet."

"You're right about that, Marco. Are you having second thoughts?"

"Not on your life."

We drove up to the Hotel Dell Oro, which was also a dance club and casino and buzzing with flashy-looking twenty-somethings, mostly tourists, I guessed. All were spending their money like water and being extremely unconscious of all the dangers around them. The local police worked hard to make sure crime against tourists, at least, was kept to a minimum. It was, after all, Cape Verde's largest source of income. The tourist industry had been severely hampered by the recent pandemics and waves of economic boom and bust. It was digging itself out of debt, and several large construction projects were being built, apparently sponsored by foreign governments. I was impressed there was so much new building going on.

"I didn't pick you for a gambler, Carson." I looked at him out of the corner of my eye.

"I wasn't quite prepared for this scene. I wasn't told the casino had reopened. But I think it's a good cover. We have the pent-house on top and two adjacent rooms. I'll let you figure out how you want to allocate them. Will your friend be here now?"

"He better be. I was supposed to be here last night."

We begged off baggage handlers who offered to assist us with the large bags and the hard cases, instead picking up a rusty red cart and stacking everything up nearly four feet tall. It took the two of us to balance the load while we precariously pushed it into the lobby.

The smell of sweaty bodies and alcohol, mixed with the sounds of casino life, was oddly comforting. I knew I wasn't going to see anything like this when we got to the continent, so I drank it in. Checking my surroundings, I didn't spot Sven or the other two men I'd sent over. I followed Carson to the reception desk.

Carson spoke in a dialect I didn't understand, which sounded like a pidgin Spanish or Portuguese. He signed a piece of paper and gave the second copy to me, along with an envelope with my name on it.

"You owe my office. We'll send a bill," Carson said without humor.

"Fair enough. It's what we agreed." I opened the envelope. It was a letter from Sven.

Marco,

I am coming, but when I found out you were going to be delayed a day, I took a short trip to the other side of the island. I'm presuming you'll get in late, so I'll see you as soon as I arrive back tonight. Don't plan on dinner for me. I met your

two boys there, and they're with me. All is well. Here's my
sat phone.

Sven had signed his name, and underneath it was an eleven-digit phone number I quickly copied into my phone.

Carson peered over the top of the letter. "Everything okay?"

"Yup. They should be here soon. All three of them are together, which is good."

I thanked my lucky stars I didn't have to go pull people out of bars or establishments as I sometimes had to with some of these mercenary types. Sven was a straight shooter. And the two other fellows I hired were all business. I couldn't afford to work with anyone who wasn't focused on getting in and out quickly.

"Does he say anything about your colleagues in Nigeria?" Carson asked.

"No. When we get to the room, I'm going to call Senator Campbell's office."

"Good idea." He held up the room cards. "I'll take the front."

He grabbed the handles on the cart and pulled it behind him while I pushed. The behemoth pile barely fit into the elevator, and we turned away others who wanted to share. At the top floor, the doors opened to a beautiful vista of downtown city lights framed in a picture window just as we stepped out of the elevator. I was impressed. It seemed like Cape Verde had sprouted civilization everywhere. It was looking more prosperous than I remembered.

Just before we got to the double doors at the end of the hall leading to the penthouse, I heard my name being called behind us.

"Hey there, Marco!" Sven yelled. "I actually thought I was going to beat you."

Behind Sven was Riley Murphy, a young chap I'd met on an op who came from Dublin, and Juan Correia, who was of Spanish descent but lived on the island. Juan had been hired several times by various contractors for security, and while I had only met him socially, he also came highly recommended. Riley was a drone operator, sort of an Internet geek, and a sharpshooter. Basically, if there was a gadget involved, Riley was all over it. He also built small, ultralight airplanes in his spare time.

"Riley, Juan, good to see you fellas." I embraced all three of them one by one, slapped their backs, and introduced them to Carson. They helped us bring the enormous pile of bags into the penthouse suite.

"Jeez, Marco, are we going to start a small war or something?" said Sven.

"Not if I can help it. I'm not quite sure what we're going to need. I'm limited on the number of personnel, but I don't want to limit myself on the equipment. We're going to need everything we can stand to carry."

"My stuff's downstairs locked up. I'll go get it in a bit," Sven said.

Riley spoke up next. "Well, I think it's better to be prepared than to fall short. I myself am a little knackered. We're leaving early in the morning, right?"

"We are."

"If it's all the same to you, Boss, I'd like to have our short meet and greet and then hit the bed."

I nodded to all four of them. "That's exactly what I'm going to do, although I have some calls to make. But let's not unpack these things. Let's just sit, and I'll give you a lay of what's going on."

Carson offered the fruit and drinks that had been left on the table for us, I assumed compliments of the United Nations.

"You help yourselves here while I make a couple of calls. And then I'll keep it short, ten minutes max, okay?"

Sven and the two new members nodded. Carson returned a blank stare. He wasn't finished with his read on the newcomers.

I went into the bedroom and closed the door, retrieving my sat phone. I activated it and first tried to call Shannon. It sounded like the line was going through, and then it went dead. I began another call, but before I could make a connection, she had called me back.

"Oh, Marco, I'm so glad to hear from you. Does this mean you've arrived?"

"No, sweetheart. We're in Cape Verde. Picked up a couple of guys, and then we're headed over first thing in the morning, very early."

"How do things look? Is there any news?" she asked me.

"No, I'm sorry. I'm going to make some calls right now, but in case I don't get in touch tomorrow, as long as you don't hear anything negative, everything's a go and everything's good. It's going to be a long day tomorrow, and we start really early."

"Well, it's just getting to be dusk here. It must be 2:00 AM there."

"A little after midnight here."

"Well, I know you've got a lot to do, and you're probably tired. If I hear anything tomorrow at the office or anyone tries to get hold of me or you to relay a message, do I text you or do I call you?"

"No, you call me. Use this number. No messages, no texts, please."

"Can I just tell you a little bit about what I did today?"

I didn't want to be short with her, but I had just a sliver of time to get done what I needed to do. It was not something I liked doing, but I had to put her off.

"Sweetheart, I've got another call to make, and then I'm going to have a meeting with the guys. I'm afraid I can't right now. Everybody's exhausted, and I still have work to do. If you don't mind, I promise, the next time we talk, I'll give you a chance to catch me up to date. But if anything comes through about Karin or the pilots, you let me know. You call me anytime you need to, okay?"

"Understood. I love you, Marco. I know you'll be safe, and I want you to be rested and ready for anything. I'll be thinking about you, and don't worry about me. I'm doing great, and I'm actually feeling useful and having a good time. You take care of yourself, take care of business, and I'll talk to you maybe tomorrow. Love you."

"Love you."

I disconnected the call and got Senator Campbell's office on the first ring. The senator answered the phone himself.

"Oh my God, just the person I need to talk to," he said. "Are you there yet?"

"Not quite, Senator. I was delayed in New York, as you know, and then we needed to pick people up here in Cape Verde, so we're spending the night and leaving early in the morning."

"Jeez, it's taken you two days to get over there."

"It's seventeen hours of straight flights, Senator." I added, "I got to ask you, have you heard anything at all about my people?"

"Not specifically. We confirmed there's a red Nigerian brigade, a paramilitary group—it's one of those offshoots, but not controlled by the government—pushing their way in to try to drive a coup or something. It's not very stable there, and all of a sudden, we've heard an escalation in chatter and tension. But no, no ransom demands, no threats. It's like complete radio silence on that score. We have been putting our feelers out, and of course, State is working overtime, double overtime, to get any information on Karin. So far, I think all our sources are truncated or located in other portions of the country. I just don't have anybody in that western district. It's heavily impacted by the jungle and there's practically no civilization there. It's about forty miles outside of the capital. I understand you're going to be dropping in. Is that right?"

"That's right. It's just a quick insertion, and then he's going to turn around and take off. I think that's the best. Otherwise, we'd be hiking through that terrain."

"Who's flying anyway?"

"Carson arranged it. It's a marked plane, but I think the registry is from Spain. Nothing fancy. Sort of nondescript. That's the way Carson wants it to be. Even though they may know I'm coming, or at least Carson thinks they know, we don't want to broadcast I'm here for some kind of a hostage negotiation. But we'll know more tomorrow once we get there."

"Okay, son. We're counting on you. I'm working on a couple

of things and will talk to you later about that. You make sure you let me know when you arrive. You're going to want to ping me as soon as you land, so we can get some eyes on you electronically."

"Will do." I hesitated, but I had to ask. "Senator, do you think they're still alive? I mean, is there any kind of buzz about any of this going on there? I'm getting nothing but happy updates from State, but are you hearing anything different than that? I don't want to have smoke blown up my ass, especially since I'm about to expose four very worthy and valuable gentlemen here to the thrills and chills of Africa. Are you hearing anything that I need to know about even if it's a guess?"

I knew Senator Campbell would probably reveal to me if he'd learned anything at all, and I was trusting he would keep his word to me.

"Not a thing, Marco. But then we don't usually talk about that. We're talking about rescue until we have to talk about recovery. Until then, it's all rescue, my man. You be safe, and I'm going to call you if I hear a thing. You do the same."

"Agreed."

I used my personal phone to scan through some of the messages I'd received, since the beginning of our flight. The plane didn't have Wi-Fi capabilities, and I chose not to activate the sat phone until we landed in Cape Verde. There wasn't anything of note, except for a rather cryptic message from Karin's brother.

I didn't know she had a brother!

'I'm okay. Time is short. Hope to make the wedding. Make sure you bring a Bible.'

I'd never heard of such a message. The first thing I was going to do was see if any of those clues would help Carson discern where they might be located. Just before I switched off my phone, I checked the number one more time. It had an area code from somewhere in France. The avatar was just the letter K for Karin, underneath a purple circle, that read *Karin's brother*. I was pretty sure it was from Karin herself.

"Hang in there, kid," I whispered, more to myself than to her.

CHAPTER 8

Shannon

I PUT ON my running shorts and shoes, wore a long-sleeve zip-up fleece for a top, and put my hair in a ponytail for my morning run at the beach. The sun was just beginning to crack over the mountains to the east of me, and the warmth felt good on my legs. I set my watch for one hour and then an interim alarm for thirty minutes so I could turn around and come back the opposite direction. I headed north, mingling with seabirds, and observed several pelicans out for an early morning dive. I even thought I saw the fins of a porpoise out to sea. People were starting to see them more frequently as the months got closer to the end of hurricane season.

The beach was more or less deserted, except for a couple of diehard fishermen and a group of pink ladies, as I called them. They always had big smiles, a hearty wave, and wore pink fleeces, probably cancer survivors. Or at least that's what I told myself. I quickly passed them, turned and waved, and knew I'd see them on the return trip.

The bay was fairly calm. White and grayish billowy clouds scooted across the sky quickly. A breeze had picked up, and it threatened to rain. I'd checked the forecast when I woke up, and there was still not supposed to be any rain in sight. But we were on borrowed time. October could be very wet and sometimes very dangerous.

Several other joggers passed me going the opposite direction, and we nodded. I saw a couple walking hand in hand slowly, looking for shells and picking up debris. It looked like there was a community college class with a professor studying the yellow taped-off area where the sea turtles had buried their eggs. I could see him pointing at several mounds, perhaps seeing signs of life. Very rarely did the hatchlings come out in the early morning hours. It was usually at night. I made a mental note to turn my porch light off so the little beings could find their way out to the safety and their new life in the gulf.

I felt good, productive, and I was proud of the meeting Rebecca and I had with the planning director. There was still something about his demeanor that bothered me, but my active imagination often got me into trouble. I decided to file it away in the back of my head and continue on with my plans for the day. That way, I wouldn't be sitting by the phone waiting for a call that might not come today or tomorrow or even the next.

I almost didn't notice the huge looming structure with its completed first floor off to the right, facing due west. It was our dream home. Marco had stopped the construction on it until he could be around to catch little flaws or make adjustments to the plans as we went along. And with travel looming soon, he didn't want anything to go forward without him present. I recalled the beautiful dinner and the night we spent on the bed he had brought up to the floor so we could watch the stars and listen to the sounds of the birds and the ocean. That was such a magical night. I couldn't wait until he got back to do it again.

The upper floor walls had started to be framed since the first floor was done in cinder block. Large vertical steel bars ascended from the block wall downstairs through the floor joists of the second story, extending up into the sky as if they were lightning catchers or metal sunflowers trying to touch the stars.

As of now, any storms that popped up this month or perhaps next would completely drench our construction site. It couldn't be helped, and there was no sense trying to cover it up, since the heavy rains and winds would blow tarps and coverings from here to Tampa.

I kept running as the house slid past my line of vision until it was behind me. A short time later, my alarm went off, and I turned, touched my toes, sprinkled my fingers in the water, stretched, and began to run in the opposite direction back toward my bungalow. As I ran past our house site, I noticed a lone figure sitting at the top of the sand dune just south of our lot. His head was buried in his arms as he slumped over his knees, as if shielding himself from the brightness of the morning sun. I was concerned that perhaps he was ill or was in some kind of distress. And although it wasn't wise and I had promised Marco I wouldn't, I just had to check on him. I wasn't worried that he was trespassing on our property as much as I wanted to make sure that he was well.

I walked slowly across the fluffy white sand until I was about twenty feet from his seated position. He looked up quickly, and when he saw me, fear flashed in his eyes behind a few glistening tears. He abruptly scrambled to his feet, wiped his face on the sleeve of his right forearm, and apologized.

"It's okay. I just came over to see if you're all right. Is there something bothering you? Do you need anything?" I asked him.

He looked down at his feet and shook his head. That's when I noticed his shoes were worn. One of the shoelaces had been broken and tied and then retied several times to mend it. He was wearing pajama bottoms in a navy blue and white plaid pattern. He had on a jacket that was made for a man clearly two or three sizes larger than he was. He was skinny, and his hair looked like it hadn't been combed in days. I went no further to give him space.

And that's when I smelled the alcohol.

I didn't see evidence of a bottle or can, but I knew he'd been drinking. With my dad's issue after Em's death, I knew what a drunk looked and smelled like. This young man was clearly a drunk. And it was a tragedy he was so young.

I decided to take the cautious approach and didn't step any closer to him.

"I do have my cell phone with me. If you'd like, I can call someone. It looks to me like you need to find some place where you can get a shower and a hot meal?"

"Not interested." He did not make eye contact with me. I saw his sunburned cheeks and his nose and realized that he probably had been sleeping on the beach. I had seen a few homeless men during the months since I moved here, and oftentimes they would find their breakfast in the back alleys, rummaging through garbage of several of the local restaurants. I figured that's probably where he was headed next.

"I hope you find what you want. And I hope you will let somebody help you."

I turned and walked back toward the surf. I heard him shout at a distance behind me, "Thank you."

Without looking at him or putting him on the spot further, I waved with my left hand and resumed my jog.

THE OFFICE WAS nearly deserted, but I knew people would start dribbling in at 8:30 and it would be a full crew by 9:00. I made coffee, poured myself some in Marco's favorite Navy SEAL mug, added the fresh half-and-half I insisted the office stock at all times, and went to my desk. The boxes they had brought in yesterday were still neatly tucked to the right side of my desk. Two of them were empty, and two of them still had files in them. I decided to put the empty files out in the hallway for recycle, and sat down to start going over some of the old files that I probably needed to purge. Marco had given me so much information about the project and the project's history, I really hadn't had time to study everything yet.

I stumbled across some communication that he'd had with the seller of the property. This was before he and I were dating, just after he'd gotten his divorce from Rebecca. The property had been owned by an elderly woman who had no family, and was in a rest home. It was being handled by an estate attorney, and she was donating the proceeds to charity, upon her death.

That gave me an idea. I wondered if she'd be interested in becoming a donor for our Trident Towers project. Checking the phone number in the documents, I called the attorney and left a message for him to return my call. On my laptop I did a search of the woman's name, and didn't see an obituary posted. Of course, she could have moved, she could have passed away elsewhere, but there was no record of anything but the transfer of the property from her, Maryann Sussman, to Marco. My finger glided over his name on the deed, which read, *Marco Gambini, an unmarried man.*

"Not for long, my love," I whispered into the early morning air.

I set the file aside.

The rest of the files contained some miscellaneous office bills, payroll reports, several of them relating to the sale of Marco's office building in Manhattan, and fees and profit and loss statements or proformas for projects he didn't buy. Most of these were generated by consultants and engineers, planners and artists that he had hired over the past several years.

The bottom line was, I didn't find anything I could really toss. It all needed Marco's approval to dispose of. So, I placed the box with all the files in them next to the file cabinet, out of the way. I had done my due diligence, tried to purge them, and wasn't comfortable with doing away with them just yet.

Armed with a fresh cup of coffee, I made my to do list, and began working on it. I would be visiting the sultan sometime this afternoon, and had been invited to dinner. I was looking forward to it, even though I would be peppered with questions about Marco and the crew stuck in Nigeria.

I added "Promo Blurb" for the Town Hall meeting scheduled since the station would need it to start advertising it for a good turnout. Jared wanted cameras present, which I wasn't keen on, but probably couldn't stop. I knew Marco would hate that idea.

I needed to update Tyler Mason, Warren's assistant planning director, so I could control the narrative, in case the full story hadn't gotten to him yet. I still considered him an ally.

There were a few wedding details I would take care of, but were added to the bottom of the list.

Always at the top of my list, but not written down, was an update from either Marco, the Senator or both. I worried that two days had just zoomed by, and they still hadn't made contact with the parties who held Karin and the others hostage.

I got a text message from Rebecca.

Can you call me Shannon?

I texted her back. *Calling now.*

It rang twice and then she answered, out of breath.

"Are you okay? You sound like you must have been exercising."

"Oh I was. I was on the treadmill. I spilled my water, and made a mess right after I read your text. I nearly did a faceplant. I'm sorry about that."

"So what's up?"

"I have started to get a couple of strange phone calls, Shannon and I just thought I'd tell you about it."

"Oh? You think this has something to do with the project?"

"Well at this point, I'm not going to rule it out."

"Strange, as in how?" I asked.

"It's just someone that breathes my name. Like oh, I don't know. It almost sounds like a crank caller to me. Like somebody's just you know, trying to mess with me a little bit. But I wanted to tell you one thing that this particular person said to me that really kind of involves you."

My blood turned to ice. I held my breath, bracing myself. "Go on."

"Well he said, and Shannon this doesn't really make any sense, but he said, 'I think you're the pretty one.'"

"I don't think that means anything to me. The pretty one? As in prettier than whom?"

Then I realized she thought it did have something to do with me and I remembered our on-air interview.

"Wait a minute. You mean you think this was somebody that perhaps saw our interview on TV?"

"I think so. What do you think I should do, Shannon? Do you think I should call the police?"

"Yes. As a matter of fact, I think you should go over there and meet with them. If you call them I'm just afraid it's going to get lost in the shuffle, it'll get passed on to somebody as a message and since it's not urgent and I know they're extremely busy, you may not get the attention you need. But, in light of the bombing, and I mean we're getting pretty high profile here, it could be someone who is trying to scare us off."

"That's what I thought, too."

My mind raced to think of all the preparation we were doing for the Town Hall Meeting, which heightened the relevance. "We're going to start advertising about the meeting. Boy if there's a wacko out there who's watching my broadcast or your interviews, I sure would like to know that before we have that town hall, wouldn't you?"

"Do you want to come with me?"

I hesitated, I had so much to do. I actually thought she would do a better job on her own. But I offered to come if she absolutely felt it was necessary.

"I would appreciate it, Shannon. I mean we're all on the same team here, maybe if you were there, and you gave your opinions it would add more credibility, more weight. I've gotten calls over the years, you know those awful disgusting calls that I think they dial at random but this one seemed to be more personal."

I agreed with her and checked my schedule. "How about if I meet you over there at about 11:00. And if we're still in the mood, as a thank you Rebecca, I'll take you to lunch afterwards, how about that?"

"Shannon, you're speaking my language."

THE PINELLAS COUNTY Sheriff who sat across the table from Rebecca and I was mildly interested in the information we gave him, until we reminded him about the bombing of the Bone Frog Development Group offices several months ago and the resulting loss of life. Then he got very interested. He excused himself and brought a female officer in with him introducing her as on loan from the FBI ATF.

"It's not really all that exciting," she said. "They wrote a grant proposal, and they received some federal funds to monitor certain terrorist groups within the state of Florida. I have a broad territory to cover, but if it's a bomb or running of guns or suspected smuggling of any of those, I'm to help share the load, and give them extra resources."

"Got it," Rebecca said.

"So let me ask you, what makes you think these are related?"

Rebecca and I looked at each and she shrugged. "Well I've had a lot of firsts lately, first I've gotten divorced, okay? I'm not exactly the most liked person on the planet, it was a pretty high-profile and nasty divorce, so I'm used to hearing complaints and little things whispered behind my back. Sometimes I think I have a microphone back there or something. And then most days I just think I'm making it up. But it does feel like since we are also building this project or rather Shannon and Marco are and I'm helping as much as I can, that due to the high profile nature of it, something has gotten triggered. And I don't know what it is. But in addition to getting divorced for the first time in my life, I'm getting phone calls. I suppose next would be letters?"

Sheriff Jones inserted himself. "You say phone calls as in more than one?"

"Three. I've had three. Two last night and one this morning."

"Mrs. Gambini," the FBI liaison began, "Was there a progression in what was said between these three calls or did the person just say the same thing, and I ask this because sometimes kids, teenagers whatever, just to be malicious will take a clip or a recording and then play it and they'll play it randomly to people."

"No this was a live call. I know the difference." Rebecca spat back.

I sensed her impatience.

The agent smiled and started over. "Okay, so you knew it was a live call because why?"

"Well I heard things in the background not in every call. Like I heard a train in one of the calls and it sounds like the train that goes down—it runs from Clearwater down to St. Pete, and I think it goes further?"

Both the sheriff and the FBI agent were making notes. "Go on," she said.

"And then I heard a dog bark in one. Let's see the first time he said, well he said it all three times, 'You're the pretty one.' And at first I thought it was somebody I knew because it sounded like somebody I knew. One of my friends. I thought one of them was messing with me at first. But then, there was a lot of heavy breathing in the second call later. It was very late. Sounded like maybe he was—I don't know."

Rebecca was having difficulty saying what she was thinking. And all three of us knew what she was thinking.

"So you think perhaps he was doing something with or to his body?"

"Yes, perhaps. But I'm not sure. He just hung up the first time. The second time he said the same thing, followed by some really creepy heavy breathing." She scrunched up her nose.

I felt the need to back her up. "I think you need to know that I interviewed Rebecca yesterday at the station, and it was about the Trident Towers that we're building, and we were both on camera together. Perhaps this person thought that she was the better looking of the two of us, and I definitely think they're probably right."

"Oh stop, Shannon. We know that's not true," Rebecca said.

"No, I just I think it's someone who watched the interview. That's my point. It's someone who's fixated on her from that interview."

"So Ms. Marr, have you been contacted by anybody?"

"Absolutely not. And my fiancé is away, so I'm keenly aware of all phone calls, since I want to hear from him. But no. In light of the bomb blast, we have been asked to check everybody's ID at the office, changed our procedures completely, we even issued new badges for all the employees, and we notified our subs and some of our building contractors, that they'd have to make appointments, not just stop by. Those were all the recommendations I think your department gave us if I'm not mistaken."

I was gratified to see that both the sheriff and the FBI agent were nodding their heads slowly.

"Can you tell me what's happened with that bomb investigation?" I asked. "You know, it's been three months now? I sometimes get a call or an update, but it seems lately there's been nothing. Is the investigation still continuing or have you closed the case?"

The sheriff jumped in. "The case will never be closed, because there was the loss of life. Those cases never get shelved. Yes we have a small team on it, we're still gathering more information. Due to the fact that so much of your building was destroyed, there are lots of little pieces of evidence that frankly I'm just not sure when we're going to get through it all. But we are working on it Ms. Marr."

"Again, I'd like to know why you think this is related." The FBI agent asked Rebecca.

"Women's intuition?"

The sheriff thanked us for the report and said he would take it into a department meeting and they'd decide how they were going to pursue it. "In the meantime, Mrs. Gambini, I would change your phone number."

"Oh my God. I just can't deal with that," she said.

"Well ma'am, it's a whole lot easier to change your phone number than to get rid of a stalker. If you were my wife, that's exactly what I'd have you do. You could ignore my advice, but it's at your own risk."

CHAPTER 9

Marco

E VEN AT 4:30 in the morning, Cape Verde was still noisy as hell. Lorries and delivery trucks were making their rounds before breakfast establishments opened and ships arrived as tourists began populating some of the establishments and beaches in the little towns that dotted the coastline. Civilian traffic was heavy. Our driver took us to the private charter hanger and helped us unload.

He called a couple of workmen in the building to give him an assist. One by one, all our bags were stowed in the belly of the small prop jet we were taking. I wished that we would have more room, but it was made to seat six with two pilots, so we would be tight, but okay. I was more worried about the weight of the bags.

I had managed to bring some sidearms and two long guns. Senator Campbell's letter indicated that I was licensed by the State Department and his committee to be able to accompany and be armed while I was conducting a diplomatic mission. In a way, this was true. On top of all of that, if we were stopped or questioned, Carson's credentials would certainly help us along.

Sven had paperwork showing him as an international aid worker, Riley was licensed to carry, and had dual citizenship, identification cards showing that he also worked for the Irish government as well as for the UN. So I was fairly sure that even in the event we were stopped, we would pass the smell test.

What did have me bothered though was that we had not heard

a word from Karin or Paul or any of the others, other than the cryptic message I received. In discussing it with Carson this morning, he made the following comment. "It's obviously from her, and she said to bring a Bible. That would tell me that they're in some kind of a church or a Christian section of town. And that's unusual, because Johnny Okubo doesn't usually hang out in those areas. He hates Christians, church schools, priests. So I'm not quite sure what it means, but it could just be that they found some place that was suitable, having been at one time a church. I don't know. But that's my guess."

"What do you think she means by make the wedding?" I asked.

"Perhaps it's your wedding, Marco. Didn't you say that you've set a date for next year? Do you suppose she's referring to that?"

"But that's in January, this is October."

"Well you typically get married in churches. Maybe it's not the wedding at all. Maybe it's the timing, or has to do with how long they're going to hold her. I will say though that I'm heartened that she appears to be alive."

"Yes, I agree. Maybe it's an arraignment in January?"

"Well we know the general vicinity, when her cellphone went off the grid, and I believe your guy Riley is trying to get information on what that location was in country. Once we have that, we'll just take a look at the map and see if I can recognize something. There's been so much destruction, Marco. I may not even know some of these little villages and communities. But I think that's our biggest clue."

By the time we were ready to touch down, we saw flares that had been lit in two rows on both sides of the runway. The pilots nosed down for the landing, and all of us looked out the windows, searching for something dangerous lurking in the brush. There was a lorry at the far end of the airstrip, that looked like a malfunctioning personnel carrier.

I had been trained to look at the tires. It didn't matter how ugly or dented the vehicle looked like, if it had good tires and the engine at least started, it was a viable vehicle. And this one had decent tires. In fact, they looked almost brand new.

The co-pilot lowered the bridge door and we followed behind him, scrambling one by one down the stairway. He assisted us with some of our boxes. Out of the corner of my eye I saw the lorry begin to move toward us. I got out my pocket binoculars and looked to see who was driving.

"He's African. It looks like he's alone. One of your guys, Carson?"

"I don't think so. I was never told about this."

Our co-pilot asked us to continue working. I knew he was nervous about spending too much time on the ground, especially if there was an armored personnel carrier coming toward us. I caught Carson's expression as he rolled his eyes.

Sven whispered in my ear, "One of us has to go approach. I think it should be me. You got my back?" Sven asked.

"Okay, but are you packing?"

"Always." He patted the special pocket sewn at the rear, inside the waistband of his pants.

We continued moving the boxes into the shade while the co-pilot dashed back to the plane, retracted the stairway, and slammed the door shut. It began to turn and taxi in the opposite direction. The engines had never been cut.

Within seconds, the two were airborne once again.

Sven was waving his hand over his head shouting something to the driver. He walked at an angle so that his shooting arm was aligned with his side, so he could quickly remove his Sig behind him without drawing too much attention. A crack shot, it was guaranteed he could fire a round that would take the driver out.

None of us saw movement in the brush or heard any other vehicles, but we were all on alert as we finished stacking and sorting.

"No show of firepower, gents. We don't show anything. We're here doing research, and we're waiting for somebody to pick us up."

"Roger that, Marco," muttered Riley.

Juan put his hand over his brows and stared at the lorry again. "I think perhaps he is a local. Does this airstrip get used by farmers or small business concerns?" he asked me.

"Carson? You know this area. This is close to the coordinates where State told me to insert. What do you say?"

"I don't think any of the farmers here have the money for any airdrops unless it's some kind of an emergency. Or a dignitary of some kind. But nobody like that would ride in that truck." He said.

Sven was chatting incessantly, and I could tell he was nervous.

"He's speaking Portuguese," Carson whispered.

"I was just going to say that. But he speaks it with an African dialect," added Juan.

Finally, we heard our forward scout say, "All right, all right. That's good. You stay right there. Let me ask my colleagues." Sven carefully turned, again shielding his shooting side. And walked with his angled body toward us.

Sven's face was sweating already, bright red, dirty streaks of orange dust making lines along his hairline in front of his ears and down into his shirt collar. "He says that he was instructed to meet us at the airstrip. I asked him who gave the order and he said he was told to come. He said it was a gentleman from the big house, as he put it. What do you think?"

"I don't know. I think maybe let's find out where he's going to take us and let's make the motions at least that we're loading up," I instructed.

Sven motioned to the driver to come forward toward us.

All of a sudden, Carson grabbed my forearm, "Wait. He needs to check the back first. I want to make sure that it's empty."

"Sven, did you hear that?" I shouted back to him.

Disgusted, Sven angled his way back to the driver holding out both hands to the side as if he was surrendering. We could hear some of the conversation and then the driver stepped out of the van. He walked around to the back side and opened the doors. There were no windows in the back of the lorry, and I considered that to be a good thing since the windows in the front were all busted out. We saw Sven nod his head, and then come running back to us.

"It's completely empty. I don't see anything there that looks suspicious. Some old rags, just some tools, nothing. I honestly think he doesn't know anything about this, he's just sent to pick us up."

"Where is he taking us to?" I asked.

"He said it's a big house, just a few clicks down the road. He speaks Portuguese, but he's African. He said that a house has been provided for us to stay. And there is a doctor waiting there for us, should we need it."

Carson and I exchanged glances.

"Riley as soon as we can, I want you to ping. Here's my phone. I want you to ping this number, and I want you to keep it on. That's going to give a location to Senator Campbell's office, and they're going to make sure they position the satellites so that they can hone in on where we are."

Riley grabbed the phone, pushed the button to deliver the call, and tucked it carefully in the deep pocket of his Flak vest. "We're good to go now, sir. Let's get these damn boxes out of the sun. My red hair and peachy complexion hate this weather."

We were loaded, the driver not lifting a finger to help. Both Carson and I rode up front. Carson sat next to him and I rode in the junior seat behind. The rest of the men and the luggage, equipment, were in the back. I was hoping that Riley was able to get some kind of intel with his computer if he could connect the link to the satellite. But with the number of potholes and deep gouges in the red earth and trail, I had my doubts.

I turned to our driver and asked him if he lived nearby. It was a dumb question.

He looked at me and shook his head. He said something in a dialect I didn't recognize, an African dialect, but it also sounded slightly Portuguese. He looked like he was scared as hell.

Carson gave me an explanation. "He doesn't understand you. But I think the answer is yes. And even if he did understand you, he wouldn't tell you. He's a one and done and he's being paid to keep quiet."

"So who arranged the house?" I asked.

"I think your Senator is working on things behind the scenes. I'm not sure. It's not something we do. But I'm glad. It means we can sort of disappear. We won't be as exposed as we'd be in the jungle."

"So when villagers or people see these types of planes come in and land and then turn around and take off, what do they think? I mean isn't that a red flag?"

"It depends on what their job is. If they're a lookout sure. But there's so much going on between the drugs and the human trafficking, gun-running, most of the locals who aren't involved in any of that stay as far away from it as possible. Out here, they're exposed, there's no big city or police force that will protect them, they're on their own. And people who live out here know how to protect themselves. But they also know how to keep quiet. We're just going to have to pray that God is looking favorably on our mission, Marco."

We came to a fork in the road, and after several hundred yards crossed a small stream. The natural beauty of the land, devoid of bombed out buildings and broken-down vehicles was beautiful. It was lush and green unlike closer to the coast where the ground was more arid and desert-like. There were colorful birds calling back and forth, and the whole region looked like nobody had ever been there before, except for the obvious evidence of the road. It looked to me like the Garden of Eden.

And there wasn't a single piece of rusted corrugated metal in sight.

As we rounded a turn to the right, a large pink villa was nestled in the side of a small foothill. It was surrounded by a high fence, that was electrified. Inside the compound, through the wire fencing, I could see banana trees and other tropical fruits being grown. The grounds were extremely well-tended. Not abandoned. There was no evidence of any armed guards, which was what I expected at the gated entrance. But as the driver stopped, we heard a buzzing sound and a gate slid to the left electronically. It closed behind us as we made our way toward the large porch that wrapped around the front of the house.

It looked to me like an old building from Colonial times, a grand house that once belonged to a governor or perhaps a provincial leader of some kind. It didn't look African at all, but more like something I'd seen in Mexico or Central America, owned by a wealthy businessman, probably a drug cartel boss. I did see two black Mercedes vehicles parked in front of a two-car garage on the side, and a four-door brand new four-wheel-drive pickup, with some kind of a logo on the driver door.

"Do you recognize this?" I asked Carson.

Carson barked some questions of the driver who answered him back rapidly.

"He says it all belongs to a gentleman who owns a fruit company. He is also a banker in the capital. I have heard of this place. I have never seen it but I have heard of it. At one time, it was overrun by a militia but that was maybe five, ten years ago. This belongs to a Western man. This is not an African's house."

"I'm struck with how lush and beautiful the gardens are and yet I don't see anybody working," I added.

"I'm sure all will be revealed." He barked a few other comments to the driver who responded, nodding his head and giving an answer. The two of them bantered back and forth, then Carson laughed. I waited because I didn't want to ask but I needed to know what they'd been discussing.

"He says this place is his honeymoon palace. He brings his girlfriends here. I think this is where he has his little liaisons. His name is Malcolm McConnell, McConnell Co. Fruit, Ltd. and he is not originally from here. He lives in London."

I had already deduced the same. I was still confused and waited for more explanation.

Carson leaned into the seat and asked the driver one last question, and the driver nodded his head. "Si, si."

"So the kid's from Portugal?" I asked, noting his thick African-Portuguese accent.

"His mother was from Brazil. I believe the owner of the fruit company is from the U.K., but originally from Scotland. His wife was Brazilian and this was her favorite place in the whole world. Now that she is gone, he brings his favorite girlfriends here and only stays but a few days out of the month. Our driver here is one of his sons."

I had a new respect for the situation I was walking in to. If McConnell was a wealthy businessman, and he paid off the right people, and he didn't cause problems for the government, he could probably more or less do whatever he wanted here. But the gentleman would still have one problem. And that was Mr. Johnny Okubo.

I suspected that part of the reason for his cooperation was due to the fact that Okubo hated westerners and was murdering as many of them as he could before his days were done. If that was what the gentleman wanted, to be rid of Johnny Okubo, I would make sure he got his wish, in exchange for a safe house to bring my people to when we rescued them.

And his Uncle Sam would also be very, very grateful.

CHAPTER 10

Shannon

REBECCA AND I opted for grouper tacos at one of my favorite family-run restaurants on Gulf Boulevard. The place was packed with snowbirds coming back to the beach, before the onset of cold weather on the upper East Coast. It was a cycle repeated every year.

The tourists came from January through April and then dwindled somewhat as the hot summer months went by. People who owned property elsewhere but vacationed in Florida, came in the months of September, October, November and December, after the hot weather was over and liked to leave before the crowds started in January. So, this was a slow time for most of the shops and restaurants for tourists, but a busy time for owners coming down to avoid the cold, and fix up their rentals.

I reflected on our meeting with the sheriff and FBI agent.

"That was sort of an interesting interview with the two of them, don't you think?" I asked Rebecca.

"Yes, it confirms what I've always thought. The sheriff here is pretty good. You don't hear many complaints, and they staff their stations better than just about any other place in the country. I just can't for the life of me understand why it's taken so long to conclude their investigation about the bombing. That was three months ago now."

I watched her features carefully. "I know, and I'm sure the families of the ones we lost would like some closure. But it is what it is. If enough people work on it, they'll eventually catch a break. But it does seem like an inordinate length of time. They're usually on top of it and get things solved right away."

"I agree. That's been my experience all along."

Our order arrived, and as I dug into the delicious taco, I thought about Rebecca's phone call.

"What are the odds of me having a stalker and then you getting a stalker a few months later? Doesn't that just sound a little too convenient?" I asked her.

She wiped her mouth on a napkin. "It does. You don't read about that very often."

"And the bombing is another crime entirely. It's not a stalking crime. It's something else, don't you agree?"

"I sure do. And they already caught your guy. He's serving time."

She stopped eating and set down the taco. For a few seconds, we just stared at each other as something came to mind to both of us at the same time.

"And he's still out there, isn't he, Shannon?" she said it first.

"That's right. I don't think any of the victims were the target. I'm not even sure Marco was the target, even though he was injured."

"And that means it's possible he's not done, but we won't know that until we know the motive," Rebecca added.

"No wonder the department is having such a tough time. Along with all the forensic evidence, there just aren't any clues," I said.

"They asked if anyone in the company had a grudge, didn't they? They asked that of me."

"Yes, they did. But there wasn't a note, a statement, anything to tell anyone why it was planted."

Rebecca whispered, "Which means, to me, he's not done. He didn't get what he wanted."

I had a sudden flash of realization. "I think he wanted to delay or stop the project, Rebecca. I think that was the motive."

"And look at us. We're still trying to go forward."

A chill went down my spine.

We finished our lunch and waited for the bill. "Are you going to change your number?"

"I guess so. It's just going to be such a pain in the butt, re-entering in all my contacts. Oh my gosh."

"You know, what I would do is call your carrier or one of the phone companies, and see if there's a way you can import your contacts list on a new phone. Just get a new phone with a different plan and a different number but keep your contacts. There has to be a way somebody could figure that out. I'll bet one of our guys at the office, one of the young guys, or maybe even the interns would know how to do that."

"That's a good idea, Shannon. I think you just saved me a whole lot of headache."

We kept the conversation light. I didn't bring up Marco's name, and she didn't ask me anything about him. If we remained on this kind of casual level with the discussions between us and the very beginnings of perhaps a friendship, it would work out. And anything I could do to help take something that was a problem for Marco off his shoulders was a good thing. I was certainly not the type to get so jealous I couldn't understand they'd had something together to be married for all that length of time. But I wasn't going to let it interfere with my relationship with him, and if we kept him out of our conversation, it was safer, and we could be friends.

I paid for our lunch, and we prepared to leave.

"So you're headed out to the beach to see your friend?" I asked.

"Yup."

I noticed she didn't make eye contact with me, and that felt a little weird, but then we were just getting to know one another. As we walked out to our respective cars, she stopped and sighed.

"Okay, I wasn't going to do this, but this is an old boyfriend. He's an investor, wealthy fellow, and he's going to be looking for some property out this way, and I offered to show him around a little bit."

"Ah, well, don't worry. I was just curious, but your personal life is your personal life, after all. We're sort of connected in this weird way, but you can tell me things like that and if it makes you feel funny I can promise I won't tell Marco if you think that's a requirement."

"No, not really. But you know it's just weird like you said."

"Well, let's just make it *not* weird then. And you don't have to tell me about this stuff. I shouldn't have inquired."

"How about you? Any old boyfriends that sometimes come around?"

"No. I was pretty darn inexperienced, Rebecca. You'd be actually shocked if you—well, I'll just tell you. I can count on one hand the number of men I've slept with. That's how bad it was." I wrinkled my nose, and she matched my expression.

"Gotcha. I would never have guessed that. But you got the prize, right?"

I didn't like the tone of her voice. "Now that's getting a little over the top. Can we not do that?"

She was nodding her head before I even had to say it. "Duly noted and it won't happen again."

I checked my phone for the time. "I better get going. I've got a little bit more work to do at the office, and then I have that dinner tonight with the sultan."

"Oh, that'll be interesting. Does he know about Marco yet?"

"No. And that's another one of those things I probably shouldn't have even brought it up. We shouldn't talk about that, either." I allowed my lower lip to protrude a bit. "I guess this is going to be a little bit harder than I thought it was going to be. I'm sorry."

"Me too. But we'll just keep starting over. We'll get it right one of these days. I liked you the very first time I met you. That night when you interviewed me in the penthouse, and we drank all that booze, you remember that?"

"I'm still feeling the hangover, Rebecca." I laughed, and she joined me.

"I saw in you a younger friend maybe like a younger sister. I don't want to intrude on your sister's territory, but I'd be honored if you'd consider me like a sister. And I'll behave. I'm starting to learn my lesson, and I'm starting to enjoy myself. It's really not a lot of fun to make enemies everywhere you go."

"Boy isn't that the truth? Even when you don't try to you make enemies sometimes. What a crazy place the world is."

"Well you have a productive afternoon and good luck with your party tonight."

I gave her the hug I had been wanting to give her since yesterday. As I gripped her shoulders, I added, "Thanks Rebecca. I know you mean well, and I think we can be friends. Nobody will ever take Emily's place, but the two of you are about as different as night and day. I hope you have a good time tonight. You'll probably have a much better time than I'm going to have."

She giggled and put her hand over her mouth.

I released her shoulders and headed to my car.

THREE HOURS LATER, when I drove up to the beautiful home on the beach, I pretended this was the finished home Marco and I were going to someday inhabit. I knew that was going to be a huge day for me. It would be the culmination of so much and it would mean that all our big problems were behind us.

Tonight, as I looked at the lights shining through the huge place and heard the dancing music inside wafting out over the paver tile driveway and probably extending way out over the beach on the other side, I was struck by how close this family was. It was a huge family, and they rejoiced and celebrated together, cared for one another, and there was really very little argument. In fact, even when the boys misbehaved, the sultan was easy on them.

Their world was wrapped in laughter, beautiful colors, traditions, spicy foods, gossip, being together—doing everything together including bathing and cooking. It was just unlike any culture I'd ever been exposed to. And tonight, I was missing my sister. I was missing Marco. I was missing the relationship I didn't have any longer with my parents. This was going to be a wonderful substitute.

I had stopped by to get some chocolate and vanilla ice cream, which I knew to be the sultan's favorites. I also brought three key lime pies, a rhubarb pie, and a box of pink pineapples imported from Costa Rica. It was piled up in the back of my car, so I brought all the boxes together and set them at the base of the stairs. I knew once the servants found out about them, they would do all the heavy lifting.

"There you are, Shannon." The sultan's wife number one greeted me warmly at the door. "I have been waiting to show you some things for the last two hours."

One of the younger wives came up behind her wrapping her arms around her as if she were her mother, not her sister-wife. "She's been going to the door looking out the window about every five minutes, Shannon. Wait until you see what she's going to show you."

"Well, let's not hang around here. Show me. I want to see this."

The young wife directed several of the servants to go down and pick up all the boxes at the base of the stairs while I handed the three key lime pies in a cellophane bag to another servant to take to the kitchen. The smells of spiced curry and unusual meats filled the whole house. It was delightful to me, but I had a feeling the landlord was going to say something about it when they moved out. After all, the sultan was supposed to stay nearly two months. In two month's time, the smell of the curry and all the vegetables and spices, would probably never leave the fabric or the walls of this property.

The older wife took my hand and drew me to the bedroom. On the king-size bed, there was a black one-piece bathing suit with a deeply plunging neckline and legs cut so high, I was sure it was designed so that the wearer's butt cheeks would be fully exposed. I couldn't believe my eyes. My hand came up to my mouth, and I could feel my cheeks redden.

"Oh my God. Is this yours?"

"Yes!" She bent over and picked up the suit running around the room with it attached to her front. "I'm going to wear this by moonlight tonight. The sultan and I are going to take a walk. Doesn't it sound romantic?"

I laughed. I was touched by how his number one wife was so accommodating, was so happy to bring him pleasure. She was simply the easiest person in the world to live around. I suspected with many wives, part of the reason they all got along was because of her. She was an enormous gift to them all. I appreciated how she treated me as well. It was as if I had been part of this family, just as Marco was.

"You are so brave. I can't wait to see that tonight. I'm going to stay, until I see you walk down the beach at sunset."

"I want to thank you, Shannon, for making him come here. Do you know he put on a bathing suit for the very first time in his life today?"

"I didn't know that. So did all of you go shopping today for bathing suits?"

"Yes, those that plan to wear them. Not everybody will, of course."

"Of course."

I returned to the main party, which was equally divided between the enormous two-story ocean-view living room, and the patio with steps leading down to the sugar sand beach. I was looking for the sultan, figuring it would be safer to talk to him when there was a crowd around us, and I could beg for discretion. He would understand that. Besides, I didn't have much I could tell him. But he needed to hear it from me, since Marco wasn't here.

I found him encircled by a group of his wives and both his sons. Just like his number one wife had predicted, he was wearing a pair of yellow Florida swim trunks with pink flamingos on it. I'd remembered his fondness for the birds from our last visit to his island kingdom of Bonin.

He wore a matching shirt in all-yellow, with a Flamingo stitched on the vest pocket. Glancing down, I saw his skinny legs sprouted from his more than ample belly, adorned with yellow flip-flops. His entire outfit was straight out of one of those beach shops lining Gulf Boulevard, and I could just imagine the time they must have had with everyone running around picking out things he would buy. The fact that he didn't shop exclusive also impressed me. He could have easily afforded to buy the entire store several times over.

He caught me entertaining myself with his vision and smiled, holding up his umbrella drink. It was pink, of course, and even matched the pink toenail polish one of his wives must have done for him.

I wanted to take a picture to send to Marco, but I knew photos were not allowed without permission. I approached, since he was knit rather tightly with his entourage.

"Welcome, Shannon. What do you think?" he asked, spreading his arms to the sides.

"I'd say Florida looks good on you. You fit right in, along with the partying." I leaned in and whispered in his ear, "It warms my heart to see you so happy."

"Thank you."

He placed one arm over Absalom's shoulder.

"My boys have been good tour guides. Please don't feel offended, but we've been doing lots of exploring on our own. Tomorrow, they have arranged to take me fishing on a charter boat."

I was surprised he didn't have more concerns about security or that there hadn't been restrictions placed by Marco's team. I made a note to ask him if and when I could.

"You fit in nicely." I glanced up at Absalom and raised my eyebrows. "Make sure to take good care of your father. Everything here isn't always as it seems."

He nodded, which made the sultan frown.

"I talked with Ryan at the office, and he gave me some advice on that. We're staying to places with lots of people around, nothing too private. That was his suggestion. And, of course, we are not dressed like we are at home."

"But all the same, be careful. I know Marco would—"

And then I realized my mistake.

"Where is Marco?" the sultan asked, searching the crowd.

This was the moment I had been dreading. "Marco had to go help the team in Africa. They've had some issues with the permits, and—"

"But surely something he could send someone else to do. You are left here, all alone? I was hoping to spend some time with him this week."

I could see the veiled question about whether he should return home in light of Marco's absence. I decided to nip that one in the bud. So, I lied.

"He told me you'd want to chicken out on him. He said to just wait it out. We have, I think, one month and another month extension on this house—already paid for. He promises he'll be back in the next few days."

"Few days? That sounds like a week!"

I was really treading water here and didn't want to ruin the friendship, or Marco's business relationship with this very dear client, but I was walking on thin ice.

"My opinion is—and again this is only my opinion—you must do what you think best. Could be he will be home in maybe four days. I can't imagine it could take that long to pay those that are expecting it and get paperwork filed. From what I know of the business, it shouldn't be long."

I was fully prepared to fall on my sword if it should come to that.

"Please tell me that you are not going to reject his hospitality. He went to great lengths to get you the best property in all of Indian Rocks Beach. And you're close to the site of the Towers buildings, the one your boys are working on."

I felt bad sticking that little knife blade into him, but I was getting more and more used to making ruthless and perhaps irresponsible decisions. If I was going to fail, I would fail forward and take the blame, if it was necessary.

I hoped it wouldn't be.

I was pushed out by the throng surrounding the sultan, who wanted to run down to the beach and dip their toes in the surf, which gave me the ability to wander back into the house and visit with several of the wives and some guests they'd invited. I watched the cooking being done, the meddling of the wives from time to time, being shooed away by the catering staff who were annoyed and trying to maintain control. It was an impossible task.

Yet everything flowed in that high energy way, with that aura that always surrounded the sultan and his family. They lived larger than life in every aspect that could be measured.

I was beginning to become fond of it.

One of the younger wives approached me, dragging me out of the kitchen.

"We've laughed and chattered about it all day, watching him walk around in his flip-flops and his swimsuit. He is like a different man, Shannon. I love him no matter where he lives, but this new side of him, this zest for life, this is what you and Marco have brought him."

"Thank you. That's kind of you to say that."

"I mean it. When the sultan is unhappy, the whole household is sad, dreary. When he's happy, life springs abundant. We were truly made to celebrate, don't you think?"

I smiled at her perception. There was a kind of wholesome innocence to her approach to life, and it stemmed from the man himself. I found the same endearing qualities in Marco when he could relax to enjoy it. I also realized the sultan could not do what he did without someone like Marco to help support and protect his boys. Just as I was trying to take a load off Marco's shoulders, so was he trying to do the same for the sultan.

I wandered the crowd until the sun began to set, and, sure enough, I watched as the sultan took his number one wife, hand in hand, in his flip-flops and flamingo-covered bathing suit and she in her black rather racy one, walking in the surf with the pink sky raging above them. She had a butt I knew I'd have some day, and the suit revealed all of it. But at that moment, she was the most beautiful woman in the world, and her love and devotion were large enough to fill the whole sky.

A good distance behind them, where their whispers and conversations could be kept private, walked the cluster of wives both in and out of their new suits, holding hands and chattering, watching their sultan take his Florida stroll.

I saw the young wife I had spoken to earlier in that group. Her comments had touched my heart. I was sure the sultan had not confided in her or any of them, as he had with us, that his cancer was terminal and he had less than a year to live. It was not my place to tell them. It was only my place to help them all celebrate the life that was left.

CHAPTER 11

Marco

MALCOLM MCCONNELL WAS a big man, probably standing taller than 6'4". He made an impressive statue, perched on the top step of his huge veranda at the front of the villa. He was wearing a pair of blue jeans and a white dress shirt rolled up to the elbows. He was relaxed, and as he leaned against one of the pillars on the porch, I could see that he was extremely well built and fit.

I made a point to be the first one to greet him, giving him a handshake. "You must be McConnell."

"And you must be Marco Gambini. I have followed your success, for years. You're actually one of the few I do."

I was surprised he knew who I was, except for whatever background information the senator had given him. "Good to know. And it's nice to have a friend in faraway places such as this."

"Indeed."

He studied me carefully and then turned his gaze on the collection of men unloading the back of the lorry. Without looking at me, he asked, "Did you have any trouble?"

"Well, I was never given the information we would be staying with you. I was only told someone would meet us at the airport. But other than the fact that Carson here has a couple of men we couldn't pick up in Benin because we came straight here from Cape Verde, everything's cool, and we have our equipment, and we're ready to go. But I have very little in the way of intel, sir, and I'm more than a little worried about it. I'm hoping you have a lot more."

He peered up at the sky, searching the tree line carefully. "Let's get you inside, since some of our unfriendlies are getting a little more sophisticated, and we have to watch out for aerial surveillance."

That spurred me into rushing everyone's timeline. I shouted commands until I was hoarse. Sven was starting to sneer at me with attitude.

I pointed to the sky, and he nodded.

We left all the equipment in McConnell's living room, while he insisted on having a feast at a large round table in his dining area, which was covered with more exotic and tropical fruits than I had ever seen before. Living in Florida, I was used to seeing all kinds of strange things, but here, other than the papaya and bananas and dragon fruit, I didn't see anything I could even name.

The group dove into the fruit like it was their last meal. McConnell said he drank chai tea, and he had one taker for that, but the rest of us drank freshly ground and French press coffee with cream. I felt like I was back in the states. I could handle anything with a good cup of coffee and some cream.

"I see you met Cristobal, and he managed to get you here safely, without getting stuck. No broken axles this time?" he asked as he put his arm around the boy.

I saw the family resemblance. My guess was that McConnell's wife, now deceased, was a beauty.

"He did a good job, didn't let on who he was until we were nearly here. Thanks for sending him."

I was wondering where his other staff would be since I hadn't seen any.

"Things are getting a little squirrelly here. I find a single driver truck doesn't draw a lot of attention. But please be careful, and I would prefer that you only use sat phones, not landlines or cell. I'm not sure if I'm being monitored, but it wouldn't surprise me. The rebels have had a lot of help from some countries that are fairly sophisticated electronically and only too willing to help."

It was just a little hint, but I picked up the danger signal well enough. McConnell was handling things his way, or at least the way he used to. And perhaps that way of life was being threatened.

Actually, I knew it was being threatened.

As we were standing, leaning over and placing fruit on our plates, he instructed us to sit right where we were.

I really wanted to kick off my shoes, put some shorts on, and go for a swim. Or walk along the beach, but being in the beautiful house with all this fresh fruit was the next best thing.

McConnell sat after filling his plate with pineapple. "So I'm going to fill you in on what I know, and incidentally, I have been in contact with Senator Campbell, Marco."

That was obvious. "Good. And what's the news?"

"Well, as you know, they blew up your airplane. It actually didn't even make it in the newspapers or on any of the capital television stations, because the government didn't want the general public to know, since it gets the population nervous. But people find out anyway."

I understood that and told him so. "Keeping a total lid on the media, social media, is next to impossible."

"Yes, and we have a prime minister who is barely hanging on, guarded nearly twenty-four seven, but it's beginning to look a little more like a house arrest to me. In these strange days, people's loyalties can shift depending on whether or not they think they're keeping their family safe, and that is the driver for most the common people."

"Not just the common people," I objected. "When connected people lose their security, it happens there too."

"I agree. Makes for some strange characters whom you thought you could count on."

So far, this wasn't anything I hadn't expected.

Sven had a question for him. "Do you know where the team is?"

"I do. And I believe they have set a trap, using them as bait. Marco, I believe they're very interested in capturing you. I was disappointed to hear you were going to come yourself, but after what I knew about you and your history on the teams, I understood why. You need to know you have to question everything. If it looks like it's going to be easy, you've overlooked something grave. If it looks impossible, you've probably correctly figured it out."

"That's kind of like our motto 'The only easy day was yesterday.' I hate that motto."

The group laughed.

"There is a *haunted* mission city, a place where a horrible massacre developed about a year and a half ago. We think there were something like three hundred people slaughtered there, buried in a mass grave. The leader—"

Carson Odingo interrupted him, "You've got Johnny Okubo, Red Johnny, don't you?"

McConnell nodded in Carson's direction. "You are well informed."

"So do you know where the bulk of the militia is actually staying, the soldiers, the fighters?" I asked.

"They are dispersed in several neighboring villages, and Johnny is being rather cagey about it. He is said to move his base every night to a different village. And he randomly changes his mind. He rules ruthlessly, and many of his own men have suffered horrible atrocities, not only the civilian population. He seems to thrive on shedding blood, and he's showing no signs of slowing down."

I couldn't wait to get my hands on this guy. I knew Sven and several of the others felt the same.

"They've laid this trap for you. They bring young girls they have kidnapped from other villages to this sacred spot where they are either married to one of his henchmen, or the girl and her entire family is beheaded in front of everyone. We call this the bride spot."

Carson looked at me. "*Making the wedding.* That was what she said."

I nodded. I said to McConnell's puzzled expression, "My representative sent a cryptic message about bringing a Bible and hoping to make a wedding. What you're saying about this place, that it was a church complex at one time and a place he performs weddings, fits right in with that."

"She has a telephone?"

"Riley's trying to track it. Might be she was able to borrow it. We don't know that it's on her. But she did leave the message. I don't want to put her in danger by messaging her back."

Sven spoke up next. "There may be no other way, Marco. We're going to have to take some chances here. Just my opinion. We don't have a lot of time."

"Your friend is very perceptive. But here's why I'm concerned. We understand your colleague is to be presented as a bride herself in two days. If she does not submit, she will be killed. Johnny's men are good at starting rumors, and they did their job well. Cristobel overhead a discussion of some villagers. What he also learned is he intends to kill your pilots and the rest of her team. And we believe one of your group is missing, so one may have been sacrificed to ensure the cooperation of the others. You need to be prepared for that."

My guts turned inside out. The danger I was fearing now become all too real. "Who's missing?"

"You have an Indian pilot? A Veejay somebody?"

"Paul. Paul Vijay. He's missing or dead?"

"Missing. My son was told he hasn't been seen since the day of their capture. Word has it that he was murdered trying to escape."

McConnell said something to his son I didn't understand. The boy left the room.

Each of us was dealing with the knowledge of the loss of Paul. But I had to stay in action or I'd go crazy. Juan was the only one in our group who didn't know what a fine man he was.

My eyes were downcast, but I knew McConnell was watching me carefully. I wanted to know how he handled the danger his son was in. It was one thing to lose a man who had signed up for it, but a son, his flesh and blood, I knew it must weigh on him ten times worse.

"It must be difficult for you here, with your son. Have you thought about taking him to London, where it might be safer?" I asked McConnell.

"I have. I begged him. He doesn't want to leave. This is the only home he's known. And he misses his mother, who loved this house with all her heart."

"The first thing I wondered when I drove up was where is all your security?"

Several others at the table nodded.

Sven inserted his thoughts.

"Either your security guards are wearing jungle costumes or you have such a healthy containment system here, that you're completely safe."

McConnell chose his words slowly. "I have friends here. I have a life here. I am good for business here. However, you are right. Things are changing. And I am increasingly worried about our safety. I know most of the population don't want to submit to these militia groups. They will, if they must, but people here worry that if too much attention is given to their homes and their own personal protection, it will come across as a sign of resistance. Somebody will come through and destroy them. It makes little difference whether it's the government or an independent militia. Nobody here wants to be the center of conflict. It never works for the people who occupy that space, does it?"

McConnell was very perceptive, and it underscored my previous thoughts that he was going to help Uncle Sam, because Uncle Sam was possibly going to do him a favor.

"What happened to your wife?"

"Unfortunately, she was caught up in a raid of a village about fifty kilometers away. She was helping a woman deliver a baby. None of them made it out alive."

"I'm so sorry. Still, why don't you both leave? You could have a good life in London."

"Well, now that opportunity has slipped away. I was informed by the Secretary of Commerce I was not allowed to leave the country. On the one hand, I have enemies in the militia groups, on the other hand, I have friends in the government who will restrict my movements and activities. I think you call this between a rock and a hard place?"

Everybody nodded but kept their thoughts to themselves.

The boy came in and brought a folder, laying it in front of McConnell's seat. Carefully, he pulled out several glossy photographs, and I identified them as surveillance photos taken by a drone.

"You have a drone?" I asked.

Riley leaned over and picked up the photo, his eyes wide as he studied the photo. "Yeah, he fucking has a drone. This is awesome work. Tell me you didn't build this yourself?" he asked.

"No, this was provided to me by a friend. Unfortunately, this drone was shot down. Luckily, I was advised to rig it with an explosive device, so it wouldn't be captured and then traced back to me. But these images were generated before the self-destruct. You'll see there is a chapel at the corner and many school buildings or offices making up the perimeter of the complex. I believe your people are somewhere in one of these buildings."

I scanned through the several photographs and, except for pictures of paramilitary type males, saw no evidence of civilians.

"Is this one day's pictures or do you have more?" I asked.

"Unfortunately, this is all I have. It was taken two days ago. I was hoping—" He turned to Riley—"Hoping that you had triangulated the text you had received from her. Were you able to do that?"

Riley shook his head. "I don't have everything I need. But we were being tracked by Washington for the first hour or so of our journey here. I didn't want to run his battery down, so turned it off, and we're recharging. I'm thinking Norfolk or our friends in DC can use their equipment to get me a location, possibly even the name of the owner if they're good enough."

"Riley's right. The quality of these pictures is phenomenal. I mean, I can see that gentleman there with a rifle…he's wearing a shirt from the Afrika Korps," I pointed out.

McConnell agreed. "That happens all the time. They raid and keep whatever they can. They especially like uniforms because it allows them to pose as some kind of official authority. They look for patches and medals and things they can wear, take as trophies."

I asked Riley to make a phone call on my behalf to Senator Campbell, giving him the phone number that came from Karin's text message. "See if you can get them to get us some info STAT. And also verify they're still tracking this."

Riley agreed, looked around him, chose a small dark portion of the living room where he could have some privacy, and began making his call.

Juan spoke up. "I still don't understand how you get all this done. I don't see gardeners, housekeepers. I don't see anybody. You have no security here. I would think you would be extremely vulnerable. You must have somebody you call when you need to."

"Up until two days ago, yes. But I lost part of my security team in an ambush. I do feel that Johnny Okubo is beginning to close in on me. And he's destroying everything in his path."

Riley came running into the room with our first piece of good news.

"The senator says their tracking is fine. They've located where the militia group is camping tonight, even have satellite tracking on these grounds and the church yard. He's authorized us to go in and do a look see. He also said whoever owns this cellphone still has the ability to make text or receive calls. It is registered to a deceased member of the Africa Korps who grew up in Paris."

"Hot damn. I say we rock and roll tonight, boys." My exuberance was catching.

I looked into the faces of our little team. It was totally crazy, but these guys actually sprang to life, juiced with this new possibility of starting a war.

It was what we all lived for.

CHAPTER 12

Shannon

"IS THIS SHANNON Marr?"

"Yes sir, it is. Can I help you?"

"I mean *the* Shannon Marr, the TV reporter?"

"Yes, and who is this please?"

"Well, I'm returning your call. I'm Grantham Webb, and I understand you have some paperwork that shows I handled the estate of Maryann Sussman?"

I sat up, taking my feet off the desk and placing them firmly on the ground. My blood pressure rose as my stomach churned.

"Yes, I called you yesterday. I was going through some files of my fiancé, Marco Gambini?"

"A very nice gentleman, my compliments to you, ma'am."

"Well, as you know, he purchased the property from the estate, and you helped handle the transaction. I noticed when I was reading the terms of her estate that she was invoking a tax break so she could leave her proceeds to charity when she passed on. Since we are building a housing project for disabled veterans, I was just wondering if she would consider donating to our project, and I think it would qualify. None of the money—"

"I must stop you there because it's a little premature. Ms. Sussman is currently still alive. She's in twenty-four hour care at a facility here in Tampa. She's ninety-one years old, so I don't know how much longer she will live. But she is not of the capacity to be able to make that decision, unfortunately."

I knew there had to be a provision in her estate allowing someone else to make that determination, and I also knew that, in many cases, the attorneys handling the estate would be the logical choice to do this.

"In the event she is incapacitated, who is it that can make decisions for her?"

"Well, let's see here—I've got her file in front of me."

I heard rustling of papers.

"There was a great-grandnephew or someone who was out in…I believe it was California perhaps?"

"But I thought she didn't have any heirs."

"Well, technically, yes, because he was not made a part of her estate. But in the event she was not able to manage her affairs, she designated her sister as the responsible party, and she passed away shortly after the sale. This boy is the last remaining relative. So anything we did with the proceeds after her passing would have to be approved by him."

"I don't understand. You mean you were able to sell the property and put the money what into a trust account somewhere?"

"That's standard, ma'am."

"What makes a difference if she passes on then?"

"Oh, I see what you mean. Well, in this case, she was in full agreement of selling the property to Marco, your fiancé. She wanted to sell it to him, and I believe she knew what he was going to do with it. I was carrying out her wishes. She didn't have the knowledge to handle it herself, and she had used me for trust work in the past, so she asked me to handle the sale. All she did, if you look at the deed, is sign off on it. That's her signature. It's not mine."

I didn't know where I'd put copies of the paperwork, but I knew I had a folder somewhere and had missed that important detail. But this situation was becoming confusing. At the same time, I didn't really doubt the attorney. I just wanted to verify it. Without Marco being here, it was just one more piece of information I needed.

"If I were to present a proposal to you, could you get it to the grandnephew?"

"I could, except that he's suing me."

My distrust of attorneys was making my stomach churn.

"May I ask what's he suing you for?"

"He claims I shouldn't have sold the property."

So there was a possible enemy.

I didn't want to spook the attorney any further by suggesting this. Marco definitely didn't know about it, and he needed to. So did the police.

"And I can't comment or do anything on this estate. It will have to go through some pretty expensive litigation now, since I cannot afford to lose my license. However, at the time, I knew nothing about the relative, nor did I expect her sister would pass away so suddenly. The estate has significant assets, so the boy will inherit a fortune, eventually."

"What happens to all the money then, if the litigation goes on for a number of years after she passes?"

"It sits in the bank. It waits, collecting interest, until that determination is made. Do you know how long some farmers took to get their money with the water dispute between California and the neighboring states claiming water rights to the Colorado River?"

I'd never heard of this. "No. I'm sorry. I don't follow such things."

"Well, as a reporter, you should. It was kind of a rip-off. Several of those farmers who objected to the sale held up the proceeds for everybody for almost forty-two years. That's how long it took. Do you know how many depositions were taken, how many truckloads of files there were?"

"I imagine it would fill a garage or two."

"Oh, more than that. The court reporter who handled the case became independently wealthy just from selling the transcripts alone. Every law school in the United States that teaches property, especially eminent domain law, gets copies of those transcripts.

And there are a lot of them. That court reporter is set for life. All she has to do is keep copying and sending out digitals these days. In the old days, she had to actually buy a Xerox machine. Times have changed, Shannon. It's an interesting story. You should look into it."

"You know, Mr. Webb, I'm finding all kinds of interesting things every single day. For instance, my fiancé has told me about the different warring jurisdictions, especially when it has to do with maritime law and what happens. I didn't know it makes a difference where a ship sinks."

"That's a fact. That's another one. Lots of fun stories. I'm afraid I'm not at liberty to help you. You would have to wait first until she passes away, and then you could contact him. I am not willing to do so. Now if you hired another attorney who could look into where this gentleman lives and find out his address and approach him, it's possible you could get something that way, but it's very risky, and you'd be burning up lots of attorney's fees with no guarantee you would have a good outcome. His lawsuit is public record, so that part wouldn't be too hard to determine. But, even if he agreed to it before she passes away, once she passes away all bets are off. It's like it resets to zero. He can't give future value to a decision that has to be made after her death, because he made the agreement before he had the capacity to own the assets."

"Well, thank you, sir. If you hear anything new about her situation, or the lawsuit against you or anything at all that would help me, I'd appreciate a return call."

"Absolutely. Personally, I think she would have loved making a contribution to your project. I've been watching it in the paper, of course. I can't help it. I was never a veteran, but a lot of the wealth and security I have today was paid for in blood by young men and women just like your fiancé, who sacrificed themselves to help make us safe. I owe them everything. You tell Marco that. And if some miracle should happen and she wakes up one day and says I've changed my mind and this is what I want you to do, well, then, I'll call you first thing."

After lunch, I received a call from the Pinellas County Sheriff.

"Ms. Marr? This is Rodney Watson from the Pinellas County Sheriff's Department. We met yesterday at the station?"

"Yes sir, you have some news for me?"

"As a matter of fact, I do. We have located a surveillance camera for the business across the street from your office building, and we have a couple of pretty clear images of people going and coming from your building, as well as other buildings. We have a person of interest, and I was wondering if I could bring the clip over to your office and show it to a few of your people who were there that day. Would that be all right?"

"Absolutely. Can you tell me a little bit about this person?"

"I'm just going to have to bring it and let you look at the people who came in and out of the building to see if you can identify them. I'm thinking, if you can tell me who some of your legitimate contractors and vendors are that came in that day, that would help us eliminate having to track them down, at least initially. I'm hoping we'll have five or six people we can't identify, and then we can use our resources better to just focus on them. How does that sound?"

"Sounds good to me. I'm not going to tell you how to do your job, but making it more efficient? I'm all about that. I have two people gone plus my fiancé, and I have three others on extended leave."

I hated to call the absence of Karin and Paul and Ron and several of the others on the team as extended leaves, especially since three of them were there that day. But it was true. Two of the interns were running down some material costs and checking subcontractors. Otherwise, everyone else was present.

"I'll be right down."

I located Dax and let her know what was happening.

"I'll make sure nobody leaves. You want everybody? Even the interns?"

"I think we ought to have everybody interviewed who was present at the old offices, even the interns. I mean, who knows?"

"What do I tell people then?"

"Tell them that Pinellas County Sheriff's Department wants to show them some electronic photographs. Just to see if they can identify anybody. I think that's all you need to say. We don't have a suspect yet. We're cooperating. So we're just fishing. No one should object."

"You got it."

As I turned to go, Dax asked to my back, "Have you heard anything from Marco since yesterday?"

"Not a word. I was out late last night after dinner anyway, but I didn't get a message last night and I didn't get one this morning or today. He'll call when he can. Unfortunately, that probably means he's still in transit."

"He asked me once if Rhea and I would like to go run a project in Africa. You know, after all this shit that's gone on—sorry Shannon—Rhea and I just don't think we could put up with it. I mean why go over there when things are so good here?"

I understood how Dax felt, and I didn't judge her. But I wanted to make a point. "Not everybody does things for safety or for money. Sometimes people want to do things because they want to leave the world a better place. I think you do that every day, Dax. And there's lots of ways people can show it. I just think the sultan, our client, wants to make a statement. If it were just Marco and me, trust me, I would stay as far away as possible. I have no interest in getting involved in things like that. But when somebody good wants to do something worthy and needs help or protection, that's what Marco does so well. I understand it. And he's proud of the work. We need to remember that. We need to help him be able to do that, because that's part of who he is."

As I walked out of Dax' office, I reminded myself I needed to stop emulating my preacher grandfather. I was becoming unbearable, even to myself.

SHERIFF WATSON WAITED in the small conference room as, one by one, all of the employees of Bone Frog Development, filed through, sat with him, and reviewed the video surveillance. He was composing a list of subcontractors, and he had already gone through two pages of names, single-spaced.

"Okay, that's Ernie, Ernie from—oh, I'm just drawing a blank now," Rhea said. "I could go ask Dax?"

"Ray Townsend from Townsend Plumbing?" he asked her.

"That's it. Ray Townsend."

I watched the Sheriff play the clip again. Rhea was watching even people walking past casually on the sidewalk.

"That's funny."

"What?" We both asked in unison.

"Put that back just a few seconds and stop it. I'll tell you when," Rhea instructed.

As we all looked at the stopped footage, Rhea said, "Isn't that one of our interns? Isn't that Rory? You know Rory, the kid from FSU?"

I angled my face down toward the laptop and played the little clip back and forth several times. It didn't look, at first, like Rory was interested in the building at all, but just before he stepped out of view, I saw him turn around and look at the front doors over his shoulders. Then he left the scene. I was shocked I hadn't recognized the young intern before, but it was unmistakable that it was Rory.

"What are we looking at here?" Watson asked.

"This kid here is one of our interns. He works here. But he didn't come to work here until about thirty days ago. He wasn't working here at the time of the bomb blast. I guess it's just coincidence that he walked by the building, but I would have thought he would be in school. I don't know. It's just odd."

"Then you'll want to see this." Watson forwarded a tape to later that day, and I watched a young man, about the same build, with a baseball cap on, carrying a box and walking through the front doors. The hair color sticking out from under his cap was dark, though, extending into a ponytail down his back.

"He's the same build, but wrong hair color," said Rhea.

"That can be faked. It could have been attached to the cap. Bank robbers do it all the time," Watson said.

"Are you sure we're not just chasing windmills here?" I asked. "I've been accused of doing that a time or two."

"Maybe to you. But what we do is different. We don't have the manpower to chase down everything, but we must. There's enough here for me to question him further, just to be sure. So, if you're finished with everything here, Rhea, I'd like to question this Rory kid, if you don't mind?"

She stood, "I'll go get him. I'm sure there's an explanation."

Several minutes later, Rhea escorted Rory to the conference room, which was empty except for Sheriff Watson.

"Rory, this is Rodney Watson of the Pinellas Sheriff's Department," I began. "You want to take a seat here, and he's going to show you something and ask you some questions. Is that okay with you?"

Rory shrugged.

I focused on his hair, blond and streaked with bleach. That wasn't uncommon in the Florida area, especially amongst young people, but I'd remembered his hair being a light brown instead of a blond on the video.

Watson's voice was calm, not giving away any of his concerns or suspicions.

"Rory, this is how it goes. I want you to look at all the people going and coming. I've got just a little clip here for you to look at. I know you weren't working here at the time but we're making everybody go through this list and see if they can catch something they didn't see before. Okay?"

"Sure thing."

He played the forward button, and Rory watched, angling his head to the left and then the right as he fiddled with a coin in his fingers. All of a sudden, he stopped his fiddling. Other than that, his body didn't change one bit. But the coin dropped to the ground. He bent down to pick it up and slipped it in his pocket quickly.

"So do you see anybody in these pictures that you recognize?" Watson asked.

"Yes. I used to walk past that building all the time, and I think I saw myself there."

His baby face and innocent looks were deceiving, I thought. And there was something else about him that looked familiar.

"Yeah? What were you doing that day?" Watson asked.

"Well, let's see, I think I was maybe grabbing some lunch. I went down there a lot just to buy stuff. I'm always checking out the surf shops. I like the sandwiches down there. I don't know what I was doing that day. That was a long time ago."

"Think real hard, Rory."

"I don't know. I honestly can't help you."

Watson stood up, adjusted his belt, and looked over Rory to me. "Okay, let me see if there's anything else that's come over from the office that I'm supposed to show you. So just have a seat, and I'm going to talk to Shannon a bit about something and see if she has the right equipment for me to use," Watson added, patting the young man's shoulder.

Rory shrugged and then turned to me. "Could I have a bottle of water?"

"Absolutely I'll go get one. Sorry I didn't ask," I lied.

Watson closed the door behind us, and drew me further into the hallway, positioned so that Rory couldn't see us. He made a request of me.

"Have someone else bring him some water please. I'd like you to show me his file if you have one. An application? Can I get a copy?"

"Of course. What are you looking for?"

"I'd like to see what he puts as references. An address. Let's go to your office. Is that where the files are kept?"

"No, the interns' files are kept in Rhea's office. Follow me."

I directed Rhea to bring Rory some water. While she left, I opened the drawer with all the internship contracts in it. Going through all the tabs, we found Rory's folder, and pulled it out.

Opening the manilla folder up, I was surprised to find nothing in there.

Watson was quicker than I was. He bolted out of the office and ran down the hall to the conference room with the door that had been left ajar. I stood behind him as we saw the space was completely vacant. An unopened bottle of water sat on the table.

He looked at me. "We said somebody from inside, didn't we?"

"You did. You both did."

"I don't know how the hell he got in here, but I think he's our man."

CHAPTER 13

Marco

RILEY DEMONSTRATED HOW the drones he'd brought were able to track and record even directions that faced the sun, and unlike a lot of other drones, that used a heat signature, these were accurate from a mile up. It made them harder to detect.

I was impressed with this new technology.

"Yeah they developed these lenses for satellites that orbit the sun, because they need to photograph sunspots and sometimes objects that are on the backside. There's no way to avoid the sun's light, so they devised these to bend it and then send it back up, scrubbed of all the limiting rays. It's really cool what they're doing these days," Riley said.

He had brought one large drone and seven small ones, and he explained the smaller drones were actually more expensive. "You're not going to like the bill for these, Marco."

"Then bring them back. Make sure you get them all back. I'll sell them back to you."

McConnell had also been fascinated not only with the drones themselves but the computer controllers he brought as well.

"I think I've invested in the wrong business. Fruit only has a shelf life of about a week—longer if it's refrigerated. But this stuff, all the components and upgrades they're doing these days, man, this is a wide-open field."

"Yeah, and since so much of the technology from China is frowned upon, although it's technically very good, there's a lot of room for UK-based or US-based companies to really make some money and capitalize on it. Notwithstanding the security aspect of it, of course."

"Of course."

Riley explained he was going to send two up at a time, and then recycle them so there were always two in the air with the others back in their perch, uploading their information.

"The screen you have here, which is recording, is not of the quality that the data is going to be when they send it to Marco's computer or Norfolk. And right now, I've got it set to just send to your computer, Marco. You want me to ask Campbell if he's got a secure server we can send it to in DC?"

"Do it. I think he should have it."

"Okay let me take care of this. It's going to take me about ten minutes, and I should be good to go. I'll give him a call and see if I can get all the links."

McConnell and I walked to the side of the living room. I needed some advice.

"My inclination is to insert as soon as we've got the information analyzed and we're sure where we're going and how to get there. I need to ask, are you willing to put your son in harm's way to get us there? I mean, he's a local kid. People have probably seen him with the truck. Unless you think he's under suspicion? I don't want to get your family in any more trouble than they're already in."

"I think we're okay with him. He has a friend though, Abdallah. His father was a policeman in the capital who was gunned down. Abdallah lives with his mother and sisters here, and they're the best of friends. I think he's sympathetic to our side of things, and if asked, I think he would help us. I'd feel better if we did that."

"Of course. You get your son to bring him over. I want to vet him first."

"I would expect nothing less."

It wasn't more than an hour before we were packed and loaded. I had verified all the proper links were downloading to my laptop. We would leave it behind at McConnell's residence, but I was going to take my hand-held, which would give me a mirror image of what the drones were recording. Riley was going to stay behind, as well, to man the birds. We'd have to use the sat phone because the INVISIOs wouldn't reach that far. After speaking with Abdallah, I was satisfied we could trust him. He was eager to be of service. The kid was about the same age as Cristobel but was roughly three inches shorter. Cristobel, on the other hand, took after his father.

Each man had their own duty bag with their choice of fire power and ammunition. We carried enough food for two days, in case we needed it, plus water, two sat phones amongst us, and each man had an INVISIO com, so we could whisper instructions to each other.

Abdallah explained we would be going through the brush for approximately two miles. Then we would come to a clearing, which was a favorite roundabout for people practicing with ATVs, trucks, even some limited drag racing sort of activity the local kids did. The ground was pockmarked and devoid of vegetation, unlike the rest of the area on route to their designated meetup.

"This is the most dangerous part because we have to go across this clearing. Otherwise, we have to go to the river and the river, is not safe." He shook his head for emphasis.

His English was rather spotty and his dialect so strong it made it difficult to understand him. But after he repeated himself a couple of times, the group all nodded their heads in agreement. I told them I was going to walk point with Abdallah after we arrived and stashed the lorry. I told Sven to carry up the rear. Juan was responsible for keeping an eye on the sides and the sky so that hopefully we had all our bases covered.

It was still very hot at 1:00 in the afternoon, and in about thirty minutes, my shirt and pants were completely drenched with sweat. I also had picked up some bug bites when I passed under a tall tree with banana-type fronds that seemed to just grip the side of my face and neck. Something got deposited in my shirt and I wiggled until I got rid of it. But I knew I was going to have a pretty sizeable welt that was going to itch or worse for days.

The drone footage that was forwarded to the small laptop was a little grainy today. But it had the capability of showing our location in relation to where we were headed, and that was a tremendous help, since it also identified barriers, streams, large structures, or abandoned vehicles. The one thing we didn't see, was burned out and damaged villages. I guessed Abdallah probably tried to avoid those so the chances of engagement of any kind was eliminated.

We came to the clearing just as Abdallah had told us, and everything was eerily quiet. We heard the sounds of birds and other noisy animals—lizards, crickets and insects of all kinds—but nothing was heard once we hit the clearing, almost as if we had entered a dead zone.

"We walk carefully straight across." Abdallah said. "We go two, one, one?"

Everybody nodded.

"If you hear something, just stop. You do not run, until you know who is coming. You stop briefly to listen to where it's coming from, and then you continue on your forward direction like you're going where you always go and you don't have anything to fear." I said.

We were adequately armed but not so anyone would notice. Juan had stuffed his long gun in his backpack in two pieces, Sven had a short barrel Uzi-type machine gun, Israeli made, and everyone had a side arm and several knives. Abdallah did not carry a weapon other than a machete, an ax, and a very long bladed, serrated knife looking similar to a K-bar.

Abdallah and I walked across the clearing, choosing an area at the tip of the clearing instead of crossing at the widest point. Listening for sounds of anything around us, we walked normal speed and buried ourselves in the brush at the other end, waiting for the rest of the team. Juan was the next to follow, and he did not follow the same path that Abdallah and I did, seemingly going off into the east instead of going north. In several minutes, he found us in the brush and joined us. I directed Sven.

"Okay, my friend, your turn."

"Hey, Marco, I hear something behind me. There's a truck coming. I think I should wait."

"Is it a large truck or a vehicle of some kind, a sedan?"

"It sounds like one of those three-wheeled delivery vehicles? It has a tiny engine. But I hear some talking so there's more than one."

"Get down and wait. You have some good cover?"

"Will do."

Our team of three laid flat against the ground on our side of the clearing and waited. A group of three scooters with small trailers attached entered the clearing, picking up speed as soon as they hit the edge. The first scooter turned abruptly and did several wheelies in the middle. Red dirt flew everywhere until our vision was completely obscured. There were shouts and cheers as the other two watched the antics of the first one.

Then the other two took their turns. One rolled his and was able to right the machine himself without any help. He was laughed at and called names. They played in the red dirt for nearly an hour, while I checked in with Sven several times to make sure he was okay.

Finally, the friends all left the scene, headed in the same direction Abdallah and I had headed.

"We're going to take a course correction chance. I don't want to run into these guys again. So we're going to head east, and then we'll get back on a direct route to the camp. You're good to go Sven."

Several minutes later Sven entered the clearing from the south, dodging again the widest part and instead slicing off the area to limit his visibility time. I saw him check the sky, and then Sven leapt over a rock and disappeared. Nobody moved.

Abdallah whispered in my ear, "Drone."

It was one of Riley's, since I could barely hear it.

While we were watching the clearing, Sven came up behind me and surprised us all.

"Did you hear a drone?" I asked.

"I thought I did. It kind of sounded a little bit like a very light-weight RPG. But there's no blast so I guess we're good to go."

We resumed our trek, headed east first and then corrected it to follow north. Abdallah was clearing the brush and moved us into the thickest part of the jungle, our actions and sounds would be muffled. We encountered wild fruits, including a beautiful banana tree with bright red ripe bananas that probably was forty feet tall. There were colorful butterflies and birds, even a monkey colony with red faces.

I followed the map and stopped everyone about a half mile from the site.

I pointed to the screen and did not say a word. I put my hands up, cupping one ear to indicate I wanted them to listen.

I'd been trained to listen and smell, to take in my surroundings, as if I was a blind person. I had done hundreds of exercises blindfolded, so I could learn to spatially orient. It came in handy, even though this was in the middle of the day. I could smell smoke from a campfire in three different directions. I also smelled something of a chemical nature like turpentine or pitch, perhaps somebody repairing a roof or creating a tar seal. I didn't hear any mechanical machinery, no trucks or motors of any kind and there were surprisingly no airplanes flying overhead.

Very slowly, we moved toward the red square on the box that was our target. At last, through the jungle foliage, we could see buildings patched together with concrete block and corrugated iron. There was evidence of recent tree removal, including fresh hack marks and leaves being harvested. I also located a campfire pit that had been used in the past.

We passed a burn pit loaded with pieces of clothing, a rubber tire that smoked, nothing I wanted to look too closely at for fear I'd see remains of a body there. Sven didn't seem to have that same problem and rummaged through with a stick, whispering, "It's just a trash dump. Nothing bad here."

I called Riley on my sat.

"Anything on your end, Riley? We're in position."

I heard the crackle on the other end and then Riley's voice smoothing out. "No, but we got some really good visuals here. The senator's monitors in DC have not come up with any large groups heading your way, but it does appear there is a large personnel carrier on the backside farthest away from you. It could have brought in several militia units, that we haven't seen. So be careful. They have the capacity to truck in or out maybe thirty or so."

"Good to know. We don't hear any motors. But we'll watch for that."

"Senator wants to know if your accommodations are satisfactory."

I chuckled. "Probably one of the nicest safe houses I've stayed at. Tell my 'uncle' I appreciate it. I'm just not sure how long it's safe to stay there. But he's got a full medical facility there, and if we have someone injured, we can take care of them properly. You just ask him to keep us visible. Okay?"

"Will do."

I heard McConnell's voice. "Everything good with Abdallah?"

"Tell Cristobel he's fine. Thanks."

I disconnected the call but left the sat phone turned on. I checked the handheld backup computer and saw a miniaturized version of what Riley was looking at. Riley magnified the area, and lowered the drone a bit so he could see a little more detail of the houses in the perimeter. He scanned the steeple of the church, expanding the magnification, enough to see two well-armed soldiers, sleeping in the afternoon heat.

"Okay, so we got two. Let's see if we can determine what's in those buildings."

I dialed Riley again. "Can you get down to look in some of those windows? You see any traffic or evidence of traffic in and out?"

"Just watch. I didn't notice it, but I could have missed it."

We both watched in tandem as the drone dipped, magnifying the size of the buildings so I could count every crack, every rust mark, every divot created by gunfire. The drone came to one wall opposite the church that had been made of sunbaked stone. Sprays of automatic gunfire divots crisscrossed the stone wall, hundreds of them. The dark stains on the wall indicated it had been a site of some carnage.

Most of the dirt area in the central courtyard between the buildings, looked like it was fresh tilled or worked over soil. I decided not to tell the team I suspected a mass grave or burial site underneath, but I guessed many of my team were already thinking that.

Remembering what McConnell had told me, I knew the presence of a sleepy little church with some outbuildings was something that might not flag most people's attention, but it was exactly what he had described. This was not what it seemed, and it was dangerous.

Just then, a section of the dirt in the center courtyard began to move, and slowly, a trap door opened in two halves, the dusty metal pieces falling to the sides. Up from the center of the bowels of the courtyard came the sounds of heavy steps on a metal rail. Riley must have seen the same thing because the drone focused in on the faces of the soldiers coming out of the opening.

There were three, one of them sporting a bandage across an eye that was bleeding and a wound on his forehead. But behind the three militants, I saw the unmistakable form of Karin Atkins. Her face was nearly unrecognizable. Her eyes were so swollen they were nearly shut. Her lip was cut. Her hands were bound with dirty rags in front of her, but her feet were not. Her hair was matted and caked with mud. Behind Karin, I saw Ron Hansen and then two others.

All the hostages followed the three soldiers, with one dropping behind to kick Ron Hansen in the butt several times to speed him up. They had all been beaten, but they were walking.

And they were alive!

As they marched toward the old church, the one thing I didn't see, was the presence of Paul Vijay.

Rest in peace brother.

CHAPTER 14

Shannon

THE PINELLAS COUNTY Sheriff's Department sprang into action, like nothing I'd ever expected. They sent two staff over to my office, helping Rhea and some of the other assistants look for any kind of paperwork that had information on Rory's whereabouts. His application and contract were already mailed out to the school, and, after I called them, they would be looking for it. But right now, the copy that was supposed to be retained on our end, was missing. He must have known this was coming.

We had always thought our biggest security issue was not people who worked here, but people who came in from the outside.

Watson asked me my opinion about why Rory would be so interested in our project.

"I have no idea. I really hadn't had very much contact with him, and I know you're interviewing the other interns, but it's nothing I expected. So I didn't look into it. I'm so sorry we don't have the paperwork for you."

"Let's hope some of your other kids know him a little bit better. Sometimes that happens."

I had forgotten to mention my call with attorney Grantham Webb and kicked myself for it.

"I need to tell you about a conversation I had with an attorney. Maybe this is related, maybe it's not, but I was looking into the paperwork for when my fiancé purchased the Towers property, and I noticed that an attorney had handled the sale. I called him up to see if perhaps they wanted to donate some of the proceeds. From looking at the paperwork, it appeared the elderly lady who sold the property was going to be donating, and I thought perhaps she might be interested in being one of our benefactors." I shrugged my shoulders, realizing that perhaps it had been a hare-brained idea, and he laughed.

"What does this have to do with Rory?"

"Well, the attorney told me there was an heir that was not named in this lady's instructions. In fact, the estate was to be donated, but disposition of the estate after she died, was going to be given to her sister. Apparently, her sister has recently passed, but there is another relative, and he explained to me it's a young man. He's suing the attorney for handling of the sale. Do you think he could be this Rory fellow?"

Watson wanted the name of the attorney, which I gladly gave him. I also told him about how he might get an address from the lawsuit.

"He told me it's public record, so easy to find, if someone knows how to look."

"I got people who can do that, no problem. You be sure to tell me if you hear anything else. This information might be useful, Shannon."

"No problem. I want to help anyway I can. I'm as anxious as the rest of you to get this all behind us."

"Did your guy seem that smart, that devious?" he asked me.

"Not really, but I guess I never suspected a college kid would have such deep-seated feelings of revenge and hate."

"You haven't seen enough of the world, Shannon. A lot of our kids fall through the cracks. Just look at the school shooters. Mostly males, mostly young. You take a kid like this, if it is this kid, without a family around him to monitor or perhaps send up a red flag, well, they can think up some pretty devious things. If no one reports them, they slide under the radar."

"Maybe he's not this guy."

"We can't take that chance. We cover all the bases. Thanks.

I was feeling like a fifth wheel. My insides were shaking from this new information. The worst thing about it was we had to suspect everyone in the office now. That's what one of the investigators told me. That meant I had to be careful of what I said to even people like Dax and Rhea—people I'd trust with my life.

Not hearing from Marco was also driving me crazy. I felt like I was waging a war on two fronts. I was right about his trip; I should have insisted I go along.

I wanted to get out of here, go for a run on the beach, except now the beach might not be my happy, safe place, either. It really bothered me I never suspected Rory and that he got so close to me, to all of us. It was so easy for him to worm his way into our company. No one would have suspected him of planting a bomb.

I knew Marco was going to want a full rundown, and I wished I had his ear to be able to at least discuss with him what we discovered. He'd be excited about perhaps solving the issue of the bomber, but I was really unclear about this purchase, and I realized there could be some factors he knew about that I didn't. It just was frustrating for me not to have all the details.

The sheriff and his task force were able to get information on the lawsuit, and while being partially stonewalled by the attorney representing the young man, it was finally confirmed. Rory was in fact individual who had brought the lawsuit against the estate attorney. They had an address, finally. Things were piling up and an all-out effort was being made to locate him, as well as any of the places he might have hung out.

Everybody on staff was alerted to the fact that he was a suspect and they weren't to talk to the media or each other about the case or the situation. If they ran across Rory, they were not to try to contact him in any way and needed to inform the sheriff immediately. The entire office was allowed to leave after the sheriff's technicians finished their search.

I contacted our head of security and requested an escort so I could go home and change. My clothes smelled and my armpits were even making me sick to my stomach.

"I'm ready to go home. I need to take a shower, and I want to do a run on the beach. I need to get all this out of my head. I haven't heard from Marco. I hope he is okay, but I just need some alone time, but I don't want to be totally alone. Can somebody accompany me there?"

"Absolutely, ma'am. We have orders to do whatever it is that you require. I'll have one of my female security people accompany you. Should she meet you here?"

"I'm going to head home now. Why don't you have her meet me at my house, and then we can just go for a run up and down the beach? I can shower, put on a fresh set of clothes, and then get back here. How does that sound?"

"I'll have her meet you there in fifteen, maybe twenty minutes. Her name is Andie, and she'll put you through your paces. She's quite competitive."

"I'm not feeling like running any races, but it probably would be good to take my mind off this stuff. Thanks."

I indicated to the task force, who were staying behind, in our large conference room as their base of operation, that I was headed home and had a security detail with me. I told them that I'd be back in a little more than an hour.

Dax approached me. "You sure that's wise, Shannon? I mean, I think it's better if you stay here."

"But all you people are going to be going home. I mean I'm sure they're not going to want all of you to have guards, I'll be fine. I think this is just a kid working on his own. I'm sure he doesn't have resources or a crew, I don't think he's after me. I think he's trying to figure out a way to get in and botch this project."

"All right. I've said my piece. Now I'll shut up." She gave me a hug. I brought my things to the car and started my drive home.

My phone rang, and I was surprised to find the planning director himself on the other end.

"Mr. Warren? You have some good news for me, I hope?"

"I wish it was good news. Listen, I have a situation I want to talk to you about in private. It involves the son of a former friend of mine. I kind of consider him a stepson."

My mind raced. With all the details going on around me, the last thing I needed to do was give the planning director, who was giving us fits with our project, some kind of parenting advice. I hoped my irritation didn't show up in my voice.

"You know, now is not a really good time for me. We've got a lot going on at the office. I'm not allowed to say anything, but I just need to maybe clear some space here for an hour or two. How about if I call you back this afternoon?"

"I'm concerned about him and I think he is going off the rails."

He got my attention all right. "Who are we talking about here, Mr. Warren?"

"We're talking about my stepson, Rory Gibbs. I believe he is an intern at your office?"

"Rory Gibbs is your stepson? Why didn't you tell me this before?"

"I didn't realize he was working at your office. I knew he was very bitter about the sale of the property, but I had no idea he was actually working in your office or that he was so fixated on this land your fiancé has purchased. I don't know what he's up to, but my neighbor called me to say the police were at my house today. Do you know anything about that?"

I wasn't supposed to talk to anyone about the case. My frustration was at the boiling point. I decided to violate my agreement with the Sheriff's Department. "The Sheriff's Department thinks he's our bomber."

"Oh my God. It's worse than I thought."

"Mr. Warren, what are you not telling me?"

"I didn't want to tell you because I thought you'd suspect I was just delaying the process. But I think he intends to make some kind of a statement at the town hall meeting, and I wanted to postpone it. He is extremely bitter, and he feels his birthright has been stolen from him, even though he's really not been a part of the family. He was sort of a bad seed. I was in love with his mother, and she passed when he was in high school. I took on responsibility of looking after him a little bit because I knew my former girlfriend would've wanted me to, and I've tried to treat him as a stepson just as if we were married. But my girlfriend suspected him of doing some dangerous things. And now, in hindsight, I'm convinced she was right."

"You need to talk to Rodney Watson of the Pinellas County Sheriff's Department. You need to call him right away. I have his number—let me just pull over to get it for you."

I set the phone down and rummaged through my purse to see if I could find the card from the sheriff. I found it in an outer pocket. I gave the planning director the phone number for his direct line. "I believe he's at our offices right now, but if you know any information about Rory, for his own protection, you need to let Sheriff Watson know about it. All right?"

"Thank you. And be careful please, Shannon. I feel somewhat responsible that I didn't tell you about all of this. I wanted to, but I just didn't think it would come to this."

"I understand. I sort of thought something was afoot, but I understand, and you're doing the right thing now. Please, please call Watson. That's the only thing right now that you can do that will help."

"I will."

I was getting a very troubling feeling, now that I was out of the office and on my own. I wished I'd had the security detail with me. It was a stupid mistake on my part, but rather than drive back to the office and pick someone else up, I decided to just make it to my house and then get that run on the beach. Parking my car, I walked past one of the navy-blue security cars parked in the spot Marco usually parked in.

Thank God she's here, I thought.

Unlocking my front door, I was unprepared for what I saw in front of me. The young guard had been gagged, bound hand and foot, and was suffering from a gunshot wound. At least she was breathing!

I quickly scanned the room, backing up, looking for a weapon or something to defend myself, feeling my skin beginning to prickle all over with the realization that perhaps whoever did this, possibly Rory, was still in the house. I hit the fireplace wall, searching the shadows of my little place. Remembering my fireplace set, I reached carefully around to the back and pulled out the poker. It wasn't much, and it wasn't going to save me from a bullet, but I might be able to hit someone with it or defend myself somehow. I didn't carry a gun, and I kicked myself for not having done that. Marco had told me over and over again I needed to get some kind of defensive tool in my handbag, and I'd ignored him.

Listening, I didn't hear a sound, so slipped my hand into my purse and dialed Watson. Hearing his voice, I whispered into the phone.

"Help. I'm at home. My detail is shot. Please—"

"Stay safe. We're already on the way. Can you clear the house?"

"Let me try."

I sidestepped, still clutching the poker in my right hand, and holding my cell in my left. I backed into the doorway, kicked it open, and ran out into the parking lot.

"I'm in the parking lot."

"You're gonna hear sirens. They're two blocks away."

"Thank God."

I moved to the sidewalk on Gulf, lots of cars racing by, people walking. I wanted to be in the middle of all of it. I didn't want to be left alone.

At last, the paramedics and two sheriff cars arrived. I was in shock, shaking, pointing to the house. One of the officers carefully removed the poker from my hand with a smirk. She gently led me to the side of the cruiser as the deputies cleared the house. It did nothing to make me relax.

I waited until they had searched the little place, including the bathroom, closets, kitchen, even under the bed in my bedroom.

They searched everywhere. They stepped out onto the patio that overlooked the beach. One of the officers asked me, "Do you leave this door unlocked normally?"

Fear was again beginning to grip me, and I began to tremble. I answered by shaking my head from side to side. "No."

I was sure I locked it because it was just something I wouldn't forget.

I was done with the idea of taking a run, and I figured since the person who did this was obviously out on the beach, that would be the last place I should go. I didn't know how the sheriff's office was going to search the entire beach, but it's likely they were going to be closing several of the access points so they could try. But it would be next to impossible to find this person now, not knowing how far they may have run.

I asked for permission to get back to the office. They asked me to stay. I waited until Watson came himself.

"Any news on anything? Did you get anything from the attorney?" I asked.

"Jeez, Shannon. Are you okay?"

"No, I'm not okay! I've had about enough of this! I'm not safe anywhere." I was furious with his question, but grateful, since it was like splashing cold water on my face and I began to fight back.

He watched me. "I gotta hand it to you. You're one tough lady, Shannon." He waited while I took several deep breaths. "I got quite a bit from the attorney. And we're looking. I think we're going to find him very soon."

This surprised me. "You think he's somewhere around here?" Then I remembered the young man who I had seen on the beach by our house.

"You know, I think perhaps I saw him when I was running on the beach back a few days ago. He was up by the house Marco and I are building. He was very distraught, and I offered to get him some help, asked if he needed anything, and he begged me off. I just turned around and ran away. Maybe he's up by the property we own up there. It's the construction site on Gulf."

I gave him the address, and Watson asked that someone go check. It was also relayed back to the station.

"You think he was there to cause you harm or what? Did he threaten you in any way?"

"No. He was just a mess. He looked like he'd been drinking for quite some time."

"So you took him for a homeless person?"

"Yes. He didn't look anything like the intern we have at the office. He didn't look like Rory. I didn't recognize him!"

"I'm going to recommend you not stay here tonight. Do you have someone else you could stay with?"

I thought of Jared, but I quickly dismissed it. I didn't want to put any burden on any of the staff like Dax or Rhea. I decided that there really wasn't anybody I felt like staying with.

"I'll just stay at the office. It's got great security. We've got guards around the clock, and I've got some blankets there. I'm sure I can find some pillows. I'll be fine. I'll even ask for a couple of security people to stay with me if you like. I agree with you. I don't feel safe here."

"I'm going to drive you back to the office myself."

"No, I want to drive. I need to have my own car."

"Nope, not tonight. I don't want you driving."

What was one more restriction on my movements when I'd already had so many today? I resigned myself to the fact that until they caught this guy, life as I knew it would totally be changed. I hoped it happened soon.

As the afternoon turned into evening, we ordered some food for the remaining staff who stayed behind, and for the officers who were running the task force. I spread out the comforter I'd found, and used a couple of pillows from the waiting room, and decided I could spend the night on the couch in Marco's office.

I wanted to call Marco, but I didn't want to cause worry. He probably had more than enough on his mind already. I knew it would frustrate him to be clear across the world, and not be able to do anything to take care of me. The best option was just to stay where it was safe, and this was the safest place I could think of.

About eight o'clock at night, I felt exhausted. The windows of the building showed that outside had turned dark, and even though I'd had a gallon of coffee, I was having a hard time keeping my eyes open. I kept waiting for news from somewhere—from Marco, from Senator Campbell, from Watson and the task force lady. Nobody had anything for me at the present time.

I slipped off my shoes, changed into a pair of exercise-type tights and a top from my gym bag, and nestled down in the comforter on the couch. The faint smell of Marco's scent, his cologne, the occasional good cigar he would smoke, all those little things I began to pick up, reassured me, he was really very close by. I told myself if he reached out, he could touch me right now.

And because I was near him, I was safe.

Just before I dozed off to sleep, Rhea came running into my office.

"Boss, they got him!"

CHAPTER 15

Marco

O NE OF THE messages I'd received from Senator Campbell's office was approval to engage the enemy. If I was active, I'd have to ask permission also from my handlers at the Navy, and sometimes there was a delay that cost us a mission, or an easy chance to get something done became a big cluster fuck.

I liked it better this way.

"Riley, you let them know we're going to hit the hornet's nest."

"Roger that, Marco. Godspeed."

Because we were all miked up, everyone on the team heard this, and knew what was coming next. I could do it, but I was going to give Juan the chance to earn his creds with the team. Sven and I had our explosive rounds out, and Sven also had some smoke bombs. Carson would second anything missed. Abdullah was handed my handheld.

Juan already had his long gun out, hooked up, and loaded. He was sited and waiting for my command. I liked this kid a lot. He would have made a great SEAL, and I was going to recommend him, if he was interested.

"Juan, your show."

Three rapid bursts crossed the clearing, each one landing on their mark. Carson handled a second shot when there was still movement. Sven threw the incendiary devices and one smoke bomb without waiting to see if we needed it.

The shots and explosions echoed throughout the jungle, and I was sure it could be heard all the way to the capital. Karin and Ron Hansen turned around to face opposite to us and ducked to avoid any resultant rounds. Ron knocked the other prisoner down where he tumbled like a sack of rocks.

I ordered Abdullah to stay put, and make sure everything was being captured on Riley's drone, and let us know if something else was happening outside our vision. We went in to get the three, all covered up in Kevlar, with extra sheets for the prisoners.

The two men in the bell tower began shooting and hit one of their own. I could hear a radio warning going out.

"Juan?" I pointed up, and with two quick bursts, they were neutralized. But of course, I knew the rest of the group was on its way.

I untied Karin, who was astonished we were there.

"Marco—"

"Quiet. We're not out of the woods yet. Or did you plan on staying to be some asshole's bride?"

"No. I was going to sacrifice myself."

"Not on my watch. Are we ready?" I asked Carson and Sven.

"We're good to go. We got one injury here," said Sven. "Nothing we can't handle when we get back."

We were joined by Abdullah and raced through the jungle. Karin had been trying to talk to me, but she was so weak just running even with my assistance was proving difficult.

The clearing was the next hurdle. We could hear trucks behind us, and the unmistakable buzz of a large drone, that was not one of ours.

"I got it," yelled Juan, as he dropped his hostage into Abdullah's arms and sited the bird. "Piece of cake."

It was a Hollywood movie-type scene. As the drone splintered into a million pieces, I understood it had been armed and ready to deliver a welcome package we'd not recover from. But it also meant that someone on the other side was looking at us, however briefly, on their own screen, and would know right where to go.

Then we heard a truck motor ahead of us, and my spirits sank.

We were surrounded.

"We head east. Carson, you direct us, please."

He took charge until we came to the river. We followed along the muddy bank through thick, sticky brush until I heard Riley's squawk on the sat phone.

"Don't order dinner yet," I told him.

"You want *to* run to the sound of the truck. That's Paul driving the lorry. He's coming right for you."

"Can you direct him? If he doesn't change course, he's going to run right into the group. We can hear a half dozen or more vehicles—big ones."

"I'm marking his spot. You get there like yesterday."

No fuckin' problem.

We zigzagged through the brush, came the long way around to be sure we were not leading them to the lorry, and, at last, found him on the other side of the clearing. We had to make a run for it, straight across, and we'd be exposed for too long, but there wasn't any other way to do it. We had to get these people to the vehicle, because it wasn't sustainable for us to carry the load any longer.

Dodging a hail of gunfire from somewhere on the north side, Sven lobbed an explosive device right in the middle of the nest. For thirty glorious seconds, all was quiet except the panting and beating of our hearts. I felt something warm running down my chest and noticed Karin had been hit, and she was not able to use her legs any longer.

Paul ran from the lorry and grabbed her from my arms, depositing her in the back, then resumed the wheel.

"You're my pilot, not my driver," I yelled.

"I thought you'd say, 'Nice to see you, Paul,' or something like that. But my real talents lie elsewhere today. You ever try to travel the streets of Mumbai at rush hour? I've been driving since I was thirteen."

We took off, and this time, there would be no detours. We had to get back to McConnell's fast or we'd lose Karin. Sven was attending to her and had placed a tourniquet to her upper arm.

"It's her right arm. Shattered the bone," he informed us.

I was grateful she had passed out and wasn't feeling the pain just yet. But she would not stay that way for long.

Riley buzzed on the sat phone, giving us kudos. We weren't out of the clear yet, and I nearly turned the damned thing off I was so annoyed. Time for celebration was long into the future, I thought, if it was coming at all. I wasn't sure the lorry would handle the trip through jungle, crisscrossing across cattle trails and narrow pedestrian paths without losing an axle or tire or having an engine malfunction.

"Riley, you better let the senator know McConnel's place might not be safe for long, if at all. I'd like to see some sort of help on evac. I can't scramble this much equipment with so little notice, not clear over there."

"He's already working on it. Just get over here, and we'll see what can be done."

I knew McConnell had heard that.

"You guys better start packing up, just in case."

That shut him up. Paul was doing a great job maneuvering around tree stumps, small creeks, large rocks, and mud bogs. Several times, he nearly got stuck, but each time, he managed to scissor his way out of it.

"Where were you the last two days?" I asked him. "We were told you were killed trying to escape."

"No. I wasn't the one killed. I got the trackers before they were able to call in their positions. Luckily, they had water and some dried fruit that tasted like shit on them. It kept me hydrated and alive. I had weapons, backpacks and extra rations. I watched the clearing, saw where you ditched the lorry, and hung around to protect it. I just missed being able to connect with you due to those kids. I prayed to God you guys would return as I had no clue how to get out of this hellhole."

As we drove up to the compound, the gates opened McConnell, Riley and Cristobel came running to help off-load the hostages. Sven had a somber look on his face.

"Marco, she's lost a lot of blood. She's got to be evacuated."

Karin had been a highly decorated asset with the State Department, not one of the desk jockeys who ordered everyone else to do the dangerous stuff. Perhaps it was due to that, perhaps it was due to something McDowell had to offer, but we were informed the Navy was sending a chopper near midnight.

We were told to hang tight, as if there was somewhere else to go.

CHAPTER 16

Shannon

I WAS AWAKENED by shouts and cheers coming from the lobby, and as I opened Marco's office door and saw the crowd dancing, even the sheriff deputies and ATF agents, I was delighted that something great had happened.

"He's coming home, Shannon. The Navy's sending him home," Dax said, hugging everyone she could find.

While the Navy might have helped extract him, there was no way in hell he'd be traveling that flight from Africa to New York or Washington DC or wherever they planned to put him, in a Navy clunker. He was going to go with one of his jets.

"Where's he landing?"

Nobody seemed to know yet.

I nodded to the crowd. "Check with the pilots. Somebody knows, trust me!"

The news also was celebrated that Paul Vijay had survived the kidnapping, at one time being thought of as murdered. I was so happy for him and his loving family. The next person I wanted to talk to was the sultan to give him the good news, but neither the brothers nor the sultan and his family were really clued in to the dangerous rescue mission in Africa. There was probably lots to be done yet going forward, but at least the team was safe, and they were on their way back.

All of a sudden, my mood completely did backflips. I could think about things like a future, like redecorating the office to put in a more comfortable couch in for Marco, like beginning to look at my wedding plans. Those simple little ordinary things that I liked to do every day that I had put aside for this emergency, came flooding back to me. They were things I had resented at one time. I'd been so busy and maxed out with the big projects I hadn't enjoyed the little things that made my life *mine*. Made my life with Marco the miracle that it really was.

This one was a close one, I knew. And I'd have to have that conversation with him as far as how many more of these he was going to go on. Wasn't it time for him to stop being a Boy Scout? He had said that to me early on in our dating when he talked about leaving the Teams. But he just couldn't let go of it when it came to his businesses. No, he couldn't.

Well, maybe now he could.

Watkins and several of his negotiating team returned to the office a short time later to interview me and catch me up to date on the progress they'd had with our intern.

"He is a nutcase all right, Shannon. Very good at worming his way into people's hearts one way or the other. Apparently, he spent quite a bit of time as a teen under counseling, probably should have been treated a little more aggressively, in my opinion. The family kept all that a secret, and he lived in some group settings, homes for troubled teens. Since he had never broken the law, the walkaways and the rejections of programs and his meds never grew to a serious level. His case wasn't elevated to a higher authority. The system failed him, failed his whole family. His stepfather—"

"You know, I know him. He's the head planning director for Pinellas County. You think he hid all this from the rest of us?"

"I think he knew a lot more than what he was telling you, Shannon. Did he do the right thing? He did. In the end. But it was almost too late. He knew the problems the kid had had, but it's one of those things... He loved the mother, and he thought it would break her heart. After she was gone there was nobody to control him. That's where he should have flagged somebody.

Mental illness is such a problem, and families think they can handle it on their own, but they need support. They need help. It's not something you can just deal with and everything will be fine. There are some people in this world that continue to spiral out of control until something sets them off if they don't get professional help."

"I imagine no one wants to think their kid is damaged. It's a hard thing to accept," I added.

"You have broken homes. In his case, there wasn't a strong family unit around him. He was left to sort of grow up on his own. I think this guy was fixated on Marco's purchase of land he for some reason felt he had a right to. And it's too bad there wasn't somebody really there for him in the family. There was a vacuum, and left to his own devices, with what little money he had inherited from his mother, he wasted it all on the lawsuit and devising a devious plan to try to get even. He was totally driven by revenge. Very twisted."

"The night I saw him at the beach, crying and upset, he just looked like a vulnerable young man, down on his luck, and didn't look like a dangerous individual at all. I'm shocked I spent time around him here in the office. The other kids did too, and nobody picked up on it—nobody."

"If only he could have used his people skills for good, Shannon. But sometimes really sick people are very talented at masking their pain, as well as their rotting insides. This guy was crying out for help in lots of different ways, and nobody caught him until now. Hopefully, he'll be placed somewhere where he can get care, so he can't harm himself or others. He doesn't belong in the prison system, because that will only make his situation worse. He needs a lot of care."

I realized I needed to call Grantham Webb, the attorney who had handled the estate. I wasn't sure what the status of the lawsuit would be, but I thought he might like to hear what was going on. I asked Watkins if I could share a little bit with him, and he agreed.

"Nothing about the case, where he was found, any of the evidence. Nothing about that, Shannon. But you can certainly tell him that Rory's in custody, and that we're going to make sure he gets the treatment he needs, as much as we can."

I went back into Marco's office and placed that call to Webb.

"I had a feeling you were going to get this rat's nest untangled, dearie. I knew it was something I couldn't do. I've done a lot of good things for people, but this stuff you're talking about with the kid and how he came after me so tenaciously, this was way beyond my league. Hopefully, they can get him some help, some serious help."

"I just wanted you to know, and I thank you again for the information you gave me."

"Well, Maryanne is hanging in there, and let's hope she hangs in there for a long, long time. In a way I hope she doesn't wake up. I don't want her to know about all this. But we'll see."

"I feel good about the outcome. I hope you get some relief from the lawsuit. Maybe it'll take a while, but I hope that happens."

"Oh, I already got a call from his attorney. I already know some of what's gone on. I appreciate your call though. He's dropping out of the case, and I'm just not sure there's going to be an attorney who's going to want to take on this job, but who knows, people do strange things. I'm not going to hold my breath, but I do feel a little bit better about things. You take care, and I hope you find the rest of your donors for your project. And get that thing built for some mighty fine people who gave a lot to our country."

"I will let Marco know. And thank you."

Before I hung up, I had another thought.

"By the way, would you be willing to serve on an advisory board? We are going to have civic leaders since part of our project will be a not-for-profit organization. We want people on our board that are of good reputation, who have the same calling to help these men and women who need it."

"Sweetheart, it would be my honor, as long as they don't yank my license. You can count me in."

We chuckled, and I was touched with how strange the world was.

I was going to join the rest of the crowd when my cell phone rang again. I didn't recognize the number. But it was one of those eleven-digit sat numbers.

"Hello?"

"Shannon, sweetheart. I'm just heading across the Atlantic. I can't wait to see you."

"Marco! Oh my God, I've worried so much about you. Are you injured at all? Is everybody okay?"

I kept babbling on with questions and knew it was pure nerves driving me. He chuckled and interrupted me, and I didn't mind a bit.

"I'm fine. A little tired and dehydrated, and I got some enormous bites, welts that go all the way down my stomach."

"Poor baby. Get your butt over here and I promise to make it better."

"I plan on doing just that. Promise you won't tease me for all my new scratches and bites. They're really gross."

"I refuse to believe that."

"I'm going to have my first nice glass of wine, try to rest and knock down some vitamins and things I've been given. I just want you to know I am coming home and hopefully will be there later tonight or early in the morning. Probably more likely in the morning."

"Where do you fly into?"

"JFK, of course."

"Of course. You're on your own charter, aren't you?"

"Well, I had a chance at picking up one of those puddle jumpers, landing in Norfolk, maybe taking another transport plane to Tampa. All that would be on Uncle Sam's dime, but I would have had to wait for the connection. So while they were arranging things, and I just said forget it. When we landed in Cape Verde, I had my plane delivered, and we're all safely on board."

"Good. I'm glad you did that. So all your hostages are okay?"

"Karin Atkin got shot. She's in pretty bad shape, but she was airlifted to Germany to repair her shattered arm. She was pretty close there, and Sven has decided to stay until she's ready to come home. I needed to get back to Florida to see you, to see everything. And we've got the sultan still there? Is that right? He must be having kittens by now."

"As of yesterday, he was still there. And, oh my gosh, what a time they're having. They're going to be the talk of the surf shops along Gulf Boulevard for years. They're going to talk about the sultan who went in and bought boogie boards and swimsuits and towels for people who had never owned one before, just like they talk about his trip to Cartier when he brought all those jewels and had them made into necklaces and bracelets for his harem. It's such a treat to see the childish delight in his eyes, Marco. I have had several wives tell me what a change it's been for him. I know he loves his kingdom and I know he loves his palace, but if you were to ask me, I think he'd enjoy living here."

"Well, that will never happen, Shannon, but I understand. And I'm glad we've expanded his world a bit. We needed to give him something like that, didn't we?"

"You bet. It was the right thing to do. And the boys? They've been wonderful. Happy, they feel like tour guides. It is really something to watch, that family."

I didn't want to bring up my concerns about them working in Africa. I would be devastated if something were to happen there, but it was going to be beyond me to try to talk them out of their housing project there in Nigeria. That was something Marco was going to have to deal with.

I was glad it wasn't on my plate.

SECURITY WAS TIGHTER than ever, on direct instructions coming from Marco. I was allowed to go home, but I was escorted every-where. I showered, put on the prettiest dress I could find, straightened the little bungalow, brought in some fresh fruit and flowers, and decided to wait for Marco there. The guards were going to take turns, and they'd instructed me not to take a run without one of them at my side. Nobody knew for sure that Rory didn't have accomplices, and although it was unlikely, nobody wanted to take that chance. Marco expressly forbid me to go anywhere without the team.

His overly protective nature and the look on the team's faces as they explained to me Marco's instructions warmed my heart. I was so excited that he cared so much about my health, and unlike before when I sort of resented having to have all these protectors, I felt his love wrap around my arms with his edicts and instructions, just as if he'd whispered something sweet in my ear. I was important to him, I knew I was, but everything Marco did showed me further how much he loved me. I knew that now. I would never question that again.

I served a light dinner to the two guards who were leaving as two others arrived to take their place. I hadn't received any updates yet, but I'd checked with the office several times, and things were beginning to get back to normal. Rebecca had been in to help plan the town hall meeting, which was still scheduled for Friday night. I was delighted Marco would be back in time to actually lead the meeting himself.

I got out a blanket and laid it on the couch with a pillow. I wanted to be in the living room when he arrived home. The two guards monitored the outside, made sure that all my doors and windows were locked before they left. Around one o'clock in the morning, I heard a driver pull up. I ran to the door, opened it a crack, and saw Marco pull himself out of the back seat of the Mercedes, lugging a big briefcase with him. The driver came round and deposited four large duffle bags at the doorway.

Marco finally looked up and saw me. Dropping his briefcase, he ran, picked me up in his arms, and held me tight.

"God, I missed you. I miss everything about you," he whispered.

"I was so scared this time, Marco. I am so grateful that you came back, that you saved those people. You did what you had to do. I'm so proud of you, but God my heart was just—"

He interrupted my thoughts with a kiss. I attempted to pull away, but he continued to hold onto me, squeezing my upper torso into him and whispering in my ear, "I'm here. We're together, Shannon. I wish I could marry you tomorrow. Shall we just run off and do that?"

"I can't do that to the sultan!" I leaned away from him.

He rolled his eyes and dropped his hands briefly from my waist. "Oh! The sultan. I see our loyalties have been a little bit altered?"

"You should hear what they've got planned, Marco. I mean, it's like they're buying all the flamingos in all of the Indian Ocean to completely cover the island or something. They've got some ideas that I have never even thought of. I couldn't stop him—from all of them having the celebration he wants to have for us. But I do understand. If it was just you and me, I'd marry you tonight!"

He reached over to my chin, held it up, and kissed me again.

We heard the driver clear his throat and give a short cough. Marco whispered in my ear, "Oops."

The driver was standing with hands clasped together in front, feet apart staring at a point about two feet from the tips of his toes. "Will there be something else sir?"

"No, thank you."

Marco pulled a couple of bills out of his wallet, making the driver's eyes widen with shock.

"Thank *you*, sir!"

Marco patted him on the shoulder and said, "Thanks, I can take it from here."

I helped him bring the heavy bags inside as Marco searched the house.

"Where the hell are the guards?"

"They're out there. I asked them not to be too obvious, if you don't mind."

He drew me into his arms again, "I don't mind at all. I'm

thinking of all the things I want to do tonight with you—"

I put my fingers over his mouth. "This morning. It's morning, Marco."

"It sure will be morning by the time we're done."

"Counting on it, been thinking about nothing else ever since we got the call you were safe."

"I'm going to go check on them now, and then I'm all yours." He took my hand, and we walked through the sliding glass door onto the patio.

"Okay, I know you're out there. Somebody want to show their face?"

One of the security guards walked forward, in full battle gear, including a bulletproof vest, night vision goggles on top of his baseball cap. He stepped under the light so we could see his face and shook Marco's hand.

"Glad you're home, sir. Carter's over on the other side. We're laying low; we got the message." He looked over at me and winked.

"In the morning, I'd like to take my fiancée for a nice morning walk on the beach. I think if you stay a decent distance away, and I'd prefer that you wear swim trunks instead of this get-up, would you accompany us?"

"Yes sir. There's a couple of new fellows coming over. They'll probably be the ones, but I'll let them know to bring their trunks."

"And I'll make a nice breakfast for us. I've got all the fixings for crab omelets," I said proudly.

"I'm sorry I'll miss that, ma'am. But perhaps another time." He saluted again casually, and disappeared into the foliage.

"Boy, you really run a tight ship my dear." Marco said to me as we walked inside.

He locked the door and then turned to pull me into his arms again.

"Absolutely. I'm not going to let anything in the world spoil our happily ever after. I've waited a long time for this, Marco, and—"

He interrupted me again, like he so often did, with a deep penetrating kiss. It had all the possibilities of the next three or four hours of fantastic bed play. That would be only the beginning.

And I couldn't wait.

LEGACY

Bone Frog Bachelor Series
Book Four

SHARON HAMILTON

CHAPTER 1

"T HEY ARE LOVELY to look at, aren't they, Marco?" the Sultan of Bonin asked me.

He was dressed in a bright white cotton tunic with gray slacks beneath. I wondered if he had ever owned a pair of real leather shoes, because I only saw him in sandals or flip-flops. And in Florida, it was always flip-flops, the brighter the better.

Shannon was at the shoreline splashing water with all of the ladies from the sultan's harem joining in. They were laughing and acting like a bunch of school girls, completely oblivious to proto-col, customs, or any danger that might lurk in the shadows. It was a brief reprieve in an otherwise very dangerous year, but we were headed to the altar, come Hell or high water. I greatly looked forward to the lavish wedding at the Pink Palace, complete with a pink beach in the sultan's private island kingdom on invitation and organized by him and his incredible family.

I'd been looking forward to it since the evening Shannon agreed to marry me, this old bucket of bones, former Navy SEAL, former multi-billionaire, but now just a billionaire. And that was good enough for her, so it was good enough for me. I'd been doing a lot of adjusting these days.

For the first time in my life, I wasn't kicking and screaming along the way. I was choosing a higher path, perhaps, and looking for contentment, even though I was a man of action.

Never had I ever thought this could happen.

I was getting married for the *rest* of my life, which meant forever.

"They are just that, aren't they?" I said. "Angels, sent here to bring us both multitudes of pleasure and satisfaction, making our lives richer and full of magic."

He grumbled a deep guttural chuckle, nodding. "Agreed."

"I don't think I've ever seen Shannon so happy. Your wives are marvelous guests. I was trying to show you what our life is like here, but your ladies have transformed this place—so unfamiliar— with their joy. They have made such an impact on the whole area. They bring their own magic, and here I thought it was Florida. They are going to take home a part of the Florida Gulf Coast with them."

I studied his eyes as he focused on the women down below our balcony. His nod was barely perceptible. His breathing was a bit ragged, his eyes a little droopy, but other than that, no one would suspect the man was gravely ill.

"A gift for a dying man? Would you say that?"

"No, Sultan. I didn't mean that at all."

"Ah, but I took it that way. It is unfortunate that we have to die. But if we are to die, we should all be so lucky as to die happy, like I am."

"Truer words were never spoken, my sultan."

"In my case, it actually is fortunate to know that I have little time left. I am grateful to be able to spend the last days of my life planning a wedding for you and Shannon. It's like a bit of me will always be with you as long as you are together, because I'm helping to create that memorable bond between you by hosting you at my palace. I am going to be forever grateful. And long after I'm gone, I'm hoping your wedding will be the talk of the kingdom."

My Navy SEAL training kicked in on red alert. I had only allowed myself to shed a tear a handful of times. It was usually at funerals for one of my teammates or one of their close family members. But the sultan's strong words hit me in the solar plexus, throwing me off balance for a moment, and before long, I felt the moisture in my eyes threatening to spill over and run down my cheeks. I inhaled deeply and willed my eyes to clear.

Most of the time, I could make it hold back.

This time, it worked.

"My friend, if this in any way is going to shorten your life, you know I would call a halt to it. A significant portion of the work will be done by others, but if I get any inkling that this is going to be hard on you physically, I must insist that we postpone or conduct the ceremony elsewhere so that it's not so taxing to you. But I understand, even if it was so, you would probably lie to me and make me believe that it wasn't."

He had a sparkle in his eye as he looked up at me, smiled, and then returned his gaze to the women.

"I didn't use to be so transparent, Marco. You've changed that in me as well. It's funny how life teaches you, as it's slipping away, what's really important. Our bodies go away, our soul transports, and what remains, what's truly important, are the memories and the friendships and the love we've created. You can't participate in that if you don't *feel*. And part of that extreme connection and feeling creates pain. There's no way to avoid it, is there?"

I doubted I had changed him as much as my association with him had changed me. He was far more to me now than just my client, my sometimes investor or benefactor. "Friendship" didn't do it justice. Even "family" didn't describe it fully. If I wasn't careful, I'd start bawling like a baby.

I locked my jaw and cleared my throat.

"You mean loss, my sultan?"

"Yes. I used to want to be famous, planned to get richer and richer as the years went by, wanted to have the jewels and gold fall from my fingers like rain and watch others squeal with joy at being given some of my kingdom's bounty."

He stopped. So I had to ask him.

"And now? What's changed?"

"Now, from where I'm sitting, I'm just enjoying being a beach bum in a multi-million-dollar house rented by my friend." He smiled at this, placing his arm on my shoulder with a smile. "And my desire is that I will leave a big hole. That I will be missed, not thought of as successful, leaving his kingdom in good shape or growing his wealth, assets, children, families, taking on more wives. I just want to be *missed*."

"You will be. I guarantee it. I know Shannon and I will miss you."

I wrestled my wits back into that cool, deadly column of steel that could defeat anything, including death. I continued in a new vein.

"But I don't want to talk about those times. I have no idea how many years I have myself. None of us do. But I want to spend whatever time we do have together living, not watching each other die. Because we die a little bit every day, don't we?"

He frowned, again nodding. His eyes had filled with water he didn't try to cover up.

"Yes. Even the children. Even the most beautiful and coveted wither and die, sometimes fast. But it is an adventure we can never escape."

I was feeling morose suddenly, even with the idyllic laughter and the sounds of splashing water below us. There was nothing I could do to stop the passage of time, the inevitable that was going to befall all of us. I didn't like the idea of having something taken away from me, even though I knew we couldn't hold on to everything, especially as we were leaving this world. But the feeling of being vulnerable and not able to control the end—to have a say in it but not really be able to control it—that was difficult for me.

I'd always prided myself on having such excellent control over all my business activities. Yet, over the past two years, life had been the most difficult, with the divorce from Rebecca, the bombing of my office building, and almost losing Shannon. The world still was a dangerous place, and I knew, even here at the Gulf Coast of Florida, danger lingered. I would have to be vigilant in my protection of this special family.

I had something I'd wanted to speak to him in private since his arrival in Florida for his first-ever vacation in Florida. Probably his last.

"As long as we are talking about futures and spending our time in the living side of the ledger, I wanted to ask you why you don't consider building your housing projects in some location other than those war-torn areas in Nigeria. I know you purchased the property, made promises. I know you've invested quite a bit already."

I was worried how he'd take my question, but I had no option now but to continue.

"Don't you think there are other places you could build where you could do good and where your legacy would have a chance of standing for longer than just a few months or years?"

"I want to build it for those people because of how those people have suffered. Everything they've had has been taken away from them. Even their culture has been robbed of them, shredded by evil men doing unspeakable things."

"But what's the point of building something the militia groups are just going to bomb and tear apart? What's the point of making people see there is good and hope in the world and then have them experience everything being destroyed and taken away again? Maybe that part of the world is so overrun with hate and these competing groups that it can't be fixed for a century, many years. Perhaps it's too soon to do this. Shouldn't we have peace first? Order? Remove the chaos?"

"Ah, I anticipated this, Marco. I knew this question was coming."

He wasn't smiling this time, and I knew I was cruising close to the edge of what he would accept hearing.

"What's the benefit in just adding fuel to the bonfire?" I asked him.

"You mean my project becomes a new target for them to attack?"

"Yes. Exactly. I mean, why do it there?"

"Because it's what I can do. I can try and make a difference."

"But don't you suppose there are other places where you could do good and it would last? Do you have to take it to absolutely the most dangerous place in the world? Don't get me wrong, Sultan. I will build your project anywhere you say you want to, but I question whether it's worth the risk to your sons, since your legacy may not survive the attack. Your boys could be hurt or worse."

"Am I to assume, Marco, that you have lost some of your nerve?"

"No, sir. It's not my nerve. I've gained more knowledge. It's just hit me plain as day that I think it's a mistake to build it in Nigeria. I can teach your boys building projects and how to run big companies here in Florida or some other place in the United States where the experience would be much different than Africa, and you could do good."

"But this is the land of opportunity, the land of plenty. I wanted to give something to people who don't have that. Who have nothing to live for."

I thought very carefully for several minutes before I spoke. I knew I was about to make a huge shift in our priorities. I needed to make this point to him.

"My sultan, I'm going to show you some people who have lost everything."

I drove the two of us in my red Bentley convertible with the top down. We were the picture of opulence and abundance. With the sunshine on our faces, the warm Florida gulf breeze rearranging our hair, and wearing matching Aviators sunglasses, we were spending a day few other people on the planet got to experience. We were lucky. Yes, I admit I felt entitled too.

We scooted down Gulf Boulevard and turned onto the causeway crossing the dark blue waters of Tampa Bay. We were headed east away from the Gulf. After several minutes of complete silence, we finally pulled off the highway and onto a side street that led to the complex I wanted to visit. At a stoplight, we heard the surrounding noises of cars, blaring country music, the barking of talk radio soaring to the heavens, construction work, sirens, businesses, and airplanes. In the middle of all of that, he turned to me and asked, "Where are we going, Marco?"

He trusted me, but he did appear slightly worried. I knew he didn't like hospitals. I anticipated this.

"I'm going to show you something you've never seen before. You're going to have to trust me on that. It's safe, but I'm going to show you something that you're never going to forget."

When the light changed, we turned into a complex shaded by enormous trees on both sides of the roadway with trunks that were five or more feet in diameter, interspersed with palm trees and grassy knolls and walkways. We passed a large cemetery with two navy blue tents readying for a funeral, American flags flying opulently everywhere we looked.

The setting was gorgeous. Old sandstone-colored buildings with tile roofs looked like they could have been built for a Spanish garrison. The entire complex had been built probably prior to World War II, the quarters resembling those I'd stayed at in Hawaii at Pearl Harbor. Newer buildings had been built and added to the main halls, and as we headed down the street, we stopped in front of a large brand-new hospital several stories high, sparkling like a diamond in the sunlight in front of us. A huge American flag flew in the lawn in front of the parking lot that almost dwarfed the building itself. Several smaller flags, depicting the different branches of service and the State of Florida, stood nearby, as witness to the greatness of our flag.

I was filled with pride.

In his white tunic, his starched and pressed gray slacks, and his bright orange flip-flops, he followed me with short stubby steps, gripping the bronze handrails, until we climbed the four concrete stairs to the main lobby. Adjacent the stairway was a ramp, bordered with handrails on both sides for the sick or disabled.

Inside, elevator music played. The steel-colored travertine floor was inlaid with scrolling flowers on vines, butterflies, and several eagles. It echoed noisily and reflected every little bit of activity in the enormous rotunda we were standing in. An information desk at one end of the hall gave us the guidance I needed.

I made my inquiry and then took the sultan's arm, and we walked down the center corridor and around the corner to a special laboratory I'd helped fund.

"This is a government facility?" he asked.

"It's the Veteran's Administration Hospital. This is where they treat our wounded servicemen, mostly those who are residents of Florida and other Southern states. They are some of the best doctors and technicians in the world here, and I want you to see what they do. I have helped fund a new orthotics lab, something I'm very proud of. It was out of working with these people that my vision for the Trident Towers was born."

I could see his eyes squint, but his skepticism appeared to be waning.

I opened the frosted glass door, etched with the Trident logo of my company. Once inside, we saw machinery, drills, saws, and equipment dangling from cords hung from the ceiling. Tables were strewn with artificial parts, from flesh-colored prosthetic hands to forearms, legs, ankles, and toes. There was a casting room. Someone polished a metal brace with a grinder that let out a high-pitched squeal that almost hurt my ears. I could smell some of the polymer and plaster materials that they used. Several other technicians were assembling components for artificial limbs. They tested and examined their handiwork, bent the artificial knees, and moved the artificial ankles and feet slowly to adjust for anything that was needed.

Looking over at the sultan, who I had nearly forgotten was there, I saw his eyes widen and his jaw drop. The overall effect on him was greater than I thought it would be. He was clearly in shock.

I spotted someone I wanted to visit with, so I directed us to walk to the other end of the room where a gentleman in a wheelchair had just returned from a private, curtained dressing area. The man was missing both legs, one arm, and part of the right side of his face and ear, obvious to most people that he'd been a victim of a bomb blast of some kind.

The orthotist he was working with was fitting him for an arm to give him more mobility, and I was privy to the fact that he would also be fitted with two legs. I had taken a special interest in this young Navy man because he had, like me, passed his BUD/S training, but he needed to serve one more rotation before he could complete the rest of his SEAL training, and was injured before he could finish.

I had given him one of my gold Tridents on a visit earlier in the year, and he wore it proudly on his T-shirt.

"Hey, Sam, nice to see you again," I said to the young lieutenant.

"Marco! This is going to be a great day. I come in with just one appendage, and I'm going to leave with two. Soon I'll have all four. God-willing, I can begin to run again! That's pretty good, don't you think?"

He was still handsome even though the skin around his eye was shriveled and scarred. He'd lost his ear, but luckily not his vision. His smile was slightly crooked, but it gave him character and didn't bother me one bit.

"Hell yeah, it's a good day. Any day we're alive is a good day."

We fist-bumped our lefts.

"I have someone I want you to meet, Sam. This here is the Sultan of Bonin, a friend of mine, who is also hiring me to build a housing project. I came to show him some of the work we're doing here, and I wanted him to meet a real-life hero."

Sam grinned from ear to ear, extending his left hand instead of his non-existent right and shook hands with the sultan awkwardly. "Nice to meet you, sir. You'll have to forgive me, but I don't know where your kingdom is. Where is Bonin anyway?" he asked.

"It's a tiny island inside the Indian Ocean. Independent of India, but very dependent on trade with her. Our kingdom used to have several other islands, more like atolls, but India has taken them back. I have the best and the largest of the bunch."

He smiled and released Sam's hand carefully.

I noticed the sultan suddenly squinting a bit as the technician removed the sheet covering young Sam's leg stumps where he'd been surgically repaired just below both hips. This also exposed a very scarred upper arm and a small pointed fleshy protrusion at the end of the stump instead of an elbow joint. That protrusion was being fitted into a plastic custom-formed cast and strapped with Velcro straps around his chest and crisscrossing down his back for support.

Sam was attempting to move the arm but hadn't quite figured out how to do so. It stiffly sat on the edge of his chair and then into his lap. He attempted to reach the table and pick up a pen, which quickly dropped. The technician was patient, working with him to adjust the prosthesis so he could control the movements more efficiently.

The sultan's eyes were transfixed on the young Navy lieutenant. I could see he wanted to ask questions.

"Go ahead. Ask him anything you like," I blurted out.

"Thank you, Marco. Were you involved in a bomb blast or what caused this unfortunate accident?"

"Yes, we were broadsided by a fishing boat carrying arms to the enemy. Part of the armaments blew up while we were trying to offload people to safety. The boat had drifted without a motor, and we had picked up a distress call, but they had decided to scuttle our ship or try to take us all hostage, which didn't work, but some of us were injured in the process."

"Tell him, Sam, where it happened," I asked him.

"Off the west coast of Africa, below the bulge." Sam shifted between the sultan's eyes and mine, sensing there was some significance to my question. And indeed it had the effect I was looking for.

I knew from conversations with Sam that he had considered suicide. He was regretting seeing his family and initially didn't want them to visit, but when his girlfriend finally came to Germany, his attitude about living began to change as well. It was that little taste of honey he needed to get him back on track. I wasn't going to reveal his private life, perhaps saving it for when I had full permission. So I improvised.

"Sam and I have spent a lot of time talking about all this. It was through my acquaintance with him that I discovered veterans needed equipment, and they were not getting this from the federal government. In response, we set up a grant that I underwrote so I could donate to the hospital. They could get their equipment, and it didn't raise the conflict of government-private partnership. I'm very proud of this clinic, because it's one of the best in the whole United States."

"I had no idea, Marco, but this is so like you. Never leave anybody behind, right?"

"Hooyah, S.O. Gambini!" Sam boomed, raising his left hand in a fist.

As we walked away, the sultan kept looking back, watching Sam and his orthotist work on the arm. Each time Sam caught his gaze and waved, the sultan smiled a little more.

"These are the people who have come home after doing their duty, who gave more than just their time. They left part of their bodies behind on the battlefield. They were injured by men of pure evil, and this is the least I can do for them."

"I understand now, Marco."

"These are really the people who have nothing."

CHAPTER 2

T HE WOMEN HAD congregated around the swimming pool after their morning frolic in the ocean, several of them braiding each other's hair or painting toes and fingernails. A couple of the younger wives were dancing to Western music—or at least attempting to dance to Western music, which was something totally unfamiliar to them.

Shannon had just dipped in the water to cool off and was handed a large beach towel by the sultan's number one wife.

"I have something I've wanted to show you ever since I got here. Would you come up to my bedroom please?" the attractive older woman, the first of his wives, asked.

"Of course. Let me continue to dry off, and then I'll be right up there."

"I'll wait," she quipped with a wink.

As Shannon dried off, three other wives approached, requesting permission to accompany them. Not having a clue what this was all about, Shannon agreed after glancing at the older woman.

"This is all very mysterious," she said to the wives.

Most of what Shannon got back were titters and giggles. They were such a tight-knit group that each of them was extremely involved in everyone else's life. Gossip was commonplace, and it was more a communal relationship, a true sisterhood rather than some kind of competitive show for the sultan's attention. They didn't try to belittle each other or encourage his advances too obviously, being very conscious of their sister wives' feelings.

Shannon was fascinated with the whole makeup of their arrangement.

With the towel slung around her waist, she slipped on her sandals and followed the older woman upstairs to the bedroom.

She was instructed to sit on the edge of the bed while the older woman and two others opened the massive closet doors and brought out five large cardboard boxes. When the lid was removed on the first box, Shannon could now see what the purpose of the meeting was all about. Pulled from inside each box, delicately draped over well-tanned arms and freshly painted pink, red, and purple fingernails, were yards and yards of beautiful silk saris. Some were edged with ribbons of silver and gold, glistening in the noonday sun. The bright, vibrant colors of turquoise, purple, fuchsia, reds, and oranges were almost a shock to the system. In the Florida atmosphere, the brilliant colors seemed to fit very well.

She was encouraged to stand as the wives busied themselves wrapping her in the beautiful silks, including trying several different saris for her head and around her shoulders as a shawl for windy weather. Some were wrapped strapless or over one shoulder, designed for warmer climates. The wives drew out over thirty beautiful hand-made saris. Marco had told Shannon that often these works of art could cost many thousands of dollars.

The hand stitching and detail, applique, and patchwork designs of exotic flowers, birds, and vine blossoms of all colors splashed across the silks, nearly giving her a headache. She was in complete awe.

His number one wife commanded, "So your job is to choose which ones of these are your favorites. I'm giving these to you as a gift. You choose as many as you like. Your wedding is to be a feast that will continue for several days, and you will need morning saris. You will need afternoon tea saris, and you will need romantic saris for midnight walks on the beach. You are going to need many, many costumes, and it is our custom that wearing the same sari twice during your wedding week is bad luck for the marriage. So you wear them each one time. Then you fold them up, and we pass them on."

Shannon was embarrassed with the opulence and the generosity of the women in front of her.

"These are stunning. I don't know what to say. I've never seen such beautiful fabric and such vibrant colors. I'm so afraid to wear them, that I'll spill something on them—and I know they can cost a small fortune. I truly don't deserve such a gift."

"Nonsense, dear Shannon. Just like when we made you up to dress as a dancing girl, to be alluring for your husband, it is our job to make sure you make a stunning entrance, that you are the center of all the attention, that you wear robes fit for a queen. Because you are a queen. You're Marco's queen."

"I am speechless. Thank you." Shannon hugged each of the women one by one. "I feel like I'm going to need a dolly or a crane to bring back some of these. These are simply amazing."

The sultan's first wife chuckled. "We will bring them back with us after you choose today. You'll see them again on the island for your big day, and they will be washed and pressed and prepared for you—scented, of course—so that you don't have to travel with them. But we do need to narrow it down. Otherwise, all these boxes, we're going to use all of them. You'll see. You can go through quite a few."

One of the younger wives added, "And Marco is not to see you wear any of these prior to the wedding day, which is why we are showing them to you today. You are not to allow a man's eyes to fall upon you when you wear these gowns, or it is again considered bad luck for your marriage."

It took Shannon all of two minutes to remove her bathing suit and put on the silk slip undergarment they gave her. One by one, they tried on nearly all the saris in the boxes, setting aside certain ones as a definite yes, placing some on the other side of the bed when they couldn't decide, and a third pile for saris that Shannon didn't particularly care for color-wise, but the wives were going to try to overrule her decisions.

The women worked like bees, wrapping and unwrapping, examining folds, tying sashes, layering and positioning the precious silks.

"And we haven't even gotten to the jewelry yet. You will have to wear coins, of course, and we will create folds in your gowns so you can accept gifts. If you are asked to dance, it is customary that the man should give you an envelope of cash," blushed one of the younger wives.

"Unless he brings coins. Coins work!" one of the other wives said.

There was general agreement between the women. Shannon understood that perhaps the gold was more preferable. She wondered if the wives even had an opportunity to spend any money they would receive. And if they did receive cash, how would they spend it?

At last, every sari was unfolded, wrapped around her, and examined next to her skin to find the most flattering colors and textures for her complexion. She chose colors she enjoyed wearing or that made her happy. She stooped to count them neatly folded on the right side of the bed and discovered that they had selected twenty-two.

"A very auspicious number, twenty-two," the older wife said. "It is a balanced number. It is private and intimate, a perfect pair, just like a honeymoon should be. Twenty-two is a very good choice, my dear. I can't wait to see you all dressed up, your makeup just so, and your hair scented with jasmine and lavender. We are going to have such a wonderful time, Shannon."

"I have a question for you and perhaps a request," Shannon stated.

"Yes? What is it?" responded wife number one.

"Well, there is my friend, Rebecca. And—"

"Not Marco's former wife. You don't mean *that* Rebecca, do you?" the older woman asked. Several of the others in the group gasped at the thought.

"Well, as a matter of fact, yes. She and I have become friends. I'm just finding her cooperation and help to be useful. And I think even though Marco doesn't trust her—"

"He is wise, Shannon. You should take heed."

"Yes, I'm being careful. But I would like to have you have a session with her. I would like her to be pampered as well. Can that be done? And I have friends coming, as is customary here in the States. We call them bridesmaids here, and it's very common for the entire wedding party to have their hair, nails, and their makeup done all together as a group, going somewhere to be styled and made up for the wedding. Would it be possible I could have my friends, my bridesmaids as well? Or is that asking too much?"

The older woman's eyes grew wide. Her lips formed a straight line, and Shannon wasn't sure if there was disapproval or just confusion.

"Anything you ask of us, we will do, if we can. I am delighted to say that your girlfriends, your bridesmaids as you call them, would be most welcome. But Shannon, I am afraid I cannot bring Rebecca into our harem. The sultan has told us that she is not to be invited to the wedding. I hope you haven't asked her."

"I did, sort of. So I guess I'll have to fix that," Shannon said.

She felt awful and didn't approve of the opinion of Rebecca, but she understood where the sultan was coming from, and her attempt to ruin Marco's financial status was something she would not be forgiven by Marco or any of the staff at the office. But Rebecca was proving to be useful and was working hard to try to get back into everyone's good graces. She was trying.

"This is not a debate, Shannon. It is simply not possible. Don't even ask, because even if Marco asked, the sultan would never allow it. He has to be careful who he invites to the island, and everybody will have to be vetted. I'm sure Marco is going to help with that process. But no matter how long it takes, Rebecca will never be allowed."

The reveal didn't sit very well in Shannon's stomach, but after all, the generosity of the sultan and his palace was so overwhelming, it softened the disappointment of not being able to include

Rebecca. There was no way she could do anything but agree with them.

ALL AFTERNOON, THE women poured over other details of the many receptions and parties that were going to be hosted. There were certain of the wives who had daughters who would help with preparing the food, as well as taking care of guests, especially the children, on the guest list.

Shannon was shown pictures of some of the dishes they were going to be serving, foods she could never recall eating before even during her previous stay at the palace. It was explained to her also that she and Marco would not be spending their wedding night in the palace itself.

"There is a small cottage nestled in some mangroves and huge palm trees. It's a beautiful spot, and it has an unobstructed view of the bright turquoise ocean and pink sand." The young wife showed her a picture of a huge house, certainly not a cottage, of modern style with a metal roof adorned with cupolas and statues of various deities mounted in the eaves. All around the property was a bright green manicured lawn almost looking like it had been cut with scissors instead of a mower. Flowers bloomed, trees were trimmed, and benches and walks were available for walking at night by torch.

"You will love it there, and we only use the wedding house for newly married couples. No one lives there as a rule. It's very special, and it has lots of spirit."

"This doesn't look like a cottage. It must be three thousand square feet at least," Shannon said.

"I don't know," the older wife shrugged. "It's quite spacious inside with lots of light. With the jungle and the lush foliage and trees all around, it's like living in the middle of an exotic jungle. We are bringing pink doves and coral-colored parrots to release at the reception. I'm sure a few will manage to escape over to your side of the island. But other than those, you won't be intruded upon at all. It will be your own private paradise. Your meals will be provided. You can choose when they come and what you wish to eat."

"What if I want to cook?"

The group whispered amongst themselves in hushed tones. "My dear, your job is to please your husband. If you please him with your cooking, then yes, you may." Her eyes sparkled as she smiled.

In the background. Several of the other wives giggled, covering their mouths.

Shannon was fascinated with the culture that was going to be wrapped around her regardless of how she felt about it. She decided she was going to enjoy this time, because she knew that nothing like this wedding, the reception, the feast, or the parties would ever occur in her lifetime again.

As she glanced again at the boxes with their lids loosely reset, at the pictures, and the colors of decorations, flowers, the birds, and the grounds, she felt like she was living in the middle of a fairy tale. She was excited that this event, the start of her new married life, joined by the man of her dreams, her prince charming, would be remembered and talked about for years.

Her heart was filled with love and gratitude for the new family she'd acquired with the sultan and his wives.

She was the luckiest woman in the whole world.

CHAPTER 3

I WAS EXCITED to call our working group meeting, assembling the whole team in charge of the Trident Towers. After my meeting with the sultan, I had some fantastic news to share with everyone, and I had a feeling it was going to be extremely popular.

I took my time, examined the faces of my handpicked staff, and finally landed with a smile that was warmly returned from my beloved fiancé, Shannon. Everyone was sitting in rapt attention, waiting for me to announce the good news.

"Today is a very special day for all of us, not just for me but for all of us. I have worked on the Trident Towers project for the past five years, eventually bringing this project to the attention of the public where we've received great support, in spite of the threats and the bombing of our office building earlier this year. The community has really embraced us, and it appears that most of, if not all, the obstacles that were in our way have been removed. We are greenlight, full speed ahead, mates!"

The cheering went on for nearly a full minute before I could break in and add the rest of my news.

"Let me also tell you, in addition to the fact that we are moving full tilt on this project, that I have received the backing of one very important person."

I turned behind me and out from my office stepped the Sultan of Bonin. I had forgotten how small he was, and in his illness and present condition, which he hid very well, he looked even smaller and more shriveled. But his smile was wide, almost looking embarrassed as he bowed in greeting. Both his sons, who were seated at the long project table, stood out of respect for their father, but also for their sultan. The room clapped to welcome the sultan.

"So here's what we're going to do. The sultan and I have discussed his project in West Africa, and we both have come to the conclusion that now is probably not the best time to build there. It is an unsettled area, and it's getting worse by the month, with no clear dominant presence and no stable government to negotiate with for our protection and safety. We had a close call with Karin and our pilots and crew, a little too close for me. I'm not willing to jump right back in there again."

Karin looked down on her folded hands, a worried frown seizing the lower part of her face. I suspected that perhaps the remembrance of what she'd had to go through haunted her—being yanked off the plane and held hostage, all the money she brought for setting up the pre-construction phase of the project, paying for permissions and bribes, and not knowing if she would ever be able to return home in one piece. I considered that perhaps I wasn't being fair to her.

"Karin, we've made this shift, partly because of the sacrifice you made on that trip two months ago. I know how close it was, and we thought we were prepared, but we were blindsided. I would not forgive myself if I allowed anything like that to happen again, and since I'm also responsible for Khalil and Absalom, the sultan's two sons, I can't afford to fail. So, after a long discussion with the sultan, he has finally agreed instead to back our Trident Towers, which means that Khalil and Absalom will become co-project managers, overseen by Dax and the rest of our crew."

The group around the table clapped. Karin did not. But she bravely looked up to me and spoke. "I really did think I'd bought it that time, Marco. When you must face death like that, or the possibility of being held captive or prisoner for years, it changes you. I was prepared to tell you if you were going to be building in Nigeria that I was going to have to separate from the company."

The audience, several of the members who sat close to her, touched her shoulders or patted her hands. Karin was a highly skilled negotiator, fluent in several African languages, as well as Chinese and Russian, and had been a fearless standard bearer of our company. But I could see that her close encounter was life altering. I was delighted I wasn't going to have to ask her to do that again.

"We all understand your sacrifice, Karin. It could have been any one of us in that same situation. And that's why this makes so much more sense. We will not have to take out a bank loan, which will reduce our costs, since the sultan has been very generous with us on the terms. His boys will be trained. They'll learn a great deal about building projects and how we do things here, as well as become familiar with the disabled population, particularly the community of wounded Navy SEALs. We're going to use them as much as possible so that they can help sell the project to others. I want the brothers to understand why it's important that we provide housing for these wounded heroes, and I know all of us will feel a great sense of pride when the project is finally done."

I stared at Karin until she returned my gaze again.

"In many ways, Karin, this is for you." I began to clap out of respect for the woman who almost gave her life for the chance to represent my company in an unstable environment. I'd known it was risky as hell, but yet I didn't follow my gut instinct, that knot in my stomach I should have paid attention to. I told her and the group that it was my miscalculation that caused their near-fatal capture.

"I feel I owe you an apology, but what I really want to say, Karin, is that I am filled with gratitude, and I'm honored to be able to work alongside you."

"Here, here," said Paul Vijay. "To the toughest broad I know, unstoppable, unsinkable, who refused to give up even against all the odds. You are the example of dedication and resolve, just like you are too, Marco."

The crowd clapped again. I noticed Shannon's eyes were filled with tears. I could see the sense of pride residing there, and I hoped that during our hopefully long married life, she would always look at me the way she was today. I drank in the admiration beaming from her beautiful face.

Several others made comments. Somebody asked the sultan when he might return to Nigeria. I knew the answer to that but couldn't reveal it.

"Well," he began, "that's a long painful subject, and I'm not sure it's worth the money and risk involved. Like Marco, I would feel very responsible if something happened to one of you. And since Marco is the expert, and he flatly could not guarantee my sons' safety, I really was in a way relieved. I had promised, and I wanted to keep that promise. But Marco showed me how we could still be a force for good, just not have to risk so much to do it."

The room agreed with his comments and let him know.

"I took the sultan over to the VA hospital in Tampa. He was much impressed with the orthotics lab there. I've arranged to hire a retired former Navy Lieutenant, Sam Connors, who lost both legs and an arm—"

"And an ear, don't forget the ear," the sultan interrupted.

"Yes, and an ear. I've hired him as a consultant on ADA requirements and to help be the liaison for some of the family members of disabled warriors we'll be working with. We're going to be customizing these homes so that they are retrofitted for whatever they need. For some, they may need altered cabinets and countertop heights, ramps, wide doorways for wheelchair access, elevators, and special appliances that can be operated with limited use of arms or legs. We want to make this experience as close to a normal living situation as is possible. It's our way of saying thank you to these men and women. And in honoring them, we become better human beings ourselves."

The new scope of the project was well received, and Shannon and Dax quickly removed themselves to the kitchen and brought out several bottles of champagne that we uncorked and passed around in small paper cups.

"To taking care of people who have lost everything but their hope and their will to live," said the sultan as he raised his glass.

It was worth drinking to, even if the cups were paper.

"You didn't breathe a word of this, Marco. You kept me completely in the dark."

Shannon's arms were crossed at her chest. We were driving back to the construction site for our new home on the Gulf. I could tell from the corner of my eye she was stifling a grin.

"I have to have some secrets, don't I?"

"No, I don't think so," she said.

"I thought you like strong men who are mysterious, who do honorable things, but don't talk a lot about them."

"Oh, it's true, Marco. I hate salesmen. You don't have to sell me on you being a hero. I can tell there are some times you'd like to brag, but you don't do that."

"That's because I've seen a lot of the dark side of it. Going after evil is all-consuming sometimes. I'm not sure it's always heroic, but it is necessary. And the fact is, people like me, we're created to do that. I also knew you would like this change of venue."

"Oh, how so?"

"Shannon, don't play with me." I gave her a mock frown. "Would you rather that I head off to Africa and try to pick up where Karin left off, invest another two or three million, and possibly risk my life and not get back in time for the wedding? You honestly think I would do that?"

I could see her smile, her little mouth puckering at the edges. So sexy and so utterly kissable. I was about ready to pull the car over to the side and just ravish the heck out of her. But I decided to wait till later this evening instead.

"I think it's a wonderful idea, Marco. And I'm glad you were able to talk him out of the project in Africa. Florida is going to be a great place for the boys to learn their trade. And I have a feeling based on the past few days I spent with his wives that they were going to want to come over and inspect the process as well.

They're going to miss Florida, Marco. I'm certain of it."

"I wouldn't mind entertaining the sultan and his group again. They can come as often as they like. But I'm just not sure how much time he has left. I think this is also a better solution for him. God forbid something happen to one of the boys. He'd have to spend his final days mourning instead of being able to reflect on a life well lived and a job, a worthy job, well done."

With her seatbelt still attached, she turned toward me, bringing her knees up onto the leather seat, leaned over, and kissed me. With her fingers, she rubbed the sides of my right temple, traced a finger lazily back and forth against my lower lip, and gave me a pre-dinner hard-on I knew I was going to have to take care of. That meant we'd be late for dinner, but oh my God, it would be so worth it.

It had been a good day. It was time to start celebrating.

And I was in the mood for some love.

CHAPTER 4

ALMOST A MONTH had passed since the sultan and his entourage returned to India, and Shannon corresponded with several of his wives through Harry. He'd procured a computer in secret and showed them how to find all the tutorials he wanted them to follow and how to navigate the web.

There were dozens of decisions that had to be made about the reception and the guest list, questions about seating and making sure we anticipated any problem that could pop up during the several days' events. Marco insisted that security be beefed up, so he sent over some of his best men, as well as a few new hires of recent retirees from the ranks of the Special Forces. He hired the best marksmen, men who were born protectors with years of experience navigating the dangerous arenas of the world.

So it was alarming when, with a little more than thirty days until the actual wedding event was to occur, Marco got the call telling him the sultan had taken ill and was bedridden—possibly would remain bedridden for good. He decided, once he consulted with the sultan's doctors and Harry, as well as his wife number one, that a special hematologist would be flown over to help diagnose what was happening, monitor him, and guide the sultan back to some semblance of health, or at least help make him comfortable so he could conduct his affairs, tie up loose ends, and have a relatively pain-free existence. There was no question that his body was shutting down. No one was hiding the fact any longer. The sultan was gravely ill. It was hard to miss.

When the entourage had left in early November, Shannon had cried as she hugged all of the wives one by one and thanked the servants, the cooks, the dressers, and the dancers. The large boxes of saris were loaded, along with all the other luggage and trunks of new clothes they'd accumulated. They had taken private transportation hired by Marco's company.

It'd taken Shannon several days to get over the fact that these women, who had become like sisters to her, were halfway across the world and not accessible anymore.

So on this morning, Shannon and Marco both got up at dawn to make their way to the private airport at Tampa. From Tampa, they would have to hop to New York City for a refueling and then fly directly to Mumbai, where they would travel the rest of the way by helicopter or water taxi. Shannon was instructed to pack lightly, since they were planning to stay only a few days. The hematologist they brought had a very busy, high-demand practice in Tampa and would not be available longer than a week. But he did agree to give Marco and the sultan that week.

Shannon loved flying on private planes. She loved the freedom of walking into the private jet terminal, waiting while the jet was fueled and inspected for flight, avoiding all the traffic of the normal airport milieu. But the best thing about flying private on his jet was that the food was wonderful and the bed in the back was extremely comfortable. She didn't have to sit strapped into a seat the whole time. She could rest, sip gourmet wines, even take a bubble bath if she so desired, and have a leisurely, stress-free trip.

Dr. Tramel had brought one of his medical student trainees and an expert nurse who had spent twenty years in the Army doing battle surgeries in field hospitals all over the globe. She was in high demand, especially in the specialized emergency rooms in the Tampa area.

But she preferred to work for Dr. Tramel. This crack medical team was legendary.

Dr. Tramel was reviewing the sultan's records, making comments to the other two professionals, pointing out several things he wanted them to check out and consider, watch for. That gave Marco and Shannon time to slip to the back for a little bit of privacy and, if lucky, perhaps a lovemaking session.

The bedroom had been redecorated in calming shades of blue and green. The mattress was replaced with a foam pad that was so comfortable she nearly fell asleep just lying on the bed.

"Miss Marr, soon to be Mrs. Gambini, can I interest you in some whiskey perhaps?" Marco asked, holding up his bottle of Uncle Nearest.

"Of course. Are you trying to get me drunk?"

"Just warmed up a bit. Not that you need it. But I thought we could enjoy a little bit of private time over whiskey. What do you think?" he answered, giving her a kiss.

"I'm game."

As she sipped on the amber liquid in the small tumbler with one large ice cube circling the bottom, she thought about how much her life had changed since those days long ago when she was twelve years old and her older sister was alive. Marco was the shining prince, her fiancé. She thought about Emily and all that she'd missed out on, her death in the auto accident tragically taking everything from her. All their lives had changed overnight. Everything was different, forever altered by Em's death. Shannon felt like she was completing a circle of some kind, that she was finishing the job that had been started so long ago, that the love Emily had for this man was also the love Shannon shared with him as well.

It was nothing short of a miracle.

Marco set his glass on the bedside table and attended to the front of her blouse, unbuttoning each little pearl button carefully, almost delicately. His strong hands were scarred, and as he reached inside to touch the soft tissues of her chest, she felt the calluses on his palms and fingers, felt the results of his war years and the years thereafter, the scars that altered his flesh forever. As he touched her tenderly, she shivered with pleasure, ripples sparking down her spine, traveling along the backside of her thighs and then all the way down to her toes.

She needed him so badly.

Being the object of Marco's desire was an incredible experience for her every time they made love. This strong man knew how to be relentless and yet very tender and caring. His strong muscles and conditioned body held hers until she shattered, was totally spent, falling back to the mattress, covered in the sweat of their lovemaking. She was exhausted but still needed more. And it seemed like the more they were together, the more she couldn't be without him. The addiction for him was growing stronger. She wondered if something were to happen to him, would she lose the will to live?

Pushing those negative thoughts from her head, she set her sights on entering this doorway of her new married life. The team would do everything it could to repair the sultan's health. She'd finish making those last plans with the women of his household and then prepare herself to walk boldly into the rest of her future without regret.

She knew her life would be forever changed by the ceremony, her hand in his, the exchanging of rings, the commitment they would make to each other in front of everybody who was dear to them. She was ready to fully embrace this and the magic that came with it.

The shower they took afterward spurred another lovemaking session. She indulged in the scents of lavender and lemons, feeling the strength of his fingers shampooing her hair and covering her whole body with wet kisses.

Rubbing her head with a towel afterwards and wrapped in his big blue terry cloth robe with nothing on underneath, she had dangerous thoughts, perhaps trying to entice him a third time, and he very nicely kissed her neck and urged her to wait just a bit longer until they landed in New York. Reluctantly, she agreed.

Like everything else Marco asked her to do, she found it impossible to refuse him.

They joined the rest of their party just twenty minutes before they began their descent into New York. If the doctor and his assistants suspected anything was going on in the back bedroom, they didn't let on. But Shannon still had a hard time looking them in the eyes without blushing.

On the ground for barely a half an hour, several catered meals were brought on board. The jet was prepared for takeoff, and shortly thereafter, they were in the sky again. They traveled with the sun to their backs until the dark night sky was pierced with twinkling lights and partially obscured by gray wispy clouds. The droning of the engines and Shannon's earlier exertions sent her into a deep sleep. She awoke just as they landed. Mumbai at sunrise sparkled like a golden jewel in the middle of the blue Indian Ocean.

They caught their limo driver, who also helped with the equipment Dr. Tramel brought as well as their luggage. He dropped them off at the water taxi port.

From there, they crossed the very still Indian Ocean. Shannon had never seen it so smooth and glassy before. It was as if they were sailing across an arctic lake, on a new adventure of some kind, to an undiscovered country or province. With the sun in their faces, they confronted the expectations of a dying man. Shannon braced for what she hoped would not be a sad encounter with him.

She had hope.

Shannon could tell just by the way Marco's distracted behavior manifested itself, Marco was concerned about the same thing.

As the Pink Palace and the coral pink sands of his island kingdom came into view, she was suddenly excited for the big day coming up in January, when she would become Mrs. Marco Gambini.

But first, there was work to do. She needed to be with an old friend and help his family begin the process of grieving.

CHAPTER 5

I KNEW THE instant our water taxi tied off that something was wrong. It was often something I felt on missions when I was a SEAL, just something in the air. It might be the certain call of a bird, the lack of noise, or a certain pungent smell, as if something evil or dangerous lurked in the bushes.

With the security detail I knew the sultan had, I doubted that could be a possibility. My men, and they were ten of my best, were spread out all along the island both on the shore and on the interior.

Shannon knew we were going to honeymoon in the new house the sultan had built on the opposite side, the north side. But I neglected to tell her we would be watched constantly. I knew she wouldn't like it, but I was hoping their skills would keep them from being discovered. Her life was far more important than her acceptance of some of my decisions.

My body was stiff, and the hair at the back of my neck stood out, scratching against my polo shirt. It was like I had some preternatural remnants of an early warning system hardwired into my body from millions of years of evolution. Some would call it the remnants of early man's lizard brain. Many of my SEAL buddies claimed to feel the same thing.

It did interfere with us going on with our regular lives, since we saw danger everywhere we looked. We had to. It kept us alive.

Shannon was babbling on about something she'd been discussing with the nurse accompanying our hematologist. Two of the sultan's men took our luggage, and we boarded the small six-passenger golf cart while the luggage came behind in the small pickup. Along the peach-colored path of shells and sand, used as trails leading us to the palace, I searched the sky for evidence of a drone or sniper hiding in one of the tall palms, even a lookout hive that perhaps I wasn't aware of. I saw no evidence of cameras, lights, drones, satellites, or safe stations anywhere. But I still wasn't relieved.

There was something wrong, and I wasn't going to rest until I discovered what it was.

"Are you okay, Marco?" Shannon asked me. The sultan's driver moved our cart at a good clip, as it bounced and hummed taking small divots and crushing rocks beneath its tiny tires. The doctor and his two associates whispered amongst themselves from the third seat.

Shannon and I sat behind the driver, and my laptop was on the bench seat between us.

I looked over at her and realized I'd never answered her question, and she was not going to give up. She wanted an answer, and she would wait until I gave her one. I thought over the choices and decided, damn, I had to come clean. There was no way in the world I was going to have a better chance than now to explain how I felt.

I reached over and grabbed her hand, placing it on top of my thigh. I pressed both my palms against it. Leaning in toward her ear, I first kissed her earlobe and then whispered, "I'm just feeling something, and it doesn't feel right. I will figure it out, and then I'll let you know."

"Like what?" she said loudly, her voice carrying over the hum of the engine.

The doctor and his two assistants turned to study us.

I rolled my eyes and whispered in her ear again, "Please, Shannon, this needs to be quiet. I don't want you to draw attention to it. I promise I will let you know once I find out."

Shannon was quiet the rest of the trip to the palace.

There was a major construction project going on in the front entrance, a large waterfall made with statues in coral and black granite, depicting beautiful naked women underwater, swimming, bathing, in various erotic poses that I feared some of Shannon's relatives wouldn't approve of. My team would love it, but Shannon's family could be easily offended.

The doctor whistled and scratched his beard. "Man, oh man, are you sure you're not taking me to a bordello, Marco?"

"You've seen the records, Doc. You've seen his pictures and his tests, and you know he has a harem of… I think it's still twelve or thirteen. Plus, he has a special someone in Brooklyn as well. Someone he never married. The man has appetites maybe you and I would fantasize about, but it seems to serve him well."

I could see the doctor wasn't buying any of it.

"He says he doesn't take any pills for performance enhancement, but somehow, I don't believe him. Do you know for sure?"

"Haven't got a clue. I doubt it, honestly. I mean why take a pill when you've got all these lovely ladies who can perform unspeakable acts of erotic fantasy—lovemaking and passion. He lives for those sessions, I know. I don't think the sultan would be capable of holding down a job ever. He likes women. It's his hobby, his passion, and I say, what the Hell. If you can afford it, then why not?"

The doc shook his head, skepticism making his jawline tense. His lips rolled down, and big worry lines developed at the bridge of his nose and on his forehead. He cocked his head at an angle and flicked his tongue, making a little ticking sound that was irritating as Hell.

"I've never quite run across a patient like him. In some ways, he's extremely well-preserved. He has a very strong heart, and his lungs are strong, although he's been developing some fluid, which is what happens with this form of cancer. Without much exercise, either. God, he must have a good diet is all I can say. All his other vitals are pretty darn normal. You'd think a man of his size, the opulence, and the way he lived would have Type II diabetes. On that score, he's healthy as a horse."

I found that funny.

"You're forgetting that he may not take walks or ride a treadmill or bicycle, but I'm willing to bet you he has sex perhaps three or four times a day, and I've heard through flimsy walls things I shouldn't have. I think he's got me beat."

We both laughed this time, the doctor placing his hand on my right shoulder.

Shannon trailed behind, and since I was carrying her heavy bag, she was carrying my briefcase containing my computer and sat phone.

The doors opened, and instead of my rotund friend, the sultan, we were greeted by a trio of younger wives, their eyes red and faces sad. I saw the house staff standing to the side, obviously pushed away so the women could greet me themselves, which was the custom for honored guests. It was remarkable that even in the face of such tragedy they still subscribed to some of these ancient rules.

Looking at the three women, all my fears were confirmed.

"So where is he? I presume he's in the bedroom?"

Like the three monkeys sitting in a tree, they all nodded quickly. The silver and gold jewelry jingled. They wore bangles on their ankles, bells on their wrists, and bright-colored saris that left a wide muscled midriff exposed. They were dressed for highbrow company, and it was important for the family to show their respect.

"I have brought the doctor, and we would like to examine him now if we could."

"Ah, Marco, I am so glad you have arrived!" It was Harry's voice I heard next, which completely shocked me.

"Harry? I didn't realize you were coming. Is—"

"No. The answer to your question, which I do not want you to ask, is no."

That's when I knew the beautiful Salima, his mother, wasn't coming or had not yet arrived. Harry was the lovechild of the sultan and the beautiful Salima. I figured she was back in Brooklyn, where the sultan had purchased them a brownstone.

Harry spoke up next. "Come this way. He's most anxious to see you. Maybe you can talk some of these women into leaving the room. Honestly, there are so many little noises and squeals and rattling of coins and bells and chains I don't see how he could sleep. And he needs his rest."

"Harry, I didn't introduce you to the doctor. Dr. Tramel, this is Harry, the sultan's private secretary." I winked after I said that, and Dr. Tramel appeared to recall the little story I'd told him about how the family didn't formally recognize Harry's paternity. It was going to have to stay that way.

After the two men chatted and Harry was introduced to the doctor's assistants, we were led into the huge chamber with the round bed atop a three-stepped dais strewn with exquisite throw carpets, barely covering some of the beautiful light pink and veined granite marble in the floor. The huge bed dwarfed the sultan as he lay in a relatively plain cotton nightshirt, although adorned with pearlescent stitching and tiny shell buttons. He was dozing in and out of consciousness and didn't seem to recognize we had entered the room.

"May I?" Dr. Tramel asked Harry.

Harry deferred to the sultan's first wife, who stood, released the sultan's hand from her grip, bowed, and stepped backwards to allow the doctor to examine her husband.

I moved to the other side of the bed, holding Shannon's hand, our fingers laced tightly together. I felt the large green, emerald ring that I'd given her recently. Her delicate floral scent was the right kind of intoxicating to me. I also detected the faint scent of our lavender shower gel from the plane.

It brought a smile to my face.

She leaned her head against my shoulder and watched as the doctor pulled the gown from the front of his chest, opened it carefully, listened to his heart, examined his eyes, and checked the tips of his fingers and his fingernails. Then he pulled aside the covers to examine his feet. Both ankles were extremely swollen to the point that, if the sultan were to stand, the flesh would roll over his ankles. His toes were stuck in a reflexive strained, pointed position that looked painful. Occasionally, his legs jerked.

The skin at the back of his heels was separated, cracking and infected, showing an angry shade of red. These issues with his legs and toes hadn't appeared when we were in Florida. Perhaps walking on the beach and the saltwater had healed him in some respect. But here, it looked to me like he was getting very weak and might not be well enough to even sit up or walk.

Dr. Tramel came over to me quietly and, as he put his arm around Harry's shoulders, whispered to the two of us, "I'm not sure exactly what is going on, but it appears he is fighting some kind of an internal infection. He also has involuntary muscle spasms. And that's not the cancer. There's something else going on. It's almost like an allergic reaction that's taken hold of his body. His heartbeat is strong, but his pulse is faster than I'd like it to be. I don't see where he's ever been on blood pressure medication so perhaps that could help. I'd also like to put him on a water pill for those ankles but want to see a blood test first. At the least, he's going to have to have some treatment because leaving those ankles and toes and nails as they are will lead to further infection, and he risks amputation. Somehow blood is not getting to his extremities. His fingers, the tips of them are blue if you notice."

"Doc, does he appear dehydrated?" Harry asked. "Because he's been drinking lots of water. He seems to want water more than anything else. The water seems to stop the spasms slightly."

"Well, I have some ideas about that, but this doesn't look like a long-term reaction to any of his cancer medications or his long-term treatment. This is something else. And it almost feels like some foreign substance he's been exposed to."

The question that immediately rose in my mind was if he'd been poisoned, and I whispered such to the doctor.

"Yes, Marco, I think you could be right. It's not arsenic. His breath doesn't have that almond smell. But somehow, he's leaching out nutrients from his body, and maybe the thirst is coming from that. His body is trying to heal itself, but these spasms are worrisome. I'm going to have to run some tests. I researched and found a lab in Mumbai that will do things on a twenty-four-hour turnaround, unless the tests take longer. It's expensive, but they will send a helicopter to pick up any lab work that I have and promised I could have the results within hours. I think I better start by taking some labs, maybe a urine sample if we can get it, and then we'll have to go from there."

He looked at the sultan's number one wife, who had been conversing with a small cluster of wives in the corner. She approached, apprehension showing in her face.

"You have news for me? Please tell me it's good news."

"Ma'am, you know he has a chronic condition from which he will not survive. But this sudden turn is caused by something else. I want you to limit and insist on it—" He looked at me and then back to the woman. "I want only certain people to handle him. We'll need to bathe him."

"Oh, we can do that, that's our job."

"Okay, as long as everybody bathes before and after they handle him. I can't be sure that he hasn't picked up some kind of toxin in his system. It might be transmitted if you aren't careful."

"Yes, we will do that. We will take shifts. And when they bring in the food, we will feed him. We won't let anybody else feed him," she said as she shook her head, dangling her hoop earrings and making the bells around her neck chatter.

"Listen, it's not only who gets to feed him, I want to make sure his food's being prepared properly. I would feel a whole lot better, Marco, if we could bring in somebody else from the outside to prepare his meals. With the swelling and the deterioration of his circulation, I'm feeling like there's something that he's ingested internally. But I won't know for sure until we do the blood tests."

"That can be arranged," I said.

"We can do that," his wife added. "We want to take care of him, and he has daughters who can help in the kitchen. We don't need to bring anybody else from the outside. We can use the kitchen staff to help prepare things we're going to need for the wedding."

Shannon squeezed my hand at the mention of the wedding. That got me to chuckle. "Oh, so it's okay if they poison us and the guests at our wedding, but it's not okay for them to serve the sultan, is that what you're saying?"

"Not at all, Marco. There is much to do to prepare. We will be his servants, his cooks. We will bathe him, protect him from the outside world. Frankly, I wouldn't feel right if he passed away under any other circumstance. I would feel horribly guilty. We need to take care of him. It's our mission. Centuries ago, if he were to die, we would all die with him. In a way, not much has changed. Our loyalty to our sultan is a primary concern. Even the children and grandchildren feel the same way."

The doctor had begun the process of drawing blood, and even that didn't rouse the sultan from his fitful sleep. Dr. Tramel's emergency nurse was on the satellite phone, probably to the lab in Mumbai arranging the lab work pickup. I slipped out of the bedroom and into the hallway, examining who was watching the sultan's door. I was surprised that there were no guards posted at his bedroom door, which is what I had asked. This was just one more thing that didn't make sense to me. Had these people disobeyed me? Or was there some change of plans?

Shannon walked up behind me and placed her arms around my waist, pressing her forehead into my back between my shoulder blades.

"Oh God, Marco, I hate seeing him like that. I'm hoping, whatever is going on, that he can recover. I don't want to put these people through a wedding when he's so sick. Do you think we should make other arrangements?"

I turned around, matching her arms around my waist by doing the same to hers. I tipped her chin up and gave her a gentle kiss, whispering, "The invitations have all been sent out. The wedding is here. He would be furious if we canceled it. It has nothing to do with whether it's easy. It is what one good friend does for another to honor the doorway we are to walk through. This isn't just a celebration. It's a mark in time, a mark in history, a point from which we go forward."

She melted into my arms, leaning against my chest, mumbling her agreement and understanding.

To the top of her head, I added, "We'll sort it out, Shannon. Let's not worry yet. We have lots of things to do while we're here, and if someone has done something despicable, I promise you, they will pay for it with their life."

CHAPTER 6

T HE FOLLOWING MORNING, Shannon and the entire team were relieved the sultan appeared to be improving. They awaited the results of testing that had been ordered and flown to Mumbai for analysis. The sultan was still delirious, wild-eyed, and occasionally had fits of agitation and muscle tenseness. It made sense to Shannon that he had been exposed to something rather than this being the result of his cancer treatments or something related to his other illnesses.

Marco approached her tenderly, taking her in his arms.

"Why don't you go with a couple of the wives and take a tour of the cottage, maybe go explore the rest of the island? I'll send one of my guys with you."

Marco had used his fingers to put quote marks around the word *cottage*. It really wasn't a cottage at all but a massive, contemporary glass and steel architecturally-designed home with stunning views of the blue Indian Ocean.

It was a tempting offer.

"We still don't have the results, and I know that his family is going to want to know as soon as possible. I am heartened that he's better, but he's still not out of the woods, Marco. I think I better stay."

"Well, then if we get some news, I think you should wander a bit, just have them entertain you. I'm going to need some serious discussions with the sultan once he's more coherent. And if he is not getting significantly better or if this is the result of something else more serious, then of course I'm going to ask the boys to fly over as well."

"I think that's a good plan. The boys' mother doesn't want them to come over, worrying them unless it's absolutely necessary," she answered.

Shannon knew Marco was all about the planning, the contingency planning, and the backup planning. And until the immediate family and household could be eliminated from suspicion, he had some serious interviews to conduct.

He pressed his palm to her cheek. "I wish I could spend more time, but we knew this wasn't a vacation. I can't wait for our big day, and I'm hoping nothing will stop that from happening."

"Me too, Marco. And I understand. I think perhaps I'll take a nap, and then let's see what the day brings. I could just hang out in their quarters, but I've developed a little jet lag."

She smirked at him and then smiled.

"That's your fault, sir," she said as she pointed to his chest.

"Guilty as charged." His raspy, sexy voice tickled her insides deliciously.

"And I have a few office things I need to take care of. We've set up some interviews, and if I'm not going to be there, I'm going to ask Rebecca if she can fill in."

Marco growled. She was on delicate ground.

She'd decided yesterday to approach the subject of inviting Rebecca to the wedding.

"Marco, I wanted to talk to you about—"

"The answer's no, Shannon. She's not coming. I still don't trust her. If you think that the sultan or his family will accept her, you're extremely naïve. Be warned, if you push the subject, you're only going to alienate them. So please, Shannon, drop it. Figure out another way you and Rebecca can resume your friendship, but she is not going to attend this wedding, and I don't care if you promised it to her or not. She's not allowed on this island or anywhere close to this island, and she's not going to be a part of our ceremony. I really need you to understand that, Shannon."

With his hands on Shannon's shoulders, he stared directly down into her eyes. She could see that it was useless to try to argue with him and relented, for now.

"I won't make a scene. I promise. I got your message, and I will fully comply."

Marco wiggled his eyebrows at her last comment.

"Fully comply? Hmm… Just what did you have in mind?"

She pushed his chest with both her palms, throwing him off balance. But with one step backwards, he became a concrete wall again. She needed to change the subject.

"It's wonderful that you were able to convince him to do the project in Florida. It was a worry and a concern hanging over my head, and I knew it would hang over my head the entire pre-planning and the parties and the wedding itself. Even the honeymoon was going to be spoiled by the possibility you might have to leave to go to a part of the world where the odds were extremely high you and the rest of the team could be injured. So, thank you, Marco. Thank you for taking care of it in such a professional manner. I honestly think it was the best way this whole building project could have developed. And I'm going to work my damnedest to make sure we pull it off with all the bells and whistles and all the hopes and dreams you originally had for the project, and more."

He embraced her in his strong arms, kissing her neck, the side of her cheek, and her hairline. His soft lips began grazing across hers, setting her libido on fire. And then finally he planted a deep kiss on her lips, which turned her knees and toes to butter. She squeezed him tightly, moved her arms up around his neck, and whispered, "I love you so much, Marco. We have so much to look forward to."

TWO HOURS LATER, with the sun well down toward the horizon, Shannon was awakened by noises coming from downstairs. The women were agitated, and there was arguing occurring in the great hall, stretching all the way down the hallway to the harem quarters. With the beautiful marble and travertine floors and the jewel encrusted inlaid columns in the grand ballroom they called their living room, the whole place echoed with worried and anxious voices. She knew something important had happened.

She slipped on her leather sandals and flew down the twisted stairwell to the ground floor, coming upon a group of several of the wives clustered in front of the doors to the sultan's bedroom.

She examined the faces of the women and sensed there was news about the sultan.

She asked one of the younger wives. "What's happened?"

"He is much better. The doctor has prescribed an anti-toxin and other things to help flush his system out. They have discovered from the tests that he has been poisoned. It's strychnine."

"Strychnine? How could he be poisoned with strychnine?"

"Apparently, very easily. I guess the house uses it for pest control. It grows wild here, all over India as well. The seeds, when ground into a fine powder or poultice, are very toxic.

"Is there a traitor in the house?" Shannon asked.

"Marco is interviewing several of the staff, especially the cooks."

"Will he recover fully?" Shannon asked.

One of the other wives inserted herself. "We're not exactly sure, but we are relieved to know the doctor says he will recover. As to recovering fully, that we have to wait and see."

The younger of the two wives looked terrified. She was being very brave but finally her nose puckered as her upper lip quivered, and then Shannon noticed the tears overflowing, spilling over her colorful cheeks, making streaks in her makeup. She collapsed in Shannon's arms.

Stroking the young wife's beautiful hair, Shannon whispered, "It's going to be fine. You'll see. He has the very best doctors, and they will figure out what needs to happen. You need to be strong for him, right?"

The young wife nodded her head with resignation and left to gather a couple of children who had migrated to the hallway near the sultan's bedroom.

Shannon wanted to visit with the sultan, but she knew the doctors were probably with him and, in time, Marco would fill her in completely. One by one, the wives faded back into their private wing, and eventually, the sultan's number one wife exited the door, closing it softly behind her. She gave Shannon a brave smile.

"Have you heard?"

"One of your sisters told me it was poison. Are we suspecting anybody, anybody on the palace staff?"

"Marco is interviewing the kitchen help now. It definitely is something he ingested, and the doctor says he will not remember what made him sick. We are hoping there will be no lasting issues, in light of his already weakened state."

Her shoulders were stooped over, her shiny black hair wrapped in a tight bun shielded in a colorful headscarf tied at the back of her neck.

Shannon touched her hands. "You should go get some rest. I'm sure if there's any change they will come get you."

She nodded. "I am exhausted, I admit it. But that was wonderful news finding out that he can recover. I just hope we got it in time. First, I am going to see what kind of mess our kitchen is, and then I'm going to turn in early."

"Is he with the doctor, anyone else with him?" Shannon asked.

"Yes, just the three of them. We bathed him, as apparently that helps with the healing as he sweats out the poison. I have to bathe again and thoroughly clean these clothes or perhaps burn them."

She held out to the sides the colorful sari she was wearing, and Shannon regretted the fact that perhaps this beautiful item would have to be destroyed.

"So we don't know if others have been contaminated?"

"That's correct. There is a team coming from your Navy, I believe—a HAZMAT team. They're going to do a thorough sweep of the palace, the kitchen, the water supply. We have to bring in food and water for now because we have to find out where this came from first. But it's most likely ingested through his food or perhaps the water he drank, although strychnine is supposed to be a very bitter substance. The doctor thinks it was probably laced into some food prepared for him that would be rather spicy so he wouldn't notice. He loves his yellow curry and eats it almost every day. And so far none of the children or the wives or myself have any symptoms. I think he was targeted for some particular reason."

She rubbed her eyes and sighed again. "Why in God's name would anyone want to harm him?"

Shannon whispered to the wife, "Perhaps it had to do with those men the boys were dealing with, with the drug smugglers with the stolen boat?"

"It's hard to say. It almost feels like it's personal, though, doesn't it?" she answered.

Shannon agreed. "You go check on the kitchen. I'm going to wait in the living room until somebody comes to get me. I don't want to be in anybody's way."

As the sultan's first wife wafted away amid sounds of silks and bangles, Shannon tried to make herself comfortable in the great hall. She brought out her cell phone, nestling herself in a red leather couch facing the fireplace. It seemed silly to have a fire in such a warm part of the world, but the fire and the spiced wood they burned was like incense, which soothed her nerves. She was grateful for it.

Dialing the office, she was put through to Dax so she could update everyone on their discovery.

"Jeez, Shannon, the hits just keep on coming, don't they?" Dax said.

"Well, that's true, and I suppose I will find out more later, but I just wanted to ease everybody's mind. It looks like he will pull through, although I haven't seen him, and I haven't been able to talk to Marco. But hearing from some of the sultan's family here, they seem to think he will make a full recovery."

"Thank God!."

"What kind of a weakened condition he will remain is yet to be seen. I'd like you to get hold of the boys and let them know. I don't want them to worry."

"Oh, you got it, Shannon. Hey, those guys have been working really hard. I wasn't sure at first it was going to be something I could tolerate. They've been raised so different, but every single task I have given them, they've willingly tackled. I have to remind them to ask questions, because they are so smart they want to figure it all out themselves. Sometimes, it's actually better if you ask questions so you can get it done right the first time, know what I mean?"

"Point taken. You keep bugging them until they learn."

"And they are learning. I like their attitude too. There's been a big shift, and I'm sure you've noticed it as well."

"I have. Is there any other news?" Shannon asked.

"Well, we've got some really good bids on the flooring, and I'm supposed to pick up the preliminary electrical and plumbing permits tomorrow morning. We already got the underground just before you left, but people are most anxious to get to work here, and we're getting lots of really good labor prices. Wish I could say the same for the materials, but that's a work in progress. I actually think we're going to come in under budget. I really do."

Shannon was pleased. "That's great news. Marco is going to love hearing that." She hesitated and then asked, "And Rebecca? How's she behaving?"

"I've not seen much of her, thank God. I'm not sure whether she really has a place in this organization. I admire you for trying, but without you here, Rebecca just seems to be hanging on to an old life she doesn't own any longer. She needs to find her own gig."

Shannon knew Dax was telling the truth. She had a keen sense of reading human nature, and Shannon had grown to respect that.

"So we're still a go for January then?"

"Yes, Dax, the wedding's still going forward as planned. Can't wait for you to see all their beautiful preparations here."

"So when do you think you guys will come back, or are you

going to stay?"

"Oh no, we'll be back in a few days I'm sure. We've got way too much to do. The last thing I want is have to be checking in with the office while we're on our honeymoon. If I don't do the work before the wedding, that's what's going to happen, and you know it."

"Damn right about that. Well, I think we're in good shape. Did you meet the young Navy lieutenant, Sam?"

"Yes! Marco introduced me to him once. How's he working out?"

"He's a dynamo. I mean he has some really good friends that are very well connected in the community, not only with the SEALs but in the disabled community. There are lots of grants available and companies that might be willing to underwrite part of the project in exchange for promotional opportunities. Sam is looking into that for some of our costs. We had a large electrical contractor from Orlando approach us about donating their fees, their labor. That would be huge. That will probably save us if it comes through nearly three hundred thousand, Shannon."

"Fantastic, Dax. And Sam has done all this?"

"He has. He attended a dedication for a children's hospital in the Orlando area where this electrical contractor donated their services to that cause. It was for children of service members—police, fire, and first responders—who lost their lives in their line of duty, and the children's hospital specializes in cancer treatment and makes sure that the widow and children of the fallen warrior never have to pay a hospital bill again. This program that Marco started here with the Trident Towers, it's right up their alley. It's perfect for them."

"That's awesome. Well, as soon as I'm finished here, I can't wait to get back and finish work on my to-do list, which is steadily getting larger instead of smaller. I'm going to try to make contact with Rebecca now, but in case I don't, if she comes in, would you tell her I'm trying to reach her?"

"Will do, Boss. You take care, and give the big fella a hug and kiss from me, okay?"

"Absolutely. And I'll give one to the sultan too. Especially the sultan, from you."

The last thing Shannon heard as she disconnected the phone was Dax's laughter. It warmed Shannon's heart.

She sat in the great room, feeling like a princess in the kingdom of make-believe. She'd never imagined she'd someday get married on an exotic island, in a pink palace with a jewel-encrusted room, with Prince Charming himself at her side.

They had come so far, had endured so much in these months, it would have been horrible if everything they'd worked for evaporated in a puff of smoke, like waking up from a magical dream. Everyone looked to Marco as the leader of the project, the chief strategist, but Shannon began to realize the sultan was actually the glue that held everybody together.

He was their host for the wedding, he was their largest benefactor, and he was probably Marco's best friend at this point. Marco was one hundred percent dedicated to making sure the sultan was going to leave a legacy in the world.

Shannon loved her husband-to-be more and more every day, because Marco's life was larger and more meaningful than Shannon had ever thought possible.

And the more she spent time with Marco, the better person she became as well.

Something slipped into her mind which made her smile. She thought of a phrase she could use to describe her life now.

She was going to call it Marco's magic.

CHAPTER 7

T HE KITCHEN, PREP, and wait staff were lined up next to a wall leading to the courtyard garden at the side of the sultan's palace. They consisted mostly of men, but there were several women in the group of twelve. I could see they were terrified of the possibility they'd be interrogated or perhaps accused of being an accomplice to the poisoning.

"I just want to find out who's responsible for this and why, and I'm starting with the group of you here who are the kitchen staff and the wait staff, but I'm going to check everybody who could have had contact with the poison materials and the sultan. First of all, I'm going to call you in one by one and ask a series of questions. You have nothing to fear if you have no responsibility for any of this. But trust me, if you know anything or suspect anything and you don't inform me, it will go very badly for you. I am not here to dole out punishment or to beat you into giving a confession. But I warn you, the sultan is going to survive this attack, and his methods may not be as kind as mine."

I paced in front of them, staring each person straight-on, hoping to put the fear of God in their souls.

"So look upon me as your last chance to avoid very unpleasant circumstances."

The staff sometimes looked amongst themselves and sometimes looked down at their hands or feet, but I didn't notice anybody who had an attitude that stood out from all the rest. Culturally, they came from many different countries in the Indian basin, even parts of Africa. I had their files. While some had been in the sultan's employ for generations, nearly considered family members, there were a handful who were fairly new hires. I was going to focus on those first, thinking it would likely be the best method of catching the probable culprit or culprits.

There was going to be no kitchen preparation today, and several trusted servants were dispatched to obtain food elsewhere off-island. As soon as the Navy team arrived, the entire kitchen would be searched—every crack in the tile countertops, behind stoves. In short, every square inch of the place would be thoroughly inspected and tested for the presence of strychnine. Later, we'd test the grounds and the residences of all the people living here. They were to take hair samples from families, even the pets would undergo testing.

I was told only two people were not present today who had worked this week for the sultan's family. We were in the process of retrieving them, but they were said to be off-island. That concerned me. But I knew we'd find them.

After the kitchen staff, I was going to interview the housekeeping staff, the groundskeepers, and some of the carpenters and workmen, although those individuals were typically second-, third-, or fourth-generation employees of the sultan's family and really would have nothing to gain from his demise. I suspected there was some personal motive, not a huge smuggling operation or political assassination attempt at work here, as the sultan had few enemies and he protected his kingdom well. I needed to find out the motive.

The head chef's office was vacated so I could conduct my interviews. Several of the staff members who were going to be interviewed first did not speak English. We chose—at the suggestion of the sultan's number one wife—one of his other wives who was most fluent in several languages, more than a dozen at least, to be our translator. She sat next to me behind the mahogany desk. I made sure the chair the interviewee was sitting on was two or three inches shorter than mine, was uncomfortable, and squeaked with the slightest movement.

The sister-wife introduced me, and I tried to repeat the man's name but of course butchered it. She smiled and proceeded to tell me what the background of the employee's family was. He was an older gentleman who appeared to be about the sultan's age.

"He is the brother of a childhood playmate of my sultan, Marco. Sadly, his brother was killed in a fishing accident several years before, and the family came into hard times. Sultan hired him about a year ago, as he was well-known in the southern ports of India for being an excellent cook for some of the big houses there."

"Thank you, that was very complete." I looked over the file that had his picture, writing I couldn't interpret, and a tiny scrawled signature almost resembling an X. Perhaps he was not someone who had attended school and could read or write.

"If you will translate for me, I'm going to ask him several questions. Please explain this to him."

She did as she was told, and the cook nodded in agreement. His eyes darted back and forth, and I could see his chest was shiny with beads of sweat.

As I spoke, she translated.

"Just as I said earlier, you have nothing to fear if you have nothing to hide. I'm going to ask you several times if you have observed anything or if you know anything about the poisoning of the sultan. Are you familiar with poisons?"

He spoke back to the wife, shaking his head.

"He says that, in his village, which was not the same village the sultan's friend was raised in, they were brothers but not raised together, several holy men knew how to make potions. He had no taste for any of that, and he felt, as a Hindu, he was commanded to be respectful of all peoples and all beings."

"Okay, so would you know what a poisonous plant or seeds would look like? Have you ever seen anything someone has told you is poisonous?"

The gentleman nodded his head yes.

"He says they have rats on the island, and there is bait for the black traps that are here. There also are snakes and other animals that get into the garbage. It is a problem on this island, but the bait and traps seem to keep it under control. He says he is not the one who prepares the traps."

"Ask him where the poison is for these traps."

"He says he does not know. He does know where some of the traps are placed, but he does not know who prepares them or where the poison is stored."

"Ask him who does know?"

"He says he believes it is the prep chef, the woman they know as Seema."

I searched the files and saw that Seema was indeed someone I was going to be interviewing at the front of the line.

I continued. "Where has he worked in the past?"

As we kept up our translated dialogue, the man seemed to relax slightly, revealing more and more about his family, his past, and some of the incredible misfortunes that he had experienced as a young child and a young man. He showed his left foot, which was turned to the side, giving him a noticeable limp, a deformity he said from birth. He tried to work as kitchen staff several places before he landed several good jobs working for wealthy families. But one by one, as the family dynasties changed and financial situations were altered by events, he was either relieved of his duties or absorbed into another household where occasionally the owner would beat them.

"He found that as a disabled cook, he was often the brunt of everybody else's scorn."

I was not familiar with his culture, but there was something in the look of him, in his eyes, that I trusted. I decided that he was not going to benefit from killing the sultan, had no animosity, and actually had much to lose if he were to be terminated from this particular job. He had no wife or children to support, so living on the island in a modest house was probably the best he could ever hope for. There would be no reason he would want to disturb that.

We interviewed three others, all with similar stories, several recounting how the sultan had been kind to them when they were either sick in the hospital or had suffered a family tragedy. I began to see a pattern, which I should have guessed, but had never known before. The sultan liked to do things for people who'd not been as fortunate as he had. It was completely consistent with what I knew of the man himself.

When I interviewed Seema, she reflected the same nervousness initially that all the rest of the kitchen staff I'd interviewed displayed. She was difficult to open up, but when she did, she volunteered that she was aware the poison for the rat traps was something that would be harmful to pets and to humans. And she kept the poison in a special closet in her cottage, under lock and key. She said she had checked the closet after word got out that it was strychnine poising, and nothing appeared to be out of the ordinary.

"As far as she understood, no one else had a key to the storage closet."

"You can see how it looks for you, Seema. You can see that you have access to what may have poisoned him. We aren't sure, but you can see that. Have you ever seen any of that substance in the kitchen or outside of your home, or have you ever seen any of the traps missing or broken apart?"

That seemed to elicit a reaction. Her eyes lit up as she recounted that several nights ago she went to replace the bait in several of the boxes and could not find one. It had been placed along the path they took to empty the garbage, the path where things were burned and not allowed to attract pests from the jungle. She didn't like to walk through the dense foliage because of snakes and other predators out there, so she didn't go search for it. And she didn't consider that there was anything out of the ordinary, so she didn't report it. But she took a new box out there and to the best of her knowledge, that box was still in place today.

It was a very lucky break, if in fact that turned out to be the source of the poison. But I still didn't have the motive. One thing that did relieve me, however, was that this was something that one person could do by themself. It wouldn't require a whole team, or a group of conspirators to pull off. And that made it even more likely my hunch was correct. This act was personal.

As I did with all the interviewees, I always ended the conversation by asking them who they would suspect. And like all the others, she shook her head, wished she could help, but said she had absolutely no inkling that someone would want to do him harm.

In between appointments, my security team informed me they had located both of the employees who were not here today but had been working during the time the sultan was poisoned. I was told they would be brought in tomorrow morning, early.

I finished the interviews late. Those who traveled by boat off the island at night were told to remain on the grounds, and a facility was provided for them. Those individuals were monitored and watched even more closely than the residents of the island. I received word that the Navy team was going to arrive first thing in the morning, near dawn. I made a list of all my questions and the places I wanted them to search first, gathered my notes together along with the files of the men and women of the staff, and asked for permission to begin interviewing the housekeeping staff in the morning.

Harry greeted me, handing me a longneck beer, which I was grateful for. I mockingly wiped the top of it off and examined it closely before I took a sip.

"Oh, so I see you're going to interview me too then, is that right, Marco?"

"I'm just messing with you, Harry. So how is your mom?"

"She's worried. She wants to come to your wedding, but I just—I don't know if that's going to be possible. She also wants to say goodbye. I'm hoping he will allow it."

"That would be nice, but politically, well, I've had no experience on that score since I'm only married to one woman at a time, but I certainly wouldn't want to be the one to straighten all that out. Does she have any friends among the wives?"

"I think the younger ones are more open-minded. But his number one wife will not be happy. She would put her foot down, and he would have to honor her request. I think if we are able to arrange it, if he's agreeable to it, it's going to have to be kept from her. I hate to do that, but I think that's the only way it'll happen. My mother may not want to press it. And maybe that would be the best."

I felt for Harry, living in one world, roots in another, robbed of a father, who nonetheless provided for him. He was lucky to have such a worldly and giving mother, who loved him absolutely to the ends of the earth. But Harry was, even though a US citizen, very connected to the sultan. He was proud of his heritage, and I could see his father's passing was going to be tough for him, perhaps even harder than it would be on his mother. For his mother had experienced the sultan's love, knew that she was his favorite even though he'd never married her. Harry never got to experience that. For his own safety, he was raised clear across to the other side of the globe in a Brooklyn brownstone.

I needed to get to bed, and after conferring with Dr. Tramel and getting his update, I was satisfied that the sultan was going to be up and walking tomorrow. He advised me not to visit, since they'd finally gotten him to the point where his muscle cramping had stopped. I learned this was a symptom of strychnine poisoning, and often patients died not from the poisoning itself but from cardiac arrest because they could never rest their bodies. They were in constant motion until it just literally wore them out.

As prescribed, the sultan was drinking huge quantities of water, which was good, and the lab in Mumbai had delivered a portable testing kit so he could monitor the sultan's blood with a finger prick and test for the presence of the poison. Dr. Tramel told me that his count was coming down quickly. He thought there would be very little trace of it left within three days.

"Are you any closer to finding out who did this?" he asked.

"I'll see what the Navy boys say. But I think the easiest possibility would be a rodent bait set out by the garbage dump. The purpose is to kill rats and snakes that might come to feed off the garbage. I've identified who prepares the traps, and we've also verified that one of the kits is missing. So it could be a crime of opportunity. I'd be surprised if that wasn't the source."

"Good work, Marco. It doesn't take very much to kill a person, about a half cup. But I think what may have happened is the first dose didn't kill him, so it was given again and again, possibly for several days. The chemical is quite bitter, very difficult to disguise, so they would have to be careful not to get exposed. That said, it's just a guess. But I think we are dealing with an inexperienced person who found a way to do this, not someone who planned it long-term or was a trained assassin."

"Well, Doc, I'm bushed. And if I'm ever going to get married, I better get upstairs and see my lovely fiancée before she decides, 'Hey, maybe I'll go home with the doc instead.'"

We both had a good laugh at that.

I climbed the staircase, my eyes traveling over the great hall— the hallway down to the women's quarters, the area off to the right where the kitchen and the staff would normally be busily washing dishes and preparing food for the next day. I glanced at the torches lit in the hallway leading to the sultan's room and was satisfied there were two of my men outside his door, both armed and extremely lethal. The doctor had told me that his number one wife was spending the night with him in bed. Which was only allowed after they stripped and burned the sheets, changed his nightshirt, and bathed him. The doctor had told me he thought it was safe.

I had done all I could at this point, and I knew there would be a lot more to discover tomorrow when the team arrived. But we were getting closer.

I opened the door to the bedroom and instantly was transported to another world. She lay naked on the bed, her hands above her head, tied to the ornate bedframe with red silk sashes. She had lit candles all around the room, and I saw a chilled bottle of champagne next to the dresser. She'd probably waited there for me for a long time, because several of the candles had dripped onto the furniture and floor. She'd fallen asleep against her arm. I quietly closed the door and locked it. Without taking my eyes off of Shannon's beautiful body, I slowly stripped off my clothes, my hard-on swollen and almost painful. I very gently climbed onto the bed, placed my knees over her hips, leaned into her face, and kissed her.

Her body responded immediately as she moaned and began to writhe on the bed beneath me. "Are you all done, Marco?" she whispered, her lips calling me.

"No, sweetheart. I've only just begun."

CHAPTER 8

WHEN SHANNON AWOKE in the morning, Marco had already left to go meet with the Navy advance team. She arched up, stretching her arms to the headboard, fingering the red silk bonds he had lovingly tightened and then released during their hours-long lovemaking session. Her total exhaustion was delicious. She would miss him, knew he'd be busy all day today, and ached for him to return.

All in due time.

She knew she had to be patient.

She slipped on her clothes, enjoying the casual feel of her khaki pants and the leather flip-flops, then ran down the stairs to ask questions and seek information. Her belly was starved and gurgling.

She heard noises in the kitchen and smelled fresh coffee so made her way through the doorway and was greeted with several smiling faces. A mug of coffee with cream was placed in her hands. She greeted the staff, took a sip, and declared it excellent. Her thumbs-up was returned.

She was shown to a seat at the table where she was brought some eggs and some fruit. An overflowing bowl containing colorful fruits from all over the island had been placed in the middle of the long table that could easily feed thirty. Other than bananas and papayas, she didn't recognize anything.

One of the sultan's younger wives marched past to get some coffee herself.

"I've already had my sip, and these eggs are fantastic, so I guess the kitchen's been tested and it's clean?" she asked the wife.

"Yes, they were here nearly two hours ago, Shannon. They found no trace of the chemical. They're outside working on the grounds. I think they're going to do some of the other rooms and cottages later. Are you feeling well?"

"Yes." Shannon smiled, then blushed, and closed her eyes.

Her companion at the table giggled, placing her red painted fingernails over her mouth. "I see. I'm happy for you."

Shannon wondered if any of the women in the harem ever had boyfriends outside of the palace. She had never considered that before, but it would be logical for the women to do so. She made a note to ask Marco about it.

"So he is better, I take it?"

"Oh yes. I've heard he's already had an argument with somebody."

"With who?"

"One of us. I'm not sure what it was about, not anything important, of course. It happens. We rarely fight for very long, but sometimes things happen. I know my sultan is back when he gets cranky."

"I understand that one. I really do," Shannon replied.

"Are you wanting a tour of the honeymoon home? Marco told me that perhaps you'd like to take a walk through the gardens, and we could take the little cart over to the house or we could walk. It's about a mile and a half. I was told we'd have to take one of Marco's men, but there are a handful of us who would like to go with you if you're up to it."

"I would love to. Just as soon as I'm done here, I'm ready."

She took her mug, promising to return with the ladies.

"I'll find out who I'm supposed to take as security. I'm sure he's going to have a preference."

Marco entered the hall with four well-built younger men, and she guessed they were the Navy contingent he'd been waiting for.

"There she is, my princess," Marco said.

"I was wondering where you were. Are you going to introduce me to your friends?" Shannon asked as she stood.

One by one, they were introduced, the last one had to remove his latex gloves before he would shake hands with her.

"Sorry, we've been handling stuff I don't want to contaminate you with. But it's very nice to meet you, ma'am," the young blonde boy said.

"You guys all look so young!"

"They *are* young. They look young because I'm old. Remember, Shannon, you're marrying an old guy."

The Navy group laughed, and Shannon could tell there was quite a bit of camaraderie between all of them.

"I'm going take your suggestion, Marco, and go for a walk to find the honeymoon house. Several of the wives want to come along. I understand we're supposed to take a guard, so can you arrange that for me?"

He stepped over to her, and she could tell he wanted to grab her around the waist and press her hard against him, but wanted to show more respect in front of their new audience. He gave her a gentle peck on the cheek. "What, pray tell, are you going to do for me?"

There were whoops and hollers from the Navy men behind him. Shannon stared into Marco's eyes and whispered, "Oh, I think something involving red sashes, some wonderful creams, and maybe a bottle of whiskey this time. I sure do wish they had a hot tub here." She smiled, and his smile mirrored hers.

"As a matter of fact, they do. It's over at the Honeymoon House, but you're going to have to wait on that one."

The men continued to call out comments.

"Then I guess we'll have to do without. We'll improvise, Marco," she whispered.

"Well, you heard it yourselves, gents. My future wife is planning a party for this evening. And I'm going to be very frank, you're not invited."

SHANNON, THE WIVES, and Gary, one of Marco's security detail, walked through the jungles and garden path past fragrant flowers and vines that twisted around palm trees and other flowering trees. She could hear birds calling and remembered being told they had imported some coral-colored parrots for their event. She thought she could hear some.

"No, those are the fruit parrots. Those are green," said one of the wives.

The guard Marco had assigned had just recently detached from the military and was going to be helping run security at the Trident Towers. He stayed behind ten feet or more and checked in by a small microphone attached to his jacket every five minutes. He answered calls or questions that came over his earpiece. Shannon felt secure, although it was distracting to hear some of the squawks and the conversations said in code.

"We have a lagoon over off this way if we follow this path, and it's wonderful for swimming," one of the wives motioned.

"I want to see the house first. Can we do that?" Shannon asked.

"Of course."

About forty-five minutes later, the pathway arched to the left. Through the foliage, as they got closer and closer, a huge structure was revealed. It had a metal roof and was designed in such a way that it looked out of place on this exotic island. It contained more glass than concrete. The outside was finished in a stucco-type material that was embedded with pieces of coral and shells, giving it a pink palace look with a modern twist. The colors were stunning, and beyond the home to the side, she could see the ocean peeking through the trees.

One of the wives had a key to the front door, so she opened it and allowed Shannon to be the first one to walk in.

She felt like she was walking into a cathedral in Europe. The foyer was nearly three stories tall leading to a grand living room with windows decorated in stained glass shedding bright colors all over the marble and travertine floors. Everywhere she looked were carvings and inlay of birds, vines, flowers, and some scenes depicting the ocean surf and the pink beach beyond. There was one stunning window up high that was a sunset done in peaches and roses and reds. She was left without words.

The size of the home was enormous, yet it only had two bedrooms, one grand bedroom which was probably the master suite with a beautiful pink marble bathroom and a second on the reverse side of the house done in light gray marble, with its own electronic features such as a large screen TV and an old-fashioned music box. There were musical instruments left behind, and the bedroom also was large enough to contain a billiard table. She turned and looked back at the group from the doorway. "His and hers? A honeymoon house where he sleeps here and she sleeps there?"

The wives tittered and giggled.

One of them came up to her and said, "But isn't it nice to keep the mystery alive? Like sometimes you can be in his room, sometimes you can be in her room. The change of scenery is good for your sex life, madam."

She was very young. Shannon knew she was several years younger than her, but her bright eyes and sweet smile showed Shannon that she was indeed experienced in the art of lovemaking, as all the women in his harem were.

She winked at the young wife, adding, "You're right. I've learned something. It's variety, right?"

Several of the women giggled, pulling their saris across their mouths, and nodded their heads.

The young Navy guard frowned. "I got to see this. Do you mind?" He walked through the entrance to the gray bathroom and whistled. "The size of the closet in here is as big as my apartment back home. This is your honeymoon house? This is where you'll spend your honeymoon?" he asked.

"Indeed, it is. Pretty nice, right?"

Several of the wives had walked out to the backyard off of the lanai patio that stretched fifty feet or more before the porch covering ended. With very shallow steps, they made their way down to the sandy shore and watched the bright blue ocean undulate in the sunlight. It was one of the most beautiful views Shannon had ever seen.

There was a hammock built for two or three hanging between two palm trees to the right and a small cupola with a screened area that contained a pool, like a hot tub. "This is beautiful. I think I've died and gone to heaven," she exclaimed.

The group walked along the shoreline, noticing far out in the distance several fishing boats. One was passing by, and two were anchored. Beyond them, a large container ship slowly sailed by. Other than that, there wasn't any evidence of civilization any-where. Several islands covered in greenery sat in a chain to the left, but no structures or power lines were seen, no boats hitched. Beneath the turquoise water, Shannon noticed a shallow area with a coral reef, which would be perfect snorkeling. She made a note to ask about getting some equipment to do that.

"So how long do people usually stay here, and who stays here?" she asked.

"It was built several years ago, about five years, I think. When he took his last wife, he had the house built so they had some privacy. Of course he's had daughters who have been married and family sometimes from the staff, depending. This is only used for people to celebrate their honeymoon. It's not a vacation home, and no children are ever allowed."

"It's just a special place just for honeymoons then?" she asked.

"Yes. Very special. Very private and very special."

They locked the house up after Shannon had a tour of the gar-dens. Someone had decorated the rose garden with statues of naked women, which made Shannon chuckle. The sultan's touch and choices were everywhere around them. She had not seen roses, but beneath one large water statue was a vase containing a half dozen gorgeous red, pink, and white roses, extremely fragrant and perfectly pruned. "If you wish, I have something you can clip some roses and bring back to your room. It is allowed," one of the wives said.

"Thank you. Yes, I'd like that." She asked for Shannon to point to the flowers she'd like to take, and after she was given the bouquet of half a dozen beautiful fully blooming roses and buds ready to burst, they began their trip back down the shell pathway on their way back to the palace. When the turnoff to the lagoon came up again, they decided to take that trail, and the wives showed her the beautiful swimming hole that had been created with flat soapstone slabs and rocks. They told her they often used the place for swimming and bathing.

Again, with the jungle foliage so thick around them, it was a private location. There were several paths that led into the lagoon area. "Where do these go?"

"Some of them lead back to the houses where family lives. If you go not very far in this direction, you come to the ocean again. There's a small bay there where boats that bring supplies or pleasure crafts can be docked."

"Is that where we came off the taxi?"

She shook her head no.

Shannon began walking down one particular path until she heard the rustling sound of the surf and the waves of the ocean. Birds called, and in the jungle were sounds of scurrying small animals and birds getting out of the way as the women and their chaperone passed. Just before they came to the beach, they heard voices.

Shannon carefully hid herself behind a large palm tree and peered around to see if she could identify the people talking. She saw one of the sultan's wives speaking to a young man in rolled up dirty pants and no shirt. They appeared to be arguing, and then she burst into tears, hiding her face. "Oh dear. That is not allowed," said one of the older wives.

"Who is she?" asked Shannon. She didn't recognize her.

"That's Meera. She is one of his newer wives. She comes from another island, formerly an island kingdom that was dissolved, absorbed by India some years ago. Her family came into disfavor with the Indian government, and she was orphaned when she lost her parents when she was small. The sultan took her in. Because, well—"

Shannon could see there was something delicate the wife didn't want to say.

One of the other wives spoke up. "She was defiled. Victim of rape. It is difficult to be married into a good home, a good house if this has happened. The sultan took her as one of his wives."

"That must be a brother or something. Maybe she does have family left," said Shannon.

One of the older wives motioned for them to leave, and as Shannon was the last, she turned around and saw the young couple embrace in an erotic kiss that was not remotely familial.

She knew she was going to have to let Marco know about this right away.

CHAPTER 9

I WAS IN the middle of discussing several items with the sweep team from the Navy when Shannon and several of the wives bolted in and came running straight for me.

"Marco! You have to hear about this!"

The women behind Shannon were whispering amongst themselves and discussing with other members of the staff. I immediately put my hands up and stopped all the conversation.

"Whoa, whoa, whoa! Let's hold it right there. If we have some information about what's going on, I want it said in private. I do not want gossip to be spread throughout this kingdom. It's important that we do this the right way. Nobody leaves this room until Shannon tells her story. Do you understand?"

My security detail had stood as soon as the ladies entered, ready for whatever was to come next. The wives immediately nodded their heads, as well as three of the housekeeping staff who had been waiting on us during our meeting. I took Shannon's hand and sat her next to me on the big red leather couch.

"Okay, Shannon, tell me what's going on."

She caught her breath, her face pale white with what I took to be fear.

"Well, we went over to the honeymoon house, and oh, Marco, it's lovely."

"I'm sure it is. But let's get to the story, okay?"

"Yes, yes, of course. We walked over to the bathing pool, I think they call it the lagoon, and it had several trails that went off in different directions, and I was just exploring one of the trails. They told me it led to the beach. We walked through the jungle forest, and gradually, I could hear the water and sounds of the surf, and then we heard voices. So very carefully, we listened and crept through the foliage until we saw two people on the beach talking, a man and a woman. It appeared the man had arrived by boat, a small boat. Their conversation was very heated—looked like arguing."

"Who? Are these people from this household?" I demanded, needing to get to the point.

Shannon looked to the group of wives.

"Yes. One of the sultan's wives and another gentleman—they were both young." Again, she looked to the women. "I believe she is one of his newer wives."

"How do you know this? Did you recognize her?"

"No, I was told. But we assumed she was speaking to her brother."

I stood up and put my hands on my hips and turned. "So? That's not unusual. What made you think it was suspicious activity?" I studied the women, cowering in the corner.

"Because—"

"Sir," one of the younger wives spoke up boldly. "Whether or not she was with her brother, it makes no difference. It is forbidden for her to speak to a man unaccompanied. This is not allowed."

"Who is this woman? Is she one of his wives? Are you sure?" I asked her.

"Her name is Meera, and she has been married to the sultan about five years, came to live with us then," she told me.

I was furious that a member of his party walked without an accompaniment to the other side of the island. And since I knew that area to be a major pickup and drop off area, it was also unsafe. I wondered if he was there to assist her in an escape.

Shannon spoke up again.

"They were arguing, Marco. We started to move away, and

when I turned around to look at them, they had embraced and they kissed. And it wasn't like they were brother and sister. It was an intimate kiss. Swear to God, Marco, it's not my imagination."

Although I was glad that we were getting closer to perhaps the bottom of the plot, I was still struggling with a reason or motivation for the sultan's poisoning. But Shannon apparently thought they were connected. I knew I had to do some checking with the sultan and his number one wife. But I threw down some ultimatums to the room first.

"Who knows her well?"

The wife who spoke to me earlier stepped forward. "She sometimes confides in me."

"Is her reputation solid in this household? Have you had any problems with her in the past?"

All three of the women again answered without speaking, by shaking their heads no.

"Do you know who she was talking to? Does he work here in the kingdom?"

"No. But I do believe he could have been her former betrothed. They were promised to each other as children through their families. I don't know all of the story."

"I need to talk to her right away. I would like one of you to go to the harem quarters and see if you can find her. Bring her to me. Do not tell anybody. Just tell her that the sultan would like to see her, but bring her here to me."

As perhaps the youngest of the three scampered off down the hallway toward their quarters, I addressed the other two.

"Not a word of this to anyone. I'm sure the sultan and his number one will ask you questions, and that's okay. But there is to be no gossip, and until she's thoroughly vetted, she may not be the suspect, but neither is she innocent. Do you understand?"

Again, they agreed.

"Everyone stays right here until we find her. No one leaves this room." I addressed the wait staff as well. "Unfortunately, I can't let you go, either. You've seen more than I wanted you to see here, and you're going to have to stay until we get this resolved. And no one is to leave the island, is that clear?"

I turned to my Navy boys, who agreed.

"We'll get the word out, Marco," said Darius, who I permitted to leave.

"Does anyone know anything else about this wife and the man she may be speaking to today?"

One of the waitstaff stepped forward. "The man she was with was likely her betrothed, many years ago. As children, they were committed to each other, as has been said. I believe he has been recently returned, having been sent to the military. I believe I overheard this when we were unloading supplies. Perhaps he feels he has a right to claim her."

"But she's married to the sultan. That's a contract." I was worried that breaking the marriage contract was grounds for imprisonment or worse in this society. The sultan didn't have a prison on his island, but the Indian authorities would certainly intervene, and her life would be made quite difficult.

We didn't have to wait long. The wife I sent to retrieve Meera came back, holding her hand, bringing her in tow. They stopped just in front of me.

Meera was glancing around her, at the congregation of the American men seated at the table with Shannon, her sister-wives, and me. She looked genuinely confused. Speaking to her sister-wife, it was translated for us.

"She says she was summoned to meet with the sultan. She came specifically to meet him here. Is this the meeting place or—?"

"Have a seat please," I interrupted, motioning to the chair.

She delicately set her frame down, her back ramrod stiff and her eyes frightened and unable to contact mine or any of the other sister-wives. At last, she placed her hands in her lap and looked down, waiting for instructions.

I motioned to the other wife to translate for us, and she quickly rose, standing beside Meera.

"You were seen with a young man at the beach today. Who is this person, and why did you disobey the sultan's rules about wandering the island without protection?"

She waited for the translation and then began. "He is a friend from many years ago, before I was married. He has been insisting that I meet with him. I did not invite him. I requested that he leave."

"But you met with him anyway," I insisted.

"He found me, threatened to make a scene if I wouldn't meet with him in private. I had to take that risk for his own safety, as well as mine. I knew if he were caught he would get in trouble. So I agreed to meet him at the dock."

I knew it was possible, of course, but I needed to find out if she was involved in the poisoning.

"Is he responsible for poisoning the sultan?"

I noted that the idea was foreign to her, but as she considered it, I could see some clarity come to her face. Then she put her hand to her mouth, bent over, and began to cry.

"Where is he now?"

The sister-wife asked her three or four times the same question, and Meera refused to answer. Behind me, I heard rustling and noted that Number One had entered. I turned, backing away so she could address the woman herself. She stepped within two feet of the young wife, waited until the girl looked up to her, and then slapped her across the face. I didn't want to physically restrain his number one wife, but a fight would risk everyone else's existence if they got involved in it. I moved to block his number one and asked the young wife where her friend was.

Number One blurted out. "He lives in the camp down by the docks, isn't that right, Meera?"

The translator spoke to her and then, in perfect English, gave the bride's answer.

"I am so sorry, sir. I have broken the rules, and I am not worthy of all that has been given me. He is not well, and I only thought if I met with him, perhaps I could stop him from doing something I was afraid of, or perhaps hurting me or one of the other wives. It didn't occur to me that he would be the person to try to take the sultan's life. I really didn't think he would do that."

Number One spoke up, spitting as she did so, showing her disgust. "So you sit here and tell us that even when the sultan was poisoned, you didn't think to tell us about this person? The person you thought could create harm? His life was in grave danger, but you never thought to try to protect him with this information? Meera, where are your loyalties? Where is your moral compass?"

"I am so sorry. What is he going to do to me?" Meera asked, her eyes wide and filling with tears.

"There will be no mercy shown you here," said Number One. "This will be taken up with the Indian authorities, if you are involved."

"But I didn't know he would—"

"You failed to report it," I added. "You are not to be trusted, Meera."

"It will go better for you if you help Marco find him. After that, it's up to the Indian authorities. I am not sure what this will entail or what they will do. But we need to find him. It'll be way more dangerous for you if we do not, and it's very dangerous for him, either way."

"I will. I promise to help you find him. I owe that to the sultan," she said through her tears.

The rest of the afternoon was spent organizing a team to scour the sea village across the channel, looking for Meera's former boyfriend. I sent one from the Naval research team to verify the presence of any strychnine at his home, if we found it, and I had several others accompany them in addition to one of the other wives. My men were instructed to get in, find him, and get him out before they were noticed.

Again I admonished them to not discuss the situation with anyone and then dismissed them.

Shannon was beside herself.

"How did he even get in touch with her? You know, Marco,

she must have had help from somebody on the outside?"

Number One stepped into our conversation.

"We do occasionally receive deliveries and visitors, and he could have posed as one of those. We have been bringing in lots of fresh food, now that the kitchen is safe. The sooner we locate him, the better we can find out how he did it."

I now had a whole team of other people to interview, families of the staff who worked there, some of the delivery people. We had easily a hundred people left to interview. Time was not our friend, and until then, the sultan was being guarded round the clock. I had been told he was beginning to object to all the scrutiny and his lack of privacy.

That was a good sign.

The sultan was up and about, speaking with several of his wives and the staff, and looked to be much better. His skin coloring was nearly back to normal. He said his bones ached, but he told me that was his condition before he got sick.

At dusk, the team brought the unfortunate young man to us, with the report that he'd confessed to the poisoning out of jealousy and revenge. The young man was pushed down onto the marble floor and thrown at the sultan's feet.

The sultan yelled at him with a voice that rattled windows in the great hall. "You come into my household and threaten these women, these people, their livelihoods. You threaten me? All I have done is help Meera. I was there for her when you were gone. You abandoned her after you defiled her. What would have happened if you'd left her with child?"

The boy mumbled to the floor. "But she was to be my wife. She was promised—"

"You took permission where you were given none. You took what was not yours. I could have you rot in prison for the rest of your life if I decided to. What kind of a life for her is that? Bringing you water and fruits and candies and screwing all the guards at the prison for the chance to see you? Just so she could have a few minutes alone with you? How dare you place her in such danger. I saved her from an outcast life of poverty, and this is how you show your respect for what I have done?"

He didn't look up but kept his body touching the floor, his forehead kissing the marble, his hands at the sides of his head, knees tucked, his butt in the air.

"I am sorry, my sultan. I am so sorry."

"I am not your sultan. I am merely the person who showed compassion for someone who had been harmed by your actions. She doesn't belong with you, but thanks to you, she will no longer have a home here, food to eat, or the sisterhood around her. She will be cast out again. You have done this."

The man on the floor began to wail. The sultan got up and was going to kick him in the gut but looked at me as he tried to get his balance to make the kick. I was not encouraging. In fact, I really didn't want him to do any physical damage to the man or it would lighten our case.

"What can I do? Please, what can I do to save Meera from that fate?" the man mumbled.

I stepped in, hoping to calm the waters.

"You can help her situation if you cooperate and tell us how you managed the poisoning? Tell me the truth, and you have a chance to save some of your dignity."

The sultan flopped down on the leather couch with a growl. He acted like a wounded bear.

"I came on the island and lived by the lagoon for two days before I saw Meera. I planned to take her back to my village, but she rejected me, told me to leave. I stole from the garbage, foraged for food for myself. I believed I could convince her to leave with me, but she refused, over and over again. Then I watched as your helper baited the box for the rats by the scrapyard, and I realized that if I took that poison I could use it to make you sick. I stole the box and pried open. I waited for the right opportunity and mixed it in with some cooked peppers and curry that were cooling in the outside kitchen area. I had been told it was your favorite dish. I only wanted to make you sick, I didn't intend to take your life."

The whole room drew their attention to the sultan.

He surveyed the faces of his family and staff, his eyes finally resting on Meera. "What would you have me do, Meera?"

"You will never trust me again. I have broken my promise, and I don't think you should ever trust me to be in your house. I have greatly enjoyed it here. I wish I had not acted behind your back to meet him, but I promise I never meant to cause you harm. You have been good to me."

"Do you love him?"

"My sultan, sadly, no. It is delusional on his part to think that I would spend a life with him. But my mistake was not informing you or your Number One. And for that, I should pay."

"I regret that you will have to leave my household, Meera. I only hope that you will at some future date learn how to live on the right path. But I cannot take the chance you would harm me or anyone else in this household. You have lost your opportunity and your position."

The sultan looked over at the young man. "You will be taken to the police in Cochin, and you will be turned over to them for a trial and sentencing. If Meera testifies on your behalf, perhaps that can help your situation. But I wash my hands of you, and if you ever were to return to this kingdom again, we will not be so lenient. But I will not push for a harsh sentence."

The young man's jaw was rigid, anger and resentment seething from his eyes. "You are a snake," he said to the sultan. The crowd was aghast.

"You reject the gift of compassion? You truly are a troubled young man and not worthy to take a bride from anywhere. Perhaps you shall die like one, my son. And you shall never have the love of your dreams, but you will die knowing that you ruined someone else's life as well. For Meera no longer will have a life coveted by so many. You've destroyed her chance at happiness. You can die knowing that you gave me the poison, but you poisoned Meera's life too."

CHAPTER 10

SHANNON SPENT THE following day attending to last-minute preparations for the wedding. As the Navy team continued sweeping through the island properties, they set up monitoring devices and camera surveillance that could be maintained and operated off the island, a highly sophisticated system that Marco had found for him and agreed to update and monitor for as long as the sultan desired.

The sultan had recovered remarkably well. Most of the laughter and happiness of the household was gone, however. Everyone was keenly aware of the impact the sultan's health had on the family. And Shannon realized for the first time that he really was the hub where all the spokes of the wheel joined. And he was not going to be able to quickly transfer that to anyone else. Even his sons were not trained to take over running a kingdom.

It was the one thing Shannon felt the sultan had ignored, and now that he was faced with an impending end, there wasn't the time to really fix it. So the household was filled with sadness and thoughts of the inevitable demise of the great man. She knew her future husband, even though he would do anything for the sultan, also was incapable of truly fixing this. There was nothing to be done now.

She spoke to Marco privately when they were alone. They were planning to leave the following day.

"Has he given any thought to what will happen once he goes? I mean, who will keep this household, who will run it?" she asked.

"I've tried to talk to him about it, Shannon. He refuses to discuss it. I know he doesn't want to send everybody into chaos, but I'm afraid he's resigned himself to someone else solving it for him. And as close as I am to him, even I can't do it. He's not going to give the power to either one of his sons or his wives, especially now."

"So what'll happen with Meera and her wanna-be lover?" Shannon asked.

"He's facing many, many years in prison. Perhaps some kind of clemency would be granted after the sultan's death, but there's no guarantee on that. The government of India, who is responsible for certain security matters of the kingdom, since it's within its sphere, really doesn't have the capacity to handle it. I'm guessing there are politicians in India who have their sights on the island someday. This whole way of life that we're witnessing is probably also going to fade, just like he will."

"Then I'm glad he will die before he has to see all that happen," she said.

"These are the stories of all the great maharajas and islands that are in the Indian Ocean as, one by one, they became hotels or luxury resorts, places where the rich and famous could rent a castle, a villa, or a palace for themselves and their entourage. There will always be people who want that. But the number of people who are in this world able to afford maintaining it and keeping it, that number's dwindling. There used to be a thousand islands with kingdoms on them. And they used to pitch wars against each other hundreds of years ago. Now, they're just paper tigers."

Shannon felt her eyes moisten as she mourned, in advance, the death of a lifestyle.

"We have to learn to adapt, sweetheart. We have to learn to take what the world gives us and, if anything, learn from this. We can't be stuck in one place, treasuring a lifestyle or trying to hang on to something that is not going to last. We have to be adaptable. We have to notice the trends and the people out there, and at some point, we have to know, just like the song says, when to hold them and when to fold them. I don't think it's possible for the sultan to ever be able to make that decision. And some people are just like that."

He gently pressed his palm against her cheek.

"But don't grieve, Shannon. Enjoy what's here. Enjoy the fantasy, the life of a small little clutch of family members, a dying kingdom. Enjoy it, and then like a butterfly, let it go. Let it fly off."

Shannon was reminded of what she had to do with one of her friends who was cleaning out her mother's closets and things after she passed away.

"I'm thinking about my friend Judie and what we had to do after her mother died. She kept saying over and over again, why did mom not get rid of all this stuff? Her mother just didn't want to come to the point where she had to let go of this stuff, she just couldn't do it, and so she passed away leaving that to somebody else. I don't want to do that to our kids. I don't want to make them have to go through that."

"I've experienced that going through things I had to ship home when I had someone on the teams who passed. It was left up to me to decide what to keep and what not to. Most of it, I kept because it wasn't my decision, and I figured if my SEAL buddy kept it, there was a reason in there somewhere, although most of the time it wasn't clear. I remember talking to a widow when it had been several weeks since her husband passed away. I called on her. I was asked to by the Navy to see if I could help, and she took me outside to her backyard, which was filled with sand, piles of wood here and there, plants in pots, and some that were needing to be planted. A huge concrete mixer and bags of concrete covered in plastic was the focal point of the backyard. So much stuff the kids couldn't even play out there."

"Did you help?"

"Yup. When he went off with SEAL Team 3, that fateful day six months before, it was supposed to be a temporary TDI, and he'd be back in a week or two. Except he never came back. And he left this big yard filled with a mess. His unfinished project."

"So what did you do?"

"I promised her we'd take care of it. I asked her if she would allow me to complete it for him. And so we got together a regular party, you know, one of my SEAL team parties. We got about twenty guys, their wives, their friends, the kids, everybody got into it. We had kids bringing in pallets of lawn and laying them out and stamping on them, watering plants. We had wives hauling wheelbarrows, digging holes, and trimming trees. We had some of the youngsters hauling big black bags of cuttings and trash out to the curb to be picked up. It took us all weekend, but in the end, on Sunday night, we all stood there in the middle of his garden, and we knew that we had finished his vision."

Shannon had a hard time stifling back tears. "That's one of the most amazing stories I think I've ever heard you tell, Marco. I can't imagine how grateful she must have been."

"She was. And a few weeks later, in the team building, there was a big fight."

"What over?"

"Well, you know how it is, when one warrior passes away, the rest of us take it upon ourselves to take care of the wife and kids. We knew he'd want someone else to raise his children who had the same ethos and honor he did. And so within the next few weeks, it was decided what the pecking order would be. We gave the chosen man our best, and he spent the summer wooing the widow, asked her to marry him, and then did."

"That's the way it is with police and fire, too, sometimes; I've talked to widows who almost have to refuse men from their husband's force stopping by bringing flowers and casseroles and little gifts for the kids. I had one woman I interviewed who was angry about it."

"Well, that's because she probably hadn't finished grieving. It's hard to let go and to think about a future. Especially since the whole center of your life is gone. I had to do that on a limited basis with Emily. I didn't have time to grieve. I was still running missions at that time, and then I decided to do something else with my life. I jumped into my relationship with Rebecca, and I was off to the races again. This time, Shannon, you came to me. And that's probably the only way it would've happened. You healed me."

"I think what you're saying is we all have to find our futures, and that means everybody here at the palace, they'll have stories to tell. The kids will talk about it, won't they?" she asked him.

"Yep, there'll be lots of stories told, and some of them will even be true."

He put his arm around her. "I think getting married here is the greatest gift we could give the sultan. I was so worried he wasn't going to make it, but now that he is, we're putting double and triple into his safety here so that we can have our day and the sultan can have his one last party. He doesn't want to say it's a goodbye party. He wants to say that it's our wedding celebration, but it really is a goodbye party, Shannon. And I can't think of anybody else I'd rather walk through that doorway to the future with than you. Lots of stories to tell our children, right?"

"Absolutely. Thank you, Marco. That puts it all in perspective."

Saying goodbye that next day was difficult for Shannon. There were many tears shed and still some uneasy nerves. The sultan himself appeared to be in a great mood, starting to get back his usual laughing self, but nobody else was really feeling a tremendous amount of joy, especially since Marco and Shannon were leaving. But Marco had assured everybody that the detail he was leaving behind would lay down their lives for any one of them. The kingdom had been way more vulnerable than he thought, and they were going to do everything in their power to make sure they were protected, but not feeling like they were cooped up in a military prison somewhere. Shannon knew that security was an issue for the women.

Sultan's wife number one confided in Shannon the day they left that he promised her he was not going to marry again. Of course, the two women knew that he didn't have much chance of living very long past the wedding, but it was important for him to tell her that she was his most important wife, his number one wife, and that he was done marrying.

Shannon realized it was way more important to wife number one than it was to anybody else. Maybe it was his way of telling her he had always loved her and perhaps loved her most. The household had been turned into a hospital of sorts with the sultan's treatments, and they knew he was going to be sick while receiving some of these treatments, so rather than spending time worrying about sexual favors, she knew the women were going to be more like nursemaids for him. Which was what his needs were.

They took the helicopter up and away after Marco gave his last-minute instructions to his team leader, and everyone waved as the two of them ascended into the sky. They took a limo shuttle to Mumbai where they caught a commercial liner back to New York and then took the flight down to Tampa. It was a long day when they arrived back at Indian Rocks Beach, but as soon as they got off the plane, she felt she was truly home. It was an adventure she would never forget. It would heighten the tension but also the enjoyment of the wedding. It was the acknowledgment of a life well lived for a man worthy of praise. And it was something Marco wanted to do with her by his side. That was the most important thing of all.

On the second day they were home, they drove out at sunset to watch the beautiful orange and yellow and rose-colored clouds, sitting in the shell of their home which had been closed in but wasn't complete. The balcony had yet to be built but the platform was there. And that's where they sat and ate some Indian takeout they'd picked up along the way, watching the sunset and the waves and the beach.

She angled her head a little bit and was considering something when Marco asked her what she was thinking about.

"I don't know whether I like pink sand or white sand. I think I like the white sand better."

"My dear, if that is your opinion, you are commanded to keep it to yourself."

"Yes, sir. Anything you want."

"Anything?" he asked.

She held his face between her hands, kissed him, and said, "Anything."

CHAPTER 11

ABOUT SEVEN DAYS after we returned back to Florida, we were finally able to have the groundbreaking ceremony I'd wanted to have for nearly six months. There had been so much going on, especially with the trip to the kingdom. Everything had gotten delayed, and it was looking like we might have to postpone the whole thing until after the wedding sometime in January or February.

What I wasn't prepared for was the fact that everyone came together on this thing, the contractors really pushed themselves to try to do things ahead of time. It was the most cooperative and successful planning and start to a project I'd ever experienced. And I'd done plenty of complexes.

Sam's input was invaluable. Whenever we ran into some kind of an issue we had to solve, he was the first person we called. We asked him how it would impact a disabled person, how would someone who needed to cook and clean and rest and use the bathroom be able to use a space or a stairway or a ramp, and I think because it was centered on the disabled the project almost became a living, breathing thing. We were honoring something that was bigger and way beyond ourselves. It was a wonderful lesson in how well people could work together.

We did have our detractors. We occasionally got hit pieces written in magazines and newspapers, but whenever they went digging, they couldn't find any dirt, because everything was not being done for profit. And we could prove it too. Today, as I stood next to Shannon, we had the governor, the mayors of several little beach towns, the mayor of Tampa, the heads of our local police and first responders, the fire department, and presidents of three local hospitals all working in sync, where they were normally competitors to each other.

I wanted the picture of all of us standing together with the shovel in my hand so that I could remember there was a day in December before Christmas when the whole community came together. Each of us took a shovel full of dirt and tossed it into the center, the crowd clapping and the photographs clicking. We all went to dinner at a catered Oddfellows Hall, overlooking the ocean in St. Petersburg.

The place had been an old fisherman hall, back in the days when early settlers built the coastal towns, set up their big houses, and conducted their fishing operations on individual piers, depending on what they could afford at the time. Most of the buildings that were used in those days were gone, but this one, built in the 1840s, remained. I was told it was the only one that did. Hurricanes had a way of leveling the playing field and just like roofs for houses weren't expected to last more than ten or twelve years, no matter what the material, piers and big wooden halls would always fall victim to angry wind and rain.

We were exhausted from all the preparations, and even though some of our civic leaders wanted to continue to party into the night, Shannon and I said our goodbyes and left.

I was looking forward to my first day back at the office.

"Boss!" said Dax. "I tried to straighten things up as best I could, but I'm just not talented like you are. I'm afraid you're going to find things a mess. I wasn't quite sure what day you'd be in. I mean, everything's in good shape. It's just not clean."

"I'm okay with that, Dax. I know you guys are working hard. Let's just see what you got. And judging from the pile of papers on my desk, looks like I better start at the top and go down."

"Well, we tried to send you messages on everything, and we've made a booklet of the change orders and the contracts. I really think you ought to review all those first. Your CFO signed and arranged for certain advanced payments that you agreed to, but I really want you to look at all the contracts. And maybe you'll see something we all missed."

"Sounds good to me."

She motioned for me to go into the conference room since my desk didn't have very much room for stacking files and going through paperwork. I had forgotten how beautiful the room was, looking out into the blue ocean, with the big billowy white and gray clouds out in the distance. I could see we were going to have rain soon, and I had noted a large population of dragonflies around Shannon's house and around our new home site, which always indicated there was going to be a change in weather soon. We even had butterflies this time of year, but I knew they would be done very soon.

She plopped several folders that were tabbed and held together with brads right in the center of the table in front of me.

"There you go. I've got all the underground orders, all the sub-contractors and the general engineering contracts for the project. On a separate file over here, I've got all their employment requirements that the county has asked us to make sure they adhere to. We want to hire veterans as much as possible, and we are to hire long-term unemployed for spaces we can."

"I understand. I knew that was going to be the case, and I totally approve."

"And then this book over here, the brown one, has a copy of all the building permits we've pulled, and I have tabs for each of the phases. You heard about the electrical contractor, right?"

"Yes, I think you told me."

"These guys are amazing. I mean they're like 'can we come over and just do this and can we get compensation to make an order.' I think they have pretty much all the materials they're going to need for the whole project. They've rented a storage facility in Tampa so they could store everything, and it's guarded twenty-four seven. I didn't realize this, but there have been a recent spate of break-ins at warehouses for construction yards, with supplies being limited. There's a pretty healthy trade in stealing other people's stuff."

I laughed at her commentary. "Other people's stuff, huh?"

"You know what I mean."

"I'll look these over. Are you going to be around in case I have questions?"

"I am, and if I'm not," she pulled out her cell phone, "just give me a ring."

"How are the wedding plans coming?"

Dax blushed before she added, "Well, we kind of were waiting for yours to be over first, because everything had to be working around this project and that trip. We've kind of put it on hold, just doing minimal amounts of things."

"You have a date?"

"Not yet, Boss. We're going to do that soon. I think we want to look and see what you guys do, and maybe we'll get some ideas."

I threw my head back and laughed at that suggestion. I didn't want to make fun of her, but I knew there wasn't going to be any possibility her wedding was going to look anything like ours. But I knew she liked to dream, and I considered it a good thing.

I went through over half of the early project permits, and I read all the proposals for contracts that weren't signed yet. We tried to do a competitive bidding process, but there were certain cases where it was going to be particularly good to choose one contractor over another. The biggest determination would be whether or not they had disabled employees. We had a steel fabricator who climbed all over tall office buildings in downtown Tampa as they were being built, ten- and twelve-story skyscrapers, and was disabled. He had no legs and used a rigging system to get up and down off of the buildings. I had read an article about that guy, and even though his price was a little higher than the two other bids we got, I put a note to make sure he was the one who got the job. And I didn't want anyone pressuring him to lower his price.

I received a call from Senator Campbell in Washington, DC.

"Senator, what can I do you for?"

"I understand you had quite a party yesterday. Everything going well?"

"Yes, I've got enough paperwork to choke a horse, but nothing like what you guys have, of course."

"Oh, tell me about it. Our rules for the budget committee this year are nearly eight inches thick. Those are just the rules. The regulations are, I think, about as thick as well. Honest to God, I think we'd be a greater country if we didn't put so much in writing."

"Damn, Senator, don't let anybody hear you say that."

"Oh, I'm well aware. You know, I learned a lot about butterflies after you took those pictures of some of the butterflies you have there in Florida. I was reading that the monarch has to eat milkweed. If the monarch lays her eggs on anything but a milkweed plant, the little baby caterpillar will die because that's the only plant it can eat. I got to thinking about that when I was looking at the piles of paper I had to send off to the shredder. After we review it and mark things up, then we have to get rid of it in a secure manner. But as I saw that huge cart, taking two big, strong guys to push, I thought to myself, we're just like monarch butterflies. We live on paperwork, right?"

"That's funny. Well, as long as you don't eat it, that is."

"It's the stuff we do. We live on it. I don't have to eat it to live on it."

"So how's your family? And you run into any more hotspots?"

"Well, I have to say I was a little disappointed that you weren't going to Nigeria. It's not gotten any better, but we could have used your intel, and it was good cover for some of our guys, but I don't blame you, and it's not exactly something that's going to work itself out right away. So yeah, it's still there, new ones coming all along. We've got some issues with drugs and human trafficking, just like before, but now we've run across several celebrity-type militia men in several of those countries who are targeting wealthy

Saudis and European businessmen. Even a Russian oligarch. Did you read about that?"

"I did. And their Wagner group wasn't even able to help, despite being ruthless themselves."

"Damn right. So there's big money in going after people like that. I think the trade is changing a bit. And high-value targets... I mean, let's face it, Marco. If somebody could kidnap the president of the United States, don't you think somebody might pay some money instead of telling everybody we don't negotiate with terrorists?"

I thought about that for a second. It was a horrible idea, but desperate times were creating desperate people.

"Well, until 9/11, nobody thought they would've flown planes into buildings and have them coordinated so well. At each level, they seem to up the game a bit, don't they, Senator?"

"It's hard to combat that, which means you're probably in a pretty good field. I mean, we're going to need guys like you forever. The world isn't going to go back to some utopian little small-town farm corncob pipe dream with everybody eating apple pie and vegetables out of their garden, right? We live in dangerous times. And the best we can do for our wives and daughters and families, the innocents, is to keep them prepared. Keep talking about it. We aren't going to be able to get them all."

"But they aren't going to be able to get all of us, either. And there are enough people like you and me, Senator. We're never going to quit."

"Okay, well, I'm going to try to get down and see you before you go overseas again, and you did get our RSVP for the wedding?"

"Yes, I saw it there. Is there anybody I forgot to invite that you think I should?"

"Well, knowing how you plan a party and knowing how the sultan is, I don't suppose you would mind one more couple. Would you mind inviting my son-in-law?"

"Your son-in-law? I don't think I've met him."

"Oh, he's on our committee. He graduated from law school but had a specialty in business, sharp kid. Now don't steal him, Marco, because we need him on the committee. But his jaw still drops when he breezes past the president or the vice president, and I think he would be tickled pink if he could come to that wedding. Of course, I'm paying for everything. I'm not allowing the sultan to bankroll that."

"I didn't know he was offering that. Really?"

"Yes, he did. Now don't tell anybody, because I don't know if he's offered it to others. But Beth and I, we're really looking forward to your wedding, and I really think I want this show of respect for the sultan, in light of his health. And you do know that I know he's on his last legs?"

"I figured. Not much gets by you, Senator."

"So his name is Dan Shay, and you can send him the invitation in care of the committee. Don't put any stupid notes on it like you forgot or anything like that. I'll just handle that myself and claim I have no idea why it came late. Maybe I'll tell him that it was there all along and I forgot to give it to him or something. But anyway, my daughter and my son-in-law would be forever grateful if they could come."

"You got it. So tell me about Africa. Who are the players then, anybody we've known from before?"

"Well, you did a pretty good job on the last bunch there, and we've had fairly good cooperation with a few of the militia leaders, bringing them some business. They're all anxious to get off the watch list and be able to do business in the United States. But the crazies are coming in. I think they get hopped up on something, and I'm not into that, so I have no idea what it is. The CIA tells us that it's a good thing and a bad thing. We have some of the bad guys dying from Fentanyl as well. But these people are ruthless. They are not necessarily the worst… they're just plain, ordinary garden variety criminals, but they get worse and worse. They're not doing it to protest or demand something. They're just doing it because they can, because they love to cheat and steal and ruin people's lives. If they could bring down a government or two, it's like a notch in their belt. Crazy people, really crazy people."

"So it sounds like maybe next year I might have another mission or two."

"You could be right. Don't hold your breath, though, but in my book, Marco, you're the best. I know there's competition, but there's no substitute for the best."

I returned a call from Dr. Tramel, who had left a message while I was on the phone with the senator.

"Marco, I'm just calling to give you an update. It appears that all his blood work is normal. And I've been in close contact with your Navy team over there, and they haven't seen a trace of strychnine pop into the palace for about ten days. So they were asking me if they should maybe come home. They're not my team, but because I think this particular scare is over, it might be a good idea. But it's up to you."

"Yeah, I think they can come home. What does the sultan want?"

"Oh my gosh, I'm trying to get him to go on a diet. He's feeling pretty good about himself, and he eats too much fat and too much Western food for his Indian insides. That little problem with them with the yellow curry kind of took his appetite away from curry for a while, but it'll probably come back. But he's eating steak and mashed potatoes and all kinds of things I guess you introduced him to here in Florida. He doesn't much like fish, but he loves crab. I understand they've been flying over blue crabs and grouper and all kinds of things so he could keep his Florida vacation going a little bit longer. It's kind of funny when you think about it, though."

"I get you. Well, I think he should enjoy himself. His ETA still about a month, two months?"

"I think he might have a little longer than that, but it all depends on what happens. He might get a cold, flu, or COVID. I'm most worried about the wedding and the crowd there. I'm not worried about the crowd turning on him and trying to kill him or anything, but I'm worried about what he could pick up. You're going to have people from all over the world there, Marco. You know that, right?"

"I do. And I noticed you're not on the reservation list, so are you coming or not?"

"I've got a conflict, but I think I'm going to try to make it. I don't think my wife will, but I'll come. I feel like I should. I want to give him a checkup, and I also want to double-check the lab in Mumbai."

"The lab? Why?"

"Well, I've understood there is a Chinese concern that has been purchasing laboratories, and we had a group here in Tampa try to purchase a string of labs. They do a lot of DNA testing. We're kind of concerned about the medical database that's being created by some of these organizations. I just want to walk through the lab and actually look at them, because since this transfer happened about two weeks ago, the communication's been totally different. They're not as quick to get back to me, and I'm not getting my questions answered. So I'm going to stop by for a day and just do a tour, just have them show me what they do. They send out these medical devices and kits, and I recommended them to someone who was doing some work in South America, and the kits were a mess. They came partially broken, incomplete. It was bad. And I think the guy spent over ten thousand dollars ordering this stuff. So something's happened over there, and I'm going to check it out."

"Well, I don't like the sound of that, Doc. You better go with somebody."

"A couple of your guys there said they'd be happy to do it. And I think that's what I'll do. Thanks, if you can allow that to happen."

"No problem. I'm all for it. So will I see you before the wedding or are you just going to show up?"

"No, I think I'll see you there. You take care. If you hear anything concerning the sultan, because I'm not sure he tells me everything… If you get any information from any of those wives that love you so much—"

"Watch it, Doc. You know I'm not that way."

"Yes, I know, but they might tell you something they may not tell me. So if you get an inkling about anything, you let me know, okay?"

"Absolutely. It's a deal. I'm going to sit down with you. We'll put our feet in the water and have a nice longneck beer when I see you next. How about that?"

"You got it, Marco. Take care."

CHAPTER 12

AFTER THE GROUNDBREAKING ceremony, Shannon noticed a big uptick in "drop by" appearances, unannounced by media and their staff. Videos and photographs were taken at the site as they began their first pours. There were offers of TV interviews, and even Shannon's former Tampa television station begged her to come back and do some exclusive interviews. She was going to ask Rebecca if perhaps she'd like to do that, figuring it might be good for her to get out of the office.

She'd noticed Marco's ex had been not her usual self and appeared to be mildly depressed. At best, quiet. But she wasn't sure and certainly didn't want to ask.

With all the increased scrutiny, Marco wisely put extra details on all of them. Shannon was getting used to the idea of waking up and going for a run on the beach with two former Navy SEALs at her side. In her old days, she would have relished the opportunity to get to know some handsome, young fit men. But now it made her feel embarrassed. They were extremely well-behaved, and she suspected that they knew exactly how she felt.

Marco must be having a field day watching me.

There were new faces around the office, as several additional staffers were added, especially to deal with the public scrutiny. They hired a media copy editor to handle press releases. Various officials from all the little towns up and down the Gulf Coast made an appearance, had to be seen shaking Marco's hand with the cranes and cement trucks in the background.

While she was pleased that support for the Trident Towers had skyrocketed, she wasn't so sure she was ready for all the notoriety.

When she came into the office in the morning, Rebecca was waiting for her.

"Can I have a little bit of your attention please? Alone?" Rebecca said, eyeing the handsome fellow to Shannon's right.

He was quick to understand without making them feel awkward.

"Listen, let me go get you guys some waters or do you want coffee or tea?" he asked.

"Coffee, and I think, Rebecca, you want coffee, as well?"

"Absolutely. Overdo it with the cream."

After her security detail left, Rebecca leaned into Shannon, whispering, "How do you get them to do that? Nice as all get out, handsome, built, and just decent. You know, in my younger days, I wouldn't have been interested in that type. Now that I'm older? I could do without the drama."

"I've heard stories, Rebecca."

"I'll bet you have. But, boy, I enjoyed myself way back then."

Shannon smiled. "Come on in. We'll leave the door open so he can bring our coffee."

They situated themselves on either side of Shannon's messy desk. Their coffee was served, the door closed, and they were finally alone.

"What's on your mind, Rebecca?"

Shannon was wondering if she was going to make a request about the wedding and the fact that she did not get an invitation. She was not looking forward to having to explain it to her but promised herself she would own up and be straightforward. Rebecca was not welcome at the sultan's palace, and Marco didn't want to have anything to do with her, either.

"I'm sure you've noticed things here have changed quite a bit. And I'm happy with that. I'm happy for all of you." Rebecca hesitated.

"But you are not happy here?" Shannon asked her.

"Well, I do have a history quite different than yours, Shannon. And I'm just not sure it's my thing. I mean, I like the attention; I get that it's important in order to get the support we need for the project, but I'm just not feeling this is where I need to be. I've decided I want to go back to New York."

Shannon was shocked. "New York?"

"Oh, come on now. You know I love New York. I always will love New York. I need the city. You don't see me running around here in flip-flops and shorts, and I certainly don't wear a skimpy bathing suit at my age." Rebecca laughed as she named all the things she didn't enjoy about Florida.

"Nor do I," ventured Shannon. "Flip-flops, yes, but a skimpy bathing suit? No, thanks."

"Hanging out at the bar and having older men in their sixties hit on me, drunk and in need of sex, is not my idea of meeting somebody new. I love the city life there. I love the restaurants. Sure, here you have a lot of casual restaurants, but it's just not New York, is it?"

"It definitely is not New York. You've got me there."

"I'm going to head out. And in anticipation of this discussion, I went over all my files with my number two, and I think Connie's going to do a great job in my place, if that's what you decide to do. In any event, she's up to speed. She probably knows some of the things better than I do. She's got a good flare for space and texture and design, and she spends way more time with those SEALs than I do these days, so I think she's a better choice to run your design team."

"I'm really surprised, Rebecca. I thought you wanted to be part of this project."

"Well, that was before we got all this media attention. You forget, I have a past. It kind of follows me around a bit."

Shannon knew what she was talking about. When they'd offered Rebecca to be interviewed, there was a string of reporters who refused to take it due to how she had treated them in the past. She was known to beat up the press, belittling them, and didn't seem to mind the flack she got as a result. As far as being a spokesperson, their PR person, she wasn't really helping the project that much. But still, Shannon was surprised.

"What will you do?" Rebecca gave her a stare like she was made from a pile of rotten banana peels. Shannon corrected herself, sat up straight, and added, "Not that there aren't hundreds and hundreds of jobs you could take, Rebecca. I just mean, what is it that makes you excited about going back there? Surely it must be some kind of job situation or some kind of opportunity."

Rebecca nodded. She finished her coffee, set it down on the saucer, and placed the saucer at the edge of Shannon's desk. Crossing her legs, she folded her hands together. "I'm going to go into the consulting business. Design renovation, that sort of thing. I have a nest egg to work with, and I may even decide to buy and renovate office buildings, office complexes with good bones that need help. Perhaps become a commercial landlord. Or design, fix them up, and sell them. I'm not sure. I could be a consultant for others wanting to spruce up their image or their look. I think I have a taste for that. I'm also hungering to work with other people in business."

Shannon got the implication that perhaps their beachfront-casual company was not really something she enjoyed much. She'd never considered that.

"So do you have some clients in mind?"

"Not yet. I haven't really started putting feelers out. I needed to talk to you first. I want to make sure we're okay, the two of us. Marco and I will never be okay, and I understand he will never trust me, and that's probably a good thing. Given the opportunity, who knows, I might go back to that blood sport."

This alarmed Shannon.

Rebecca must have noticed her change in demeanor.

"Oh, don't get scared, Shannon. I'm just messing with you a little bit. I like fighting. But I like to win if I fight. There is no winning in this game with Marco, only losing. And I have a feeling I would be the one to lose. With you though, it's not a game like that. You've always accepted me straight on, even when everybody else didn't. And I appreciate that."

"Thank you, Rebecca. That's very kind."

"But that can be a flaw. Be careful, Shannon. Don't trust everybody you think you can."

"Are you saying there's something I need to know here?"

"No, nothing of the kind. But your trusting nature makes you naïve. Being naïve sometimes makes you less powerful. I think you're okay with it, because that's not what you seek. You're basically a healer, a support person. You can take the lead, but you prefer to be the one behind the leader, don't you?"

Shannon knew most women would take offense at that comment. She did not. "I think you've got me pegged correctly."

"I, on the other hand, like to be in charge. Running my own company will be a lot more fun than ruining Marco's. I want to make a name for myself on my own. And I think this is a good time; this is my opportunity to do that."

Shannon completely understood and agreed with her.

"I'm going to miss you, Rebecca. I think you're doing the right thing. And I wish you all the success in the world. If there's anything I can do to help you, just let me know."

They both stood, like professional businesswomen, shaking hands—no hugs, no kisses or crying. Just a clean break, a separation, each side maintaining the dignity they'd earned.

And regardless of who got to marry Marco, Shannon knew that both of them loved him dearly.

I truly hope she'll find that special someone like I have.

CHAPTER 13

I WAS AT the jobsite meeting early with several subcontractors. I helped figure out the source of a couple of problems with scheduling. We readjusted two due dates, and then I wrote down the notes so I could update the computer program back at the office. I was scanning the site for the two brothers and came up empty.

Sam was sitting in his wheelchair, talking to two vets who had asked for a little pre-tour.

"Hey, Sam, have you seen Absalom and Khalil yet this morning?"

He straightened himself up in the wheelchair. "No, they were out last night, celebrating. You know that they got the bride-price settled for the girl, right?"

"Yes, I heard that, and I'm relieved it finally happened."

I had wanted them to officially pay the fee demanded when the boys left India with the young dancer. Well, it wasn't really a kidnapping, but they had offered her money to travel with them to the United States from India for a chance at a better life. She was a beautiful, exotic Indian troupe dancer, and Khalil had fallen head over heels in love with her, although there was quite a difference in their upbringing.

The sultan had been furious with his son but didn't have the heart to separate them. I knew that a bride-price would be requested, and I also knew that, if they didn't accept the terms offered, the boys would be in deep trouble. The sultan could possibly make her go home. Nobody wanted that.

They'd negotiated the deal, and I was under the impression that, with my security detail, they had arranged the payment details. They invited me to the celebration, but I declined. The dancing and drinking until all hours of the morning wasn't something I was really interested in doing.

"So do you think it has to do with that, Marco?"

It hit me that it could be a definite possibility and kicked myself for not thinking about it earlier. Here, we'd just gotten over the sultan's poisoning, and now we might have a situation with his sons. I was sickened at the thought.

"I think that's a bridge too far." But inside, my gut was telling me something else.

I had promised my support and protection and had five of my best guys on those three, practically showering and sleeping with everybody. They were never to be out of my detail's sight. If something occurred, that meant maybe my guys were in danger as well.

"Have you seen Kurt, Reggie, or Connor?" I asked.

"Nope. But you know, maybe they're just sleeping it off somewhere. They've been late before."

"Yeah, but not after negotiating a bride-price with a bunch of bandits in India. I don't like this. I'm going to call a team meeting. If you hear anything, give me a call please," I asked Sam.

"You got it."

Before I turned to go, I nodded to the two wheelchaired vets in front of me. "I'm sorry I didn't introduce myself. I'm Marco Gambini, and it will be our pleasure to design you a home far beyond your wildest dreams. That's our mission. Unfortunately, that also means we have to work with a lot of people, and things fall through the cracks occasionally. I'm sure this is just a minor hiccup."

"Before my accident, I worked construction from the time I was about ten," said the younger of the two. He was a bright towhead with big blue eyes. His light complected skin was already getting red from the sun. "I've always wanted to live in Florida. And when I found out about this project, I chose to come down and shack up with my buddy here. And he got me in the door."

"Well, good for you. Good day, gents."

While I was running to my car, I made texts to the detail team without an answer and got on the phone with my head of security.

"I'm getting a bad feeling about Khalil and Absalom being missing this morning from the jobsite. Tell me you know something about it that makes sense," I said to Jeffrey.

"Marco, I wish I did. I know they were partying, and you know how those guys get. But they've been better lately. Have you tried to get the detail team?"

"Yeah, I just tried on my way over here. Nobody is picking up. Where were they last night, do you know?"

"Let's see. I think it was the Blue Crab Grill?"

"Okay, I've got the number. You let me know if you hear anything please, and I want you to call your entire team, put the word out. Anybody knows anything, I want to hear about it right away. Can we meet back at the office in about an hour?"

"You want everybody or just the heads?"

"If they're on assignment, they stay where they are. But they check in with you, okay? Otherwise, I'd like all the heads of your departments who are not assigned. I need some extra eyes and ears, and I need some good ideas and fast. If this breaks into a full-scale hostage situation, I've already lost time."

I called several other team guys and had someone run over to the house Khalil and Absalom lived in, who reported back that it didn't look like anybody had been there since last night. The beds were not made, but the showers were dry. The detail team and their two cars were also gone.

Once I arrived at the office, without greeting anyone, including Shannon, I closed my office door and sat, placing a call to Bonin. My head of security there picked it up before it rang twice.

"Everything okay over there?" I asked him.

"Yep. But that kind of a question means it's not okay over

there. Or am I making things up?"

"I can't find Khalil and Absalom. And the three guys I had with them last night are missing as well. I'm fearing something bad. Please tell me I'm being stupid about this."

"No, you're not being stupid about it, Marco. You probably have the best sixth sense of anybody I've ever worked for. But if you're looking for something here that might have spilled over to your part of the world, I don't see it. Everything's been quiet. He's been taking good care of himself. The women seem to be fine, a little quiet too, but busy with the wedding details and attending to their spaces. They have big plans to decorate the great hall, their quarters, the sultan's bedroom, and the honeymoon house."

"Any changes in the staff or anybody being squirrelly? And whatever happened with the kid and Meera?"

"They didn't call you?"

"No, they sure didn't. Who was supposed to call me?"

"Well, the imperial guard in Cochin agreed to place him in a safer prison situation than he normally would've been thrown in. I'm not sure whether it was the sultan's doing or Meera herself pleading for his health. But in any event, the trial was quick, two days, and he was sentenced to twenty years for attempted murder."

"Oh my God, twenty years?"

"Yep. We all expected hanging. I guess the fact that he'd been conscripted to serve in the military saved his life. It's just a guess. You want to know the rest of it?"

"They didn't give time to Meera, did they?"

"It was a shakedown. She was fined, and my understanding is one of the sultan's wives paid the fine."

I knew what that meant. The sultan paid it himself.

"So is she staying in Cochin or going back to her family in Mumbai?"

"She's gone to Mumbai to be with her family, those that are left. I believe she has a job working for a large house."

"As staff?"

"Marco, you know how this goes. She was the wife of the sultan, for a certain period of time, and she did the unthinkable. But the problem, the boy, he's locked up, so there really is no problem anymore. One of the sultan's friends, a wealthy businessman from Mumbai, has taken her into his household, yes, as staff. But I doubt she'll ever have to wash a diaper or clean a window."

Marco knew that's the way it was. No wonder no one from his house informed him of the trial or about Meera. Things were worked out. People didn't talk about it upfront. It was just done as a backroom deal, as a favor, sort of a saving of face. She did pay the price for her indiscretion, although it was slight. She would never be given the kind of responsibility she had at one time or the opportunity. But this assured her that she didn't have to starve or beg or do something awful on the streets of Mumbai. She would've been better off to go to prison than have to do that.

"I want to hear when she's located, okay? And I also would like you to maintain contact with somebody at the prison. I want to make sure that he stays there. It's part of our responsibility with the sultan that if he should ever be let free, we are alerted to it immediately so we can take precautions."

"I understand completely. We will do that."

"Well, I need to go," Marco said as he looked downstairs at the plaza right outside the front doors of the office building. A messenger was bringing a leather pouch into the lobby. He was a private courier service, and he knew that pouch would be searched thoroughly.

"I think I'm about to get some kind of news. I don't think I'm going to like it," said Marco.

"Let's hope and pray you're wrong. But let me know please. If there's anything you want me to do or not do, please tell me."

"You are not to tell the sultan or any of the wives yet. You can tell a few of the trusted team leaders, but no word to any of the staff or the wives or the sultan until I give the okay. Is that understood?"

"Absolutely, sir."

I walked to the doorway, opening it, and watched as the courier made his way through our upstairs lobby quarters, accompanied by my front office receptionist.

"Marco, this gentleman has a special letter that needs to be hand-delivered to you." The attractive older woman had unmistakable worry lines in her forehead, the edges of her eyes squinting, her upper lip curled up slightly in disgust.

"That's okay. Let's give the gentleman a chance to do his duty." I turned to the young man. "What do you have for me?"

"I have a letter, and I need a signature from Marco Gambini."

"That's me. Do you need to see identification?"

"Yes, please."

I reached into my back pocket and produced my Florida license and also showed him my concealed carry permit. "Do you want to see my insurance card, my blood type, or my passport?"

The boy didn't comment, wrote down the number of my driver's license on a clipboard, put an X in a box, and handed it to me. "Sir, if you will sign right there where I've indicated, I will give you the letter."

I did so and was handed the cream-colored expensive stationery I knew didn't come from an office supply store. Then he handed me his business card. The gentleman turned around and my receptionist accompanied him back to the elevator. Once I opened the thick cotton velum, three single lines of typing jumped out at me, with no signature block underneath. I read the lines carefully.

We have Khalil and Absalom.

They are as yet unharmed, but we have three injured security detail who say they work for you.

We will be in touch as to the terms we will require in order to return the two brothers to their father.

I noted they didn't say anything about my security team members.

CHAPTER 14

T HE SECOND-FLOOR OFFICE building complex was turned into a command center almost immediately. After having spent years working together, both inside the company and as part of SEAL Team 3 in Marco's early days, the group of men who set things up worked together as one cohesive hive unit. Very little was said. They showed each other certain things as they sat down together at a table to troubleshoot what had to be done. There was the spirit of cooperation and working to connect the cables, to load the data, to print out and analyze the information very quietly. No shouting, no arguing, no bosses, just a group of men working together to put the network in play.

Shannon could see how their SEAL training had created the environment for them to trust each other and learn how to fit in where they could. They didn't have to be perfect at everything, but they learned to fit in and do what they could do without worrying about what they couldn't.

Shannon was stunned at the humility and the lack of confrontation, even though the situation was extremely stressful.

She stayed out of Marco's way, only because she didn't want to distract him. But on several occasions, he came up to her, rubbed her shoulders, or gave her a kiss on the neck, just to let her know he was grateful for her help.

It didn't take long before they identified the players of the kidnap group who had been canvassing the office building, the construction site, and the homes that Khalil and Absalom lived at for several days prior. But they still didn't know who they were.

Marco had tagged the cars and the cell phones of his security team. He also had installed a locator chip in Absalom and Khalil's cell phones. The surveillance cameras outside of their houses were extremely helpful, giving them great facial and physical detail of some of the players.

After pouring over the material, it became obvious to Marco's team that the crew was a hired group of professional mercenaries. Shannon heard the team talking about possibilities, discussing the various groups they'd encountered before, and trying to pin one. Several spoke about how they were an imported group from outside the US, perhaps Russia or China, and that they were expert at hostage removal and negotiation.

"Let's hope they don't know who they're dealing with," Marco whispered over one man's shoulder as they studied a surveillance tape.

One of the men commented, "I've seen these guys before."

"Where?"

"Nigeria. About two years ago. Ruthless guys. Ice water in their veins. Leave a lot of bodies behind. But they are effective through the use of violence and intimidation."

"Sounds like the Wagner Group to me," said another team guy.

"This is a little far for them to travel," mentioned another.

Shannon knew the Wagner Group were paid mercenaries from Russia, war-torn areas of the Eastern Bloc countries, and the worst of the worst from Africa.

Marco paced behind the screens. "Okay, so if we have the Wagner Group, then I need to call Washington."

He grabbed Shannon by the arm and took her into his office, closing the door. "Been wanting to do this all day and just haven't found the time," he said as he kissed her. Shannon was swooning, her knees wobbling from his deep passionate kiss that left her breathless.

He dialed Senator Campbell, who picked up right away. Marco

was direct. "So we've got the Wagner Group involved in the kidnapping of the sultan's two sons here in Indian Rocks. I may need some help, and I sure as Hell could use some advice."

"Oh my God, that's not good. I would normally ask how they got into the country, but as we all know, we've got a problem that way. You're by the Gulf, so I'm guessing they might have even made a landing underwater. What do you think, Marco?"

"Yeah, that would be possible. It's also probably a good way to extract. We've been monitoring the surveillance footage we set up. These guys are well-trained, have plenty of sophisticated equipment, and know how to use it. Now my question to you is these guys are hired killers, so if some of them, one of them, two of them, all of them wind up meeting their end, what kind of a problem is that going to be for us? Do I have to capture them or are we licensed to kill?"

"I'm going to have to check on that. My authorization doesn't quite go that high, but I would say definitely if you have to defend yourself or you feel there's an imminent danger to one of your team or to the boys, take your shot. And we'll do the best we can to back you up. What I don't want is some big explosion or firefight in the middle of Crabby Bill's or down at the flea market on a weekend morning, scaring the tourists like crazy. That's what I don't want."

"Understood. I'll keep you informed. We may need some support from the air? Any chance we could get some surveillance pictures? You got any drones flying over here?"

"Think you guys probably have better ones than we do, but I will see if I can arrange some big eyes for you. Any reason to assume this is something other than just a straight hostage situation?"

"You mean like smuggling humans, drugs, or something like that?" Marco asked.

"That's right. Might give our Coasties a little chance to insert themselves if that was the case. Of course, you could always suspect it and then wind up being wrong. That'd be another way to do it, but keep us posted and let me know what you need, and I'll see what I can do. I'll start alerting and setting fires over here."

Marco told Shannon he was very grateful he'd cultivated such a powerful friend, and he hoped that if, unofficially, part of the US government could help back him up, he would have a better chance of pulling this off.

"Have you ever run across these guys before?" she asked.

"Not when I was on the Teams. They weren't created yet. But as a civilian, we have. Sometimes it's hard to tell since they are a secret group and they get in and out quietly, not like a militia group who just shoot and blast their way into an arena." He paused. "How you holding up, sweetheart?"

"Don't think my heart has stopped lobbing inside and outside my chest. Wish I could be as calm as you are. All of you—"

"That's how we do it," he said, brushing across her lips. "Come on. Let's get back and see what they've come up with."

After the surveillance footage was analyzed, one of the technicians determined that the computers Khalil and Absalom had used to communicate with the office had been hacked. An unknown I.P. address had been inserted, which was worrisome, but also gave them an opportunity. First, this indicated their level of skill was higher than they'd expected, but it also gave them an address the team could go after, to trace and perhaps pull that thread to find out information about the enemy.

"They've been watching all of their communications and also the negotiations," someone said to Marco.

Another engineer brought up his theory. "Could just be they wanted to make sure there was no back-channel way they were going to sabotage the money exchange. Maybe they just wanted to confirm the cops weren't involved or the federal government wasn't going to jump in on them? Could be as innocent as that?"

"It could be," Marco sighed. "But we have to assume they have compromising information. We are not doing anything defense-wise luckily, with this project, but we're going to have to break all communication with this office so they don't get access to personal files for any outside jobs we are doing elsewhere in the world. I can't risk our data centers being compromised. And these guys are good at it."

It was added to the to-do list, not something that was going to get the boys back, but it was something they were going to have to deal with after everything either blew up or worked out.

One of the surveillance videos showed two men unloading scuba gear, including rebreathers, leaving the equipment selectively around foliage and sand dunes that edged the Gulf. In the back of the van, they noticed what looked like ammunition and the unmistakable shape of a .50 cal already set up on its stand. That told Marco, and he demonstrated it to the whole team, that loss of life wasn't out of the question for these guys. Perhaps their final farewell parting gift was going to be the elimination of as many people on the team as possible, including the boys.

"How much was the bride-price, Marco?" someone asked.

Marco asked his head of security to help him out.

"Four million. They brought it in cash and were to deliver it just before they went to dinner. Connor sent me a picture of the drop, and none of the guys who took possession of the cash are in any of this footage. It's another team altogether."

"That makes sense. So they got away with the money, then."

Shannon offered to prepare some coffee, which was welcome. She asked if she should have some food brought in or if they wanted to work straight through. She knew sometimes Marco wouldn't eat for days while he was trying to solve a problem.

The group agreed that an order for food would be fantastic. Shannon took two of the men downstairs to the storage room where they had bottles of water and other supplies, including medical kits, and had them brought up to the second floor, where they also created a quiet room out of one vacant office, adding several cots. Marco had explained people could be taking turns resting and watching until they worked out a solution.

She ordered some pizzas, a bunch of hand-held snacks, and a few sandwiches from a local deli. She was going to go pick them up, but Marco wouldn't allow her to leave the building. It would all be delivered to the downstairs center and received by members of the team.

As the unit pieced together what they could, one by one, little details became clear. The puzzle was being solved. The group determined that all the cell phones had been destroyed at the same time. So there was no back-channel way for them to follow or tag them, and there was no way they could activate the listening devices to hear conversations even while the phone was turned off.

The grounds over at the brothers' houses were searched by another unit of three men, and while sorting through bits of trash and cigarette butts planted around the perimeter, someone found a wrapper from mints at a restaurant. This restaurant overlooked the water in Clearwater, right next to the marina, which was chock-full of huge yachts and motorboats. There was a flotilla or race set up for the weekend, so the area was unusually packed with imported boaters and audience.

"That's a good lead. Go search the restaurant; see if they've seen any of these guys." Marco then sent them photos of various members of the group caught on surveillance video.

Shannon arranged the food on their beautiful conference room table, placing the waters out next to a tray with ice. She also made pitchers of ice water as well as two pitchers of iced tea. The blackout shades were pulled so that there would be no lights showing from the outside. They wanted to keep hidden all the activity going on for now to not make themselves a target, unless they already were.

Marco received another call from Senator Campbell and retired to his office to take it.

Shannon walked behind the desks and the monitors, watched telemetry results, heat signatures, and images she wasn't used to seeing. It was an incredible array of equipment. And she had no idea that Marco possessed all these things. She knew everything was stored in the equipment room downstairs, but she had never had an opportunity to see it.

Then she thought about Rebecca and wondered if she'd made it to New York, hoping that somehow she didn't get snagged. She figured Marco wouldn't mind her making the call, but she decided to ask anyway.

"Yeah, you can call her, it's probably what you would've done normally, but just don't tell her anything about this. This information isn't to get outside this room."

"I figured as much. So I'm going to go in my office and do it."

She left the beehive and sat at her own desk after closing the door, relieved to have some peace and quiet at last. Dialing Rebecca's number, Marco's feisty ex picked up on the first ring.

"I hope you haven't changed your mind about letting me go, but you probably know there's nothing you could do to make me stay. Or maybe I'm just being egotistical. How are you doing, Shannon?" Rebecca asked.

Shannon stumbled a bit but managed to get out, "Oh, I'm good. I just wanted to make sure you got to New York and that you're safe."

"I am, and what makes you concerned for my safety? What's going on?"

"Oh, nothing. Well, Marco's working late, and I just thought I'd give you a call and make sure you got there. That's all."

"I'm staying at the Waldorf. It's no secret. If you need to reach me later, and my cell doesn't answer, you can leave a message at the hotel. My rental isn't ready until the end of the month so I'll be staying here a while. I can't wait to get out, walk the streets, and enjoy the sites again. I have to admit I feel a sense of freedom."

"I'm glad."

Relieved that everything appeared to be in order, she decided to make sure the food was fully stocked and asked Marco again if there was anything she could do.

"I think we're going to be here awhile. More coffee. And would you mind whipping up a miracle or two?"

"You think everyone is still alive?"

"For now. When they don't need them is when we start to worry. But we gotta find them first. We're on it."

CHAPTER 15

T HE RESTAURANT TURNED out to be just as I'd thought, a really smart tip. Several staffers, recognizing several faces on the videos, indicated there had been a group of men who had dined with them and also took several meals in take-out. One of the staffers recalled two of the group wandered down the plankway of the boat harbor but didn't see if they returned or jumped on board a boat there.

I directed six more assets, who approached the restaurant and harbor, one of them releasing a small, hand-held drone. I was pleased with footage that came back. The drone was small and nearly silent, looking like a medium-sized bird as it sailed up and down the pier, taking shots of the interior of several of the larger crafts who might be able to stow away equipment and prisoners. They got several heat signatures, but one nearly forty-foot ocean-worthy yacht showed five stationery figures lying prone. It was impossible to see much detail, but they had five live bodies show-ing up.

Despite the unaccounted for body, the team at the office went wild.

I directed the team to search the surrounding area, since the harbor was bordered by a City of Clearwater public park, filled with foliage and tall trees casting shadows. We were searching for snipers, extra men tasked with protection of the vessel. We already knew there were two armed men on deck, inside. Time was of the essence, since from afar, the protection team might have been able to see or detect the drone. I was worried they'd get word to the men holding the hostages or, worse, call in a bigger team for defense.

The sky was turning bright rose-orange but was devoid of clouds this night, and as soon as it was dark, we'd hit.

I got word the team had spotted a sniper on top of a building in a small strip mall of boutique shops. He was Target 1. Two others were identified in the park. One was sitting, the other casually jogging but craning his neck toward the boat on too many occasions. He ran past the bench-sitter twice before the team identified him as one of the men loading scuba gear. So he was Target 2. The benchwarmer became Target 3. Another man was identified sitting in a parked car facing the harbor, using a powerful single scope and surveilling the waterway and crafts in front of him. When he spoke into a collar wire, he became Target 4.

I knew there should be more. Darkness was beginning to descend on the area. The restaurant was closing, and the lights inside were turned off. As the staff left, the team scrutinized the help, matching them to the numbers they knew were there from their visit earlier.

I waited, planning on waiting thirty minutes, which made me nervous as all hell. But then a flashlight was spotted inside the restaurant, coming from the kitchen area, and I knew we had the other man, who apparently had slipped in during their dinner and found a hiding place until closing time.

He was labeled Target 5.

"Draper, you ready at the restaurant?"

"Roger that, sir."

"On my mark, gents. We go in five. Be locked and loaded."

Now was not the time for questions, and I was relieved nobody had one. They knew what to do. Lethal force would only be used if it was necessary. Stealth and silence were our primary goals, eliminating the threat to our team who was going to breach the ship and rescue the hostages.

I felt the command center holding their collective breaths.

Shannon sat next to me, handing me a cold water bottle I pushed away. I checked my watch. It was go time.

"On my mark—three, two, one, go."

Instantly, the team acted as one unit. Simultaneously, the benchwarmer, the jogger, and the man in the car were overtaken, each doused with a tranquilizer shot to the neck. The sniper caught wind something was going on, adjusted his site toward the park, and tapped his earpiece just before my man hit the side of his head, shattering the device and probably giving him a nice-sized concussion before he could utter a word.

Draper reported in since we had no visual on him. Target 5 was neutralized.

I ordered the team to breach, and within thirty seconds, a con-cussive flash device had been lobbed through an open window in the cabin. The two semi-conscious guards were also dosed, hogtied, and gagged.

I held my breath as the report came in. Indeed, Absalom, Kha-lil, and the girl were alive but drugged. They would have to be carried out. On the other side, two of my men remained, both wounded. A third was missing, and my stomach fell to my ankles. I hoped it wasn't the scenario I had envisioned. But until I got proof, I wasn't going to assume anything.

I ordered more assets in, plus the van. The detail was loaded inside, all seven of them headed for the FBI complex in Tampa.

My two men were transported for medical treatment at Mor-ton Plant hospital, one of them being shot. Both had lost a lot of blood.

But the hostages were unharmed, as the caller had said. We needed to find that caller, as perhaps my man's life was at stake.

The brothers and Absalom's four-million-dollar future love-dancer-turned-bride were being escorted back to the office building.

It was too early to celebrate, because we were still down one man with no idea where to search. But, shortly after arriving at the FBI building, one of the men admitted to being a new member of the Wagner Group. In exchange for some kind of deal, he revealed the location of my injured team guy and the caller. I was asked to stand down and allow the FBI to handle the raid, which I had to comply with, but waited with baited breath.

But we were hopeful.

It took over an hour before we got the news that the subject had been placed under FBI custody, and my man had been badly injured and left for dead. He was taken to the Level 1 trauma center at Tampa General and was expected to live.

The cheering started almost immediately after we heard word. I allowed a few moments of mirth to creep into my body before I had the task of making my list of the people I had to call. Of course, Senator Campbell was at the top. I would let my team call first, and then I'd follow up calling the families of my men in the hospital.

Shannon wrapped her arms around me and hugged me from behind.

"You did it, Marco. I got to see it all."

I turned. "No, we did it. I'm nothing without this team. These things never happen like we plan, but we plan every which way from Sunday, and hopefully, it's enough. Tonight, we were lucky."

LUCKY. I KNEW that we'd been lucky. It was all too easy, almost as if it had been a setup. But we had been prepared. We had tripled our security presence, and we had installed surveillance every-where. I was glad we didn't have to call on the Navy or the Coast Guard or even the local police or Feds, except for detaining the Wagner guys. The State Department was going to be interested in interviewing them, and I knew that they were going to have to be the ones to determine why they got hired and by whom.

But the looming question in my mind was how was this going to affect the sultan, long-term. I began to realize why he hadn't made a big thing about passing on his kingdom to his kids, because now I saw that, although he had been a very powerful ruler and his family unbelievably wealthy for generations, each new generation adding to the wealth of the previous, the world had changed. Even though the sultan had done everything right to protect his legacy, it would not be possible to keep him completely safe. And I didn't like admitting that. Because we weren't talking about somebody's safety on a mission or during a project or a battle. What we were talking about was making sure that wherever they came after the sultan and tried to hit him, that we were prepared. And there was just no fucking way that could happen. The bad guys always had a vote. They always got to change their mind, and they got to act when they felt like it, not when we were ready to take them on.

So I knew it was something I had to discuss with the sultan. And I wasn't necessarily excited about it. I needed to think about it a little bit more.

Maybe he knew this, maybe that's why he invited us to have the wedding at his palace. Perhaps he knew I wasn't going to be able to take on a job like his protection for the rest of his life or to ensure there would be something left for everybody else. I think he understood the impossibility of what he really wanted.

And now, for the first time, I saw it as well.

I'd always thought he'd been too casual about things and too worried about others.

I'd noticed a change in him when I invited him to come to Florida. Ten years ago, when we first began working together, he would've never considered taking a trip like that or walking on the beach with number one, the other wives trailing behind. But he was doing lots of things he didn't used to do. Because he knew he wouldn't be here for the second phase of the operation.

"I'll be God-damned. You son of a bitch. You're smarter than I am, aren't you?" I said.

The imaginary sultan I was talking to laughed in my face.

"Who are you talking to, Marco?" Shannon asked.

"I'm rehearsing a speech. No worries. Hey, listen, I have some calls to make. Can I have a couple of guys take you home? I don't know how long I'll be."

"I'd rather stay."

"The excitement's over. Now comes the paperwork. You don't need to stay for that."

I was lying, of course. But I wanted to be free to express myself to the team and to my callers, and some of what I was going to say, I knew she wouldn't understand.

Shannon agreed.

Before I called the sultan, I dialed Senator Campbell.

"I was relieved to hear it went well, Marco. On the issue of the Wagner Group, it definitely indicates an escalation. I even had a discussion with the Secretary of Defense, and I won't allow this to be quoted, but he seemed to think this was a pre-operational ruse, a foil. He thinks they hired a B team just to see what they'd be experiencing, and when they hire the A team, they'll know better what to do."

Now my apprehension about how we'd been too lucky returned, but there was a valid reason for it.

"What you're saying is this is going to be their plan of attack then? This is going to be how they destabilize certain factions, scare the population?"

"Exactly. They have many ways to get into this country, and we've been advertising it pretty much twenty-four seven in the news. But they can get in by boat, plane, or walk right across the border. They can come from Canada, and they will. The Secretary says he's gotten good intel that small teams are being trained to come in by submarine. They've been spotted all year just far enough off of the coast, primarily the Eastern coast of the United States, where their radar can jam. There are, especially in the Florida coast, so many shipwrecks and coral reefs that they can maneuver undetected if they're small enough. I wish we could've gotten you guys in the water, but I'm sure there will be a next time, Marco. We're still guessing until we have the proof, and we're working on it."

"Hope those B teamers give you good intel. Maybe some of them will fill in the blanks for you."

"Believe me, our guys are going to work these guys over and get what they can. But he thinks, and I agree, these aren't the top picks. These people were never going to get out alive. They were either going to kill all the hostages and then get killed themselves, or they were going to get captured, and they don't particularly care about them. So they can rot in a cell in Virginia or Kansas or Guantanamo forever."

"Suits me fine."

"Oh, and by the way, we did manage to get the money back. I'm not sure what happens to the bride-price now."

"The girl was frightened to death. I wouldn't be a bit surprised if she wants to go home."

Senator Campbell chuckled. "Well, the United States is a dangerous country, after all, isn't it? That's what they keep saying. Perhaps that's the best solution for everyone. It will break a certain heart, though."

I knew he was right. "So I have to ask some blunt questions, Senator. Is there some kind of favor that the sultan can do for Uncle Sam to perhaps get some protection? I'm trying to wrap my head around how I can keep this from happening again and again and again. He can't even stay holed up on his island. He's so vulnerable. But he's a friend of ours, and is there something he can do to help?"

"Well, we certainly aren't going to fucking put a base on his island, although it's not big enough anyway. I think him being involved in some of the politics in India, with that, he could be our ears to the ground. But, Marco, that's a pipe dream that he can be protected. And I think you better level with the man. He probably already knows it."

"So when I explained to him about these groups and about what's perhaps coming down the line—"

"You do not attribute those to me or to the Secretary, do you understand?"

"Of course. If I explained to him that's our theory, and I explained to him that there is no way anyone can tell him he's safe or his family is safe, then what do I do?"

"I suggest you be prepared for whatever he says. I know you don't want to abandon him. But you can't do this forever, Marco. At some point, you must get off the horse and do something else. I'm wondering if you could ever do that."

"So you're done with me then?"

"Not saying that, Marco. A man has to have a life, you know that."

"And you don't want me to kill myself trying."

"I would never want you to die for Uncle Sam. Why would I want you to die for a sultan in the middle of the Indian Ocean on a tiny island with a pink palace and pink sand beach? That's like what you read in children's books. I'm surprised it's even there anymore."

"So it's up to him then. I just give him the facts, and then he decides what he wants to do."

"That's my advice. It's a free world, not just a free country, with certain exceptions here and there. We have the right to do what we want. We have the right to live, and we have the right to die. Some people think living is more important. Some people think the way you die is the most important."

That sent chills down my spine. I knew men on the Teams who felt that way every time they went out.

"Does this mean you're not coming to the wedding?"

"No, I'm coming. You couldn't keep me away now. But, Marco, you got to figure out when it's time to quit. You got to know that. Otherwise, you might lose something more precious than life itself."

We both said it in unison. "Shannon."

I got home past 10:00, and I was unhappy it was becoming my routine. I knew eventually she was going to say something about it. It didn't matter what I was doing was important. Of course she worried, and a wife *should* worry if they loved their husbands. I didn't want her to. I knew my limits, and I wasn't sure exactly what I could promise. But I could promise to tell her the truth.

I put off my call to the sultan till tomorrow, leaving a message with their time difference, that I was exhausted and needed to get to bed, and I would make contact with them the next day.

I unlocked our front door, waved to our detail who was just settling in for the night in our driveway, entered our small living room, and looked out through the sliding glass window. The beach beyond was lit by a full moon spilling into the rippling water of the bay, the Gulf of Mexico. I just stood there and watched as the water lapped in the surf, as clouds were strewn about the sky, occasionally covering the full moon. I even heard the cicadas in the distance, screaming so loud that I could hear them through the closed glass door.

This was the place I belonged. This was the magical place I'd always dreamt about. But the more I spent time here, the more I realized that this place wasn't as safe as I thought it was. And that created a dichotomy for me.

While I wasn't going to make that commitment to the sultan, I could make that commitment to Shannon—the commitment to keep her safe forever. That was something I could do and would be willing to risk my life for. But I was done doing that for other people. And although the sultan was my best friend, as close to a father as I could have wanted, he had his own family, and he had his own empire that he needed to watch over. While I might help him, I couldn't do it for him. My responsibility was Shannon. Our life together. The children we hoped to have.

I turned from the window and found Shannon leaning in the doorway of our bedroom. She had on one of those long, silky, black negligees. In the darkness, all I could see was beautiful, smooth skin popping out from it here and there, a long leg, her graceful arms and hands, and one shoulder shone in the moonlight. She was all the things I'd ever wanted in a woman, not only physically but emotionally. Just the right kind of naïve, the right kind of innocence matched with that adventurous and stubborn spirit of hers. And she was so much more. I hoped today hadn't scared her or driven her away.

On my way over to embrace her, I apologized.

"Apology accepted," she quickly answered.

She waited for me to touch her before she spoke again.

"Marco, I missed you. I can't do this without you."

"I understand. And I want to tell you that tonight was just a special thing, but unfortunately, sweetheart, it may happen again. I'm going to try not to make it happen, but it could happen again. I just want you to know I see it, and I will never choose to guard someone else or be someone else's protection at the expense of yours. You must understand that. And I will be doing dangerous things. I'm not ready to give that up."

"I know you aren't. I watched you. I saw it in you. You love it. It's who you are."

I angled my head and chuckled. "Now, I never would've come up with that. Where did you get that idea?"

"Your face. You love what you do. You love putting it on the line. And I love that you love it. But I still miss you. I ache for you. And I think, until you've broken all the bones in your body and you can no longer be mobile, you'll probably be running around shooing people away with your cane or trying to ram some bad guy with your car—maybe running people off the road in your golf cart."

"What did I ever do to deserve you?"

"Well, why don't you step inside here, and I'll tell you a few things about that. No, I'm going to correct myself. I'm going to show you."

"Sounds good to me."

I TELEPHONED THE sultan first thing in the morning. He was irritated I had waited so long to give him the update.

"These are my boys, Marco. I was told everybody came out okay, but these are my boys, and I expected more."

"They could have called you themselves, Sultan, but I take it, and I accept your criticism. I was exhausted, and I need to have a very frank conversation with you. I'm not looking forward to this."

"Oh, so you and Shannon have decided to go get married in Las Vegas with an Elvis priest, right?"

"That's funny. I would never do that to you. Never, never, never."

"Then what is it?"

"I learned with this last operation that there's no such thing as being completely safe. I think you should actually take some martial arts training, and I think your harem should know how to defend themselves as well. As should your staff. If they're going to be there and protect you when I can't be, that has to happen."

"What are you saying, Marco?"

"I'm saying it's impossible for me to guarantee your safety. I can do it for blocks of time, but I can't watch you and your whole family twenty-four seven. It's just not a possibility. We have to operate in a different fashion to keep you safe. But we can't always be there to defend you. It's indefensible."

"But I pay you to do the impossible."

"And I've been able to do that so far. But we've also been very lucky. As you know, the world is changing."

"So you're telling me you're refusing to work for me then? You've never had problems taking a paycheck before."

I bristled at that a bit.

"It wasn't always for the paycheck. You are my friend, probably my best friend. I realize that. And I'm willing to take on the responsibility of helping get you trained and supplying the men and assets to help keep you safe, but I don't want to promise you I can keep doing this—rescue people or sort out whatever it is that you and your family gets into. This thing with the girl, for instance, and the boat that Absalom and Khalil tried to purchase. You and your family have to start taking some responsibility for this. I cannot do it all."

"You didn't mention the poisoning."

"That comes from a different place. That was a wrong committed against someone else five years ago. You married a young woman to save her, but that woman was what someone else wanted. And think about it, you have more money, you have a big palace, you have wives, you have the perfect life for some."

"So am I to believe that you are quitting?"

"No, I'm not quitting. But I am getting married, and my loyalty to Shannon is going to be first and forever first. And I won't be doing anything that would jeopardize that. So I will help you get as ready as you can, but I cannot do it at the sacrifice of the woman I love."

I was surprised and pleased that it had been that easy to explain my thoughts to him. He seemed to take it well, although with the sultan, I never was sure of what he was thinking.

We still needed to go over the list of suspects, who was the most likely to have launched the attack on the boys, and I knew it would take a while to identify the right person. I hoped the interviews with the FBI were fruitful, but without it, we might never know. I felt good about the fact that I didn't promise something I couldn't deliver. I owed Shannon to give her everything she deserved. She was going to be my main priority.

Working for the sultan was going to give us the money to travel and to experience the whole world. It was my vehicle to the life I wanted to live, not the goal, not the destination.

I was happy with that choice.

CHAPTER 16

S HANNON HAD GROWN up watching old BBC movies, fascinated at following the treks of some of the explorers during the latter part of the 19th century and early 20th century. She loved movies that depicted exotic places and huge expeditions or treks. One of the movies that, of course, was haunting her now was "A Passage to India."

She was reminded of all the helpers, trunks, and luggage and how much of a process it was to travel during those days. She was also reminded of the differences between the classes. There were those who traveled well, those who worked for those who traveled well, and everybody else. Although much had changed and India was now a democracy, there were still old traditions kept, old ways of doing things which would die hard. In short, many people who worked for the sultan, and even the US government, were the lucky ones. They had a steady paycheck and didn't have to worry as much about their future. As long as they did their job, it was a benevolent arrangement.

But it wasn't that way for everybody, and with the wars in Africa and the violence spreading all over the world, it made her realize the time was ripe for mayhem, and she needed to be conscious of it. There wasn't much she could do to solve the problems, but she didn't want to become one of those problems, one of the hostages like the sultan's two sons had been now twice. She didn't want to make people risk their lives to save her, if she could save herself.

She renewed her commitment to herself to learn how to use a variety of weapons and get some martial arts training.

Sitting in the jet terminal in New York, she looked at all the baggage they had brought. And she did feel like one of those women traveling with three or four camels behind them lugging all their possessions. She didn't know why she brought so much, except she had gifts for everybody. She had gifts for wives, children, helpers, servants, and everybody in between. She even had a special gift for the sultan.

"I can't believe you brought so much. You could have just not brought any clothes at all, would've been fine with me." Her husband-to-be was always a prankster.

"I was just thinking the same thing, Marco. But the reality is two-thirds of these are gifts I'm bringing over from Florida. I have so many people to thank for this wonderful affair."

"Well, you forget, usually people come to a wedding and they bring you gifts."

"You're right. But like you told me the other night, I'm stubborn, aren't I?"

He laughed, and she noticed how visibly relaxed he was, now that they were actually underway. She remembered as a child when her family would go on a camping trip, to Disney World, or to one of the national parks, they were so excited to pack up the car. They had so much stuff they could hardly sit in it. It had been the same when she tried that one year in college. And she sure remembered Em when she had so much in her little car their dad had remarked, as she was pulling out of the driveway, that the rear tires looked like they were flat. He admonished her about getting them checked out at her first gas stop.

It was exciting to be on a great adventure. And she knew it would be. She was glad, because all the problems for not only the project but the safety of the men and women who worked on the project, as well as the sultan's family, were past. But as Marco reminded her, they had to keep ever vigilant. And she sure had learned that one full tilt.

Their jet arrived, and Marco had ordered a larger one this time. He explained that it was going to remain in Mumbai until they were ready to come home. That way he could have it serviced, have a team who would lock it down and keep it safe for them. He mentioned that it had two bedrooms, but she wasn't worried about that. They only needed one.

"I like your choice today, Marco."

He smiled at her and gave her a wink. "We're still limited staff on board, but I just wanted to be sure you were comfortable, my dear."

"This is a special day. I may wind up sleeping, because I doubt I'll be able to once we get on the island."

"I'd be happy to help you with that, my bride-to-be." He took her hand and kissed her palm, tenderly repeating the movement several times. "Shall we go?"

This was the part in a movie where the orchestra would play. Like the time they went on a helicopter ride in Hawaii with a former Air Force fighter pilot who liked to rock and roll that helicopter like it was his personal warship, they'd risen straight up off the ground. Then, as they had flown slowly over to the canyon, he turned on the "Star Wars" theme full force. Suddenly they had dipped down into the green cut of the lush jungle, and she'd left her stomach on the roof of the copter.

She had never been so scared in her life. Their fearless pilot had been probably the same age as Marco right now, a handsome hunk of a guy with aviators. His white teeth had grinned, especially at her. Em and her mom had seemed to take it all in good stride, but Shannon had been terrified.

Walking across the tarmac, she carried her computer and Marco carried his. They greeted the staff, took their seats inside, and received the briefing from the captain. She immediately slipped off her shoes and tucked them under the seat, preparing for takeoff.

The flight to New York had been choppy, mostly because Marco decided to take a commercial jet, seating them in first class instead of renting one of his planes. He had explained that some of the exclusive behavior that they'd been doing out of Tampa and Clearwater airports might catch the eye of some of the bad guys who were always out there looking for somebody they could fleece, a millionaire they could kidnap, or a wife they could take away and hold for ransom. She was beginning to believe him. At first when he began speaking of it, months ago before they were engaged, she hadn't believed him at all.

They held hands and were given their choice of wine, whiskey, or champagne.

"I'll have champagne," she said.

"And you, sir?"

"I'm going to have some single barrel Jack Daniels. Or do we have any Gentleman Jack on board?"

"For you, Mr. Gambini, we have just about the whole line. Is it Gentleman Jack or is it single barrel?"

Marco looked at Shannon and then said, "Gentleman Jack, please."

He used to be a wine drinker, which was her drink of choice usually. In recent days, he'd taken to purchasing some of the finest whiskey he could buy. Shannon occasionally indulged in that as well.

He expanded his seat to lie back slightly, and they both put their feet together on the leather cushion provided.

"I never thought I would live this way. I never thought I would be going to an exotic island palace. I never thought I'd have Prince Charming sitting next to me, holding my hand, and being, well, charming."

"What did you think of me when you were younger? I know I've probably asked you before but tell me the story again? The story of that day," he asked.

"Of course I was still devastated with Emily's death. And at the funeral, my parents were in complete shock. I knew it was the end of our happy family life as we knew it. Being twelve years old, I was trying to suck it up, but my lower lip was huge, puckering and wobbling, and I couldn't stop sniveling and sneezing, eyes pouring out tears that just would not stop. People kept giving me Kleenexes and handkerchiefs, and I refused all of that help and wiped my face clean with my sleeve. I got in trouble with my mother for it. My dress was black velvet and brand new for the occasion. But it wasn't an occasion I wanted to be celebrating."

"I get it. Now I understand your expression."

"My expression?"

"You had the look of defiance on you. You were fighting demons way back then."

"I was fighting for my family. I knew so much was going to be on my shoulders, because my parents, especially my father, loved Emily so much. I knew I wasn't going to be the substitute he needed. His life was forever going to be a big expansive void. I wasn't going to be able to fill that void ever."

"Perhaps that's not true. You know what they say, circumstances reveal a person. They don't make a person. Maybe that's exactly what you needed to do, which was rise up out of the ashes and be strong. Sometimes we have to change our environment. As a twelve-year-old girl, you didn't have that luxury. So look what you did. You took charge of your life, you went to school, you tried acting and modeling, and you got a job in a place that you love. And look what else happened. Because you made all those choices."

"Okay, so what about you then?"

"I knew I had to get out of that place after I said goodbye. There was nothing for me there."

Her heart jumped with a little pang. Shannon wanted to tell him, "But I was there, Marco."

She didn't.

"I needed to go be with the guys who would have my back. I needed to risk everything. Maybe I was headed off to battle because I didn't feel like I deserved to live. Em had been begging me to marry before I deployed, and I wanted to have my full concentration on my first tour. And look what happened. I didn't."

"So you weren't conscious of all the people around you, were you?"

"No, that's not true. I looked at your parents, and I saw that they were unreachable. I think even though she was the one who died, I think your father wished it had been me. I had a buddy from the team—"

"Carter, right?"

"That's right. Boy, you have a good memory."

"I met him later, remember?"

"That's right. I forgot about that. Well, anyway I was glad Carter was there, and I knew there was nothing else there for me, except I saw this cute little girl with braces and pigtails standing strong. You looked like your fist would punch me in the nose if I said something wrong, and I thought about what I could possibly tell you that would make you feel better. I was destined to fail at that, but I wanted to try for some reason. It just didn't seem fair, because I knew as soon as I left, nobody was going to be there for you."

She wiped her eyes, as the story was getting to her. She had not heard this part before.

"I looked at the casket and the beautiful pink and white roses that I had sent covering the entire top. The roses were going to wither and die on top of her grave after she was buried there, so I plucked the prettiest bud and brought it over to you, didn't I?"

"You did. That's a memory forever embedded in my brain. There's no way in the world I could ever forget that."

"If you were a boy, I might have given you a memento of my service, but that's not what you wanted. I gave you the prettiest rose, and I told you that I loved your sister with all my heart. And I was telling the truth, Shannon. I think I still love her, and I hope that doesn't upset you."

"No. Of course, I love her as well. I loved my parents even though life with them was changed, and I never really had the relationship I wanted. But that's why I had to come see you,

Marco. That man who stood in front of me that day in his white uniform, handsome and tall, the man my sister was going to devote her life to, thought enough of me, a little twelve-year-old girl with braces, to be kind. I had to come see if that was really you or if you were putting on a show."

He wrapped his arm around her shoulder and pulled her to him. "Sweetheart, if this is too painful—"

"No, I'm glad we're talking about it. The only thing that had been unresolved for me until the night we met again and slept together was whether or not you were the real deal. I thought I'd come just to kind of prove that maybe you were some asshole big buff billionaire military man, and perhaps I'd spent my whole teenage and early college years being enamored with somebody who was a fake. I had to find out for myself if that feeling inside my gut that told me you were a man worthy of my love was true or if it was false. And even if I discovered it was false, I had to know that before I could go on with the rest of my life. It sounds stupid, I know—"

Marco reached across, pulled her mouth to his, and planted a deep kiss.

"Always, Shannon. I'll always be here for you. This is how it goes. This is how the fairytale begins. This part here is not imagination." As he nibbled on her lips, he added, "This is real."

They arrived in Mumbai and traveled by limo down to Cochin, there catching Marco's Sikorsky. She was concerned about the luggage, but he informed her that everything had arrived there ahead of them. It had been put on a boat in Mumbai heading straight for the kingdom.

"I hope they have a better track record than the airlines."

"You better believe they do. Their livelihood depends on it."

As they landed, they saw the palace had gone through a huge renovation. Garlands of flowers hung all over the entranceway, and fresh rose petals, which had to have been imported from Europe or a large grower in Mumbai, were laid out across the shell pathway leading to the grand entrance. With the flowers and the rose petals all around, the trees also had been sprayed with rose petals, and in the breeze, it looked like pink snow. It was such a magical wonderland of a place already, Shannon wanted to remember this moment for the rest of her life.

The staff greeted them in brand new uniforms, trimmed in gold, each wearing a significant piece of jewelry, which she took to mean the sultan had been generous. Even the staff's children were present, wearing silks and fineries she had never seen them wear before. Shannon and Marco were greeted like royalty. They could have been the queen and king of England, and they wouldn't have gotten a better reception.

Shannon was having a hard time keeping the tears from running down her face. She kept bowing, placing her hands together, and saying thank you over and over again. She probably said it nearly a hundred times before she got to the front door.

Marco, she could tell, was touched as well. As they entered the great hall, the sultan was waiting for them, standing but leaning slightly against a pillar, which was new. She could see he had some lines on his face and perhaps was experiencing some pain. But nothing would stop him from giving them a grand, wide grin, removing himself from his perch, and coming over to hug them dearly.

"My friends, you honor me with your presence."

Marco grabbed the man, as much to stabilize him as to hug him. "My dear, dear friend. No one in the whole world could ever have done this for us. No one has been more kind, more generous. I am going to be eternally grateful."

The sultan winked and put his finger to his nose. "I'm glad to hear you say that, my pretend son. I want you to think of me until we greet each other someday in another place, in another palace, at another time."

Marco hung on to him, but it was more for the reaction that it caused inside his own body than to stabilize the sultan. He was so moved, she heard him gasp several times, clearing his throat and trying not to let his nose run too much. One of the little girls dressed in a white sari with rose-colored cummerbund brought him a little satin pillow with several pieces of tissue on it. She bowed and handed it up to him.

Someone else had noticed what Shannon had.

They were shown to their quarters after they greeted all the wives, looking as beautiful as they'd ever seen them. The whole banister leading up to the guest room, the room where Marco and Shannon had first loved each other in this palace, was wrapped in garland. The inside of the bedroom was decorated like a forest filled with flowering trees, but the garlands were hand-strung, and they had even brought butterflies into the room so that white-, yellow-, and peach-colored little insects with happy hearts flew everywhere around them. It was a magical touch Shannon didn't think she would ever forget. Where they found so many butter-flies, she would never know, but she hoped, in the morning, she would wake up and they'd be all over her.

They embraced and decided they would freshen up and then join everyone downstairs for a toast, which was on the agenda. They had just enough time to tease each other with a nice warm lavender shower but saved the sex for later.

A white sari had been left for Shannon, not one of the ones she had chosen, but all the rest of them were safely folded and tucked into the large cabinet with the carved doors just on the other side of the bedroom. She had some slippers set out that were lined in gold with upturned toes fitting her feet perfectly. She put the silk slip undergarment on and then proceeded to wrap the sari around herself, asking Marco for some help. The white gold-stitched slippers with the curled toes were incredibly soft and comfortable. She applied some jasmine and lavender oils behind her ear, spritzed on some of her favorite perfume, Audrey Hepburn's favorite blend, and looked at herself in the mirror. She gasped as she saw her face.

She was playing "Breakfast at Tiffany's." She was in "A Passage to India." Shannon was a queen in quest for a kingdom. She was a bride waiting for her happily ever after with her Prince Charming.

It was all in her imagination, and it lifted her and filled her with unspeakable pleasure.

They went downstairs and celebrated with the small group, and then several of the guests who had arrived earlier began to come in where a large buffet was set. People were informally seated and served. She noted that Dr. Tramel had arrived, alone, as well as several of Marco's men from his security team, all dressed to the nines in white tuxes.

The afternoon and early evening was luscious, and she tried not to drink too much and not to eat too much. Number one wife came over to her, whispering, "So now it is your time, Shannon. We've come to prepare you for tomorrow."

Shannon looked at her with questions in her eyes, then glanced over at Marco talking to the sultan. He'd noticed the conversation and toasted her with his champagne and a wink.

"So this has all been planned then?" Shannon asked her.

"You need to go through the ritual bathing. We will clean your skin, wash your hair, and make you feel beautiful for your day tomorrow. Please allow us this gift."

She had planned on spending a wonderful evening with Marco, but she could see that perhaps that was going to be postponed until the big day. Shannon looked at him as if asking for permission. He nodded and toasted her again.

"Well, then I guess I'm all yours."

She would never forget the way their hands lovingly massaged her and removed just about every hair on her body, which was a little painful at times. Her hair was infused with oils, conditioned, and then shampooed with loving strokes, relaxing her head and neck. Several times during the ritual cleansing, she fell asleep.

They had dipped in the saltwater pool and then the cold pool before the process began. All the wives came in with her, and she appreciated the sisterhood, the laughing, and the camaraderie they had for each other, for their position, for the wonderful life that they had there. She was moved they wanted to share it with her. She was not going to live like this, far from it in fact. But it was a gift they could give her that no one else in the whole world ever could.

Oiled and her hair washed, she was sent upstairs with a special pre-wedding gown and instructed not to have sex with her husband-to-be, which she thought was an unusual request.

As she opened the doors, the butterflies fluttered about her. Marco was sitting under the covers with a light green silk robe on.

"Look at you. You are a vision. How do you feel, sweetheart?"

"I feel like a queen, Marco. But—"

He was up in an instant, taking me in his arms and whispering, "I know, I know. The sultan warned me. Let's dispense with tradition, shall we?"

"Oh, yes, I was hoping you'd say that."

CHAPTER 17

I WAS GLAD that the household staff allowed Shannon and me to sleep in slightly, which was to say we slept until eight o'clock. I brought her coffee in bed, and soon the wives showed up to begin her bridal gown preparations. I excused myself, got quickly dressed, and headed downstairs.

Several new people had arrived either late last night or very early this morning, including Senator Campbell. But we also had the US ambassador to India attend and several other senior State Department officials, as well as most of my team at the office in Indian Rocks. Sam was in attendance as well, telling me he wouldn't have missed it for the world. Several of Shannon's relatives were there, people I had never met before, but sadly, her parents weren't among them.

The house, if it could be called that, was opulently decorated in garlands with flowers and hanging jewels. The rugs were all new, sparkling in their gold and silver threads. The pillars of the great hall were inlaid with lapis and gold, the jewels were polished to a fine patina, chairs were set up in the hall and adorned with white and pink roses. Some of the butterflies from our bedroom must have escaped, because here and there, we would find the happy creatures fluttering over a flower, a fern, or even landing on people's heads. It was quite a conversation starter.

The sultan saw me commenting on the details and took me aside, smiling.

"Look out here. You can see the parrots I brought over."

Through the glass, I saw more than a hundred salmon-and-pink-colored parrots flying around several large banana trees, foraging off the ground and perching on various feeders where some of their favorite delicacies sat.

"You'd be best to stay away from them, however. They are eating much fruit today, especially bananas and figs, their favorite. You do know what happens to the system," the sultan said to me with a wink. "But they are such beautiful creatures, and just like the butterflies, I think they were made out of magic. Don't you?"

"Absolutely, I would've never thought of this. Your imagination is—"

"Oh no, this wasn't me. My wives, they love doing this. They live for it, I think. But this is a special day, because they honor me by how they honor you."

I made the rounds of several other dignitaries, sat out in the garden with several of our team members, and found a way to ask a few technical questions, but I didn't fill the day with work. I knew we were safely being protected, and probably there would be a video of the entire occasion from many, many different angles, mostly because we had surveillance every place but the honeymoon house. I had strictly given instructions that it not be included in any surveillance other than the outside.

The group began to gather in the hallway in the great hall. A small trio played ancient instruments in the front of the hall by the altar. The music was unusual, a combination of Indian harp and some unfamiliar reed or flute. It was befitting the great hall and echoed, flowing melodic charm throughout the whole place. I was given the instructions to stand toward the front near the altar on one side, and I noticed the audience was spread out evenly with half of the wives on my side and half of the wives on Shannon's side. The sultan was not there yet as he was going to escort Shannon down the aisle.

One by one, several of the employees and SEAL team members I'd served with agreed to show people to their seats and then joined me. Most of them wore uniforms. However, I chose to wear a white tux. I had the option, of course, but I left the honor to the men who were on active duty.

The harp music began to change pace, and I realized we were getting close to the start of the ceremony. If someone were to ask me if I was nervous, I would say no, but then being perfectly honest, I had as many butterflies in my belly as I saw in the palace.

This was a forever life-changing event, more momentous than anything I'd ever done on the teams or in my business life. It was perhaps the beginning of one story and the end of another. And I was going to move through it with grace and dignity and help my bride in the process. I knew what this meant, that my loyalty would forever be with Shannon.

The music stopped briefly, and then a trio of harpists began a beautiful rendering of a hymn I didn't know the title to. As the audience turned, the vision appeared of the sultan with his fine white tunic, all the medals of his station, the ambassadorships he'd had, the awards he'd received, and one of my tridents I had given him, which technically was a violation but a violation I allowed him graciously.

As the music began, Shannon stepped forward, her white sari highlighting the beautiful curves of her body. Her warm red lips called to me, her smile made me feel like I was riding on a carpet. The wives had done up her hair with braids, interspersed with lace, silk, and flowers. Little pink rosebuds were woven in between as well, perfectly framing her lovely face. Her bouquet was made of pink, white, and cream roses plus several fragrant flowers from the island.

I was transported full circle to the first day I remembered seeing her up close, as I held the rose to her nose and, in my own way, pledged to forever be her warrior prince.

And yet, I didn't realize it until years later.

I gulped in air, watching as she walked carefully next to the sultan, clutching his arm firmly. I suspected perhaps he was doing the same. Both were beaming, nodding to guests along the way as they walked down the gold-threaded carpet to where I was standing. Shannon's delicate scent engulfed me, lighting a fire inside which completely took my breath away. I could hardly speak.

"You are so beautiful. Are you sure I'm good enough?" My voice was scratchy as I tried to force it out so she could hear. I thought I had whispered, but several people in the front rows began to titter.

She gave me a strange look. "Of course you are. You always were, Marco. I will never ever leave you. I will never, ever love anyone as much as I love you. I humbly ask you to forgive all my transgressions, my stubbornness, and—"

I put my hand over her mouth, and again, the front rows began to giggle.

"I will never cause you to want to leave. And I will I protect you until my last breath." I kissed her, and then the reverend we had selected cleared his throat.

That brought us back to real time, and he began the service, reciting an ancient Rumi text on love.

"I choose to love you in silence…

For in silence

I find no rejection,

I choose to love you in loneliness…

For in loneliness no one owns you but me,

I choose to adore you from a distance…

For distance will shield me from pain,

I choose to kiss you in the wind…

For the wind is gentler than my lips.

I choose to hold you

In my dreams…

For in my dreams, you have no end."

The vows were taken, questions asked, and the small personal gifts exchanged, which was their custom. I gave her a small perfect pink shell. She gave me a dark gray pearl.

Our clergy wrapped our hands together in a gold cord, allowed for the preparation and placing of rings. I kissed her palm and then held it to my cheek. I could hear sniffles in the audience, and I knew we were making quite a few people either sad or extremely happy. She kissed her fingertip and then spread it over my lower lip. She took her tears and repeated the motion, which I eagerly tasted.

The reverend announced that we were now joined as one, man and wife, and motioned for me to kiss the bride.

She didn't have time to give her bouquet away, which was what was supposed to happen, so she clutched it at the back of my neck as I grabbed her firmly around the waist and kissed her hard, not letting go, not being appropriate, not holding back at all. She laughed into my ear. It felt so good to feel and touch her in such a happy mood and to hear her joyful sigh.

With my hands on her face and her palms on mine, I said it again, "Forever."

She repeated it to me. "Forever."

We made our way very slowly back down the aisle, hugging guests, taking our time on that long walk back across to the reception area. It was customary for the husband and wife to make one toast and then to disappear, which I was thrilled with.

Two pink crystal goblets were handed to us with pink champagne, and we held them up to the assembly with thanks.

The sultan was the first to speak.

"To romance. To falling in love, living a life of magic and hope forever after. Let us all commit to finding that beautiful place in our lives, where love grows, where all the magic of the world resides."

He turned to us. "To Marco and Shannon, two people joined forever and ever. My dearest friends. May your kingdom last forever."

He raised his glass, and everyone else partook.

I would often remember that day. It was hard to hold it all in my head, but little bits and pieces of it came back to me in the days and weeks that followed. No matter what I was doing, I'd stop to think about how I felt that day, dedicating my life to something and someone new. Dedicated to making myself a better man for it all.

It was as much for the women of the sultan's family as anyone else when they helped Shannon down the pathway, made sure her beautiful sari didn't get snagged in the stones, the shells, or the foliage. We had chosen to walk the mile and a half to the honeymoon house instead of taking the cart, but the cart had been decorated nonetheless, just in case we changed our minds.

At the front door, also adorned with garlands of flowers we knew came from exotic far away locations, a white silk ribbon was cut, and we were, at last, officially on our honeymoon, the doors closing silently behind us.

The candles were scented, infused with scents of vanilla, lavender, citrus, and lime. Some butterflies lingered there. The blue ocean was brighter than I'd remembered seeing before. Night was beginning to form, transforming the whole area into a warm rosy glow.

I took her in my arms and brought her to the bedroom. As we disrobed, the glow of the distant dying sun shone on our faces. I carefully removed the clips and tiny rosebuds and let her hair fall around her shoulders. Without all the adornments, the flowers or the gold threads, with her bare body beneath mine, just the sparkle in her eyes and the ruby redness of her lips were all the garnish that was required.

My life was now perfect. I'd never thought or said that before.

But I now believed in happily ever after.

ABOUT THE AUTHOR

 NYT and USA/Today Bestselling Author Sharon Hamilton's SEAL Brotherhood series have earned her author rankings of #1 in Romantic Suspense, Military Romance and Contemporary Romance. Her other *Brotherhood* stand-alone series are: Bad Boys of SEAL Team 3, Band of Bachelors, True Blue SEALs, Nashville SEALs, Bone Frog Brotherhood, Sunset SEALs, Bone Frog Bachelor Series and SEAL Brotherhood Legacy Series. She is a contributing author to the very popular Shadow SEALs multi-author series.

Her SEALs and former SEALs have invested in two wineries, a lavender farm and a brewery in Sonoma County, which have become part of the new stories. They also have expanded to include Veteran-benefit projects on the Florida Gulf Coast, as well as projects in Africa and the Maldives. One of the SEAL wives has even launched her own women's fiction series. But old characters, as well as children of these SEAL heroes keep returning to all the newer books.

Sharon also writes sexy paranormals in two series: Golden Vampires of Tuscany and The Guardians.

A lifelong organic vegetable and flower gardener, Sharon and her husband lived for fifty years in the Wine Country of Northern California, where many of her stories take place. Recently, they have moved to the beautiful Gulf Coast of Florida, with stories of shipwrecks, the white sugar-sand beaches of Sunset, Treasure Island and Indian Rocks Beaches.

She loves hearing from fans through her website: authorsharonhamilton.com

Find out more about Sharon, her upcoming releases, appearances and news when you sign up for Sharon's newsletter.

Facebook:
facebook.com/SharonHamiltonAuthor

Twitter:
twitter.com/sharonlhamilton

Pinterest:
pinterest.com/AuthorSharonH

Amazon:
amazon.com/Sharon-Hamilton/e/B004FQQMAC

BookBub:
bookbub.com/authors/sharon-hamilton

Youtube:
youtube.com/channel/UCDInkxXFpXp_4Vnq08ZxMBQ

Soundcloud:
soundcloud.com/sharon-hamilton-1

Sharon Hamilton's Rockin' Romance Readers:
facebook.com/groups/sealteamromance

Sharon Hamilton's Goodreads Group:
goodreads.com/group/show/199125-sharon-hamilton-readers-group

Visit Sharon's Online Store:
sharon-hamilton-author.myshopify.com

Join Sharon's Review Teams:

eBook Reviews:
sharonhamiltonassistant@gmail.com

Audio Reviews:
sharonhamiltonassistant@gmail.com

Life *is one fool thing after another.*
Love *is two fool things after each other.*

REVIEWS

accept the turning to become a vampire. Either way she and Lionel can never be together since it is forbidden.

I enjoyed this story and I am looking forward to the next installment."

"A hauntingly romantic read. Old love lost and new love found. Family, heart, intrigue and vampires. Grabbed my attention and couldn't put down. Would definitely recommend."

PRAISE FOR THE
SEAL BROTHERHOOD SERIES

"Fans of Navy SEAL romance, I found a new author to feed your addiction. Finely written and loaded delicious with moments, Sharon Hamilton's storytelling satisfies like a thick bar of chocolate." —Marliss Melton, bestselling author of the *Team Twelve* Navy SEALs series

"Sharon Hamilton does an EXCELLENT job of fitting all the characters into a brotherhood of SEALS that may not be real but sure makes you feel that you have entered the circle and security of their world. The stories intertwine with each book before…and each book after and THAT is what makes Sharon Hamilton's SEAL Brotherhood Series so very interesting. You won't want to put down ANY of her books and they will keep you reading into the night when you should be sleeping. Start with this book…and you will not want to stop until you've read the whole series and then…you will be waiting for Sharon to write the next one." (5 Star Review)

"Kyle and Christy explode all over the pages in this first book, *[Accidental SEAL]*, in a whole new series of SEALs. If the twist and turns don't get your heart jumping, then maybe the suspense will. This is a must read for those that are looking for love and adventure with a little sloppy love thrown in for good measure." (5 Star Review)

and proud of those who serve to keep us safe. This is an author who writes amazing stories that you love and cry with the characters. Fans of Jessica Scott and Marliss Melton will want to add Sharon Hamilton to their list of realistic military romance writers." (5 Star Review)

"Dear FATHER IN HEAVEN,

If I may respectfully say so sometimes you are a strange God. Though you love all mankind,

It seems you have special predilections too.

You seem to love those men who can stand up alone who face impossible odds, Who challenge every bully and every tyrant ~

Those men who know the heat and loneliness of Calvary. Possibly you cherish men of this stamp because you recognize the mark of your only son in them.

Since this unique group of men known as the SEALs know Calvary and suffering, teach them now the mystery of the resurrection ~ that they are indestructible, that they will live forever because of their deep faith in you.

And when they do come to heaven, may I respectfully warn you, Dear Father, they also know how to celebrate. So please be ready for them when they insert under your pearly gates.

Bless them, their devoted Families and their Country on this glorious occasion.

We ask this through the merits of your Son, Christ Jesus the Lord, Amen."

By Reverend E.J. McMalhon S.J. LCDR, CHC, USN
Awards Ceremony SEAL Team One
1975 At NAB, Coronado